Jennifer Weiner lives in Philadelphia with her husband, daughter and her rat terrier, Wendell. To find out more visit her website on www.jenniferweiner.com

Good in Bed

In Her Shoes

JENNIFER WEINER

POCKET
BOOKS

LONDON · SYDNEY · NEW YORK · TORONTO

This Jennifer Weiner omnibus edition first published
in Great Britain by Pocket Books, 2004
An imprint of Simon & Schuster UK Ltd
A Viacom Company

Copyright © Jennifer Weiner, 2004

Good in Bed first published in Great Britain by Pocket Books, 2001
A Viacom Company
Copyright © Jennifer Weiner, 2001

In Her Shoes first published in Great Britain by Pocket Books, 2003
A Viacom Company
Copyright © Jennifer Weiner, 2002

1 3 5 7 9 10 8 6 4 2

Simon & Schuster UK Ltd
Africa House
64–78 Kingsway
London WC2B 6AH

www.simonsays.co.uk

Simon & Schuster Australia
Sydney

A CIP catalogue record for this book is available from the British Library

ISBN 1 4165 0205 X

Printed and bound in Great Britain by
Cox & Wyman Ltd, Reading, Berks

Good in Bed

For my family

Home is so sad. It stays as it was left,
Shaped to the comfort of the last to go
As if to win them back. Instead, bereft
Of anyone to please, it withers so,
Having no heart to put aside the theft
And turn again to what it started as,
A joyous shot at how things ought to be,
Long fallen wide. You can see how it was:
Look at the pictures and the cutlery.
The music in the piano stool. That vase.
—Philip Larkin

Love is nothing, nothing, nothing like they say.
—Liz Phair

PART ONE

Good in Bed

ONE

"Have you seen it?" asked Samantha.

I leaned close to my computer so my editor wouldn't hear me on a personal call.

"Seen what?"

"Oh, nothing. Never mind. We'll talk when you get home."

"Seen what?" I asked again.

"Nothing," Samantha repeated.

"Samantha, you have never once called me in the middle of the day about nothing. Now come on. Spill."

Samantha sighed. "Okay, but remember: Don't shoot the messenger."

Now I was getting worried.

"*Moxie.* The new issue. Cannie, you have to go get one right now."

"Why? What's up? Am I one of the Fashion Faux Pas?"

"Just go to the lobby and get it. I'll hold."

This was important. Samantha was, in addition to being my best friend, also an associate at Lewis, Dommel, and Fenick. Samantha put people on hold, or had her assistant tell them she was in a meeting. Samantha herself did not hold. "It's a sign of weakness," she'd told me. I felt a small twinge of anxiety work its way down my spine.

3

I took the elevator to the lobby of the *Philadelphia Examiner,* waved at the security guard, and walked to the small newsstand, where I found *Moxie* on the rack next to its sister publications, *Cosmo* and *Glamour* and *Mademoiselle.* It was hard to miss, what with the supermodel in sequins beneath headlines blaring "Come Again: Multiple Orgasm Made Easy!" and "Ass-Tastic! Four Butt Blasters to Get your Rear in Gear!" After a quick minute of deliberation, I grabbed a small bag of chocolate M&M's, paid the gum-chomping cashier, and went back upstairs.

Samantha was still holding. "Page 132," she said.

I sat, eased a few M&M's into my mouth, and flipped to page 132, which turned out to be "Good in Bed," *Moxie's* regular male-written feature designed to help the average reader understand what her boyfriend was up to . . . or wasn't up to, as the case might be. At first my eyes wouldn't make sense of the letters. Finally, they unscrambled. "Loving a Larger Woman," said the headline, "By Bruce Guberman." Bruce Guberman had been my boyfriend for just over three years, until we'd decided to take a break three months ago. And the Larger Woman, I could only assume, was me.

You know how in scary books a character will say, "I felt my heart stop?" Well, I did. Really. Then I felt it start to pound again, in my wrists, my throat, my fingertips. The hair at the back of my neck stood up. My hands felt icy. I could hear the blood roaring in my ears, as I read the first line of the article: "I'll never forget the day I found out my girlfriend weighed more than I did."

Samantha's voice sounded like it was coming from far, far away. "Cannie? Cannie, are you there?"

"I'll kill him!" I choked.

"Take deep breaths," Samantha counseled. "In through the nose, out through the mouth."

Betsy, my editor, cast a puzzled look across the partition that separated our desks. *"Are you all right?"* she mouthed. I squeezed my eyes shut. My headset had somehow landed on the carpet. "Breathe!" I could hear Samantha say, her voice a tinny echo from the floor. I was wheezing, gasping. I could feel chocolate and bits of candy shell on my teeth. I could see the quote they'd lifted, in bold-faced pink letters that screamed out from the center of the page. "Loving a larger woman," Bruce had written, "is an act of courage in our world."

"I can't believe this! I can't believe he did this! I'll kill him!"

By now Betsy had circled around to my desk and was trying to peer over my shoulder at the magazine in my lap, and Gabby, my evil coworker, was looking our way, her beady brown eyes squinting for signs of trouble, thick fingers poised over her keyboard so that she could instantly e-mail the bad news to her pals. I slammed the magazine closed. I took a successful deep breath, and waved Betsy back to her seat.

Samantha was waiting. "You didn't know?"

"Didn't know what? That he thought dating me was an act of courage?" I attempted a sardonic snort. "He should try *being* me."

"So you didn't know he got a job at *Moxie.*"

I flipped to the front, where Contributors were listed in thumbnail profiles beneath arty black-and-white head shots. And there was Bruce, with his shoulder-length hair blowing in what was assuredly artificial wind. He looked, I thought uncharitably, like Yanni. "'Good in Bed' columnist Bruce Guberman joins the staff of *Moxie* this month. A freelance writer from New Jersey, Guberman is currently at work on his first novel."

"His first *novel?*" I said. Well, shrieked, maybe. Heads turned. Over the partition, Betsy was looking worried again, and Gabby had started typing. "That lying sack of shit!"

"I didn't know he was writing a novel," said Samantha, no doubt desperate to change the subject.

"He can barely write a thank-you note," I said, flipping back to page 132.

"I never thought of myself as a chubby chaser," I read. "But when I met C., I fell for her wit, her laugh, her sparkling eyes. Her body, I decided, was something I could learn to live with."

"I'll KILL HIM!"

"So kill him already and shut up about it," muttered Gabby, shoving her inch-thick glasses up her nose.

Betsy was on her feet again, and my hands were shaking, and suddenly somehow there were M&M's all over the floor, crunching beneath the rollers of my chair.

"I gotta go," I told Samantha, and hung up.

"I'm fine," I said to Betsy. She gave me a worried look, then retreated.

It took me three tries to get Bruce's number right, and when his voice mail calmly informed me that he wasn't available to take my call, I lost my nerve, hung up, and called Samantha back.

"Good in bed, my ass," I said. "I ought to call his editor. It's false advertising. I mean, did they check his references? Nobody called me."

"That's the anger talking," said Samantha. Ever since she started dating her yoga instructor, she's become very philosophical.

"Chubby chaser?" I said. I could feel tears prickling behind my eyelids. "How could he do this to me?"

"Did you read the whole thing?"

"Just the first little bit."

"Maybe you better not read any more."

"It gets worse?"

Samantha sighed. "Do you really want to know?"

"No. Yes. No." I waited. Samantha waited. "Yes. Tell me."

Samantha sighed again. "He calls you. . . . Lewinsky-esque."

"With regards to my body or my blow jobs?" I tried to laugh, but it came out as a strangled sob.

"And he goes on and on about your . . . let me find it. Your 'amplitude.' "

"Oh, God."

"He said you were succulent," Samantha said helpfully. "And zaftig. That's not a bad word, is it?"

"God, the whole time we went out, he never said anything . . ."

"You dumped him. He's mad at you," said Samantha.

"I didn't dump him!" I cried. "We were just taking a break! And he agreed that it was a good idea!"

"Well, what else could he do?" asked Samantha. "You say, 'I think we need some time apart,' and he either agrees with you and walks away clinging to whatever shreds of dignity he's got left, or begs you not to leave him, and looks pathetic. He chose the dignity cling."

I ran my hands through my chin-length brown hair and tried to gauge the devastation. Who else had seen this? Who else knew that C. was me? Had he shown all his friends? Had my sister seen it? Had, God forbid, my mother?

"I gotta go," I told Samantha again. I set down my headset and got to my feet, surveying the *Philadelphia Examiner* newsroom—dozens of mostly middle-aged, mostly white people, tapping away at their computers, or clustered around the television sets watching CNN.

"Does anybody know anything about getting a gun in this state?" I inquired of the room at large.

"We're working on a series," said Larry the city editor—a small, bearded, perplexed-looking man who took everything absolutely seriously. "But I think the laws are pretty lenient."

"There's a two-week waiting period," piped up one of the sports reporters.

"That's only if you're under twenty-five," added an assistant features editor.

"You're thinking of rental cars," said the sports guy scornfully.

"We'll get back to you, Cannie," said Larry. "Are you in a rush?"

"Kind of." I sat down, then stood back up again. "Pennsylvania has the death penalty, right?"

"We're working on a series," Larry said without smiling.

"Oh, never mind," I said, and sat back down and called Samantha again.

"You know what? I'm not going to kill him. Death's too good for him."

"Whatever you want," Samantha said loyally.

"Come with me tonight? We'll ambush him in his parking lot."

"And do what?"

"I'll figure that out between now and then," I said.

I had met Bruce Guberman at a party, in what felt like a scene from somebody else's life. I'd never met a guy at a social gathering who'd been so taken with me that he actually asked me for a date on the spot. My typical m.o. is to wear down their resistence with my wit, my charm, and usually a home-cooked dinner starring kosher chicken with garlic and rosemary. Bruce did not require a chicken. Bruce was easy.

I was stationed in the corner of the living room, where I had a good view of the room, plus easy access to the hot artichoke dip. I was doing my best imitation of my mother's life partner, Tanya, trying to eat an Alaskan king crab leg with her arm in a sling. So the first time I saw Bruce, I had one of my arms jammed against my chest, sling-style, and my mouth wide open, and my neck twisted at a particularly grotesque angle as I tried to suck the imaginary meat out of the imaginary claw. I was just getting to the part where I accidentally jammed the crab leg up my right nostril, and I think there might have been hot artichoke dip on my cheek, when Bruce walked up. He was tall, and tanned, with a goatee and a dirty-blond ponytail, and soft brown eyes.

"Um, excuse me," he said, "are you okay?"

I raised my eyebrows at him. "Fine."

"You just looked kind of . . ." His voice—a nice voice, if a little high—trailed off.

"Weird?"

"I saw somebody having a stroke once," he told me. "It started off like that."

By now my friend Brianna had collected herself. Wiping her eyes, she grabbed his hand. "Bruce, this is Cannie," she said. "Cannie was just doing an imitation."

"Oh," said Bruce, and stood there, obviously feeling foolish.

"Not to worry," I said. "It's a good thing you stopped me. I was being unkind."

"Oh," said Bruce again.

I kept talking. "See, I'm trying to be nicer. It's my New Year's resolution."

"It's February," he pointed out.

"I'm a slow starter."

"Well," he said, "at least you're trying." He smiled at me, and walked away.

I spent the rest of the party getting the scoop. He'd come with a guy Brianna knew from graduate school. The good news: He was a graduate student, which meant reasonably smart, and Jewish, just like me. He was twenty-seven. I was twenty-five. It fit. "He's funny, too," said Brianna, before delivering the bad news: Bruce had been working on his dissertation for three years, possibly longer, and he lived in central New Jersey, more than an hour away from us, picking up freelance writing work and teaching the occasional bunch of freshmen, subsisting on stipends, a small scholarship, and, mostly, his parents' money.

"Geographically undesirable," Brianna pronounced.

"Nice hands," I countered. "Nice teeth."

"He's a vegetarian," she said.

I winced. "For how long?"

"Since college."

"Hmph. Well, maybe I can work with it."

"He's . . ." Brianna trailed off.

"On parole?" I joked. "Addicted to painkillers?"

"Kind of immature," she finally said.

"He's a guy," I said, shrugging. "Aren't they all?"

She laughed. "And he's a good guy," she said. "Talk to him. You'll see."

That whole night, I watched him, and I felt him watching me. But he didn't say anything until after the party broke up, and I was walking home, feeling more than a little disappointed. It had been a while since I'd even seen someone who'd caught my fancy, and tall, nice hands, nice-white-teeth grad student Bruce appeared, at least from the outside, to be a possibility.

But when I heard footsteps behind me, I wasn't thinking about him. I was thinking what every woman who lives in a city thinks when she hears quick footsteps coming up behind her and it's after midnight and she's between streetlights. I took a quick glance at my surroundings while fumbling for the Mace attached to my keychain. There was a streetlight on the corner, a car parked underneath. I figured I'd Mace whoever it was into temporary immobility, smash one of the car windows, hoping the alarm would go off, scream bloody murder, and run.

"Cannie?"

I whirled around. And there he was, smiling at me shyly. "Hey," he said, laughing a little bit at my obvious fear. He walked me home. I gave him my number. He called me the next night, and we talked for three hours, about everything: college, parents, his dissertation, the future of newspapers. "I want to see you," he told me at one in the morning, when I was thinking that if we kept talking I was going to be a wreck at work the next day. "So we'll meet," I said.

"No," said Bruce. "Now."

And two hours later, after a wrong turn coming off the Ben Franklin Bridge, he was at my door again: bigger than I'd remembered, somehow, in a plaid shirt and sweatpants, carrying a rolled-up sleeping bag that smelled like summer camp in one hand, smiling shyly. And that was that.

And now, more than three years after our first kiss, three months after our let's-take-a-break talk, and four hours after I'd found out that he'd told the entire magazine-reading world that I was a Larger Woman, Bruce squinted at me across the parking lot in front of his apartment where he'd agreed to meet me. He was blinking double-time, the way he did when he was nervous. His arms were full of things. There was the blue plastic dog-food dish I'd kept in his apartment for my dog, Nifkin. There, in a red wooden frame, was the picture of us on top of a bluff at Block Island. There was a silver hoop earring that had been sitting on his night table for months. There were three socks, a half-empty bottle of Chanel. Tampons. A toothbrush. Three years' worth of odds and ends, kicked under the bed, worked down into a crack in the couch. Evidently, Bruce saw our rendezvous as a chance to kill two birds with one stone—endure my wrath over the "Good in Bed" column and give me back my stuff. And it felt like being punched in the chest, looking at my girlie items all jumbled up in a cardboard Chivas box he'd probably picked up at the liquor store on his way home from work—the physical evidence that we were really, truly over.

"Cannie," he said coolly, still squinching his eyes open and shut in a way I found particularly revolting.

"Bruce," I said, trying to keep my voice from shaking. "How's that novel coming? Will I be starring in that, too?"

He raised his eyebrow, but said nothing. "Remind me," I said. "At what point in our relationship did I agree to let you share intimate details of our time together with a few million readers?"

Bruce shrugged. "We don't have a relationship anymore."

"We were taking a break," I said.

Bruce gave me a small, condescending smile. "Come on, Cannie. We both know what that meant."

"I meant what I said," I said, glaring at him. "Which makes one of us, it seems."

"Whatever," said Bruce, attempting to shove the stuff into my arms. "I don't know why you're so upset. I didn't say anything bad." He straightened his shoulders. "I actually thought the column was pretty nice."

For one of the few times in my adult life, I was literally speechless. "Are you high?" I asked. With Bruce, that was more than a rhetorical question.

"You called me fat in a magazine. You turned me into a joke. You don't think you did anything wrong?"

"Face it, Cannie," he said. "You are fat." He bent his head. "But that doesn't mean I didn't love you."

The box of tampons bounced off his forehead and spilled into the parking lot.

"Oh, that's nice," said Bruce.

"You absolute bastard." I licked my lips, breathing hard. My hands were shaking. My aim was off. The picture glanced off his shoulder, then shattered on the ground. "I can't believe I ever thought seriously for even one second about marrying you."

Bruce shrugged, bending down, scooping feminine protection and shards of wood and glass into his hands and dumping them back into the box. Our picture he left lying there.

"This is the meanest thing anyone's ever done to me," I said, through my tear-clogged throat. "I want you to know that." But even as the words were leaving my mouth, I knew it wasn't true. In the grand, historical scheme of things, my father leaving us was doubtlessly worse. Which is one of the many things that sucked about my father—he forever robbed me of the possibility of telling another man, *This is the worst thing that's ever happened to me,* and meaning it.

Bruce shrugged again. "I don't have to worry about how you feel anymore. You made that clear." He straightened up. I hoped he'd be angry—passionate, even—but all I got was this maddening, patronizing calm. "You were the one who wanted this, remember?"

"I wanted a break. I wanted time to think about things. I should have just dumped you," I said. "You're . . ." And I stood, speechless again, thinking of the worst thing I could say to him, the word that would make him feel even a fraction as horrible and furious and ashamed as I did. "You're small," I finally said, imbuing that word with every hateful nuance I could muster, so that he'd know I meant small in spirit, and everywhere else, too.

He didn't say anything. He didn't even look at me. He just turned around and walked away.

Samantha had kept the car running. "Are you okay?" she asked as I slid into the passenger's seat clutching the box to my chest. I nodded silently. Samantha probably thought I was ridiculous. But this wasn't a situation I expected her to sympathize with. At five foot ten, with inky black hair, pale skin, and high, sculpted cheekbones, Samantha looks like a young Anjelica Huston. And she's thin. Effortlessly, endlessly thin. Given a choice of any food in the world, she'd probably pick a perfect fresh peach and Rya crispbreads. If she wasn't my best friend, I'd hate her, and even though she is my best friend, it's sometimes hard not to be envious of someone who can take food or leave it, whereas I mostly take it, and then take hers, too, when she doesn't want any more. The only problem her face and figure had ever caused her was too much male attention. I could never make her feel what it was like to live in a body like mine.

She glanced at me quickly. "So, um, I'm guessing that things with you two are over?"

"Good guess," I said dully. My mouth tasted ashy, my skin,

reflected in the passenger's side window, looked pale and waxen. I stared into the cardboard box, at my earrings, my books, the tube of MAC lipstick that I thought I'd lost forever.

"You okay?" asked Samantha gently.

"I'm fine."

"Do you want to get a drink? Some dinner, maybe? Want to go see a movie?"

I held the box tighter and closed my eyes so I wouldn't have to see where we were, so I wouldn't have to follow the car's progress back down the roads that used to lead me to him. "I think I just want to go home."

My answering machine was blinking triple-time when I got back to my apartment. I ignored it. I shucked off my work clothes, pulled on my overalls and a T-shirt, and padded, barefoot, into the kitchen. From the freezer I retrieved a canister of frozen Minute Maid lemonade. From the top shelf of the pantry I pulled down a pint of tequila. I dumped both in a mixing bowl, grabbed a spoon, took a deep breath, a big slurp, settled myself on my blue denim couch, and forced myself to start reading.

Loving a Larger Woman

by Bruce Guberman

I'll never forget the day I found out my girlfriend weighed more than I did.

She was out on a bike ride, and I was home watching football, leafing through the magazines on her coffee table, when I found her Weight Watchers folder—a palm-sized folio with notations for what she'd eaten, and when, and what she planned to eat next, and whether she'd been drinking her eight glasses of water a day. There was her name. Her identification number. And her weight, which I am too much of a gentleman to reveal here. Suffice it to say that the number shocked me.

I knew that C. was a big girl. Certainly bigger than any of

the women I'd seen on TV, bouncing in bathing suits or drifting, reedlike, through sitcoms and medical dramas. Definitely bigger than any of the women I'd ever dated before.

What, I thought scornfully. Both of them?

I never thought of myself as a chubby chaser. But when I met C., I fell for her wit, her laugh, her sparkling eyes. Her body, I decided, was something I could learn to live with.

Her shoulders were as broad as mine, her hands were almost as big, and from her breasts to her belly, from her hips down the slope of her thighs, she was all sweet curves and warm welcome. Holding her felt like a safe haven. It felt like coming home.

But being out with her didn't feel nearly as comfortable. Maybe it was the way I'd absorbed society's expectations, its dictates of what men are supposed to want and how women are supposed to appear. More likely, it was the way she had. C. was a dedicated foot soldier in the body wars. At five foot ten inches, with a linebacker's build and a weight that would have put her right at home on a pro football team's roster, C. couldn't make herself invisible.

But I know that if it were possible, if all the slouching and slumping and shapeless black jumpers could have erased her from the physical world, she would have gone in an instant. She took no pleasure from the very things I loved, from her size, her amplitude, her luscious, zaftig heft.

As many times as I told her she was beautiful, I know that she never believed me. As many times as I said it didn't matter, I knew that to her it did. I was just one voice, and the world's voice was louder. I could feel her shame like a palpable thing, walking beside us on the street, crouched down between us in a movie theater, coiled up and waiting for someone to say what to her was the dirtiest word in the world: *fat.*

And I knew it wasn't paranoia. You hear, over and over, how

fat is the last acceptable prejudice, that fat people are the only safe targets in our politically correct world. Date a queen-sized woman and you'll find out how true it is. You'll see the way people look at her, and look at you for being with her. You'll try to buy her lingerie for Valentine's Day and realize the sizes stop before she starts. Every time you go out to eat you'll watch her agonize, balancing what she wants against what she'll let herself have, what she'll let herself have against what she'll be seen eating in public.

And what she'll let herself say.

I remember when the Monica Lewinsky story broke and C., a newspaper reporter, wrote a passionate defense of the White House intern who'd been betrayed by Linda Tripp in Washington, and betrayed even worse by her friends in Beverly Hills, who were busily selling their high-school memories of Monica to *Inside Edition* and *People* magazine. After her article was printed, C. got lots of hate mail, including one letter from a guy who began: "I can tell by what you wrote that you are overweight and that nobody loves you." And it was that let-ter—that word—that bothered her more than anything else anyone said. It seemed that if it were true—the "overweight" part—then the "nobody loves you" part would have to be true as well. As if being Lewinsky-esque was worse than being a betrayer, or even someone who was dumb. As if being fat were somehow a crime.

Loving a larger woman is an act of courage in this world, and maybe it's even an act of futility. Because, in loving C., I knew I was loving someone who didn't believe that she herself was worthy of anyone's love.

And now that it's over, I don't know where to direct my anger and my sorrow. At a world that made her feel the way she did about her body—no, herself—and whether she was desirable. At C., for not being strong enough to overcome what the world told her. Or at myself, for not loving C. enough to make her believe in herself.

I wept straight through Celebrity Weddings, slumped on the floor in front of the couch, tears rolling off my chin and soaking my shirt as one tissue-thin supermodel after another said "I do." I cried for Bruce, who had understood me far more than I'd given him credit for and maybe had loved me more than I'd deserved. He could have been everything I'd wanted, everything I'd hoped for. He could have been my husband. And I'd chucked it.

And I'd lost him forever. Him and his family—one of the things I'd loved best about Bruce. His parents were what June and Ward would have been if they were Jewish and living in New Jersey in the nineties. His father, who had perpetually whiskered cheeks and eyes as kind as Bruce's, was a dermatologist. His family was his delight. I don't know how else to say it, or how much it astonished me. Given my experience with my own dad, watching Bernard Guberman was like looking at an alien from Mars. *He actually likes his child!* I would marvel. *He really wants to be with him! He remembers things about Bruce's life!* That Bernard Guberman seemed to like me, too, might have had less to do with his feelings about me as a person and more to do with my being a), Jewish, and hence a marriage prospect; b), gainfully employed, and thus not an overt gold digger; and c), a source of happiness for his son. But I didn't care why he was so nice to me. I just basked in his kindness whenever I could.

Bruce's mother, Audrey, had been the tiniest bit intimdating, with manicured fingernails painted whatever shade I'd be reading about in *Vogue* the next month, and perfectly styled hair, and a house full of glass and wall-to-wall white carpeting and seven bathrooms, each kept immaculately clean. The Ever-Tasteful Audrey, I called her to my friends. But once you got past the manicure, Audrey was nice, too. She'd been trained as a teacher, but by the time I met Audrey her working-for-a-living days were long past and she was a full-time wife, mother, and volunteer—the perenniel PTA mom, Cub Scout leader, and Hadassah president, the one who could always be counted on to organize the synagogue's annual food drive or the Sisterhood's winter ball.

The downside of parents like that, I used to think, was that it killed your ambition. With my divorced parents and my college debts I was always scrambling for the next rung on the ladder, the next job, the next freelance assignment; for more money, more recognition, for fame, insofar as you could be famous when your job was telling other people's stories. When I started at a small newspaper in the middle of nowhere, covering car crashes and sewage board meetings, I was desperate to get to a bigger one, and when I finally got to a bigger one, I wasn't there two weeks before I was already plotting how to move on.

Bruce had been content to drift through graduate school, picking up a teaching assignment here, a freelance writing gig there, making approximately half of what I did, letting his parents pick up the tab for his car insurance (and his car, for that matter), and "help" with his rent and subsidize his lifestyle with $100 handouts every time he saw them, plus jaw-droppingly generous checks on birthdays, Chanukah, and sometimes just because. "Slow down," he'd tell me, when I'd slip out of bed early to work on a short story, or go into work on a Saturday to send out query letters to magazine editors in New York. "You need to enjoy life more, Cannie."

I thought sometimes that he liked to imagine himself as one of the lead characters in an early Springsteen song—some furious, passionate nineteen-year-old romantic, raging against the world at large and his father in particular, looking for one girl to save him. The trouble was, Bruce's parents had given him nothing to rebel against—no numbing factory job, no stern, judgmental patriarch, certainly no poverty. And a Springsteen song lasted only three minutes, including chorus and theme and thundering guitar-charged climax, and never took into account the dirty dishes, the unwashed laundry and unmade bed, the thousand tiny acts of consideration and goodwill that actually maintaining a relationship called for. My Bruce preferred to drift through life, lingering over the Sunday paper, smoking high-quality dope, dreaming of bigger papers and better assignments without doing much to get them. Once, early in our relationship, he'd sent his clips to the *Examiner,* and gotten a curt "try us in five years" postcard in response. He'd shoved the letter in a shoebox, and we'd never discussed it again.

But he was happy. "Head's all empty, I don't care," he'd sing to me, quoting the Grateful Dead, and I'd force a smile, thinking that my head was never empty and that if it ever was, you could be darn sure I'd care.

And what had all my hustle gotten me, I mused, now slurping the boozy slush straight from the bowl. What did it matter. He didn't love me anymore.

I woke up after midnight, drooling on the couch. There was a pounding in my head. Then I realized it was someone pounding at the door.

"Cannie?

I sat up, taking a moment to locate my hands and my feet.

"Cannie, open this door right now. I'm worried about you."

My mother. Please God no.

"Cannie!"

I curled tight onto the couch, remembering that she'd called me in the morning, a million years ago, to tell me she'd be in town that night for Gay Bingo, and that she and Tanya would stop by when it was over. I got to my feet, flicking off the halogen lamp as quietly as I could, which wasn't very quietly, considering that I managed to knock the lamp over in the process. Nifkin howled and scrambled onto the armchair, glaring at me reproachfully. My mother started pounding again.

"Cannie!"

"Go 'way," I called weakly. "I'm . . . naked."

"Oh, you are not! You're wearing your overalls, and you're drinking tequila, and you're watching *The Sound of Music*."

All of which was true. What can I say? I like musicals. I especially like *The Sound of Music*—particularly the scene where Maria gathers the motherless Von Trapp brood onto her bed during the thunderstorm and sings "My Favorite Things." It looked so cozy, so safe—the way my own family had been, for a minute, once upon a time, a long time ago.

I heard a muttered consultation outside my door—my mother's voice, then another, in a lower register, like Marlboro smoke filtered through gravel. Tanya. She of the sling and the crab leg.

"Cannie, open up!"

I struggled back into a sitting position and heaved myself into the bathroom, where I flicked on the light and stared at myself, reviewing the situation, and my appearance. Tear-streaked face, check. Hair, light brown with streaks of copper, cut in a basic bob and shoved behind my ears, also present. No makeup. Hint—well, actuality—of a double chin. Full cheeks, round, sloping shoulders, double D-cup breasts, fat fingers, thick hips, big ass, thighs solidly muscled beneath a quivering blanket of lard. My eyes looked especially small, like they were trying to hide in the flesh of my face, and there was something avid and hungry and desperate about them. Eyes exactly the color of the ocean in the Menemsha harbor in Martha's Vineyard, a beautiful grapey green. My best feature, I thought ruefully. Pretty green eyes and a wry, cockeyed smile. "Such a pretty face," my grandmother would say, cupping my chin in her hand, then shaking her head, not even bothering to say the rest.

So here I am. Twenty-eight years old, with thirty looming on the horizon. Drunk. Fat. Alone. Unloved. And, worst of all, a cliché, Ally McBeal and Bridget Jones put together, which was probably about how much I weighed, and there were two determined lesbians banging on my door. My best option, I decided, was hiding in the closet and feigning death.

"I've got a key," my mother threatened.

I wrested the tequila bowl away from Nifkin. "Hang on," I yelled. I picked up the lamp and opened the door a crack. My mother and Tanya stared at me, wearing identical L.L. Bean hooded sweatshirts and expressions of concern.

"Look," I said. "I'm fine. I'm just sleepy, so I'm going to sleep. We can talk about this tomorrow."

"Look, we saw the *Moxie* article," said my mother. "Lucy brought it over."

Thank you, Lucy, I thought. "I'm fine," I said again. "Fine, fine, fine, fine."

My mother, clutching her bingo dauber, looked skeptical. Tanya, as usual, just looked like she wanted a cigarette, and a drink, and for me and my siblings never to have been born, so that she could have my mother all to herself and they could relocate to a commune in Northampton.

"You'll call me tomorrow?" my mother asked.

"I'll call," I said, and closed the door.

My bed looked like an oasis in the desert, like a sandbar in the stormy sea. I lurched toward it, flung myself down, on my back, my arms and legs splayed out, like a size-sixteen starfish stapled to the comforter. I loved my bed—the pretty light blue down comforter, the soft pink sheets, the pile of pillows, each in a bright slipcover—one purple, one orange, one pale yellow, and one cream. I loved the Laura Ashley dust ruffle and the red wool blanket that I'd had since I was a girl. Bed, I thought, was about the only thing I had going for me right now, as Nifkin bounded up and joined me, and I stared at the ceiling, which was spinning in a most alarming way.

I wished I'd never told Bruce I wanted a break. I wished I'd never met him. I wished that I'd kept running that night, just kept running and never looked back.

I wished I wasn't a reporter. I wished that my job was baking muffins in a muffin shop, where all I'd have to do was crack eggs and measure flour and make change, and nobody could abuse me, and where they'd even expect me to be fat. Every flab roll and cellulite crinkle would serve as testimony to the excellence of my baked goods.

I wished I could trade places with the guy who wore the "FRESH SUSHI" sandwich board and walked up and down Pine Street at lunch hour, handing out sushi coupons for World of Wasabi. I wished I could be anonymous and invisible. Maybe dead.

I pictured myself lying in the bathtub, taping a note to the mirror, taking a razor blade to my wrists. Then I pictured Nifkin, whining and looking puzzled, scraping his nails against the rim of the bathtub and wondering why I wasn't getting up. And I pictured my mother having to go through my things and finding the somewhat battered copy of *Best of Penthouse Letters* in my top dresser drawer, plus the pink fur-lined handcuffs Bruce had given me for Valentine's Day. Finally, I pictured the paramedics trying to maneuver my dead, wet body down three flights of stairs. "We've got a big one here," I imagined one of them saying.

Okay. So suicide was out, I thought, rolling myself into the comforter and arranging the orange pillows under my head. The muffin shop/sandwich board scenario, while tempting, was probably not going to happen. I couldn't see how to spin it in the alumni magazine. Princeton graduates who stepped off the fast track tended to own the muffin shops, which they would then turn into a chain of successful muffin shops, which would then go public and make millions. And the muffin shops would only be a diversion for a few years, something to do while raising their kids, who would invariably appear in the alumni magazine clad in eensy-beansy black-and-orange outfits with "Class of 2012!" written on their precocious little chests.

What I wanted, I thought, pressing my pillow hard against my face, was to be a girl again. To be on my bed in the house I'd grown up in, tucked underneath the brown and red paisley comforter, reading even though it was past my bedtime, hearing the door open and my father walk inside, feel him standing over me silently, feeling the weight of his pride and his love like it was a tangible thing, like warm water. I wanted him to put his hand on my head the way he had then, to hear the smile in his voice when he'd say, "Still reading, Cannie?" To be little, and loved. And thin. I wanted that.

I rolled over, groped for my nightstand, grabbed a pen and paper. *Lose weight,* I wrote, then stopped and thought. *Find new boyfriend,* I added. *Sell screenplay. Buy large house with garden and fenced yard. Find mother more acceptable girlfriend.* Somewhere between writing *Get and maintain stylish haircut* and thinking *Make Bruce sorry,* I finally fell asleep.

Good in bed. Ha! He had a lot of nerve, putting his name on a column about sexual expertise, given how few people he'd even been with, and how little he'd known before he'd met me.

I had slept with four people—three long-term boyfriends and one ill-considered freshman year fling—when Bruce and I hooked up, and

I'd fooled around extensively with another half-dozen. I might've been a big girl, but I'd been reading *Cosmopolitan* since I was thirteen, and I knew my way around the various pieces of equipment. At least I'd never had any complaints.

So I was experienced. And Bruce . . . wasn't. He'd had a few harsh turn-downs in high school, when he'd had really bad skin, and before he'd discovered that pot and a ponytail could reliably attract a certain kind of girl.

When he'd shown up that first night, with his sleeping bag and his plaid shirt, he wasn't a virgin, but he'd never been in a real relationship, and he'd certainly never been in love. So he was looking for his lady fair, and I, while not averse to stumbling into Mr. Right, was mostly looking for . . . well, call it affection, attention. Actually, call it sex.

We started off on the couch, sitting side by side. I reached for his hand. It was ice-cold and clammy. And when I casually slung an arm over his shoulder, then eased my thigh against his, I could feel him shaking. Which touched me. I wanted to be gentle with him, I wanted to be kind. I took both of his hands in mine and tugged him off the couch. "Let's lie down," I said.

We walked to my bedroom hand in hand, and he lay on my futon, flat on his back, his eyes wide open and gleaming in the dark, looking a bit like a man in a dentist's chair. I propped myself up on my elbow and let the loose ends of my hair trail gently across his cheek. When I kissed the side of his neck he gasped as if I'd burned him, and when I eased one hand inside his shirt and gently tugged at the hair on his chest, he sighed, "Ah, Cannie," in the tenderest voice I'd ever heard.

But his kisses were horrible, slobbery things, all bludgeoning tongue and lips that felt as if they were somehow collapsing when they met mine, so that I was left with a choice between teeth and mustache. His hands were stiff and clumsy. "Lie still," I whispered.

"I'm sorry," he whispered back unhappily. "I'm all wrong, aren't I?"

"Shh," I breathed, my lips against his neck once more, the tender skin right where his beard ended. I slid one hand down his chest, lightly feathered it over his crotch. Nothing doing. I pressed my breasts into his side, kissed his forehead, his eyelids, the tip of his nose, and tried again. Still nothing. Well, this was curious. I decided to show him a trick, to teach him how to make me happy whether he could get hard or not. He moved me enormously, this six-foot-tall guy with a ponytail and a look on his face like I might electrocute him instead of . . . this. I wrapped both of my legs around one of his, took his hand, and slid it into my panties. His eyes met mine and he smiled when he felt how wet I was. I put his fingers where I needed them, with my hand over his, pressing his fingers against myself, showing him what to do, and I moved against him, letting him feel me sweat and breathe hard and moan when I came. And then I pressed my face into his neck again, and moved my lips up to his ear. "Thank you," I whispered. I tasted salt. Sweat? Tears, maybe? But it was dark, and I didn't look.

We fell asleep in that position: me, wearing just a T-shirt and panties, wrapped around him; him, with only his shirt unbuttoned, only halfway, still in underwear, sweatpants, socks. And when the light crept through my windows, when we opened our eyes and looked at each other, it felt like we had known each other much longer than just one night. As if we could never have been strangers. "Good morning," I whispered.

"You're beautiful," he said.

I decided that I could get used to hearing that in the mornings. Bruce decided that he was in love. We were together for the next three years, and we learned things with each other. Eventually, he told me the whole story, about his limited experience, about always being either drunk or stoned and always very shy, about how he'd been turned down a few times his first year in college and just decided to be patient. "I knew I'd meet the right girl someday," he said, smiling at me, cradling me close. We figured it out—the things he liked, the things I liked, the things we both liked. Some of it was straightforward. Some of it would have been raunchy enough to raise eyebrows even in *Moxie*, where they ran regular features on new "sizzling sexy secrets!"

But the thing that galled me, that chewed at my heart as I tossed and turned, feeling clammy and cotton-mouthed from the previous night's tequila binge, was the column's title. "Good in Bed." It was a lie. It wasn't that he'd been some kind of sexual savant, a boy wonder under the sheets . . . it was that we had loved each other, once. We'd been good in bed together.

TWO

I woke up on Saturday morning to the sound of the telephone. Three rings, then silence. A ten-second pause, then three more rings, followed by more silence. My mother was not a fan of answering machines, so if she either knew or believed that I was home, she'd just keep calling until I picked up. Resistance was futile.

"This is so obnoxious," I said, in lieu of "hello."

"This would be your mom," said my mother.

"I'm shocked. Could you call me back later? Please? It's very early. I'm very tired."

"Oh, quit whining," she said briskly. "You're just hung over. Pick me up in an hour. We'll go to the cooking demonstration at Reading Terminal."

"No," I said. "Absolutely not." Knowing, even as I said it, that I could protest and complain and come up with seventeen different excuses, and, come noon, I'd still be in the Reading Terminal, cringing as my mother offered a high-volume play-by-play critique of the hapless chef's menu selection and cooking skills.

"Drink some water. Take some aspirin," she said. "I'll see you in an hour."

"Ma, please . . ."

"I'm assuming you read Bruce's article," she said. My mother is not big on elaborate transitions.

"Yeah," I said, knowing, without having to ask, that she had, too. My sister Lucy, a charter subscriber to *Moxie* and eager reader of any and all things related to femininity, still had her copy delivered to our house. After last night's door-pounding debacle, I could only assume that she'd pointed it out to my mother . . . or that Bruce had. The very thought of that conversation—"I'm just calling to let you know that I had an article published this month and I think Cannie's pretty upset by it"—made me want to hide under the bed. If I could even fit. I didn't want to walk around in a world where *Moxie* was on the newsstands, in mailboxes. I felt scalded by shame, like I was wearing a gigantic crimson C., like everyone who saw me would know that I was the girl from "Good in Bed," and that I was fat and that I'd dumped some guy who'd tried to understand and love me.

"Well, I know you're upset. . . ."

"I'm not upset," I snapped. "I'm fine."

"Oh," she said. This, obviously, was not the response she was expecting. "I thought it was kind of crummy of him."

"He's a crummy guy," I said.

"He wasn't a crummy guy. That's why it was so surprising."

I slumped against my pillows. My head hurt. "Are we going to debate his crumminess now?"

"Maybe later," said my mother. "I'll see you soon."

There are two kinds of houses in the neighborhood where I grew up— the ones where the parents stayed married, and the ones where they didn't.

Given only a cursory glance, both kinds of houses look the same— big, rambling, four- and five-bedroom colonials set well back from the sidewalk-less streets, each on an acre of land. Most are painted conservative colors, with contrasting shutters and trim—a slate-gray house with blue shutters, for example, or a pale beige house with a red door. Most have long driveways, done in gravel, and many have in-ground pools out back.

But look closer—or, better yet, stay a while—and you'll start to see the difference.

The divorce houses are the ones where the Chem-Lawn truck doesn't stop anymore, the ones the plowing guy drives past on the mornings after winter storms. Watch, and you'll see either a procession of sullen-faced teenagers, or sometimes even the lady of the house, emerge to do the raking, mowing, shoveling, trimming, themselves. They're the houses where Mom's Camry or Accord or minivan doesn't get replaced every year, but just keeps getting older and older, and where the second car, if there is one, is more likely some fourth-hand piece of automotive detritus purchased from the *Examiner*'s classified ads than the time-honored stripped-down but brand-new Honda Civic or, if the kid's really lucky, Dad's cast-off midlife crisis sports car.

There's no fancy landscaping, no big pool parties in the summer, no construction crews making a racket at seven A.M. adding on that new home office or master bedroom suite. The paint job lasts for four or five years instead of two or three, and is more than a little bit flaky by the time it gets redone.

But mostly, you could tell on Saturday mornings, when what my friends and I dubbed the Daddy Parade began. At about ten or eleven o'clock every other Saturday, the driveways up and down our street, and the neighboring streets, would fill with the cars of the men who used to live in these big four- and five-bedroom houses. One by one, they'd exit their cars, trudge up the walkways, ring the bells of the homes where they used to sleep, and collect their kids for the weekends. The days, my friends would tell me, would be full of every kind of extravagance—shopping excursions, trips to the mall, the zoo, the circus, lunch out, dinner out, a movie before and after. Anything to keep the time passing, to fill the dead minutes between children and parents who suddenly had very little to say to each other once they'd got done either mouthing pleasantries (in the cordial no-fault cases) or spitting vitriol (in the contested cases, where the parents paraded each other's shortcomings and infidelities in front of a judge—and, by extension, in front of a gossipy public, and, eventually, their children as well).

My friends all knew the drill. My brother and sister and I did it a few times in the early days of my parents' split, before my father announced that he wanted to be less like a father, more like an uncle, and that our weekend visits didn't fit in with his vision. Saturday nights would be spent on a pullout bed in his condo across town—a small, dusty space full of too much expensive stereo equipment and top-of-the-line TVs, and either too many pictures of the children, or, eventually, none at all. At my dad's place Lucy and I would huddle on the thin mattress of the pullout couch, feeling the metal frame poke us all night long, while Josh would sleep beside us in a sleeping bag on the floor. Meals would be taken in restaurants exclusively. Few of the newly single dads had the skills to cook, or the desire to learn. Most of them, it turned out, were just waiting for a replacement wife or girlfriend to come along, to stock the refrigerators and have dinner waiting every night.

And on Sunday morning, in time for church or Hebrew school, the parade would begin again, only in reverse: the cars pulling up and disgorging the kids, who'd hustle up the driveway trying not to run or look too relieved, and the fathers trying not to drive away too fast, trying to remember that this was supposed to be a pleasure, not a duty. For two years, three years, four years they'd come. Then they'd vanish—remarried, mostly, or moved away.

It wasn't that bad, really—not third-world bad, not Appalachia bad. There was no physical pain, no real hunger. Even with the drop in the standard of living, the suburbs of Philadelphia were still a damn sight better than the way most people in the world—or the country—lived. Even if our cars were older and our vacations less lavish and our in-ground swimming pools less than pristine, we still had cars, and vacations, pools in the backyards, and roofs over our heads.

And the mothers and children learned how to lean on each other. Divorce taught us how to deal with stuff, whether it was reduced circumstances, or what to say when the Girl Scout leader asked what you'd like to bring to the Father/Daughter banquet. ("A father," was the preferred answer.) My girlfriends and I learned to be flippant and tough, a posse of junior cynics, all before we hit sixteen.

I always wondered, though, what the fathers felt as they drove up the street they used to drive down every night, and whether they really saw their former houses, whether they noticed how things got frayed and flaky around the edges now that they were gone. I wondered it again as I pulled up to the house I'd grown up in. It was, I noticed, looking even more Joad-like than usual. Neither my mother nor the dread life partner, Tanya, was much into yard work, and so the lawn was littered with drifts of dead brown leaves. The gravel on the driveway was as thin as an old man's hair combed across an age-spotted scalp, and as I parked I could make out the faint glitter of old metal from behind the little toolshed. We used to park our bikes in there. Tanya had "cleaned" it by dragging all the old bikes, from tricycles to discarded ten-speeds, out behind the shed, and leaving them there to rust. "Think of it as found art," my mother had urged us when Josh complained that the bike pile made us look like trailer trash. I wonder if my father ever drove by, if he knew about my mother and her new situation, if he thought about us at all, or whether he was content to have his three children out there in the world, all grown up, and strangers.

My mother was waiting in the driveway. Like me, she's tall, and heavy (a Larger Woman, I heard Bruce's voice taunt in my head). But whereas I am an hourglass (an extremely full hourglass), my mother is shaped like an apple—a round midsection on toned and muscular legs. A former high-school standout in tennis, basketball, and field hockey, and the current star of the Switch Hitters (her inevitable lesbian softball team), Ann Goldblum Shapiro has retained both the carriage and the sensibilities of a onetime jock, a woman who believes there's no problem that can't be solved, and no situation that can't be improved, by a good brisk walk or a few laps in the pool.

She wears her hair short and lets it stay gray and dresses in comfortable clothes in shades of gray and beige and pale pink. Her eyes are the same green as mine, but wider and less anxious, and she smiles a lot. She's the kind of person who's constantly being approached by strangers—for directions, for advice, for honest assessments of whether bathing suits made the would-be wearer's butt look big in the communal dressing room at Loehmann's.

Today, she was dressed for our outing in wide-legged pale pink sweatpants, a blue turtleneck sweater, one of her fourteen pairs of activity-specific sneakers, and a windbreaker accented with a small triangular, rainbow-colored pin. She wore no makeup—she never wore it—and her hair was in its usual air-dried spikes. She looked happy as she climbed into the car. For her, the free cooking demonstrations at Philadelphia's premiere downtown food market *cum* meeting place were better than standup comedy. They weren't intended to be participatory, but nobody bothered to tell her that.

"Subtle," I said, pointing at her pin.

"You like?" she asked, oblivious. "Tanya and I picked them up in New Hope last weekend."

"Did you get me one?" I asked.

"No," she said, refusing to take the bait. "We got you this." She handed me a small rectangle wrapped in purple tissue paper. I unwrapped it at a red light, to find a magnet depicting a cartoon girl with squiggly curled hair and glasses. "I'm not gay, but my mother is," it read. Perfect.

I fiddled with the radio and kept quiet during the half hour drive back to town. My mother sat quietly beside me, obviously waiting for me to bring up Bruce's latest opus. On the way into the Terminal, in between the vegetable vendor and the fresh fish counter, I finally did.

"Good in bed," I snorted. "Hah!"

My mother gave me a sideways glance. "So I take it he wasn't?"

"I don't want to be having this conversation with you," I grumbled, as we worked our way past the bakeries and the Thai and Mexican food stalls and found seats in front of the demonstration kitchen. The chef—a semiregular I remembered from the Southern Favorites lesson three weeks before—blanched as my mother sat down.

She shrugged at me, and stared at the blackboard. This week it was American Classics with Five Easy Ingredients. The chef launched into his spiel. One of his assistants—a gangly, pimply kid from The Restaurant School—started hacking away at a head of cabbage. "He's going to cut his finger off," my mother predicted.

"Shh!" I said, as the front-row regulars—mostly senior citizens who took these sessions way too seriously—scowled at us.

"Well, he is," said my mother. "He's holding the knife all wrong. Now, getting back to Bruce . . ."

"I don't want to talk about it," I said. The chef melted a gigantic glob of butter in a pan. Then he added bacon. My mother gasped as if she'd witnessed a beheading, and raised her hand.

"Is there a heart-healthy modification for this recipe?" she inquired. The chef sighed and started talking about olive oil. My mother returned her attention to me. "Forget Bruce," she said. "You can do better."

"Mother!"

"Shh!" hissed the front-row foodies. My mother shook her head. "I can't believe this."

"What?"

"Would you look at the size of that pan? That pan's not big enough." Sure enough, the chef-in-training was cramming way too much imperfectly chopped cabbage into a shallow frying pan. My mother raised her hand. I yanked it down.

"Just let it go."

"How's he going to learn anything if nobody tells him when he's making a mistake?" she complained, squinting at the stage. "That's right," agreed the woman sitting next to her.

"And if he's going to dredge the chicken in that flour," my mother continued, "I really think he needs to season it first."

"You ever try cayenne pepper?" asked an elderly man in the row ahead. "Not too much, you understand, but just a pinch gives it a really nice flavor."

"Thyme's nice, too," said my mother.

"Okay, Julia Child." I closed my eyes, slumping lower in my folding chair as the chef moved on to candied sweet potatoes and apple fritters, and my mother continued to quiz him about substitutions, modifications, techniques that she'd learned in her years as a homemaker, while offering running commentary to the bemusement of the people sitting near her and the fury of the entire front row.

Later, over cappuccinos and hot buttered pretzels from the Amish pretzel stand, she gave me the speech I was sure she'd been preparing since last night. "I know your feelings are hurt right now," she began. "But there are a lot of guys out there."

"Yeah, right," I muttered, keeping my eyes on my cup.

"Women, too," my mother continued helpfully.

"Ma, how many times do I have to tell you? I'm not a lesbian! I'm not interested."

She shook her head in mock sadness. "I had such high hopes for you," she fake-sighed, and pointed toward one of the fish stalls, where pike and carp were stacked on top of each other, open-mouthed and googly-eyed, their scales gleaming silver under the lights. "This is an object lesson," she said.

"This is a fish stall," I corrected.

"This is telling you that there are plenty of fish in the sea," she said. She walked over and tapped one fingernail on the glass case. I followed her reluctantly. "You see that?" she said. "Think of each one of those fish as a single guy."

I stared at the fish. The fish, stacked six high on the crushed ice, seemed to gape back. "They have better manners," I observed. "Some of them are probably better conversationalists, too."

"You want fish?" asked a short Asian woman in a floor-length rubber apron. She had a filleting knife in one hand. I thought, briefly, about asking to borrow it, and what it would feel like to gut Bruce. "Good fish," she urged.

"No thanks," I said. My mother led me back to the table.

"You shouldn't be so upset," she said. "That article will be lining birdcages by next month. . . ."

"What an uplifting thought to share with a journalist," I said.

"Don't be sarcastic," she said.

"I don't have any other way to be." I sighed.

We sat down again. My mother picked up her coffee cup. "Is it because he got a job at a magazine?" she ventured.

I took a deep breath. "Maybe," I acknowledged. And it was true, seeing Bruce's star rise while mine just stayed in place would have hurt even if his first story hadn't been about me.

"You're doing fine," said my mother. "Your day will come."

"What if it doesn't?" I demanded. "What if I never get another job, or another boyfriend. . . ."

My mother waved her hand dismissively, as if this was too silly to even consider.

"But what if I don't?" I asked raggedly. "He's got this column, he's writing a novel. . . ."

"He says he's writing a novel," said my mother. "Doesn't mean it's true."

"I'm never going to meet anyone else," I said flatly.

My mother sighed. "You know, I think some of this is my fault," she finally said.

That got my attention.

"When your father used to say things . . ."

This was definitely a turn I didn't want the conversation to take. "Mom . . ."

"No, no, Cannie, let me finish." She took a deep breath. "He was awful," she said. "Mean and awful, and I let him get away with way too much, and I let it go on for too long."

"Water under the bridge," I said.

"I'm sorry," said my mother. I had heard her say this before, of course, but it hurt every time, because every time it made me remember just what she was apologizing for, and how bad it had been. "I'm sorry because I know it's what's made you this way."

I stood up, grabbing her cup and mine, our used napkins, the remains of the pretzels, and headed off to find a garbage can. She followed behind me. "Made me how?" I asked.

She thought about it. "Well, you're not great with criticism."

"Tell me about it."

"You don't seem very comfortable with how you look."

"Show me a woman who is," I shot back. "It's just that not all of us get to enjoy having our insecurities exploited for millions of *Moxie* readers."

"And I wish . . ." She looked ruefully toward the tables at the center of the market, where families were gathered, having sandwiches or coffee, passing sections of the *Examiner* back and forth. "I wish you believed in yourself more. Like with . . . romantic stuff."

Yet another conversation I didn't want to be having with my late-in-life-lesbian mother.

"You'll find the right guy," she said.

"I've been underwhelmed by the choices so far."

"You stayed with Bruce too long. . . ."

"Ma, please!"

"He was a nice guy. But I knew you didn't love him that way."

"I thought you were out of the heterosexual advice-giving arena."

"I'm making a special guest appearance on an as-needed basis," she said cheerfully. Outside, by the car, she gave me a rough hug—a big step for her, I knew. My mother is a great cook, a sympathetic listener, and a good judge of character, but she's never been big on touchy-feely stuff. "I love you," she said, which was also out of character for her. But I wasn't going to object. I needed all the love I could get.

THREE

On Monday morning I sat in a waiting room full of women too big to cross their legs, all of us wedged into inadequate armchairs on the seventh floor of the University of Philadelphia Weight and Eating Disorders Center, thinking that if I ran the place I'd make sure to have couches.

"A few surveys," the smiling, skinny secretary behind the desk had said, handing me a half-inch thick slab of forms, a clipboard, and a pen. "There's breakfast," she added chirpily, pointing at a stack of desiccated bagels, a tub of fat-free cream cheese, and a pitcher of orange juice with a thick film of pulp floating on the top. Like anyone would eat in here, I thought, bypassing the bagels and sitting down with my forms beneath a poster that read "Taking it off . . . one day at a time!" and depicted a model in a leotard romping through a field full of flowers, which was not something I planned on doing, no matter how skinny I got.

Name. That was easy. Height. No problem. Current weight. Ack. Lowest weight maintained as an adult. Did fourteen count as an adult? Reason for wanting to lose weight. I thought for a minute, than scribbled, *Was humiliated in national publication.* I thought for a minute, than added, *Would like to feel better about myself.*

Next page. Diet history. Highest weights, lowest weights, programs I'd enrolled in, how much I'd lost, how long I'd kept it off. "Please use reverse side if more space is needed," read the form. I needed. In fact, judging from a quick glance around the room, everybody needed. One woman even had to ask for extra paper.

Page three. Parents' weights. Grandparents' weights. Siblings' weights. I took guesses for all of them. These weren't things that were discussed around the table at family gatherings. Did I binge and purge, fast, abuse laxatives, exercise compulsively? If I did, I thought, would I look like this?

Please list your five favorite restaurants. Well, this would be easy. I could just walk down my street and pass five fabulous places to eat—everything from spring rolls to tiramisu before I'd gone three blocks. Philadelphia still lived in the shadow of New York City and often had the character of a sulky second sister who'd never made the honor roll or the homecoming court. But our restaurant renaissance was for real, and I lived in the neighborhood that boasted the first crêperie, the first soba noodle shop, and the first drag show dinner theater (so-so female impersonators, divine calamari). We also had the obligatory two coffee shops per block, which had hooked me on three-dollar lattes and chocolate-chip scones. Not, I knew, the breakfast of champions, but what was a girl to do, except try to compensate by avoiding the cheesesteak shops on every corner? Plus which, Andy, the one real friend I'd made at the paper, was the food critic, whom I often accompanied on review meals, eating foie gras and rabbit rillettes and veal and venison and pan-seared sea bass at the finest restaurants in town while Andy murmured into the microphone wire running through his collar.

Five favorite foods. Now this was getting tricky. Desserts, in my opinion, were an entirely separate category from main dishes, and breakfast was another thing altogether, and the five best things I could cook bore no relation to the five best things I could buy. Mashed potatoes and roast chicken were my go-to comfort foods, but could I really compare them to the chocolate tarts and crème brûlée from the Parisian bakery on Lombard Street? Or the grilled stuffed grape leaves at Viet Nam, the fried chicken at Delilah's, and the brownies from Le

Bus? I scribbled, crossed out, remembered the chocolate bread pudding at the Silk City Diner, heated and with fresh whipped cream, and had to start again.

Seven pages of physical history. Did I have a heart murmur, high blood pressure, glaucoma? Was I pregnant? No, no, and a thousand times no. Six pages of emotional history. Did I eat when I was upset? Yes. Did I eat when I was happy? Yes. Would I be tearing through those bagels and that funky-looking cream cheese at this very moment, were it not for the present company? You betcha.

On to the psychology pages. Was I frequently depressed? I circled *sometimes*. Did I have thoughts of suicide? I winced, then circled *rarely*. Insomnia? No. Feelings of worthlessness? Yes, even though I knew I wasn't worthless. Did I ever fantasize about cutting off fleshy or flabby areas of my body? What, doesn't everyone? Please add any additional thoughts. I wrote, *I am happy with every aspect of my life except my appearance.* Then I added, *And my love life.*

I laughed a little bit. The woman stuffed into the seat next to mine gave me a tentative smile. She was wearing one of those outfits I always thought of as fat-lady chic: leggings and a tunic top in a soft, periwinkle blue, with silk-screened daisies across her chest. A beautiful outfit, and not cheap, either, but play clothes. It's as if the fashion designers decided that once a woman hit a certain weight, she'd have no need for business suits, for skirts and blazers, for anything except glorified sweatsuits, and they tried to apologize for dressing us like overaged Teletubbies by silk-screening daisies on the tops.

"I'm laughing to keep from crying," I explained.

"Gotcha," she said. "I'm Lily."

"I'm Candace. Cannie."

"Not Candy?"

"I think my parents decided not to give the kids on the playground any extra ammunition," I said. She smiled. She had glossy black hair twisted back with lacquered chopstick-y things, and diamond studs the size of cocktail peanuts in her ears.

"Do you think this will work?" I asked. She shrugged her thick shoulders.

"I was on phen-fen," she said. "I lost eighty pounds." She reached into her purse. I knew what was coming. Regular women carry pictures of their babies, their husbands, their summer houses. Fat ladies carry pictures of themselves at their skinniest. Lily showed me the full-figure view, in a black suit, and then the side profile, in a miniskirt and sweater. Sure enough, she looked terrific. "Phen-fen," she said, and sighed gigantically. Her bosom looked like something governed by tides and gravity, not mere human will. "I was doing so great," she said. Her eyes took on a faraway look. "I was never hungry. It was like flying."

"Speed'll do that to you," I observed.

Lily wasn't listening. "I cried the day they took it off the market. I tried and tried, but I gained everything back in, like, ten minutes." She narrowed her eyes. "I would kill to get more phen-fen."

"But . . . ," I said hesitantly. "Wasn't it supposed to cause heart problems?"

Lily snorted. "Given a choice between being this big and being dead, I swear I'd have to think about it. It's ridiculous! I could walk down two blocks and buy crack cocaine on the corner, but I can't get phen-fen for love or money."

"Oh." I couldn't think of anything else to say.

"You never tried phen-fen?"

"No. Just Weight Watchers."

That brought a chorus of complaints and rolled eyes from the women sitting around me.

"*Weight* Watchers!"

"That's a crock."

"Expensive crock."

"Standing in line so some skinny thing can weigh you. . . ."

"And those scales were never right," said Lily, to a chorus of enthusiastic *uh-huhs!* The size six behind the desk was looking worried. Fat lady insurrection! I grinned, imagining us surging down the hall, a righteous, stretch-pant-wearing army, tipping over the scales, toppling the blood-pressure machine, tearing the height-weight charts off the walls and making all the skinny clinicians eat them, while we feasted on bagels and fat-free cream cheese.

"Candace Shapiro?"

A tall doctor with an extremely deep voice was calling my name. Lily squeezed my hand.

"Good luck," she whispered. "And if he's got any samples of phen-fen in there, grab 'em!"

The doctor was fortyish, thin (of course), and going gray at the temples, with a warm handshake and big brown eyes. He was also extremely tall. Even in my thick-soled Doc Martens I barely came up to his shoulders, which meant he had to be at least six and a half feet. His name sounded like Dr. Krushelevsky, only with more syllables. "You can call me Dr. K," he said, in his absurdly deep, absurdly slow voice. I kept waiting for him to drop what I took for a misguided Barry White impression and talk normally, but he didn't, so I guessed that basso profundo was the way he did talk. I sat, holding my purse against my chest, while he flipped through my forms, squinting at a few answers, laughing out loud at others. I looked around, trying to relax. His office was nice. Leather couches, a comfortably cluttered desk, a real-looking Oriental rug covered with piles of books, papers, magazines, and a television/VCR in one corner, a small refrigerator with a coffee machine perched on top in another. I wondered if he'd ever slept there . . . if maybe the couch unfolded into a bed. It looked like the kind of place you'd want to stay in.

"Humiliated in national publication?" he read out loud. "What happened?"

"Ugh," I said. "You don't want to know."

"No, really. I do. I think that's the most unusual answer anyone's ever given."

"Well, my boyfriend . . ." I winced. "Ex-boyfriend. Excuse me. He's writing this column for *Moxie*. . . ."

"Good in Bed?" asked the doctor.

"Why, yes, I like to think so."

The doctor blushed. "No . . . I mean . . ."

"Yeah, that's the column Bruce writes. Don't tell me you read it," I said, thinking, if some fortysomething diet doctor had seen it, I could pretty much assume that everyone else in my life had, too.

"I actually clipped it out," he told me. "I thought our patients might enjoy it."

"What? Why?"

"Well, it was actually a fairly sensitive appreciation of . . . of . . ."

"A fat lady?"

The doctor smiled. "He never called you that."

"Just everything but."

"So you're in here because of the article?"

"Partly."

The doctor looked at me.

"Okay, mostly. It's just, I don't . . . I never thought of myself . . . that way. As a larger woman. I mean, I know I am . . . larger . . . and I know I should lose weight. I mean, it's not like I'm blind, or oblivious to the culture, and how Americans expect women to look . . ."

"So you're here because of America's expectations?"

"I want to be thin." He looked at me, waiting. "Well, thinner, any-how."

He flipped through my forms. "Your parents are overweight," he said.

"Well . . . kind of. My mom's a little heavy. My father, I haven't seen in years. He had kind of a belly when he left, but . . ." I paused. The truth was, I didn't know where my father was living, and it was always awkward when it came up. "I have no idea what he looks like now."

The doctor looked up. "You don't see him?"

"No."

He scribbled a note. "How about your siblings?"

"Both skinny." I sighed. "I'm the only one who got hit with the fat stick."

The doctor laughed. "Hit with the fat stick. I've never heard it put quite that way."

"Yeah, well, I got a million more of 'em."

He flipped some more. "You're a reporter?"

I nodded. He flipped back. "Candace Shapiro . . . I've seen your byline."

"Really?" This was a surprise. Most civilians skipped right over the bylines.

"You write about television sometimes." I nodded. "You're very funny. Do you like your job?"

"I love my job," I said, and meant it. When I wasn't obsessing over the high-pressure, in-the-public-eye nature of being a reporter, or scrapping for good assignments with territorial coworkers, and entertaining dreams of the muffin shop, I managed to have a good time. "It's really fun. Interesting, challenging . . . all those things."

He wrote something down in the folder. "And do you feel like your weight affects your job performance . . . how much money you make, how far you've advanced?"

I thought for a minute. "Not really. I mean, sometimes, some of the people I interview . . . you know, they're thin, I'm not, I get a little jealous, maybe, or wonder if they think I'm lazy or whatever, and then I have to be careful when I write the articles, not to let the way I'm feeling affect what I say about them. But I'm good at my job. People respect me. Some of them even fear me. And it's a union paper, so financially I'm okay."

He laughed, and kept flipping, slowing at the psychology page.

"You were in therapy last year?"

"For about eight weeks," I said.

"May I ask what for?"

I thought for a minute. There is no easy way to say to someone you'd just met that your mother had announced, at fifty-six, that she was gay. Especially not to someone who sounded like a thin, white James Earl Jones, and would probably be so tickled he'd repeat it out loud. Possibly even more than once.

"Family things," I finally said.

He just looked at me.

"My mother was . . . in a new relationship, that was moving very quickly, and it kind of freaked me out."

"And did the therapy help?"

I thought of the woman my HMO assigned me to, a mousy woman with Little Orphan Annie curls who wore her glasses chained around her neck and seemed a little bit afraid of me. Maybe hearing about the newly lesbian mother and my absent father within the first five minutes of taking my history was more than she'd planned on. She always had this vaguely cringing look, as if she feared that at any moment I would charge across her desk, knock her box of Kleenex to the floor, and try to throttle her.

"I guess so. The therapist's main point was that I can't change things other people in my family do, but I can change how I react to them."

He scratched something in my folder. I tried to do a subtle lean so I could make some of it out, but he had the page tilted at a difficult angle. "Was that good advice?"

I shuddered inwardly, remembering how Tanya moved in six weeks after she and my mother had started dating, and her first act of residence was to move all of the furniture out of what had been my bedroom and replace it with her rainbow-striped sun catchers and self-help books, plus her two-ton loom. By way of saying thanks, she wove Nifkin a small striped sweater. Nifkin wore it once, then ate it.

"I guess so. I mean, the situation's not perfect, but I'm sort of getting used to it."

"Well, good," he said, and flipped my folder closed. "Here's the thing, Candace."

"Cannie," I said. "They only call me Candace when I'm in trouble."

"Cannie, then," he said. "We're running a year-long study of a drug called sibutramin, which works somewhat the way phen-fen did. Did you ever take phen-fen?"

"No," I said, "but there's a lady in the lobby who misses it sorely."

He smiled again. He had, I noticed, a dimple in his left cheek. "I consider myself warned," he said. "Now, sibutramin's a lot milder than phen-fen, but it does the same thing, which is basically to fool your brain into thinking that you're full longer. The good news is, it doesn't have the same health risks and potential complications that have been associated with phen-fen. We're looking for women who are at least thirty percent above their ideal weight . . ."

". . . and you're delighted to inform me that I qualify," I said sourly.

He smiled. "Now, the studies that have been done already show patients losing between five and ten percent of their body weight in a year's time."

I did some quick calculations. Losing ten percent of my body weight was still not going to put me anywhere near the weight I wanted to be.

"Does that disappoint you?"

Was he kidding? It was so frustrating! We had the technology to replace hearts, to put septuagenarians on the moon, to give old geezers erections, and the best modern science could do for me was a lousy ten percent?

"I guess it's better than nothing," I said.

"Ten percent is a lot better than nothing," he said seriously. "Studies show that even losing as little as eight pounds can have a dramatic effect on blood pressure and cholesterol."

"I'm twenty-eight years old. My blood pressure and cholesterol are fine. I'm not worried about my health." I heard my voice rising. "I want to be thin. I need to be thin."

"Candace . . . Cannie . . ."

I took a deep breath and rested my forehead in my hands. "I'm sorry."

He put his hand on my arm. It felt nice. It was probably something they'd taught him to do in medical school: If patient becomes hysterical at prospect of relatively minute weight loss, place one hand gently on forearm. . . . I moved my arm away.

"Look," he said. "Realistically, given your heredity, and your frame, it may be that you were just never meant to be a thin person. And that's not the worst thing in the world."

I didn't lift my head. "Oh, no?"

"You're not sick. You're not in any pain. . . ."

I bit my lip. He had no idea. I remember when I was fourteen or so, on summer vacation somewhere by the beach, walking down a sidewalk with my sister, my slender sister, Lucy. We were wearing baseball caps and shorts and bathing suits and flip-flops. We were eating ice-cream cones. I could close my eyes and see the way my tanned legs looked against my white shorts, the sensation of the ice cream melting on my tongue. A kindly-looking white-haired lady had approached us with a smile. I thought she'd say something like how we reminded her of her granddaughters, or made her miss her own sister and the fun they'd had together. Instead, she nodded at my sister, walked up to me, and pointed at the ice cream cone. "You don't need that, dearie," she'd said. "You should be on a diet." I remembered things like that. A lifetime's accretion of unkindnesses, all of those little lingering hurts that I carried around like stones sewn into my pockets. The price you paid for being a Larger Woman. *You don't need that.* Not in pain, he'd said. What a joke.

The doctor cleared his throat. "Let's talk about motivation for a minute."

"Oh, I'm very motivated." I lifted my head, managed a small, crooked smile. "Can't you tell?"

He smiled back. "We're also looking for people who have the right kind of motivation." He shut my folder and crossed his hands over his nonexistent belly. "You probably know this already, but people who have the best long-term success with weight management decide to lose weight for themselves. Not for their spouses, or their parents, or because their high-school reunion's coming up, or they're embarrassed over something that somebody wrote."

We stared at each other silently.

"I'd like to see," he said, "if you can come up with some reasons to lose weight, other than the fact that you're angry and upset right now."

"I'm not angry," I said angrily.

He didn't smile. "Can you think of other reasons?"

"I'm miserable," I blurted. "I'm lonely. Nobody's going to date me looking like this. I'm going to die alone, and my dog's going to eat my face, and no one will find us until the smell seeps out under the door."

"I find that highly unlikely," he said with a smile.

"You don't know my dog," I said. "So am I in? Do I get drugs? Can I have some now?"

He smiled at me. "We'll be in touch." I stood up. He pulled a stethoscope around his neck and patted the examining table. "They'll draw some blood on your way out. I just need to listen to your heart for a minute. Hop up here for me, please."

I sat up straight on the crinkly white paper on top of the table and closed my eyes as his hands moved against my back. The first time a man had touched me with any regard or kindness since Bruce. The thought made my eyes fill. Don't do it, I thought fiercely, don't cry now.

"Breathe in," Dr. K. said calmly. If he had any idea what was going on, he didn't let on. "Nice deep breath . . . and hold it . . . and let it out."

"Is it still there?" I asked, staring at his head, bent over, as he wedged the stethoscope beneath my left breast. And then, before I could stop myself, "Does it sound broken?"

He straightened up, smiling. "Still there. Not broken. In fact, it sounds like you have a strong and healthy heart." He offered his hand. "I think you're going to be fine," he said. "We'll be in touch."

Out in the lobby, Lily the daisy-shirt woman was still wedged into her chair, half of a plain bagel balanced on one knee. "So?" she asked.

"They're going to let me know," I said. There was a piece of paper in her hand. I was unsurprised to see that it was a Xeroxed copy of "Loving a Larger Woman" by Bruce Guberman. "You seen this?" she asked me.

I nodded.

"This is great," she said. "This guy really gets it." She shifted as much as her seat would allow and looked me right in the eye. "Can you imagine the idiot who'd let someone like this get away?"

FOUR

I think every person who is single should have a dog. I think the government should step in and intervene: If you're not married or coupled up, whether you've been dumped or divorced or widowed or whatever, they should require you to proceed immediately to the pound nearest you and select an animal companion.

Dogs give your days a rhythm and a purpose. You can't sleep ridiculously late, or stay out all day and all night, when there's a dog depending on you.

Every morning, no matter what I'd drunk, what I'd done, or whether or not my heart had been broken, Nifkin woke me up by gently applying his nose to my eyelids. He is a remarkably understanding little dog, willing to sit patiently on the couch with his paws crossed gracefully in front of him while I sang along to *My Fair Lady* or clipped recipes from *Family Circle*, which I subscribed to even though, as I liked to joke, I had neither family nor circle.

Nifkin is a small and neatly made rat terrier, white with black spots and brown markings on his long, spindly legs. He weighs precisely ten pounds and looks like an anorexic and extremely high-strung Jack Russell, with a Doberman pinscher's ears, pointing permanently upright, tacked onto his head. He's a secondhand dog. I inherited him from three sportswriters I knew at my first paper. They were renting a house, and they decided that a house required a dog. So they got Nifkin from the pound believing that he was actually a Doberman pinscher puppy. Of course, he was no such thing . . . just a full-grown rat terrier with oversized ears. Truthfully, he looks like pieces of a few different dogs that someone put together as a joke. And he's got a permanent, Elvis-like sneer on his face—the result, the story goes, from when his mother bit him when he was a puppy. But I refrain from remarking on his shortcomings when he's within earshot. He's also very sensitive about his looks. Just like his mother.

The sportswriters spent six months alternately showering him with attention, letting him lap beer out of his water bowl, or leaving him penned up in their kitchen, completely ignored, all the while waiting for him to grow into his Doberman pinscher-hood. Then one of them got a job at the *Fort Lauderdale Sun-Sentinel,* and the other two decided to split up and move to their own apartments. Neither one wanted to take along anxious little Nifkin, who did not in any way resemble a Doberman pinscher.

Employees could run free classified ads in the paper, and their ad, "One dog, small, spotted, free to a good home" ran for two weeks with no takers. Desperate, with their bags packed and security deposits already paid on their new places, the sportswriters double-teamed me in the company cafeteria. "It's you or the pound again," they said.

"Is he housebroken?"

They exchanged an uneasy look. "Kind of," said one. "For the most part," said the other.

"Does he chew things?"

Another uneasy look. "He likes rawhide," said one. The other one kept his mouth shut, from which I inferred that Nifkin probably also enjoyed shoes, belts, wallets, and anything else that came his way.

"And has he learned to walk on a leash, or is he still pulling all the time? And do you think he'd answer to something other than Nifkin?"

The guys looked at each other. "Look, Cannie," one of them finally said, "you know what happens to dogs in the pound . . . unless they can convince somebody else that he's a Doberman pinscher. And that's unlikely."

I took him in. And, of course, Nifkin spent the first months of our time together pooping furtively in a corner of the living room, chewing a hole in my couch, and acting like a spastic rabbit whenever his leash was attached to his collar. When I moved to Philadelphia I decided that things would be different. I put Nifkin on a rigorous schedule: a walk at 7:30 A.M., another one at 4 P.M., for which I paid the kid next door $20 a week, then a brief constitutional before I went to sleep. We did six months of obedience boot camp, after which point he'd pretty much stopped chewing, was thoroughly housebroken, and was generally content to walk politely beside me, unless a squirrel or a skateboarder distracted him. For his progress, he was allowed on the furniture. He sat beside me on the couch while I watched TV, and slept curled up on a pillow next to my head every night.

"You love that dog more than me," Bruce would complain, and it was true that Nifkin was spoiled rotten, with all manner of fluffy toys, rawhide bones, small fleece sweaters, and gourmet treats, and, I am embarrassed to say, a small dog-size sofa, upholstered in the same denim as my couch, where he sleeps when I'm at work. (It was also true that Bruce had no use for Nifkin, and couldn't be bothered to walk him. I'd come home from the gym, or a bike ride, or a long day at work, to find Bruce sprawled on my couch—frequently with his bong nearby—and Nifkin perched, quivering, on one of the pillows, looking as if he were going to explode. "Has he been out?" I'd ask, and Bruce would shrug shamefacedly. After this happened a dozen times or so I just quit asking). Nifkin's picture is my screen saver at work, and I subscribe to the online newsletter *Ratter Chatter,* although I've managed to refrain from sending in his picture—so far.

In bed together, Bruce and I used to make up stories about Nifkin's history. I was of the opinion that Nifkin had been born into a well-to-do British family, but that his father had disowned him after catching him in a compromising position in the hayloft with one of the stable boys, and banished him to America.

"Maybe he worked as a window dresser," Bruce had mused, cupping one hand over my head.

"Hand hat," I cooed, and snuggled into him. "I'll bet he hung out at Studio 54."

"He probably knew Truman."

"And he'd wear custom-made suits, and carry a cane."

Nifkin looked at both of us as if we were nuts, then strolled off to the living room. I tilted my head up for a kiss, and Bruce and I were off to the races again.

But as much as I'd rescued Nifkin from the sportswriters, the classified ads, and the pound, he had rescued me, too. He kept me from being lonely, he gave me a reason to get up every morning, and he loved me. Or maybe he just loved the fact that I had opposable thumbs and could work a can opener. Whatever. When he laid his little muzzle next to my head at night and sighed and closed his eyes, it was enough.

The morning after my appointment at the weight management clinic I hitched Nifkin to his extend-o-leash, tucked a plastic Wal-Mart bag into my right pocket, four small dog biscuits and a tennis ball into my left. Nikfin was jumping about crazily, caroming from my couch to his couch, down the hall to the bedroom and back again at warp speed, pausing only to dart a lick toward my nose. Every morning, to him, is a celebration. Yay! he seems to say. It's morning! I love morning! Morning! Let's go for a walk! I finally got him out the door, but he kept prancing at my side as I fished my sunglasses out of my pocket and put them on. We proceeded down the street, Nifkin practically dancing, me dragging behind.

The park was almost empty. Just a pair of golden retrievers sniffing at the bushes, and a haughty cocker spaniel in the corner. I unleashed my dog, who promptly and without provocation made a beeline for the cocker spaniel, barking frantically.

"Nifkin!" I hollered, knowing that as soon as he got within a foot or two of the other dog he'd stop, give a deep, disdainful sniff, perhaps bark a few more times, and then leave the other dog alone. I knew that, Nifkin knew that, and it was more than likely that the cocker spaniel knew it, too (it's been my experience that other dogs mostly ignore the Nif when he goes into his attack mode, probably because he's very small and not all that menacing, even when he's trying). But the dog's owner looked alarmed as he saw a spotted, sneering rat terrier missile streaking toward his pet.

"Nifkin!" I called again, and my dog for once listened to me, stopping dead in his tracks. I hurried over, trying to look dignified, and scooped Nifkin into my arms, holding him by his scruff, looking into his eyes and saying, "No," and "Bad," the way I'd learned in Remedial Obedience. Nifkin whined and looked disgruntled at having his fun interrupted. The cocker spaniel wagged his tail hesitantly.

The cocker spaniel guy was looking amused.

"Nifkin?" he asked. I could see he was getting ready to pop the question. I wondered if he'd have the nerve. I made myself a bet that he would.

"Do you know what a nifkin is?" he asked. Score 1, Cannie. A nifkin, according to my brother's fraternity friends, is the area between a guy's balls and his ass. The sportswriters had named him.

I put on my best puzzled look. "Huh? It's his name. Does it mean something?"

The guy blushed. "Uh, yeah. It's, um . . . it's kind of a slang term."

"For what?" I asked, trying to look innocent. The guy shuffled his feet. I looked at him expectantly. So did Nifkin.

"Um," said the guy, and stopped. I decided to have mercy.

"Yes, I know what a nifkin is," I said. "He's a secondhand dog." I gave him the abbreviated version of the sportswriter story. "And by the time I figured out what a nifkin was, it was too late. I tried calling him Nifty . . . and Napkin . . . and Ripken . . . and, like, everything else I could think of. But he won't respond to anything but Nifkin."

"That is rough," said the guy, laughing. "I'm Steve," he said.

"I'm Cannie. What's your dog's name?"

"Sunny," he said. Nifkin and Sunny sniffed each other tentatively as Steve and I shook hands.

"I just moved here, from New York," he said. "I'm an engineer. . . ."

"Family in town?"

"Nope. The single guy." He had nice legs. Tanned, slightly furry.

And those dumb Velcro-strapped sandals that everyone was wearing that summer. Khaki shorts, a gray T-shirt. Cute.

"Would you like to have a beer maybe sometime?" he asked.

Cute, and evidently not averse to the sweaty, queen-size woman.

"Sure. That'd be great."

He smiled at me from under his baseball cap. I gave him my number, trying not to get my hopes up, but feeling pleased with myself nonetheless.

Back home, I gave Nifkin a cup of Small Bites kibble, ate my Special K, then gargled, flossed, and took deep, calming breaths, preparing for my interview with Jane Sloan, lady director extraordinaire who I'd be profiling for next Sunday's paper. In deference to her fame, and because we'd be lunching at the *très chic* Four Seasons, I took extra care with my clothes, struggling into both a panty girdle and control-top pantyhose. Once my midsection was secured, I pulled on my ice-blue skirt, ice-blue jacket with funky star-shaped buttons, the requisite chunky black loafers, uniform shoe of twentysomething would-be hipsters. I prayed for strength and composure, and for Bruce's fingers to be broken in some bizarre industrial accident guaranteeing that he'd never write again. Then I called a cab, grabbed my notebook, and headed to the Four Seasons for lunch.

I cover Hollywood for the *Philadelphia Examiner*. This is not as easy as you'd think, because Hollywood is in California, and I, alas, am not.

Still, I persist. I write about trends, about gossip, the mating habits of stars and starlets. I do reviews, and even the occasional interview with the handful of celebrities who deign to stop by the East Coast on their promotional juggernauts.

I wandered into journalism after graduating from college with an English degree and no real plans. I wanted to write. Newspapers were one of the few places I could locate that would pay me to do it. So, the September after graduation, I was hired at a very small newspaper in central Pennsylvania. The average age of a reporter was twenty-two. Our combined years of professional experience were less than two years, and boy, did it show.

At the *Central Valley Times*, I covered five school districts, plus assorted fires, car crashes, and whatever features I could find time to churn out. For this I was paid the princely sum of $300 a week— enough to live on, just barely, if nothing went wrong. And of course, something was always going wrong.

Then there were the wedding announcements. The *CVT* was one of the last newspapers in the country that still ran, free of charge, lengthy descriptions of weddings—and, woe to me, of wedding dresses. Princess seams, alençon lace, French embroidery, illusion veils, beaded headpieces, gathered bustles . . . all of these were terms I found myself typing so often that I put them on a save-get key. Just one key- stroke, and out would pop complete phrases: *freshwater pearl embroidery*, or *ivory taffeta pouf*.

One day I was wearily typing the wedding announcements and musing on the injustice of it all when I came across a word I couldn't read. Many of our brides filled their forms in by hand. This particular bride had written in looping cursive, in purple ink, a word that looked like CFORM.

I carried the form over to Raji, another cub reporter. "What's this say?"

He squinted at the purple. "C-FORM," he read slowly. "Like MDOS, or something."

"For a dress, though?"

Raji shrugged. He'd grown up in New York City, then attended Columbia Journalism School. The ways of Central Pennsylvanians were strange to him. I headed back to my desk; Raji went back to his dread chore, typing in a week's worth of school lunch menus. "Tater Tot," I heard him sigh. "Always, the Tater Tot."

Which left me with C-FORM. Under "contact for questions" the bride had scribbled her home phone number. I picked up the phone, and dialed.

"Hello?" answered a cheerful-sounding woman.

"Hello," I said, "this is Candace Shapiro calling from the *Valley Times*. I'm trying to reach Sandra Garry. . . ."

"This is Sandy," chirped the woman.

"Hi, Sandy. Listen, I do the wedding announcements here, and I'm reading your form and there's a word . . . C-FORM?"

"Seafoam," she answered promptly. In the background I could hear a kid screaming, "Ma!" and what sounded like a soap opera on TV. "That's the color of my dress."

"Oh," I said, "well, that's what I needed to know, so thanks. . . ."

"Except, well, maybe . . . I mean, do you think people will know what seafoam is? Like, what do you think of when you think of seafoam?"

"Green?" I ventured. I really wanted to get off the phone. I had three baskets of laundry reposing in the trunk of my car. I wanted to get out of the office, go to the gym, wash my clothes, buy some milk. "Like a pale green, I guess."

Sandy sighed. "See, that's not it," she said. "It's really more blue, I think. The girl at the Bridal Barn said the color's called seafoam, but that's really more of a green-sounding thing, I think."

"We could say blue," I said. Another sigh from Sandy. "Light blue?" I essayed.

"See, but it's not really blue," she said. "You say blue, and people think, you know, blue like the sky, or navy blue, and it's not, like, dark or anything . . ."

"Pale blue?" I offered, running through my bridal announcement-gleaned gamut of synonyms. "Ice blue? Robin's egg blue?"

"I just don't think any of those are quite right," Sandy said primly.

"Hmm," I said. "Well, if you want to think about it and call me back . . ."

Which was when Sandy started to cry. I could hear her sobbing on the other end of the phone as the soap opera droned in the background and the child, who I imagined, had sticky cheeks and possibly a stubbed toe, continued to whine, "Ma!"

"I want it to be right," she said between her sobs. "You know, I waited so long for this day . . . I want everything to be perfect . . . and I can't even say what color my dress is. . . ."

"Oh, now," I said, feeling ridiculously ineffectual. "Oh, listen, it's not that bad. . . ."

"Maybe you could come here," she said, still crying. "You're a reporter, right? Maybe you could look at the dress and say what's right."

I thought of my laundry, my plans for the night.

"Please?" asked Sandy, in a tiny, pleading voice.

I sighed. The laundry could wait, I supposed. And now I was curious. Who was this woman, and how did someone who couldn't spell seafoam find love?

I asked her for directions, mentally cursed myself for being such a softie, and told her I'd be there in an hour.

To be perfectly honest, I was expecting a trailer park. Central Pennsylvania has plenty of those. But Sandy lived in an actual house, a small white Cape Cod with black shutters and the proverbial picket fence out front. The backyard boasted a plastic orange SuperSoaker, an abandoned Big Wheel, a new-looking swingset. There was a shiny black truck parked in the driveway, and Sandy stood at the door— thirtyish, tired-looking around her eyes, but with a tremulous species of hope there, too. Her hair was pale blond, fine as spun sugar, and she had the tiny snub nose and wide cornflower-blue eyes of a painted figurine.

I got out of the car with my notebook in my hand. Sandy smiled through the screen door. I could see two small hands clutching her thigh, a child's face peeping around her leg, then vanishing behind it.

The house was cheaply furnished, but neat and clean, with stacks of magazines on the pine-veneer coffee table: *Guns & Ammo, Road & Track, Sport & Field*. The ampersand collection, I thought to myself. Powder-blue wall-to-wall carpet lined the living room floor; fresh white linoleum—the kind you roll down in a single sheet, with patterns stamped on it to make it look like separate tiles—covered the kitchen. "Do you want a soda? I was just about to have one myself," she said shyly.

I didn't want soda. I wanted to see the dress, come up with an adjective, hit the road, and be good & gone by the time *Melrose Place* was on. But she seemed desperate, and I was thirsty, so I sat down at her kitchen table under the stitched sampler that read "Bless This Home," with my notebook at my side.

Sandy took a gulp of her drink, burped gently against the back of her hand, closed her eyes, and shook her head. "Excuse me, please."

"Are you nervous about the wedding?" I asked.

"Nervous," she repeated, and laughed a little. "Honey, I'm terrified!"

"Is it . . ." I wanted to tread carefully here, "have you done the whole wedding thing before?"

Sandy shook her head. "Not like this. My first time I eloped. That was when I found out I was pregnant with Trevor. Justice of the peace over in Bald Eagle," she said. "I wore my prom dress to that one."

"Oh," said I.

"Second time," she continued, "there never was a wedding at all. That was Dylan's daddy, who I guess you could call my common-law husband. We were together seven years."

"Dylan, that's me!" piped up a little voice from underneath the table. A small, sleek blond head peeked out. "My daddy's in the army."

"That's right, honey," said Sandy, absently tousling Dylan's hair with one hand. She raised her eyebrows significantly toward me, shook her head, and whispered, "J-a-i-l."

"Oh," I said again.

"For stealing cars," she whispered. "Not anything, you know, too bad. I actually met Bryan, my fiancé, when I went visiting Dylan's dad," she said.

"So Bryan's . . ." I was just starting to learn how the long pause could sometimes be a reporter's best friend.

"Going to be paroled tomorrow," Sandy said. "He was in for fraud."

Which, I guessed from the pride in her voice, was a step up even from grand theft auto.

"So you met him in prison?"

"We were actually corresponding for some time before then," Sandy said. "He put an ad in the classified section . . . here, I saved it!"

She hopped up, causing our soda glasses to rattle, and came up with a laminated piece of paper no bigger than a postage stamp. "Christian gentleman, tall, athletic build, Leo, seeks sensitive pen-pal for letters and maybe more," it read.

"He got twelve responses," Sandy said, beaming. "He said he liked my letter the best."

"What did you tell him?"

"I was real honest," she said. "I explained my situation. How I was a single mother. How I wanted a role model for my boys."

"And you think . . ."

"He'll be a good daddy," she said. She sat down again, staring into her glass like it contained the mysteries of the ages instead of flat generic cola. "I believe in love," she said, her voice strong and clear.

"Did your parents . . ." I began. She waved one hand in the air, as if to shoo away the very idea.

"My father left when I was four, I think," she said. "Then it was just my mom and one boyfriend after another. Daddy Rick, Daddy Sam, Daddy Aaron. I swore it wasn't gonna go that way for me. And it's not," she said. "I think . . . I know . . . that this time I got it right."

"Mom?" Dylan was back, his lips dyed Kool-Aid red, holding his brother's hand. Where Dylan was small and fine-boned and blond, this boy—Trevor, I guessed—was darker and sturdier, with a thoughtful look on his face.

Sandy stood up and shot me a tentative smile. "You wait right here," she said. "Boys, you come with me. Let's show the reporter lady momma's pretty dress!"

After all of that—the prison, the husbands, the Christian classified ad—I was prepared for something dreadful, some off-the-rack horror show of a dress. The Bridal Barn specialized in those.

But Sandy's dress was beautiful. Tightly fitted on top, a fairytale princess boned bodice spangled with snowflake-sized crystals that caught the light, a deeply scooped neckline that showed off the creamy skin of her chest, swelling into a wave of tulle that swished around her feet. Her cheeks were flushed, her blue eyes sparkled. She looked like Cinderella's fairy godmother, like Glinda the good witch. Trevor held her hand solemnly as she made her way into the kitchen, humming "Here Comes the Bride." Dylan had appropriated her veil and popped it on his own head.

Sandy stood under the kitchen light and twirled. The edge of her skirt whispered along the floor. Dylan laughed and clapped his hands, and Trevor stared up at his mother, how her bare arms and shoulders rose out of the dress, how her hair fell against her skin. She twirled and twirled and her sons stared at her as if they were under a spell, until finally she stopped. "What do you think?" she asked. Her cheeks were flushed, and she was breathing hard. I could see each breath make her bosom swell against the tight-fitted scalloped edges of the bodice. She turned once more, and I could see tiny cloth rosebuds stitched all down the back, tight as a baby's pursed lips. "Is it blue? Green?"

I looked at her for a long moment, her pink cheeks and milky skin, and her sons' delighted eyes.

"I'm actually not sure," I said. "But I'll figure something out."

I missed the deadline, of course. The city editor was long gone by the time I made it back to the newsroom, after Sandy had shown me her pictures of Bryan, and told me all about their honeymoon plans, after I'd watched her read her sons *Where the Wild Things Are,* and kiss their foreheads and their cheeks, and add a finger's worth of bourbon to her soda, and half as much to mine. "He's a good man," she'd said dreamily. Her lit cigarette moved through the room like a firefly.

I had three inches to fill, and I had to write to fit, write only enough to fill the allotted space beneath the blurry picture of Sandy's smiling face. I sat at my computer, my head spinning a little, and keyed up my fill-in-the-blank marriage form, the one with spaces: bride's name, groom's name, attendants' names, description of dress. Then I pressed the "escape" key, cleared the screen, took a deep breath, and wrote:

Tomorrow Sandra Louise Garry will marry Bryan Perreault in Our Lady of Mercy Church on Old College Road. She will walk down the aisle with antique rhinestone combs in her hair and will promise to love and to honor and cherish Bryan, whose letters she keeps folded beneath her pillow, each one read so many times it's worn thin as a butterfly's wing.

"I believe in love," she says, even though a cynic might say there's every indication that she shouldn't. Her first husband left her, her second is in jail—the same jail where she met Bryan, whose parole begins two days before the wedding. In his letters, he calls her his little dove, his perfect angel. In her kitchen, the last of the three cigarettes she allows herself each night burning between her fingers, she says he is a prince.

Her sons, Dylan and Trevor, will attend the bride. Her dress is a color called seafoam, a color perfectly balanced between the palest blue and the palest green. It isn't white, a color for a virgin, a teenager with her head full of sugar-spun romances, or ivory, which is white tinged with resignation. Her dress is the color of dreams.

Well. A little florid, a little overwritten and overwrought. A dress the color of dreams? The whole thing had "Recent Graduate of College Creative Writing Workshop" stamped on every syllable. The next morning I came to work and there was a copy of the page splayed over my keyboard, the offending passage circled in red copy-editor's grease-paint pencil. "SEE ME," said the two-word message scrawled in the margin, in the unmistakable hand of Chris, the executive editor, an easily distractible Southerner who'd been lured to Pennsylvania with the promise of moving on to a bigger, better paper in the chain (that, plus unparalleled trout fishing). I knocked timidly at his office door. He beckoned me inside. A second copy of my story was opened on his desk.

"This," he said, pointing with one spindly finger. "What was this, exactly?"

I shrugged. "It was just . . . well, I met this woman. I was typing her announcement and there was a word I couldn't read, so I called her, then I met her, and then . . ." My voice trailed off. "I guess I thought it sounded like a story."

He looked up at me. "You were right," he said. "Want to do it again?"

And a star was born . . . well, sort of. Every other week I'd find a bride and write a short column about her—who she was, her dress, the church and the music and the party afterward. But most of all, I wrote about *how*: how my brides decided to get married, to stand up in front of a minister or rabbi or justice of the peace and promise forever.

I saw young brides and old brides, blind and deaf brides, teenage brides pledging themselves to their first loves and cynical twentysome-things taking vows with the men they called their baby's fathers. I attended first, second, third, fourth, and a single fifth wedding. I saw eight-hundred-guest extravangazas (an Orthodox wedding, where the men and women danced in separate ballrooms and there were a total of eight rabbis in attendance, all wearing Tina Turner–style glitter wigs by the end of the night). I saw a couple get married in adjoining hospital beds after a car accident that had left her a quadriplegic. I saw a bride left at the altar, watched her face crumple when the best man, his face pale and grave, made his way down the aisle and whispered, first into her mother's ear, and then into hers.

It was ironic, I knew, even then. While my peers were writing hip, sarcastic first-person columns for nascent online magazines about being single in the nation's big cities, I was toiling at a little local newspaper—a dinosaur, quivering on the tar pit of extinction in the evolutionary scale of the media—investigating marriage, of all things. How quaint! How charming!

But I couldn't have written about myself the way my classmates did, even if I'd wanted to. The truth was, I didn't have the brio to chronicle my own sex life. Nor did I have the kind of body I'd be com-fortable exposing, even in print. And sex didn't interest me the way marriage did. I wanted to understand how to be part of a couple, how to get brave enough to take someone's hand and leap across the chasm. I would take each bride's story, each halting narrative of how they met and where they went and when they knew, and turn them over and over in my mind, looking for the loose thread, the invisible seam, the crack I could pry open so I could turn the story inside out and figure out the truth.

If you read that little paper in the early 1990s, you could probably see me at the edges of a hundred different wedding pictures, in the blue linen dress that I wore—plain, so as not to call attention to myself, but dressy, in deference to the solemnity of the occasion. See me in the aisle seats, my notebook tucked into my pocket, staring at a hundred different brides—old, young, black, white, thin, not thin—looking for answers. How do you know when a guy is the right guy? How can you be sure enough to promise someone forever and mean it? How can you believe in love?

After two-and-a-half years of the wedding beat, my clips happened to cross the right editor's desk at the precise moment that my home-town's big daily paper, the *Philadelphia Examiner,* had, as an institution, decided that attracting Generation X readers was of utmost importance, and that a young reporter would, by her very existence, draw those readers in. So they invited me to move back to the city of my birth and be their eyes and ears on twentysomething Philadelphia.

Two weeks later, the *Examiner* decided as an institution that attracting Generation X readers mattered not a whit, and went back to desperately trying to shore up circulation among soccer moms in the suburbs. But the damage had been done. I'd been hired. Life was good. Well, mostly.

From the start, the single biggest drawback to my job was Gabby Gardiner. Gabby is a massive, ancient woman, with a cap of bluish-tinged white curls and smeary, thick glasses. If I'm big, she's super-size. You'd think we would enjoy some solidarity because of our shared oppression, our common struggle to survive in a world that deems any woman above a size twelve grotesque and laughable. You would think wrong.

Gabby is the entertainment columnist for the *Philadelphia Examiner* and has filled that post, as she's fond of reminding me and anyone else within earshot, "for longer than you've been alive." This is both her strength and her weakness. She's got a network of contacts that spans both coasts and two decades. Unfortunately, those decades were the 1960s and 1970s. She stopped paying attention somewhere between Reagan's election and the advent of cable, so there's a whole universe of stuff, from MTV on down, that simply doesn't register on her radar the way, say, Elizabeth Taylor does.

Gabby's age could be anywhere from sixty on up. She has no children, no husband, no discernible hint of sexuality or hint of any life at all outside of the office. Her lifeblood is Hollywood gossip, and her attitude toward her subjects is rarely anything less than reverential. She talks about the stars she covers, mostly thirdhand, in reprinted bits of regurgitated gossip from the New York City tabloids and *Variety,* as if they are her intimates, her friends. Which would be pathetic if Gabby Gardiner were the least little bit likable. And she's not.

She is, however, lucky. Lucky that most of the *Examiner's* readers are over forty and not interested in learning anything new, so her "Gabbing with Gabby" column remains one of the most popular parts of our section—another fact that she frequently remarks upon, at top volume (allegedly she shouts because she's deaf, but I'm convinced that she does it because it's more annoying than simply talking).

For my first few years at the *Examiner* we left each other alone. Unfortunately, things escalated last summer, when Gabby took a two-month leave to address some nasty-sounding medical problem ("polyps" was the only word I caught, before Gabby and her friends shot me laser-beam hate looks, and I scurried out of the mailroom without even having retrieved my copy of *Teen People)*. In her absence, I got to write her daily column. She lost the war, but won the battle: They kept calling the damn thing "Gabbing with Gabby," appending a short note in an embarrassingly small font about how Gabby was "on assignment" and that *"Examiner* staff writer Candace Shapiro is filling in."

"Good luck, kid," Gabby had said grandly, waddling over to my desk for her farewell, beaming as if she hadn't spent the past two weeks lobbying for the editors to run wire copy instead of giving me a chance while she was off, presumably being de-polyped. "Now, I told all my best sources to call you."

Terrific, I thought. Hot gossip about Walter Cronkite. Can't wait.

That should have been the end of it, but it wasn't. Every morning, Monday through Friday, I could look forward to my daily call from Gabby.

"Ben Affleck?" she'd rasp. "What's a Ben Affleck?"

Or, *Comedy Central?* Nobody watches it."

Or, pointedly, "Saw something on Elizabeth on *ET* last night. Why didn't we have it?"

I tried to ignore her—to be pleasant on the phone and every once in a while, when she got particularly crabby, to toss in a line about "Gabby Gardiner will return at the end of September" at the end of the column.

But then one morning she called and I wasn't there to pick up my phone, so Gabby got my voice mail, which was basically me saying, "Hello, you've reached Candace Shapiro, entertainment columnist at the *Philadelphia Examiner.*" I didn't realize my misstep until the paper's executive editor stopped by my desk.

"Have you been telling people you're the entertainment columnist?" he asked.

"No," I said. "I'm not. I'm just filling in."

"I got a very irate call from Gabby last night. Late last night," he emphasized, with the expression of a man who did not appreciate having his sleep interrupted. "She thinks you're giving people the impression that she's gone for good and you've taken over."

Now I was confused. "I don't know what she's talking about."

He sighed again. "Your voice mail," he said. "I don't know what it says, and, frankly, I don't want to know what it says. Just fix it so Gabby isn't waking up my wife and kids anymore."

I went home and wept to Samantha ("She's completely insecure," she observed, and passed me a pint of half-melted sorbet as I moped on her couch). I raged on the phone to Bruce ("Just change the damn thing, Cannie!"). So I took his advice, altering my voice mail to say, "You've reached Candace Shapiro, temporary, transient, impermanent, just-filling-in, in-no-way-here-for-good entertainment columnist." Gabby called the next morning. "Love the message, kid," she said.

But the damage was done. When Gabby returned from her break

she took to calling me "Eve"—as in *All About*—when she spoke to me at all. I just tried to ignore her, and focus on my extracurricular activities: short stories, scraps of a novel, and *Star Struck,* the screenplay I'd been laboring over for months. *Star Struck* was a romantic comedy about a big-city reporter who falls for one of the stars she interviews. They meet cute (after she falls off a bar stool ogling him at the hotel bar), get off on the wrong foot (after he assumes she's just another plus-size groupie), fall for each other, and, after the appropriate Act Three complications, end up in each other's arms as the credits roll.

The star was based on Adrian Stadt, a cute comedian on *Saturday Night!* whose sense of humor seemed in sync with my own—even when he was doing his memorable three-month stint as the Projectile Vomiting Pilot. He was the guy I'd watched all through college and beyond and thought, if he were here, or if I were there, we'd probably get along. The reporter, of course, was me, only I named her Josie, made her a redhead, and gave her stable, straight, still-married parents.

The screenplay was what I'd pinned my dreams on. It was my answer to all of my good grades, to every teacher who'd ever told me I was talented, to every professor who'd ever said I had potential. Best of all, it was a hundred-page response to a world (and to my own secret fears) that told me that plus-size women couldn't have adventures, or fall in love. And today I was going to do something gutsy. Today, over lunch at the Four Seasons, I was interviewing actor Nicholas Kaye, star of the forthcoming *Belch Brothers,* a teen-pleasing comedy featuring twin brothers whose gas gives them magical powers. More importantly, I was also interviewing Jane Sloan, who'd executive-produced the movie (with one hand holding her nose, I figured). Jane Sloan was a hero of mine, who, before her slide toward the crassly commercial, had written and directed some of the sharpest, funniest films Hollywood had ever seen. Better yet, they were films with sharp, funny women in them. For weeks I'd been distracting myself from the missing-Bruce blues by constructing an elaborate daydream of how we'd meet and she'd immediately recognize me as a kindred spirit and potential collaborator, slipping me her business card and insisting that I contact her the moment I turned my attention from journalism to screenwriting. I even smiled a little, imagining the look of delight on her face when I modestly confessed that I had indeed penned a screenplay, and that I'd send it to her if she liked.

She was a writer, I was a writer. She was funny, I figured, and I'm funny, too. True, Jane Sloan was also rich and famous, successful beyond my wildest dreams, and about the size of one of my thighs, but sisterhood, I reminded myself, is powerful.

Almost an hour after I arrived, forty-five minutes after we were scheduled to meet, Jane Sloan seated herself across from me and laid a large mirror and a larger bottle of Evian next to her plate. "Hello," she said, her throaty voice emerging through her clenched teeth, and proceeded to give her face a few healthy squirts. I squinted at her, waiting for the punch line, waiting for her to crack up and say she was kidding. She didn't. Nicholas Kaye sat down beside her and shot me an apologetic grin. Jane Sloan finally put the mirror and bottle down.

"I'm sorry we're late," said Nicholas Kaye, who looked much like he did on TV—cute as a button.

Jane Sloan shoved the butter dish aggressively across the table. She picked up her napkin, which had been folded into the shape of a swan, opened it with one dismissive flick of her wrist, and carefully wiped her face with it. Only after she'd set the napkin, now stained ecru and crimson and mascara-black, onto the table, did she deign to speak.

"This city," she pronounced, "is wreaking havoc on my pores."

"I'm sorry," I said, feeling stupid as soon as the apology had left my mouth. What was I sorry for? I wasn't doing anything to her pores.

Jane waved one pale hand languorously, as if my apology for Philadelphia was of no more consequence then a mold spore, then picked up her silver butter knife and started poking at the flower-shaped butter pat in the dish she'd just banished to my side of the table. "What do you need to know?" she asked, without looking up.

"Umm," I said, fumbling for my pen and my notebook. I had a whole list of questions ready, questions about everything from how she'd cast the movie to who her influences were, and what she liked on TV, but all I could think of was, "Where'd you get the idea?"

Without lifting her eyes from the butter, she said, "Saw it on TV."

"That late-night sketch comedy show on HBO?" Nicholas Kaye said helpfully.

"I called the director. Said I thought it should be a movie. He agreed."

Great. So that was how movies got made. Strange little butter-averse pint-size Elvira with squirt bottle makes phone call, and voilà, instant film!

"So . . . you wrote the script?"

Another wave of that ghostlike hand. "I just oversaw."

"We hired a few guys from *Saturday Night!*," said Nicholas Kaye.

Double great. Not only did I not work for *Saturday Night!*, I wasn't even a guy. I quietly abandoned my plan of telling her that I'd written a screenplay. They'd probably laugh me all the way to Pittsburgh.

The waiter approached. Both Jane and Nicholas scowled at their menus in silence. The waiter shot me a desperate look.

"I'll have the osso bucco," I said.

"Excellent choice," he said, beaming.

"I'll have . . ." said Nicholas. Long, long pause. The waiter waited, pen poised. Jane poked at the butter. I felt a drop of sweat descend from the nape of my neck, down my back, and into my underwear. "This salad," he finally said, pointing. The waiter leaned in for a look. "Very good, sir," he said, relieved.

"And for the lady?"

"Lettuce," Jane Sloan mumbled.

"A salad?" the waiter ventured.

"Lettuce," she repeated. "Red leaf, if you have it. Washed. With vinegar on the side. And I don't want the leaves cut in any way," she continued. "I want them torn. By hand."

The waiter scribbled and fled. Jane Sloan slowly lifted her eyes. I fumbled my notebook open again.

"Umm . . ."

Lettuce, I was thinking. Jane Sloan is eating lettuce for lunch, and I'm going to sit here and suck down veal in front of her. And, worse yet, I couldn't think of a thing to ask.

"Tell me your favorite scene in the movie," I finally managed. A horrible question, a freshman-at-the-school-paper question, but better than nothing, I thought.

She smiled, finally—faintly, fleetingly, but still, it was undeniably a smile. Then she shook her head.

"Can't," she said. "Too personal."

Oh, God, help me. Rescue me. Send a tornado shrieking through the Four Seasons, uprooting businessmen, sending fine china flying. I'm dying here. "So what's up next?"

Jane just shrugged and looked mysterious. I felt the waistband of my control-top pantyhose give up the fight and slide down my mid-section, coming to rest at the top of my thighs.

"We're working on something new together," Nicholas Kaye volunteered. "I'm going to write . . .with a couple of my friends from college . . . and Jane's going to show it to the studios. Would you like to hear about that?"

He launched into an enthusiastic description of what sounded like the world's dumbest movie—something about a guy who inherits his father's whoopie cushion factory, and how his father's partner double-crosses him, and how he and the spunky cleaning lady triumph in the end. I took notes without hearing, my right hand moving mechanically over the page as my left hand ferried food to my mouth. Meanwhile, Jane was dividing her lettuce into two piles—one of mostly leaf pieces, the other of mostly stem pieces. Once this division was complete, she proceeded to dip the top third of the tines of her fork into the vinegar pot, then carefully spear a single piece of lettuce from the mostly leaf side and place it precisely in her mouth. After exactly six bites—during which time Nicholas polished off his salad and two pieces of bread and I downed half my osso bucco, which was, all things considered, delicious—she patted her lips dry with her napkin, picked up her butter knife, and started poking the butter again.

I reached over and pulled the butter dish away, thinking that I couldn't stand to see this, and, also, that I had to try something, because the interview was going down the crapper. "Cut it out," I said sternly. "That butter hasn't done anything to you."

There was a pause. A pregnant pause. An icy, yawning crevasse of a pause. Jane Sloan stared at me with her dead black eyes.

"Dairy," she said, as if it were a curse.

"Third largest industry in Pennsylvania," I countered, without any idea of whether it was true. It sounded about right, though. Whenever I went for a bike ride that took me more than a few miles out of the city, I saw cows.

"Jane's allergic," Nicholas said quickly. He smiled at his director, and took her hand, and then it hit me: They're a couple. Even though he is twenty-seven and she is . . . well, God, at least fifteen years older than that. Even though he is recognizably human and she . . . isn't. "What else?"

"Tell me . . . ," I stammered, my mind stuck on blank at the sight of their interlaced fingers. "Tell me something about the movie that not everybody knows."

"Part of it was shot where they shot *Showgirls,*" offered Nicholas.

"That's in the press packet," Jane said suddenly. I knew that, but I'd decided to be polite, take the quote, and get the hell out of Dodge before I found out what a woman who ate six lettuce leaves for lunch did when they asked if she wanted dessert.

"I'll tell you something," she said. "The girl in the flower shop? She's my daughter."

"Really?"

"Her first role," Jane said, sounding almost proud, almost shy. Almost real. "I've been discouraging her . . . she's already obsessing over the way she looks. . . ."

Wonder where she gets that, I thought, but said nothing.

"I haven't told anyone else that," Jane said. The corners of her lips twitched. "But I like you."

Heaven help the reporters you don't like, I thought, and was trying to construct a reasonable response when she suddenly stood up, taking Nicholas along with her. "Good luck," she murmured, and they swept out the door. Just as the dessert cart arrived.

"Something for mademoiselle?" said the waiter sympathetically.

Can you blame me if I said yes?

* * *

"So?" asked Samantha, on the phone that afternoon.

"She ate lettuce for lunch," I moaned.

"A salad?"

"Lettuce. Plain lettuce. With vinegar on the side. I almost died."

"Just lettuce?"

"Lettuce," I repeated. "Red leaf lettuce. She specified a variety. And she kept squirting her face with Evian."

"Cannie, you're making this up."

"I'm not! I swear! My Hollywood idol, and she's this lettuce-eating freak, this, this miniature Elvira with tattooed eyeliner. . . ."

Samantha listened dispassionately. "You're crying."

"I am not," I lied. "I'm just disappointed. I thought . . . you know . . . I had this idea that we'd hit it off. And I'd send her the screenplay, but I'm never going to get to give anyone the screenplay, because I didn't go to college with a single cast member of *Saturday Night!*, and those are the guys who get their scripts read." I glanced down at myself. More bad news. "Also I got osso bucco on my jacket."

Samantha sighed. "I think you need an agent."

"I can't get an agent! Believe me, I've tried! They won't even look at your stuff unless you've had something produced, and you can't get producers to look at something unless it comes from an agent." I wiped my eyes viciously. "This week sucks."

"Mail call!" said Gabby gleefully. She dropped a stack of papers on my desk and waddled off. I said good-bye to Sam, and turned to my correspondence. Press release. Press release. Fax, fax, fax. Envelope with my name carefully lettered in the handwriting I had long since learned to identify as Old Person, Angry. I ripped the envelope open.

"Dear Miss Shapiro," read the shaky letters. "Your article on Celine Dion's special was the filthiest, nastiest smear piece of garbage I have seen in my fifty-seven years as a loyal *Examiner* reader. Bad enough that you mocked Celine's music as "bombastic, overblown ballads," but then you had to go and make fun of her looks! I'll bet you're no Cindy Crawford yourself. Sincerely, Mr. E. P. Deiffinger."

"Hey, Cannie."

Jesus Christ. Gabby was forever sneaking up behind me. For being massive, and old, and deaf, she could be quiet as a cat when it suited her. I turned around and there she was, squinting over my shoulder at the letter in my lap.

"Did you get something wrong?" she asked, her voice full of sympathy as thick, and fake, as Cheez Whiz. "Do we need to run a correction?"

"No, Gabby," I said, trying not to scream. "Just a little opposing viewpoint."

I tossed the letter in the trash can and shoved my chair back so fast I almost ran over Gabby's toes.

"Jeez!" she hissed and retreated.

"Dear Mr. Deiffinger," I composed in my head. "I may not be a supermodel, but at least I've got enough working brain cells to know what sucks when I hear it."

"Dear Mr. Deiffinger," I thought, walking the mile and a half from work to the Weight and Eating Disorders office where my first Fat Class was meeting. "Sorry you took offense at my description of Celine Dion's work, but I actually thought I was being charitable."

I stomped into the conference room, seated myself at the table, and looked around. There was Lily, from the waiting room, and an older black woman, about my size, with a bulging briefcase beside her, poking away at one of those hand-held e-mail readers. There was a blond teenager, her long hair swept off her face in a hairband, her body hidden beneath a bulky oversized sweatshirt and gigantic droopy jeans. And there was a woman of perhaps sixty who had to weigh at least four hundred pounds. She followed me into the room, walking with the aid of a cane, and surveyed the seats carefully, measuring her bulk against their parameters, before easing herself down.

"Hey, Cannie," said Lily.

"Hey," I grumbled. The words *Portion Control* were written on a white wipable message board, and there was a poster of the food pyramid on one wall. This shit again, I thought, wondering if I could place out of the class. I'd been to Weight Watchers, after all. I knew all about portion control.

The skinny nurse I remembered from the waiting room walked through the door, her hands full of bowls, measuring cups, a small plastic replica of a four-ounce pork chop.

"Good evening, everyone," she said, and wrote her name—Sarah Pritchard, R.N.—on the board. We went around the table, introducing ourselves. The blond girl was Bonnie, the black woman was Anita, and the very large woman was Esther from West Oak Lane.

"I'm having a flashback of college," whispered Lily, as Nurse Sarah distributed booklets full of calorie counts, and packets of printouts on behavior modification.

"I'm having a flashback of Weight Watchers," I whispered back.

"Did you try that?" asked Bonnie the blond girl, edging closer to us.

"Last year," I said.

"Was that the One Two Three Success program?"

"Fat and Fiber," I whispered back.

"Isn't that a cereal?" asked Esther, who had a surprisingly lovely voice—very low, and warm, and free of the dread Philadelphia accent that causes natives to swallow their consonants like they're made of warm taffy.

"That's Fruit and Fiber," the blond girl said.

"Fat and Fiber was where you had to count the grams of fat and the grams of fiber in every food, and you were supposed to eat a certain number of grams of fiber, and not go over a certain number of grams of fat," I explained.

"Did it work?" asked Anita, setting down her Palm Pilot.

"Nah," I said. "But that was probably my fault. I kept mixing up which number I was supposed to stay below and which one I was supposed to go above . . . and then I found, like, these really high-fiber brownies that were made with iron filings or something. . . ."

Lily cracked up.

"They had a zillion calories apiece but I figured it didn't matter because they were very low in fat and very high in fiber. . . ."

"A common mistake," said Nurse Sarah cheerfully. "Fat and fiber are both important, but so is the total number of calories you take in.

It's very simple, really," she said, turning back to the board and scribbling the kind of equation that had confounded me in eleventh grade. "Calories taken in versus calories expended. If you take in more calories than you burn, you'll gain weight."

"Really?" I asked, my eyes wide.

The nurse looked at me suspiciously.

"Are you serious? It's that simple?"

"Um," she began. I suspected that she was probably used to fat ladies sitting meekly in the chairs, like overfed sheep, smiling and nodding and being grateful for the wisdom she was imparting, staring at her with abashed, admiring eyes, all because she'd had the good fortune of being born thin. The thought infuriated me.

"So if I eat fewer calories than I burn . . ." I slapped my forehead. "My God! I finally get it! I understand! I'm cured!" I stood up and pumped my hands in the air as Lily snickered. "Healed! Saved! Thank you, Jesus, and the Weight and Eating Disorders Center, for taking the blinders from my eyes!"

"Okay," said the nurse. "You've made your point."

"Damn," I said, resuming my seat. "I was going to ask if I could be excused."

The nurse sighed. "Look," she said. "The truth of it is, there're a lot of complicating factors . . . and science doesn't even understand all of them. We know about metabolic rates, and how some people's bodies just seem to want to hang on to excess weight more than other people's do. We know this isn't easy. I would never tell you that it was."

She stared at us, breathing rapidly. We stared right back.

"I'm sorry," I finally said into the silence. "I was being fresh. It's just that . . . well, I don't want to speak for anybody else, but I've had this explained to me before."

"Uh-huh," said Anita.

"Me, too," said Bonnie.

"Fat people aren't stupid," I continued. "But every single weight-loss program I've ever been to treats us like we are—as if as soon as they explain that broiled chicken is better than fried, and frozen yogurt's better than ice cream, and that if you take a hot bath instead of eating pizza, we're going to all turn into Courteney Cox."

"That's right," said Lily.

The nurse looked frustrated. "I'd certainly never mean to suggest that any of you are stupid," she said. "Diet is part of it," she added. "Exercise is part of it, too, although probably not as big a part as we used to believe."

I frowned. That was just my luck. With all of the biking and walking I did, plus regular workouts at the gym with Samantha, exercise was the one part of a healthy lifestyle that I had down pat.

"Now today," she continued, "we're going to be talking about portion size. Did you know that most restaurants serve portions that are well over the recommended USDA guidelines of what most women require over an entire day?"

I groaned softly to myself as the nurse arrayed the plates and cups and little plastic pork chop on the table. "The correct portion of protein," she said, speaking in the slow, loud, careful voice commonly employed by kindergarten teachers, "is four ounces. Now, can anyone tell me about how much that is?"

"Size of your palm," muttered Anita. "Jenny Craig," she said to the nurse's surprised look.

Nurse Sarah took a deep breath. "Very good!" she said, making a visible effort to sound happy and upbeat. "Now, how about a portion of fat?"

"Tip of your thumb," I muttered. Her eyes widened. "Look," I said, "I think we all know this stuff. . . am I right?"

I looked around the table. Everyone nodded. "The only thing we're here for, the only thing that this program has to offer us, is the drugs. Now, are we going to get them today, or do we have to sit here and act like you're telling us things we don't already know?"

The nurse's face went from frustrated (and slightly dismissive) to angry (and more than slightly scared). "There's a procedure to this," she said. "We explained it. Four weeks of behavior-modification classes . . ."

Lily started thumping her fist on the table. "Drugs . . . drugs . . . drugs . . ." she chanted.

"We can't just hand out prescription medication. . . ."

"Drugs . . . drugs . . . drugs . . ." Now Bonnie the blond girl and Esther were chanting along as well. The nurse opened her mouth, then closed it again. "I'll get the doctor," she said, and bolted. The five of us stared at each other for a moment. Then we all burst out laughing.

"She was scared!" Lily hooted.

"Probably thought we'd crush her," I muttered.

"Sit on her!" gasped Bonnie.

"I hate skinny people," I said.

Anita looked very serious. "Don't say that," she said. "You shouldn't hate anyone."

"Agh," I sighed. Just then, Dr. K. stuck his head through the door, with the chastened-looking nurse right behind him, practically clinging to the hem of his white coat.

"I understand there's a problem," he rumbled.

"Drugs!" said Lily.

The doctor had the look of a man who wanted very badly to laugh and was trying very hard not to.

"Is there a movement spokeswoman?" he asked.

Everyone looked at me. I got to my feet, smoothed my shirt, and cleared my throat. "I think that it's the feeling of the group that we've all been through different lectures and courses and support groups concerning behavior modification." I looked around the table. Everyone seemed to be nodding in agreement. "It's our feeling that we've tried to change our behavior, and eat less, and exercise more, and all of those things that they tell you to do, and what we'd really like . . . what we're really here for, what we've all paid for, is something new. Namely, drugs," I concluded, and sat back in my seat.

"Well, I know how you feel," he said.

"I doubt that very much," I shot back.

"Well, maybe you can tell me," he said mildly. "Look," he said. "It's not like I know the secrets to lifelong weight loss and I'm here to tell them to you. Think of this as a journey . . . think of it as something we're in on together."

"Except that our journey led us to the wonderful world of plus-size shopping and lonely nights," I grumbled.

The doctor smiled at me—a very disarming grin. "Let's forget about fat or thin for a minute," he said. "If you guys already know the calorie counts of everything, and what a serving of pasta's supposed to look like, then I'm sure you all know that most diets don't work. Not over the long term, anyhow."

Now he had our attention. It was true, we'd all figured this out (from bitter personal experiences, in most cases), but to hear an authority figure, a doctor, a doctor who was running a weight-loss program say it . . . well, that was practically heresy. I half expected security guards to come rushing through the door and drag him off to be re-brainwashed.

"I think," he continued, "that we'll all have much better luck—and we'll be happier—if we think instead about small lifestyle changes—little things that we can do every day that won't prove unsustainable over the long term. If we think about getting healthier, and feeling happier with ourselves, instead of looking like Courteney . . ."

He looked at me, eyebrows raised.

"Cox," I supplied. "Actually, Cox-Arquette. She got married."

"Right. Her. Forget her. Let's concentrate on the attainable, instead. And I promise that nobody here will treat you like you're stupid, no matter what your size is."

I found I was touched in spite of myself. The guy was actually making sense. Better yet, he wasn't talking down to us. It was . . . well, revolutionary, really.

The nurse gave us one last disgruntled glance and scurried away. The doctor closed the door and took a seat. "I'd like to do an exercise with you," he said. He looked around the table. "How many of you ever eat when you're not hungry?"

Dead silence. I closed my eyes. Emotional eating. I'd been through this lecture, too.

"How many of you eat breakfast, and then maybe you come to the office and there's a box of doughnuts and they look good and you'll have one just because they're there?"

More silence. "Dunkin' Donuts or Krispy Kremes?" I finally asked.
The doctor pursed his full lips. "I hadn't thought about it."

"Well, it makes a difference," I said.

"Dunkin' Donuts," he said.

"Chocolate? Jelly? Glazed that somebody from Accounting ripped in half, so there's only half a doughnut left?"

"Krispy Kremes are better," said Bonnie.

"Especially the warm ones," said Esther.

I licked my lips.

"The last time I had doughnuts," said Esther, "someone brought them to work, just like we're talking about, and I picked out one that looked like a Boston cream . . . you know, it had the chocolate on top?"

We nodded. We all probably knew how to recognize a Boston cream doughnut on sight.

"Then I bit into it," Esther continued, "and it was . . ." Her lips curled. "Lemon."

"Ick," said Bonnie. "I hate lemon!"

"Okay," said the doctor, laughing. "My point is, they could be the best doughnuts in the world. They could be the Platonic ideal of doughnut-ness. But if you've already had breakfast, and you aren't really hungry, ideally, you should be able to walk right by."

We thought about this for a minute. "As if," Lily finally said.

"Maybe you could try telling yourself that when you are really hungry, if what you're really hungry for is a doughnut, then you can go get one."

We thought again. "Nope," said Lily. "I'm still eating the free doughnuts."

"And how do you know what you're really hungry for?" asked Bonnie. "Like, me . . . I'm always hungry for the stuff I know I shouldn't be eating. But, like, give me a bag of baby carrots and I'm all, like, whatever."

"Did you ever try boiling them and mashing them with ginger and orange rind?" asked Lily. Bonnie wrinkled her nose.

"I don't like carrots," said Anita, "but I do like butternut squash."

"That's not a vegetable, though. It's a starch," I said.

Anita looked confused. "How can it not be a vegetable?"

"It's a starchy vegetable. Like a potato. I learned that in Weight Watchers."

"On Fat and Fiber?" asked Lily.

"Okay then!" said the doctor. I could tell from his eyes that the unruly chatter of five veterans of Weight Watchers, Jenny Craig, Pritikin, Atkins, et al., was starting to get to him. It couldn't be fun.

"Let's try something," he said. He walked to the door and flicked off the lights. The room dimmed. Bonnie giggled. "I want you all to close your eyes," he said, "and try to figure out how you feel right now, right this minute. Are you hungry? Tired? Are you sad, or happy, or anxious? Try to really concentrate, and then, try to really separate the physical sensations from what's happening emotionally."

We all closed our eyes.

"Anita?" asked the doctor.

"I'm tired," she said immediately.

"Bonnie?"

"Oh, maybe tired. Maybe a little hungry, too," she said.

"And emotionally?" he prodded.

Bonnie sighed. "I'm sick of my school," she finally muttered. "The kids say rotten things to me." I snuck a peek at her. Her eyes were still tightly screwed shut, and her hands were clenched into fists on top of her oversized jeans. High school, evidently, had not gotten any kinder or gentler since my own attendance ten years prior. I wished I could put my hand on her shoulder. Tell her that things would get better . . . except, given recent events in my own life, I wasn't sure it was the truth.

"Lily?"

"Starving," Lily said promptly.

"And emotionally?"

"Umm . . . okay," she said.

"Just okay?" asked the doctor.

"There's a new episode of *ER* on tonight," she said. "I can't be anything less than okay."

"Esther?"

"I'm ashamed," said Esther, and burst into tears. I opened my eyes. The doctor pulled a small packet of Kleenex out of his pocket and handed it over.

"Why ashamed?" he asked gently.

Esther smiled weakly. "'Cause before we started I was looking at the plastic pork chop, and I was thinking that it didn't look half bad."

That broke the tension. We all started laughing, even the doctor. Esther sniffled, wiping her eyes.

"Don't worry," Lily said. "I was thinking the exact same thing about the pat of butter on the food pyramid."

The doctor cleared his throat. "And Candace?" he asked.

"Cannie," I said.

"How are you?"

I closed my eyes, but only for a second and what I saw was Bruce's face, Bruce's brown eyes close to mine. Bruce saying that he loved me. Then I opened them and looked right at him. "Fine," I said, even though it wasn't true. "I'm fine."

"So how'd it go?" asked Samantha. We were panting on side-by-side StairMasters that night at the gym.

"So far, not bad," I said. "No drugs yet. The doctor who's leading the class seems okay."

We climbed in silence for a few minutes, the belts grinding and squeaking beneath our feet as a Funky Fitness class blared away beside us. Our gym seemed determined to attract new members by offering every flavor-of-the-week fitness class, so we had Pilates, gospel aerobics, interval spinning, and something called the Fireman's Full-Body Workout, complete with hoses, ladders, and a one-hundred-pound mannequin to be hauled up and down the stairs. Meanwhile, the roof leaked, the air conditioners were iffy, and the Jacuzzi always seemed to be under repair.

"And how was the rest of your day, dear?" asked Sam, wiping her face with her sleeve. I told her about Mr. Deiffenger's angry defense of Celine Dion.

"I hate readers," I gasped, as my StairMaster kicked into a higher gear. "Why do they have to get so personal?"

"I guess he probably figures that you were messing with Celine, so you deserve it."

"Yeah, but she's public property. I'm just me."

"But not to him, you're not. Your name's in the paper. That makes you public property, just like Celine."

"Only bigger."

"And with better taste. And not," said Samantha sternly, "with any plans to marry your seventy-year-old manager who's known you since you were twelve."

"Oh, now who's being critical?" I asked.

"Damn Canadians," said Samantha. She'd spent a few years working in Montreal, had endured a disastrous love affair with a man there, and never had anything nice to say about our neighbors to the North, including Peter Jennings, whom she steadfastly refused to watch, arguing that he'd taken a job that should have rightfully gone to an American—"someone who knows how to say the word *about*."

After forty miserable minutes, we adjourned to the steam room, wrapped ourselves in towels, and assumed prone positions on the benches.

"How's the Yoga King?" I inquired. Sam gave a satisfied-looking smile and raised her arms above her head, reaching toward the ceiling.

"I'm feeling very flexible," she said smugly. I threw my towel at her head.

"Don't torture me," I said. "I'm probably never going to have sex again."

"Oh, cut it out, Cannie," said Samantha. "And you know this won't last. Mine never do." Which was true. Sam's love life, of late, had been uniquely cursed. She'd meet a guy and go out with him once, and everything would be wonderful. They'd meet again, and things would be clicking along. And then, on the third date, there'd be some horrible awkward moment, some unbelievable revelation, something that would basically make it impossible for Sam to see the guy again. Her last guy, a Jewish doctor with a fabulous résumé and enviable physique, had looked like a contender until Date #3, when he'd taken Sam home for dinner and she'd been disturbed to find a picture of his sister prominently displayed in the entryway hall.

"What's wrong with that?" I'd asked.

"She was topless," Samantha'd replied. Exit Dr. Right, enter the Yoga King.

"Look at it this way," said Samantha. "It was a lousy day, but now it's over."

"I just wish I could talk to him."

Samantha brushed her hair back over her shoulders, propped her head on an elbow, and stared down at me from her perch on one of the upper tiers of wooden benches. "To Mr. Deiffledorf?"

"Deiffinger. No, not him." I ladled more water on the hot rocks so the steam billowed around us. "To Bruce."

Samantha squinted at me through the haze. "Bruce? I don't get it."

"What if . . . ," I said slowly. "What if I made a mistake?"

She sighed. "Cannie, I listened to you for months talk about how things weren't right, how things weren't getting better, how you knew that taking a break would be the right thing to do in the long run. And even though you were upset right after it happened, I never heard you say that you'd made the wrong decision."

"What if I think something different now?"

"Well, what changed your mind?"

I thought about my answer. The article was part of it. Bruce and I had never talked about my whole weight thing. Maybe if we had . . . if he had some sense of how I felt, if I had some inkling of how much he understood . . . maybe things could have been different.

But more than that, I missed talking to him, telling him how my day went, blowing off steam about Gabby's latest salvos, reading him potential leads for my stories, scenes from my screenplays.

"I just miss him," I said lamely.

"Even after what he wrote about you?" asked Sam.

"Maybe it wasn't so bad," I muttered. "I mean, he didn't say that he didn't find me . . . you know . . . desirable."

"Of course he found you desirable," Sam said. "You didn't find *him* desirable. You found him lazy, and immature, and a slob, and you told me not three months ago lying on this very bench that if he left one more used piece of Kleenex in your bed you were going to kill him and leave his body on a New Jersey Transit bus."

I winced. I couldn't remember the line exactly, but it sure sounded like something I'd say.

"And if you called him," Samantha continued, "what would you say?"

"Hi, how are you, planning on humiliating me in print again anytime soon?" I'd actually had a monthlong reprieve. Bruce's October "Good in Bed" had been called "Love and the Glove." Someone— Gabby, I was practically sure—had left a copy on my desk at work the day before, and I'd read it as fast as I could, with my heart in my throat, until I'd determined that there wasn't a word about C. Not this month, at least.

Real men wear condoms, was his first line. Which was a hoot, considering that during our three years together Bruce had been almost completely spared the indignities of latex. We'd both tested clean, and I went on the pill after a handful of dismaying times when his erection would wilt the instant I produced the Trojans. That minor detail was, of course, notably absent from the story, along with the fact that I'd wound up putting the thing on him—an act that left me feeling like an overprotective mother tying her little boy's shoes. *Donning the glove is more than a mere duty,* he'd lectured *Moxie's* readers. *It's a sign of devotion, of maturity, a sign of respect for all womankind—and a sign of his love for you.*

Now, the memory of the way he'd really been regarding condoms seemed too tender to even consider. And the thought of Bruce and I in bed together made me cringe, because of the thought that came dashing in on its heels: *We'll never be like that again.*

"Don't call him," said Sam. "I know it feels awful right now, but you'll get through it. You'll survive."

"Thank you, Gloria Gaynor," I grumbled, and went to take a shower.

When I got home, my answering machine was blinking. I hit "play" and heard Steve. "Remember me? The guy in the park? Listen, I was just wondering if you'd like to get that beer this week or maybe dinner. Give me a call."

I smiled as I walked Nifkin, grinned when I cooked myself a chicken breast and a sweet potato and spinach for dinner, beamed all through my twenty-minute consultation with Sam on the question of Steve, Cute Guy from the Park. At nine o'clock precisely I dialed his number. He sounded glad to hear from me. He sounded . . . great, in fact. Funny. Considerate. Interested in what I did. We quickly covered the basics of each other's lives: ages, colleges, oh-did-you-know-Janie-from-my-high-school, a little bit about parents and family (I left out the whole lesbian mother thing, in order to have something to talk about in the event of a second date), and a little bit about why-we're-single-right-now (I gave the two-sentence synopsis of the Bruce denouement. He told me he'd had a girlfriend back in Atlanta, but she'd gone to nursing school and he'd moved here). I told him about covering the Pillsbury bake-off. He told me that he'd taken up kayaking. We decided to meet for dinner on Saturday night at the Latest Dish and maybe catch a movie after that.

"So maybe this will be okay," I told Nifkin, who didn't seem to care much, one way or the other. He turned three times and settled himself on a pillow. I put on my nightgown, trying to avoid glimpses of my body in the bathroom mirror, and went to sleep feeling cautiously optimistic that there was at least a chance that I wouldn't die alone.

Samantha and I had long since identified Azafran as our designated first date restaurant. It had all the advantages: It was right around the corner from her house and my apartment. The food was good, it wasn't too expensive, it was BYOB, which gave us the chance to a) impress the guy by bringing a good bottle of wine, and b) eliminate the possibility of the guy getting blotto, because there'd be nothing more than the single bottle. And, best of all, Azafran had floor-to-ceiling windows, and waitresses who worked out at our gym, who knew us, and who would obligingly seat us at the window tables—our backs to the street, with the guy facing forward—so that whichever one of us didn't have the date could stroll by with Nifkin and scope out the prospect.

I was congratulating myself, because Steve looked eminently scopable. Short-sleeved polo shirt, neat khakis that looked as though he might actually have ironed them, and a pleasant whiff of cologne. A nice change from Bruce, who was given to stained T-shirts and droopy shorts and who could, absent frequent reminders on my part, be somewhat haphazard in his deodorant use.

I smiled at Steve. He smiled back. Our fingers brushed over the calamari. The wine was delicious, perfectly chilled, and it was a perfect night, with a clear, starry sky and just a hint of fall in the wind.

"So what did you do today?" he asked me.

"Went for a bike ride, up to Chestnut Hill," I said. "Thought about you . . ."

Something flickered across his face then. Something bad.

"Look," he said quietly. "I ought to tell you something. When I asked if you wanted to have a beer with me . . . well, I told you I was new to the neighborhood . . . I mean, I was really just looking for . . . you know. For friends. For people to hang out with."

The calamari turned into a lead ball in my stomach. "Oh."

"And I guess I didn't make that clear enough . . . that, I mean that this isn't a date or anything . . . oh, God," he said. "Don't look at me like that."

Don't cry, I told myself. Don't cry don't cry don't cry. How had I misread this so badly? I was pathetic. A walking joke. I wanted Bruce back. Hell, I wanted my mother. Don't cry don't cry don't cry.

"Your eyes," he said softly. "Your eyes are killing me."

"I'm sorry," I said dumbly. Apologizing as always. This cannot get any worse, I thought. Steve stared over my head, out the window.

"Hey," he said, "isn't that your dog?"

I turned, and, sure enough, there was Samantha, and Nifkin, both peering through the window. Sam looked impressed. As I stared, she flashed me a quick thumbs-up.

"Will you excuse me?" I murmured. I stood up, forcing my feet to move. In the ladies' room I splashed cold water on my face, concentrating on not breathing, feeling the tears I couldn't cry mass behind my forehead and instantly transform themselves into a headache. I considered the night ahead: dinner, then we were supposed to go see the latest world-ending disaster flick at the multiplex. But I couldn't. I couldn't spend the whole night sitting next to a guy who'd just declared himself an un-date. And maybe that made me too sensitive, or ridiculous, but the truth was, I couldn't do it.

I went to the kitchen and found our waitress.

"Almost ready," she said, then looked at my face. "Oh, God . . . what? He's gay. He's an escaped convict. He used to date your mother."

"Along those lines," I said.

"Want me to tell him you're sick?"

"Yeah," I said, then thought again. "No. Tell you what . . . pack up the food, and don't tell him anything. Let's see how long he sits there."

She rolled her eyes. "That bad?"

"There's another way out of here, right?"

She pointed to the fire exit, which was propped open by a chair containing a busboy on a break. "Go for it," she said, and a minute later, clutching two to-go containers and what remained of my pride, I slunk past the busboy and out into the night. My head was pounding. Fool, I thought fiercely. Idiot. Stupid, stupid idiot to think that somebody who looks like that would be interested in someone who looks like you.

I got upstairs, dumped the food, took off my dress, pulled on my ratty overalls, thinking furiously that I probably looked like Andrea Dworkin. I stomped down the stairs, out the door, and started walking, first down to the river, then north, toward Society Hill and Old City, and finally west toward Rittenhouse Square.

Part of me—the reasonable part—was thinking that this was not a big thing, just a minor bump on life's bicycle path, and that he was the idiot, not me. *The single guy,* he'd said. Was I wrong to think that he was asking me out on a bona fide date? And so what if this wasn't a date after all? I'd had dates before. I'd even had boyfriends. It was completely reasonable to think that I'd have them both again, and this guy wasn't worth another second of my time.

But another part—the shrill, hysterical, hypercritical, and, unfortunately, much louder part—was saying something else entirely.

That I was dumb. That I was fat. That I was so fat that nobody would ever love me again and so dense that I couldn't see it. That I'd been a fool, or, worse, been made a fool of. That Steve, the Teva-wearing engineer, was probably sitting at an empty table, eating calamari and laughing to himself about big, dumb Cannie.

And who was I going to tell? Who could comfort me?

Not my mother. I couldn't really talk to her about my love life after I'd made it so clear that I didn't approve of hers. And plus, with Bruce's column, she'd learned enough about my after-dark activities for the time being.

I could tell Samantha, certainly, but she'd think I was crazy. "Why are you assuming this is about the way you look?" she'd demand, and I'd mutter that it could probably have been about something else, or just a plain old misunderstanding, all the while feeling the truth in my bones, the Gospel according to my father: I was fat and I was ugly and nobody would ever love me. And it would be embarrassing. I wanted my friends to think of me as someone who was smart and funny and capable. I didn't want them to feel sorry for me.

What I wanted to do was call Bruce. I wouldn't tell him about this latest humiliation—I didn't want his pity, either, or for him to think I'd come crawling back, or was planning to, simply because some fuzzy-legged jerk had rejected me—but I wanted to hear his voice. No matter what he'd said in *Moxie,* no matter how he'd shamed me. After three years, he knew me better than probably anyone else in the world, except Samantha, and at that moment, standing on the sidewalk on 17th and Walnut, I wanted to talk to him so badly that I got weak in the knees.

I hurried home and heaved myself up the stairs two at a time. Sweaty, hands shaking, I sprawled on the bed and reached for the phone, punching in his number as fast as I could. He picked up instantly.

"Hey, Bruce," I began.

"Cannie?" His voice sounded strange. "I was just going to call you."

"Really?" I felt a small spark of hopefulness flare in my chest.

"I just wanted to let you know," he began, and his voice dissolved into harsh, ragged sobs. "My father died this morning."

I don't remember what I said then. I remember that he told me the details: He'd had a stroke and he'd died in the hospital. It had been very fast.

I was crying, Bruce was crying. I couldn't remember when I'd felt so horrible about something. It was so unfair. Bruce's father was a wonderful man. He had loved his family. He had even, I thought, maybe loved me, too.

But even as I was feeling horrible, I felt the spark growing. *He'll get it now,* a voice in my head whispered. Once you've had a loss like that, doesn't it change the way you see the world? And wouldn't it change the way he saw me, my own fractured family, my own lost father? Plus, he'd need me. He'd needed me once before, to rescue him from loneliness, from sexual ignorance and shame . . . and surely he would need me again to help him get through this.

I imagined us at the funeral, and how I'd hold his hand, how I'd help him, hold him up, be there for him to lean on, the way I wished I could have leaned on him. I imagined him looking at me with new respect and understanding, new consideration, with the eyes of a man, not a boy.

"Let me help. How can I help?" I said. "Do you want me to come over?"

His reply was dismayingly instant. "No," he said. "I'm going home, and there's a ton of people there now. It would be weird. Could you come to the funeral tomorrow?"

"Of course," I said. "Of course. I love you," I said, the words out of my mouth almost before I'd finished thinking them.

"What does that mean?" he asked me, still crying.

To my credit, I recovered fast. "That I want to be there for you . . . and help you any way I can."

"Just come tomorrow," he said dully. "That's all you can do right now."

But something perverse in me persisted.

"I love you," I said again, and left the words hanging there. Bruce sighed, knowing what I wanted, and unwilling, or unable, to give it to me.

"I have to go," he said. "I'm sorry, Cannie."

PART TWO

Reconsider Me

FIVE

Thinking back, there was probably some way I could have felt worse at Bernard Guberman's funeral. Like if I'd killed him myself.

The service started at two o'clock. I got there early, but the parking lot was already full, with cars backed down the driveway, spilling onto the highway. I finally parked across the street, dashed across four lanes of traffic and straight into a cluster of Bruce's friends. They were standing in the vestibule, in what were surely their interview suits, hands in their pockets, talking quietly and looking at their feet. It was a brilliantly sunny fall afternoon—a day to look at leaves, to buy apple cider and build the first fire of the year. Not a day for this.

"Hey, Cannie," George said softly.

"How's he doing?" I asked.

George shrugged. "He's inside," he said.

Bruce was sitting in a little vestibule, holding a bottle of Evian water and a handkerchief in his right hand. He was wearing the same blue suit he'd worn on Yom Kippur, when we'd sat side by side in temple. It was still too tight, the tie still too short, and he was wearing canvas sneakers that he'd decorated with drawings of stars and swirls during some particularly boring lecture. The second I saw him it was as if our recent history fell away—my decision to ask for a break, his decision to describe my body in print. It was as if nothing was left but our connection—and his pain. His mother stood above him with one hand on his shoulder. There were people everywhere. Everyone was crying.

I went over to Bruce, knelt down, and hugged him.

"Thank you for coming," he said, coolly. Formally. I kissed his cheek, scratchy with what looked like three days' growth of beard. He didn't appear to notice. The hug his mother gave me was warmer, her words a marked contrast to his. "Cannie," she whispered. "I'm glad you're here."

I knew it was going to be bad. I knew I'd feel terrible, being there, even after our parking-lot breakup, even though, of course, there was no earthly way I could have known that this would happen.

But it wasn't just bad. It was agony. Agony when the rabbi, whom I'd seen at Bruce's house at dinner a few times, talked about how Bernard Leonard Guberman had lived for his wife and his son. About how he'd take Audrey to toy stores, even though they didn't have grandchildren. "Just to be ready," he'd say. Which was when I lost it, knowing that I was the one who was supposed to produce those grandchildren, and how much the kids would have loved him, and how lucky I would have been to have that kind of love in my life.

And I sat there on the hard wooden bench in that funeral parlor, eight rows back from Bruce, who was supposed to have been my husband, thinking how all I wanted was to be beside him, and how I'd never felt farther away.

"He really loved you," Bruce's Aunt Barbara whispered to me as we stood washing our hands outside the house. There were cars double-parked in the cul-de-sac, cars circling the block, so many cars that they'd had to station a policeman outside the cemetery for the burial service. Bruce's father had been active in the temple, and had had a thriving practice as a dermatologist. Judging from the throngs, it looked like every Jew or teenager with a skin condition had shown up to pay their respects.

"He was a wonderful man," I said.

She looked at me curiously. "Was?"

Which was when I realized that she was talking about Bruce, who was still alive.

Barbara wrapped her maroon fingernails around my forearm and dragged me into the immaculate, Downy-scented laundry room.

"I know you and Bruce broke up," she said. "Was it because he didn't propose?"

"No," I said. "I guess . . . I just felt more and more that maybe we weren't a good fit."

It was as if she hadn't heard.

"Audrey always told me that Bernie said how happy he'd be to have you in the family," she said. "He always said, 'If Cannie wants a ring, she'll have a ring in a minute.'"

Oh, God. I felt tears starting to build behind my eyes. Again. I'd wept during the service, when Bruce stood on the bimah and talked about how his father taught him to catch a ball and drive, and I'd cried at the cemetery when Audrey sobbed over the open grave and said, over and over, "It isn't fair, isn't fair."

Aunt Barbara handed me a handkerchief.

"Bruce needs you," she whispered, and I nodded, knowing that I couldn't trust my voice. "Go," she said, pushing me into the kitchen. I wiped my eyes and went.

Bruce was sitting on the porch with his friends around him in a forbidding-looking circle. When I approached, he squinted at me, observing me like a specimen on a slide.

"Hey," I said softly. "Is there anything I can do for you?"

He shook his head and looked away. There was someone in every chair on the porch, and nobody looked like they were moving. As gracefully as I could, I squatted down on the step behind them, just outside of the circle, and sat there, holding my knees. I was cold, and hungry, but I hadn't brought a jacket, and there wasn't anywhere to balance a plate. I listened to them talk about nothing—about sports, and concerts, and their jobs, such as they were. I watched as Bruce's mother's friends' daughters, a trio of interchangeable twentysome-things, made their way onto the porch with paper plates full of petit fours, and gave Bruce their condolences, and their smooth cheeks to kiss. It felt like swallowing sand, watching him go out of his way to smile at them and show how he'd remembered all their names, when he could barely spare me a glance. Sure, I knew when—if—we decided to break up, he'd most likely find somebody else. I just never thought I'd have to suffer through a preview. I sat on my hands feeling wretched.

When Bruce finally stood up, I got up to follow him, but my leg had fallen asleep, and I stumbled and went sprawling, wincing as a splinter dug its way into my palm.

Bruce helped me up. Reluctantly, I thought.

"Do you want to take a walk?" I asked him. He shrugged. We walked. Down the driveway, down the street, where more cars were massing.

"I'm so sorry," I told him. Bruce said nothing. I reached for his hand, my fingertips brushing the back of his palm. He didn't reach back. "Look," I said, feeling desperate, "I know things have been . . . I know that we . . ." My voice trailed off. Bruce looked at me coldly.

"You aren't my girlfriend anymore," he said. "You were the one who wanted a break, remember? And I'm small," he practically spat.

"I want to be your friend," I said.

"I've got friends."

"I noticed," I told him. "Mannerly bunch."

He shrugged.

"Look," I told him. "Could we . . . could we just . . ." I put my fist against my lips. Words were failing me. All I had left were sobs. I swallowed hard. Get through this, I told myself. "Whatever happened between us, however you're feeling about me, I want you to know that your father was a wonderful man. I loved him. He was the best father I ever saw, and I'm sorry he's gone, and I just feel so terrible about all of this . . ." Bruce just stared at me. "And if you want to call me . . ." I finally managed.

"Thanks," he finally said. He turned to walk toward the house, and after a moment I turned to follow him, like a chastened dog, walking numbly behind him with my head hanging down.

I should have just left, but I didn't. I stayed on through the evening prayers, when men with tallits over their shoulders crowded

Audrey's living room, bumping their knees on the hard wooden mourning benches, pressing their shoulders against the covered mirrors. I stayed when Bruce and his friends gathered in the white-and-chrome kitchen to pick over deli trays and make small talk. I hung on the edge of the group, so full of sadness I thought I would burst, right there on Audrey's Spanish-tiled floor. Bruce never looked at me. Not even once.

The sun set. The house slowly emptied. Bruce collected his friends and took us up to his bedroom, where he sat down on his bed. Eric and Neil and Neil's hugely pregnant wife took the couch. George took the chair at Bruce's desk. I folded myself up on the floor, outside of the circle, thinking with some small and primitive part of my brain that he'd have to talk to me again, he'd have to let me comfort him, if our years together were to have meant anything.

Bruce unfastened his ponytail, shook out his hair, and tied it back again. "I've been a child my whole life," he announced. Nobody seemed to know quite how to respond to that, so they did what I supposed they normally did, up in Bruce's room. Eric filled the bong, and George fished a lighter out of his suit jacket pocket, and Neil shoved a towel under the door. Unbelievable, I thought, biting back a burst of hysterical laughter. They cope with death the exact same way they cope with a Saturday night when there's nothing good on cable.

Eric passed the bong to Neil without even asking me if I wanted it. I didn't, and he probably knew it. The only thing pot ever did for me was make me want to sleep and eat even more than I already did. Not exactly the kind of drug I needed. Still, it would have been nice if he'd offered.

"Your father was really cool," George mumbled, and everyone else mumbled his assent, except for Neil's pregnant wife, who made a big production of heaving herself to her feet and walking out the door. Or maybe it's always a production to get up and go when you're that pregnant. Who knows? Neil gazed at his sneakers. Eric and George said again how sorry they were. Then everybody started talking about the playoffs.

Always a child, I thought, looking at Bruce through the haze. For a minute, I caught his eye, and we looked right at each other. He tilted the bong toward me: Want some? I shook my head no, and took a deep breath into the silence.

"Remember when the swimming pool was finished?" I asked.

Bruce gave me a small but encouraging nod.

"Your father was so happy," I said. I looked at his friends. "You guys should have seen it. Dr. Guberman couldn't swim . . ."

". . . he never learned how," Bruce added.

"But he insisted—absolutely insisted—that this house have a swimming pool. 'My kids aren't going to sweat for another summer!'"

Bruce laughed a little bit.

"So the day the pool was finished, he threw this gigantic party." Now George was nodding. He'd been there. "He had it catered. He ordered, like, a dozen watermelon baskets . . ."

". . . and a keg," said Bruce, laughing.

"And he walked around all afternoon in this monogrammed bathrobe that he'd bought just for the occasion, smoking this gigantic cigar, and looking like a king," I concluded. "There must have been a hundred people here . . ." My voice trailed off. I was remembering Bruce's father in the hot tub, a steaming cigar clenched between his teeth, a Dixie cup full of beer sweating on the ledge beside him, and the full moon hanging like a circle of gold in the sky.

And finally I felt that I was on more stable ground. I couldn't smoke pot, and he wouldn't let me kiss him, but I could tell stories all night long. "He looked so happy," I said to Bruce, "because you were happy."

Bruce started to cry quietly, and when I got up and crossed the room and sat beside him, he didn't say anything. Not even when I reached for him. When I put my arm around his shoulders he leaned into me, holding me and crying. I closed my eyes so I only heard his friends getting up and filing out the door.

"Ah, Cannie," he said.

"Shh," I said, and rocked him, moving him back and forth with my whole body, easing him back onto the bed, beneath a shelf lined with his Little League trophies and perfect attendance plaques from

Hebrew school. His friends were gone. We were finally alone. "Sshh now, shh now." I kissed his wet cheek. He didn't resist. His lips were cool underneath mine. He wasn't kissing me back, but he wasn't pushing me away, either. It was a start.

"What do you want?" he whispered to me.

"I would do whatever you wanted," I said. "Even . . . if you wanted that . . . I'd do it for you. I love you . . ." I said.

"Don't say anything," he whispered, sliding his hands up under my shirt.

"Oh, Bruce," I breathed, unwilling to believe that this was happening, that he wanted me, too.

"Shh," he said, shushing me the way I'd quieted him moments before. His hands were fumbling with the many clasps of my bra.

"Lock the door," I whispered.

"I don't want to let you go," he said.

"You don't have to," I told him, tucking my face into his neck, breathing in the smell of him, sweet smoke and shaving cream and shampoo, glorying in the feel of his arms around me, thinking that this was what I wanted, was what I'd always wanted—the love of a man who was wonderful and sweet and who, best of all, understood me. "You don't have to ever again."

I tried to make it good for him, to touch him in his favorite places, to move the way that I remembered he liked. It felt wonderful to me, to be with him again, and I thought, holding his shoulders as he thrust himself into me and moaned, that we could start over; that we *were* starting over. The *Moxie* article I was willing to write off as water under the bridge, provided he'd swear a solemn oath to never again mention my body in print. And the rest of it, his father's death, we'd get through as a couple. Together. "I love you so much," I whispered, kissing the side of his face, holding him close, trying to quiet the small voice inside of me that noticed, even in the throes of passion, that he wasn't saying anything back.

Afterward, with my head on his shoulder and my fingertips tracing circles on his chest, I thought that nothing had ever felt so right. I thought that maybe I'd been a child, a girl, but now I was ready to step up to the plate, to do the right thing, to be a woman, and to stand beside him, holding him up, starting tonight.

Bruce, evidently, had other thoughts. "You should get going," he said, removing himself from my arms and walking into the bathroom without looking back at the bed.

This was unexpected. "I can stay," I called.

Bruce came out of the bathroom with a towel wrapped around his waist. "I've got to go to temple with my mom in the morning, and I think it would, um, complicate things if . . ." His voice trailed off.

"Okay," I said, remembering my vow, to be an adult, to think of what he needed instead of what I wanted, even though what I wanted was more along the lines of a long, slow, sweet snuggle, followed by both of us drifting gently off to sleep—not this hasty retreat. "No problem," I said, and pulled my clothes back on. No sooner had I straightened my panties then Bruce was grabbing my elbow and walking me toward the door, hustling me past the kitchen and the living room, where, presumably, his mother was waiting and his friends had regrouped.

"Give me a call," I said, hearing my voice trembling, "whenever you want."

He looked away. "I'm going to be kind of busy," he said.

I took a deep breath, willing the panic to subside. "Okay," I said. "Just know that I'm there for you."

He nodded gravely. "I appreciate that, Cannie," he said, as if I'd just offered him financial planning advice instead of my heart on a platter. I went to kiss him. He offered me his cheek. Fine, I thought, getting into the car, gripping the steering wheel tightly so he wouldn't see my hands shake. I can be patient. I can be mature. I can wait for him. He loved me so much, I thought, speeding home through the dark. He'll love me again.

SIX

When I took Psychology 101, the professor taught us about random reinforcement. Put three groups of rats in three separate cages, each equipped with a bar. The first group of rats got a pellet every time they pressed the bar. The second group never got pellets, no matter how often they pressed. And the third group got pellets just once in a while.

The first group, the professor said, eventually gets bored with the guaranteed reward and the rats who never get treats give up, too. But the random rats will press on that bar forever, hoping each time they press that this time the magic will happen, that this time they'll get lucky. It was at that moment in class that I realized that I had become my father's rat.

He'd loved me once. I remembered it. I had a handful of mental pictures, postcards that had gotten soft around the edges from being handled so often. Scene one: Cannie, age three, snug in her father's lap, her head against his chest, feeling his voice rumble through her as he read *Where the Wild Things Are*. Scene two: Cannie, age six, holding hands with her daddy as he led her through the doors of the elementary school on a warm summer Saturday to take her first grade readiness test. "Don't be shy," he tells her, kissing both her cheeks. "You'll do great."

I remember being ten years old spending whole days with my father, running errands, meeting his secretary, and Mrs. Yee at the dry cleaners who did his shirts, the salesman at the clothing store who looked at my father with respect as he paid for his suits. We'd pick up brie at the fancy cheese shop that smelled wonderfully of freshly roasted coffee beans, and jazz records at Old Vinyl. Everyone knew my father's name. "Dr. Shapiro," they'd greet him, smiling at him, at us, lined up in a row, from oldest to youngest, with me at the head of the line. He'd put one big warm hand on my head, stroking my ponytail. "This is Cannie, my oldest," he'd say. And all of them, from the clerks at the cheese store to the security guards in his building, seemed to know not just who he was, but who I was, too. "Your father says you're very smart," they'd say, and I'd stand there, smiling, trying to look smart.

But days like that became rare as I got older. The truth was, my father mostly ignored me. He ignored all of us—Lucy, and Josh, and even my mother. He came home late, he left home early, he spent his weekends in the office or on long drives "to clear my head." Whatever affection we got, whatever notice he paid us, was parceled out in small doses, administered infrequently. But oh, when he loved me, when he put his hand on my head, when I leaned my own head against him . . . there was no feeling in the world that could beat it. I felt important. I felt cherished. And I would do whatever it took, press the bar until my hands bled, to get that feeling again.

He left us for the first time when I turned twelve. I came home from school and there he was, unexpectedly, in the bedroom, piling undershirts and sock balls into a suitcase. "Dad?" I asked him, startled to see him in the daytime. "Are you . . . are we . . ." I wanted to ask if we were going somewhere—a trip, maybe? His eyes were heavy and hooded. "Ask your mother," he said. "She'll explain."

And my mother did explain it—that both she and my father loved us very much, but they couldn't work things out between the two of them. I was still numb from the shock of that when I found out the truth of what was going on from Hallie Cinti, one of the popular girls. Hallie was on my soccer team, but in a completely different league socially. On the field she frequently looked as though she'd prefer that I not pass to her, as if my foot on the ball could transmit my own personal taint and send nerd-germs creeping through her cleats. Three years later she'd be infamous for administering restorative blow-jobs to three of the five starters on the boys' basketball team during halftime of the state play-offs, and we'd all be calling her Hallie Cunti, but I didn't know that yet.

"Heard about your father," she said, plunking herself down at my table, which was in a corner of the lunchroom where Hallie Cinti and her ilk rarely ventured. The chess club kids and my friends from Junior Debaters stared, open-mouthed, as Hallie and her friend Jenna Lind slung their purses over the backs of two plastic chairs and stared at me.

"Heard what?" I asked warily. I didn't trust Hallie, who'd ignored me through six years of school, or Jenna, whose hair was always perfectly feathered.

Hallie, as it turned out, couldn't wait to tell me. "I heard my Mom talking about it last night. He moved in with some dental technician on Copper Hill Road."

I toyed with my peanut butter sandwich, buying time. Was this true? How could Hallie's mother know? And why was she talking about it? My mind was fluttering with questions, plus the half-remembered faces of all the women who'd ever scraped my teeth.

Jenna leaned in to deliver the coup de grace. "We heard," she said, "that she's only twenty-seven."

Well. So that would explain the gossip. Hallie and Jenna stared at me, and my debate-team friends stared at them staring. I felt like I'd been suddenly thrust onstage, and I didn't know my lines, or even what I was supposed to be performing.

"So is it true?" Hallie asked impatiently.

"It's no big deal," said Jenna, evidently hoping to get me to spill via sympathy. "My parents are divorced."

Divorced, I thought, tasting the word. Was this really what was happening? Would my Dad do this to us?

I lifted my eyes to the popular girls. "Go away," I told them. I heard one of my debate friends gasp. Nobody talked to Jenna and Hallie that way. "Leave me alone. Go away!"

Jenna rolled her eyes. Hallie shoved her seat back. "You're a big fat loser," she opined, before scurrying back to the popular kids' tables, where everyone's shirts had little alligators, and all the girls ever had for lunch was Diet Coke.

I walked home slowly and found my mother in the kitchen, with about ten half-unpacked bags of groceries arrayed on the counters and dining room table. "Is Dad living with someone else?" I blurted. She shoved three packages of chicken breasts into the freezer and sighed, her hands on her hips.

"I didn't want you to find out like this," she murmured.

"Hallie Cinti told me," I said.

My mother sighed again.

"But she doesn't know anything," I said, hoping my mother would agree.

Instead she sat at the kitchen table and motioned for me to join her. "Mrs. Cinti works at the same hospital as your Dad," she said.

So it was true.

"You can tell me things. I'm not a little kid." But at that moment, I wished that I was a little kid—the kind whose parents still read to her in bed and held her hands when she crossed the streets.

My mother sighed. "I think this might be for your father to tell you."

But that conversation never happened, and two nights later, my father had moved back. Josh and Lucy and I stood in the backyard and watched him pull the suitcase out of the trunk of his little red sports car. Lucy was crying, and Josh was trying not to. My father never even looked at us as he crossed the gravel driveway, the heels of his boots crunching with each step.

"Cannie?" Lucy sniffled. "If he's back now, that's good, isn't it? He won't leave anymore, right?"

I stared at the door, watching it slowly close behind him. "I don't know," I said. I needed answers. My father was unapproachable, my mother was no help. "Don't worry," she scolded me. Her own face was etched with lines of sleeplessness. "Everything's going to be fine, honey." This from my mother, who never called me honey. As much as I dreaded it, I would have to go right to the source.

I found Hallie Cinti in the girls' room the next Monday afternoon. She was standing at the mirror, squinted as she reapplied Bonnie Belle lip gloss. I cleared my throat. She ignored me. I tapped her on her shoulder and she turned to face me, her lips pursed in distaste.

"What?" she spat.

I cleared my throat as she glared at me. "Um . . . that thing . . . about my father," I began.

Hallie rolled her eyes and pulled a pink plastic comb out of her purse.

"He moved back," I said.

"How swell for you," said Hallie, now combing her bangs.

"I thought maybe you might have heard why. From your mom."

"Why should I tell you anything?" she sneered.

I'd spent the whole weekend planning for this contingency. What could I, plump and unpopular Cannie Shapiro, offer sleek, beautiful Hallie? I pulled two items out of my backpack. The first was a five-page paper on light and dark imagery in *Romeo and Juliet*. The other was a fifth of vodka that I'd swiped from my parents' liquor cabinet that morning. Hallie and her crew might not have been as academically advanced as I was, but they made up for it in other fields of endeavor.

Hallie snatched the bottle out of my hands, checked to see that the seal was unbroken, then reached for the paper. I yanked it back.

"First, tell me."

She gave a little shrug, slipped the bottle into her purse, and turned back toward the mirror. "I heard my mother talking on the phone. She said that his dental friend told him that she wanted children," she said. "And I guess your father doesn't want any more. And looking at you," she continued, "I can understand why." She turned to me, smirking, extending her hand for the paper.

I threw it at her. "Just copy it over in your own handwriting. I put in some spelling mistakes, so they'll know it's you, not me."

Hallie took the paper and I went back to class. *No more children.* Well, the way he treated us, that made sense.

He stayed with us for almost six years after that, but he wasn't the same. The little moments of kindness and love, the nights he'd read to us in bed, the Saturday afternoon ice-cream cones and the Sunday afternoon drives, were gone. It was as if my father had fallen asleep, alone, on a bus or a train, and woken up twenty years later, surrounded by strangers: my mother, my sister, my brother, and me, all wanting things—help with the dishes, a ride to band practice, $10 for the movies, his approval, his attention, his love. He looked out at us, mild brown eyes swimming with confusion, then hardening with anger. Who are these people? he seemed to be wondering. How long will I have to travel beside them? And why do they think I owe them anything?

He went from being loving, in an absent-minded, occasional way, to being mean. Was it because I knew his secret—that he didn't want more children, that he'd probably never wanted us? Was it that he missed the other woman, that she was his one true love, forever denied to him? I thought that was some of it. But there were other things, too.

My father was—is, I suppose—a plastic surgeon. He started off in the Army, working with burn victims, wounded soldiers, men who'd come back from the war with their skin pink and puckery from chemicals, or lumpy and disfigured from shrapnel.

But he discovered his true genius after we moved to Pennsylvania. There, the bulk of his practice involved not soldiers but society ladies, women whose only wounds were invisible and who were willing to drop thousands of dollars on a discreet, skilled surgeon who'd make their bellies tight, their eyelids less droopy, who'd eliminate saddlebags and double chins with a few deft strokes of the scalpel.

He was successful. By the time he left us for the first time Larry Shapiro was known as the man to see in the greater Philadelphia area for tummy tucks, chin lifts, nose jobs, boob jobs. We had the requisite big house, the curved driveway, the in-ground swimming pool with hot tub in the back. My father drove a Porsche (although, thankfully, my mother was able to talk him out of the NOSEDOC vanity plates). My mom drove an Audi. We had a maid clean twice a week; my parents threw catered dinner parties every other month, and we went on vacations to Colorado (for skiing) and Florida (for sun).

And then he left, and came back, and our lives fell apart, like a well-loved book that you'd read and read again, until one night you picked it up to read yourself to sleep and the binding collapsed, sending dozens of pages spiraling toward the floor. He didn't want this life. That much was clear. He was miserable tethered to this suburb, to the never-ending schedule of soccer games and spelling bees and Hebrew schools, tied down by mortgage payments and car payments, habit and obligation. And he took his misery out on all of us—and, for some reason, on me especially.

Suddenly, it was as if he couldn't bear to look at me. And nothing I could do was right, or even close.

"Look at this!" he'd thunder, of my B+ in algebra. He was sitting at the dining room table, a familiar glass of scotch at his elbow. I was skulking in the doorway, trying to hide myself in the shadows. "What is your excuse for this?"

"I don't like math," I'd tell him. In truth, I was just as ashamed of the grade as he was angry about it. I'd never gotten anything less than an A in my life. But no matter how hard I tried, or how much extra help I got, algebra confounded me.

"Do you think I liked medical school?" he snarled. "Do you have any idea how much potential you have? Do you have any inkling what a waste it is to squander your gifts?"

"I don't care what my gifts are. I don't like math."

"Fine," he'd say with a shrug, flinging the report card across the table like it had suddenly acquired an offensive smell. "Be a secretary. See if I care."

He was like that with all of us—snarly, surly, dismissive, and rude. He'd come home from work, drop his briefcase in the hall, pour himself the first in a series of scotch on the rocks, and storm by us, upstairs into the bedroom, locking the door behind him. He'd either stay up there, or retreat to the living room, with the lights turned low, listening to Mahler's symphonies. Even at thirteen, even without the benefit of a basic music appreciation class, I knew that nonstop Mahler, backed by the rattle of ice cubes in his glass, could portend nothing good.

And when he did bother to speak to us, it was only to complain: how tired he was, how little appreciated; how hard he worked to provide things for us, "you little snobs," he'd slur, "with your skis and your swimming pool."

"I hate to ski," said Josh, who did. One run and he'd head back to the lodge to drink hot chocolate and fret, and if we forced him back out he'd convince the Ski Patrol that he was suffering from imminent frostbite, and we'd have to collect him at the first aid cabin, stripped down to his long underwear and basting under the heat lamps.

"I'd rather swim with the other kids at the Rec Center," said Lucy, which was true. She had more friends than the rest of us put together. The phone was always ringing. Another sore spot with my father. "That goddamn phone!" he'd yell when it rang during dinner. But we weren't allowed to take it off the hook. It could be his office, after all.

"If you hate us so much, why did you even have kids?" I'd scream at him, taunting him with what I knew was the truth. He never had an answer—just more insults, more anger, more scalding, punishing rage. Josh, just six, was "a baby." Lucy, who was twelve, he either ignored or berated. "Stupid," he'd say, shaking his head at her grades, "Clumsy," when she'd drop a glass. And, at thirteen, I became "the dog."

It's true, thirteen was not the year when I was looking my best. In addition to the breasts and hips I'd sprouted, seemingly overnight, I had acquired a mouthful of complicated-looking metal and rubber bands to correct my overbite. I had a *de rigeur* Dorothy Hamill haircut, which wasn't doing my full face any favors. I bought clothes in two sizes—baggy and baggier—and spent the whole year in a perpetual stoop, trying to hide my chest. I looked like the Hunchback of Notre Dame, only with zits and braces. I felt like a walking affront, like a collection of the things my father spent his days waging war against. He was all about beauty—its creation, its maintenance, its perfection. Having a wife who'd fallen short of the mark and hadn't stayed thin was one thing, I supposed . . . but a daughter who'd failed so flagrantly was, evidently, unforgivable. And I had failed. There was nothing beautiful about me at thirteen, nothing at all, and I could feel that fact confirmed in the hard, hateful way he looked at me, and in all the things he said.

"Cannie's very bright," I heard him tell one of his golf buddies. "She'll be able to take care of herself. Not a beauty," he said, "but smart."

I stood there, hardly believing what I'd heard, and when I finally believed it, I crumpled inside, like a tin can under a car's wheels. I wasn't stupid, and I wasn't blind, and I knew that there were many ways in which I differed from Farrah Fawcett, from girls in movies and on posters in boys' bedrooms. But I'd remembered his hand on my head, his beard tickling my cheek as he kissed me. I was his daughter, his little girl. He was supposed to love me. Now he thought I was ugly. *Not a beauty* . . . but what father doesn't think his little girl is beautiful? Except I wasn't little. And, I guessed, I wasn't his girl anymore.

When I look at pictures of myself from that time—and, understandably, there are only about four—there's this horrible desperate look in my eyes. *Please like me,* I'm pleading, even as I'm trying to hide myself behind a row of cousins at a bar mitzvah, beneath the hot tub bubbles during a pool party, with my lips drawn in a pained smile, stretched tight over my braces, ducking my head into my neck, hunching my shoulders, slouching to make myself shorter, smaller. Trying to disappear.

Years later, in college, when a friend was recounting some bit of suburban childhood horror, I tried to explain how it was with my father. "He was a monster," I blurted. I was an English major, versed in Chaucer and Shakespeare, Joyce and Proust by then. I still hadn't found a better word than that.

My friend's face got very serious. "Did he molest you?" she asked. I almost laughed. Given how much of my father's conversation with me revolved around how ugly, how fat, how hideous I was, molestation was the last thing I would have expected.

"Did he abuse you?" she asked.

"He drank too much," I said. "He left us." But he never hit me. He never hit any of us. It would have been easier if he had. Then there would have been a name we could give it, a box to put it in, a label for the box. There would have been laws, authorities, shelters, TV talk shows where reporters gravely discussed what we were enduring, a built-in recognition of what we'd experienced, to help us through.

But he never raised a finger. And, at thirteen, at fourteen, I had no words for what he was doing to us. I didn't even know how to start that conversation. What would I have said? "He's mean?" Mean meant being grounded, meant no television after dinner, not the kind of daily verbal assault my father would routinely deliver over the dinner table, a scathing recitation of all the ways I'd failed to live up to my potential, the walking tour of the places that I had failed.

And who would have believed me? My father was always charm personified to my friends. He remembered their names, and their boyfriend's names, he would inquire courteously about summer plans and college visits. They wouldn't have believed me, and if they had they would have wanted me to explain. And I had no explanation, no answers. When you're on a battleground, you don't have the luxury of time to dwell on the various historical factors and sociopolitical influences that caused the war. You just keep your head down and try to survive it, to shove the pages back in the book, close the covers and pretend that nothing's broken, nothing's wrong.

The summer before my senior year of high school, my mother took Josh and Lucy to Martha's Vineyard for the weekend. A friend had a rental house, she was itching to get out of Avondale. I had my first summer job, as a lifeguard at a local country club. I told my Mom that I'd stay home, watch the dogs, hold down the fort. I figured it would be fine: I could have the house to myself, entertain my twenty-three-year-old boyfriend away from her watchful eye, come and go as I pleased.

For the first three days it was fine. Then I came home in the predawn hours of the fourth morning, and it was as if I were twelve again. There was my father in the bedroom, the suitcase on the bed, the stacks of white T-shirts and the piles of black socks—maybe the same ones, I thought wildly, that he'd taken the last time.

I stared at them, and then at him. My father looked at me for a long moment. Then he sighed.

"I'll call," he said, "when I have my new number."

I shrugged. "Whatever," I said.

"Don't talk to me like that!" he said. He hated when we were flip. He demanded respect, even—especially—when he didn't deserve it.

"What's her name?" I asked. He narrowed his eyes.

"Why do you want to know?"

I looked at him and couldn't think of an answer. Did I imagine that it made any difference? Could a name even matter?

"Tell your mother," he began. I shook my head.

"Oh, no," I said. "Don't make me do your dirty work. If you've got something to say, tell her yourself."

He shrugged, like it didn't matter. He added a few more shirts, a fistful of ties.

"I'm glad you're leaving. Do you know that?" I said. My voice was too loud in the early-morning quiet of the house. "We'll be better off without you," I said.

He looked at me. Then he nodded. "Yes," he said, "I think maybe you will."

He went back to his packing. I went back to my bedroom. I lay on the bed—the bed where my father had read to me, a million years ago—and closed my eyes. I'd been waiting for this, after all. I'd known it was coming. I thought it would feel the way it does when a scab over an old wound finally falls off—a momentary pang, a little bit of pain, a sense of absence. Then nothing. Just nothing at all. That was what I was supposed to feel, that was all I wanted to feel, I thought fiercely, tossing and turning on my bed, trying to find comfort. It didn't matter, I told myself, over and over again. I just couldn't figure out why I was crying.

I went to Princeton because he told me to, in one of his last acts of hands-on parenting. I'd wanted to go to Smith. I liked the campus, liked the crew coach, liked the idea of an all-girls' school, where the focus would be on learning, where I could be free to be who I was: your basic late-eighties model nerd with her nose in a book.

"Forget it," my father pronounced over the table. He'd been gone for six months by then: relocated to a new suburb, living in a brand-new, shiny condo with a brand-new shiny girlfriend. He'd agreed to meet us for dinner, then cancelled and rescheduled twice. "I'm not sending you to some dyke school."

"Larry," said my mother, her voice quiet and hopeless. All of her good humor and cheer had been leeched from her by then. It would be years—and Tayna—before she laughed and smiled easily.

My father ignored her, glaring at me suspiciously, a forkful of steak raised halfway to his mouth. "You aren't a dyke, are you?"

"No, Dad," I said, "I actually prefer threesomes."

He chewed. Swallowed. Patted his lips with his napkin. "That's two more people than I'd have thought would be interested in seeing you naked," he said.

As much as I'd liked Smith, I hadn't liked Princeton. The campus looked like the staging ground for a very successful eugenics experiment: everyone was blond, preppy, and perfect, except for the dark-haired girls who were sleek, exotic, and perfect. During the weekend I'd spent there I hadn't seen a single fat person, or anyone with bad skin. Just acres of shiny hair, straight white teeth, and perfect bodies in perfect clothes arrayed beneath the perfect willow trees that grew beneath perfectly Gothic stone halls.

I said I'd be miserable. My father said he didn't care. I dug my heels in. He told me it was Princeton or nothing. And by the time I'd been packed off to Campbell Hall and stayed long enough to start classes and have my graduation-present mountain bike stolen from the library bicycle rack, the divorce was final, and he was gone for good, sticking us with a tuition bill of which he'd paid just enough to make it impractical for me to start over anywhere else. So I quit the crew team—no big loss to me, or the team, I suspect, since I'd gained the requisite Freshman Fifteen, plus the fifteen pounds my roommate should have gained but didn't, thanks to her diligent bulimia—and got a job with the Department of Food Services, affectionately known as Doofus to its employees.

If college is supposed to be the best years of your life, then it's safe to say that I spent the best years of my life in a hairnet, dishing out reconstituted scrambled eggs and limp bacon, loading dirty dishes on the conveyor belt, mopping the floors, looking at my classmates out of the corner of my eyes and thinking that they were all so much more beautiful, graceful, comfortable in their own skins than I could ever be. They all had better haircuts. And all of them were thin. True, many of them were thin because they were sticking their fingers down their throats after every meal, but at times that seemed like a small price to pay for having basically everything a woman could want—brains, beauty, and a way to eat ice cream and cherry Danishes and still stay skinny.

"Good Hair" was the first article I wrote for the campus alternative newspaper. I was a freshman, and the editor-in-chief, a junior named Gretel whose own hair was kept in a paramilitary blond brush cut, asked me to write more. By sophomore year I was a columnist. By junior year I was a senior writer, spending every hour I wasn't slinging hash or pushing a mop in the *Nassau Weekly*'s cramped, dusty offices in Aaron Burr Hall, and I'd decided that this was what I wanted to do with my life.

Writing let me escape. It let me escape Princeton, where everyone was chic and stylish and, in the case of the guy down the hall, the future ruler of some minor Middle Eastern principality. It let me escape the insistent tug of my family, and its ongoing misery. Writing was like slipping into the ocean, a place where I could move easily, where I could be graceful, and playful, and invisible and visible all at once—a byline, not a body. Sitting in front of the computer, with the screen blank and the cursor blinking, was the best escape I knew.

And there was plenty to escape from. In the four years I was at Princeton, my father remarried and had two more children. Daniel and Rebecca. He had the nerve to send me pictures, and birth announcements. Did he think I'd be happy, seeing their squinched-up baby faces and tiny baby footprints? It felt like being kicked. It wasn't that he didn't want children, I realized sadly. It was that he hadn't wanted us.

My mother went back to work, and her weekly telephone calls were full of complaints about how schools, and kids, had changed since she got her teaching certificate. The subtext was clear: This wasn't the life she signed up for. This wasn't where she expected to be, at fifty, making ends meet on alimony and what the local school board paid permanent substitutes.

Meanwhile, Lucy had flunked out of her first year at school in Boston, and was living at home, attending community college haphazardly, and majoring in unsuitable men. Josh was spending three hours a day in the gym, lifting weights so frequently that his upper body looked inflated, and had pretty much stopped talking except for a series of tonal grunts and the occasional "Whatever."

"Just get your education," my mother would say wearily, after the latest recitation of how my father's checks were late again, of how her car had broken down, of how my sister hadn't come home for two nights in a row. "Just finish up. We'll be fine."

Then—finally—it was the June of my graduation.

Except for a handful of strained lunches during the summer and Christmas breaks, I hadn't seen my father. He sent birthday cards (usually on time), and tuition checks (almost always late) and usually for about half of what they were supposed to be. I felt like I'd become just one more unremarkable item on his to-do list. I hadn't expected him to come to my graduation. I never thought he'd care. But he called me a week in advance of the much-longed-for date, saying that he was looking forward to it. Him, and his new wife, whom I'd never met.

"I'm not sure . . . I don't think . . . ," I stammered.

"Cannie," he said. "I'm your father. And Christine's never seen Princeton!"

"So tell Christine you'll send her a postcard," my mother said sourly. I had dreaded telling my mother that he'd be there, but I couldn't figure out how to tell him no. He'd said the magic words, the

pellet words. *I'm your father.* After everything—his distance, his deser-
tion, the new wife and new kids—I was, it seems, still starving for his
love.

My father, with new wife and kids in tow, arrived during the
English Department's reception. I'd won some small award for creative writing, but they came too late to hear my name called.
Christine was a petite little thing, with an aerobicized hard body and a
blond perm. The children were adorable. My floral Laura Ashley dress
had looked just fine in the dorm. Now it looked like a slipcover, I
thought dismally. And I looked like a sofa.

"Cannie," said my father, looking me up and down. "I see college
cuisine's agreed with you."

I clutched my stupid plaque tightly against me. "Thanks so
much," I said. My father rolled his eyes at his new wife as if to say, *Can
you believe how touchy she is?*

"I was just teasing you," he said, as his new adorable children
stared at me, as if I were an animal in a zoo for the oversized.

"I, um, got you tickets for the ceremony." I didn't mention that
I'd had to beg, borrow, and finally pay $100 I couldn't spare to score
the tickets. Each senior was issued a total of four. The administration
at Princeton hadn't yet made accomodations for those of us struggling
with reconstructed families that included stepmothers, stepfathers,
new half-siblings, and the like.

My father shook his head. "Won't be necessary. We're leaving in
the morning."

"Leaving?" I repeated. "But you'll miss graduation!"

"We've got tickets to Sesame Place," chirped his little wife, Christine.

"Sesame Place!" repeated the little girl for emphasis.

"So Princeton was sort of on our way."

"That's . . . um . . . well." And suddenly I was blinking back tears.
I bit my lip as hard as I could, and squeezed the plaque against me so
tightly that I had an eight-by-twelve bruise on my midsection for the
next week and a half. "Thanks for stopping by."

My father nodded, and moved as if he was going to hug me, but
wound up merely grasping my shoulders and giving me the kind of

shake that coaches routinely administer to underperforming athletes—a "buck up, camper" kind of shake. "Congratulations," he said. "I'm very proud of you." But when he kissed me his lips never even touched my skin, and I knew the whole time that his eyes were on the door.

Somehow I made it through the ceremony, the dismantling of my dorm room, the long ride home. I hung my diploma on my bedroom wall and tried to figure out what I'd do next. Graduate school was out of the question. Even after all those breakfasts I'd worked, all those drooly pieces of bacon and curdled scrambled eggs, I was still $20,000 or so in debt. I couldn't see borrowing more money. So I lined up job interviews with the handful of small papers who were willing to even consider a college graduate with no real-world experience, in the middle of a recession, and spent the summer driving up and down the Northeast in the thirdhand van I'd bought with some of my food-service dollars. When I loaded up the car to head out for my job interviews, I made myself a promise—I wasn't going to be my father's rat anymore. I was going to walk away from the pellet bar. He could bring me nothing but unhappiness, and I didn't need more unhappiness in my life.

I heard from my brother that our father had moved out West, but I didn't ask for specifics, and nobody offered them. Ten years after the divorce he no longer had to pay child support or alimony. The checks stopped coming. So did the birthday cards, or any acknowledgment that we even existed. Lucy's graduation came and went, and when Josh sent a card announcing his, it came back returned to sender. Our father had moved on, it seemed, without telling us where.

"We could find him on the Internet or something," I offered. Josh glared at me.

"Why?"

And I couldn't think of an answer. If we found him, would he come? Would he care? Probably not. We agreed, the three of us, to let it be. If our father wanted to stay gone, we would let him.

And we struggled into our twenties without him. Josh overcame his fear of the slopes and spent a year and a half drifting from one ski-resort town to another, and Lucy ran off briefly to Arizona with a guy she claimed was a former professional hockey player. As evidence, she'd had him remove his bridge in the middle of dinner and show that he was missing all his teeth.

And that was that, pretty much.

I know that what had happened with my father—his insults, his criticism, the way he made me feel that I was defective and deformed—had hurt me. I'd encountered enough of those self-help articles in women's magazines to know that you don't go through that kind of cruelty unscathed. With every man I met I'd watch myself carefully. Did I really like that editor, I'd wonder, or am I just searching for Daddy? Do I love this guy, I'd ask myself, or do I just think he'd never leave me, the way my father did?

And where had all the care I'd taken gotten me, I wondered? I was alone. A man who'd liked me enough to want me in his family was dead, and I couldn't even say how sorry I was properly. And now that it was possible—now that it was likely, even—that Bruce had finally gotten to the point in his life where he could understand me, where he could sympathize with what I'd been through because of what he'd gone through—he wouldn't even talk to me. It felt like the cruelest joke, like a rug being yanked out from under me—in other words, like the way my father made me feel, all over again.

SEVEN

The scales at the University of Philadelphia's Weight and Eating Disorders Center looked like meat carts. The platforms were about four times the size of normal scales, with railings all around them. It was hard not to feel like livestock when you climbed aboard, as I had every other week since September.

"That's very unusual," said Dr. K, gazing down at the red digital printout on the scale. "You lost eight pounds."

"I can't eat," I said numbly.

"You mean you're eating less," he said.

"No, I mean every time I put something in my mouth I puke."

He looked at me sharply, then back at the scale. The numbers were the same. "Let's step into my office," he suggested.

And there we were again: me in the chair, him at his desk, my ever-thickening folder spread in front of him. He was tanner than when I'd seen him last, and possibly even thinner, floating in his white laboratory coat. It had been six weeks since I'd last seen Bruce, and things were not proceeding as I'd hoped.

"Most patients gain weight before we start them on the sibutramine," he said. "They have a kind of last hurrah. So, as I said, this is unusual."

"Something happened," I said.

He looked at me sharply. "Another article?"

"Bruce's father died," I said. "Bruce, my boyfriend . . . ex-boyfriend. His dad died last month."

He looked down at his hands, at his folder, then, finally, up at me. "I'm sorry to hear that."

"And he called me . . . and told me . . . and asked me to go to the funeral . . . but he wouldn't let me stay. Wouldn't let me stay with him. He was so awful . . . and it was so sad . . . and the rabbi said how he used to go to toy stores, and I feel so terrible . . ."

I blinked hard against the tears. Wordlessly, Dr. K. handed me a box of Kleenex. He took off his glasses and pressed two fingers against the bridge of his nose.

"I'm a bad person," I blubbered. He looked at me kindly.

"Why? Because you broke up with him? That's silly. How could you know this was going to happen?"

"No," I said. "I know I couldn't. But now, it's like . . . all I want is to be there for him, and love him, and he won't let me, and I feel so . . . alone. . . ."

He sighed. "It's hard when things end. Even if nobody dies, even if you part on the best possible terms, and there's nobody else involved. Even if you're the one who lets go first. It's never easy. It always hurts."

"I just feel like I made this huge mistake. Like I didn't think things through. I thought I knew . . . how it would feel to be apart from him. But I didn't. I couldn't. I never imagined anything like this. And all I do is miss him. . . ." I swallowed hard, choking on another sob. I couldn't explain it—that I'd been waiting my whole life for a guy who would get me, who would understand my pain. I thought I'd known what pain was, but I knew now I'd never hurt this way.

He focused his eyes on a spot on the wall over my head as I wept. Then he opened a drawer, pulled a pad out of his desk, and started writing.

"Am I out of the study?" I asked.

"No," he said. "Of course, you're going to have to start eating again soon. But I think it might be a good idea for you to have someone to talk to."

"Oh, no," I said. "Not therapy."

He gave me a crooked smile. "Am I sensing a little antipathy here?"

"No, I don't have anything against it, but I just know it won't help," I told him. "I'm looking at the situation realistically. I made a huge mistake. I wasn't sure that I loved him enough, and now I know that I do, and his father's dead and he doesn't love me anymore." I straightened my back and wiped my face. "But I still want to do this. I really want to do this. I want to have one thing in my life I can feel good about. I want to feel like I'm doing something right."

He sat me on the examination table again, his hands gentle on my back and my arms as he tied a piece of rubber tubing around my bicep and told me to make a fist. I looked away when he slid the needle in, but he'd done it so skillfully I could barely feel it. Both of us watched the glass vial filling up with my blood. I wondered what he was thinking. "Almost done," he said quietly, before deftly removing the needle and pressing a piece of gauze over the wound.

"Do I get a lollipop?" I joked. He handed me a Band-Aid instead, and the piece of paper where he'd written two names, two phone numbers. "Take it," he said. "And, Cannie, you've got to eat, and if you find that you can't, you have to call us, and then I'd really suggest calling one of these counselors."

"I'm so huge, do you really think a few more days is going to kill me?"

"It's really not healthy," he said seriously. "It can have an adverse impact on your metabolism. My suggestion is to start off with easy stuff . . . toast, bananas, flat ginger ale."

Out in the lobby, he gave me a sheaf of papers easily three inches thick. "Keep exercising, too," he said. "It'll help you feel better."

"You sound like my mother," I said, tucking everything into my purse.

"And Cannie?" He put his hand on my forearm. "Try not to take it so hard."

"I know," I said. "I just wish things were different."

"You'll be fine," he told me firmly. "And . . ."

His voice trailed off. He looked uncomfortable.

"You know how you said you were a bad person?"

"Oh," I said, embarrassed. "Sorry. I just have this tendency to get a little melodramatic. . . ."

"No, no. That's okay. I just meant . . . I wanted to tell you . . ."

The elevator doors slid open, and the people on it looked at me. I looked at the doctor and stepped backward.

"You aren't," he told me. "I'll see you in class."

I went home and lunged for the telephone. My one message was from Samantha.

"Hi, Cannie, it's Sam . . . no, not Bruce, so get that pathetic look off your puss and call me if you feel like going for a walk. I'll buy you an iced coffee. It'll be great. Better than a boyfriend. 'Bye."

I set down the phone, and picked it up again when it started ringing. Maybe it was Bruce this time, I thought.

Instead, it was my mother.

"Where have you been?" she demanded. "I've been calling and calling."

"You didn't leave a message," I pointed out.

"I knew I'd get you eventually," she said. "How's it going?"

"Oh, you know . . . ," I said, my voice trailing off. My mother had really been making an effort since Bruce's father had died. She'd sent a card to the family and made a donation to the temple. She'd been calling me every night, and insisted that I come to her softball league's play-off series and watch the Switch Hitters take on Nine Women Out. It was all attention I could have done without, but I knew she meant well.

"Are you walking?" she asked me. "Are you riding your bike?"

"A little bit," I sighed, remembering how Bruce used to complain that spending time at my house was more like triathlon training sessions than a vacation, because my mother was always trying to organize a walk, a bike ride, two-on-two basketball at the Jewish Center, where she'd gleefully body-check my brother under the boards while I sweated on a StairMaster and Bruce read the sports section in the Seniors' Lounge.

"I'm walking," I said. "I take Nifkin out every day."

"Cannie, that's not enough! You should come home," she said. "You'll be in for Thanksgiving, right? Are you going to come Wednesday, or the day of?"

Ugh. Thanksgiving. Last year Tanya had invited another couple—both women, of course. One of them wouldn't touch meat, and referred to heterosexual people as "breeders," while her girlfriend, whose buzz cut and broad shoulders gave her a disconcerting resemblance to my senior prom date, sat beside her looking embarrassed, then vanished into the family room, where we found her, hours later, watching a football game. Tanya, whose Marlboro habit had rendered her tastebuds defunct, spent the entire meal hustling from the kitchen to the table, bearing one bowl of overcooked, overmashed, oversalted side dishes after another, plus something called Tofurkey for the vegetarian. Josh had cut out early on Thursday night, muttering something about finals, and Lucy spent the entire time on the phone with a mysterious boyfriend, who, we would later learn, was both married and twenty years her senior.

"Never again," I'd whispered to Bruce that night as I tried to find a comfortable position on the lumpy couch while Nifkin trembled behind a stereo speaker. Tanya's loom occupied the space that had formerly housed my bed, and whenever we came home I had to camp out in the living room. Plus, her two evil cats, Gertrude and Alice, took turns stalking the Nif.

"Why don't you come home for the weekend?" my mother asked.

"I'm busy," I said.

"You're obsessed," she corrected. "I'll bet you're sitting there, reading old love letters Bruce sent you and hoping I'll get off the phone in case he calls you."

Damn. How does she do that?

"I am not," I told her. "I've got call waiting."

"Waste of money," said my mother. "Look, Cannie. He's obviously angry with you. He's not going to come running back just yet. . . ."

"I'm aware of that," I said frostily.

"So what's the problem?"

"I miss him," I said.

"Why? What do you miss so much?"

I didn't say anything for a minute.

"Let me ask you something," my mother had said gently. "Have you talked to him?"

"Yeah. We talk." In truth, I'd broken down and called him twice. Both calls had lasted less than five minutes, both had ended when he told me, politely, that there were things he needed to do.

My mother persisted. "Is he calling you?"

"Not so much. Not exactly."

"And who's ending the calls? You or him?"

This was getting touchy. "I see you've returned to the heterosexual advice-giving arena."

"I'm allowed," my mother said cheerfully. "Now: Who's hanging up?"

"Depends," I lied. In truth, it was Bruce. Always Bruce. It was like Sam had said. I was pathetic, and I knew it, and I couldn't stop myself, which was even worse.

"Cannie," she said. "Why don't you give him a break? Give yourself a break, too. Come home."

"I'm busy," I demurred, but I could feel myself weakening.

"We'll bake cookies," she wheedled. "We'll go for long walks. We'll go for a bike ride. Maybe we'll go to New York for the day . . ."

"With Tanya, of course."

My mother sighed. "Cannie," she said, "I know you don't like her, but she is my partner . . . Can't you at least try to be nice?"

I thought about it. "No. Sorry."

"We can have some mother/daughter time, if you really want it."

"Maybe," I said. "It's busy here. And I've got to go to New York next weekend. Did I tell you? I'm interviewing Maxi Ryder."

"Really? Ooh, she was great in that Scottish movie."

"I'll tell her you said so."

"And listen, Cannie. Don't call him anymore. Just give him some time."

I knew she was right, of course. A), I wasn't stupid, and b), I'd been hearing it from Samantha, and from every single one of my friends and acquaintances who had an even passing familiarity with the situation, and I'd probably be hearing it from Nifkin, too, if only he could talk. But somehow I couldn't stop. I had turned into someone that I would have pitied in another life; someone who searched for signs, who analyzed patterns, who went over every word in a conversation looking for hidden meanings, secret signals, the subtext that said, *Yes, I still love you, of course I still love you.*

"I'd like to see you," I'd told him shyly, during Five Minute Phone Conversation #2. Bruce had sighed.

"I think we should wait," he said. "I don't just want to jump right back in again."

"But we'll see each other sometime?" I said, in a tiny little voice that was utterly unlike anything I'd normally use for conversation, and he'd sighed again.

"I don't know, Cannie," he said, "I just don't know."

But "I don't know" wasn't a "no," I'd reasoned, and once I had a chance to be with him, to tell him how sorry I was, to show him how much I had to give, how much I wanted to be back with him . . . well, then he'd take me back. Of course he would. Wasn't he the one who'd said "I love you" first, three years ago, as we'd held each other in my bed? And hadn't he been the one who was always bringing up marriage, always stopping on our walks to admire babies, always steering me toward jewelry shop windows when we walked on Sansom Street, and kissing my ring finger and telling me how we'd always be together?

It was inevitable, I tried to tell myself. Just a matter of time.

"Let me ask you something," I began.

Andy the food critic shoved his glasses up his nose and murmured into his sleeve. "The walls are painted pale green, with gilt on the moldings," he said softly. "It's very French."

"It's like being inside a Fabergé egg," I volunteered, looking around.

"Like being inside a Fabergé egg," Andy repeated. I heard a muted click as he turned off the tape recorder he had concealed in his pocket.

"Explain men," I said.

"Can we do the menu first?" Andy cajoled. This was our standard deal: first, the food, then, my questions about men and married life. Today we were casing the latest crêperie for a possible review.

Andy perused the menu. "I'm interested in the paté, the escargot, the greens with pear and warm Gorgonzola, and the mushroom in puff pastry to start with," he instructed. "You can get any kind of crêpe you want for a main course, except not the plain cheese."

"Ellen?" I guessed. Andy nodded. In one of life's supreme ironies, Andy's wife, Ellen, was possessed of the least adventurous palate of all time. She eschewed sauces, spices, most ethnic cuisines, and was constantly frowning over the menus, desperately scanning them for things like plain baked chicken breasts and mashed potatoes that weren't truffled, garlicked, or otherwise gussied up. Her ideal evening, she'd once told me, consisted of rented movies and frozen waffles "with the kind of syrup that has absolutely nothing maple about it." Andy adored her . . . even when she was screwing up his review meals by ordering yet another Caesar salad or plain piece of fish.

Our waiter ambled over to refill our water glasses. "Any questions?" he drawled. From his offhand manner, plus the blue paint caked under his fingernails, I had him pegged as a waiter by day, artiste by night. He seemed hugely, supremely, unassailably indifferent. *Pay attention,* I tried to tell him telepathically. It didn't seem to work.

I ordered the escargot and a crêpe with shrimp, tomatoes, and creamed spinach. Andy took the paté and the salad, and a crêpe with wild mushrooms, goat cheese, and toasted almonds. We each had a glass of white wine.

"Now," he said, as the waiter loped back to the kitchen. "How can I help you?"

"How can they . . ." I began. Andy raised his hand.

"Are we speaking in the abstract or the specific here?"

"It's Bruce," I acknowledged. Andy rolled his eyes. Andy was not a fan of Bruce . . . not since the first and last review dinner he'd come out for. Bruce was even worse than Ellen. "A picky vegetarian," Andy had messaged me at work the next day, "is basically a food critic's worst nightmare." In addition to not finding a single thing he wanted to eat, Bruce also managed to tip his menu far enough toward the candle that lit our table to actually set the menu on fire, bringing three waiters plus the sommelier running and sending Andy, a stickler for anonymity, dashing into the men's room lest he risk discovery. "It's hard to keep a low profile," he carefully pointed out the next day, "when you're being sprayed with a fire extinguisher."

"I just want to know," I said. "I mean, the thing that I don't understand . . ."

"Spit it out, Cannie," Andy urged. The waiter returned, dumped my escargot in front of Andy, Andy's paté in front of me, and hastily departed. "Excuse me," I called toward his back. "Could I have some more water? When you get a minute? Please?" The waiter's whole body seemed to sigh as he reached for the pitcher.

Once our glasses were filled, Andy and I traded plates, and I waited for him to describe, and taste, before continuing.

"Well, it's like, okay, I know that I was the one who wanted to take a break, and now I miss him, and it's like, this pain . . ."

"Is it a sharp stabbing pain, or more of a constant throbbing ache?"

"Are you making fun of me?"

Andy stared into my eyes, his own brown eyes wide and innocent behind his gold-rimmed glasses. "Well, maybe a little bit," he finally said.

"He's completely forgotten me," I grumbled, spearing a snail. "It's as if I never even mattered . . . like I never meant anything to him."

"I'm confused," said Andy. "Do you want him back, or are you just concerned about your legacy?"

"Both," I said. "I just want to know . . ." I gulped a mouthful of wine to stave off tears. "I just want to know that I meant something, somehow."

"Just because he's acting like you didn't mean anything doesn't mean that you really didn't," said Andy. "It's probably just an act."

"You think?"

"The guy adored you," Andy said. "That wasn't an act."

"But how can he not even want to talk to me now? How can it just be so completely . . ." I sliced one hand through the air to indicate a violent and absolute ending.

Andy sighed. "For some guys, it's just like that."

"For you?" I asked.

He paused, then nodded. "For me, when it was over, it was always over."

Over his shoulder, I could see our waiter approaching . . . our waiter, plus two other waiters, trailed by an anxious-looking dark-haired man with an apron tied over his suit. The manager, I presumed. Which could only mean the one thing that Andy dreaded most— namely, someone had figured out who he was.

"Monsieur!" the man in the suit began, as our waiter set down our entrées, another one poured us fresh water, and a third waiter carefully decrumbed our not-very-crumby table. "Is everything to your liking?"

"Just fine," said Andy weakly, as Waiter One set fresh silverware beside our plates, Waiter Two whisked fresh bread and butter to the center of the table, and Waiter Three hustled over with a lit candle.

"Please let us know if there's anything else we can bring you. Anything!" the manager fervently concluded.

"I will," Andy said, as the three waiters lined up and stared at us, looking anxious and vaguely resentful, before finally retreating to the corners of the restaurant where they watched our every mouthful.

I didn't even care. "I just think that I made a mistake," I said. "Did you ever break up with someone and think you made a mistake?"

Andy shook his head, wordlessly offering me a bite of his crêpe.

"What should I do?"

He munched, looking thoughtful. "I don't know if these are actual wild mushrooms. They taste kind of domestic to me."

"You're changing the subject," I grumbled. "You're . . . oh, God. I'm boring, aren't I?"

"Never," said Andy loyally.

"No, I am. I've turned into one of those horrible people that just talks about their ex-boyfriend all the time, until nobody can stand to be around them and they don't have any friends . . ."

"Cannie . . ."

". . . and they start drinking alone, and talking to their pets, which I do anyway . . . oh, God," I said, only half-faking a collapse into the bread dish. "This is a disaster."

The manager hurried over. "Madame!" he cried. "Is everything all right?"

I straightened myself up, flicking bits of bread from my sweater. "Just fine," I said. He bustled off, and I turned back to Andy.

"When did I become a madame?" I asked mournfully. "I swear, the last time I was at a French restaurant they called me Mademoiselle."

"Cheer up," said Andy, handing me the last of the paté. "You're going to find someone much better than Bruce, and he won't be a vegetarian, and you'll be happy, and I'll be happy, and everything's going to be fine."

EIGHT

I tried. Really, I did. But I found myself so preoccupied with Bruce misery that it was hard to get anything done at work. This is what I considered as I sat on an Amtrak Metroliner bound for New York and Maxi Ryder, famously ringletted and frequently dumped costar of last year's Oscar-nominated romantic drama, *Trembling*, in which she'd played a brilliant brain surgeon who eventually succumbs to Parkinson's disease.

Maxi Ryder was British, twenty-seven or twenty-nine, depending on which magazines you believed, and had been known, early in her career, as something of an ugly duckling until, through the miracle of rigorous diet, Pilates, and the Zone (plus, it was whispered, some discreet plastic surgery), she'd managed to transform herself into a size-two swan. In fact, she'd been a size two to start off with, and a beauty to boot, but had gained twenty pounds for her breakthrough role in a foreign film called *Advanced Placement*, playing a shy Scottish schoolgirl who has a torrid affair with her headmistress. By the time that film had reached the States, she'd shed the twenty pounds, dyed her hair auburn, ditched her British manager, hooked up with the hottest agency in Hollywood, founded the inevitable production company (Maxi'd Out, she'd called it), and been featured in a *Vanity Fair* spread of homes of the stars, wearing only a black feather boa, curled seductively beneath the headline "Maxi's Pad." Maxi, in other words, had arrived.

But for all her talent and her beauty, Maxi Ryder kept getting dumped, in the most public ways you could think of.

She'd done the typical starlet-in-her-twenties thing, popularized by Julia Roberts and practiced by the generation that followed, which was to fall in love with her costars. But while Julia would have them yanking her toward the altar, poor Maxi just got her heart broken, again and again and again. And it didn't happen quietly, either. The assistant director she'd fallen for on *Advanced Placement* showed up at the Golden Globes sucking face with one of the girls from *Baywatch*. Her costar on *Trembling*—the one with whom she'd played a half-dozen torrid love scenes, where the chemistry between them was so palpable it practically soaked your popcorn—had broken the news to her, and the rest of the world at the same time, during a Barbara Walters' "Ten Most Fascinating People" interview. And the nineteen-year-old rock star she'd picked up on the rebound had gotten married in Vegas two weeks after they met to a woman who was not Maxi.

"It's a wonder she's doing any press at all," Roberto, the publicist at Midnight Oil, had told me the week before. Midnight Oil was a very small, somewhat obscure New York PR firm—leagues below the big agencies that Maxi'd typically deal with. But between *Advanced Placement* and *Trembling,* she'd spent six weeks in Israel making a tiny little movie, a period piece about a kibbutz during the Seven Day War . . . and tiny little movies generally had small-time publicity agencies, which was where Roberto came in.

Seven Day Soldier would probably never even have made it to American art houses, had it not been for the Oscar nomination Maxi had gotten for *Trembling*. And Maxi would probably never have done any publicity for the movie, except she'd signed on to it before she'd made it big, which meant she'd agreed to be paid bupkes, and to publicize the film "in any way the producers deem appropriate."

So, needless to say, the producers saw a chance to at least have an enormous opening weekend based on the strength of Maxi buzz. They'd flown her in from a shoot in Australia, set her up in the penthouse of the Regency on the Upper East Side, and invited in what Roberto referred to as "a select group of reporters" to enjoy twenty-minute audiences with her. And Roberto, bless his loyal heart, had called me first.

"Are you interested?" he'd asked.

Of course I was, and Betsy was thrilled in the way that editors usually are when plummy scoops fall into their laps, even though Gabby grumbled about one-hit wonders and flashes in the pan.

I was happy. Roberto was happy. Then Maxi's personal publicist got in on the act.

There I was, moping at my desk, counting the days since Bruce and I had spoken (ten), the length in minutes of the conversation (four), and contemplating making an appointment with a numerologist to figure out if the future held anything good for us, when the phone rang.

"This is April from NGH," rapped the voice on the other end. "We understand you're interested in speaking with Maxi Ryder?"

Interested? "I'm interviewing her Saturday at ten in the morning," I told April. "Roberto from Midnight Oil set it up."

"Yes. Well. We have a few questions before we sign off."

"Who are you again?" I asked.

"April. From NGH." NGH was one of the hugest and most notorious public relations firms in Hollywood. They were the people you called if you were famous, under forty, found yourself in the midst of some kind of unsavory and/or illegal mess and wanted to keep all but the most fawning and tractable press far, far away. Robert Downey hired NGH after he passed out in someone else's bedroom in a heroin haze. Courtney Love had NGH redo her image after she'd redone her nose, her breasts, and her fashion, and they smoothed her transition from foul-mouthed grunge goddess to couture-clad sylph. At the *Examiner*, we called them Not Gonna Happen . . . as in, that interview you were hoping for, that profile you wanted to write? Not Gonna Happen. Now, evidently, Maxi Ryder had enlisted their assistance as well.

"We would like your assurance," April from NGH began, "that this interview will focus exclusively on Maxi's work."

"Her work?"

"Her roles," said April. "Her acting. Not her personal life."

"She's a celebrity," I said mildly. Or at least I thought it came out that way. "I consider that her work. Being a famous person."

April's voice could have frozen hot fudge. "Her work is acting," she said. "Any attention that she gets is only because of that work."

Normally I would have let it drop—just gritted my teeth and grinned and agreed to whatever ridiculous conditions they wanted to impose. But I hadn't slept the night before, and this April was pushing all the wrong buttons. "Oh, come on!" I said. "Every time I open *People* magazine I see her in a slit skirt and big, dark, don't-look-at-me glasses. And you're telling me she just wants to be known as an actor?"

I'd hope that April would take my remarks in the half-joking manner I'd intended them. But I wasn't sensing a thaw.

"You cannot ask her about her love life," April said sternly.

I sighed. "Fine," I said. "Terrific. Whatever. We'll talk about the movie."

"So you're agreeing to the conditions?"

"Yes. I'm agreeing. No love life. No skirts. No nothing."

"Then I'll see what I can do."

"I told you, Roberto already set up the interview!"

But I was talking to a dead line.

Two weeks later, when I finally left for the interview, it was a gray, drizzly Saturday morning in late November, the kind of day where it looks like everyone with means and money has fled the city and gone to the Bahamas, or their country cottage in the Poconos, and the streets are populated with the people they'd left behind: pockmarked delivery boys, black girls with braids, scruffy-looking dreadlocked white kids on bikes. Secretaries. Japanese tourists. A guy with a wart on his chin with two hairs sprouting from it, long, curly hairs that reached almost to his chest. He smiled and stroked them as I walked by. My lucky day.

I spent the twenty-block walk uptown trying not to think of Bruce and trying not to let my hair get too wet. The lobby of the Regency was huge, marble, blessedly quiet and mirror-lined, which let me appreciate, from three different angles, the zit that had sprouted on my forehead.

I was early, so I decided to loiter. The hotel gift shop boasted the typical assortment of overpriced bathrobes, $5 toothbrushes, and magazines in many languages, one of which happened to be the November *Moxie*. I grabbed it and flipped to Bruce's column. "Going Down," I read. "One Man's Oral Adventures." Hah! "Oral adventures" had not been Bruce's forte. He had a little problem with excessive saliva. In a moment of margarita-soaked weakness I'd once referred to him as "the human bidet." It had been that bad at the beginning. Of course, there was no way he'd mention that, I thought smugly, any more than he'd mention that I'd been the only girl he'd ever attempted that particular maneuver upon. And I flipped back to his column. *"I once overheard my girlfriend refer to me as the human bidet,"* read the pull-quote. He'd heard that? My face flamed.

"Miss? Are you planning to purchase that?" asked the woman behind the counter. So I did, with a pack of Juicy Fruit gum and a $4 bottle of water. Then I parked myself on one of the plush couches in the icy-cool lobby and began:

Going Down

When I was fifteen and a virgin, when I wore braces and the tighty whities my mother bought me, my friends and I used to laugh ourselves sick over a Sam Kinison routine.

"Women!" he'd rant, tossing his hair over his shoulder, stalking the stage like a small, rotund, beret-wearing trapped animal. "Tell us what you want! Why," he'd say, and drop to one knee, beseeching, "why is it so HARD to say YES, right THERE, that's GOOD, or NO, not THAT. TELL US WHAT YOU WANT!" he'd shriek, as the audience erupted, "WE'LL DO IT!"

We laughed without knowing precisely what made this so hysterical. What could be so hard? we wondered. Sex, insofar as we'd experienced it, did not involve much mystery. Lather, rinse, repeat. That was our repertoire. No fuss, no muss, and certainly no confusion.

When C. parted her legs and then parted herself with her fingertips . . .

Oh . . . my . . . God, I thought. It was as if he'd shoved a mirror between my legs and broadcasted the image to the whole world. I swallowed hard and kept reading.

. . . I felt a sudden and complete sympathy with every man who'd ever pumped his fist to Kinison's lament. It was like looking at a face with no features, was the best thing I could think. Hair and belly and hands above, creamy thighs to the left and the right, but in front of me, a mystery, curves and tucks and protrusions that bore, it seemed, little resemblance to the air-brushed pornography I'd seen since I was fifteen. Or maybe it was just the proximity. Or maybe it was just my nerves. Being confronted with a mystery is a scary thing.

"Tell me what you want," I whispered to her, and I remember how far away her head seemed at that moment. "Tell me what you want and I'll do it." But then I realized that by telling me what she wanted, she'd be as much as admitting that . . . well, that she knew what she wanted. That someone else had stared into this strange, unknowable heart, had learned the geography, had unfurled her secrets. And even though I knew she'd had other lovers, that seemed somehow different, more intimate. She'd let someone else see her here, like this. And I, being male and a former Sam Kinison listener to boot, resolved to bring her to paradise, to make her mewl like a sated kitty, to obliterate every trace of memory of the He Who'd Gone Before.

Strange unknowable heart, I snorted. He Who'd Gone Before. Somebody get me a shovel!

And she tried, and I tried, too. She demonstrated with her fingertips, with words, with gentle pressure and gasps and sighs. And I tried, too. But a tongue isn't like a finger. My goatee drove her crazy, in precisely the opposite of the way she wanted to be driven crazy. And when I heard her on the phone once refer to me as the Human Bidet, well, it seemed easier to rely on the things I knew I could do better.

Do any of us know what we're doing? Does any man? I ask my friends, and at first they all guffaw and swear they have to scrape their women off the ceiling. I buy them beer and keep their glasses full, and in a few hours I have my more perfect truth: We're all clueless. Every single one of us.

"She says she's coming," says Eric mournfully. "But I dunno, man . . ."

"It isn't obvious," says George. "How are we supposed to know?"

How, indeed? We're men. We need reliability, we need hard (or even liquid) evidence, we need diagrams and how-to guides, we need the mystery explicated.

And when I close my eyes I can see her, still, as she lay that first time, furled tight like the wings of a tiny bird, seashell pink, tasting like the rich ocean water, full of tiny lives, things I'll never see, let alone understand. I wish I could. I wish I had.

"Okay, Jacques Cousteau," I muttered, and struggled to my feet. When he closed his eyes he could still see me, he'd written. Well, what did that mean? And when had he written it? And if he still missed me, then why wasn't he calling? Maybe, I thought, there was hope after all. Maybe I'd call him later. Maybe we still had a chance.

I took the elevator up to the hospitality suite on the twentieth floor, where a variety of young, larva-pale publicists in variations on black stretch pants, black bodysuits, and black boots sat on couches and smoked.

"I'm Cannie Shapiro from the *Philadelphia Examiner*," I said, to the one sitting beneath a life-size cardboard cutout of Maxi Ryder in battle fatigues, brandishing an Uzi.

Larva Girl paged languidly through some pages full of names.

"I don't see you," she said.

Great. "Is Roberto here?"

"He stepped out for a minute," she said, flip-flopping one hand toward the door.

"Did he say when he'd be back?"

She shrugged, apparently having exhausted her vocabulary.

I peered at the pages, trying to read upside-down. There was my name: Candace Shapiro. And there was a thick black line through it. "NGH" read the note in the margin.

Just then Roberto hustled in.

"Cannie," he said, "what are you doing here?"

"You tell me," I said, trying for a smile. "Last I heard I was interviewing Maxi Ryder."

"Oh, God," he said. "Nobody called you?"

"About what?"

"Maxi decided to, um, scale way back on the print interviews. She's only doing the *Times*. And *USA Today*."

"Well, nobody told me." I shrugged. "I'm here. Betsy's expecting a story."

"Cannie, I'm so sorry. . ."

Don't be sorry, you idiot, I was thinking. Do something!

". . . but there's nothing I can do."

I gave him my best smile. My most charming smile, which I hoped was underscored with my I-work-for-a-large-important-newspaper steel. "Roberto," I said, "I was planning to talk to her. We saved the space. We're counting on the story. Nobody called me . . . and I schlepped all the way up here on a Saturday, which is my day off . . ."

Roberto started wringing his hands.

". . . and I would really, really appreciate it if we could maybe just get even fifteen minutes with her."

Now Roberto was wringing his hands and biting his lip at the same time, plus shifting from foot to foot. Bad signs all.

"Listen," I said softly, leaning toward him, "I watched every single one of her movies, even the direct-to-video ones. I'm, like, the complete Maxi expert. Isn't there anything we can do?" I saw him start to waver, when the cell phone on his belt shrilled.

"April?" he said. *April,* he mouthed to me. Roberto was a sweetheart, but not the sharpest knife in the drawer.

"Can I talk to her?" I whispered, but Roberto was already reholstering his phone.

"She said they weren't comfortable with your, um, compliance."

"What? Roberto, I agreed to every single one of her conditions. . . ." My voice was rising. The larval creatures on the couch were starting to look vaguely alarmed. As was Roberto, who was edging out into the hallway.

"Let me talk to April," I pleaded, holding out my hand for his cell phone. Roberto shook his head. "Roberto," I said, hearing my voice breaking, imagining Gabby's gloating grin when I came back to the office empty-handed. "I can't go back without a story!"

"Look, Cannie, I am so, so sorry . . ."

He was wavering. I saw he was. And that's when a tiny woman in high-heeled calf-length black leather boots came trip-trapping down the long marble hall. There was a cell phone in one hand, a walkie-talkie in the other, and a no-nonsense look on her unlined, carefully made-up face. She could have been a very mature twenty-eight or forty-five with a great plastic surgeon. This, undoubtedly, was April.

She took me in—my zit, my anger, my black dress and sandals from last summer, far less fashionable than anything any one of the couch larvae were wearing, in one cool, dismissive glance. Then she turned to Roberto.

"Is there a problem?" she said.

"This is Candace," he said, pointing weakly at me. "From the *Examiner.*"

She stared at me. I felt—actually felt—my zit expanding beneath her gaze.

"Is there a problem?" she repeated.

"There wasn't until a few minutes ago," I said, struggling to keep my voice calm. "I had an interview scheduled for two o'clock. Roberto tells me it's been cancelled."

"That's right," she said pleasantly. "We decided to limit our print interviews to major newspapers."

"The *Examiner* has a circulation of 700,000 on Sundays, which is when we'd planned the story for," I said. "We're the fourth-largest city on the East Coast. And nobody bothered to tell me the interview was off."

"That was Roberto's responsibility," she said, raking him with her gaze.

This was clearly news to Roberto, but he wasn't going to contradict Miss Kitten with a Whip. "Sorry," he muttered to me.

"I appreciate the apologies," I said, "but as I told Roberto, we've now got a hole in our Sunday newspaper, and I've wasted my day off." Which wasn't technically true. Stories fell through all the time, as April probably knew, and we'd just pop something else in the hole. And as for wasting my day off, any time I got a free ticket to New York, I always found something to do there.

But I was furious. The nerve of these people, to treat me so rudely, and to be so patently, completely not sorry about it!

"Isn't there any way she can see me for a few minutes? Since I'm here?"

April's tone was becoming decidedly less pleasant. "She's running late as it is, and she's flying right back to location this afternoon. To Australia," she emphasized, as if this was a place a country mouse such as myself had most likely never heard of. "And," she continued, snapping a small notebook open, "we've already scheduled a telephone interview with your boss."

My boss? It was inconceivable that Betsy would do this, beyond inconceivable that she'd do this and not tell me.

"With Gabby Gardiner," April concluded.

I was stunned. "Gabby's not my boss!"

"I'm sorry," April said, sounding not sorry at all, "but those are the arrangements we've made."

I backed into the hospitality suite and plopped into a chair by the window. "Look," I said. "I'm here, and I'm sure you'd agree that it would be better for all of us to do an in-person interview—even a quick one—with someone who's seen all of Maxi's movies, who took the time to prepare for this—than something over the phone. I'm happy to wait."

April stood in the hall for a moment. "Do I have to call security?" she finally asked.

"I don't see why," I said. "I'll just sit here until Ms. Ryder finishes up with whoever she's in with, and if it happens that she's got a minute or two to spare before she has to go rushing back to Australia, I will conduct the interview that I was promised." I clenched my hands into fists so she wouldn't see how I was shaking, and played my final card. "Of course, if it should turn out that Ms. Ryder doesn't have a few minutes for me," I said sweetly, "then I'll be writing a thirty-inch story about what's happened to me here. And by the way, what's your last name?"

April glared at me. Roberto sidled closer to her, flicking his eyes back and forth between us, as if we were playing a very fast game of tennis. I stared right back at April.

"It's impossible," she said.

"Interesting last name," I said. "Is it one of those Ellis Island specials?"

"I'm sorry," she said, for what would be the last time, "but Ms. Ryder's not going to be speaking to you. You were sarcastic to me on the phone . . ."

"Ooh, a sarcastic reporter! Bet you've never seen one of those before!"

". . . and Ms. Ryder doesn't need your kind of attention . . ."

"Which is fine," I exploded, "but couldn't one of your lackeys or flunkies or interns have had the courtesy to call me before I came all the way up here?"

"Roberto was supposed to," she said again.

"Well, he didn't," I told her, and crossed my arms. Standoff. She stood and glared at me for a minute. I glared right back. Roberto leaned against the wall, actually shaking. The larvae stood in a row, their eyes darting back and forth.

"Call security," April finally said, and turned on her heel. She looked back over her shoulder at me. "You," she said. "Write whatever you want. We don't care."

And with that, they were gone: Roberto, shooting me a final, desperately apologetic look over his shoulder, the larvae, all in black boots, and April, and whatever chance I had of meeting Maxi Ryder. I sat there, until they'd all piled into an elevator. Only then did I let myself cry.

Generally speaking, hotel lobby bathrooms are great places to have breakdowns. People registered at the hotel are mostly using the bathrooms in their rooms. People on the streets don't always know that they can breeze right in to the lobby of even the fanciest hotel and almost always use the toilet unmolested. And the bathrooms tend to be spacious and fancy, with all the amenities from hairspray and tampons to actual towels for wiping your tears and drying your hands. Sometimes there's even a couch to collapse on.

I staggered down the hall, into the elevator, and through the gold door reading "Ladies" in elaborate script, heading for the handicapped stall and peace, quiet, and solitude, grabbing two neatly rolled towels on my way in. "Fucking Maxi Ryder!" I hissed, and slammed the door, sat down, and pressed my fists against my eyes.

"Huh?" said a familiar voice from somewhere over my head. "Why?"

I looked up. A face was peeking over the top of the stall.

"Why?" Maxi Ryder said again. She was just as adorable in person as she was on the big screen, with her saucer-wide blue eyes, her lightly freckled, creamy skin, her cascade of auburn curls, seemingly brighter and more glossy than standard-issue human hair was meant to be. She was gripping a slim cigarette in one tiny blue-veined hand, and as I watched she took a generous drag and blew it out toward the ceiling.

"Don't smoke in here," I told her. It was the first thing I could think of. "You'll set off the alarms."

"You're cursing me because I'm smoking?"

"No. I'm cursing you because you stood me up."

"What?"

Two sneaker-clad feet plunked lightly onto the marble and came to rest outside my stall. "Open up," she said, rapping at the door. "I want some explanation."

I slumped down on the toilet seat. First April, now this! Reluctantly I leaned forward and unlocked the door. Maxi stood outside the stall, arms crossed on her chest, waiting for her answers. "I'm from the *Philadelphia Examiner,*" I began. "I was supposed to interview you. Your little Gestapo-ette told me, after I came all the way up here, that the interview had been canceled and rescheduled with this woman at my office who's just . . ." I gulped. "Vomitous," I arrived at. "So it kind of ruined my day. Not to mention our Sunday section." I sighed. "But it's not your fault, I guess. So I'm sorry. I shouldn't have cursed at you."

"Bloody April," said Maxi. "She never even told me."

"I'm not surprised."

"I'm hiding," said Maxi Ryder, and gave a nervous giggle. "From April, actually."

In person her voice was soft, cultured. She was wearing bell-bottomed jeans and a scoop-necked pink T-shirt. Her hair was piled into the kind of artless updo that probably took a hairdresser half an hour to construct, ornamented with tiny, sparkling butterfly clips. Like most young female stars I'd met, she was thin to the point of unreality. I could make out the bones of her wrists and forearms, the pale blue tracery of veins along her neck.

Her pouty lips were painted scarlet. Her eyes were carefully lined and shadowed. And her cheeks were streaked with tears.

"Sorry about your interview," she said.

"It wasn't your fault," I said again. "So what brings you to these parts? Don't you have your own bathroom somewhere else?" I asked.

"Oh," she said, and drew a long, shuddering breath. "You know."

"Well, actually, not being a thin, rich, successful movie star, I probably don't."

One corner of her mouth quirked upward, then drew down again into a trembling crimson bow. "Ever had your heart broken?" she asked in a shaky voice.

"Actually, yes," I said.

She closed her eyes. Impossibly long lashes rested against her pale freckled cheeks, and tears slid out from beneath them.

"It's unbearable," she said. "I know how that sounds . . ."

"No. No. I know what you mean. I know that it feels like that."

I handed her one of the rolled-up towels I'd grabbed on the way in. She took it, then looked at me. It was, I thought, a test.

"My house is full of things he gave me," I began, and she nodded vigorously, curls bouncing.

"That's it," she said, "that's right."

"And it hurts to look at them, and it hurts to put them away."

Maxi slumped to the bathroom floor and leaned her cheek against the cool marble wall. After a moment's hesitation, I joined her, struck by the absurdity of it all, and how it would make a great opening for an article: *Maxi Ryder, one of the most acclaimed young actresses of her generation, is crying on the bathroom floor.*

"My mother always says that it's better to have loved and lost than never to have loved at all," I said.

"Do you believe that?" she asked.

I only had to think about it for a minute. "No. I don't even think she believes it. I wish I'd never loved him. I wish I'd never met him. Because I think that as good as the good times were, it isn't worth feeling like this."

We sat for a minute, side by side.

"What's your name?"

"Candace Shapiro. Cannie."

"What was his name?"

"Bruce. And you?"

"I'm Maxi Ryder.

"I know that. I meant, what was his name?"

She made a horrible face. "Oh, don't tell me you don't know! Everybody knows! *Entertainment Weekly* did a whole story. With a flow chart!"

"Well, I was very explicitly forbidden from even mentioning it." Plus, there was more than one candidate, but it didn't seem prudent to say so.

"Kevin," she whispered. Which would be Kevin Britton, her costar from *Trembling.*

"Still Kevin?"

"Still Kevin, always Kevin," she said sadly, fumbling for another cigarette. "Kevin who I can't forget, even after I've tried everything. Drink . . . drugs . . . work . . . other men . . ."

Jeez. I suddenly felt very innocent.

"What do you do?"

I knew what she was asking me. "Oh, you know. Probably the same kinds of things as you." I laid one hand across my forehead, affecting world-weary hauteur. "I started by running off to my private island with Brad Pitt, trying to forget the pain by buying up llama ranches in New England . . ."

She punched my arm. Her clenched fist felt like a puff of air. "Seriously! Maybe it'll be something I haven't thought of."

"Probably just more stuff that doesn't really work. Baths, showers, bike rides . . ."

"I can't go for bike rides," she said morosely.

"Because of the paparazzi?"

"No. I never learned how."

"Really? Bruce, my ex-boyfriend, couldn't ride a bike either . . ." My voice trailed off.

"God, don't you hate that?" she asked.

"The way even completely unrelated things remind you of the person you're trying to forget? Yes. I hate it." I looked at her. With her face framed by the bathroom wall marble, she looked ready for her close-up. Whereas I was probably a blotchy-faced, runny-nosed wreck. No justice, I thought. "What do you do?" I asked.

"Invest," Maxi said instantly. "Manage my money. And my parents' money, too." She sighed. "I used to manage Kevin's money. I wish he'd given me a little notice that he was going to dump me. I'd have sunk him so deep into Planet Hollywood that he'd be taking guest-shots on the WB just to make his rent."

I considered Maxi with newfound respect. "So you, like . . ." I racked my brains for the appropriate vocabulary. "Day-trade?'

She shook her head. "Nope. I don't have time to be geeking around on computers all day. I pick stocks, and I look for investment opportunities." She stood and stretched, her hands on her nonexistent hips. "I buy real estate."

My respect was turning into awe. "Like houses?"

"Yup. Buy them, have a crew renovate them, sell them at a profit, or live in them a while, if I'm between movies."

I felt my fingers reaching for my pen and notebook, creeping almost of their own accord. Maxi as real-estate mogul was something I hadn't read in any of the innumerable profiles I'd plowed through. It would make great copy. "Hey," I ventured. "Do you think . . . I mean, I know they said you were busy, but maybe . . . could we talk for a few minutes? So I can write my story?"

"Sure," said Maxi, shrugging, and looked around as if realizing for the first time that we were in a bathroom. "Let's get out of here. Want to?"

"Aren't you supposed to be heading to Australia? That's what April said."

Maxi looked exasperated. "I'm not leaving till tomorrow. April's a liar."

"Imagine that," I said.

"No, really . . . oh. Oh, I see. You're kidding." And she smiled at me. "I forget how people are."

"Well, generally, they're bigger than you."

She sighed, gazed at herself, and dragged deeply on her cigarette. "When I turn forty," she said, "I swear, I'm giving this all up, and I'm going to build a fortress on an island with a moat and electrified fences, and I'm going to let my hair go gray and eat custard until I have fourteen chins."

"That was not," I pointed out, "what you told *Mirabella*. You told them you wanted to appear in one quality movie a year, and raise your children in a country farmhouse."

She raised an eyebrow. "You read that?"

"I've read everything about you," I told her.

"Lies. All lies," she said, almost cheerfully. "Today, for example. I'm to go to some place called Mooma . . ."

"Moomba," I corrected.

". . . and have drinks with Matt Damon, or Ben Affleck. Or maybe both. And we're supposed to look very secretive and lovey, and somebody's going to call Page 6, and we're to be photographed, and then we're going to go to some restaurant that probably paid April off to have dinner, except of course I can't actually have dinner, because, God forbid, I ever get photographed with something actually in my mouth, or with my mouth open, or basically in any manner that could give any suggestion that I ever do anything with my mouth besides kiss men . . ."

". . . and smoke."

"Not that, either. The cancer lobby, you know. Which is how I got away from April. Told her I needed a cig."

"So you really want to pass up drinks and dinner with Ben . . . or Matt. . . ."

"Oh, it doesn't stop there. Then I'm supposed to be seen out dancing at some bar with pigs in its name . . ."

"Hogs and Heifers?"

"That's it. Dancing there till some ungodly hour, and then, and only then, am I permitted some sleep. And that's after I take off my brassiere and dance on the bar while I'm twirling it over my head."

"Wow. They really, um, arrange all that for you?"

She pulled a crumpled piece of paper out of her pocket. Sure enough: 4 P.M., Moomba; 7 P.M., Tandoor; 11–?, Hogs and Heifers. She reached into another pocket and produced a very small black lace Wonderbra. She wrapped the Wonderbra around her hand and started swinging it around her head while pumping her hips in a parody of a party girl's bump and grind. "See," she said, "they even made me practice. If it was up to me I'd sleep all day . . ."

"Me, too. And watch *Iron Chef.*"

Maxi looked puzzled. "What's that?"

"Spoken like someone who's never been home alone on a Friday night. It's this TV show where there's this reclusive millionaire, and he's got these three chefs . . ."

"The Iron Chefs," Maxi guessed.

"Right. And every week they have cooking battles with some

challenger chef who comes in, and the eccentric millionaire gives them a theme ingredient that they have to cook with, and half the time it's something that starts off alive, like squid or giant eel . . ."

Maxi was smiling, and nodding, and looking like she couldn't wait to see the first episode. Or maybe she was just acting, I reminded myself. That was, after all, her job. Maybe she acted this excited and friendly and, well, nice, every time she met someone new, and then forgot they'd ever existed as soon as she moved on to the next movie.

"It's fun," I concluded. "Also free. Cheaper than renting a movie. I taped it last night, and I'm going to watch it when I get home."

"I'm never home on Fridays or Saturdays," she said sadly.

"Well, I almost always am. Believe me, you're not missing much."

Maxi Ryder grinned at me. "Cannie," she said, "know what I really want to do?"

And that was how I wound up in the Bliss day spa, naked on my belly, next to one of the most acclaimed young movie stars of my generation, talking about my failed love life while a man named Ricardo slathered Active Green Clay Mud all over my back.

Maxi and I had slipped out a back door of the hotel and caught a cab to the spa, where the receptionist very snippily informed us that they were booked all day, were booked for weeks, in fact, until Maxi slipped off her sunglasses and made about three seconds' worth of significant eye contact and the service improved by about 3,000 percent.

"This is so great," I told her, for about the fifth time. And it really was. The bed was cushioned with about half a dozen towels, and each one of them was easily as thick as my comforter. Soothing music played so softly in the background I thought it was a CD, until I'd opened my eyes long enough to see that there was an actual woman with an actual harp in the corner, half-hidden behind a lacy billow of curtains.

Maxi nodded. "Wait until they start with the showers and the salt rub." She closed her eyes. "I'm so tired," she murmured. "All I want to do is sleep."

"I can't sleep," I told her. "I mean, I start, but then I wake up . . ."

". . . and the bed's so empty."

"Well, I actually have a little dog, so the bed isn't empty."

"Oh, I'd love a dog! But I can't. Too much travel."

"You can come hang out with Nifkin any time," I said, knowing that it was highly unlikely that Maxi would be dropping by for an iced cappuccino and a frolic in the dog-crap-studded South Philadelphia dog park. Then again, I reasoned, as Ricardo gently rolled me over and started smearing my front, this was pretty unlikely, too.

"So what's next?" I asked. "Are you blowing off your entire agenda?"

"I think I am," she said. "I just want one day and one night to live like a normal person."

This hardly seemed like to the time to point out that normal people did not get to drop a thousand dollars on a single trip to a spa.

"What else do you want to do?"

Maxi considered. "I don't know. It's been so long . . . what would you do if you had a day to kill in New York?"

"Am I me in this scenario, or am I you?"

"What's the difference?"

"Well, do I have unlimited resources and recognition issues, or am I just plain old me?"

"Let's do plain old you first."

"Hmm. Well, I'd go to the ticket outlet in Times Square and try to get a half-price ticket for a Broadway show tonight. Then I'd go to the Steve Madden store in Chelsea and see what was on sale. And I'd look in all the galleries, and I'd buy six-for-a-dollar barrettes at the flea market on Columbus, and I'd have dinner at Virgil's, and go to the show."

"That sounds fantastic! Let's do it!" Maxi sat straight up, naked, covered in mud, with something thick slicking back her hair, and pulled the cucumber slices off her eyes. "Where are my shoes?" She looked down at herself. "Where are my clothes?"

"Lie down," I said with a laugh. Maxi lay down again.

"What's Steve Madden?"

"It's a great shoe store. One time I wandered in there, and it was the No Big Feet sale. All the size tens were half-price. I think it was the happiest day of my life, footwear-wise."

"That sounds so great," Maxi said dreamily. "Now, then. What's Virgil's?"

"Barbecue," I said. "They do these great ribs and fried chicken, and biscuits with maple butter . . . but you're a vegetarian, right?"

"Only on the record," said Maxi. "I love ribs."

"Do you think we can do it? I mean, won't people recognize you? And what about April?" I looked at her shyly. "And . . . I mean, not to pressure you or anything, but if we could talk about your movie for a little while . . . so I can write my story, and my editor doesn't kill me."

"But of course," said Maxi grandly. "Ask me anything at all."

"Later," I said. "I don't want to take advantage."

"Oh, go 'head!" She giggled merrily, and started writing my article: "Maxi Ryder is naked in a downtown spa, doused in aromatic extracts, musing on her lost love."

I heaved myself onto one elbow so that I could look at her.

"Do you really want to get into the lost love thing? I mean, that was the one thing that April was a demon about. She only wanted reporters to ask you about your work."

"But the thing about being an actor is that you get to take your life—your pain—and make it work for you." She took what sounded like a deep cleansing breath. "All things serve a purpose," she said. "I know that if I'm ever called upon to play a woman scorned . . . say, dumped publicly on a talk show . . . I'll be ready."

"You think that's bad? My ex-boyfriend writes the men's sex column for *Moxie.*"

"Really?" she asked. "I was in *Moxie* last fall. 'Maxi on *Moxie.*' It was pretty stupid. Does your ex ever write about you?"

I sighed miserably. "I'm his favorite topic. It's not a lot of fun."

"What?" asked Maxi. "Did he talk about something personal?"

"Yeah," I said. "My weight, for starters."

Maxi sat straight up again. "'Loving a Larger Woman?' That was you?"

Damn. Had everyone in the world read that stupid thing?

"That was me."

"Wow." Maxi looked at me—not, I hope, to try to figure out how much I weighed, and whether it could genuinely have been more than Bruce. "I read it on the plane," she said apologetically. "I don't read *Moxie,* normally, but it was a really long flight, and I got bored, so I read, like, three months' worth. . . ."

"You don't have to apologize," I said. "I'm sure a lot of people read it."

She lay down again. "Were you the one who called him the human bidet?" she asked.

Even under the mud, I was blushing again. "Never to his face," I said.

"Well, it could be worse. I got dumped on a Barbara Walters special," said Maxi.

"I know," I said. "I saw."

We lay in silence as the attendants sprayed the mud off of us with a half-dozen hoses. I felt like a very pampered, very exotic pet . . . that, or a particularly expensive cut of meat. Then we were covered with coarse salt, scrubbed down, showered off again, then wrapped in warm robes and sent off for facials.

"I think you had it worse than I did," I reasoned, as we let our clay masks dry. "I mean, when Kevin talked about ending a long relationship, everyone who watched knew that he meant you. But with the article, the only people who knew that C. was me were . . ."

"Everyone who knew you," said Maxi.

"Yeah. Pretty much." I sighed. Between the seaweed and the salt and the New Age music and the warm and gentle almond-oiled hands of Charles the masseur, I felt like I was wrapped in some delicious cloud, miles above the world, away from telephones that didn't ring and resentful coworkers and snooty publicists. Away from my weight . . . so much so that I wasn't even worried what Charles & Company were thinking as they rubbed and oiled and rolled me around. There was just me and the sadness, but even that didn't feel very heavy just then. It just felt there, like my nose, like the scar over my belly button I got from picking at a chicken pox scab when I was six. Just another part of me.

Maxi grabbed my hand. "We're friends, right?" she said. And I thought, for a moment, that she probably didn't mean it—that this was a version of her quickie, six-week, movie-set friendships. But I didn't care.

I squeezed back. "Yes," I said. "We're friends."

"You know what I think?" Maxi asked me. She raised a single fingertip. Instantly, there were four more shots of tequila in front of us, each one paid for, no doubt, by a different adoring guy. She picked up a glass and looked at me. I did the same, and we gulped tequila. I set the glass down, wincing at the burn. We'd wound up at Hogs and Heifers after all. We'd had a late lunch at Virgil's, where we'd sampled ribs, barbecued chicken, banana pudding, and cheese grits. Then we'd each bought about six pairs of Steve Madden shoes, reasoning that although we might feel fat, our feet didn't. Then it was on to the Beauty Bar, where we'd bought all manner of cosmetics (I stuck mostly to sand-colored eyeshadow and concealing cream. Maxi splurged on everything with glitter). It all added up to much more than I'd planned on spending on either shoes or makeup in the next year, and possibly even the next several years, but I figured, when's the next time I'll be shopping with a movie star?

"You know what I think?" Maxi repeated.

"What's that?"

"I think that we actually have a lot in common. It's the body thing," she said.

I squinted at her. "Huh?"

"We're ruled by our bodies," she pronounced, and sipped at a beer that someone had sent over. To me, this sounded very profound. This, perhaps, was because I was profoundly drunk. "You're stuck with a body that you think men don't want . . ."

"It's a little more than a theory at this point," I said, but Maxi wasn't about to have her monologue interrupted.

"And I'm afraid that if I start eating things I like, I'll stop looking the way I look, and nobody will want me. Worse than that," she said, glaring through the cigarette haze, "nobody will pay me. So I'm stuck, too. But what we're really trapped by is perceptions. You think you need to lose weight for someone to love you. I think if I gain weight, no one will love me. What we really need," she said, pounding the bar for emphasis, "is to just stop thinking of ourselves as bodies and start thinking of ourselves as people."

I stared at her admiringly. "Thass very deep."

Maxi took a deep swallow of beer. "Heard it on Oprah."

I did another shot. "Oprah's deep. But I have to say that all things considered, I'd rather be trapped in your body than mine. At least I could wear bikinis."

"But don't you see? We're both in prison. Prisons of Flesh."

I giggled. Maxi looked offended. "What, you don't agree?"

"No," I said, snorting, "I just think that Prisons of Flesh sounds like the name of a porno movie."

"Fine," Maxi said when she'd stopped laughing. "But I have a valid point."

"Of course you do," I told her. "I know that I shouldn't feel the way I do about how I look. I want to live in a world where people are judged by who they are instead of what size they wear." I sighed. "But you know what I want even more than that?" Maxi looked at me expectantly. I hesitated, then took another tequila. "I want to forget about Bruce."

"I have a theory about that, too," Maxi announced triumphantly. "My theory," she said, "is that hate works." She clinked her glass against mine. We did the shot, and upended the glasses on the sticky bar top, beneath the gently swaying clothesline of brassieres that had once cupped the breasts of the famous.

"I can't hate him," I said sadly. Suddenly my lips felt as though they were forming words a good foot or two away from my face, like they'd decided to just detach themselves and head for greener pastures. It was a common side effect when I'd been enjoying too many libations. That, and a liquid sensation in my knees and wrists and elbows, like my joints were coming unhinged. When I got drunk I started remembering things. And right now, because there was Grateful Dead on the jukebox ("Cassidy," I thought), what I was remembering was how we'd gone to pick up Bruce's friend George to go to a Dead show, and while we were waiting we'd slipped into the study and I'd given him a very quick, extremely hot blow job underneath the stuffed deer's head mounted on the wall. Physically I was sitting at Hogs and Heifers, but in my head I was on my knees in front of him, my hands cupping his ass, his knees pressing my chest as he trembled and gasped that he loved me, thinking that I was made for this, made for nothing but this.

"Sure you can," Maxi urged, yanking me out of the basement and into the tequila-soaked present. "Tell me the worst thing about him."

"He was really sloppy."

She crinkled her nose adorably. "That's not that bad."

"Oh, you have no idea! He had all this hair, see, and it would get in the shower drain, and he'd never clean his shower, but every once in a while he'd just, like, scoop up a clump of this disgusting, awful, soap-scummy hair and, like, park it in a corner of the tub. The first time I saw it I screamed."

We did another shot. Maxi's cheeks were flushed bright, her eyes were gleaming.

"Also," I continued, "also he had disgusting toenails." I burped, as delicately as I could, against the back of my hand. "They were all yellow and thick and raggedy . . ."

"Fungus," said Maxi knowledgeably.

"And then there was his minibar," I said, warming to the task. "Every time his parents went on a plane, they'd bring him those minibottles of vodka and scotch. He'd keep them in a shoebox, and whenever anyone would come over for a drink, he'd say, 'Have something from the minibar.'" I paused, considering. "Actually, that was kind of cute."

"I was going to say," agreed Maxi.

"But it got annoying after a while. I mean, I'd come over, I'd have a terrible headache, I'd just want a vodka and tonic, and off he'd go to the minibar. I think he was just too cheap to shell out for an actual bottle of his own."

"Tell me," asked Maxi. "Was he really good in bed?"

I tried to prop my head in my hand, but my elbow wasn't doing its job, and I wound up almost bouncing my forehead off the bar. Maxi laughed at me. The bartender scowled. I asked for a glass of water. "You wanna know the truth?"

"No, I want you to lie to me. I'm a movie star. Everyone else does."

"The truth," I said, "the truth is that . . ."

Maxi was laughing, leaning in close. "C'mon, Cannie, let me have it."

"Well, he was very willing to try new things, which I appreciated . . ."

"Come on. No editori . . . editorial . . ." She closed her eyes, and her mouth. "No spin. I asked a simple question. Was he any good?"

"The truth. . . ." I tried again. "The truth is that he was very . . . small."

Her eyes widened. "Small, you mean . . . down there?"

"Small," I repeated. "Tiny. Microscopic. Infinitesimal!" There. If I could say that word, I couldn't be as wasted as I thought I was. "I mean, not when it was hard. When it was hard it was pretty normal-sized. But when it was soft, it was like it telescoped back into his body, and it just looked like this little . . ." I tried to say it, but I was laughing too hard.

"What? C'mon, Cannie. Stop laughing. Sit up straight. Tell me!"

"Hairy acorn," I finally managed. Maxi whooped. Tears came to her eyes, and somehow I was sideways, my head in her lap. "Hairy acorn!" she repeated.

"Shh!" I shushed her, trying to maneuver myself upright.

"Hairy acorn!"

"Maxi!"

"What? Do you think he's going to hear me?"

"He lives in New Jersey," I said very seriously.

Maxi climbed onto the bar and cupped her hands around her mouth. "Attention, bar patrons," she called. "Hairy Acorn resides in New Jersey."

"If you're not gonna show us your tits, then get off the bar!" shouted a drunk guy in a cowboy hat. Maxi very elegantly gave him the finger, then climbed down.

"It could almost be a proper name," she said. "Harry Acorn. Harry A. Corn."

"You can't tell anynone. Anyone," I slurred.

"Don't worry. I won't. And I seriously doubt that me and Mr. Corn travel in the same circles."

"He lives in New Jersey," I said again, and Maxi laughed until tequila came out of her nose.

"So basically," she said, once she'd stopped spluttering, "you're pining for a guy with a small willy who treated you badly?"

"He didn't treat me badly," I said. "He was very sweet . . . and attentive . . . and . . ."

But she wasn't listening. "Sweet and attentive are a dime a dozen. And so, I'm sorry to inform you, are small willies. You can do better."

"I have to get over him."

"So get over him! I insist!"

"What's the secret?"

"Hate!" said Maxi. "Like I said before."

But I couldn't hate him. I wanted to, but I couldn't. Against my will, I remembered something tremendously tender. How once, around Christmas, I'd told him to pretend he was Santa Claus, and I pretended I had come to the mall to have my picture taken. How I'd perched on his lap, taking care to plant my feet firmly on the floor so I wouldn't rest all my weight on him, and whispered in his ear, "Is it true that Santa comes just once a year?" How he'd laughed, and how he'd gasped when I put one hand against his chest and shoved him flat back on the bed and snuggled against him while he performed an impromptu and doubtlessly off-key rendition of "All I Want for Christmas Is You."

"Here," said Maxi, shoving a shot of tequila into my hand. "Medicine."

I gulped it down. She grabbed my chin and stared into my eyes. It looked like there were two of her—saucer-blue eyes, cascading hair, the geometrically perfect sprinkling of freckles, the chin just a shade too pointed, so that she wouldn't be perfect, but overwhelmingly endearing instead. I blinked, and she turned into one person again.

Maxi studied me carefully. "You still love him," she said. I bowed my head. "Yes," I whispered.

She let go of my chin. My head hit the bar. Maxi pulled me back upright by my barrettes. The bartender was looking concerned. "I think maybe she's had enough," he said. Maxi ignored him.

"Maybe you should call him," she said.

"I can't," I told her, suddenly acutely aware that I was very, very drunk. "I'll make a fool of myself."

"There are worse things than just looking foolish," she said.

"Like what?"

"Losing someone you love, because you're too proud to call and lay it on the line," she said. "That's worse. Now: What's his number?"

"Maxi . . ."

"Give me the number."

"This is a really bad idea."

"Why?"

"Because . . ." I sighed, suddenly feeling all the tequila pressing against my skull. "Because what if he doesn't want me?"

"Then it's better that you know that, once and for all. We can go in like surgeons and cauterize the wound. And I'll teach you the restorative powers of hating his guts." She held out the phone. "Now. The number."

I took the phone. It was a tiny thing, a toy of a telephone, no longer than my thumb. I unfolded it clumsily, and squinted, poking at the digits with my pinkie.

He picked up on the first ring. "Hello?"

"Hey, Bruce. It's Cannie."

"Hi-ii," he said slowly, sounding surprised.

"I know this is kinda weird, but I'm in New York, in this bar, and you'll never guess who I'm here with . . ."

I paused for a breath. He didn't say anything.

"I have to tell you something . . ."

"Um, Cannie . . ."

"No, I just want, I just need . . . you just have to lishen. Listen," I finally managed. The words came in a rush. "Breaking up with you was a mistake. I know that now. And Bruce, I'm so sorry . . . and I miss you so much, and it's just getting worse and worse every day, and I know I don't deserve it, but if you could gimme 'nother chance I'd be so good to you . . ."

I could hear the springs creak as he shifted his weight on the bed. And someone else's voice in the background. A female voice.

I squinted at the clock on the wall, behind the dangling bras. It was one in the morning.

"But I'm innerupting," I said dumbly.

"Hey, Cannie, this actually isn't such a good time . . ."

"I thought you needed space," I said, "because of your father dying. But that's not it, is it? It's me. You don't want me."

I heard a bumping sound, then a far-off, murmured conversation. He'd probably put his hand over the receiver.

"Who is she?" I yelled.

"Look, is there a good time when I can call you back?" Bruce asked.

"Are you gonna write about her?" I cried. "Does she get to be an initial in your wonderful, fabulous column? Is she good in bed?"

"Cannie," Bruce said slowly, "let me call you back.".

"Don't. Don't worry. You don't have to," I said, and started stabbing at buttons on the telephone until I found the one that switched it off.

I handed the phone back to Maxi, who was staring at me gravely.

"That didn't sound good," she said.

I felt the room spinning. I felt like I was going to throw up. I felt like I'd never be able to smile again in my life, that, somewhere in my heart it was always going to be one o'clock in the morning, and I'd be calling the man I loved, and there'd be another woman in his bed.

"Cannie? Can you hear me? Cannie, what should I do?"

I lifted my head from the bar. I rubbed my eyes with my fist. I drew a deep shuddering breath. "Get me more tequila," I said, "and teach me how to hate."

Later—much later—in the cab back to the hotel, I leaned my head on Maxi's shoulder, mostly because I couldn't hold it up. I knew that this was it: the point where I had nothing left to lose, nothing left at all. Or maybe it was that I'd lost the most important thing already. And what did it matter? I thought. I reached into my purse, fumbling for the somewhat tequila-sticky copy of my screenplay that I'd tucked inside a million years ago, thinking that I'd revise the final scenes on the train ride home.

"Here," I slurred, shoving the screenplay into Maxi's hands.

"Oh, really, for me?" Maxi cooed, going into what sounded like her standard accepting-a-gift-from-a-stranger spiel. "Really, Cannie, you shouldn't have."

"No," I said, as a brief ray of sense poked through the alcohol fog. "No, I probably shouldn't have, but I'm gonna."

Maxi, meanwhile, was leafing drunkenly through the pages. "Whazzis?"

I hiccuped and figured, since I've come this far, why lie? "It's a screenplay that I wrote. I thought maybe you would like to read it, like maybe on the plane if you get bored again." I hiccuped some more. "I don't wanna impose . . ."

Maxi's eyelids had drooped to half-mast. She shoved the screenplay into her little black backpack, mangling the first thirty pages in the process. "Don' worry about it."

"You don't have to read it if you don't want to," I said. "And if you read it and you don't like it, you can tell me. Don't worry about hurting my feelings." I sighed. "Nobody else does."

Maxi leaned over and enfolded me in a clumsy hug. I could feel the bones of her elbows jabbing me as she gripped me tightly. "Poor Cannie," she said. "Don't you worry. I'm gonna take care of you."

I stared at her, as dubious as I was drunk. "You are?"

She nodded violently, with her ringlets bouncing around her face. "I'll take care of you," she said, "if you'll take care of me. If you'll be my friend, then we'll take care of each other."

NINE

I woke up in a hotel suite, in a very large bed, in my unfashionable black dress. Someone had taken off my sandals and set them neatly on the floor.

Sun was slanting through the windows, making bright stripes on the ivory-colored carpet and the pink down comforter that felt light as a kiss on my body. I lifted my head. Youch. Big mistake. I gingerly set my head back down on the pillows and closed my eyes again. It felt like someone had welded an iron band around my scalp and was tightening it slowly. It felt like my face was shrinking. It felt like there was something taped to my forehead.

I lifted my hands, removed a piece of paper that had, indeed, been taped to my forehead, and began to read.

Dear Cannie,

Sorry I had to leave you in such a state, but my plane left very early this morning (and April is livid with me . . . but that's okay. It was worth it!).

I feel very badly about what happened last night. I know that I pushed you into calling him, and that it was terrible news to receive. I can imagine how you're feeling now. I have been there myself (in terms of the tequila and the heartbreak both!).

Why don't you call me tomorrow, when you're back home and, I hope, feeling better? My number's below. I do hope you'll forgive me, and that we are still friends.

There will be a car waiting for you out front all day long, to take you home—my treat. (Actually, April's!) Please call soon.

Sincerely,
Maxi Ryder

And then there were a string of telephone numbers: Australia. Office. England. Pager. Cell phone. Fax. Alternate Fax. E-mail.

I made my way gingerly to the bathroom, where I was noisily and thoroughly sick. Maxi had left aspirin on the sink, along with what looked like several hundred dollars of unopened Kiehl's grooming products, and two large bottles of Evian water, still chilled. I swallowed three aspirin, sipped carefully at the water, and caught a glimpse of myself in the mirror. Ugh. Not good. Pale, pasty, blotchy skin, greasy hair, black-circled eyes, and all the makeup I'd tried at the Beauty Bar had smeared everywhere. I was weighing the pain-to-benefit ratio of a long hot shower when there was a gentle knock at the door.

"Room service," said the waiter, and wheeled in a cart. Hot coffee, hot tea, four kinds of juice, and dry toast. "Feel better," he said sympathetically. "And Ms. Ryder made arrangements for late checkout."

"How late?" I asked. My voice sounded creaky.

"Late as you like," he said. "Take your time. Enjoy."

He opened the curtains, displaying a panoramic view of the city.

"Wow," I said. The sunlight felt like it was stabbing my eyes, but the power of that view was undeniable. I could see Central Park spread out below me, dotted with people and trees, with their leaves turning orange and gold. The the stretch of high-rises in the distance. Then the river. Then New Jersey. *"He lives in New Jersey,"* I heard myself saying.

"It's the penthouse suite," he said, and left me there.

I poured myself a cup of tea, added sugar, attempted a few bites of toast. The bathtub, I observed sadly, was big enough for two—in fact, it was probably big enough for three, if the occupants were so inclined. The rich are different, I reasoned, and ran the water as hot as I could stand it, dumped in some frothing lotion guaranteed to possess so many restorative powers that I should rise from the tub reborn, or at least much better looking, and pulled my sundress off over my head.

My second mistake of the morning. There were mirrors all over the bathroom, mirrors offering views you couldn't usually find outside of a department store. And the terrain was not looking good. I closed my eyes to blot out the vision of stretch marks and cellulite. "I have strong tanned legs," I recited to myself. We'd practiced positive self-talk the week before in Fat Class. "I have beautiful shoulders." Then I slipped into the tub.

So, I thought bitterly. So he had someone else. So what did I think would happen? He's Jewish, he's got an education, he's tall and he's straight and he's easy on the eyes, and somebody was bound to snatch him up.

I rolled over, sending a cascade of water to the bathroom floor.

But he loved me, I thought. And was always telling me so. He thought I was perfect . . . that we were perfect together. And ten minutes later he's got someone else in his bed? Doing the things he swore he only ever wanted me to do?

The voice returned, implacable. *But you were the one who wanted a break.* And, *What did you expect?*

"Philadelphia, right, miss?" The driver was Russian, and was actually wearing a chauffeur's cap. The car, as it turned out, was a limousine, with a backseat bigger than my bed, and probably bigger than my bedroom, too. I peeked inside. There was the requisite television set, a VCR, a fancy-looking stereo . . . and, of course, a bar. Different liquors glittering in cut-crystal decanters, and a row of empty glasses. My stomach rolled over lazily.

"Could you excuse me?" I asked, and hurried back into the lobby. Hotel lobby bathrooms are also great places to get sick.

The chauffeur looked amused when I made it back to the car. "You want to take the Turnpike?"

"Whatever's easiest," I said, slipping into the seat, while he held the door open and loaded my backpack, shoe boxes, and shopping bags from the Beauty Bar into the trunk. There was a telephone in the backseat, next to the stereo and the television set, and I grabbed it, suddenly, sweatily desperate to know whether Bruce had tried to get in touch with me last night. There was a single message on my machine. "Hey, Cannie, it's Bruce, returning your call. I'm going home for a few days, so maybe I'll try you later this week." No *I'm sorry*. No *It was all a bad dream*. The call had come at eleven in the morning, probably after he'd had time for a morning go-round and a Belgian waffle with Miss Squeaky Springs, who would, thanks to my training, never refer to him as the Human Bidet, and who probably did not weigh more than he did.

I closed my eyes. It hurt so much.

I set the phone back as we barreled down the New Jersey Turnpike at eighty miles an hour, right past the exit that would take me to his door. I tapped two of my fingers against the window as we sped past. Hello and good-bye.

Sunday passed in a blur of tears and vomit at Samantha's house, where Nifkin and I had decamped, the better not to hear the telephone not ringing. Samantha, I could tell, was doing her damndest not to say she'd told me so. She lasted longer than I would have—all the way until Sunday night, when she finally ran out of questions to ask about Maxi and turned to the topic of Bruce, and the disastrous telephone call.

"You wanted to take a break for a reason," she told me. We were sitting at the Pink Rose Pastry Shop. She was nibbling a macaroon. I was forking my way through a baseball-shaped and baseball-sized éclair, the best legal antidote for human misery I'd found, figuring that it didn't matter, because I hadn't eaten anything since the afternoon before, in New York, with Maxi.

"I know," I said, "I just can't remember what it was anymore."

"And you did think things through before you did it, right?"

I nodded.

"So you had to at least consider the possibility that he'd find somebody else?"

It felt like an impossibly long time ago, but I had considered it.
At one point I'd even hoped for it, hoped for him to find some cute little Deadhead girl with ankle bracelets and armpit hair who'd stay up
late and get high with him while I worked hard, sold my screenplays,
and made *Time* magazine's "Thirty Under Thirty" list. Once upon a
time, I'd been able to contemplate that scenario without tears, nausea,
and/or feelings that I wanted to die, wanted to kill him, or wanted to
kill him and then die.

"There were reasons things weren't working out," Samantha said.

"Tell me again what they were."

"He didn't like to go to movies," said Samantha.

"I go to movies with you."

"He didn't like to go anywhere!"

"So it'd kill me to stay home?" I poked the éclair so hard it top-
pled over, oozing custard. "He was a really good guy. A good, sweet
guy. And I was a fool."

"Cannie, he compared you to Monica Lewinsky in a national magazine!"

"Well, that's not the worst thing in the world. It's not like he
cheated on me."

"I know what this is about," said Samantha.

"What?"

"It's about wanting what you can't have. It's the law of the universe:
He loved you, you felt bored and suffocated. Now he's moved on, and
you're desperate to have him back. But think about it, Cannie . . . has
anything really changed?"

I wanted to tell her that I had—that I'd gotten an up-close look at
what else was out there in my personal dating universe, and that its
name was Steve, it wore Tevas, and it didn't even consider a night out
with me to be a date.

"You'd just wind up dumping him again, and that's really not fair."

"Why do I have to be fair?" I moaned. "Why can't I just be selfish and lousy and rotten, like everybody else?"

"Because you're a good person," she said. "Unfortunate as it may seem."

"How do you know?" I challenged her.

"Okay. You're walking Nifkin and you go past your car and you notice that if you pulled it up a few feet there'd be another parking space, instead of just one of those annoying gaps that looks like a parking space but isn't. Do you move the car?"

"Well, yeah . . . wouldn't you?"

"That's not the point. That's the evidence. You're a good person."

"I don't want to be a good person. I want to drive to New Jersey and kick that bitch out of his bed . . ."

"I know," she said. "But you can't."

"Why not?" I demanded.

"Because you'll wind up in jail, and I'm not going to take care of your weird little dog forever."

"Fine." I sighed.

The waiter came by, glancing at our plates. "Finished?"

I nodded. "All done. No more," I said.

Sam told me I could stay over if I wanted to, but I decided that I couldn't hide forever, so I hitched up Nifkin and went back home. I hauled myself up the stairs, with my hands full of Saturday's mail, and there he was, right in front of my door. I saw him in stages—his scuffed-up, second-best sneakers . . . then mismatched athletic socks . . . then tanned, hairy legs came into view as I ascended. Sweatpants, an old college T-shirt, his goatee, his dirty-blond ponytail, his face. Ladies and gentlemen, fresh from his engagement with the Spring Squeaker, Bruce Guberman.

"Cannie?"

I felt so strange, as if my heart were trying to sink and rise at the same time. Or maybe it was just more nausea.

"Look," he said, "I, um, I'm sorry about last night."

"Nothing to apologize for," I said breezily, shouldering past him and unlocking the door. "What brings you here?"

He walked inside, keeping his eyes on his shoelaces and his hands in his pockets. "I'm on my way down to Baltimore, actually."

"How nice for you," I said, giving Nifkin a stern look in hopes that it would stop him from jumping up toward Bruce, his tail wagging triple-time. "I wanted to talk to you," he said.

"How nice for me," I replied.

"I was going to tell you. I wanted to tell you before you read about it," he said.

Oh, terrific. I was going to have to live it and read about it, too? "Read about it where?" I asked.

"In *Moxie*," he said.

"Actually, *Moxie*'s not high on my reading list," I told him. "I already know how to give a good blow job. As you may remember."

He took a deep breath, and I knew what it was, knew what was coming, the way you can feel the air pressure change and know that a storm's on the way. "I wanted to tell you that I'm kind of seeing somebody."

"Oh, really? You mean you didn't have your eyes shut the whole time last night?"

He didn't laugh.

"What's her name?"

"Cannie," he said gently.

"I refuse to believe that you found another girl named Cannie. Now tell me. C'mon. Age? Rank? Serial number?" I asked jokingly, hearing my voice as if from a million miles away.

"She's thirty-one . . . she's a kindergarten teacher. She's got a dog, too."

"That's great," I said sarcastically. "I bet we have lots and lots of other things in common. Let me guess . . . I'll bet she's got breasts! And hair!"

"Cannie . . ."

And then, because it was the only thing I could think of, "Where'd she go to school?"

"Um . . . Montclair State."

Great. Older, poorer, more dependent, less intelligent. I was dying to ask if she was blond, too, just to make the run of clichés complete.

"Do you love her?" I blurted instead.

"Cannie . . ."

"Never mind. I'm sorry. I had no right to ask you that. I'm sorry." And then, before I could stop myself, I asked, "Did you tell her about me?"

He nodded. "Of course I did."

"Well, what did you say?" A horrible thought struck me. "Did you tell her about my mom?"

Bruce nodded again, looking puzzled. "Why? What's the big deal?"

I shut my eyes, assaulted by a sudden vision of Bruce and his new girl in his wide, warm bed, his arm wrapped companionably around her, telling my family secrets. "Her mother's gay, you know," he'd say, and the new girl would give a wise, professionally compassionate kindergarten-teacher nod, all the while thinking what a freak I must be.

From the bedroom, I heard choking noises. "Excuse me," I murmured, and ran into the bedroom, where Nifkin was busily regurgitating a Baggie. I cleaned up the mess and walked back to the living room. Bruce was standing in front of my couch. He hadn't sat down, hadn't so much as touched anything. I could tell just from looking at him how desperately he wanted to be back in his car with the windows rolled down and the Springsteen cranked up . . . to be away from me.

"Are you okay?"

I took a deep breath. I wish you were back with me, I thought. I wish I didn't have to hear this. I wish we'd never broken up. I wish we'd never met.

"Fine," I said. "I'm glad for you."

We were both quiet then.

"I hope we can be friends," said Bruce.

"I don't think so," I said.

"Well," he said, and paused, and I knew that he had nothing left to say to me, and that there was really only one thing he wanted to hear.

And so I said it. "Good-bye, Bruce," I said, and opened the door, and stood there, waiting, until he walked out.

Then it was Monday, and I was back at work, feeling both queasy and abidingly dumb. I was shuffling things around on my desk, half-heartedly going through my mail, which featured the usual spate of complaints from Old People, Angry, plus a collection of bitter missives from Howard Stern fans who were most displeased with the review I'd given his latest on-air venture. I was wondering whether I could simply come up with a form letter to the seventeen guys who'd accused me of being ugly, old, and jealous of Howard Stern, and signed themselves "Baba Booey," when Gabby sauntered over.

"How'd it go with Maxi Whosit?" she asked.

"Fine," I said, giving her my best bland smile.

Gabby raised her eyebrows. "'Cause I heard through the grapevine that she wasn't doing any interviews with print reporters. Just TV."

"Not to worry."

But Gabby was looking worried. Extremely worried. She'd probably scheduled Maxi as the main item for tomorrow's column—just for the sheer joy of undercutting me—and now she was going to wind up scrambling to fill the space. Scrambling was not something Gabby did well.

"So . . . you talked to her?"

"For about an hour," I said. "Great stuff. Really great. We really hit it off. I think," I said, drawing the words out to prolong the torture, "I think we might even be friends."

Gabby's mouth fell open. I could tell she was trying to figure out whether to ask if anyone had mentioned her planned chat with Maxi, or to just hope I hadn't learned about it.

"Thanks for asking, though," I said sweetly. "It's so nice of you to look out for me like this. It's almost like . . . gee! . . . like you're my boss." I pushed back my chair, got to my feet, and walked by her regally, my back straight, my head held high. Then I went into the bathroom and threw up. Again.

Back at my desk, I was groping through my drawers, searching desperately for a mint or some gum, when the phone rang.

"Features, Candace Shapiro," I said distractedly. Thumbtacks, business cards, three sizes of paperclips, and not an Altoid to be found. Story of my life, I thought.

"Candace, this is Dr. Krushelevansky from the University of Philadelphia," said a deep, familiar voice.

"Oh. Oh, hi," I said. "What's up?" I gave up on the desk drawer and started going through my purse, even though I'd already looked through there.

"There's something I need to discuss with you," he said.

That got my attention. "Yes?"

"Well, you know that last blood draw we did . . ." I remembered it well. "Something came up that I'm afraid makes you ineligible for the study."

I felt my palms go icy. "What? What is it?"

"I'd prefer to discuss this with you in person," he said.

I quickly ran through everything else that a blood test could reveal, each possibility more awful than the one before. "Do I have cancer?" I asked. "Do I have AIDS?"

"You don't have anything life-threatening," he said sternly. "And I'd prefer not playing Twenty Questions."

"Then just tell me what's wrong," I begged. "High cholesterol? Hypoglycemia? Scurvy? Gout?"

"Cannie . . ."

"Do I have rickets? Oh, God, please not rickets. I don't think I can stand being fat and bowlegged."

He started laughing. "No rickets, but I'm starting to think you might have Tourette's. How do you know all of these diseases anyhow? Do you have a physician's desk reference in front of you?"

"I'm glad you think this is amusing," I said plaintively. "I'm glad this is your idea of fun, calling up innocent reporters in the middle of the day and telling them there's something wrong with their blood."

"Your blood is fine," he said seriously. "And I'll be happy to tell you what we found, but I would prefer to do it in person."

* * *

He was sitting behind his desk when I came in, and he got to his feet to greet me. I noticed, once again, how very tall he was.

"Have a seat," he said. I dropped my purse and backpack on one chair and parked myself on another.

He fanned my folder out on his desk. "As I told you, we do a standard series of tests when we draw blood, looking for conditions that could possibly disqualify study participants. Hepatitis is one of them. AIDS, of course, is another."

I nodded, wondering if he'd ever get to the point.

"We also test for pregnancy," he said. I nodded again, thinking, *okay, already, but what's wrong with me?* And then I realized. *Pregnancy.*

"But I'm not . . ." I stammered. "I mean, I can't be."

He flipped the folder around and pointed to where something was circled in red. "I'd be happy to arrange for another test," he said, "but generally, we're very accurate."

"I . . . I don't . . ." I stood up. How had this happened? My mind was whirling. I sank back into the chair to think. I'd gone off the Pill after Bruce and I had broken up, figuring it would be a long, long time before I had the need to contracept again, and it hadn't even occurred to me that I was at risk during the shiva call. It had to have happened then.

"Oh, God," I said, jumping to my feet again. Bruce. I had to find Bruce, I had to tell Bruce, surely he'd take me back now. . . *except*, my mind whispered, *what if he didn't?* What if he told me that it was my concern, my problem, that he was with somebody else and I was on my own?

"Oh," I said, slumping once more into the seat and burying my face in my hands. It was too horrible to even think about. I hadn't even noticed that Dr. K. had left the room until the door opened and he was standing there. There were three Styrofoam cups in one of his hands, a fistful of creamers and sugar packets in the other. He set the cups down on the desk in front of me: tea, coffee, water. "I wasn't sure what you like," he said apologetically. I picked up the tea. He opened his desk drawer and produced a half-empty bear-shaped squeeze bottle of honey. "Can I get you anything else?" he asked kindly. I shook my head.

"Would you like to be alone for a bit?" he asked, and I remembered that this was the middle of a work day, that there was a world going on around me, and that he probably had other things to do, other fat ladies to see.

"You probably don't do this a lot, do you?" I asked. "Tell people that they're pregnant, I mean."

The doctor looked taken aback. "No," he finally said. "No, I guess I don't do it a lot." He frowned. "Did I do it wrong?"

I laughed weakly. "I don't know. Nobody's ever told me that I'm pregnant before, so I don't have much to compare it to."

"I'm sorry," he said tentatively. "I take it this is . . . unexpected news."

"You could say that," I said. Suddenly, I was gripped with a vivid memory of the Cannie and Maxi Tequila Tour. "Oh, my God," I said, imagining that the putative kid was probably pickled by this point. "Do you know anything about fetal alcohol syndrome?"

"Hang on," he said. I heard him moving quickly down the hall. He came back with a book in his hands. *What To Expect When You're Expecting.* "One of the nurses had it," he explained. He flipped to the index. "Page 52," he said, and handed me the book. I skimmed the salient paragraphs and learned that basically, provided I quit drinking to the point of incoherence for the duration, things would be okay. Assuming, of course, that I wanted things to be okay. And, at that moment, I had no idea what I wanted. Except, of course, not to be in this situation at all.

I put the book on his desk and gathered my purse and backpack. "I guess I should be going," I said.

"Would you like another test?" he asked.

I shook my head. "I'll do one at home, I guess, and then I'll figure out . . ." I closed my mouth. Truthfully, I didn't know what I'd figure out.

He pushed the book back toward me. "Would you like to hang onto it? In case you have other questions?"

He was being so nice to me, I thought. Why was he being so nice to me? He was probably some crazy right-to-lifer, I thought meanly, trying to trick me into staying pregnant with the beverage sampler and the free guidebooks.

"Won't the nurse want it back?" I asked.

"She's had her babies," he said lightly. "I'm sure she wouldn't mind. You're welcome to have it." He cleared his throat. "With regard to the study," he began. "If you choose to continue the pregnancy, you won't be eligible, of course."

"No thin pills?" I joked.

"They haven't been approved for use by pregnant women."

"Then I could be your guinea pig," I offered, feeling myself teetering on the edge of hysteria. "Maybe I'd have a really skinny baby. That'd be good, right?"

"Whatever you do, just let me know," he said, tucking a business card inside of the book. "I'll make sure you get a full refund if you decide not to continue."

I remembered, very clearly, somewhere in the sheaf of forms I'd filled out the first day, something stating that there would be no refunds allowed. Crazy right-to-lifer, for sure, I thought, and stood up, strapping my backpack over my shoulders.

He looked at me kindly. "Listen, if you want to talk about it . . . or if you have any other medical questions, I'd be happy to try to help."

"Thanks," I muttered. My hand was already on the doorknob.

"Take care of yourself, Cannie," he said. "And give us a call, either way."

I nodded again, turned the handle, and hustled out the door.

I made bargains with God the whole way home, the same way I'd invented letters to the Celine Dion fan, poor Mr. Deiffinger, the least of my concerns now. Dear God, if you make me not pregnant I'll volunteer at the pet shelter and the AIDS hospice and I'll never write anything nasty about anyone again. I'll be a better person. I'll do everything right, I'll go to synagogue and not just on high holy days, I won't be so mean and critical, I'll be nice to Gabby, only please, please, please, don't let this be happening to me.

I bought two tests at the drugstore on South Street, white cardboard boxes with beaming mothers-to-be on the front, and peed all over my hand doing the first one, I was shaking so hard. By then I was so convinced of the worst that I didn't need the plus sign on the EPT wand to tell me what Dr. Krushelevansky already had.

"I'm pregnant," I said to the mirror, and mimed a smile, like the woman on the box.

"Pregnant," I informed Nifkin later that night, as he bounded all over me and licked my face at Samantha's house, where I'd stashed him while I was at work. Samantha had two dogs of her own, plus a big, fenced-in yard and a pet door, so the dogs could go in and out as they pleased. Nifkin wasn't crazy about her dogs, Daisy and Mandy— I suspected that he much preferred the company of people to other pets—but he was a big fan of the premium lamb and rice kibble that Samantha served, and so, on balance, seemed happy to hang out at Sam's house.

"What did you say?" Samantha called from the kitchen.

"I'm pregnant," I called back.

"What?"

"Nothing," I yelled. Nifkin sat on my lap, looking gravely into my eyes.

"You heard me, right?" I whispered. Nifkin licked my nose and curled into my lap.

Samantha came into the living room, wiping her hands. "You were saying?"

"I said, I'm going home for Thanksgiving."

"Lesbian turkey again?" Samantha wrinkled her nose. "Didn't you tell me that I was under strict instructions to slap you if you ever mentioned spending another holiday with Tanya again?"

"I'm tired," I told her. "I'm tired and I want to go home."

She sat down beside me. "What's going on, really?"

And I wanted so badly to tell her then, to just turn to her and spill it all out, to tell her, help me, and tell me what to do. But I couldn't.

Not yet. I needed time to think, to know my own mind before the chorus started. I knew the advice she'd give me. It would be the same thing I'd tell her if she were in the same situation: young, single with a great career, knocked up by a guy who wasn't returning her phone calls. It was a no-brainer, a $500 afternoon in the doctor's office, a few days of cramps and crying, end of story.

But before I went for the obvious, I wanted some time, even just a few days. I wanted to go home, even if home had long since gone from a happy refuge to something closer to a Sapphic commune.

It wasn't hard. I called Betsy, who told me to take as much time as I needed. "You've got three weeks of vacation, five days you never took from last year, and comp time from New York," she said, in a message on my machine at home. "Have a happy Thanksgiving, and I'll see you next week."

I e-mailed Maxi. "Something has come up . . . unfortunately, not the thing I might have hoped for," I wrote. "Bruce is dating a kindergarten teacher. I am brokenhearted and going home to eat dried turkey and let my mother feel sorry for me."

"Good luck, then," she'd written back immediately, even though it had to be three in the morning there. "And never mind the teacher. She's his transition object. They never last. Call or write when you're home . . . I'll be in the States again in the spring."

I cancelled my haircut, postponed a few telephone interviews, arranged for my neighbors to pick up my papers and my mail. I didn't call Bruce. If I decided not to stay pregnant, there'd be no reason for him to know. At this stage in our non-relationship, I couldn't very well imagine him sitting beside me in a clinic tenderly holding my hand. If I did stay pregnant . . . well, I'd burn that bridge when I came to it, I thought.

I hitched my bicycle rack and mountain bike to the back of my little blue Honda, put Nifkin in his traveling case, and tossed my bag in the trunk. Ready or not, I was going home.

PART THREE

I Go Swimming

TEN

The summer between my junior and senior years at Princeton, I had an internship at the *Village Vanguard*, the oldest and most attitudinous of the alternative newsweeklies in the country.

It was a wretched three months. For one thing, it was the hottest summer in years. Manhattan was boiling. Every morning I'd start sweating the instant I exited the shower, keep sweating through the subway ride downtown, and basically continue sweating the whole day.

I worked for a horrible woman named Kiki. Six feet tall and skeletally skinny, with henna'd hair, cat-eye thrift shop eyeglasses, and a permanent scowl, Kiki's summer uniform was a miniskirt paired with thigh-high suede boots, or, alternately, the noisiest clogs in the world, topped with a tight T-shirt advertising Sammy's Rumanian Restaurant, or the Boy Scouts Gymboree, or something else so square that it was hip.

Initially, Kiki confounded me. The hipster garb made sense, and the bad attitude was par for the *Vanguard* course, but I couldn't figure out when she was getting any work done. She showed up late, left early, and took two-hour lunches in between, and seemed to spend most of her time in the office on the phone with a cadre of interchangeable-sounding friends. The mosaic nameplate on the white picket fence she'd ironically erected around her cubicle read "associate editor." And while she associated plenty, I'd never seen her edit.

She was, however, the master of delegating unpleasant chores. "I'm thinking about women and murder," she'd announce on a Tuesday afternoon, idly sipping her iced coffee while I stood before her, sweating. "Why don't you see what we've done?"

This was 1991. The back issues of the *Vanguard* weren't stored online, or even on microfilm, but in huge, dusty, falling-apart, over-sized binders that each weighed at least twenty pounds. These binders were housed along the hallway that linked the offices of columnists to the feeding pen of metal chairs and cigarette-scarred desks that served as workspace for the *Vanguard*'s lesser luminaries. I spent my days hauling the binders off the shelves, lugging them over first to my desk, then to the copying machine, all the while trying to avoid the gin breath and wandering hands of the nation's preeminent gun rights activist, whose office was right next to the shelves, and whose favorite summer hobby seemed to be accidentally on purpose brushing against the sides of my breasts when my arms were loaded down with binders.

It was miserable. After two weeks I gave up on the subway and started taking the bus. Even though it made the ride twice as long and just as hot, it kept me out of the sweltering, fetid pit that the 116th Street subway stop had become. One afternoon in early August, I was sitting on the M140, minding my own business and sweating as usual, when, just as the bus lurched past Billy's Topless, I heard a very small, perfectly calm voice that sounded as if it was coming from the precise base of my skull.

"*I know where you're going,*" said the voice. The hair on my arms and the back of my neck stood straight up. I got goosebumps, and was suddenly freezing cold, and I was completely convinced that what I was hearing was . . . not human. A voice from the spirit world, I might have said that summer, laughing it off with my friends. But really, I thought it was the voice of God.

Of course it wasn't God, just Ellyn Weiss, the small, strange, androgynous-looking *Village Vanguard* contributing writer who'd sat down behind me and decided to say, "I know where you're going" instead of "hello." But in my mind, I thought that if I ever got to hear the voice of God, it would sound exactly like that: small and still and sure.

Once you've heard the voice of God, it changes things. That day, when the preeminent gun rights activist waggled his fingertips against the side of my right breast as he made his lurching way back to his office, I accidentally on purpose dropped 1987 on his foot. "So sorry," I said, sweet as pie, when he turned the color of a dirty sheet and stumbled away, never to lay a finger on me again. And when Kiki told me, "I've been thinking about women and men, and how they're different," and asked whether I could start pulling pages, I told her a bald-faced lie. "My advisor says I won't get credit for this if all you've got me doing is photocopying," I told her. "If you can't use me, I'm sure the copy editors can." That very afternoon I slipped Kiki's skinny, angered clutches and spent the rest of the summer writing headlines, and going out for cheap drinks with my new copy-editing colleagues.

Now, seven years later, I sat cross-legged on a picnic table, my face turned up to the pale November sunshine and my bike parked beside me, waiting to hear that voice again. Waiting for God to take notice as I sat in the center of Pennwood State Park in suburban Pennsylvania five miles from the house I grew up in, for God to look down upon me and intone either, *Keep the baby,* or *Call Planned Parenthood.*

I stretched out my legs, lifted my arms over my head, breathing in through my nose, out through my mouth, the way Samantha's yoga instructor boyfriend said would rid my bloodstream of impurities and increase clear thoughts. If it had happened the way I figured—if I'd gotten pregnant the last time Bruce and I were together—then I was eight weeks along. How big was it, I wondered? The size of a fingertip, a pencil eraser, a tadpole?

I'd decided that I'd give God another ten minutes, when I heard something.

"Cannie?"

Ugh. That most definitely was not the voice of the divine. I felt the table tilt as Tanya hoisted herself on top of it, but I kept my eyes closed, hoping that maybe, for once, if I ignored her she'd go away.

"Is something wrong?"

Silly me. I was forever forgetting that Tanya was a participant in a clutch of self-help groups: one for families of alcoholics, another for sexual-abuse survivors, a third called Codependent No More!, with an exclamation point as part of its name. Leaving well enough alone wasn't even a possibility. Tanya was all about intervention.

"It might help if you talk about it," she rumbled, lighting a cigarette.

"Mm," I said. Even with my eyes shut I could feel her watching me.

"You got fired," she suddenly announced.

My eyes flew open in spite of myself. "What?"

Tanya looked inordinately pleased with herself. "I figured it out, didn't I? Hah! Your mother owes me ten bucks."

I lay on my back, waving her smoke away from me, feeling a growing annoyance. "No, I did not get fired."

"Was it Bruce? Did something else happen?"

"Tanya, I really don't feel like discussing it right now."

"Bruce, huh?" Tanya said mournfully. "Shit."

I sat up again. "Why does that bother you?"

She shrugged her shoulders. "Oh, your mother figured it was something with Bruce, so if she's right, I've got to pay her."

Great, I thought. My poor life reduced to a series of ten-dollar bets. Easy tears sprang to my eyes. It seemed these days I was crying about everything, starting with my situation and continuing relentlessly to human-interest stories that ran in the *Examiner*'s Lifestyle section and Campbell's soup commercials.

"I guess you saw that last article he wrote, huh?" said Tanya.

I'd seen it. "Love, Again," it was called, in the December issue, which had hit stands just in time to ruin my Thanksgiving. "I know I should be focusing on E. by herself," he'd written.

I know that it's wrong to compare. But there's no way to avoid it. After The First, it seems that the next woman is, necessarily, The Second. At least in the beginning, at least for a little while. And E. is in every way different from my first love: short where she was tall, fine and delicate where she was broad and solid, sweet where she was bitterly, mordantly funny.

"Rebound," my friends tell me, nodding their heads like ancient rabbis instead of twenty-nine-year-old full-time temps and graduate students. "She's your rebound girl." But what's wrong with rebound, I wonder? If there was a first and it didn't work out, then there has to be a second, a next. Eventually, you have to move on.

If first love was like exploring a new continent, I think that second love is like moving to a new neighborhood. You already know there will be streets and houses. Now you have the pleasure of learning what the houses look like inside, how the streets feel beneath your feet. You know the rules, the basic vocabulary: phone calls, Valentine's Day chocolates, how to comfort a woman when she tells you what's gone wrong in her day, in her life. Now you can fine-tune. You find her nickname, how she likes her hand held, the sweet spot just beneath the curve of her jaw : . .

And that was as far as I'd made it before running to the toilet for my second hurl of the day. Just the idea of Bruce kissing someone else on the sweet spot just beneath the curve of her jaw—even the thought of him noticing such a thing—was enough to send my already queasy stomach into revolt. He doesn't love me anymore. I had to keep reminding myself of that, and every time I thought those words, it was like hearing them for the first time, in all-capital italic letters, being boomed out by the guy who did voice-overs for movie previews: *HE DOESN'T LOVE ME ANYMORE.*

"It must be tough," mused Tanya.

"It's ridiculous," I snapped. And really, the whole situation was pretty ridiculous. After three years of resisting his pleas, his offers, his desperate importunings, and biweekly proclamations that I was the only woman he'd ever want, we were apart, I was pregnant, and he'd found somebody else, and I would, most likely, never see him again.

(*Never* was another word I'd hear in my head a lot, as in: You'll never wake up next to him again, or, You'll never talk to him on the telephone.)

"So what are you going to do?" she asked.

"That's the big question," I said, and hopped off the table and onto my bike, heading back home. Except it didn't feel like home anymore and, thanks to Tanya's invasion, I wasn't sure it ever would again.

The less you know about your parents' sex lives, the better. Sure, you figure, they had to have done it at least once, to get you, and then maybe a few more times, if you had brothers and sisters, but that was procreation; that was duty, and the thought of them using their various openings and attachments for fun, for pleasure—in short, in the manner you, their child, would like to be using yours—was nothing short of sick-making. Particularly if they were having the kind of trendy, cutting-edge love life that was all the rage in the late 1990s. You don't need to know about your parents having sex, and you especially don't need to know about them having hipper sex than you are.

Unfortunately, thanks to Tanya's self-help training, and my mother's being rendered senseless by love, I got the whole story.

It started when my brother, Josh, came home from college and was rummaging in my mother's bathroom for the toenail clippers, when he came across a small stack of Hallmark greeting cards—the kind with abstract watercolors of birds and trees on the front, and florid calligraphy'd sentiments inside. "Thinking of you," read the front of one, and inside, beneath the rhymed Hallmark couplet, someone had written, "Annie, after three months, the fire still burns strong." No signature.

"I think they're from this woman," said Josh.

"What woman?" I asked.

"The one who's living here," said Josh. "Mom says she's her swim coach."

A live-in swim coach? This was the first I'd heard of it.

"It's probably nothing," I told Josh.

"It's probably nothing," Bruce told me, when I'd talked to him that night.

And that was how I started my conversation with my mother when she called at work two days later: "This is probably nothing, but . . ."

"Yes?" asked my mother.

"Is there, um, someone else . . . living there?"

"My swim coach," she said.

"You know, the Olympics were last year," I said, playing along.

"Tanya's a friend of mine from the Jewish Community Center. She's between apartments, and she's staying in Josh's room for a few days."

This sounded slightly suspect. My mother didn't have friends who lived in apartments, let alone who slept over because they were between them. Her friends all lived in the houses their ex-husbands had left, just like she did. But I let it go until the next time I called home and an unfamiliar voice answered the telephone.

"H'lo?" the strange voice growled. It was, at first, impossible to tell whether I was talking to a woman or a man. But whoever it was sounded as if they'd just gotten out of bed, even though it was almost eight o'clock on a Friday night.

"I'm sorry," I said politely, "I think I have the wrong number."

"Is this Cannie?" demanded the voice.

"Yes. Who's this, please?"

"Tanya," she said proudly. "I'm a friend of your mother's."

"Oh," I said. "Oh. Hi."

"Your mother's told me a lot about you."

"Well, that's . . .that's good," I said. My mind was churning. Who was this person, and what was she doing answering our telephone?

"But she's not here right now," Tanya continued. "She's playing bridge. With her bridge group."

"Right."

"Do you want me to have her call you?"

"No," I said, "no, that's okay."

That was Friday. I didn't speak to my mother again until she called on Monday afternoon at work.

"Is there something you want to tell me?" I asked her, expecting her to say some variation of "No." Instead, she took a deep breath.

"Well, you know, Tanya . . . my friend? She's . . . well. We're in love and we're living together."

What can I say? Subtlety and discretion run in the family.

"I've got to go," I said, and hung up the phone.

I spent the whole rest of the afternoon staring blankly into space, which, believe me, did nothing to add to the quality of my article about the MTV Video Music Awards. At home, there were three messages on my machine: one from my mother ("Cannie, call me, we need to discuss this"); one from Lucy ("Mom said I have to call you and she didn't say why"); and one from Josh ("I TOLD you so!").

I ignored all of them, instead rounding up Samantha for an emergency dessert and strategy session. We went to the bar around the corner, where I ordered a shot of tequila and a slab of chocolate cake with raspberry sauce. Thus fortified, I told her what my mother had told me.

"Wow," murmured Samantha.

"Good God!" said Bruce, when I told him later that night. But it wasn't long before his initial shock turned into . . . well, call it shocked amusement. With a heavy helping of condescension. By the time he arrived at my door he was in full-blown good liberal mode. "You should be glad she's found someone to love," he lectured.

"I am," I said slowly. "I mean, I guess I am. It's just that . . ."

"Glad," Bruce repeated. He could get a little insufferable when it came to toeing the P.C. party line, and to mouthing the beliefs that were practically mandatory among graduate students in the northeast in the nineties. Most of the time I let him get away with it. But this time I wasn't going to let him make me feel like a bigot, or like I was less open-minded and accepting than he was. This time it was personal.

"How many gay friends do you have?" I asked, knowing what the answer was.

"None, but . . ."

"None that you know of," I said, and paused while he let that sink in.

"What does that mean?" he demanded.

"It means what I said. None that you know of."

"You think one of my friends is gay?"

"Bruce, I didn't even know my own mother was gay. How do you expect me to have any kind of insight about your friends' sexuality?"

"Oh," he said, mollified.

"But my point is that you don't really know any gay people. So how can you assume it's such a terrific thing for my mom? That I should be happy about it?"

"She's in love. How can that be a bad thing?"

"What about this other person? What if she's awful? What if . . ." I was starting to cry as the horrible images piled up in my head. "What if, I don't know, they're walking somewhere and someone sees them and, and, throws a beer bottle at their heads or something . . ."

"Oh, Cannie . . ."

"People are mean! That's my point! It's not that there's anything wrong with being gay, but people are mean . . . and judgmental . . . and rotten . . . and, and you know what my neighborhood's like! People won't let their kids trick or treat at our house. . . ." Of course, the truth was that nobody'd let their kids trick or treat at our house since 1985 when my father began his downhill slide by neglecting the yardwork and getting in touch with his inner artiste. He'd brought a scalpel home from the hospital and turned half a dozen pumpkins into unflatteringly accurate renditions of members of my mother's immediate family, including a truly hideous pumpkin Aunt Linda that he'd perched on our porch, topped with a platinum blond wig that he'd swiped from the hospital's lost and found. But the truth was also that Avondale wasn't an especially integrated community. No blacks, few Jews, and no openly gay people that I could recall.

"So who cares what people think?"

"I do," I sobbed. "I mean, it's nice to have ideals and hope that things will change, but we have to live in the world the way it is, and the world is . . . is . . ."

"Why are you crying?" Bruce asked. "Are you worried about your mother, or yourself?" Of course, by that time, I was crying too hard to answer, and there was also a mucus situation that needed immediate attention. I swiped my sleeve across my face and blew my nose noisily. When I looked up, Bruce was still talking. "Your mother's made her choice, Cannie, and if you're a good daughter, what you'll do is support it."

Well. Easy for him to say. It wasn't as if the Ever Tasteful Audrey had announced over one of her four-course kosher dinners that she'd decided to park on the other side of the street, as it were. I would bet a week's pay that the Ever Tasteful Audrey had never even seen another woman's vagina. She'd probably never even seen her own.

The thought of Bruce's mother in her whirlpool bathtub for two, discreetly dabbing at her own privates from beneath an Egyptian cotton washcloth with a high thread count, made me laugh a little.

"See?" said Bruce. "You just have to roll with it, Cannie."

I laughed even harder. Having discharged his boyfriendly duty, Bruce switched gears. His voice dropped from his concerned-guidance-counselor tenor to a more intimate tone. "Come here, girl," he murmured, sounding for all the world like Lionel Richie as he beckoned me beside him, tenderly kissing my forehead and not so tenderly tossing Nifkin off the bed. "I want you," he said, and placed my hand on his crotch to remove any doubt.

And so it went.

Bruce left at midnight. I fell into an uneasy sleep and woke up the morning after with the telephone shrilling on my pillow. I unglued one eyelid. 5:15. I picked up the phone. "Hello?"

"Cannie? It's Tanya."

Tanya?

"Your mother's friend."

Oh, God. Tanya.

"Hi," I said weakly. Nifkin stared at me as if to say, what is this about? Then he gave a dismissive sniff and resettled himself on the pillow. Meanwhile, Tanya was talking a blue streak.

". . . knew the first time I saw her that she could have feelings for me . . ."

I struggled to sit up, and groped for a reporter's notebook. This was too bizarre not to be recording for posterity. By the time our conversation ended, I'd filled nine pages, made myself late for work, and learned every detail about Tanya's life. I heard how she was molested by her piano teacher, how her mother died of breast cancer when she was young ("I coped with my pain with alcohol"), and how her father had remarried a not-nice book editor who refused to pay Tanya's tuition to Green Mountain Valley Community College ("they've got the third-best program in New England for art therapy"). I learned the name of Tanya's first love (Marjorie), how she wound up in Pennsylvania (job), and how she'd been in the process of ending a seven-year relationship with a woman named Janet. "She's very codependent," Tanya confided. "Maybe obsessive-compulsive, too." At this point I had retreated into full reporter mode and wasn't saying anything but "Uh-huh," or, "I see."

"So I moved out," she told me.

"Uh-huh," I said.

"And I devoted myself to weaving."

"I see."

Then it was on to how she'd met my mother (passionate glances in the ladies' locker room sauna—I'd almost been forced to put the phone down), where they'd gone on their first date (Thai food), and how Tanya had convinced my mother that her lesbian tendencies were more than a passing fancy.

"I kissed her," Tanya announced proudly. "And she tried to walk away, and I held her by the shoulders and I looked her in the eyes and I said, 'Ann, this is not going away.'"

"Uh-huh," I said. "I see."

Tanya then proceeded to the analysis and reflection portion of the speech.

"The way I see it," she began, "your mother's devoted her whole life to you kids." She said "you kids" in precisely the same tone I would have used for "you infestation of cockroaches."

"And she put up with that bastard . . ."

"Which bastard are we talking about here?" I inquired mildly.

"Your father," said Tanya, who was obviously not going to tone things down for the benefit of the bastard's offspring. "Like I was saying, she's devoted her life to you guys . . . and not that it's a bad thing. I know how much she wanted to be a mother, and have a family, and, of course, there weren't other options for dykes back then . . ."

Dykes? I could barely handle "lesbian." At what point did my mother get promoted to "dyke"?

". . . but what I think," Tanya continued, "is that now it's time for your mother to do more of what she wants. To have a life of her own."

"I see," I said. "Uh-huh."

"I'm really looking forward to meeting you," she said.

"I have to go now," I said, and hung up the phone. I didn't know whether to laugh or cry, so I wound up doing both at the same time.

"Beyond awful," I said to Samantha on the car phone.

"A freak like you wouldn't believe," I told Andy over lunch.

"Don't judge," Bruce warned me, before I'd even said a word.

"She's . . . um. She's into sharing. Lots of sharing."

"That's good," he said, doing his squinchy-blinky thing. "You should do more sharing, Cannie."

"Huh? Me?"

"You're very closed with your emotions. You keep everything so tight inside you."

"You know, you're right," I said. "Let's find a total stranger so I can tell how my piano teacher groped me."

"Huh?"

"She was molested," I said. "And she told me all the gory details."

Even Mr. Love Everyone seemed taken aback by this information. "Oh my."

"Yeah. And her mother had breast cancer, and her stepmother convinced her father not to pay her community college loans."

Bruce looked at me skeptically. "She told you all this?"

"What do you think, I drove home and read her diary? Of course she told me!" I paused to poach a few french fries off his plate. We were at the Tick Tock Diner, home of the enormous portion and the surliest waitresses south of New York. I never ordered fries there, but I used all my powers of persuasion to get Bruce to order them, so I could share. "She sounds seriously cracked."

"You probably made her uncomfortable."

"But I didn't say anything! She's never even met me! And she was the one who called me, so how could I make her uncomfortable?"

Bruce shrugged. "It's just the way you are, I guess."

I scowled at him. He reached for my hand. "Don't get mad. It's just that . . . you have this kind of judgmental thing going on."

"Says who?"

"Well, my friends, I guess."

"What, just because I think they should get jobs?"

"See, there you go. That's judgmental."

"Honey, they're slackers. Accept it. It's the truth."

"They're not slackers, Cannie. They do have jobs, you know."

"Oh, come on. What does Eric Silverberg do for a living?"

Eric, as we both knew, had a full-time temporary job at an Internet startup, where, as best we could both figure, he spent his days trading Springsteen bootleg tapes, meeting girls on one of the three online dating services he subscribed to, and arranging drug buys.

"George has a real job."

"George spends every weekend in a Civil War reenactment brigade. George owns his own musket."

"You're changing the subject," Bruce said. I could tell he was trying to stay angry, but he was starting to smile.

"I know," I said. "It's just that a guy who has his own musket is such an easy punchline."

I stood up, crossed the table, and sat down next to him on his side of the booth, squeezing his thigh and resting my head against his shoulder. "You know the only reason I'm judgmental is because I'm jealous," I said. "I wish I could have that kind of life. No college loans to pay, rent taken care of, nice, stable, married heterosexual parents who'd set me up with their slightly used furniture every time they redecorate and buy me a car for Chanukah . . ." My voice trailed off. Bruce was staring at me hard. I realized that, in addition to describing most of his friends, I'd just described him, too.

"I'm sorry," I said gently. "It's just that sometimes it feels like everybody's got things easier than I do, and that every time I get close to having things be kind of okay . . . something like this happens."

"Did you ever think that maybe these things happen to you because you're strong enough to take them?" Bruce asked. He reached down, grabbed my hand, and moved it up on his thigh. Way up. "You're so strong, Cannie," he whispered.

"I just," I said, "I wish . . ." And then he was kissing me. I could taste ketchup and salt on his lips. Then his tongue was in my mouth. I shut my eyes and let myself forget.

I spent the weekend at Bruce's apartment. It was one of those times where we got it just right: good sex, a nice meal out, lazy afternoons trading sections of the Sunday *Times,* and then I was on my way home before we started grating on each other. We talked about my mother a little bit, but mostly I got to just lose myself with him. And he gave me his favorite flannel shirt to wear home. It smelled like him, like us: like dope and sex, his skin and my shampoo. It was too tight across my chest—all of his things were—but the sleeves fell to my finger-tips, and I felt enclosed, comforted, as if he was there hugging me tight, holding my hands.

Be brave, I thought back home in my bed. I pulled Bruce's shirt tight around me, tilted my cheek toward Nifkin so he could give me an encouraging lick, and phoned home.

Thankfully, my mother answered. "Cannie!" she said, sounding relieved. "Where have you been? I've been calling and calling . . ."

"I went to Bruce's," I told her. "We had theater tickets," I lied. Bruce didn't do well in theaters. Short attention span.

"Well," she said. "Well. Um, I want to tell you that I'm sorry for springing things on you like that. I guess I should have . . . well, I know I should have waited and maybe told you in person . . ."

"Or at least not at the office," I said.

She laughed. "Right. I'm sorry."

"It's okay."

"So . . ." I could almost hear her testing half a dozen opening remarks in her head. "Do you have any questions?" she finally asked.

I took a deep breath. "Are you happy?"

"I feel like I'm in high school!" my mother said jubilantly. "I feel . . . oh, I can't even describe it."

Please, don't try, I thought.

"Tanya's really terrific. You'll see."

"How old is she?" I asked.

"Thirty-six," said my fifty-six-year-old mother.

"A younger woman," I observed. My mother giggled. You have no idea how disturbing that was. My mother has never been the giggling type.

"She does seem to have a little problem with . . . boundaries," I ventured.

My mother's voice got very serious. "What do you mean?"

"Well, she called me Friday morning . . . I guess you weren't there. . . ."

A quick intake of breath. "What did she say?"

"It might take me less time to cover what she didn't say."

"Oh, God. Oh, Cannie."

"I mean, I'm sorry she was, you know, molested . . ."

"Oh, Cannie, she didn't!" But underneath the shocked, horrified tone, my mother sounded . . . almost proud. As if underneath the anger, she was indulging a favored child in the child's favorite prank.

"Yup," I said grimly. "I got the whole saga, from the piano teacher who tickled her ivories . . ."

". . . Cannie!"

". . . and the wicked stepmother, to the obsessive-compulsive co-dependent ex-girlfriend."

"Ack," said my mother. "Jeez."

"She might want to consider some therapy," I said.

"She goes. Believe me, she goes. She's been going for years."

"And she still hasn't figured out that you don't go blurting your whole life story to a complete stranger the first time you speak to them?"

My mother sighed. "I guess not," she said.

I waited. I waited for an apology, an explanation, something that could make sense of this. Nothing came. After a moment of awkward silence, my mother changed the subject, and I went along, hoping this was a phase, a fling, a bad dream, even. No such luck. Tanya had arrived for good.

What does a lesbian bring on a second date? goes the joke. A U-Haul. What does a gay guy bring on a second date? What second date?

An old joke, true, but there's a certain amount of truth to it. After they started dating, Tanya did in fact move out of the basement of her codependent obsessive-compulsive ex-girlfriend's condominium and into an apartment of her own.

But for all intents and purposes, she'd moved in on the second date. I realized this when I came home six weeks after what my siblings and I were referring to as Mom's Outage, and saw the writing on the wall.

Well, the poster on the wall. "Inspiration," it read, above a picture of a cresting wave, "is believing we can all pull together."

"Mom?" I called, dropping my bags on the floor. Nifkin, meanwhile, was whining and cringing by my legs in a most un-Nifkin-like manner.

"In here, honey," yelled my mother.

Honey? I wondered, and walked into the family room with Nifkin cowering behind me. This time, the new poster was of frolicking dolphins. "Teamwork," it said. And beneath the dolphin poster were my mother and a woman who could only be Tanya, in matching purple sweatsuits.

"Hey!" said Tanya.

"Hey," my mother repeated.

A large tangerine-colored cat leapt off of the windowsill, stalked insolently up to Nifkin, and stretched out a paw, claws extended. Nifkin gave a shrill yip and fled.

"Gertrude! Bad cat!" called Tanya. The cat ignored her and curled up in a patch of sunlight in the center of the room.

"Nifkin!" I called. From upstairs I heard a faint whine of protest— Nifkin-speak for *no way, no day*.

"Do we have employees that we're trying to motivate?" I asked, pointing at the teamwork dolphins.

"Huh?" said Tanya.

"What?" said my mother.

"The posters," I said. "We've got the exact same ones in the printing plant at work. Right next to the "27 Days Injury Free" sign. They're, like, motivational artwork."

Tanya shrugged. I'd been expecting a standard-issue gym teacher, with sinewy calves and ropy biceps and a no-nonsense haircut. Evidently I'd been expecting wrong. Tanya was a tiny boiled pea of a woman, barely five feet tall, with an aureole of frizzy reddish hair and skin tanned the color and consistency of old leather. No chest or hips to speak of. She looked like a little kid, right down to the scabby knees and the Band-Aid wrapped around one finger. "I just like dolphins," she said shyly.

"Uh-huh," I said. "I see."

And those were just the most obvious of the changes. There was a collection of dolphin figurines above the fireplace where the family pictures had been. Plastic magazine racks were bolted to the walls, giving our family room the look of a doctor's office—the better to display Tanya's copies of *Rehabilitation* magazine. And when I went to drop my bags in my room, the door wouldn't open.

"Mom!" I called, "there's something wrong up here!"

I heard a whispered consultation going on in the kitchen: my mother's voice calm and soothing, Tanya's bass grumble rising toward hysteria. Every once in a while I could make out words. "Therapist" and "privacy" seemed to comprise a dominant theme. Finally my mother walked up the stairs, looking troubled.

"Um, actually, I was going to talk to you about this."

"About what? The door being stuck?"

"Well, the door's locked, actually."

I just stared.

"Tanya's kind of been . . . keeping some of her things in there."

"Tanya," I pointed out, "has an apartment. Can't she keep her things there?"

My mother shrugged. "Well, it's a very small apartment. An efficiency, really. And it just kind of made sense . . . maybe you can sleep in Josh's room tonight."

At this point I was getting impatient. "Ma, it's my room. I'd like to sleep in my room. What's the big deal?"

"Well, Cannie, you don't . . . you don't live here anymore."

"Of course I don't, but that doesn't mean I don't want to sleep there when I come home."

My mother sighed. "We made some changes," she murmured.

"Yeah, I noticed. So what's the big deal?"

"We, um . . . well. We kind of got rid of your bed."

I was speechless. "You got rid of . . ."

"Tanya needed the space for her loom."

"There's a loom in there?"

Indeed there was. Tanya stomped up the stairs, unbolted the door, and stomped back downstairs, looking sullen. I entered my room and saw the loom, a computer, a battered futon, a few ugly pressboard bookshelves covered with plastic walnut veneer, containing volumes with titles like *Smart Women, Foolish Choices,* and *Courage to Heal,* and *It's Not What You're Eating, It's What's Eating You.* There was a rainbow-triangle suncatcher hanging in the window and, worst of all, an ashtray on the desk.

"She smokes?"

My mother bit her lip. "She's trying to quit."

I inhaled. Sure enough, Marlboro Lights and incense. Yuck. Why did she have to plant her self-help guides and her cigarette smells in my room? And where was my stuff?

I turned toward my mother. "You know, you really could have told me about this. I could have come down and taken my things with me."

"Oh, we didn't get rid of anything, Cannie. It's all in boxes in the basement."

I rolled my eyes. "Well, that makes me feel a lot better."

"Look," she said. "I'm sorry. I'm just trying to balance things here. . . ."

"No, no," I said. "'Balance' involves taking different things into account. This," I said, sweeping my hand to indicate the loom, the ashtray, the stuffed dolphin perched upon the futon, "is taking what one person wants into account, and completely screwing the other person. This is completely selfish. This is absolutely ridiculous. This is . . ."

"Cannie," said Tanya. She'd somehow come up the stairs without my hearing.

"Excuse us, please," I said, and slammed the door in her face. I took a perverse pleasure in listening to her work at the door handle after I'd locked it with her lock.

My mother started to sit down where my bed used to be, caught herself mid-sit and settled for Tanya's desk chair. "Cannie, look. I know this is a shock. . . ."

"Have you gone completely crazy? This is ridiculous! All it would have taken was one lousy phone call. I could have come, gotten my stuff . . ."

My mother looked miserable. "I'm sorry," she said again.

I wound up not staying the night. That visit occasioned my first—and, so far, my last—stint at therapy. The *Examiner*'s health plan paid for ten visits with Dr. Blum, the smallish, Little Orphan Annie-looking woman who scribbled frantically, while I told her the whole crazy-father-bad-divorce-lesbian-mother tale. I worried about Dr. Blum. For one thing, she always looked a little scared of me. And she always seemed a few twists behind the current plot.

"Now, back up," she'd say, when I'd segue abruptly from Tanya's latest atrocity to my sister, Lucy's, inability to keep a job. "Your sister was, um, dancing topless for a living, and your parents didn't notice?'

"This was '86," I'd say. "My father was gone. And my mother somehow managed to miss the fact that I was sleeping with my substitute history teacher and I'd gained fifty pounds during my freshman year of college, so yeah, she pretty much believed that Lucy was babysitting until four every morning."

Dr. Blum would squint down at her notes. "Okay, and the history teacher was . . . James?"

"No, no. James was the guy on the crew team. Jason was the E-Z-Lube poet. And Bill was the guy in college, and Bruce is the guy right now."

"Bruce!" she'd say triumphantly, having located his name in her notes.

"But I'm really worried that I'm, you know, leading him on or something." I sighed. "I'm not sure I really love him."

"Let's go back to your sister for a minute," she'd say, flipping faster and faster through her legal pad, while I sat there and tried not to yawn.

In addition to her inability to keep up, Dr. Blum was rendered less than trustworthy by her clothes. She dressed as if she didn't know there was such a thing as the petite section. Her sleeves routinely brushed her fingertips; her skirts sagged around her ankles. I opened up as best I could, answered her questions when she asked them, but I never really trusted her. How could I trust a woman who had even less fashion sense than I did?

At the end of our ten sessions, she didn't quite pronounce me cured, but she did leave me with two pieces of advice.

"First," she said, "you can't change anything anybody else in this world does. Not your father, not your mother, not Tanya, not Lisa . . ."

". . . Lucy," I corrected.

"Right. Well, you can't control what they do, but you can control how you respond to it . . . whether you allow it to drive you crazy, or occupy all of your thoughts, or whether you note what they're doing, consider it, and make a conscious decision as to how much you'll let it affect you."

"Okay. And what's thing two?"

"Hang on to Bruce," she said seriously. "Even if you don't think he's Mr. Right. He's there for you, and he sounds like a good support, and I think you're going to need that in the coming months."

We shook hands. She wished me good luck. I thanked her for her help and told her that Ma Jolie in Manayunk was having a big sale, and that they made things in her size. And that was the end of my big therapy experience.

I wish that I could say that, in the years since Tanya and her loom and her pain and her posters moved in, that things have gotten easier. The fact is, they haven't. Tanya has the people skills of plant life. It's like a special kind of tone-deafness, only instead of not hearing the music, she's deaf to nuances, to subtleties, to euphemisms, small talk, and white lies. Ask her how she's doing, and you'll get a full and lengthy explication of her latest work/health crisis, complete with an invitation to look at her latest surgical scar. Tell her that you liked whatever she cooked (and Lord knows you'll be lying), and she'll regale you with endless recipes, each with a story behind it ("My mother cooked this for me, I remember, the night after she came home from the hospital. . . .").

At the same time, she's also incredibly thin-skinned, prone to public crying fits, and temper tantrums that conclude with her either locking herself in my ex-bedroom, if we're home, or stomping away from wherever we are, if we're out. And she dotes on my mother in the most annoying way you could imagine, following her around like a lovestruck puppy, always reaching to hold her hand, touch her hair, rub her feet, tuck a blanket around her.

"Sick," pronounced Josh.

"Immature," said Lucy.

"I don't get it," is what I said. "Having somebody treat you that way for, like, a week would be nice . . . but where's the challenge? Where's the excitement? And what do they talk about?"

"Nothing," said Lucy. The three of us had come home for Chanukah, and we were sitting around the family room after the guests had gone home and my mother and Tanya had gone to bed, all of us holding the gifts Tanya had woven for us. I had a rainbow-colored scarf ("You can wear it to the Pride Parade," Tanya offered). Josh had mittens, also in the gay-pride rainbow, and Lucy had an odd-looking bundle of yarn that Tanya had explained was a muff. "It's to keep your hands warm," she'd rumbled, but Lucy and I had already dissolved into gales of laughter, and Josh was wondering in a whisper whether such a thing could be dropped to the bottom of the pool for a little summertime muff diving.

Nifkin, who'd been given a little rainbow sweater, was in my lap, sleeping with one eye open, ready to bolt for higher ground should the evil cats Gertrude and Alice appear. Josh was on the couch, picking out what sounded like the theme song from *Beverly Hills, 90210* on his guitar.

"In fact," said Lucy, "they don't talk at all."

"Well, what would they talk about?" I asked. "I mean, Mom's educated . . . she's traveled . . ."

"Tanya puts her hand over Mom's mouth when *Jeopardy* comes on," said Josh morosely, and switched to "Sex and Candy" on the guitar.

"Ew," I said.

"Yup," confirmed Lucy. "She says it's obnoxious how Mom shouts out the answers."

"It's probably just that she doesn't know any of them herself," said Josh.

"You know," said Lucy, "the lesbian thing is okay. It would've been all right . . ."

". . . if it had been a different kind of woman," I finished, and sat there, picturing a more appropriate same-sex love: say, a chic film professor from UPenn, with tenure and a pixie haircut and interesting amber jewelry, who'd introduce us to independent film directors and take my mother to Cannes. Instead, my mother had fallen for Tanya, who was neither well-read nor chic, whose cinematic tastes ran toward the later works of Jerry Bruckheimer, and who didn't own a single piece of amber.

"So what is it?" I asked. "What's the attraction? She isn't pretty . . ."

"That's for sure," said Lucy, shuddering dramatically.

"Or smart . . . or funny . . . or interesting . . ."

We all sat, silent, as it dawned on us what the attraction might be.

"I'll bet she's got a tongue like a whale," said Lucy. Josh made retching noises. I rolled my eyes, feeling queasy.

"Like an anteater!" cried Lucy.

"Lucy, cut it out!" I said. Nifkin woke up and started growling. "Besides, even if it is just sex, that'll only get you so far."

"How would you know?" said Lucy.

"Trust me," I said. "Mom'll get bored."

We all sat for a minute, thinking that over.

"It's like she doesn't care about us anymore," Josh blurted.

"She cares," I said. But I wasn't sure. Before Tanya, my mother had liked to do things with us . . . when we were all together. She'd visit me in Philadelphia, and Josh in New York. She'd cook when we came home, call us a few times a week, keep busy with her book clubs and lecture groups, her wide circle of friends.

"All she cares about is Tanya," said Lucy bitterly.

And I didn't have an argument for that. Sure, she'd still call us . . . but not as often. She hadn't visited me in months. Her days (not to mention her nights) seemed full of Tanya—the bike trips they went on, the tea dances they attended, the weekend long Ritual of Healing that Tanya had taken my mother to as a special three-month-anniversary surprise, where they'd burned sage and prayed to the Moon Goddess.

"It won't last," I said, with more conviction than I felt. "It's just an infatuation."

"What if it isn't?" Lucy demanded. "What if it's true love?"

"It's not," I said again. But inside, I thought that maybe it was. That this was it, and we'd all be stuck, saddled with this horrible, graceless emotional wreck of a creature for the rest of our lives. Or at least the rest of our mother's life. And after . . .

"Think of the funeral," I mused. "God. I can just hear her . . ." And I dropped my voice to a Tanya rasp. "Your mother would want me to have that," I growled. "But Tanya," I said in my own voice, ". . . that's my car!"

Josh's lips twitched upward. Lucy laughed. I did the Tanya-growl again.

"She knew how much it meant to me!"

Now Josh was out-and-out smiling. "Do the poem," he said.

I shook my head.

"C'mon, Cannie!" begged my sister.

I cleared my throat, and began to recite Philip Larkin. "They fuck you up, your mum and dad. They may not mean to, but they do."

"They fill you with the faults they had . . ." continued Lucy.

"And add some extra, just for you," said Josh.

"But they were fucked up in their turn, by fools in old-style hats and coats, Who half the time were soppy-stern, and half at one another's throats."

And we joined in together, the three of us, for the last stanza—the one I couldn't even bring myself to think of in my present predicament. "Man hands on misery to man, it deepens like the coastal shelf. Get out as early as you can, and don't have any kids yourself."

Then, at Lucy's suggestion, we all got to our feet—Nifkin included—and dropped our knitted items into the fireplace.

"Begone, Tanya!" Lucy intoned.

"Return, heterosexuality!" Josh implored.

"What they said," I echoed, and watched the pride muffler burn.

Back at home, I parked my bike in the garage, next to Tanya's little green car with its "A woman needs a man like a fish needs a bicycle" bumper sticker, hauled the gigantic frozen turkey out of the garage freezer, and set it in the sink to defrost. I took a quick shower and went into the Room Formerly Known as Mine, where I'd been camped out since my arrival. In between short bike rides and long baths and showers, I'd dragged enough blankets out of the linen closet to turn Tanya's futon into a triple-lined oasis. I had also dug a crate of books out of the basement and was working my way through all the hits of my childhood: *Little House on the Prairie*, *The Phantom Tollbooth*, the Narnia chronicles, and *The Five Little Peppers and How They Grew*. I was regressing, I thought bleakly. A few more days and I'd be practically embryonic myself.

I sat at Tanya's desk and checked my e-mail. Work, work. Old Person, Angry ("Your comments about CBS being the network for viewers who like their food prechewed were disgraceful!"). And a note from Maxi. "It's 98 degrees here every day," she wrote. "I'm hot. I'm bored. Tell me about Thanksgiving. What's the cast?"

I sat down to reply. "Thanksgiving is always a production in our house," I wrote. "Start off with me, and my mother, and Tanya, and Josh and Lucy. Then there's my mother's friends, and their husbands and kids, and whichever lost souls Tanya recruits. My mother makes dried turkey. Not intentionally dried, but because she insists on cooking it on the gas grill, and she hasn't quite figured out how to cook it long enough so that it's done, but not so long that it's not leathery.

Mashed sweet potatoes. Mashed potato potatoes. Some kind of green thing. Stuffing. Gravy. Cranberry sauce from a can." My stomach turned over even as I typed. I had pretty much stopped being nauseous during the last week, but just the thought of turkey jerky, Tanya's lumpy gravy, and canned cranberry cocktail was enough to make me grab for the saltines I'd packed.

"The food's not really the point," I continued. "It's nice to see people. I've known some of them since I was a little girl. And my mom builds a fire, and the house smells like wood smoke, and we all go around the table and name one thing we're thankful for."

"What will you say?" Maxi shot back.

I sighed, wriggling my feet in the thick wool socks I'd swiped from Tanya's L.L. Bean stash, and tugged the afghan I'd lifted from the family room tighter around me. "I'm not feeling especially thankful right now," I typed back, "but I'll think of something."

ELEVEN

Thanksgiving Day dawned crisp and cold and brilliantly sunny. I dragged myself out of bed, still yawning at ten in the morning, and spent a few hours outside raking leaves with Josh and Lucy while Nifkin kept watch on us, and on the stalking cats, from the porch.

At three that afternoon, I took a shower, blew my hair into some semblance of style, and put on lipstick and mascara, plus the wide-legged black velvet pants and black cashmere sweater I'd packed, hoping that the cumulative effect would be both stylish and slimming. Lucy and I set the table, Josh boiled and peeled shrimp, and Tanya bustled around the kitchen, making more noise than food, and breaking frequently for cigarettes.

At 4:30 the guests started to arrive. My mother's friend Beth came with her husband and three tall, blond sons, the youngest of whom was sporting a nose ring right through his septum, giving him the look of a baffled Jewish bull. Beth hugged me and started sliding trays of appetizers into the oven while Ben, the pierced one, started discreetly chucking salted nuts at Tanya's cats. "You look great!" Beth said, like she always says. It wasn't even close to being true, but I appreciated the sentiment. "I loved your story about Donny and Marie's new show. When you said how they were singing with LeAnn Rimes and it looked like they wanted to suck the lifeblood out of her . . . that was so funny!"

"Thanks," I said. I love Beth. Trust her to remember the "Mormon vampires" line, the one that I'd loved, too, even if it had occasioned half a dozen angry phone calls to my editor, a fistful of furious letters ("Dear Too-Bit reporter" my favorite one began), plus an earnest visit from two nineteen-year-old Brigham Young University students who were visiting Philadelphia and promised to pray for me.

Tanya contributed green beans with the crunchy canned onions on top and a can of undiluted Campbell's Cream of Mushroom soup mixed in, then galumphed into the family room and built a blazing fire. The house filled with the sweet smell of wood smoke and roasting turkey. Nifkin and Gertrude and Alice arranged a cease-fire and curled blissfully in front of the flames, all in a row. Josh passed around the shrimp he'd prepared. Lucy mixed Manhattans—she'd perfected them during a stint as a bartender that followed the topless dancing escapade but preceded her six weeks doing phone sex.

"You look lousy," she observed, handing me a drink. Lucy herself looked great, as always. My sister is just fifteen months younger than I am. People tell us we looked like twins when we were little. Nobody says that anymore. Lucy's thin—she always has been—and she wears her wavy hair short, so that the slightly pointed tips of her ears show when she shakes her head. She's got full, lush lips and big, brown Betty Boop eyes and she presents herself to the world like the star she thinks she ought to be. It's been years since I've seen her without a full face of makeup, her lips expertly outlined and colored, her eyebrows dramatically plucked, a tiny silver stud flashing and winking from the center of her tongue. She was dressed for the Thanksgiving feast in skintight black leather pants, high-heeled black boots, and a sequined pink sweater set. She looked like she'd just stepped out of a photo shoot, or stopped in for a quick drink before heading off to someone else's much more stylish holiday festivities.

"I'm a little stressed out," I said, yawning, handing the drink back, and wishing there was time for another nap.

My mother bustled around the table with the same placecards she'd used at Passover the year before. I knew there was one that said "Bruce" somewhere in the pile, and I hoped, for my sake, that she'd discarded it rather than crossing his name off and writing in someone else's as a way to economize.

The last time he'd been here it had been winter. Josh and Lucy and Bruce and I had stood on the porch, sipping the beers that Tanya refused to let us keep in the refrigerator. ("I'm in recovery!" she'd bleat, holding the offending bottles as if they were grenades.) Then we'd gone for a walk around the block. Halfway back, it had started to snow, unexpectedly. And Bruce and I stood, holding hands with our eyes shut and our mouths wide open, feeling the flakes like tiny wet kisses on our cheeks, long after everyone else went inside.

I closed my eyes against the memory.

Lucy stared at me. "Jeez, Cannie. Are you okay?"

I blinked back the tears. "Just tired."

"Hmmph," said Lucy. "Well, I'll just mash a little something special into your potatoes."

I shrugged, and made sure to avoid the potatoes at dinner. We followed my mother's Thanksgiving tradition, going around the table and talking about what we were thankful for that year. "I'm thankful for having found so much love," rasped Tanya, as Lucy and Josh and I winced and my mother took Tanya's hand.

"I'm thankful for having my wonderful family together," said my mother. Her eyes were glistening. Tanya kissed her cheek. Josh groaned. Tanya shot him a dirty look.

"I'm thankful . . ." I had to think for a while. "I'm thankful that Nifkin survived his bout with hemorrhagic gastroenteritis last summer," I finally said. At the sound of his name, Nifkin put his paw on my lap and whined beseechingly. I slipped him a piece of turkey skin.

"Cannie!" yelled my mother, "stop feeding that dog!"

"I'm thankful I still have an appetite after hearing about Nifkin's trouble," said Ben, who, in addition to the nose ring, was irritating his parents by sporting a "What Would Jesus Do?" T-shirt.

"I'm thankful that Cannie didn't dump Bruce until after my birthday, so that I got those Phish tickets," said Josh in his deep, deadpan baritone, which went nicely with his six-foot-tall, skin-and-bones frame, and the little goatee he'd grown since I'd seen him last. "Thanks," he stage-whispered.

"Think nothing of it," I whispered back.

"And I'm thankful," concluded Lucy, "that everyone's here to hear my big news!"

My mother and I exchanged anxious glances. Lucy's last big exciting news had been a plan—thankfully aborted—to move to Uzbekistan with a guy she'd met at a bar. "He's a lawyer over there," she'd said confidently, gliding smoothly over the fact that he was a Pizza Hut delivery guy over here. Before that, there'd been the plan for the bagel bakery in Montserrat, where she'd gone to visit a friend in medical school. "Not a bagel to be had down there!" she'd said triumphantly, and got as far as filling out the papers for a small business loan before Montserrat's long-dormant volcano erupted, the island was evacuated, and Lucy's bagel dreams died a hot molten death.

"What's the news?" asked my mother, looking into Lucy's shining eyes.

"I got an agent!" she trilled. "And he got me a photo shoot!"

"Topless?" asked Josh dryly. Lucy shook her head. "No, no, I'm done with all that. This is legitimate. I'm modeling rubber gloves."

"Fetish magazine?" I asked. I couldn't help myself.

Lucy's face fell. "Why doesn't anyone believe in me?" she demanded. Knowing my family, it was just a matter of time before somebody launched into Lucy's Catalogue of Failures—from school to relationships to the jobs she'd never kept.

I leaned across the table and took my sister's hand. She jerked her hand back. "No unnecessary touch!" she said. "What's with you, anyhow?"

"I'm sorry," I said. "We weren't giving you a chance." And that's when I heard the voice. Not God's voice, unfortunately, but Bruce's. *"Good,"* he said. *"That was nice."*

I looked around, startled.

"Cannie?" said my mother.

"Thought I heard something," I said. "Never mind."

And while Lucy prattled on about her agent, her photo shoot, and what she'd wear, all the while evading my mother's increasingly pointed questions about whether she was getting paid for this or what, I ate turkey and stuffing and glutinous green bean casserole, and thought about what I'd heard. I thought about how maybe even though I'd never see Bruce again, it might be possible to keep part of him, or of what we were together, if I could be more openhearted, and kind. For all of his lecturing, for every time he was didactic and condescending, I knew that he was basically a kind person, and I . . . well, I was too, in my private life, but it could be argued that I was making my living by being unkind. But maybe I could change. And maybe he'd like that, and someday like me better . . . and love me again. Assuming, of course, we ever even saw each other again.

Underneath the table, Nifkin twitched and growled at something chasing through his dream. My eyes were clear, and my head felt cool and ordered. It wasn't as if all of my problems were gone—as if any of them were gone, really—but for the first time since I'd seen the little plus sign on the EPT stick, it felt like I might be able to see myself safely through them. I had something to hold on to, now, no matter what choice I made—*I can be a better person*, I thought. *A better sister, a better daughter, a better friend.*

"Cannie?" said my mother. "Did you say something?"

I didn't. But at that moment I thought that I felt the faintest flutter in my belly. It might have been all the food, or all of my anxiety, and I knew it was much too early to really feel anything. But it felt like something. Like something waving at me. A tiny little hand, five fingers spread like a starfish, waving through the water. Hello and good-bye.

The last day of my Thanksgiving break, before I was going to make the trek back into town and pick up the pieces of my life where I'd left them, my mother and I went swimming. It was the first time I'd been back to the Jewish Community Center since I'd learned that it was the scene of my mother's seduction. After that, the steam room had never felt quite the same.

But I'd missed swimming, I realized, as I stood in the locker room and pulled on my suit. I had missed the tang of chlorine in my nose and the old Jewish ladies who'd parade through the locker room completely naked, completely unashamed, and swap recipes and beauty tips while they got dressed. The feel of the water, holding me up, and the way I could forget almost anything but the rhythm of my breath as I swam.

My mother swam a mile every morning, moving slowly through the water with a massive kind of grace. I kept up with her for maybe half of it, then slipped into one of the empty lap lanes and did a languid sidestroke for a while, thinking of nothing. Which I knew was a luxury I couldn't afford much longer. If I wanted to get things taken care of (and that was the phrase I was using in my mind), it would have to be soon.

I flipped on my back and thought about what I'd felt at Thanksgiving dinner. That tiny hand, waving. Ridiculous, really. The thing probably didn't have hands, and if it did, it certainly couldn't wave them.

I'd always been pro-choice. I had never romanticized pregnancies, intended or otherwise. I wasn't one of those women who sees her thirtieth birthday coming and starts cooing at anything in a stroller with drool on its chin. I had a few friends who'd gotten married and started their families, but I had many more friends in their late twenties and early thirties who hadn't. I didn't hear my clock ticking. I didn't have baby fever.

I rolled back over and commenced a lazy breaststroke. The thing was, I couldn't shake the feeling that it had been somehow decided for me. As if it was out of my control now, and all I was supposed to do was sit back and let it happen.

I blew a frustrated breath into the water, watching bubbles roil around me. I'd still feel better about all of this if I could have heard God's voice again, if I knew for sure that I was doing the right thing.

"Cannie?"

My mother swam into the lane beside me. "Two more laps," she said. We finished them together, matching each other breath for breath, stroke for stroke. Then I followed her into the locker room.

"Now," my mother began, "what is going on with you?"

I looked at her, surprised. "With me?"

"Oh, Cannie. I'm your mother. I've known you for twenty-seven years."

"Twenty-eight," I corrected.

She squinted at me. "Did I forget your birthday?"

I shrugged. "I think you sent a card."

"Is that what it is?" asked my mother. "Are you worried about getting older? Are you depressed?"

I shrugged again. My mother was sounding more worried.

"Are you getting any help? Are you talking to anyone?"

I snorted, imagining how useless the little doctor, drowning in her clothes, would be in a situation like this. "Now, Bruce is your boyfriend," she'd begin, flipping through her ever-present legal pad.

"Was," I'd correct.

"And you're thinking about . . . adoption?"

"Abortion," I'd say.

"You're pregnant," said my mother.

I sat up straight, my mouth falling open. "What?"

"Cannie. I'm your mother. A mother knows these things."

I drew my towel tight around me and wondered whether it would be too much to hope that this was one of the few things my mother and Tanya hadn't made a bet about.

"And you look just like I did," she continued. "Tired all the time. When I was pregnant with you I slept fourteen hours a day."

I didn't say anything. I didn't know what to say. I knew I would have to start talking about it to someone, at some point, but I didn't have words ready.

"Have you thought about names?" my mother asked me.

I gave a short, barking laugh. "I haven't thought about anything," I said. "I haven't thought about where I'll live, or what I'll do . . ."

"But you're going to . . ." Her voice trailed off delicately.

"Seems that way," I said. There. Out loud. It was real.

"Oh, Cannie!" She sounded—if it's possible—at once thrilled and brokenhearted. Thrilled, I guess, that she'd get to be a grandmother (unlike me, my mother was prone to cooing over anything in a stroller).

And brokenhearted because this wasn't a situation you'd wish for your daughter.

But it was my situation. I saw it then, that moment, in the locker room. This was what was going to happen—I was going to have this baby, Bruce or no Bruce, broken heart or no broken heart. It felt like the right choice. More than that, it felt almost like my destiny—the way my life was supposed to unfold. I just wished that whoever had planned it would drop me a clue or two about how I was going to provide for myself and a child. But if God wasn't going to speak up, I'd figure it out myself.

My mother stood up and hugged me, which was gross, considering that we were both wet from the pool, and her towel didn't quite make it around her front. But whatever. It felt good to have someone's arms around me.

"You're not mad?" I asked.

"No, no! How could I ever be mad?"

"Because . . . well. This isn't the way I wanted it . . ." I said, briefly letting my cheek rest against her shoulder.

"It never is," she told me. "It's never just the way you think that it'll be. Do you think I wanted to have you and Lucy down in Louisiana, a million miles away from my family, with those horrible army doctors and cockroaches big as my thumb. . . ."

"At least you had a husband," I said. "And a house . . . and a plan . . ."

My mother patted my shoulder briskly. "Husbands and houses are negotiable," she said. "And as for a plan . . . we'll figure it out."

She didn't ask the $64,000 question until we were dried off and dressed and in the car on our way home.

"I'm assuming that Bruce is the father," she said.

I leaned my cheek against the cool glass. "Correct."

"And you're not back together?"

"No. It was . . ." How could I possibly explain to my mother what had happened?

"Not to worry," she said, effectively ending my attempts to think of an appropriate euphemism for sympathy fuck. We drove past the industrial park and the fruit and vegetable stand, over the mountain, on our way home. Everything looked familiar, because I'd driven past it a million times, growing up. I would swim with my mother early Saturday mornings, and we'd drive home together, watching the sleeping towns wake up, on our way to get warm bagels and fresh-squeezed orange juice and have breakfast together, the five of us.

Now, everything looked different. The trees had gotten taller, the houses looked somehow shabbier. There were new traffic lights at a few of the more dangerous intersections, new houses with raw-looking wooden walls and torn-up lawns on streets that hadn't existed when I was in high school. Still, it felt good, and comfortable, to be riding beside my mother again. I could almost pretend that Tanya had stayed in her obsessive-compulsive codependent ex-girlfriend's apartment and out of my mother's life . . . and that my father hadn't abandoned us so completely . . . and that I wasn't in my current condition.

"Are you going to tell Bruce?" she finally asked.

"I don't know. We aren't exactly talking right now. And I think . . . well, I'm sure that if I told him, he'd try to talk me out of it, and I don't want to be talked out of it." I paused, thinking it over. "And it just seems . . . I mean, if I were him, if I were in his posi-tion . . . it's a lot to burden somebody with. That they've got a child out in the world. . . ."

"Do you want him in your life?" my mother asked me.

"That's not really the issue. He's made it pretty clear that he doesn't want to be in my life. Now, whether he wants to be in . . ." I stumbled, trying to say it for the first time, "in our child's life . . ."

"Well, it's not completely up to him. He'll have to pay child support."

"Ugh," I said, imagining having to take Bruce to court and justify my behavior in front of a judge and jury.

She kept talking: about mutual funds and compound interest and some television show she'd seen where working mothers set up hidden videocameras and found their nannies neglecting their babies while they (the nannies, not the babies, I presumed) watched soap operas and made long-distance phone calls to Honduras. It reminded me of Maxi, prattling on about my financial future.

"Okay," I told my mother. My muscles felt pleasantly heavy from the swimming, and my eyelids were starting to droop. "No Honduran nannies. I promise."

"Maybe Lucy could help out some," she said, and glanced at me when we were stopped at a red light. "You've been to your ob/gyn, right?"

"Not yet," I said, and yawned again.

"Cannie!" She proceeded to lecture me on nutrition, exercise during pregnancy, and how she'd heard that vitamin E in capsule form could prevent stretch marks. I let my eyes close, lulled by the sound of her voice and the turning wheels, and I was almost asleep when we pulled into the driveway. She had to shake me awake, saying my name gently, telling me that we were home.

It was a wonder she let me go back to Philadelphia that night. And as it was, I drove home with my trunk stuffed with about ten pounds of Tupperware'd turkey and stuffing and pie, and only after giving her my solemn promise that I'd make an appointment with a doctor first thing in the morning, and that she could come visit soon.

"Wear your seat belt," she said, as I loaded a protesting Nifkin into his carrier.

"I always wear my seat belt," I said.

"Call me as soon as you know the due date."

"I'll call! I promise!"

"Okay," she said. She reached over and brushed her fingertips against my cheek. "I'm proud of you," she said. I wanted to ask her why. What had I done that anyone could be proud of? Getting knocked up by a guy who wanted nothing else to do with you wasn't exactly the stuff she could brag to her book-club friends about, or that I could send in to the *Princeton Alumni Weekly*. Single motherhood might be getting more acceptable among the movie-star set, but from what I'd seen from my divorced colleagues, it was nothing but a hardship for real-life women, and it certainly wasn't a cause for celebration, or pride.

But I didn't ask. I just started the car and drove down the drive-way, waving back at her until she disappeared.

Back in Philadelphia, everything looked different. Or maybe it was just that I was seeing it differently. I noticed the overflow of Budweiser cans in the recycling bin in front of the second-floor apart-ment as I made my way upstairs, and heard the shrill laugh track of a sitcom seeping beneath the door. Out on the street, somebody's car alarm went off, and I could hear glass breaking somewhere nearby. Just background noise, stuff I'd barely notice most of the time, but I'd have to start noticing now . . . now that I was responsible for some-body else.

Up on the third floor, my apartment had grown a thin layer of dust in the five days I'd been away, and it smelled stale. No place to raise a child, I thought, opening windows, lighting a vanilla-scented candle, and finding the broom.

I gave Nifkin fresh food and water. I swept the floors. I sorted my laundry to wash the next day, emptied the dishwasher, put the left-overs in the freezer, then rinsed and hung my bathing suit to dry. I was halfway through making a grocery list, full of skim milk and fresh apples and good things to eat, before I realized I hadn't even checked my voice mail to see if anyone . . . well, to see if Bruce . . . had called me. A long shot, I knew, but I figured I'd at least give him the benefit of the doubt.

And when I found that he hadn't called, I felt sad, but nothing like the sharp, jittery, anxious-sick sadness I'd had before, nothing like the overwhelming certainty that I would die if he didn't love me that I'd felt that night in New York with Maxi.

"He loved me," I whispered to the neatly swept room. "He loved me, but he doesn't love me anymore, and it's not the end of the world."

Nifkin raised his head from the couch, looked at me curiously, then fell back asleep. I picked up my list. "Eggs," I wrote. "Spinach. Plums."

TWELVE

"You're what?!?"

I bowed my head over my decaffeinated skim-milk latte and toasted bagel. "Pregnant. With child. Expecting. In a delicate condition. Bun in the oven. PG."

"Okay, okay, I've got it." Samantha stared at me, full lips parted, brown eyes shocked and wide-awake, even though it was only 7:30 in the morning. How?

"The usual way," I said lightly. We were in Xando, the neighborhood coffee shop that turned into a bar after six at night. Businessmen perused their *Examiner*s, harried moms with strollers gulped coffee. A good place, clean and bright. Not a place for making scenes.

"With Bruce?"

"Okay, maybe it wasn't the usual way. It was right after his father died. . . ."

Samantha gave a great exasperated sigh. "Oh, God, Cannie . . . what did I tell you about sex with the bereaved?"

"I know," I said. "It just happened."

She allowed herself another sigh, then reached for her DayTimer, all brisk efficiency, even though she was still wearing black leggings and a T-shirt from Wally's Wings advising "We Choke Our Own Chickens." "Okay," she said. "Did you call the clinic?"

"No, actually," I said. "I'm going to keep it."

Her eyes got very wide. "What? How? Why?"

"Why not? I'm twenty-eight years old, I've got enough money . . ."

Samantha was shaking her head. "You're going to ruin your life."

"I know my life's going to change. . . ."

"No. You didn't hear me. You're going to ruin your life."

I set down my coffee cup. "What do you mean?"

"Cannie . . ." She looked at me, her eyes beseeching. "A single mother . . . I mean, it's hard enough to meet decent men as it is . . . do you know what this is going to do to your social life?"

Truthfully, I hadn't given it much thought. Now that I'd gotten my mind around losing Bruce irrevocably, I hadn't even started thinking about who I might wind up with, or whether there'd ever be anybody else.

"Not just your social life," Samantha continued, "your whole life. Have you thought about how this is going to change everything?"

"Of course I have," I said.

"No more vacations," said Samantha.

"Oh, come on . . . people take babies on vacations!"

"Are you going to have money for that? I mean, I'm assuming you'll work . . ."

"Yeah. Part-time. That's what I'd figured. At least at first."

"So your income will go down, and you'll still be spending money on child care for when you are at work. That's going to have a major impact on your standard of living, Cannie. Major impact."

Well, it was true. No more three-day weekends in Miami just because USAir had a cheap flight and I felt like I needed some sun. No more weeks in Killington in a rented condo, where I'd ski all day and Bruce, a nonskiier, would smoke dope in the Jacuzzi and wait for my return. No more $200 pairs of leather boots that I absolutely had to have, no more $100 dinners, no more $80 afternoons at the spa where I'd pay some nineteen-year-old to scrub my feet and tweeze my eyebrows.

"Well, people's lives change," I said. "Things happen that you don't plan for. People get sick . . . or lose their jobs . . ."

"But those are things they don't have any control over," Samantha pointed out. "Whereas this is a situation you can control."

"I've made up my mind," I said quietly. Samantha was undeterred.

"Think about bringing a child into the world with no father," she said.

"I know," I told her, holding up my hand before she could say anything else. "I've thought about this. I know it's not ideal. It's not what I'd want, if I could choose. . . ."

"But you can choose," said Samantha. "Think about everything you're going to have to manage by yourself. How every single responsibility is going to be on your shoulders. Are you really ready for that? And is it fair to have a baby if you're not?"

"But think of all the other women who do it!"

"What, like welfare mothers? Teenage girls?"

"Sure! Them! There's lots of women who have babies, and the babies' fathers aren't around, and they're managing."

"Cannie," said Samantha, "that's no kind of life. Living hand-to-mouth . . ."

"I've got some money," I said, sounding sullen even to my own ears.

Samantha took a sip of coffee. "Is this about Bruce? About holding on to Bruce?"

I looked down at my clasped hands, at the wadded-up napkin between them. "No," I said. "I mean, I guess it involves that . . . somewhat by default . . . but it's not like I set out to get pregnant so I could get my hooks back in him."

Samantha raised her eyebrows. "Not even subconsciously?"

I shuddered. "God, I hope my subconscious isn't as unenlightened as that!"

"Enlightenment has nothing to do with it. Maybe, deep down, some part of you was hoping . . . or is hoping . . . that once Bruce finds out, he'll come back to you."

"I'm not going to tell him," I said.

"How can you not tell him?" she demanded.

"Why should I?" I shot back. "He's moved on, he's found some-body else, he doesn't want to be involved with me, or my life, so why should I tell him? I don't need his money, and I don't want whatever scraps of attention he'd feel obligated to throw me. . . ."

"But what about the baby? Doesn't the baby deserve to have a father in its life?"

"Come on, Samantha. This is Bruce we're talking about. Big, dopey Bruce? Bruce with the ponytail and the 'Legalize It' bumper sticker . . ."

"He's a good guy, Cannie. He'd probably be a really good father."

I bit my lip. This part hurt to admit or even to think about, but it was probably the truth. Bruce had been a camp counselor for years. Kids loved him, ponytail or not, dopiness or not, dope or not. Every time I'd seen him with his cousins or his former campers they were always vying with each other to sit next to him at dinner, or play bas-ketball with him, or have him help them with their homework. Even when our relationship was at its worst, I never doubted that he'd be a wonderful father.

Samantha was shaking her head. "I don't know, Cannie. I just don't know." She gave me a long, sober look. "He's going to find out, you know."

"How? We don't know any of the same people anymore . . . he lives so far away . . ."

"Oh, he'll find out. I've seen enough soap operas to guarantee you that. You'll run into him somewhere . . . he'll hear something about you . . . he'll find out. He will."

I shrugged, trying to look brave. "So he finds out I'm pregnant. It doesn't mean I have to tell him that it's his. Let him think I was sleep-ing around on him." Even though I felt struck through with grief at the thought that Bruce would ever have cause to think that. "Let him think I went to a sperm bank. The point is, he doesn't have to know." I looked at Samantha. "And you don't have to tell him."

"Cannie, don't you think he's got a right to know? He's going to be a father. . . ."

"No, he's not. . . ."

"Well, there's going to be a child born that's his. What if he wants to be a father? What if he sues you for custody?"

"Okay, I saw that Sally Jessy, too. . . ."

"I'm serious," said Samantha. "He could do that, you know."

"Oh, please." I shrugged, trying to look less worried than I was. "Bruce can barely keep track of his rolling papers. What would he want with a baby?"

Samantha shrugged. "I don't know. Maybe nothing. Or maybe he'd think that a child needs . . . you know . . . a male role model."

"So I'll let it hang around Tanya," I joked. Samantha wasn't laughing. She looked so upset I felt like offering her a hug, until I realized I'd sound just like Tanya at her most Anonymous. "It's going to be okay," I said, keeping my voice light, and convincing.

Samantha looked at me. "I hope so," she said quietly. "I really do."

"You're what?" asked Betsy, my editor. To her credit, she recovered a lot faster than Samantha did.

"Pregnant," I repeated. I was getting a little tired of playing this particular cut on the soundtrack of my life. "With child. Knocked up. Bun in the oven . . ."

"Oh. Okay. Oh, my. Um. . . ." Betsy peered at me from behind her thick glasses. "Congratulations?" she offered tentatively.

"Thanks," I said.

"Is there, um, going to be a wedding?" she asked.

"Not in the forseeable future, no," I said briskly. "Will that be a problem?"

"Oh, no, no! Of course not! I mean, of course, the paper would never discriminate, or anything. . . ."

I was suddenly very, very tired. "I know," I said. "And I know it's going to be weird for people . . ."

"The less explaining you do, the better," said Betsy. We were in the conference room with the door closed and the shades pulled, which meant I could only see my colleagues from the knees down. I recognized Frank the copy-editor's beat-up loafers slowing as they made their way to the mailroom, followed closely by Tanisha the photo clerk's stack-heeled Mary Janes, moving at a ridiculously snail-like pace. I was sure, if I had the full-body view, their heads would all be swiveling toward me, trying to figure out why Betsy and I were in here, whether I was in some kind of trouble, and what the trouble was. I was sure that once they'd made the obligatory stop at their mail-boxes, they'd make a sharp right to the desk of Alice, longtime departmental secretary and depository of all things juicy and scan-dalous. Heck, if someone else were in here with Betsy right now, I'd be doing the exact same thing. It's the downside of working with peo-ple who poke and pry and investigate for a living. You don't wind up with much of a private life.

"If I were you I wouldn't say a word," Betsy said. She was in her for-ties, a short, quick-witted woman with a shock of white-blond hair who'd lived through sexism, corporate takeovers, budget cutbacks, and half a dozen different editors in chief, all men, and all with their own unique visions of what the *Examiner* should do. She was a survivor, and my mentor at the paper, and I trusted her to give me good advice.

"Well, eventually I'm going to have to say something. . . ."

"Eventually," she said. "But for now I would say nothing." She looked at me, not unkindly. "It's hard, you know," she said.

"I know," I said.

"Will you have any . . . help?"

"If you mean, is Bruce going to ride in on a white horse and marry me, probably not. But my mother and Tanya will help out . . . and maybe my sister, too."

Betsy had come prepared. She pulled a copy of the union contract out of her briefcase, then a notebook and a calculator. "Let's see what we can do for you."

What she came up with sounded more than fair—six weeks of paid leave after the birth, and if I wanted, six more weeks of unpaid leave after that. Then I'd have to work three days a week to keep my health benefits, but Betsy said she'd be amenable to having me work one of the days from home, as long as I was reachable. She tapped out my new salary-to-be on a calculator. Oof. Worse than I thought it would be . . . but still livable. At least, that's what I hoped. How much would day care cost? And baby clothes . . . and furniture . . . and food. I saw my carefully maintained nest egg—the one I'd built up, figuring I'd need it someday to pay for a wedding, or maybe a house—dwindling down to nothing before my eyes.

"We'll work it out," Betsy told me. "Don't worry." She gathered up her papers and sighed. "At least, try not to worry more than you absolutely have to. And let me know if I can help."

"Eight weeks," said my gynecologist, in her melodious clipped British voice. "Or perhaps nine."

"Eight," I said faintly. It's hard to be emphatic when you're flat on your back, with your feet up in stirrups and your legs spread.

Gita Patel—at least, that was the name on the tag clipped on to her lab coat—set her instruments down and slid around on her wheeled stool to face me, as I struggled into a sitting position. She was about my age, I guessed, with shiny black hair pulled into a low bun at the nape of her neck. She wasn't the one I usually saw in this HMO-run hidey-hole of a doctors' office, located one level below the street on Delancey, but she had the first available appointment, and, thanks to my mother's ceaseless chorus of "Have you seen a doctor yet," I decided not to wait. So far, I thought, it was working out. Dr. Patel had gentle hands, and a pleasant way about her.

"You are feeling well?" she asked.

"Fine. Just a little tired. Well, very tired, actually."

"No nausea?" Wow. I even loved the way she said "nausea."

"Not for the last few days."

"Very well, then. Let us discuss your plans." She tilted her head ever so slightly toward the waiting room. I admired the discretion of the gesture even as I shook my head.

"No. It's just me."

"Very well," she said again, and handed me some glossy brochures. My HMO's name was emblazoned at the top. "Little Sprouts" read the title. Ugh. "Helping our members as they begin one of life's most exciting journeys!" Double ugh.

"Now then. I will see you monthly for the next five months, then every two weeks for your eighth month, and then weekly until it is time to deliver." She flipped some pages on the calendar. "I am giving you a due date of June 15 . . . understanding, of course, that babies come when they please."

I left with my purse rattling with bottles of vitamins and folic acid, my head spinning with lists of things I couldn't eat and things I'd have to buy and calls I'd have to make. Forms to fill out, birthing classes to register for, a fact sheet on episiotomies that I didn't even want to look at in my current state of mind. It was December, and the weather had finally gotten cold. A brisk wind kicked dried-up leaves into the corners as I walked, my thin jacket wrapped tight around me. I could smell snow in the air. I was tired down to my bones, and my head was spinning, but I had one more stop left.

Fat Class was just getting out when I arrived. I found my classmates, and Dr. K., exiting the Weight and Eating Disorders offices, chatting happily, bundled up in sweaters and winter coats that looked as if they were being worn for the first time that year.

"Cannie!" Dr. K. waved and walked over. He was wearing khakis, a denim shirt, and a tie. No white lab coat, for once. "How have you been?"

"Oh, okay," I told him. "I'm sorry I missed class. I meant to stop by earlier. . . ."

"Why don't we step into my office," said Dr. K.

We did. He sat behind his desk, I took the chair opposite, not realizing until I'd sat down that I wasn't just tired, I was completely exhausted.

"It's good to see you," he said again, looking at me expectantly.

I took a deep breath. Get through this, I told myself. Get through this, and you'll be able to go home and go to sleep.

"I'm going to, um . . . stay pregnant. So I have to drop out of the program," I told him. He nodded, as if this was what he'd been waiting to hear.

"I'll make arrangements for the department to send you a check," he said. "And we'll be starting new studies next fall, if you're still interested."

"I don't think I'm going to have a lot of free time," I said.

He nodded. "Well, we'll miss you in class. You really bring a certain something."

"Oh, you're just saying that. . . ."

"No, I'm not. That imitation of the female fat cell you did two weeks ago . . . you really should think about stand-up."

I sighed. "Stand-up's hard. And I've got . . . a lot of things to think about right now."

Dr. K. reached for a notebook and a pen. "You know, I actually think we might have some kind of nutrition workshop for expectant mothers," he said, clearing books and papers away, locating his telephone directory. "I mean, since you've paid already, you might as well get something . . . Or, of course, if you just want a refund, we can definitely do that. . . ."

He was being so nice. Why was he being so nice to me? "No, that's okay. I just wanted to say that I had to drop out, and that I'm sorry. . . ."

I took a deep breath, looking at him looking at me from across the desk, his eyes so kind. And then I was crying again. What was it about this room, and this poor man, that every time I sat across from him I wound up in tears?

He handed me the Kleenex. "Are you all right?"

"I'm fine. I'm fine. I'll be okay. . . . I'm sorry. . . ."

And then I was crying so hard that I couldn't speak. "I'm sorry," I said again. "I think this is one of the first-trimester things, where everything makes you cry." I patted my purse. "I've got a list in here somewhere . . . things you're supposed to take, things you're supposed to feel . . ."

He was reaching over me, pulling a white lab coat off the coat rack.

"Stand up," he said. I stood up, and he draped the coat over my shoulders. "I want to show you something," he said. "Come with me."

He led me into an elevator, then down a hall, through a door marked "Staff Only" and "Keep Out," through another door marked "Emergency Only! Alarm Will Sound!" But the alarm didn't sound as he pushed open the door. And suddenly we were outside, on the roof, with the city spilled out beneath our feet.

I could see City Hall. I was practically at eye level with the statue of Billy Penn on top. There was the PECO building, studded with glistening lights . . . the twin towers of Liberty Place, shining silver . . . tiny cars, inching down infinitesimal streets. The rows of Christmas lights and neon wreaths marching down Market Street to the waterfront. The Blue Cross RiverRink, with tiny skaters moving in slow circles. And then the Delaware River, and Camden. New Jersey. Bruce. It all looked very far away.

"What do you think?" Dr. K. asked. I think I must have jumped when he finally started talking. For a moment, I'd forgotten him . . . forgotten everything. I was so wrapped up in the view.

"I've never seen the city like this," I told him. "It's amazing."

He leaned against the door and smiled. "I think you'd have to pay a pretty hefty rent in one of the Rittenhouse Square high-rises to get a view like this," he said.

I turned toward the river again, feeling the wind blow cool on my face. The air tasted delicious. All day long—or at least since Dr. Patel had given me the pamphlet listing Common Complaints of the First Trimester—I'd noticed that I could smell everything, and that most of what I could smell made me feel sick. Car exhaust . . . a whiff of dog crap from a trash can . . . gasoline . . . even things I normally enjoyed, like the scent of coffee wafting out of the Starbucks on South Street came to me at ten times their normal intensity. But up here the air smelled like nothing, as if it had been specially filtered for me. Well, me and whatever rich balcony-lined-penthouse-dwellers were lucky enough to have regular access.

"Feeling better?" he asked.

"Yeah."

Dr. K. sat down, cross-legged, and motioned for me to join him. Being careful not to sit on his lab coat, I did.

"Do you feel like talking about it?"

I shot him a quick sideways glance. "Do you want to listen?"

He looked embarrassed. "I don't mean to pry. . . . I know it's not any of my business. . . ."

"Oh, no, no, it's not that. I just don't want to bore you." I sighed. "It's the oldest story in the world, I guess. Girl meets boy, girl loves boy, girl dumps boy for reasons she still doesn't really understand, boy's father dies, girl goes to try to comfort him, girl winds up pregnant and alone."

"Ah," he said carefully.

I rolled my eyes at him. "What, you thought it was someone else?"

He didn't say anything, but in reflected light from the streets below, I thought he looked abashed. I hunkered around until I was sitting facing him.

"No, c'mon, really. You thought I found another guy that fast? Please," I snorted. "Give me a little less credit."

"I guess I thought . . . well, I guess I really hadn't thought about it."

"Well, believe me, it takes a lot longer than a few months before I meet someone who likes me, and who wants to see me naked, and before I get comfortable enough to actually let them." I looked at him sideways again. What if he thought I was flirting? "Just FYI," I added lamely.

"I'll file that away," he said somberly. He seemed so serious, I had to laugh.

"Tell me something . . . how do people know when you're kidding? Because you always sort of sound the same way."

"Which is what? Nerdy?" He spent a long time saying the word *nerdy*, which, of course, made him sound . . . a little nerdy.

"Not exactly. Just serious all the time."

"Well, I'm not." He actually appeared to be offended. "I actually have a very fine sense of humor."

"Which I'm just somehow managing to completely miss," I teased.

"Well, considering that the handful of times we've spoken, you've been having some extravagant life crisis, I haven't been at my funniest."

Now he was definitely sounding offended.

"Point taken," I said. "I'm sure you're very funny."

He looked at me suspiciously, thick brows furrowed. "How do you know?"

"Because you said you were. People who are funny know that they're funny. People who aren't funny will say, 'My friends say I've got a great sense of humor.' Or 'My mother says I've got a great sense of humor.' That's when you know you're in trouble."

"Oh," he said. "So if you were to describe yourself, you'd say you were funny?"

"No," I sighed, looking out at the night sky. "At this point, I'd say that I was fucked."

We sat in silence for a minute. I watched the skaters turn.

"Have you thought about what you're going to do?" he finally asked. "You don't have to talk about it if you don't want to. . . ."

"No, no. I don't mind. I've only figured a few things out, really. I know that I'm going to keep it, even though it's probably not the most practical thing, and I know I'm going to cut back my schedule when the baby comes. Oh, and I know I'm going to maybe start looking for a new place to live, and see if my sister will be my birth coach."

Laid out like that, like a losing hand of cards fanned out on a table, it didn't seem like much.

"What about Bruce?" he asked.

"See, that's the part I haven't figured out yet," I said. "We haven't talked in weeks, and he's seeing someone else."

"Seriously?"

"Seriously enough for him to tell me about it. And to write about it."

The doctor considered this. "Well, that might not mean anything. He might just be trying to get back at you . . . or make you jealous."

"Yeah, well, it's working."

"But a baby . . . well, that changes everything."

"Oh, you read that pamphlet, too?" I hugged my knees into my chest. "After we broke up . . . after his father died, when I felt so miserable, and I wanted him back, and all, my friends kept telling me,

'You broke up with him, and you must have done it for a reason.' And I know that it's true. I think I did know, deep down, that we probably weren't supposed to be, you know, together for the rest of our lives. And it was probably my fault. . . . I mean, I've got this whole theory about my father, and my parents, and why I don't trust love. So I think that maybe even if he was perfect . . . or, you know, not perfect, but a good fit for me . . . that maybe I wouldn't have been able to see it, or I'd have tried to talk myself out of it. Or whatever."

"Or maybe he wasn't the right guy for you. They always taught us in medical school, when you hear hoofbeats . . ."

". . . don't look for zebras."

He grinned at me. "They said that in your medical school, too?"

I shook my head. "No. My father was a doctor. He used to say that all the time. But I don't know. I think this might actually be a zebra. I mean, I know how much I miss him, and how awful I felt when I found out he had somebody else, and I think that I blew it . . . that he was actually supposed to have been the love of my life, my husband." I swallowed hard, my throat closing around that word. "But now . . ."

"Now what?"

"I miss him all the time." I shook my head, disgusted at my own mopiness. "It's like being haunted or something. And I don't have the luxury of being haunted right now. I need to think about myself, and the baby, and how I'm going to plan and get ready."

I looked at him. He'd taken off his glasses and was watching me intently.

"Can I ask you a question?" I said.

He nodded.

"I need a male perspective. Do you have any children?"

"None that I . . . I mean, no."

"See, you were going to say, 'None that I know of,' right?"

"I was, but I stopped myself," he said. "Well, almost."

"Okay. So no kids. How would you feel, if you'd been with someone, and then you weren't with her, and she came to you and said, 'Guess what? I'm having your baby!' Would you even want to know?"

"If it were me," he said, thoughtfully. "Well, yes. If it were me I'd want to know. I would want to be a part of the child's life."

"Even if you weren't with the mother anymore?"

"I think children deserve to have two parents involved with them, and who they become, even if the parents live apart. It's hard enough to grow up in this world. I think kids need all the help they can get."

That, of course, was not what I'd wanted to hear. What I'd wanted to hear was, *You can do this, Cannie! You can go it alone!* If I was going to be apart from Bruce—and there was ample evidence that I would—I wanted every assurance that a single parent was a fine and proper thing to be. "So you think I should tell him."

"If it were me," he said thoughtfully, "I would want to be told. And no matter what you do, or what he wants, you're still the one who ultimately gets to decide. What's the worst thing that can happen?"

"He and his mother sue me for custody and try to get the baby for themselves?"

"Wasn't that on Oprah?" he asked.

"Sally Jessy," I said. It was getting colder. I pulled the lab coat tight around me.

"Do you know who you remind me of?" he asked.

"If you say Janeane Garofalo, I'll jump," I warned him. I was forever getting Janeane Garofalo.

"No," he said.

"Your mother?" I asked.

"Not my mother."

"That guy on Jerry Springer who was so fat that the paramedics had to cut a hole in his house to get him out of it?"

He was smiling and trying not to. "Be serious!" he scolded me.

"Okay. Who?"

"My sister."

"Oh." I thought about it for a minute. "Is she . . ." And then I didn't know what to say. Is she fat? Is she funny? Did she get knocked up by her ex-boyfriend?

"She looked a little bit like you," he said. He reached out, his fingertip almost brushing my face. "She had cheeks like yours, and a smile like yours."

I asked the first thing I could think of. "Was she older or younger?"

"She was older," he said, keeping his eyes straight ahead. "She died when I was nine."

"Oh."

"A lot of my patients when they meet me want to know why I got into this line of medicine. I mean, there's no obvious connection. I'm not a woman, I've never had a weight problem . . ."

"Oh, sure. Rub it in," I said. "So your sister was . . . heavy?"

"No, not really. But it made her crazy." I could only see the side of his face as he smiled. "She was always on these diets . . . hard-boiled eggs one week, watermelon the next."

"Did she, um, have an eating disorder?"

"No. Just neuroses about food. She was in a car accident . . . that's how she died. I remember my parents were at the hospital, and nobody would tell me for the longest time what was going on. Finally my aunt, my mother's sister, came to my room and said that Katie was in Heaven, and that I shouldn't be sad, because Heaven was a wonderful place where you got to do all your favorite things. I used to think that heaven was a place full of Devil Dogs and ice cream and bacon and waffles . . . all the things that Katie wanted to eat, and would never let herself have." He turned to face me. "Sounds silly, doesn't it?"

"No. No, actually, that's kind of how I imagine Heaven myself." I felt terrible as soon as I'd said it. What if he thought that I was making fun of his poor dead sister?

"You're Jewish, right?"

"Yeah."

"I am, too. I mean, I'm half. My father was. But we weren't raised as anything." He looked at me curiously. "Do Jews believe in heaven?"

"No . . . not technically." I groped for my Hebrew school lessons. "The deal is, you die, and then it's just . . . like sleep, I think. There's no real idea of an afterlife. Just sleep. And then the Messiah comes, and everyone gets to live again."

"Live in the bodies they had when they were alive?"

"I don't know. I personally intend to lobby for Heidi Klum's."

He laughed a little bit. "Would you . . ." He turned to face me. "You're cold."

I had been shivering a little bit. "No, I'm okay."

"I'm sorry," he said.

"No, it's fine! I actually like hearing about other people's, um, lives." I had almost said "problems," but I'd caught myself just in time. "This was good."

But he was already on his feet and three long-legged strides ahead of me, almost to the door. "We should get you inside," he was muttering. He held the door open. I stepped into the stairwell, but didn't move, so that when he shut the door he was standing very close to me.

"You were going to ask me something," I said. "Tell me what it was."

Now it was his turn to look flustered. "I . . . um . . . the, uh, pregnancy nutrition classes, I think. I was going to ask you if you'd consider signing up for one of those."

I knew that wasn't it. And I even had a faint inkling that it might have been something completely different. But I didn't say anything. Maybe he'd just had a brief, fleeting thought of asking me . . . something . . . because he'd been talking about his sister and he felt vulnerable. Or maybe he felt sorry for me. Or maybe I was completely wrong. After the whole Steve debacle, and now with Bruce, I wasn't feeling very trusting of my instincts.

"What time do they meet?" I asked.

"I'll check," he said, and I followed him down the stairs.

THIRTEEN

After much deliberation and about ten rough drafts, I composed, and mailed, Bruce a letter.

> *Bruce,*
>
> *There is no way to sugar-coat this, so I'll just tell you straight out that I am pregnant. It happened the last time we were together, and I've decided to keep the baby. I am due on June 15.*
>
> *This is my decision, and I made it carefully. I wanted to let you know because I want it to be your choice to what extent you are involved in this child's life.*
>
> *I am not telling you what to do, or asking for anything. I have made my choices, and you will have to make yours. If you want to spend time with the baby, I will try my best to make that work out. If you don't, I understand.*
>
> *I'm sorry that this happened. I know it isn't what you need in your life right now. But I decided that this was something you deserved to know about, so you can make the choices you think are right. The only thing I ask is that you please not write about this. I don't care if you talk about me, but there's someone else at stake now.*
>
> *Take care,*
Cannie

I wrote my telephone number, in case he'd forgotten, and mailed it off.

There was so much more that I wanted to write, like that I still pined for him. That I still had daydreams of him coming back to me, of us living together: me and Bruce, and the baby. That I was scared a lot of the time, and furious at him some of the time I wasn't scared, or so racked with love and longing and yearning that I was afraid to let myself even think his name, for fear of what I'd do, and that as much as I filled my days with things to do, with plans and lists, with painting the second bedroom a shade of yellow called Lemonade Stand and assembling the dresser I bought from Ikea, too often, I'd still find myself thinking about how much I wanted him back.

But I wrote none of those things.

I remembered when I was a senior in high school and how hard it was to wait for colleges to send out their letters and say whether they were taking you or leaving you. Trust me, waiting for the father of your unborn child to get back to you as to whether or not he's willing to be involved with you, or the baby, is a lot worse. For three days I checked my phone at home obsessively. For a week I drove home at lunchtime to check my mailbox, cursing myself for not having sent the letter via registered mail, so I'd at least know that he'd received it.

There was nothing. Day after day of nothing. I couldn't believe that he would be this cold. That he would turn his back on me—on us—so completely. But it was, it seemed, the truth of the matter. And so I gave up . . . or tried to make myself give up.

"It's like this," I addressed my belly. It was Sunday morning, two days before Christmas. I'd gone on a bike ride (I was cleared to ride until my sixth month, barring complications), put together a mobile made of brightly painted dog bones that I'd made, myself, from a book called *Simple Crafts for Kids,* and was rewarding myself with a long hot soak.

"I think that babies should have two parents. I believe that. Ideally, I'd have a father for you. But I don't. See, your, um, biological father is a really good guy, but he wasn't the right guy for me, and he's kind of having a rough time right now, and also he's seeing somebody else. . . ." This was probably more than my unborn child needed to know, but whatever. "So I'm sorry. But this is the way it is. And I'm going to try to raise you as best I can, and we'll make the best of it, and hopefully you won't wind up resenting me horribly and getting tattoos and piercings and stuff to externalize your pain, or whatever kids will be doing in about fifteen years, because I'm sorry, and I'm going to make this work."

I limped through the holidays. I made fudge and cookies for my friends instead of buying them stuff, and I tucked cash (less than I'd meted out the year before) into cards for my siblings. I drove home for my mother's annual holiday open house, where dozens of her friends, plus all of the members of the Switch Hitters and much of the roster of A League of Their Own fussed over me, offering good wishes, advice, the names of doctors and day-care centers, and a slightly used copy of *Heather Has Two Mommies* (the latter from a misguided short-stop named Dot, whom Tanya immediately took aside to inform that I wasn't a lesbian, just a dumped breeder). I stayed in the kitchen as much as I could, grating potatoes, frying latkes, listening to Lucy regale me with the story of how she and one of her girlfriends had convinced a guy they'd met at a bar to take them back to his place, then opened all the Christmas presents under his tree after he'd passed out.

"That wasn't very nice," I scolded.

"He wasn't very nice," said Lucy. "What was he doing, taking the two of us home while his wife was out of town?"

I agreed that she had a point.

"They're all dogs," Lucy continued loftily. "Of course, I don't have to tell you that." She gulped the clear liquid from her glass. Her eyes were sparkling. "I've got to get my holiday swerve on," she announced.

"Take your swerve outside," I urged her, and added another dollop of raw potato goo to the frying pan. I thought that Lucy was probably secretly delighted that it was me, not her, who'd wound up in this predicament. From Lucy, an unplanned pregnancy would have been almost expected. From me, it was shocking.

My mother poked her head into the kitchen. "Cannie? You're staying over, right?"

I nodded. Ever since Thanksgiving, I'd fallen into the pattern of spending at least one night every weekend at my mother's house. She cooked dinner, I ignored Tanya, and the next morning my mother and I would swim, slowly, side by side, before I'd stock up on groceries and whatever new-baby necessities her friends had donated, and head back to town.

My mother came to the stove and poked my latkes with a spatula. "I think the oil's too hot," she offered. I shooed her away, but she only retreated as far as the sink.

"Still nothing from Bruce?" she asked. I nodded once. "I can't believe it," she said. "It's not like him. . . ."

"Whatever," I said shortly. In truth, I thought my mother was right. This wasn't like the Bruce that I had known, and I was just as hurt and bewildered as anyone. "Evidently I've managed to bring out the worst in him."

My mother gave me a kind smile. Then she reached past me and turned the heat down. "Don't burn them," she said, and returned to the party, leaving me with a pan of half-cooked potato pancakes and all of my questions. *Doesn't he care?* I wondered. *Doesn't he care at all?*

All through the winter, I tried to keep busy. I made the rounds of my friends' parties, sipping spiced cider instead of eggnog or champagne. I went out to dinner with Andy, and went for walks with Samantha, and to birthing classes with Lucy, who'd agreed to be my birth coach "as long as I don't have to look at your coochie!" As it was, we'd almost got thrown out the first day. Lucy started hollering "Push! Push!" when all the teacher wanted to do was talk about how to pick a hospital. Ever since then, the mommy-and-daddy couples had given us a wide berth.

Dr. K. had become my new e-mail buddy. He'd write to me at the office once or twice a week, asking how I was doing, giving me updates on my friends from Fat Class. I learned that Esther had purchased a treadmill and lost forty pounds, and that Bonnie had found a boyfriend. "Let me know how you're doing," he would always write, but I never felt like telling him much, mostly because I couldn't figure out what box to put him in. Was he a doctor? A friend? I wasn't sure, so I kept things topical, telling him the latest pieces of newsroom gossip, and what I was working on, and how I was feeling.

Slowly, I started telling the people close to me what was going on, starting small, then moving in ever-widening circles—good friends, then not-so-good friends, a handful of coworkers, a half-dozen relatives. I did it in person, wherever possible, by e-mail, in Maxi's case.

"As it turns out," I began, "I am pregnant." I gave her the condensed, PG-13 version of the events. "Remember when I told you about the last time I saw Bruce, at the shiva call?" I wrote. "We had an encounter while I was at his house. That's how this happened."

Maxi's reply was instantaneous, two sentences long, and all in capital letters. "WHAT ARE YOU GOING TO DO?" she wrote. "DO YOU NEED HELP?"

I told her my plans, such as they were: have the baby, work part-time. "This isn't what I would have planned," I wrote, "but I'm trying to make the best of the situation."

"Are you happy?" Maxi e-mailed back. "Are you scared? What can I can do?"

"I'm sort of happy. I'm excited," I wrote. "I know my life will change, and I'm trying not to be too scared about how." I thought about her last question and told her that what I needed was for her to keep being my friend, to keep in touch. "Think good thoughts for me," I told her. "And hope that this all works out, somehow."

Some days, though, that didn't seem likely. Like the day I went to the drugstore to stock up on appealing pregnancy necessities including Metamucil and Preparation H and came across Bruce's latest "Good in Bed" column, a treatise on public displays of affection entitled "Oh, Oh, the Mistletoe."

"If it were up to me," he'd written, "I would hold E's hand forever. She has the most wonderful hands, tiny and slender and soft, so different from my own."

Or from mine, I'd thought sadly, staring at my own thick-fingered hands with their ragged nails and picked-over cuticles.

If it were up to me I'd kiss her on every street corner and hug her in front of live studio audiences. I don't need seasonal excuses, or random bits of greenery dangling from the ceiling as incentive. She's completely adorable, and I'm not shy about showing it.

It makes me unusual, I know. Lots of men would rather hold your shopping bags, your backpack, possibly even your purse, than hold your hand in public. They're okay kissing their mothers and sisters—years of conditioning have worn down their resistance—but they're not so great about kissing you when their friends can see. How to get your man over his hump? Don't stop trying. Brush his fingertips with yours while sharing popcorn at a movie, and hold his hand as you walk out the door. Kiss him playfully at first, and hope he'll reciprocate with more passion, eventually. Try tucking that mistletoe in your brassiere, or, better yet, that lacy garter belt you've never worn. . . .

Lacy garter belts. Oh, that hurt. I remembered how, for my birthday and for Valentine's Day, Bruce would show up with boxes full of plus-size lingerie. I refused to wear it. I told him I was shy. In truth, the stuff made me feel stupid. Regular-sized women are ashamed of their butts and bellies. How could I feel good about pouring myself into the teddies and thongs he'd somehow procured? It felt like a bad joke, like a mean trick, like a *Candid Camera* stunt, where as soon as I showed that I was dumb or gullible enough to think I'd look good in this stuff, Allen Funt and his crew would pop out of the closet, bright lights flashing and wide-angle lenses at the ready. No matter how Bruce tried to reassure me ("I wouldn't have bought it for you if I didn't want to see you wear it!") I just couldn't bring myself to even try.

I shut the magazine. I paid for my things, shoved them in my pocket, and trudged home. Even though I knew he'd written his December article months before he'd gotten my letter—if he'd gotten it at all—it still felt like a slap in my face.

Because I had no party plans (not to mention no one to kiss), I volunteered to work on New Year's Eve. I got out at 11:30, came home, bundled Nifkin in the little fleece sweatshirt he despised (in my heart, I was sure he thought it made him look silly . . . and in my heart, I had to admit he was right), and packed myself into my winter coat. I stuck a bottle of nonalcoholic grape juice into my pocket, and we walked down to Penns Landing and sat on the pier, watching the fireworks go off, as drunken teenagers and South Philly denizens screamed and groped and kissed each other all around us. It was 1999.

Then I went home and did something I probably should have done much earlier. I got a big cardboard box and started packing away all the things I had around that Bruce had given me, or the things that reminded me of him.

In went the half-melted globe candle that we'd lit together in Vermont, and in whose flickering sweetly scented light we'd made love. In went all of the letters he'd sent me, each folded neatly into its envelope. In went all the lingerie he'd bought me that I'd never worn, and the vibrator and the edible body oils and the pink fur-lined handcuffs, which were probably things I shouldn't have lying around anyhow, what with a baby on the way. In went a hand-painted glass bead necklace his mother had given me for my last birthday, and the leather bag from the birthday before that. After some deliberation I decided to hang on to the portable phone, which had managed to lose its association with Bruce . . . after all, he wasn't calling. And I kept the CDs from Ani DiFranco and Mary Chapin Carpenter, Liz Phair and Susan Werner. That was my music, not his.

I bundled it all up, taped the box, and walked it down to my storage area in the basement, thinking I could maybe sell some of the nicer stuff if it came to that, but for now, it would be out of sight, and maybe that would be enough. Or at least, a start. Then I came back upstairs and cracked open my new journal, a beautiful book with a marbled paper cover and thick lined pages. "1999," I wrote, as Nifkin hopped up and sat on the arm of the couch beside me, looking over my words with what I hoped was approval. "For my baby, whom I already love very much."

* * *

It rained through most of January and snowed almost constantly through February, turning everything white for about ten minutes, until the belching city busses and the guys hawking snot on the streets turned it gray again. I tried not to look at the red foil hearts in drugstore windows. I tried to avoid *Moxie's* red-on-pink Valentine's Day issue to which Bruce, the cover informed me, had contributed a piece entitled "Make Him Wanna Holler: 10 Sizzling New Sex Tricks for the Erotic Adventuress." One ill-fated day I'd flipped to his column while waiting in line at the convenience store, and had been assaulted with a full-page picture of Bruce wearing lipstick-red silk boxer shorts and an expression of abject bliss as he lolled on bed with a woman I sincerely hoped was a *Moxie* model as opposed to the mysterious E. I'd thrust the magazine back into the rack as if I'd been burned, and decided, after in-person consultations with Samantha ("Just let it go, Cannie,") and e-mailed debate with Maxi ("I could have him killed, if you like,") that the best thing to do would be to just ignore it, and be grateful that February was a short month.

Time passed. I developed a new and interesting set of stretch marks, and started craving the imported Stilton cheese that they sold at Chef's Market on South Street for $16 a pound. A few times, I came close to slipping a wedge in my coat pocket and slinking out of the store, but I never did. Too embarrassing, I reasoned, having to explain my cheese habit to whoever would have to come and bail me out after my inevitable arrest.

I actually felt pretty good, which was how most of the relentlessly upbeat pregnancy books I'd read described the second trimester. "You'll feel radiant and alive, full of energy!" read one, beneath a picture of a radiant and alive-looking pregnant woman walking through a field of wildflowers, hand in hand with her devoted-looking spouse. It wasn't that great, what with the occasional overwhelming sleepiness, and my breasts aching so badly some days that I had fantasies of their falling off and rolling away, and the night I ate an entire jar of mango chutney while watching a rerun of *Total Request Live* on MTV. Occasionally—well, maybe more than occasionally—I'd feel so sorry for myself that I'd cry. All of my books had pictures of pregnant ladies with their husbands (or, in the more progressive ones, partners)— someone to rub cocoa butter on your belly and fetch you ice cream and pickles, to cheer you up and urge you on and help you pick out a name. I had nobody, I would mope, conveniently ignoring Samantha and Lucy and my mother's twice-a-night phone calls and weekly sleepovers. Nobody to dispatch to the convenience store in the middle of the night, nobody who'd stay up late debating the relative merits of Alice and Abigail, nobody to tell me not to be scared of the pain and not to be scared of the future and tell me that everything would be fine.

And it felt like things were getting more complicated instead of less. For one thing, people at work were starting to notice. Nobody'd come right out and asked me yet, but I was getting the occasional stare, or hearing the occasional hushed silence when I came into the ladies' room or the cafeteria.

One afternoon Gabby cornered me by my desk. She'd been gunning for me since the fall, when my forty-inch Sunday feature on Maxi ran on the front of the Entertainment section, much to the delight of my editors. They were thrilled that we were the only East Coast paper to have secured an interview with Maxi, and even more thrilled that we had the only story in which she spoke so candidly about her life, her goals, and her failed romances. I got a nice little bonus, plus a glowing note from the editor in chief, which I kept prominently posted on my cubicle wall.

All of this was good for me, but it meant that Gabby was in an increasingly foul mood—especially since I'd gotten the nod to write about the Grammys, while she'd been consigned to prewriting Andy Rooney's obituary, lest his health take a turn for the worse.

"Are you gaining weight?" she demanded.

I tried to turn the question around, the way *Redbook*'s latest "10 Tips for Handling Difficult People" advised, aware that people's ears had pricked up. "What an unusual question," I said through numb lips. "Why are you interested?"

Gabby just stared at me, refusing to bite. "You look different," she said.

"So what I'm hearing you say," I began, per *Redbook*'s instructions, "is that it's important to you that I always look the same?"

She gave me a long, angry stare, then huffed off. That suited me fine. I hadn't decided what to tell people, or when to tell them, and for the time being I was wearing oversized shirts and leggings and hoping they'd chalk my weight gain (six pounds in the first trimester, another four since Thanksgiving) up to holiday overindulgence.

And it was true that I was eating well. I had brunch every weekend with my mother, and dinner once or twice a week with my friends, who seemed to be operating on some kind of top-secret schedule. Every night, somebody would call, and offer to come over for coffee or meet for a bagel in the morning. Every day at work, Andy would ask if I wanted to share leftovers from whichever fabulous place he'd dined at the night before, or Betsy would take me to the tiny, excellent Vietnamese luncheonette two blocks over. It was as if they were afraid to leave me alone. And I didn't even care that I was their sympathy case or their project. I sucked it all up, trying to distract myself from missing Bruce and obsessing over the things I didn't have (security, stability, a father for my unborn child, maternity clothes that didn't make me look like a small ski slope). I went to work and to see Dr. Patel, and made arrangements for all of the classes and courses a new mother-to-be could want: Breast Feeding Basics, Infant CPR, Parenting 101.

My mother put the word out, and her friends all emptied their attics and their daughters' attics. By February, I had a changing table and a Diaper Genie, a crib and a car seat and a stroller that looked more luxurious (and more complicated) than my little car. I had boxes full of footie pajamas and little knitted caps, drooled-upon copies of *Pat the Bunny* and *Goodnight Moon,* and silver rattles with teeth marks. I had bottles and nipples and a nipple sterilizer. Josh gave me a $50 gift certificate to EBaby. Lucy gave me a packet of hand-drawn coupons agreeing to baby-sit once a week when the baby came ("as long as I don't have to change number two diapers!").

I gradually turned my second bedroom from a study into a nursery. I took the time I used to devote to the composition of screenplays and short stories and query letters to *GQ* and the *New Yorker*—to bettering myself, basically—and started a series of do-it-yourself home improvement projects. And, regretfully, I started spending money. I bought a sea-green rug that went nicely with the Lemonade Stand walls, and a Beatrix Potter calendar. I trash-picked a scarred rocking chair, had the seat recaned, and spray-painted it white. I started filling the bookshelf with every children's book I could scrounge from the book editor, plus books from home, and books I bought secondhand. Every night, I read to my belly . . . just to get into the habit, plus, because I'd read somewhere that babies are sensitive to the sound of their mother's voices.

And every night, I'd dance. I'd pull the forever-dusty metal blinds down, light a few candles, kick off my shoes, crank up the music, and move. It wasn't always a happy dance. Sometimes I'd blast early Ani DiFranco and think about Bruce in spite of myself as Ani roared out "You were never very kind, and you let me way down every time . . ." But I'd try to dance happily, for the baby's sake, if not my own.

Was I lonely? Like crazy. Living without Bruce, and without the possibility of his eventual return, of even ever seeing him again, and knowing that he'd totally rejected me and our baby, felt like trying to live without oxygen. Some days I'd get angry and be furious at him for letting me stay with him so long . . . or for not coming back when I wanted him to. But I'd try to put the anger in a box, the way I'd put away his gifts, and keep moving forward.

Sometimes I couldn't help but wonder whether it was only pride that was keeping us apart, and whether it wouldn't be smarter for me to call him, or better yet, go see him, and just beg until he took me back. I wondered if maybe, despite everything he'd said, he did still love me. I'd wonder if he ever had. I'd try to make myself stop thinking these things, but my mind would churn and churn, until I'd have to get up and do something. I polished my silverware, child-proofed the cabinets, cleaned my closets. My apartment, for the first time ever, was neat, even beautiful. Too bad my head was such a mess.

FOURTEEN

"The thing that every single woman has to remember," said Samantha, as we walked along Kelly Drive on a brisk, breezy early morning in April, "is that if he wants to talk to you, he'll call. You just have to keep repeating that. 'If he wants to talk to me, he'll call.' "

"I know," I said mournfully, resting my hands on the ledge of my belly, which I could do since I had officially started showing the week before. Being pregnant was strange, but it did have a few benefits. Instead of having people—okay, men—look at me with disinterest and/or scorn because I was a Larger Woman, people looked at me with kindness, now that I was visibly pregnant. It was a nice change. It even made me feel a little bit better about my own appearance—at least for a few minutes every now and then.

"I'm actually doing better," I said. "I'm trying to be proactive. Whenever I think of him, I force myself to think of something about the baby. Something that I have to do, or buy, or sign up for."

"Sounds good. How's work going?"

"Not bad," I said. Truthfully, work was a little weird. It was strange to be doing things that would have had me so excited . . . or nervous . . . or upset . . . or happy, just a year ago, and have them feel like they barely mattered. A personal audience with Craig Kilborn over lunch in New York, to discuss his show's new direction? Eh. A

nasty spat with Gabby over which one of us was going to get to write
the postmortem on *The Nanny?* Whatever. Even my coworkers'
increasing and not-so-surreptitious glances, from my belly (burgeon-
ing) to my third left finger (bare) didn't seem to matter. Nobody'd
worked up the nerve to actually ask me anything yet, but I was ready
for the questions when they came. Yes, I'd say, I'm pregnant. No, I'd
tell them, not with the father any more. That, I thought, would
maybe hold them . . . provided I could change the subject to their
own pregnancy/birth/child-rearing stories.

"So what's on the agenda for today?" Samantha asked.

"More shopping."

Samantha groaned.

"I'm sorry, but I really just need a few more things from the
maternity place. . . ."

I knew that Samantha was trying to be a good sport about shopping with me. But I could tell it wasn't easy. For one thing, unlike any
other woman I'd ever known, she loathed shopping. For another, I was
pretty sure she was getting sick of everybody assuming we were lesbian lovers.

While Samantha was extolling the virtues of mail-order cata-
logues and Internet shopping, a guy jogged by us. Tall, lean, shorts
and a ratty-looking sweatshirt advertising some college or another.
Typical jogger on Kelly Drive on a Saturday. Except that this one
stopped.

"Hi, Cannie!"

I stopped and squinted, my hands resting protectively on my
belly. Samantha stopped, too, gaping. The Mystery Jogger pulled off
his baseball cap. It was Dr. K..

"Hey!" I said, smiling. Wow. Outside of that horrible fluorescent-
lit building, outside of his white lab coat and glasses, he was kind of
cute . . . for an older guy.

"Introduce me to your friend," Samantha practically purred.

"This is Dr. Krushelevansky." I pronounced it slowly and correctly,
I think, because he smiled at me. "From the University of Philadelphia
program I was doing."

"Peter. Please," he said.

Handshakes all around, as two rollerbladers almost crashed into us. "We'd better get moving," I said.

"I'll walk with you," he said, "if that's okay. I need to cool down. . . ."

"Oh, sure! Absolutely!" said Samantha. She gave me a short but significant look, which I took to mean, "Is he single, and is he Jewish, and if he is, what possible excuse could you have for not mentioning him to me?"

I gave her a brief shrug and raised eyebrows, which I was certain she would understand as, "I have no idea if he's single, and aren't you supposed to be taken?" Samantha seemed to have broken her bad-luck streak of third-date lunacy and was still with her yoga instructor. Many of our non-Bruce discussions revolved around whether he was too Zen to consider marrying.

Meanwhile, completely oblivious to our eyebrow-encrypted messages, Dr. K. was introducing himself to Nifkin, who'd been the object of several discussions during Fat Class.

"So you're the famous little guy," he said, as Nifkin demonstrated his vertical leap, bouncing higher and higher each time. "He should be in the circus," Dr. K. told me, rubbing Nifkin vigorously behind his ears as Nifkin preened.

"Yeah, well, a few more pounds and I'll go, too. They still hire fat ladies, right?"

Samantha glared at me.

"You look very healthy," Dr. K. pronounced. "How's work?"

"Good, actually."

"I read your piece on *The View*," he said. "I thought you were absolutely right . . . it does remind me of Thunderdome."

"Five girls enter, one girl leaves," I intoned. He laughed. Samantha looked at him, looked at me, did a few quick equations in her head, and grabbed Nifkin's leash.

"Well!" she said cheerfully. "Thanks for walking with me, Cannie, but I really need to get going." Nifkin whined as she started dragging him toward where she'd parked her car. "I'll see you later," she said. "Have fun shopping!"

"You're going shopping?" asked Dr. K.

"Yeah, I need some . . ." What I actually needed was new under-wear, as my Jockey For Her briefs were no longer covering the water-front, but I was damned if I was going to tell him that. "Groceries," I said weakly. "I was heading over to Fresh Fields. . . ."

"Would you mind if I came?" he asked. "I actually need to pick up a few things. I could drive you," he offered.

I squinted up at him in the sunshine. "Tell you what. If you can meet me in an hour, we can get breakfast, then shop," I said.

He told me that he'd lived in Philadelphia for seven years but had never been to the Morning Glory Diner, my absolute favorite breakfast spot. If there's one thing I love, it's introducing people to my food finds. I walked home, took a quick shower, pulled on a variation on my standard outfit (black velvet leggings, giant tunic top, lace-up Chuck Taylor low-tops in a subtle shade of periwinkle that I'd bought for $10), then met him at the diner, where, blessedly, there wasn't even a line—a total fluke on a weekend. I was feeling pretty good about things as we slid into a booth. He looked nice, too—he'd show-ered, I thought, and changed into khakis and a button-down plaid shirt.

"I'll bet it's weird for you, going out to eat with people," I said. "They probably feel very self-conscious about ordering what they really want."

"Yes," he said, "I have noticed some of that."

"Well, you're in for a treat," I told him, and flagged down a dread-locked waitress in a halter top with a tattoo that snaked across her exposed belly. "I'll have the neighborhood fritatta with provolone cheese and roasted peppers, a side of turkey bacon, a biscuit, and would it be possible to get potatoes and grits instead of just one or the other?"

"Sure thing," she said, and wiggled her pen toward the doctor.

"I'll have what she's having," he said

"Good boy," she said, and twitched off toward the kitchen.

"It's brunch," I said, by way of explanation. He shrugged a little bit.

"You're eating for two," he said. "How have . . . things . . . been?"

"If by 'things' you mean my situation, it's going fine. I'm actually feeling a lot better now. Still kind of tired, but that's about it. No more dizzy, no more barfing, no being so exhausted that I fall asleep on the toilet at work. . . ."

He was laughing. "Did that happen?"

"Just once," I said. "But it's better now. Even though I realize that my life has turned into one of the lesser songs in the Madonna catalogue, I limp along." I passed a hand dramatically across my brow. "Eh-lone."

He squinted at me. "Was that supposed to be Garbo?"

"Hey, don't hassle the pregnant lady."

"That was the worst Garbo imitation I have ever heard."

"Yeah, well, I do it better if I've been drinking." I sighed. "God, do I miss tequila."

"Tell me about it," said our waitress, as she deposited our heaping plates on the table. We tucked in.

"This is really good," he said between mouthfuls.

"Isn't it?" I said. "They make the best biscuits. The secret is lard."

He looked at me. "Homer Simpson."

"Very good."

"You do Homer much better than you do Garbo."

"Yeah. Wonder what that says about me?" I changed the topic before he could answer. "Do you ever think about cheese?"

"Constantly," he said. "I'm tormented, really. I lie awake at night, just thinking . . . about cheese."

"No, seriously," I said, and poked at my fritatta. "Like, who invented cheese? Who said, 'Hmm, I'll bet this milk would taste really delicious if I let it sit until a rind of mold grew around it?' Cheese had to be a mistake."

"I never thought about that," he said. "But I have wondered about Cheez Whiz."

"Philadelphia's official food!"

"Have you ever looked at the list of ingredients for Cheez Whiz?" he asked. "It's frightening."

"You want to talk about frightening, I'll show you the fact sheet on episiotomies my doctor gave me," I said. He swallowed hard. "Okay, not while you're eating," I amended. "But seriously, what is it with the medical profession? Are you guys trying to scare the human race into celibacy?"

"Are you nervous about labor?" he asked.

"Hell, yes. I'm trying to find a hospital that'll give me that Twilight Sleep thing." I looked at him hopefully "You can prescribe stuff, right? Maybe you could slip me a little something before the fun starts."

He was laughing at me. He really did have a very nice smile. His full lips were bracketed by deep laugh lines. I wondered idly how old he really was. Younger than I'd thought at first, but still probably fifteen years older than me. No wedding ring, but that didn't mean anything. Plenty of guys didn't wear them. "You'll do fine," he said.

He gave me the rest of his biscuit and didn't even flinch when I ordered hot chocolate, and insisted that brunch was his treat, and that, in fact, he really owed me for introducing him to the diner.

"Where to next?" he said.

"Oh, you can just drop me off at Fresh Fields. . . ."

"No, no. I'm at your disposal."

I looked at him sideways. "Cherry Hill Mall?" I proposed, barely hoping. The Cherry Hill Mall was over the river in New Jersey. It had a Macy's, two maternity shops, and a M.A.C. counter. And my own car was on a weekend loan to Lucy, who'd gotten a job as a singing flower delivery girl on her heartfelt assurances that yes, she could provide her own transportation, while waiting for her spokesmodel career to take off.

"Let's go."

His car was a sleek silver, some kind of heavy sedan-type thing. The doors closed with an authoritative chunk, and the motor sounded much more ostentatious than my modest little Honda ever had. The inside was immaculate, and the passenger seat looked . . . underutilized. Like the upholstery was still untouched by human buttocks.

We got on 676 and drove over the Ben Franklin Bridge, over the Delaware River, which sparkled in the sun. The trees were covered with the faintest green fuzz, and the sun was shining off the water. My legs were pleasantly tired from the walk, and I was pleasantly full from the food, and, as I rested my hands on my belly, I felt something that it took me a minute to identify. Happy, I finally figured out. I felt happy.

I warned him in the parking lot. "When we go into the stores, they might think that you're the, uh . . ."

"Father?"

"Um, yeah."

He smiled at me. "How do you want me to handle it?"

"Hmm." I actually hadn't thought that part through, so enraptured was I with being in this big, steady, powerful-sounding car, looking at springtime through the window and feeling happy. "Let's just play it by ear."

And it wasn't bad, really. At the department store, where I purchased a Pregnancy Packables kit (long dress, short dress, skirt, pants, tunic top, all in some engineered, indestructable, stretchy and guaranteed stainproof black fabric), the aisles were crowded and we were pretty much ignored. Same deal at Toys "R" Us, where I bought blocks, and at Target, where I had coupons for buy-one-get-one baby wipes and Pampers. I could feel the girl at Baby Gap looking from him to me and back again as she rang up my stuff, but she didn't say anything. Not like the woman at Pea in the Pod, who'd told me and Samantha last week that she thought we were both very brave, or the woman the week before at Ma Jolie who'd assured me that "Daddy will just love!" the leggings I was trying on.

Dr. K. was very nice to shop with. Quiet, but willing to offer an opinion when asked, and to carry all my packages and even hold my backpack. He bought me lunch at the food court (sounds tacky, but the Cherry Hill food court is actually quite nice), and didn't seem perturbed at my four bathroom stops. During the last one he even ducked into a pet store and bought a rawhide bone at least as long as Nifkin was. "So he won't feel neglected," he explained.

"He's going to love you," I said. "That's going to be a first. Nifkin usually works as my first line of elimination with . . ." Dates, I was thinking. But this wasn't a date. "New friends," I finally said.

"Did he like Bruce?"

I smiled, remembering how the two of them had existed in a fragile détente that felt like it would rupture into full-scale war if I'd only turn my back long enough. Bruce had grudgingly agreed to let Nifkin sleep in my bed, like he was used to, and Nifkin had reluctantly conceded that Bruce had a right to exist at all, but there'd been any number of raised voices, insults, and chewed shoes, belts, and wallets in between. "I think Bruce was always about two minutes from drop-kicking Nifkin somewhere far away. He wasn't exactly a dog person. And Nifkin isn't easy." I leaned back in the new-smelling car seat, feeling the late-afternoon sunshine streaming through the sunroof, warming my head.

He smiled at me. "Tired?"

"A little bit," I said, and yawned. "I'll take a nap when I'm home."

I gave him directions to my street, and he nodded approvingly as he turned onto it. "Pretty," he said. I looked at it, trying to see what he saw: the just-budding trees arcing over the sidewalks, the pots full of flowers in front of the brick townhouses.

"Yeah," I said. "I was lucky to find it."

When he offered to help me carry things upstairs, I wasn't about to turn him down, even though I was thinking, as I toted diapers up to the third floor, what my place would look like to him. He probably lived in the suburbs, in one of those grand old houses on the Main Line with, like, sixteen bedrooms and a stream running through the front yard, not to mention kitchens that did not boast Harvest Gold appliances, circa 1978. At least my place was relatively neat, I told myself. I opened the door, and Nifkin catapulted himself into the hall, hurtling into the air. Dr. K. laughed.

"Hey, Nif," he said, as Nifkin sniffed the rawhide bone through three plastic bags and went into a seizure of joy. I dumped my bags on the couch and hurried to the bathroom as Nifkin tried to burrow into the bag. "Make yourself comfortable!" I yelled.

When I emerged he was standing in the second bedroom where

I'd been trying to piece together a crib from one of my mother's friends. The crib had come to me unassembled, without directions, and possibly missing important pieces.

"This doesn't look right," he murmured. "Mind if I give it a go?"

"Sure," I said, startled and pleased. "If you actually get it together I'll owe you big-time."

He smiled at me. "You don't owe me anything," he said. "I had fun today."

Before I could think of what to make of that, the telephone rang. I excused myself, grabbed the portable, and flopped gracelessly onto the bed.

"Cannie!" bellowed a familiar British accent. "Where've you been?"

"Shopping," I said. Well, this was a surprise, too. Maxi and I had been corresponding through e-mail and the occasional telephone call at work. She talked about her travails on the set of *PlugIn,* the futuristic sci-fi thriller in which she was costarring with a hot young actor who required not one, not two, but three full-time "sobriety managers" to keep him in line, and e-mailed me investment tips and articles about how I should set up a fund for the baby. I'd write her back, talking about work, mostly, and my friends . . . and my plans, such as they were. She didn't ask many questions about the impending arrival—good manners, maybe, I thought.

"I have news," she said. "Big. Huge. The hugest. Your screenplay," she began breathlessly. I swallowed hard. Of all the things we'd talked about in the months since our meeting in New York, my screenplay hadn't come up once. I'd assumed that Maxi had forgotten about it, hadn't read it, or had read it and decided that it was so terrible it would be better for our friendship if she never spoke of it again.

"I loved it," she said. "The character of Josie is such a perfect heroine. She's smart, and stubborn, and funny, and sad and I would be honored to play her."

"Sure," I said, still not understanding what was happening. "Start eating."

"I fell in love with the part," Maxi continued, ignoring me, her words tumbling over each other, faster and faster. "And you know I've got this deal with this studio, Intermission . . . I showed the script to my agent. She showed it to them. They loved it, too . . . especially the idea of me as Josie. And so, with your permission . . . Intermission would like to buy your screenplay, for me to star in. Of course, you'd be involved the whole way through . . . I think that both of us should be able to sign off on any changes to the script, and, of course, on major casting decisions, not to mention who's going to be the director . . ."

But I wasn't listening. I lay back on the bed, my heart suddenly feeling fierce and strange and enormously excited. Making my movie, I thought to myself, a huge smile spreading over my face. Oh, my God, it's finally happening, somebody's going to make my movie! I'm a writer now, I've really made it, maybe I'll be rich!

And that's when I felt it. Like a wave cresting inside of me. Like I myself was in the ocean, being gently tumbled, over and over, by a wave. I dropped the phone and put both hands on my belly, and then came a gentle, almost inquisitive series of tap, tap, taps. Moving. My baby was moving.

"You're here," I whispered. "You're really here?"

"Cannie?" said Maxi. "Are you okay?"

"I'm fine!" I said, and started laughing. "I'm perfect."

PART FOUR

Suzie Lightning

FIFTEEN

I'd never had any luck with Hollywood. To me, the movie industry was like a guy you lusted after from across the high school cafeteria— so good-looking, so perfect, that you just knew he'd never notice you, and that if you asked him to sign your yearbook at graduation he'd stare at you blankly and grope for your name.

It was an unrequited love affair, but I'd never stopped trying. Every few months I'd importune agents with query letters asking if they were interested in my screenplay. I'd wind up with nothing to show for my troubles but a fistful of preprinted rejection postcards ("Dear aspiring writer," they'd begin), or occasionally a semipersonal letter advising me that they were no longer handling unsolicited material, unknown writers, novice writers, unproduced writers, or whatever they were using as the derogatory term du jour.

Once, the year before I met Bruce, an agent did meet with me. The thing I remember most about our appointment was that during the entire ten minutes or so he granted me, he never once said my name, or removed his sunglasses.

"I read your screenplay," he said, pushing it across the table toward me with his fingertips, as if it was too distasteful to risk full palm contact. "It was sweet."

"Sweet's not good?" I asked—the obvious conclusion one would draw from the expression on his face.

"Sweet is fine, for children's books, or TGI Fridays on ABC. For movies, well . . . we'd prefer it if your heroine blew something up." He tapped his pen across the title page. *Star Struck,* it read. Except he'd doodled little fangs coming out of the *S*'s, so they looked like snakes. "Also, I've got to tell you, there's only one fat actress in Hollywood. . . ."

"That's not true!" I exploded, abandoning my strategy of smiling politely and keeping quiet, not sure what I was more offended by—his use of the term "fat actress," or the notion that there was only one of them.

"One bankable fat actress," he amended. "And really, the reason is, nobody wants to see movies about fat people. Movies are about escape!"

Well. "So . . . what do I do now?" I asked.

He shook his head, already pushing himself back from the table, already reaching for his cell phone and his valet parking stub. "I just can't see getting involved with this project," he had told me. "I'm sorry." Another Los Angeles lie.

"We're anthropologists," I murmured to Nifkin, and to the baby, as we flew over what might have been Nebraska. I hadn't brought any of my baby books with me, but I figured, if I couldn't read, I could at least explain. "So just think of it as an adventure. And we'll be home before you know it. Back in Philadelphia, where we're appreciated."

We—me, and Nifkin, and my belly, which had gotten to the point where I pretty much regarded it as a separate thing—were in first class. Actually, as best I could tell, we were first class. Maxi'd sent a limo to my apartment, which had whisked me the nine miles to the airport, where a block of four seats had been reserved in my name and nobody so much as batted an eyelash at the presence of a small and ter-rified rat terrier in a green plastic carrying case. We were currently air-borne, at our cruising altitude of 30,000 feet, and I had my feet up on a pillow, a blanket spread over my legs, a chilled glass of Evian with a

twist of lime in my hand, and a glossy assortment of fresh magazines
fanned out on the seat beside me, beneath which Nifkin reposed.
Cosmo, Glamour, Mademoiselle, Mirabella, Moxie. The brand-new April
issue of *Moxie.*

I picked it up, hearing my heart start thumping, feeling the sick
feeling in the pit of my belly, and the familiar cold sweat at the back
of my neck.

I put it down. Why should I upset myself? I was happy, I was successful, I was flying to Hollywood first class to collect a bigger paycheck than he'd ever see in his life, not to mention the mandatory hob-
nobbing with superstars.

I picked it up. Put it down. Picked it up again.

"Shit," I muttered, to no one in particular, and flipped to "Good in
Bed."

"The Things She Left Behind," I read.

"I don't love her anymore," the article began.

When I wake up in the morning, she isn't the first thing
that I think of—whether she's here, and when I'll see her, and
when I can hold her again. I wake up and think about work,
my new girlfriend, or, more likely, my family, and my mother,
and how she'll manage in the wake of my father's recent death.

I can hear our song on the radio and not instantly punch up
another station. I can see her byline and not feel like someone
large and angry is stomping on top of my heart. I can go to the
Tick Tock Diner, where we used to go for late-night omelets
and fries, where we'd sit side by side in a booth and grin dopey
grins at each other. I can sit in that same booth without
remembering how she'd start off sitting across from me and
then, halfway through, get up and plop herself down beside
me. "I'm just being sociable," she'd say, every time. "I'm paying you a visit. Hello, neighbor!" she'd say, and kiss me, and
kiss me until the waitress with the blond bouffant and the coffee pot in each hand would stop and shake her head.

I have reclaimed the Tick Tock. Once it was our place, now

it's my place again. It's right on my way home from work, and I like the spinach and feta omelet, and I can even order it sometimes without remembering how she'd bare her teeth at me in the parking lot, demanding to know whether she had spinach stuck between them.

It's the little things that get me, every time.

Last night I was sweeping—my new girlfriend was coming over, and I wanted things to look nice—and I found a single kibble of dog food, wedged in a crack between the tiles.

I returned the obvious stuff, of course, the clothes and the jewelry, and I tossed out the rest. Her letters are boxed up in my closet, her picture's banished to the basement. But how do you guard against a single kibble's worth of her dog's Purina Small Bites that's somehow survived, undetected, for months, only to surface in your dustpan and send you reeling? How do people survive this?

Everyone has history, my girlfriend says, trying to soothe me. Everyone has baggage, everyone carries parts of their past around. She's a kindergarten teacher, a student of sociology, a professional empath; she knows the right things to say. But it makes me furious to find C.'s cherry Chap Stick in my glove box, a single blue mitten in the pocket of my winter coat. Furious, too, over the things I can't find: my tie-dye tank top and the Cheesasaurus Rex T-shirt I got for sending in three box tops from Kraft Macaroni and Cheese, because I know she's got them and I'll never get them back.

I think that when relationships end there should be Thing Amnesty Day. Not right away, when you're both still raw and broken and aching and probably prone to ill-advised sex, but down the road, when you can still be civil, but before you've completed the process of turning your former beloved into just a memory.

Turning your former beloved into a memory, I thought sadly. So that's what he's doing. Except . . . well, turning a former lover into a memory is one thing, but turning a child into a minor distraction, into something you can't even be bothered with . . . well, that was something else. Something infuriating. Ill-advised sex, indeed! What about the consequences of his little slip-up!

But for now, I hired a cleaning crew for my apartment. The floors, I told them, showing them the kibble I'd found, muttering dire predictions about bugs and mice and other assorted vermin. But really, I am haunted by memories.

I don't love her anymore. But that doesn't mean it doesn't hurt.

Oof. I leaned back in the plush, double-wide leather-clad reclining seat and closed my eyes, feeling the most potent and horrible mixture of sadness and fury—and sudden, overwhelming hope—that for a minute I thought I'd throw up. He'd written this three months ago. That was how long magazines took to print things. Had he seen my letter? Did he know I was pregnant? And what was he feeling now?

"He still misses me," I murmured, with my hand on my belly. So did that mean there was hope? I thought for a minute that maybe I'd mail him his Cheesasaurus Rex T-shirt, as a sign . . . as a peace offering. Then I remembered that the last thing I'd mailed him was news that I was having his baby, and he hadn't even bothered to pick up the phone and ask me how I was.

"He doesn't love me anymore," I reminded myself. And I wondered how E. felt, reading this . . . E. the kindergarten teacher with her sweet talk of baggage and her small, soft hands. Did she wonder why he wrote about me, after all this time? Did she wonder why he still cared? *Did* he care, or was that just my wishful thinking? And if I called, what would he say?

I turned restlessly in my seat, flipping the pillow, then scrunching it against the window and leaning against it. I closed my eyes, and when I opened them, the captain was announcing our descent into beautiful Los Angeles, where the sun was shining and the winds were from the southwest and where it was a perfect 80 degrees.

*   *   *

I got off the plane with my pockets full of little gifts the flight girls had pressed upon me, packets of Mint Milanos and foil-wrapped chocolates and complimentary eye masks and washcloths and socks. I had Nifkin's carrier in one hand, my bag in the other. In the bag was a week's worth of underwear, my Pregnancy Packable kit, minus the long skirt and tunic, which I was wearing, and a few fistfuls of assorted hygiene products that I'd thrust in at the last minute. A nightgown, some sneakers, my telephone book, my journal, and a dog-eared copy of *Your Healthy Baby*.

"How long will you be?" my mother had asked the night before I'd left. The boxes and bags of what I'd bought at the mall were still strewn in the hallway and kitchen, like fallen bodies. But the crib, I'd noticed, was put together perfectly. Dr. K. must have done it while I was on the phone with Maxi.

"Just a weekend. Maybe a few days longer." I told her.

"You told this Maxi person about the baby, right?" she'd fretted.

"Yes, Mom, I told her."

"And you'll call, right?"

I rolled my eyes, told her yes, and walked Nifkin over to Samantha's, to give her the good news.

"Details!" she demanded, handing me a cup of tea and settling on her couch.

I told her what I knew: that I'd be selling my screenplay to the studio, that I'd need to find an agent, and that I'd be meeting some of the producers. I didn't mention that Maxi had urged me to find a place to stay for a while, in case I wanted to be in California for the inevitable revisions and rewrites.

"That is completely unbelievable!" Samantha said, and hugged me. "Cannie, it's just great!"

And it was great, I mused, as I trudged down the jetway with Nifkin's case banging against my leg. "Airport," I murmured to the baby. And there, at the gate, was April. I recognized her instantly from New York. Same knee-high black leather boots, only now her hair was drawn up into a ponytail at the top center of her head, and there was something strange happening between her nose and her chin. It took me a minute to figure out that she was smiling.

"Cannie!" she said, and waved and took my hand. "It's such a pleasure to finally meet you!" She raked her eyes over me in the way that I'd remembered, lingering just a beat or two too long on my stomach, but her smile was firmly in place by the time her eyes met mine. "A towering talent," she pronounced. "Loved the screenplay. Loved it, loved it. As soon as Maxi showed it to me, I told her two things. I said, Maxi, you are Josie Weiss, and I said, I cannot wait to meet the genius who created her."

I thought briefly about telling her that we had, in fact, already met, and it had been the single worst reporting experience of that month, possibly the entire year. I wondered if she'd hear me if I whispered "hypocrite" to the baby. But then I decided, why rock the boat? Maybe she genuinely didn't recognize me. I hadn't looked pregnant the last time she'd seen me, any more than she'd been smiling.

April bent to peer into the carrying case. "And you must be little Nifty!" she cooed. Nifkin started growling. April appeared not to notice. "What a beautiful dog," she said. I snorted back laughter, and Nifkin continued to growl so hard that his cage was vibrating. Nifkin has many fine qualities, but beauty is not among them.

"How was your flight?" April asked me, blinking rapidly and smiling still. I wondered if this was how she treated her famous clients. I wondered if I was a client already, if Maxi had gone ahead and signed a pact in blood, or whatever one did to acquire the services of someone like April.

"Fine. Very nice, really. I've never been in first class before."

April linked her arm through mine like we were grade-school chums. Her forearm fit neatly below my right breast. I tried to ignore it. "Get used to it," she advised me. "Your whole life's about to change. Just sit back and enjoy the ride!"

April deposited me in a suite in the Beverly Wilshire, explaining that the studio was putting me up there for the night. Even if it was for one night only, I felt like Julia Roberts in *Pretty Woman,* if they'd gone with the indie-alterna ending, where the prostitute winds up pregnant and alone, with only her little dog for comfort.

The suite might very well be the one where they filmed *Pretty Woman*. It was big, and bright, and deluxe in every way. The walls were covered in gold and cream striped wallpaper, the floors were lined with ultra-plush beige carpeting, and the bathroom was a study in marble shot through with veins of gold. The bathroom was also, I noted, the size of my living room back home, with a bathtub big enough to accommodate a vigorous game of water polo, if I'd been so inclined.

"Fancy schmancy," I noted for the baby, and opened a pair of French doors to find a bed that looked big as a tennis court, all done in crisp white sheets, topped with a fluffy pink and gold comforter. Everything was clean and new-smelling and so gorgeous I was almost afraid to touch it. There was also an elaborate bouquet waiting for me beside the bed. "Welcome!" read the card, from Maxi.

"Bouquet," I informed the baby. "Very expensive, probably." Nifkin had bounded out of his carrier and was busily making a sniffing tour of the suite. He glanced at me briefly, then rose up on his hind legs to dip his nose toward the toilet. Once that had passed muster, he scampered into the bedroom.

I got him settled on a pillow on the bed, and took a bath, and wrapped myself in the Wilshire robe. I called room service and ordered hot tea and strawberries and fresh pineapple, and liberated some Evian and a box of Choco Leibniz, king of all cookies, from the minibar, without even blanching at the $8 price tag, which was at least triple what the cookies would have cost in Philadelphia. Then I lay back on two of the six pillows that came with the bed and clapped my hands together, laughing. "I'm here!" I crowed, as Nifkin barked to keep me company. "I did it!"

Then I called every single person I could think of.

"If you eat at any of Wolfgang Puck's restaurants, get the duck pizza," counseled Andy, in full food-critic mode.

"Fax me anything before you sign it," urged Samantha, and proceeded to spout five minutes' worth of lawyer-ese before I calmed her down.

"Take notes!" said Betsy.

"Take pictures!" said my mother.

"You brought my head shots, right?" demanded Lucy.

I promised that I'd lobby for Lucy, take notes for future columns for Betsy and pictures for Mom, fax anything legal-looking to Samantha and eat duck pizza for Andy. Then I noticed the business card propped on one of the pillows, engraved with the words *Maxi Ryder*. Under her name was the single word *Garth*, a telephone number, and an address on Ventura Boulevard. "Be there at 7 o'clock. Drinks and amusements to follow," it said.

"Drinks and amusements," I murmured, and stretched out on the bed. I could smell the fresh flowers, and could hear the faint sound of cars buzzing from thirty-two floors below. Then I closed my eyes and didn't wake up until it was 6:30. I splashed water on my face, scrambled into my shoes, and hurried out the door.

Garth turned out to be *the* Garth, hairdresser to the stars, although at first I thought the cab had dropped me off at an art gallery. It was an easy mistake to make. Garth's salon lacked the typical trappings: the row of sinks, the stacks of thumbed-through magazines, the receptionist's desk. In fact, there didn't seem to be anyone at all inside the high-ceilinged room, decorated with a single chair, a single sink, and a single floor-to-ceiling antique mirror except . . . Garth.

I sat in the chair while the man who'd put the buttery chunks into Britney Spears's tresses, who'd given Hillary her highlights and Jennifer Lopez henna, lifted and replaced sections of my hair, touching and scrutinizing it with the cool detachment of a scientist, and tried to explain myself.

"See, you're not supposed to color your hair when you're pregnant," I began. "And I wasn't expecting to get pregnant, so I'd just had my highlights done, and they've been growing out for six months and I know it looks terrible . . ."

"Who did this to you?" Garth asked mildly.

"Um, the pregnancy or the highlights?"

He smiled at me in the mirror and picked up another piece of my hair. "These weren't done . . . here?" he asked delicately.

"Oh, no. In Philadelphia." Blank look from Garth. "In Pennsylvania." Truth was, I'd gotten it done at the beauty school on Bainbridge Street, and I thought they'd done a pretty good job, but from the look on his face I could tell that Garth would not agree.

"Oh, dear," he breathed quietly. He took a comb, a little spritz-bottle of water. "Do you have any strong feelings about, um . . ." I could tell he was groping for the kindest word to describe what was happening on top of my head.

"I have lots of strong feelings, but none about my hair," I told him. "Do with me what you will."

It took him close to two hours: first cutting, then combing, then snipping the ends, then rinsing my head in a garnet-red solution he swore was completely natural, chemical free, derived from only the purest organic vegetables and absolutely guaranteed not to harm my unborn child.

"You're a screenwriter?" Garth said once I'd been rinsed. He was holding my chin, tilting my head this way and that.

"Unproduced, so far."

"Things are going to happen for you. You've got that aura."

"Oh, that's probably just the soap from the hotel."

He leaned in close and started tweezing my eyebrows. "Don't tear yourself down," he told me. He smelled of some wonderful cologne, and, even inches from my face, his skin was flawless.

Once he'd shaped my brows to his satisfaction, he rinsed out my hair, blew it dry, and spent about half an hour applying different creams and powders to my face. "I don't wear much makeup," I protested. "Chap Stick and mascara. That's pretty much it."

"Don't worry. This is going to be subtle."

I had my doubts. He'd already brushed three different shades of shadow around my eyes, including one that looked practically violet. But when he whipped the cape off me and twirled me to face the mirror, I felt sorry for even thinking about doubting him. My skin was glowing. My cheeks were the color of a perfect, ripe apricot. My lips were full, a warm wine color, curling with a faint hint of amusement even though I wasn't aware that I was smiling. And I didn't notice the eyeshadow, just my eyes, which seemed much bigger, much more compelling. I looked like myself, only more so . . . like the best, most happy version of myself.

And my hair . . .

"This is the best haircut I've ever had," I told him. I ran my fingers through it slowly. It had gone from a raggedy mouse-brown bob with a few haphazard highlights to a rich, shimmering tortoiseshell color, shot through with strands of gold and bronze and copper. He'd cut it short, the tendrils just brushing my cheeks, and let its natural wave remain in place, and he'd tucked it behind my ear on one side, giving me the look of a gamine. Sure, a pregnant gamine, but who was I to complain? "This may be the best haircut anyone's ever had."

The sound of applause came from the doorway. And there was Maxi, wearing a black slip dress with spaghetti straps and black sandals. She had diamond studs in her ears and a single diamond on a thin silver chain around her neck. The dress tied around her neck and left her back bare almost enough to display butt cleavage. I could see the tender buds of her shoulderblades, each marble-sized vertebra, the perfectly symmetrical sprinkling of freckles on her shoulders.

"Cannie! My God," she said, studying first my hair, and then my belly. "You're . . . wow."

"Did you think I was kidding?" I said, and laughed at her awed expression.

She knelt down in front of me. "Can I . . ."

"Sure," I said. She laid one hand flat on my belly, and, after a moment, the baby obligingly kicked.

"Ooh!" said Maxi, yanking her hand back as if she'd been burned.

"Don't worry. You won't hurt her. Or me."

"So it's a girl?" asked Garth.

"Nothing official. I just have a feeling," I said.

Maxi, meanwhile, was circling me as if I were a piece of property she was thinking about buying. "What does Bruce have to say about this?" she inquired.

I shook my head. "Nothing, as far as I know. I haven't heard from him."

Maxi stopped circling and stared at me, her eyes wide. "Nothing? Still?"

"Not kidding," I said.

"I could have him killed," Maxi offered. "Or even just beaten up. I could send, say, half a dozen angry rugby players with baseball bats to break his legs . . ."

"Or his bong," I suggested. "It'd probably hurt him worse."

Maxi grinned. "Do you feel okay? Are you hungry? Or sleepy? Do you feel like going out, because if you don't, that's no problem at all. . . ."

I grinned at her, and tossed my fabulous hair. "Of course I want to go out! I'm in Hollywood! I've got makeup on! Let's go!"

I offered Garth a credit card, but he shooed me away, telling me not to worry, it was all taken care of, and if I'd only promise to come back in six weeks to have my ends trimmed he'd consider that payment enough. I thanked him and thanked him until Maxi dragged me out the door. Her small silver car was pulled up to the curb. I got in carefully, aware of my shifting center of gravity . . . and aware that, next to Maxi, even with my fabulous new hair and gorgeous Garth-enhanced complexion, even in my semichic black matte tunic and skirt and not unhip black slides, I still felt like a dowdy dirigible. A gamine dirigible, at least, I thought, as Maxi zoomed across three lanes of honking cars and accelerated through a yellow light.

"I arranged for the doormen at the hotel to look in on Nifkin, in case we're out late," she shouted, as the warm night wind blew in our faces. "Also, I rented him a cabana."

"Wow. Lucky Nifkin."

It wasn't until two traffic lights later that I thought to ask where we were going. Maxi perked up instantly. "The Star Bar! It's one of my favorite places."

"Is it a party?"

"Oh, it's always a party there. Great sushi, too."

I sighed. I couldn't eat raw fish or drink alcohol. And even though I was excited to celebrate and see the stars, I knew it wouldn't be long before the thing I wanted most was the bed in that big gorgeous hotel

suite. I never liked late nights or loud parties much before I was pregnant, and I found myself liking them even less since. I'd stay for a little while, I told myself, and then plead pregnant lady exhaustion and
make a break for home.

Maxi gave me the rundown on who might be there, as well as any
pertinent back-story of which a newcomer such as myself should be
aware. The famous actor and actress, married for seven years, I learned,
were faking it. "He's gay," Maxi murmured, "and she's been getting it
on with her personal trainer for years."

"How cliché!" I whispered back. Maxi laughed and leaned in
closer. The ingenue, star of last summer's second-biggest action picture, might offer me Ecstasy in the ladies' room ("at least, she offered
it to me," said Maxi). The hip-hop princess who reportedly didn't
make a move without her Baptist, Bible-carrying mother was "a real
wild one," said Maxi. "Sleeps with boys, and girls, and both at the
same time, while Maman's off leading revivals in Virginia." The fiftyish director just got out of the Betty Ford Clinic; the fortysomething
leading man had been diagnosed as a sex addict during his last stint at
Hazelden; and the much-gossiped-about art-house director wasn't
actually a lesbian, although she was perfectly happy to feed the rumor
mill. "Straight as an arrow," said Maxi, sounding disgusted. "I think
she's even got a husband stashed in Michigan."

"The horror!" I said. Maxi giggled, grabbing my arm. The elevator doors slid open, and two gorgeous guys wearing white shorts and
white dress shirts swung open ten-foot-high glass doors, revealing a
bar that looked like it was suspended in the night sky. Windows
wrapped around the length of the room. There were dozens of small
white-cloth-covered tables for two and for four, covered with dozens of
flickering votive candles. The walls were hung with gossamer ivory
curtains that billowed gently in the night breeze. The bar was backlit
with blue neon, and the bartender was a six-foot-tall woman in a midnight-blue cat-suit, dispensing martinis with her face as gorgeous and
still as a carved African mask. Maxi gave my arm a final squeeze, whispered, "I'll be back in a jiff," and darted off to air-kiss people I'd only

seen in movies. I leaned against one of the pillars and tried not to stare.

There was the hip-hop princess, with tiny braids cascading from the crown of her head almost to her waist. There were the long-married superstars, looking for all the world like a devoted couple, and the non-lesbian art-house director, in a starched tuxedo shirt and a red bow tie. Dozens of waiters and waitresses zipped around. They all wore white—white pants, white shorts, white tank tops, and absolutely pristine white sneakers. It made the place look like the world's most chic hospital, except the staff carried oversized martinis instead of bedpans, and everyone was beautiful. My hands itched for a pen and a notebook. I had no business being at a place like this, surrounded by people like these, unless I was taking notes for a future newspaper article in which I'd quite possibly be sarcastic. I didn't belong here just as myself.

I walked to the windows, which overlooked a lit swimming pool in which nobody was swimming. There was a tiki bar with the requisite thatched roof and torches, thronged with people—all young, all gorgeous, most of them pierced and tattooed and looking like they were on their way to shoot a music video. Beyond that, smog, and Calvin Klein billboards, and the glittering lights of the city.

And there, with his back to the room, with a glass in his hand, staring off into the night, was . . . oh, God, was it? Yes. Adrian Stadt. I could recognize him from the shape of his shoulders, the set of his hips. Lord knows I'd spent enough time mooning over his pictures. His hair was cut short, and the back of his neck glimmered in the dim room.

Adrian wasn't handsome in the classic rugged-leading-man mode, and he wasn't one of the latest crop of androgynous pretty boys, either. He was more boy-next-door—medium height, regular features, unremarkable brown hair, and standard-issue brown eyes. What made him special, appearance-wise, was his smile—the sweet, crooked grin that exposed an ever-so-slightly chipped front tooth (he always told interviewers that he'd done it falling out of his treehouse at age nine). And those regular brown eyes could convey a thousand variations on bafflement, bewilderment, befuddlement—in short, all of the *b* words necessary to playing the lead in a romantic comedy. Taken by themselves, the pieces were nothing special, but put them together and you had a bona fide Hollywood hottie. At least, that's what *Moxie* called him in the "Men We Crave!" issue.

I'd been thankfully immune to teenage crushes, had never papered my locker with pictures of New Edition or anything, but I had feelings for Adrian Stadt. Watching him on *Saturday Night!* as he cringed and whined his way through impressions of Kid Picked Last for Kickball Team or sang the faux-operatic "PTA Mother's Lament," I'd felt that if we'd known each other, we could have been friends . . . or more. Of course, judging from his popularity, millions of other women felt exactly the same way. But how many of them were standing in the Star Bar on a warm spring night in Los Angeles, with the object of their affection in front of them?

I shuffled back until I was leaning against a pillar, trying to hide so I could stare, uninterrupted, at Adrian Stadt's back and trying to decide whether I'd call Lucy or Samantha first with the news. Things were going fine until a gaggle of skinny girls on stilettos surged into the room and planted themselves in front of, behind, and all around me. I felt like an elephant who'd blundered into a herd of sleek, fast, gorgeous antelope, and I couldn't see an easy way to blunder my way back out.

"Hold this a sec?" the tallest, blondest, thinnest of the girls asked me, indicating her silvery pashmina shawl. I took the shawl, then stared at her, feeling my mouth gape open. It was Bettina Vance, lead singer of the chart-topping power punk band Screaming Ophelia— one of my late-night dancing favorites when I was in a bitter mood.

"I love your music," I blurted, as Bettina snatched a martini.

She looked at me, bleary-eyed, and sighed. "If I had a nickel for every fat girl who said that to me . . ."

I felt as shocked as if she'd thrown ice water in my face. All this makeup, my great haircut, new clothes, all of my success, and all the Bettina Vances of the world would see was another fat girl, sitting alone in her room, listening to rock stars sing about lives they couldn't even dream about, lives they would never know.

I felt the baby kick then, like a little fist rapping sternly at me from the inside, like a reminder. Suddenly, I thought, the hell with her. I thought, I'm someone, too.

"Why would you need donations? Aren't you rich already?" I inquired. A few of the gazelles tittered. Bettina rolled her eyes at me. I reached into my purse and, thankfully, felt my fingers close around what I needed. "Here's your nickel," I said sweetly. "Maybe you can start saving for your next nose job."

The titters turned to outright laughter. Bettina Vance was staring at me.

"Who are you?" she hissed.

A few answers occurred: A former fan? An angry fat girl? Your worst nightmare?

Instead, I went for the simple, understated, and, not coincidentally, true answer. "I'm a writer," I said softly, forcing myself not to retreat or look away.

Bettina glared at me for what felt like an unbelievably long time. Then she snatched her shawl out of my hands and stalked off, taking her gaggle of size zeros with her. I leaned back against the pillar, shaking, and ran one hand over my belly. "Bitch," I whispered to the baby. One of the men who'd been hanging at the edge of the crowd smiled at me, then walked away before his face could really register. In the instant it took me to figure out who he was, Maxi was back at my side.

"What was that all about?" she asked.

"Adrian Stadt," I managed.

"Didn't I tell you he was here?" asked Maxi impatiently. "Jesus, what's with Bettina?"

"Never mind Bettina," I burbled. "Adrian Stadt just smiled at me! Do you know him?"

"A little bit," she said. "Do you?"

I rolled my eyes. "Oh, yeah," I said. "He's in my bowling league back in Philadelphia."

Maxi looked puzzled. "Isn't he from New York?"

"Kidding," I told her. "Of course I don't know him! But I'm a major fan." I paused, debating whether to tell Maxi that Adrian Stadt had basically inspired my screenplay. Just as Josie Weiss was me, Avery Trace was Adrian, only with a different name, and without the annoying penchant for dating supermodels. Before I'd decided what to say, she connected the dots. "You know, he'd be a perfect Avery," she murmured. "We should talk to him."

She headed toward the window. I froze. She turned around.

"What's wrong?"

"I can't just walk up to him and start talking."

"Why not?"

"Because I'm . . ." I tried to think of a nice way to say, "in a completely different league than handsome, famous movie stars." I arrived at ". . . pregnant."

"I think," said Maxi, "that pregnant people are still allowed to converse with nonpregnant people."

I hung my head. "I'm shy."

"Oh, you are not shy. You're a reporter, for heaven's sake!"

She had a point. It was true that, in my working life, I could, and have, routinely just walked up to people far more powerful or influential or better-looking than me. But not Adrian Stadt. Not the guy I'd allowed myself a one-hundred-page daydream about. What if he didn't like me? Or what if, in person, I didn't like him? Wouldn't it be better to just preserve the fantasy?

Maxi shifted from foot to foot. "Cannie . . ."

"I'm better on the phone," I finally muttered. Maxi sighed, charmingly, the way she did everything. "Wait here," she said, and hurried to the bar. When she came back there was a cell phone in her hand.

"Oh, no," I said when I saw it. "I had bad luck with that phone."

"It's a different phone," said Maxi, squinting at the numbers she'd drawn on her hand with what looked like lipliner. "Smaller. Lighter. More expensive." The phone started ringing. She handed it to me. Across the room, in front of the room-length windows, Adrian Stadt flipped his own phone open. I could see his lips moving, reflected in the glass.

"Hello?"

"Don't jump," I said. It was the first thing I could think of. As I spoke, I moved so I was standing behind a pillar draped in white silk, hidden from his view, but in a spot where I could still see his reflection in the window. "Don't jump," I said again. "Nothing could be that bad."

He gave a short, rueful laugh. "You don't know," he said.

"Sure I do," I said, with the phone in a death grip in my suddenly sweaty hand. I couldn't believe this was happening. I was talking— flirting, even!—with Adrian Stadt. "You're young, you're handsome, you're talented . . ."

"Flatterer," he said. He had a wonderful voice, low and warm. I wondered why he always spoke in that weird whiny singsong in his movies, if he really sounded like this.

"But it's true! You are. And you're in this wonderful place, and it's a beautiful night. You can see the stars."

Another bitter burst of laughter. "Stars," he sneered. "Like I'd want to."

"Not those stars," I said. "Look out the window," I told him. I watched his eyes as he did what I said. "Look up." He tilted his head. "See that bright star, just off to your right?"

Adrian squinted. "I can't see anything. Pollution," he explained. He turned from the window, scanning the crowd. "Where are you?"

I ducked even farther behind my pillar. When I swallowed, I could hear my throat click.

"Or at least tell me who you are."

"A friend."

"Are you in this room?"

"Maybe."

His voice took on a faint, teasing edge. "Can I see you?"

"No. Not yet."

"Why not?"

"Because I'm shy," I said. "And wouldn't you like to get to know me better this way?"

He smiled. I could see his lips curving in the window. "How do I know you're real?" he asked.

"You don't," I said. "I could be a figment of your imagination."

He turned around swiftly, and for a second I felt his eyes on me. I dropped the phone, picked it up, clicked it off, and handed it back to Maxi, all in one motion that I would like to think was smooth, but probably wasn't.

Instantly, the phone started ringing. Maxi flipped it open. "Hello?" I could hear Adrian's voice. "Figment? Figment, is that you?"

"Hold, please," Maxi said crisply, and handed the phone back to me. I slipped back behind my pillar.

"Star 69 is the bane of human existence in the nineties," I began. "Whatever happened to anonymity?"

"Anonymity," he repeated slowly, as if it was the first time he'd said the word.

"Just think," I continued, "of the generations of pubescent boys who are never going to be able to make hang up calls to the girls they've got crushes on. Think of how they'll be stunted."

"You're funny," he said.

"It's a defense mechanism," I replied.

"So can I see you?"

I held the phone as tightly as I could and didn't answer.

"I'm going to keep calling until you let me see you."

"Why?" I asked.

"Because you sound very nice. Can't I buy you a drink?"

"I don't drink," I said.

"Don't you ever get thirsty?" he asked, and I laughed in spite of myself.

"Let me see you," he said.

I sighed, straightened my tunic, cast a quick glance around to make sure Bettina Vance was elsewhere, then walked up behind him and tapped him on his shoulder. "Hey," I said, hoping that he'd get the full impact of my hair and makeup before getting to my belly. "Hi."

He turned, slowly. In person, he was adorable. Taller than I'd imagined, and so cute, so sweet looking. And drunk. Very, very drunk.

He smiled at me. I picked up my phone. He grabbed my wrist. "No," he said, "face-to-face."

I turned the telephone off.

He was so handsome up close. On the screen he looked cute, not gorgeous, but in the flesh he was amazing, with beautiful brown eyes, and . . .

"You're pregnant," he blurted.

Okay, not precisely a news flash, but it was something.

"Yeah," I said. "I'm pregnant. I'm Cannie."

"Cannie," he repeated. "Where's your, um . . ." And he waved one arm in the air in a vague way that I took to mean "baby's father."

"I'm here by myself," I said, deciding to let it go at that. "Actually, I'm here with Maxi Ryder. "

"I'm here alone," he said, as if he hadn't heard me. "I'm always alone."

"Now, I know that isn't true," I said. "I happen to be aware that you are dating a German medical student named Inga."

"Greta," he murmured. "We broke up. You've got some memory."

I shrugged and tried to look modest. "I'm a fan," I said. I was trying to figure out whether it would be completely tacky to ask for his autograph, when Adrian grabbed my hand.

"I have an idea," he said. "Do you want to go outside?"

"Outside?" Did I want to go outside with Adrian Stadt? Did the Pope wear a big hat? I nodded so hard I was worried I'd give myself whiplash, and darted off into the halter-topped, miniskirted masses in search of Maxi. I located her at last in the crush by the bar. "Listen," I said, "I'm going outside with Adrian Stadt for a minute."

"Oh, you are, are you?" she said archly.

"It's not like that."

"Oh, no?"

"He seems kind of . . . lonely."

"Hmph. Well, remember, he is an actor." She thought about it. "Well, actually, a comedian who makes movies."

"We're just going for a walk," I said, feeling desperate not to upset or offend her, but even more desperate to get back to Adrian.

"Whatever," she said airily. She scribbled her number on a napkin and held out her hand for the cell phone. "Give me a call from wherever you are."

I handed her the phone, tucked the number into my purse, and rolled my eyes. "Oh, right. I'll be off seducing him. It'll be very romantic. We'll be snuggling on the couch, and I'll kiss him, and he'll tell me he adores me, and then my unborn child will kick him in the ribs."

Maxi stopped looking sulky.

"And then I'll film the whole thing, and sell the rights to Fox, and they'll turn it into a special. *World's Kinkiest Threesomes.*"

Maxi laughed. "Okay. Just be careful."

I kissed her on the cheek and, unbelievably, found that Adrian Stadt was still waiting. I smiled at him, and he led me to the elevator, down and out the door, where we found ourselves standing in front of what looked like a highway. No benches, no grass, not even a lowly bus shelter, or a sidewalk to stroll on.

"Huh," I said.

Adrian, meanwhile, was looking even more tipsy than he had in the Star Bar. The fresh air didn't seem to be having the sobering effect I was hoping for. He grabbed at my hand, managing to get my wrist instead, and pulled me close to him . . . well, as close as my belly would allow.

"Kiss me," he said, and I laughed out loud at the absurdity of it. *Kiss me!* Like a line from a movie! I was looking over his shoulder for the inevitable bright lights and milling extras and director ready to yell "Cut!" when Adrian took his thumb and traced it along my cheek, then down over my lips. It was a move that I was pretty sure I'd seen him perform on screen, but I found that I didn't much care. "Cannie," he whispered. Just hearing him say my name was making me throb in places I hadn't expected to feel anything until the baby came. "Kiss me." He brought his lips down to mine, and I tilted my face up, and my body away, as his hand curved behind my neck and held my head like it was something precious. Oh, so sweet a kiss, I thought, and then his lips were back on mine, harder, his hand more insistent, as the traffic rushed by us and I felt myself melting, forgetting my resolve, my history, my name.

"Come with me," he offered, raining kisses on my cheeks, my lips, my eyelids.

"I'm staying at a hotel . . . ," I murmured weakly, realizing as soon as the words were out of my mouth that it sounded like the cheapest come-on ever. And what was going on here, anyhow? Could he really be that lonely? Did he have a thing for pregnant women? Was this perhaps his idea of a joke? "Do you want to maybe . . ." I tried to think quickly. If I were in Philadelphia, if I were standing on a street being groped by the ultimate object of my desire who was very very drunk, what would I suggest? But, of course, I couldn't think of a thing. Nothing in my life had even come close. "Go to a bar?" I finally offered. "A diner, maybe?"

Adrian reached into his pocket and produced what I figured must be a valet ticket. "How about a ride?" he said.

"Can we . . ." I thought quickly. "Can we go to see the beach? It's such a beautiful night. . . ." Which was not exactly true. It was an extremely smoggy night, but at least it was warm, and there was a breeze.

Adrian rocked back and forth on his feet and gave me a sweet, slightly dopey grin. "Sounds like a plan," he said.

First, though, there was the not inconsequential matter of getting him to surrender the keys.

"Ooh, a convertible," I cooed when a small red car arrived at the curb. "I've never driven one." I shot him my most coy and charming glance. "Could I drive it?" He handed over the keys without a word, then sat beside me quietly, not saying much except to tell me where I should turn.

When I glanced over he had his hand pressed to his forehead.

"Headache?" I asked. He nodded with his eyes shut. "Beer before liquor?"

He winced. "Ecstasy before vodka, actually," he said.

Oof. I guessed if I was going to stay in Hollywood, I'd have to get used to people casually confessing to recreational drug use. "You don't look ecstatic," I ventured.

He yawned. "Maybe I'll ask for a refund," he said, and glanced at me sideways. "So, you're, um . . . when are you . . ."

"I'm due on June fifteenth," I said.

"So your, um, husband's back in . . ."

I decided to end the game of fill-in-the-blank. "I'm from Philadelphia, and I don't have a husband. Or a boyfriend."

"Oh!" said Adrian, sounding like he felt himself to be on firmer ground. "So, your partner's back there?"

I laughed. I couldn't help it. "No partner, either. Just your classic single unwed mother." I gave him the briefest bare-bones outline of the story: me and Bruce, our breakup and twenty-minute-long reconciliation, the pregnancy, the screenplay, and my flight to California a scant twelve hours ago.

Adrian nodded, but didn't ask any questions, and I couldn't look at him to read his face. I just kept driving. Finally, after a series of twists and turns I knew I couldn't hope to remember, let alone repeat on my own, we found ourselves parked on a bluff overlooking the ocean. And in spite of the smog, it was magnificent: the smell of salt water, the rhythmic sound of the waves on the shore, the feel of all that water, all that power and motion, so close to us . . .

I turned toward Adrian. "Isn't this great?" I asked. He didn't answer. "Adrian?"

No movement. I leaned toward him slowly, like a big-game hunter approaching a lion. He didn't stir. I edged closer still. "Adrian?" I whispered. No murmured endearments, no inquiries as to the subject of my screenplay, or the nature of my life in Philadelphia. Instead, I heard snoring. Adrian Stadt had fallen asleep.

I couldn't help but laugh at myself. It was a classic Cannie Shapiro moment: out on the beach with a gorgeous movie star, with the wind whipping the waves and the moonlight gleaming on the water and a million stars in the sky, and he's passed out.

Meanwhile, I was stranded. And getting cold, too, with the wind blowing off the water. I looked in the car in vain for a blanket or a stray sweatshirt. Nothing doing. It was four in the morning, according to the glowing green hands of my watch. I decided I'd give him half an hour, and if he didn't wake up and start moving I'd . . . well, I'd figure something out.

I turned the engine on so I'd have heat, and music from the Chris Isaak CD he had in the CD player. Then I sat back, wishing I'd worn a jacket, keeping one eye on Adrian, who was snoring to beat the band, the other on my watch. It was . . . well, pathetic, really, but also a little bit funny. My big trip to Hollywood, I thought ruefully. My romance. Maybe I was the kind of girl who deserved to be mocked in magazines, I thought . . . then I shook my head. I knew how to take care of myself. I knew how to write. And I had one of the things that I wanted most in the world—I'd sold my screenplay. I'd have money, comfort, some measure of fame. And I was in Hollywood! With a movie star!

I glanced to my right. Said movie star was still not moving. I leaned closer. He was breathing harshly, and his forehead was covered in sweat.

"Adrian?" I whispered. Nothing. "Adrian?" I said in a normal voice. I didn't see as much as an eyelid twitch. I bent over and shook his shoulders lightly. Nothing happened. When I let him go he flopped bonelessly back into the bucket seat. Now I was getting worried.

I slipped one hand into his pocket, trying not to think of the potential tabloid headlines (*"Saturday Night!* Star Molested by Wannabe Screenwriter!") and found his cell phone. After a little fumbling, I produced a dial tone. Great. So now what?

Then it hit me. I reached into my purse and pulled Dr. K's business card out of my wallet. He'd told us in one Fat Class session that he didn't sleep much, and was usually in the office by 7 A.M., and it was later than that on the East Coast by now.

I held my breath and punched his numbers. "Hello?" said his deep voice.

"Hey, Dr. K. It's Cannie Shapiro."

"Cannie!" he said, sounding happy to hear from me, and not at all alarmed by the fact that I was calling long-distance in what was, for me, the wee hours of the morning. "How was your trip?"

"Just fine," I said. "Well, so far so good. Except now I seem to have a problem."

"Tell me," he said.

"Well, I, um . . ." I paused, thinking. "I made a new friend," I said.

"That's good," he said encouragingly.

"And we're at the beach, in his car, and he's kind of passed out, and I can't get him to wake up."

"That's bad," he said.

"Yeah," I agreed, "and it's not even the worst date I've been on. So normally I'd just let him sleep, except he told me before he'd been drinking and also taking Ecstasy . . ."

I paused, and heard nothing. "It's not what you think," I said weakly, even though I had no real idea what he was thinking, except that it was probably some combination of my name and words like "flaky."

"So he's passed out?" asked Dr. K.

"Well, yeah. Basically." I sighed. "And I thought I was being fairly amusing."

"But he's breathing?"

"Breathing, but sweating," I elaborated. "And not waking up."

"Touch his face, and tell me how his skin feels."

I did. "Hot," I reported. "Sweaty."

"Better than cool and clammy. We don't want that," he told me. "Try this. I want you to make a fist . . ."

"Done," I reported.

"Now rub your knuckles along his sternum. His breastbone. Do it pretty hard . . . we're trying to see if he reacts."

I leaned over and did as he instructed, pressing hard. Adrian flinched and said a word that might have been "mother." I re-settled myself in my seat and told Dr. K. what had happened.

"Very good," he said. "I think your gentleman caller is going to be just fine. But I think you should do two things."

"Go ahead," I said, tucking the phone under my chin and turning back to Adrian.

"First, turn him on his side, so in case he does vomit, he won't be in danger of aspirating any."

I nudged Adrian until he was semi-sideways. "Done," I said.

"The other thing is just to stay with him," he said. "Check on him every half hour or so. If he turns cool or starts shaking, or if his pulse becomes irregular, I'd dial 911. Otherwise, he should be fine in the morning. He might feel nauseous, or achy," he cautioned, "but there won't be any permanent damage done."

"Great," I said, cringing inwardly as I imagined what the morning would be like, when Adrian woke up with the mother of all hangovers and found himself beside me.

"You might want to take a washcloth, dip it in cool water, wring it out, and put it on his forehead," said the doctor. "That is, if you're feeling merciful."

I started laughing. I couldn't help it. "Thank you," I said. "Really. Thanks a lot."

"I hope things improve," he said cheerfully. "But it sounds like you've got this situation in hand. Will you call me and let me know how it turns out?"

"Absolutely. Thank you again," I said.

"Take care of yourself, Cannie," he said. "Call if you need anything else."

We hung up, and I considered. Washcloth? I looked in the glove compartment and found only a car lease agreement, a few CD jewel boxes, and two pens. I looked in my own purse: lipstick that Garth had given me, wallet, keys, address book, a panty liner that *What to Expect When You're Expecting* told me to carry.

I looked at Adrian. I looked at the panty liner. I figured that what he didn't know wouldn't hurt him, so I got out of the car, made my way carefully to the water, dipped the panty liner, walked back up, and laid it tenderly upon his forehead, trying not to giggle while I did it.

Adrian opened his eyes. "You're so sweet," he slurred.

"Hey, Sleeping Beauty!" I said. "You're awake! I was getting worried . . ."

Adrian appeared not to hear me. "I bet you'll be a terrific mother," he said, and closed his eyes again.

I smiled, settling myself back in my seat. A terrific mother. It was the first time I'd really thought about it—the actual act of mothering. I'd thought about giving birth, sure, about the logistics of caring for a newborn, too. But I'd never given much consideration to what kind of mother I, Cannie Shapiro, age almost twenty-nine, would be.

I cupped my hands around my belly as Adrian snored softly beside me. A good mother, I thought, bemused. But what kind? Would I be one of those cool mothers that all the kids in the neighborhood liked, the ones who served sweetened fruit punch and cookies instead of skim milk and fruit, who wore jeans and funky shoes and could actually talk to her kids, instead of just lecture them? Would I be funny? Would I be the kind of mom they'd want to be the room mother, or show up on Career Day? Or would I be one of those worried mothers, always hovering by the door, waiting for my child to come home, always running after it, clutching a sweater, a raincoat, a handful of tissues?

You'll be you, said a voice in my head. My own mother's voice. I recognized it instantly. I would be me. I had no other choice. And that wouldn't be so bad. I'd done all right by Nifkin, I reasoned. That was something.

I leaned my head against Adrian's shoulder, figuring that he wouldn't mind. And that was when I thought of something else.

I plucked his phone out of my purse, then dug out the napkin with Maxi's number, and held my breath until I heard her bright, British, "Hello."

"Hey, Maxi," I whispered.

"Cannie!" she cried. "Where are you?"

"On the beach," I said. "I'm not sure exactly where, but . . ."

"You're with Adrian?" she asked.

"Yes," I whispered. "And he's kind of passed out."

Maxi started laughing . . . and in spite of myself, I started laughing, too. "So help me out. What's the etiquette here? Do I stay? Do I go? Do I, like, leave him a note?"

"Where are you, exactly?" asked Maxi.

I looked around for a sign, for a light, for something. "I remember the last street we were on was Del Rio Way," I said. "And we're right on a bluff, maybe twenty-five yards over the water. . . ."

"I know where that is," Maxi said. "At least, I think I do. It's where he shot the love scene for *Estella's Eyes.*"

"Great," I said, trying to remember whether anyone had passed out during that particular scene. "So what should I do?"

"I'm going to give you directions to my house," she told me. "I'll be waiting."

Maxi's directions were perfect, and in twenty minutes' time we were pulling into the driveway of a small, gray-shingled house on the beach. It was the kind of place I might have picked out, given my druthers, and probably several million dollars.

Maxi herself was waiting in the kitchen. She'd swapped her dress and updo for a pair of black leggings, a T-shirt, and pigtails, which would have looked ridiculous on 99.9 percent of the female population, but looked adorable on her. "Is he still passed out?"

"Come see," I whispered. We walked back to the car where Adrian still lay in the passenger's seat, his mouth gaping open, his eyes sealed shut, and my panty liner still perched on his forehead.

Maxi burst out laughing. "What is that?"

"It was the best I could do," I said defensively.

Still giggling, Maxi grabbed a copy of *Variety* from what I took to be her recycling bin, rolled it up, and poked Adrian in the arm. Nothing. She moved the magazine lower and poked him in the belly. No response.

"Huh," said Maxi. "Well, I don't think he's dying, but maybe we should bring him inside."

Slowly and carefully, with much grunting and giggling, we maneuvered Adrian out of the car and onto Maxi's living room couch—a gorgeous white leather construction that I very much hoped Adrian would not defile.

"We should turn him on his side, in case he throws up . . ." I suggested, and stared at Adrian. "Do you really think he's okay?" I asked. "He was taking Ecstasy . . ."

"He'll probably be fine," she said dismissively. "But maybe we should stay with him." She peered at me. "You must be exhausted."

"You, too," I said. "I'm sorry about this . . ."

"Cannie, don't worry! You're doing a good deed!"

She looked at Adrian, then at me. "Slumber party?" she asked.

"Sounds like a plan," I said.

While Maxi went off, presumably to gather bedding material, I took off Adrian's shoes, then socks. I slid his belt out of its loops, unbuttoned his shirt, pulled off the panty liner and replaced it with a dishtowel I'd found in the kitchen.

Then while Maxi piled blankets and pillows on the floor, I washed the makeup off my face, struggled into a Maxi-provided T-shirt, and thought of what I could do to make myself useful.

There was a fireplace in the center of the living room—a perfect-looking, pristine fireplace with a stack of birch logs in the grate in its center. And I knew how to make fires. This was good.

I couldn't find newspaper, so I tore pages of *Variety*, twisted them into pretzels, put them underneath the wood, checked to make sure the flue was open, checked to make sure that the wood was actual wood, and not some decorator's ceramic critique of wood, then lit a match from the matchbook I'd grabbed at the Star Bar, in hopes of proving to Samantha and Andy and Lucy that I'd actually been there. The paper flared, then the logs started burning, and I rocked back on my heels, satisfied.

"Wow," said Maxi, snuggling into her pile of blankets, turning her face toward the fire's glow. "How'd you learn to do that?"

"My mother taught me," I said. She looked at me expectantly, so I told the story . . . to Maxi, and, I thought, to my baby, too, of how we'd all go fishing on Cape Cod, and how my mother would build a fire to keep us warm . . . how we'd sit in a circle—my father, my sister, my brother, and me—roasting marshmallows and watching my mother standing in the water, tossing the silvery filament of line out into the gray-black water, with her shorts rolled up and her legs strong and tanned and solid.

"Good times," Maxi repeated, rolling over and falling asleep. I lay there for a while, my eyes wide open in the darkness, listening to her deep, quiet breaths and Adrian's snoring.

Well, here you are, I told myself. The fire was dying down to embers. I could smell the smoke on my hands and in my hair, and I could hear the waves moving on the shore, and see the sky lightening from black to gray. Here you are, I thought. You Are Here. I cupped my hands around my belly. The baby turned, swimming in her sleep, executing what felt like a backflip. Her, I thought. A girl, for sure.

I sent out a good-night prayer to Nifkin, who I figured would be fine for one night on his own in a luxury hotel. Then I closed my eyes and conjured my mother's face over those Cape Cod fires, so happy and at peace. And, feeling happy and at peace myself, I finally fell asleep.

SIXTEEN

When I woke up it was 10:30 in the morning. The fire was out. So were Adrian and Maxi.

As quietly as I could I made my way to the second floor. Polished hardwood floors, modern maple shelves and dressers, mostly empty. I wondered how Maxi felt, inhabiting and abandoning a series of houses, like a caterpillar casting aside its cocoon. I wondered if it bothered her at all. I knew it would bother me.

The bathroom brimmed with all manner of plush towels and fancy soaps and shampoos in sample-sized bottles. I took a long, hot shower, brushed my teeth with one of the brand-new, still-wrapped toothbrushes I found in the medicine cabinet, then got dressed in the T-shirt and clean pajama bottoms I'd found in one of the dresser drawers. I was sure I'd need a blow dryer and possibly an assistant to even attempt to replicate what Garth had done to my hair the night before, but I didn't see either one nearby. So I pulled back sections of my hair, pinning them with the bobby pins, cementing the whole thing with a dime-sized dollop of some rich and delicious-smelling French styling potion. At least that's what I hoped it was. At my father's insistence, I'd taken Latin in high school. Useful for acing the SATs, not any good for those mornings after when you found yourself unexpectedly having to translate the names of movie star's toiletries.

When I came back downstairs Maxi was still asleep, curled like an adorable kitten on top of a pile of blankets. But where Adrian had slumbered, there was only a single sheet of notepaper.

I picked it up. "Dear Cassie," it began, and I snorted laughter. Well, I thought, at least he was close. And I'd certainly been called worse. "Thank you very much for taking care of me last night. I know that we don't know each other well . . ."

And here I snorted again. Don't know each other well! We'd barely exchanged five sentences before he'd passed out!

". . . but I know that you're a kind person. I know you'll be a wonderful mother. I'm sorry I had to leave in such a hurry, and that I won't get to see you again any time soon. I'm off to location, in Toronto, this morning. So I hope you'll enjoy this while you're in California."

This? What was this? I unfolded the note completely, and a silver key fell into what remained of my lap. A car key. "The lease is up next month," Adrian had written on the back of the piece of paper, along with the name and address of a Santa Monica car dealership. "Drop it off when you're ready to go home. And enjoy!"

I got slowly to my feet, walked to the window, and held my breath as I raised the blinds. Sure enough, there was the little red car. I looked from the key in my hand to the car in the driveway, and pinched myself, waiting to wake up and find that this was all a dream . . . that I was still asleep in my bed in Philadelphia, with a pile of pregnancy planning books on my beside table and Nifkin curled on the pillow next to my head.

Maxi yawned, rose gracefully off the floor, and came to stand at the window beside me. "What's going on?" she asked.

I showed her the car, and the key, and the note. "I feel like I'm dreaming," I said.

"Least he could do," said Maxi. "He's just lucky you didn't go through his pockets and take pictures of him naked."

I gave her a wide-eyed innocent look. "Was I not supposed to do that?"

Maxi grinned at me. "Sit tight," she said. "I'm going to fetch your dog, and then we'll plan your conquest of Hollywood."

* * *

I'd expected Maxi's cupboards to be bare, except maybe for the foods I thought that starlets subsisted on—Altoids, fizzy water, perhaps some spelt or brewer's yeast or whatever the diet gurus had decreed they should be eating.

But Maxi's shelves were stocked with all the basics, from chicken broth to flour and sugar and spices, and the refrigerator had fresh-looking apples and oranges, milk and juice, butter and cream cheese.

Quiche, I decided, and fruit salad. I was slicing kiwis and strawberries when Maxi returned. She'd changed into a pair of black pedal-pushers and a cherry-red cap-sleeved T-shirt, with big black sunglasses and what I took to be fake ruby barrettes in her hair, and Nifkin was sporting a patent-leather red collar studded with the same jewels, and a matching red leash. They both looked very grand. I served Maxi and then, in the absence of kibble, gave Nifkin a small portion of quiche.

"This is so beautiful," I said, admiring the sun glinting on the water, the fresh breeze stirring the air.

"You should stay for a while," Maxi suggested.

I shook my head. "I need to wrap things up and head back . . . ," I began, and then stopped. Really, why did I have to hurry back? Work could wait—I still had vacation time stored up. Missing a few prebaby classes wouldn't be the end of the world. A room with a view of the ocean was enticing, especially given Philadelphia's fitful, slushy spring. And Maxi was reading my mind.

"It'll be great! You can write, I'll go to work, we can have dinner parties, and fires. Nifkin can hang out . . . I'll set up a stock portfolio for you . . ."

I wanted to jump up and down with the joy of it, but I wasn't sure the baby would approve. It would be incredible out here. I could wade in the surf. Nifkin could chase seagulls. Maxi and I could cook. There had to be strings attached. I just couldn't figure out which ones, or where. And on that morning, with the sun shining and the waves rolling in, it seemed easier to let this wonderful adventure unfold than to spend much more time trying.

* * *

Things happened very quickly after that.

Maxi drove me to a skyscraper with bluish-silver glass walls and a trendy eatery on the bottom level. "I'm taking you to meet my agent," she explained, punching the button for the seventh floor.

I racked my brain for appropriate questions. "Is she . . . does she handle writers?" I asked. "Is she good?"

"Yes, and very," said Maxi, marching me down the hall. She rapped sharply on an open door and stuck her head inside.

"That's bullshit!" said a woman's voice, floating out into the hallway. "Terence, that's absolute crap. This is the project you're looking for, and he's absolutely going to have it done by next week . . ."

I peered over Maxi's shoulder, expecting the voice to belong to a chain-smoking dame with platinum hair and possibly shoulder pads, with an unfiltered cigarette in one hand and a cup of black coffee in the other . . . a female version of the reptilian sunglassed guy who'd told me there were no fat actresses in Hollywood. Instead, perched behind the giant slab of a desk was a strawberry-blond pixie with creamy skin and freckles. She wore a pale-green jumper and a lace-scalloped lilac-colored T-shirt and a pair of Keds on her child-sized feet. Her hair was gathered into a haphazard bun with a pale blue scrunchy. She looked as if she were maybe twelve years old.

"That's Violet," Maxi said proudly.

"Bull-SHIT!" said Violet again. I fought down the urge to put my hands on my belly where I imagined the baby's ears would be.

"What do you think?" Maxi whispered.

"She's . . . um," I said. "She looks like Pippi Longstocking! Is she old enough to be using language like that?"

Maxi cracked up. "Don't worry," she said. "She might look like a Girl Scout, but she's plenty tough."

With a valedictory "Bullshit," Violet hung up the phone, got to her feet, and extended her hand. "Cannie. A pleasure," she said, sounding like a regular person, not like a fire-breathing dragon who'd been channeling Andrew Dice Clay just moments before. "I really enjoyed your screenplay. Do you know what I liked best about it?"

"The curse words?" I ventured.

Violet laughed. "No, no," she said. "I loved that your lead character had such faith in herself. So many romantic comedies, it seems, the female lead has to be rescued somehow . . . by love, or by money, or a fairy godmother. I loved that Josie just rescued herself, and believed in herself the whole time."

Wow. I'd never thought about it quite that way. To me, Josie's story was wish fulfillment, pure and simple—the story of what could happen if one of the stars I interviewed in New York ever looked at me and saw more than a potential puff piece in plus-size female form.

"Women are going to fucking love this movie," Violet predicted.

"I'm so glad you think so," I said.

Violet nodded, yanked the scrunchy out of her hair, ran her fingers through it, and gathered her curls into a marginally neater version of the same bun. "We'll talk more later," she said, gathering a legal pad, a fistful of pens, a copy of my screenplay, and what looked like a copy of a contract. "For now, let's make you some money."

In the end it turned out that little Violet was an ace negotiator. Maybe it was just that the sound of that brassy voice and nonstop stream of obscenities coming out of her adorable little person was so jarring that the trio of young guys in sharp suits wound up staring more than they did contesting her assertion that my script was worth it. In the end the amount of money they gave me—one chunk to be delivered within five days of signing, the other to be handed over the day filming began, a third chunk for "first look" at whatever I wrote next—was pretty unbelievable. Maxi hugged me, and Violet hugged both of us. "Now go out there and make me proud," she said, before traipsing back to her office, looking for all the world like a fourth-grader coming in from afternoon recess.

By five o'clock that afternoon I was sitting back on Maxi's deck with a bowl of chilled grapes in my lap and a flute of nonalcoholic sparkling grape juice in my hand, feeling the most incredibly sweet relief. Now I could buy whatever house I wanted, or hire a nanny, even take a whole year off of work when the baby came. And whatever rewriting I had to do, it wouldn't be as bad as facing Gabby, and her nonstop stream criticism, both of the to-the-face and behind-the-back variety. It couldn't be as bad as straining over the seventh draft of my letter to Bruce. Those things were work. This would just be play.

I talked for hours that afternoon, screaming out the joyous news to my mother, to Lucy and Josh, to Andy and Samantha, to assorted relatives and colleagues, to anyone I could think of who'd share in my happiness. Then I called Dr. K. at his office.

"It's Cannie," I said. "I just want you to know that everything's fine."

"Your friend's feeling better?"

"Much better," I said, and explained it—how Adrian had recovered, how I'd decided to stay at Maxi's, how tiny little Violet had gotten me all of this money.

"It's going to be a great movie," Dr. K. said.

"I can't even believe it," I said, for perhaps the thirtieth time that afternoon. "It doesn't even feel real."

"Well, just enjoy it," he said. "It sounds like you're off to a wonderful start."

Maxi watched the whole thing bemusedly, and threw a tennis ball for Nifkin until he collapsed, panting, next to a pile of seaweed.

"Who's that one?" she asked, and I explained.

"He's . . . well, he was my doctor, when I was trying to lose weight, before I got pregnant. Now he's a friend, I guess. I called him last night to ask him about Adrian."

"It sounds like you like him," she said, waggling her eyebrows, Groucho Marx style. "Does he make house calls?"

"I have no idea," I said. "He's very nice. Very tall."

"Tall's good," said Maxi. "So what now?"

"Dinner?" I suggested.

"Oh, that's right," said Maxi. "I forgot that you're multitalented. You can write, and cook, too!"

"Don't get your hopes up," I said. "Let me see what else is in the fridge."

Maxi smiled. "I've got a better idea of something we should do first," she said.

* * *

The guard at the front of the jewelry store nodded at me and Maxi, and swung the heavy glass door open wide.

"What are we doing here?" I whispered.

"Buying you a treat," said Maxi. "And you don't have to whisper."

"What are you, my sugar daddy?" I scoffed.

"Oh, no," Maxi said very seriously. "You're going to buy something for yourself."

I gaped at her. "What? Why? Shouldn't you be encouraging me to save? I've got a baby on the way. . . ."

"Of course you're going to save," said Maxi, sounding eminently sensible. "But my mother always told me that every woman should have one beautiful, perfect thing that she bought for herself . . . and you, my dear, are now in a position to do just that."

I took a deep breath, like I was about to dive into deep water, rather than just walk through a jewelry store. The room was full of glass cases, at the level of what used to be my waist, and each case was full of a treasure trove of ornaments, all arranged artfully on pads of black and dove-gray velvet. There were emerald rings, sapphire rings, slender bands of platinum set with diamonds. There were dangling amber earrings and topaz brooches, bracelets of silver mesh so fine I could barely make out the links, and cuffs of hammered gold. There were glittering charm bracelets bearing tiny ballet slippers and miniature car keys . . . sterling silver earrings in the shape of plump Valentine hearts . . . interlocked bands of pink and yellow gold . . . glittering pins shaped like ladybugs and sea horses . . . diamond tennis bracelets of the kind that Bruce's mother had worn. . . . I stopped walking and leaned against a counter, feeling more than a little bit overwhelmed.

A saleswoman in a neat navy suit appeared behind it as quickly as if she'd been teleported over. "What can I show you?" she asked warmly. I pointed tentatively at smallest pair of diamond earrings that I saw. "Those, please," I asked.

Maxi peered over my shoulder. "Not those," she scoffed. "Cannie, they're tiny!"

"Shouldn't something on my body be tiny?" I asked.

Maxi looked at me, puzzled. "Why?"

"Because . . ." I said. My voice trailed off.

Maxi grabbed my hand. "You know what?" she said. "I think you look fine. I think you look wonderful. You look happy . . . and healthy . . . and, and pregnant . . ."

"Don't forget that," I said, laughing.

The saleswoman, meanwhile, was unfolding a piece of black velvet and laying earrings out on top of the case—the itsy-bitsy pair I'd requested first, then another pair about twice as large. The diamonds were each about the size of a SunMaid raisin, I thought, and cupped them in my hand, watching them sparkle, flashing blue and violet.

"They're gorgeous," I said softly, and lifted them up to my ears.

"They suit you," said the saleswoman.

"We'll take them," Maxi said, sounding very certain. "And don't bother wrapping them. She'll wear them home."

Later, in the car, with my new earrings sending spangled rainbows against the roof whenever the sunlight flashed through them, I tried to thank her—for taking me in, for buying my screenplay, for making me believe in a future where I deserved such things. But Maxi just brushed it off. "You deserve nice things," she said kindly. "It shouldn't come as a surprise, Cannie."

I took a deep breath. *Friend,* I whispered to the baby. To Maxi, I said, "I'm going to make you the best dinner you've ever had."

"I don't understand this," said my mother, who was checking in with her daily afternoon phone call/interrogation session. "And I've got five minutes to figure it out."

"Five minutes?" I tucked the phone closer to my chest and squinted at my toes, trying to decide whether it was possible to survive in Hollywood with badly chipped toenail polish, or if I'd be fined by the pedicure police. "Why are you in such a hurry?"

"Preseason softball," my mother said briskly. "We're scrimmaging the Lavender Menace."

"Are they any good?"

"They were last year. But you're changing the subject. Now, you're living with Maxi . . . ," my mother began, her voice trailing off hopefully. Or at least I thought that's what I detected.

"We're just friends, Ma," I said. "The platonic kind."

She sighed. "It's not too late, you know."

I rolled my eyes. "Sorry to disappoint."

"So what are you doing?"

"I'm having fun," I said. "I'm having a great time." I barely knew where to start. I'd been in California for almost three weeks, and every day, it seemed, Maxi and I went on some adventure, some little trip in Adrian's red convertible, which felt more and more like an enchanted chariot, or a magic carpet, every day. Last night after dinner we'd walked all the way to Santa Monica Pier, and bought greasy, salty-sweet french fries and frozen pink lemonade, which we'd eaten while dangling our feet in the water. The day before we'd gone to a farmer's market downtown, where we'd filled a backpack with raspberries and baby carrots and white peaches, which Maxi distributed to her fellow cast members (except for her costar because, she reasoned, he'd see the peaches as an invitation to make Bellinis— "and I don't want to be the one responsible for his falling off the wagon this time").

There were things in California that I still hadn't gotten used to— the uniform beauty of the women, for one, the way every other person I saw in the coffee bars or gourmet grocery stores looked vaguely familiar, like they'd played the girlfriend or the second banana's buddy on some quickly cancelled sitcom from 1996. And the car culture of the place astonished me—everyone drove everywhere, so there weren't any sidewalks or bicycle lanes, just endless traffic jams, smog as thick as marmalade, valet parking everywhere—even, unbelievably, at one of the beaches we'd visited. "I have now, officially, seen everything," I told Maxi. "No, you haven't," she'd replied. "On the Third Street Promenade there's a dachshund dressed up in a sequined leotard that's part of a juggling act. Once you've seen that, you've seen everything."

"Are you working at all?" asked my mother, who didn't sound impressed with tales of juggling dachshunds and white peaches.

"Every day," I told her, which was true. In between adventures, and outings, I was spending at least three hours a day on the deck with my laptop. Violet had sent me a script so larded with notes it was practically unreadable. "DO NOT PANIC," she'd written in lavender-colored ink on the title page. "Purple notes are mine, red notes are from a reader the studio hired, black from the guy who may or may not wind up directing this—and most of what he says is bullshit, I think. Take everything with a grain of salt, they are SUGGESTIONS ONLY!" I was gradually working through the thicket of scribbled marginalia, cross-outs, arrows, and Post-it addenda.

"So when are you coming home?" my mother asked. I bit my lip. I still didn't know, and I'd have to make up my mind—and soon. My thirtieth week was quickly approaching. After that, I'd either have to find a doctor in Los Angeles and have the baby here, or find a way to get home that didn't involve an airplane.

"Well, please let me know your plans," my mother said. "I'd be delighted to give you a ride home from the airport, and maybe even look at my grandchild before his or her first birthday . . ."

"Ma . . ."

"Just a motherly reminder!" she said, and hung up.

I got to my feet and walked down to the sand, Nifkin bouncing at my heels, hoping he'd get to chase his tennis ball into the waves.

I knew that I'd have to figure it out eventually, but things were going so well that it was hard to think of anything but the next perfect, sunny day, the next delicious meal, the next shopping trip or picnic or walk on the beach under the starry sky. Aside from the occasional memory of Bruce and our happier times together, and absent the uncertainty of not knowing what would happen next in my life, my time at the beach house was basic unmitigated bliss.

"You should stay here," Maxi would say. I never said yes, but I never said no, either. I tried to figure it out the way I'd once investigated my brides, turning the question over and over in my mind: Could this life fit me? Could I really live this way?

I thought about it at night, when my work was done and the food was cooking, and Nifkin and I would stroll along the water's edge.

"Stay or go?" I'd ask, waiting for an answer—from the dog, from the baby, from the God who had failed to instruct me back in November. But no answer came—just the waves and, eventually, the starlit night.

On my third Saturday morning in California Maxi walked into the guest bedroom, flinging open the curtains and snapping her fingers at Nifkin, who darted to her side, ears pricked up alertly, like the world's smallest guard dog. "Up and at 'em!" she said, bouncing on the balls of her feet. "We're going to the gym!"

I struggled to sit up. "Gym?" I asked. She was dressed for it, I saw. Her auburn curls were drawn up into a high ponytail, and she was wearing a form-fitting black unitard, bright white socks, and pristine white sneakers.

"Don't worry," Maxi told me. "Nothing too exerting." She sat on the side of my bed and pointed at a schedule from someplace called the Inner Light Education Center. "See . . . here?"

"Self-actualization, meditation, and visualization," read the course description.

"To be followed by masturbation?" I asked.

Maxi gave me an evil look. "Don't knock it," she said. "This stuff really works."

I went to the dresser and started searching for appropriate self-actualization wear. I figured I'd tag along, and use the meditation session to see if I couldn't come up with a plausible bit of dialogue between Josie, the heroine of my screenplay, and her soon-to-be-ex boyfriend. Or I'd contemplate my future, and what I'd do with it. Self-actualization and visualization sounded like New Age foolishness to me, but at least it wouldn't be a waste of my time.

The Inner Light Education Center was a low-slung white wood building perched on top of a hill. There were wide glass windows, and a deck lined with sea grass and pots of impatiens. There was, thankfully, no valet parking.

"You're really going to like this," said Maxi, as we made our way to the door. I'd wriggled into Maxi's oversized T-shirt, which was becoming less oversized by the day, plus a pair of leggings and sneak-

ers, and the obligatory baseball cap and shades—the one part of her
look I'd been able to adapt for myself.

"You know, in Philadelphia this place would be a cheesesteak
stand," I grumbled.

We entered a large, airy room with mirrors on the walls, a piano in
one corner, and the smell of sweat and, faintly, sandalwood incense.
Maxi and I found spots near the back, and when Maxi went to fetch us
folding foam mats, I checked out the crowd. There was a pack of
supermodel-looking stunners in the front, but also a few older women
—one with actual undyed gray hair—and a guy with a long, flowing
white beard and a T-shirt reading "I Got the Crabs at Jimmy's Crab
Shack." Definitely a long way from the Star Bar, I thought happily, as
the instructor walked through the door.

"Let's all get to our feet," she said, bending to put a compact disc
into the player.

I stared, and blinked, for there, in front of me, was a bona fide
Larger Woman . . . in a shiny electric-blue leotard and black tights, no
less. She was maybe ten years older than me, with a deep tan, and
brown hair that fell halfway down her back, held off her wide, unlined
face with a band that matched her leotard. Her body reminded me of
those little fertility dolls that archeologists dug out of ruins—sloping
breasts, wide hips, unapologetic curves. She had pink lipstick and a
tiny diamond stud in her nose, and she looked . . . comfortable.
Confident. Happy with herself. I stared at her, unable to help myself,
wondering if I'd ever looked that happy, and whether I could ever
learn how, and how I'd look with a nose-piercing.

"I'm Abigail," she announced. Abigail! I thought. My top female-
baby name contender! This had to be a sign. Of what, I wasn't sure,
but definitely something good. "And this is self-actualization, meditation, and visualization. If you're in the wrong place, please leave now."
Nobody did. Abigail smiled at us and hit a button on the stereo. The
sound of flutes and soft drumming filled the room. "We're going to
start off with some stretching and deep breathing, and then we're
going to do what's called a guided meditation. You'll all sit in whatever position you find comfortable, and you'll close your eyes, and I'm

going to guide you through imagining different situations, different possibilities. Shall we begin?"

Maxi smiled at me. I smiled back. "Okay?" she whispered, and I nodded, and before I knew it I was sitting cross-legged on a cushioned mat on the floor, with my eyes closed and the flutes and drums ringing faintly in my ears.

"Imagine a safe place," Abigail began. Her voice was low and soothing. "Don't try to choose it. Just close your eyes and see what comes."

I thought for sure I'd see Maxi's deck, or maybe her kitchen. But what I saw as Abigail repeated "safe place," was my bed . . . my bed at home. The blue comforter, the brightly colored pillows, Nifkin perched on top like a small furry hood ornament, blinking at me. I could tell by the slant of the light through the blinds that it was evening, when I'd come home from work. Time to walk the dog, time to call Samantha to see when she wanted to head to the gym, time to flip through my mail and hang up my clothes and settle in for the night. . . . And suddenly I was swept up in a wave of such wretched homesickness, such longing for my city, my apartment, my bed, that I felt faint.

I struggled to my feet. My head was full of pictures of the city— the coffee shop on the corner, where Samantha and I shared iced cappucinos and confidences and horror stories about men . . . the Reading Terminal in the morning, full of the smell of fresh flowers and cinnamon buns . . . Independence Mall on my way home from work, the wide green lawns crammed with tourists craning for a glimpse of the Liberty Bell, the dogwood trees full of pink blossoms . . . Penn's Landing on a Saturday, with Nifkin straining at his leash, trying to catch the seagulls who skimmed and dipped low over the water. My street, my apartment, my friends, my job . . . "Home," I whispered, to the baby—to myself. And I whispered "bathroom," to Maxi, and made my way outside.

I stood in the sunshine, breathing deeply. A minute later I felt a tap on my shoulder. Abigail was standing there with a glass of water in her hand.

"Are you okay?"

I nodded. "I just started feeling a little . . . well, homesick, I guess," I explained.

Abigail nodded thoughtfully. "Home," she said, and I nodded. "Well, that's good. If home's your safe place, that's a wonderful thing."

"How do you . . ." I couldn't find the words for what I wanted to ask her. How do you find happiness in a body like yours . . . like mine? How do you find the courage to follow anything anywhere if you don't feel like you fit in the world?

Abigail smiled at me. "I grew up," she said, in response to the question I hadn't asked. "I learned things. You will, too."

"Cannie?"

Maxi was squinting at me in the sunlight, looking concerned. I waved at her. Abigail nodded at both of us. "Good luck," she said, and walked back inside, hips churning, breasts wobbling, proud and unashamed. I stared after her, wishing I could whisper *role model* to the baby.

"What was that about?" asked Maxi. "Are you okay? You didn't come back, I thought you were giving birth in the stall or something . . ."

"No," I said. "No baby yet. I'm fine."

We drove back home, Maxi chattering excitedly about how she'd visualized herself winning an Oscar and tastefully, graciously, and very emphatically denouncing every single one of her rotten ex-boyfriends from the podium. "I almost started laughing when I visualized the look on Kevin's face!" she crowed, and shot me a glance at the next red light. "What'd you see, Cannie?"

I didn't want to answer her . . . didn't want to hurt her feelings by telling her that I thought my happiness lay approximately three thousand miles from the beach house and the California coastline, and from Maxi herself. "Home," I said softly.

"Well, we'll be there soon enough," Maxi said.

"Can-nie," Samantha wailed on the phone the next morning, sounded decidedly unlawyerly. "This is ridiculous! I insist that you come back.

Things are happening. I broke up with the yoga instructor and you weren't even here to hear about it . . . ."

"So tell me," I urged her, staving off a pang of guilt.

"Never mind," Sam said airily. "I'm sure whatever I'm enduring isn't as interesting as your movie-star friends and their breakups . . ."

"Now, Sam," I said, "you know that isn't true. You're my absolute best friend, and I want to hear all about the evil yoga guy . . ."

"Never mind that," said Sam. "I'd rather talk about you. What's the deal? Are you, like, on permanent vacation? Are you going to stay there forever?"

"Not forever," I said. "I just . . . I'm not sure what I'm doing, really." And I was desperate, at that moment, not to have to talk about it anymore.

"I miss you," Sam said plaintively. "I even miss your weird little dog."

"I won't be gone forever," I said. It was the only thing I knew for sure was true.

"Okay, subject change," said Samantha. "Guess who called me? That hunky doctor we ran into on Kelly Drive."

"Dr. K!" I said, feeling a sudden rush of happiness at his name, along with a twinge of guilt that I hadn't called him since the day I'd signed with Violet. "How'd he get your number?"

Samantha's voice turned chilly. "Evidently," she said, "and despite my explicit request, you once again listed me as your emergency contact when you filled out some kind of form for him."

This was a point of some contention. I always listed Samantha as my emergency contact when I went on bike trips. Samantha had been less than delighted to learn this.

"Honestly, Cannie, why don't you just list your mother?" she asked now, reiterating the complaint she'd made many times before.

"Because I'm worried that Tanya would answer the phone and have my body buried at sea," I said.

"Anyhow, he called because he wanted to know how things were going, and if I had your address; I guess he wants to send you something."

"Great!" I said, wondering what it was.

"So when are you coming home?" Sam asked again.

"Soon," I told her, relenting.

"Promise?" she demanded.

I laid my hands on my belly. "I promise," I said, to both of them.

The next afternoon, the mailbox yielded a box from Mailboxes & More on Walnut Street, Philadelphia.

I carried it out onto the deck and opened it. The first thing I saw was a postcard with a picture of a small, wide-eyed, anxious-looking Nifkin-esque dog on the front. I turned it over. "Dear Cannie," it read. "Samantha tells me you'll be in Los Angeles for a while, and I thought you might like something to read. (They do read out there, right?) I've enclosed your books, and a few things to remind you of home. Feel free to call me if you want to say hello." It was signed "Peter Krushelevansky (from the University of Philadelphia)." Under the signature was a postscript: "Samantha also tells me that Nifkin's gone West Coast, so I've sent a little something for him, too."

Inside the box I found a postcard of the Liberty Bell, and one of Independence Hall. There was a small tin of dark chocolate-covered pretzels from the Reading Terminal, and a single, slightly squashed Tastykake. At the bottom of the box my fingers encountered something round and heavy, wrapped in layers and layers of the *Philadelphia Examiner* ("Gabbing with Gabby," I noted, was devoted to Angela Lansbury's latest made-for-TV movie). Inside I found a shallow ceramic pet food bowl. The letter *N* was emblazoned on the inside, painted bright red and outlined in yellow. And around the outside of the bowl were a series of portraits of Nifkin, each accurate right down to his sneer and his spots. There was Nifkin running, Nifkin sitting, Nifkin on the floor devouring a rawhide bone. I laughed delightedly. "Nifkin!" I said, and Nifkin barked and came running.

I set the bowl down for Nifkin to sniff. Then I called Dr. K..

"Suzie Lightning!" he said, by way of greeting.

"Who?" I said. "Huh?"

"It's from a Warren Zevon song," he said.

"Huh," I said. The only Warren Zevon song I knew was the one about lawyers, guns, and money.

"It's about a girl who . . . travels a lot," he said.

"Sounds interesting," I said, making a mental note to look up the lyrics. "I'm calling to thank you for my presents. They're wonderful."

"You're welcome," he told me. "I'm glad you like them."

"Did you paint Nifkin from memory? It's amazing. You should have been an artist."

"I dabble," he acknowledged, sounding so much like Dr. Evil, of Austin Powers fame, that I burst out laughing. "Actually, your friend Samantha lent me some pictures," he explained. "But I didn't use them much. Your dog has a very distinctive look."

"You're too kind," I said truthfully.

"They opened up a paint-your-own-pottery studio around the corner from campus," he explained. "I did it there. It was some kid's fifth birthday party, so there were eight five-year-olds painting coffee mugs, and me."

I grinned, picturing it—tall, deep-voiced Dr. K. folded into a chair, painting Nifkin as the little kids gawked.

"So how are things going out there?"

I gave him the condensed version, telling him about shopping with Maxi—the cooking I'd been doing, the farmer's market I'd found. I described the little house on the beach. I told him that California felt both wonderful and unreal. I told him that I was walking every morning and working every day and how Nifkin had learned to retrieve his tennis ball from the surf.

Dr. K. made interested noises, asked pertinent follow-up questions, and proceeded directly to the big one. "So when are you coming home?"

"I'm not sure," I said. "I'm on leave right now, and I'm still fine-tuning a few things with the screenplay."

"So . . . will you give birth out there?"

"I don't know," I said slowly. "I don't think so."

"Good," was all he said. "We should have breakfast again when you come back."

"Sure," I said, feeling a pang for Sam's Morning Glory. There was no place like it out here. "That would be great." I heard Maxi's car in the garage. "Hey, I've kind of got to run . . . ."

"No problem," he said. "Call me any time."

I hung up the phone smiling. I wondered how old he was, really. I wondered if he liked me as more than a patient, as more than just another one of the big girls shuttling in and out of his office, each with her own tale of heartache. And I decided that I'd like to see him again.

The next morning Maxi proposed another trip.

"I still can't believe that you have a plastic surgeon," I grumbled, heaving myself into the low-slung little car, thinking that only in this city, at this moment in time, would a twenty-seven-year-old actress with perfect features keep a plastic surgeon on retainer.

"Necessary evil," Maxi said crisply, powering past several lesser vehicles and zooming into the fast lane.

The surgeon's office was a study in gray and mauve, all cool marble floors and glossy walls and even glossier receptionists. Maxi pulled off her oversized sunglasses and had a quiet talk with the woman behind the desk while I strolled, examining the poster-sized photographs of the doctors that lined the wall, wondering which one would have the pleasure of plumping up Maxi's lips and erasing the invisible lines around her eyes. Dr. Fisher was a Ken doll-looking blond. Dr. Rhodes was a brunette with arched eyebrows who looked about my age, but probably wasn't. Dr. Tasker was the jovial Santa Claus of the bunch—minus, of course, the roly-poly cheeks and double chin. And Dr. Shapiro . . .

I stood there, frozen, staring up at the larger-than-life picture of my father. He was thinner, and he'd shaved off his beard, but it was unquestionably him.

Maxi strolled over, her heels clicking on the floor. When she saw the look on my face, she grabbed my elbow and led me to a chair. "Cannie, what is it? Is it the baby?"

I tottered back to the wall on legs that felt like lengths of ossified wood, and pointed. "That's my dad."

Maxi stared at the picture, then at me. "You didn't know he was out here?" she asked. I shook my head.

"What should we do?"

I nodded toward the door and started walking as fast as I could. "Leave."

"So that's what's become of him," I said. Maxi and Nifkin and I were out on the deck, drinking raspberry iced tea. "Liposuction in L.A." I worked my tongue around it, trying the concept on for size. "Sounds like the beginning of a bad joke, doesn't it?"

Maxi looked away. I felt sorry for her. She'd never seen me this upset, and she didn't have any idea of how to help me. And I didn't know what to tell her.

"Sit tight," I said, getting to my feet. "I'm going to go for a walk."

I walked down by the water, passed the rollerbladers in bikinis, the volleyball games, the screaming, Popsicle-sticky kids. I passed the vendors on stilts, the piercing parlors, and the four-pairs-for-ten-dollars sock vendors, and the dreadlocked teenagers sitting on park benches, playing their guitars, and homeless people in layers and layers of clothes, splayed like corpses underneath the palm trees.

As I walked I tried to lay things out in front of me, to organize them, like they were pictures at an exhibition, framed and hung on a gallery wall.

I pictured my family as it had once been—the five of us on the lawn at Rosh Hashanah, posing in our best clothes: my father with his beard neatly trimmed and his hands on my shoulder; me with my hair twisted back in barrettes, the barest buds of breasts pushing at the front of my sweater, both of us smiling.

I pictured us all five years later: my father gone; me, fat and sullen and scared; my mother, frantic; my brother, miserable; and Lucy with her Mohawk and her piercings and late-night telephone callers.

More pictures: my college graduation. My mother and Tanya, their arms around each other's shoulders, at their softball league championship game. Josh, six feet tall and thin and solemn, carving a turkey at Thanksgiving. Years of holidays, the four of us arrayed around the dining room table, my mother at the head and my brother opposite her, various boyfriends and girlfriends showing up, fading out, all of us trying hard to look like there was nothing missing there.

I moved on. There I was, standing proudly in front of my first apartment, holding a copy of my first newspaper story, pointing at the headline "Budget Debate Postponed." Me and my first boyfriend. Me and my college sweetheart. Me and Bruce in the ocean, laughing at the camera, squinting in the sun. Bruce at a Grateful Dead concert, in a hackey-sack circle, one foot extending in mid-kick, a beer in his hand and his hair flowing loose over his shoulders. Then I made myself step back and move on.

I stood and let the ocean cool my feet and felt . . . nothing. Or maybe it was the end of love that I was feeling, the cool empty place that's left inside you where all that heat and pain and passion used to be, the slick of wet sand after the tide finally rolls back out.

Okay, I thought. Here you are. You Are Here. And you move forward because that's the way it works; that's the only place you can go. You keep going until it stops hurting, or until you find new things to hurt you worse, I guess. And that is the human condition, all of us lurching along in our own private miseries, because that's the way it is. Because, I guess, God didn't give us any choice. You grow up, I remembered Abigail telling me. You learn.

Maxi was sitting on the deck where I'd left her, waiting.

"We need to go shopping," I said.

She rose quickly to her feet. "Where?" she asked. "For what?"

I laughed, and heard the tears inside of it, and wondered if she could hear them, too. "I need to buy myself a wedding ring."

SEVENTEEN

The receptionist at my father's office didn't seem at all perturbed at the long pause before I told her why I was calling.

I had a scar, I finally explained, and I wanted Dr. Shapiro to have a look at it. I gave Maxi's cell phone number as my own and gave Lois Lane as my name, and the receptionist didn't sound the least bit curious. She just gave me a ten A.M. appointment for Friday and warned me that the traffic could be brutal.

So on Friday morning I started out early. My hair was freshly trimmed (Garth had obliged, even though it had only been four weeks, not six). And on my left hand I wore not only the plain gold band I'd imagined but a diamond of such breathtaking enormity, such improbable size, that I could barely keep my eyes on the road.

Maxi had brought it home from the set, promising that no one would miss it, and that it would be just the thing to announce to my father in general and the world at large that I'd arrived.

"But let me ask you," she began that morning, over buttermilk waffles and peach and ginger tea. "Why do you want your father to think you're married?"

I stood up and opened the curtains, looking out at the water. "I don't know, really. I don't even know if I'll wear the rings when I go see him."

"You must have thought about it," said Maxi. "You think about everything."

I looked at the rings on my fingers. "I guess it's that he said nobody would ever love me, that nobody would ever want me. And I feel like if I see him, and I'm pregnant and I'm not married . . . it'll be like he was right."

Maxi looked at me as if this were the saddest thing she'd ever heard. "But you know that's not true, right?" she asked. "You know how many people love you."

I drew a shaky breath. "Oh, sure," I said. "It's just . . . with this . . . it's hard to be reasonable." I looked at her. "It's family, you know? Who was ever reasonable about family? I just . . . I want to know why he did what he did. I want to at least be able to ask the question."

"He might not have answers," Maxi told me. "Or, if he does, they might not be the ones you want to hear."

"I just want to hear something," I said raggedly. "I just feel like . . . I mean, you only get two parents, and my mom's . . ." I gave a vague, general wave of my hand to indicate lesbianism and an inappropriate life partner. My finger flashed in the sunlight. "I just feel like I have to try."

The nurse who led me into the cubicle had breasts as symmetrical and rounded as twin halved cantaloupes. She handed me a plush terrycloth robe and a clipboard full of forms to fill out. "Doctor will be with you shortly," she said, clicking on a high-powered light and shining it on my face, where I'd invented a scar. "Huh," she said, scrutinizing the scar. "That hardly looks like anything."

"It's deep, though," I said. "I can see it in pictures. It shows up there."

She nodded as if this made perfect sense to her and backed out of the room.

I sat on a beige armchair, making up lies to put on the forms and wishing that I had a scar—some physical sign to show the world—to show him—what I'd been through, and what I'd survived. Twenty minutes later, there was a brisk knock at the door, and my father walked in.

"So what brings you here today, Ms. Lane?" he asked, his eyes on my chart. I sat quietly, saying nothing. After a moment, he looked up. There was an irritated expression on his face, a stop-wasting-my-time look that I recognized from my childhood. He stared at me for a minute with nothing registering on his face but more annoyance. Then he saw.

"Cannie?"

I nodded. "Hello."

"My God, what . . ." My father, a man with an insult for every occasion, was for once gratifyingly speechless. "What are you doing here?"

"I made an appointment," I said.

He winced, took off his glasses, and pinched the bridge of his nose—another pose I'd remembered well. It usually presaged a temper tantrum, anger of some sort.

"You just disappeared," I said. He started shaking his head and opened his mouth, but I wasn't about to let him start without saying my piece. "None of us knew where you were. How could you do that? How could you just walk out on all of us like that?" He said nothing . . . just stared at me through me—as if I were any hysterical patient, shrieking that her thighs still felt lumpy or her left nipple was higher than her right one. "Don't you care about us? Don't you have a heart? Or is that a stupid question to ask someone who sucks cellulite out of thighs for a living?"

My father glared at me. "You don't need to be condescending."

"No, what I needed was a father," I said. I hadn't realized how angry, how furious at him I was until I'd seen him, standing there in his crisp white doctor's coat, his manicured fingernails, his tan, and his heavy gold watch.

He sighed, as if the conversation bored him; as if I bored him, too. "Why are you here?"

"I didn't come here looking for you, if that's what you're asking. A friend of mine had an appointment, and I came with her. I saw your picture," I continued. "Not very smart, you know? For someone trying to stay undercover. . . ."

"I'm not trying to stay undercover," he said irascibly. "That's nonsense. Did your mother tell you that?"

"Then how come none of us know where you are?"

"You wouldn't have cared if you did," he muttered, picking up the clipboard he'd come in with.

I was so flabbergasted, he actually had his hand on the doorknob before I could think of what to say. "Are you crazy? Of course we would have cared. You're our father. . . ."

He put his glasses back on. I could see his eyes behind them, a weak, watery brown. "And you're all grown up now. All of you are."

"You think just because we're older it doesn't matter what you did to us? You think needing your parents in your life is something you outgrow, like training wheels or a high chair?"

He raised himself up to his full five feet, eight and a half inches, and gathered the cloak of authority, of Doctor-ness, around him as palpably as if he'd been pulling on a heavy winter coat. "I think," he said, speaking slowly and precisely, "that lots of people are disappointed by the lives that they wind up with."

"And that's what you want to be to us? A disappointment?"

He sighed. "I can't help you, Cannie. I don't know what you want, but I can tell you this—I've got nothing to give you. Any of you."

"We don't want your money. . . ."

He looked at me almost kindly. "I'm not talking about money."

"Why?" I asked him. My voice was cracking. "Why have kids and leave them? That's the part I don't understand. What did we do . . ." I gulped. "What did any of us do that was so awful that you never wanted to see us again?" I knew, even as I was saying the words, even as I was thinking them, that it was ridiculous. I knew that no child could be that bad, that wrong, that ugly, could be anything to cause a parent to leave. I knew that it was no fault of ours. We weren't to blame, I thought to myself. I could let it go; I could set the burden down, I could be free.

Except, of course, that knowing something in your head is different than feeling it in your heart. And I knew at that moment that Maxi had been right. Whatever my father could say, whatever answer he could provide, whatever excuse he could muster, it wouldn't be right. And it wouldn't ever be enough.

I stared at him. I waited for him to ask me something, to ask what had become of me: Where did I live, and what did I do, and whom had I decided to spend my life with? Instead he looked at me again, shook his head once, and turned toward the door.

"Hey!" I said.

He turned to look at me, and my throat closed up. What did I want to tell him? Nothing. I wanted him to ask *me* things: how are you, who are you, what's happened to you, who have you become. I stared at him, and he said nothing—just walked away.

I couldn't help myself. I reached for him, for some sign, for something, as he was walking out the door. I felt my fingertips graze the back of that crisp white coat. He never stopped walking. He never even slowed down.

When I came back, I put the rings in their little velvet box. I washed the makeup off my face and the gel out of my hair. Then I called Samantha.

"You won't believe it," I began.

"Probably not," she said. "So tell me."

And I did. "He didn't ask me a single question," I told her at the end. "He didn't want to know what I was doing out here, or what I was doing with my life. I don't even think he noticed I was pregnant. He just didn't care."

Samantha sighed. "That's awful. I can't even imagine how you must feel."

"I feel . . ." I said. I looked out at the water, then up at the sky. "I feel like I'm ready to come home."

Maxi nodded when I told her, sadly, but didn't ask me to stay.

"You're done with the screenplay?" she asked.

"I've been done for a few days," I told her. She surveyed the bed, where I'd laid my things out—my clothes and books, the teddy bear I'd bought for the baby one afternoon in Santa Monica.

"I wish we could have done more," she said with a sigh.

"We did plenty," I said, and hugged her. "And we'll talk . . . and e-mail . . . and you'll visit when the baby comes. . . ."

Maxi's eyes lit up. "Aunt Maxi," she proclaimed. "You'll have to have it call me Aunt Maxi. And I'm going to spoil it rotten!"

I smiled to myself, imagining Maxi treating little Max or Abby like a two-legged Nifkin, dressing the baby in outfits she'd picked out to match her own. "You're going to be a fabulous aunt," I said.

She insisted on driving me to the airport, helping me check my luggage, waiting with me at the gate even though everyone from the flight attendants on down were staring at her like she was the rarest exhibit in the zoo.

"This is going to wind up on *Inside Edition,*" I warned her, giggling and crying a little bit as we hugged each other for the eighteenth time. Maxi kissed my cheek, then bent down and gave my belly a little wave.

"You've got your ticket?" she asked me.

I nodded.

"Got milk money?"

"Oh, yes," I said, smiling, knowing how true it was.

"Then you're good to go," she said.

I nodded, and sniffled, and hugged her tight. "You're a wonderful friend," I told her. "You're the greatest."

"Be careful," she replied. "Travel safe. Call me as soon as you get there."

I nodded, saying nothing, because I didn't trust myself to speak, and turned away from her, toward the walkway, the plane, and home.

First class was more crowded this time than it had been on my way out. A guy about my age and exactly my height, with curly blond hair and bright blue eyes, took the seat next to me as I was struggling to get the seat belt (much tighter this time) around myself. We nodded politely at each other. Then he pulled out a sheaf of important-looking legal documents with "Confidential" stamped all over them, and I pulled out my *Entertainment Weekly*. He shot a sidelong glance at my reading matter and sighed.

"Jealous?" I asked. He smiled, nodded, and pulled a roll of candy from his pocket.

"Would you like a Mento?" he asked.

"Is that really the singular?" I replied, taking one. He gazed at the roll of Mentos, then looked at me and shrugged. "You know," he said, "that's a good question."

I reclined the seat. He was kind of cute, I mused, and clearly had a good job, or at least the paperwork to make it look like he had a good job. That was what I needed—just a regular guy with a good job, a guy who lived in Philadelphia and read books and adored me. I snuck another look at Mr. Mento and contemplated giving him my card . . . and then I pulled myself up short, hearing my mother's voice and Samantha's voice converging in my head in one loud, desperate shriek: *Are you crazy?*

Maybe in another lifetime, I decided, pulling the blanket up under my chin. But this one would work out okay. Maybe my father was never going to be my father again, maybe my mother would stay yoked to the Dread Lesbian Tanya forever. Maybe my sister would always be unstable, and maybe my brother would never learn how to smile. But I could still find good in the world. I could still find beauty. And someday, I told myself, before I fell asleep, maybe I'd even find someone else to love. "Love," I whispered to the baby. And then I closed my eyes.

If you wish for something hard enough, the fairy tales teach us, you can get it in the end. But it's hardly ever the way you thought it would be, and the endings aren't always happy ones. For months, I had been wishing for Bruce, dreaming of Bruce, conjuring a memory of his face and holding it in front of me as I fell asleep, even when I tried not to. In the end, it was almost like I'd wished him into being, that I'd dreamed so hard and so often that he couldn't help but appear before me.

It happened just the way Samantha had said it would. "You'll see him again," she'd told me that morning months ago when I told her that I was expecting. "I've seen enough soap operas to guarantee it."

I got off the plane, yawning to clear my clogged-up ears, and there, in the waiting area directly across from me, beneath a sign that read "Tampa/St. Pete's" was Bruce. I felt my heart lift, thinking that he'd come for me, that, somehow, he'd come for me, until I saw that he was with some girl I'd never seen before. Short, pale, her hair in a pageboy. Light blue jeans, a pale yellow Oxford shirt tucked in. Nondescript, fade-into-the-woodwork clothes, medium features and a medium frame. Nothing remarkable about her at all except for her thick unruly eyebrows. My replacement, I presumed.

I froze in place, paralyzed by the horrible coincidence, the outrageous misfortune of this. But if it was going to happen, this would be the place—the giant, soulless Newark International Airport, where travelers from New York, New Jersey, and Philadelphia converged in search of transatlantic flights and/or cheap domestic airfare.

For about five seconds I stood stock-still and prayed that they wouldn't see me. I tried to edge off to the side of the lounge, to skirt the entire area, thinking that there had to be some way to duck onto the escalator, grab my bags, and escape. But then Bruce's eyes locked on mine, and I knew it was too late.

He bent down, whispering something to the girl, who turned her head away before I could get a good look. Then he crossed the concourse, walking right toward me, wearing a red T-shirt that I'd snuggled up against a hundred times and blue shorts that I remembered seeing him put on, and pull off, just as often. I sent up a quick prayer of thanks for Garth's haircut, for my tan, for my diamond earrings, and endured a sudden spasm of misery that I wasn't still wearing that grand and gaudy diamond ring. It was completely superficial, I knew, but I hoped I looked good. As good as somebody seven and a half months pregnant could look after a six-hour plane trip, at least.

And then Bruce was right in front of me, looking pale and solemn. "Hey, Cannie," he said. His eyes fell to my midsection as if it were magnetized. "So you . . ."

"That's right," I said coolly. "I'm pregnant." I stood up straight and tightened my grip on Nifkin's case. Nifkin, of course, had smelled Bruce and was in the midst of trying to leap out and greet him. I could hear his tail thumping as he whined.

Bruce raised his eyes to the computerized board over the doorway I'd just passed through. "You're coming from L.A.?" he asked, showing that his reading abilities had not diminished during our time apart.

I gave another curt nod, hoping he couldn't tell how badly my knees were shaking. "What are you doing here?" I asked.

"Vacation," he said. "We're going to Florida for the weekend."

We, I thought bitterly, staring at him. He looked just the same. A little thinner, maybe, with a few more strands of gray in his ponytail, but still, same old Bruce, right down to his smell, to his smile, and the half-laced doodled-on basketball sneakers. "How nice for you," I said.

Bruce didn't take the bait. "So were you in L.A. for work?"

"I had some meetings on the coast," I said. I have always wanted to say that to someone.

"The *Examiner* sent you to California?" he asked.

"No, I had meetings about my screenplay," I said.

"You sold your screenplay?" He seemed genuinely happy for me. "Cannie, that's great!"

I said nothing, glaring at him. Of all the things I needed from him—love, support, money, the bare acknowledgment that I existed, that our baby existed, and that any of it mattered to him, his congratulations felt exceedingly paltry.

"I . . . I'm sorry," he finally managed. And with that I was furious. How rotten of him, I thought, showing up at an airport to take Little Miss Pageboy on vacation, mouthing his pathetic apology, as if it could undo the months of silence, the worry I'd gone through, the anguish of missing him and figuring out how to provide for a baby on my own. And I was furious, too, for his complacency. He didn't care—not about me, not about the baby. He'd never called, never asked, never *cared.* Just left me—left us—all alone. Who did this remind me of?

I knew, at that moment, that my anger wasn't really for him. It was for my father, of course, the Original Abandoner, the author of all of my insecurities and fears. But my father was three thousand miles away from me, with his back eternally turned. If I could only step back and look at it clearly, I'd see that Bruce was just some guy, like a thousand other guys, right down to the pot and the ponytail and the half-intended slipshod lazy life, right down to the dissertation he'd never finish, the bookshelves he'd never build, and the bathtub he'd never clean. Guys like Bruce were as common as white cotton socks sold in six-packs at the Wal-Mart, if not as clean, and all I'd have to do to acquire another one would be to show up at a Phish concert and smile.

But Bruce, as opposed to my father, was right here . . . and he was far from innocent. After all, hadn't he left me, too?

I set Nifkin down and turned to face Bruce, feeling all of my fury—years of it—curl in my chest and rise to my throat. "You're *sorry?*" I spat.

He took a step backward. "I am sorry," he said, and his voice was so sad it sounded like he was being ripped open from the inside. "I know I should have called you, but . . . I just . . ."

I narrowed my eyes. He dropped his hands. "It was just too much," he whispered. "With my father and all."

I rolled my eyes to show what I thought of that excuse, and to make it clear that he and I would not be exchanging tender reminiscences of Bernard Guberman, or anything else, anytime soon.

"I know how strong you are," he told me. "I knew you'd be okay."

"Well, I have to be, don't I, Bruce? You didn't leave me much of a choice."

"I'm sorry," Bruce said again, looking even more wretched. "I . . . I hope you'll be happy."

"I can feel those good wishes radiating right off you," I retorted. "Oh, wait. My mistake. That's just pot smoke." It felt as if a part of me had detached from my body, floated up to the ceiling, and was watching this scene unfold in terror . . . and in great sadness. *Cannie, oh, Cannie,* a little voice mourned, *this isn't who you're angry at.*

"And you know what?" I asked him. "I'm sorry about your father. He was a man. You, you're nothing but a boy with big feet and facial hair. And you're never going to be anything else. You'll never be more than a third-rate writer at a second-rate magazine, and God help you when you can't peddle any more memories of what we had together."

The girlfriend sidled up to his side and laced her fingers through his. I just kept talking. "You'll never be as good as me, and you're always going to know that I was the best you ever had."

The girlfriend attempted to say something, but I wasn't going to stop.

"You're always going to be some big goofy guy with a bunch of tapes in cardboard shoeboxes. The guy with the rolling papers. The guy with the Grateful Dead bootleg. Good old Bruce. Except that shtick gets tired after sophomore year. It gets old, the same way that you're getting old. It's unimproved, just like your writing. And you know what else?" I stepped right up to him, so we were practically toe to toe. "You're *never* going to finish that dissertation. And you're *always* going to live in New Jersey."

Bruce stood there, stunned. His mouth was literally gaping open. It wasn't a good look, emphasizing as it did his weak chin, and the network of wrinkles around his eyes.

The girlfriend looked up at me.

"Leave us alone," she said in a little squeaky voice. My new Manolo Blahnik slides gave me an extra three inches and I felt Amazonian, powerful, untroubled by this little wisp of a thing who barely cleared my shoulders. I gave her my very best shut-up-and-let-the-smart-people-talk look, the one I'd perfected over the years on my siblings. I wondered if she'd ever heard of tweezers. Sure, she could probably be looking at me and wondering whether I'd ever heard of Slim-Fast . . . or of birth control, for that matter. I found that I didn't much care.

"I don't think I was actually saying anything to you," I said, and dredged up a line from the Take Back the Night March, circa 1989. "I don't believe in blaming the victim."

That snapped Bruce back to reality. He tightened his grip on her hand. "Leave her alone," he said.

"Oh, Jesus." I sighed. "Like I'm the one doing anything to either one of you. For your information," I told the girlfriend, "I wrote him exactly one letter when I found out I was pregnant. One letter. And I won't do it again. I've got plenty of money, and a better job than he does, in case he neglected to mention that when he gave you our history, and I'm going to do just fine. I hope the two of you are very happy together." I picked up Nifkin, tossed my great hair, and breezed past a security guard. "I'd search his luggage," I said, loud enough for Bruce to hear, "he's probably holding."

And then, still being pregnant, I went to the bathroom to pee.

My knees felt like water, my cheeks were hot. Hah, I thought. Hah!

I stood, flushed, and opened the cubicle door. And there was the new girlfriend, her arms crossed against her meager chest.

"Yes?" I inquired politely. "You have a comment?"

Her mouth twisted. She had, I noticed, a bit of an overbite.

"You think you're so smart," she said. "He never really loved you. He told me he didn't." Her voice was getting higher. Squeak, squeak, squeak. She sounded like a little stuffed animal, the kind that bleated when you squeezed it.

"Whereas you," I said, "are obviously the real love of his life." I knew, deep in my heart, in my good heart, that whatever quarrel I had, it wasn't with her. But it was as if I couldn't help myself.

Her lip curled, literally curled, like Nifkin's when we played with his fluffy toys.

"Why don't you leave us alone?" she hissed.

"Leave you alone?" I repeated. "Leave you alone? See, this is the theme you keep coming back to, and I don't understand it. I'm not doing anything to either one of you. I live in Philadelphia, for heaven's sake. . . ."

And then I saw it. Something in her face, and I knew what it was.

"He's still talking about me, right?" I asked.

She opened her mouth to say something. I decided I didn't want to stay around and hear it. I was suddenly enormously tired. I ached for sleep, for home, for my bed.

"He doesn't," she began.

"I don't have time for this," I told her, cutting her off. "I've got a life." I tried to walk past her, but she was standing right by the sink, not giving me the room to pass.

"Move," I said shortly.

"No," she said. "No, you listen to me!" She put her hands on my shoulders, trying to get me to hold still, shoving me slightly. One minute I was up, trying to get past her, and the next minute my foot slipped on a puddle of water. My ankle buckled, turning underneath me. And I fell sideways, slamming my belly into the hard edge of the sink.

Bright pain flared, and I was lying on my back, lying on the floor, my ankle twisted at an angle I knew couldn't mean anything good, and she was standing above me, panting like an animal, her cheeks flushed hectic red.

I sat up, putting both palms flat on the floor, and grabbed for the sink, when I felt a sudden tearing cramp. When I looked down and saw that I was bleeding. Not a lot, but . . . well, blood is not something you want to see anywhere below the belt when you're only halfway through month seven.

Somehow I yanked myself to my feet. My ankle hurt so badly I felt sick, and I could feel blood trickling down my leg.

I stared at her. She stared back, following my gaze down to where the blood was falling in thick drips. Then she clapped one hand over her mouth, turned, and ran.

Things were starting to go fuzzy around the edges, and waves of pain were making their way through my belly. I'd read about this. I knew what it meant, and I knew that it was too early, that I was in trouble. "Help," I tried to say, but there was no one there to hear. "Help . . . ," I said again, and then the world went gray, then black.

PART FIVE

Joy

EIGHTEEN

When I opened my eyes, I was underwater. In a swimming pool? The lake at summer camp? The ocean? I wasn't sure. I could see the light above me, filtered through the water, and I could feel the pull of what was underneath me, the dark depths I couldn't make out.

I'd spent most of my life in the water swimming with my mother, but it was my father who'd taught me how, when I was little. He'd flip a silver dollar into the water, and I'd follow it down, learning how to hold my breath, how to go deeper than I thought I could, how to propel myself back to the top. "Sink or swim," my father would tell me when I'd come up empty-handed and sputtering and complaining that I couldn't, that the water was too cold or too deep. *Sink or swim.* And I'd go back into the water. I wanted the silver dollar, but, more than that, I wanted to please him.

My father. Was he here? I turned around frantically, paddling, trying to flip myself up toward where I thought the light was coming from. But I was getting dizzy. I was getting all turned around. And it was hard to keep paddling, hard to stay afloat, and I could feel the bottom of the ocean tugging at me, and I thought how nice it would be just to stop, not to move, to let myself float to the bottom, to sink into the soft silt of a thousand seashells ground down fine, to let myself sleep . . .

Sink or swim. Live or die.

I heard a voice, coming from the surface.

What is your name?

Leave me alone, I thought. *I'm tired. I'm so tired.* I could feel the darkness pulling me, and I craved it.

What is your name?

I opened my eyes, squinting in the bright white light.

Cannie, I muttered. *I'm Cannie, now leave me alone.*

Stay with us, Cannie, said the voice. I shook my head. I didn't want to be here, wherever here was. I wanted to be back in the water, where I was invisible, where I was free. I wanted to go swimming again. I shut my eyes. The silver dollar flashed and glittered in the sunlight, arcing through the air, plunging into the water, and I followed it back down.

I closed my eyes again and saw my bed. Not my bed in Philadelphia, with its soothing blue comforter and bright, pretty pillows, but my bed from when I was a little girl—narrow, neatly made, with its red and brown paisley spread tucked tight around it and a spill of hardcover books shoved underneath. I blinked and saw the girl on the bed, a sturdy, sober-faced girl with green eyes and brown hair in a ponytail that spilled over her shoulders. She was lying on her side, a book spread open before her. Me? I wondered. My daughter? I couldn't be sure.

I remembered that bed—how it had been my refuge as a little girl, how it had been the one place I felt safe as a teenager, the place my father would never come. I remember spending hours there on weekends, sitting cross-legged with a friend on the other side of the bed, with the telephone and a melting pint of ice cream between us, talking about boys, about school, about the future, and how our lives would be, and I wanted to go back there, wanted to go back so badly, before things went wrong, before my father's departure and Bruce's betrayal, before I knew how it all turned out.

I looked down, and the girl on the bed looked up from her book, up at me, and her eyes were wide and clear.

I looked at the girl, and she smiled at me. *Mom,* she said.

* * *

Cannie?

I groaned as if waking from the most delicious dream and slitted my eyes open again.

Squeeze my hand if you can hear this, Cannie.

I squeezed weakly. I could hear voices burbling above me, heard something about blood type, something else about fetal monitor. Maybe this was the dream, and the girl on the bed was real? Or the water? Maybe I really had gone swimming, maybe I'd swum out too far, gotten tired, maybe I was drowning right now, and the picture of my bed was just a little something my brain had whipped up by way of last-minute entertainment.

Cannie? said the voice again, sounding almost frantic. *Stay with us!*

But I didn't want to be there. I wanted to be back in the bed.

The third time I closed my eyes I saw my father. I was back in his office in California, sitting up straight on his white examining table. I could feel the weight of diamonds on my finger, in my ears. I could feel the weight of his gaze upon me—warm and full of love, like I remembered it from twenty years ago. He was sitting across from me, in his white doctor's coat, smiling at me. *Tell me how you've been,* he says. *Tell me how you turned out.*

I'm going to have a baby, I told him, and he nodded. *Cannie, that's wonderful!*

I'm a newspaper reporter. I wrote a movie, I told him. *I have friends. A dog. I live in the city.*

My father smiled. *I'm so proud of you.*

I reached for him and he took my hand and held it. *Why didn't you say so before?* I asked. *It would have changed everything, if I'd just known you cared. . . .*

He smiled at me, looking puzzled, like I'd stopped speaking English, or like he'd stopped understanding it. And when he took his hands away I opened mine and found a silver dollar in my palm. *It's yours,* he said. *You found it. You always did. You always could.*

But even as he spoke he was turning away.

I want to ask you something, I said. He was at the door, like I remembered, his hand on the knob, but this time he turned and looked at me.

I stared at him, feeling my throat go dry, saying nothing.

How could you? is what I thought. *How could you leave your own children?* Lucy was just fifteen, and Josh was only nine. How could you do that; how could you walk away?

Tears slid down my face. My father walked back to me. He pulled a carefully folded handkerchief from his breast pocket, where he always kept them. It smelled like the cologne he always wore, like lemons, and the starch the Chinese laundry place put in, like they always did. Very carefully, my father bent down and wiped away my tears.

Then there was the darkness below me again, and the light above.

Sink or swim, I thought ruefully. And what if I wanted to sink? What was there to keep me afloat?

I thought of my father's hand on my cheek, and I thought of the steady green-eyed gaze of the girl on the bed. I thought about what it felt to take a warm shower after a long bike ride, to slip into the ocean on a hot summer day. I thought about the taste of the tiny strawberries Maxi and I had found at the farmer's market. I thought about my friends, and Nifkin. I thought about my own bed, lined with flannel sheets softened from many trips through the dryer, with a book on the pillow and Nifkin perched beside me. And I thought for a minute about Bruce . . . not about Bruce specifically, but the feeling of falling in love, of being loved, of being worthy. *Treasured,* I heard Maxi say.

So okay, I thought. Fine. I'll swim. For myself, and for my daughter. For all the things I love, and everyone who loves me.

When I woke up again I heard voices.

"That doesn't look right," said one. "Are you sure it's hanging the right way?"

My mother, I thought. Who else?

"What's this yellow stuff?" demanded another voice—young, female, crabby. Lucy. "Probably pudding."

"It's not pudding," I heard in a raspy growl. Tanya.

Then: "Lucy! Get your finger out of your sister's lunch!"

"She's not going to eat it," Lucy said sulkily.

"I don't know why they even brought food," Tanya rumbled.

"Find some ginger ale," said my mother. "And some ice cubes. They said she can have ice cubes when she wakes up."

My mother leaned close. I could smell her—a combination of Chloe and sunscreen and Pert shampoo. "Cannie?" she murmured. I opened my eyes—for real this time—and saw that I wasn't underwater, or in my old bedroom, or in my father's office. I was in a hospital, in a bed. There was an IV taped to the back of my hand, a plastic bracelet with my name on it around my wrist, a semicircle of machines beeping and chirping around me. I lifted my head and saw down to my toes—no belly looming up between my face and my feet.

"Baby," I said. My voice sounded strange and squeaky. Someone stepped out of the shadows. Bruce.

"Hey, Cannie," he said, sounding sheepish, looking wretched, and horribly ashamed.

I waved him away with the hand that didn't have a needle stuck in it. "Not you," I said. "My baby."

"I'll get the doctor," said my mother.

"No, let me," said Tanya. The two of them looked at each other, then hustled out of the room as if by mutual agreement. Lucy shot me a quick unreadable look and dashed out behind them. Which left just me and Bruce.

"What happened?" I asked.

Bruce swallowed hard. "I think maybe the doctor better tell you that."

Now I was starting to remember—the airport, the bathroom, his new girlfriend. Falling. And then blood.

I tried to sit up. Hands eased me back onto the bed.

"What happened?" I demanded, my voice spiraling toward hysteria. "Where am I? Where's my baby? What happened?"

A face leaned into my line of sight—a doctor, no doubt, in a white coat with the obligatory stethoscope and plastic name tag.

"I see you're awake!" he said heartily. I scowled at him. "Tell me your name," he said.

I took a deep breath, suddenly aware that I was hurting. From my belly button on down it felt like I'd been torn open and sewn back together sloppily. My ankle throbbed in time with my heartbeat. "I'm Candace Shapiro," I began, "and I was pregnant . . ." My voice caught in my throat. "What happened?" I begged. "Is my baby okay?"

The doctor cleared his throat. "You had what's known as placenta abruptio," he began. "Which means that your placenta separated from your uterus all at once. That's what caused the bleeding . . . and the premature labor."

"So my baby . . . ," I whispered.

The doctor looked somber.

"Your baby was in distress when they brought you in here. We did a cesarean section, but because we didn't have the fetal monitor in place, we aren't sure whether she was deprived of oxygen, and if so, for how long."

He kept talking. Low birth weight. Premature. Underdeveloped lungs. Ventilator. NICU. He told me that my uterus was torn during the delivery, that I was bleeding so badly, they had to take "radical steps." Radical as in my uterus was now gone. "We hate to have to do this to young women," he said gravely, "but the circumstances left us no choice."

He droned on and on about counseling, therapy, adoption, egg harvesting, and surrogates until I wanted to scream, to claw at his throat, to force him to give me the answer to the only question I cared about anymore. I looked at my mother, who bit her lip and looked away as I struggled to sit up. The doctor looked alarmed, and tried to ease me back down onto my back, but I wasn't going. "My baby," I said. "Is it a boy or girl?"

"A girl," he said—reluctantly, I thought.

"Girl," I repeated, and started to cry. My daughter, I thought, my poor daughter whom I couldn't keep safe, not even on her way into the world. I looked at my mother, who'd come back and was leaning against the wall, blowing her nose. Bruce put his hand awkwardly on my arm.

"Cannie," he said, "I'm sorry."

"Get away from me," I wept. "Just go." I wiped my eyes, shoved my matted hair behind my ears, and looked at the doctor. "I want to see my baby."

They eased me into a wheelchair, sore and stitched up, hurting all over, and wheeled me to the Neonatal Intensive Care Unit. I couldn't go in, they explained, but I could see her through the window. A nurse pointed her out. "There," she said, gesturing.

I leaned so close my forehead pressed on the glass. She was so small. A wrinkled pink grapefruit. Limbs no bigger than my pinky, hands the size of my thumbnail, a head the size of a smallish nectarine. Tiny eyes squinched shut, a look of outrage on her face. A dusting of black fuzz on top of her head, a nondescript beige-ish hat on top of that. "She weighs almost three pounds," the nurse who was pushing me said.

Baby, I whispered, and tapped my fingers against the windows, drumming a soft rhythm. She hadn't been moving, but when I tapped she pinwheeled her arms. Waving at me, I imagined. *Hi, baby,* I said.

The nurse watched me closely. "You okay?"

"She needs a better hat," I said. My throat felt thick, clotted with grief, and there were tears running down my face, but I wasn't crying. It was more like leaking. As if I was so full of sadness and a strange, doomed kind of hope that there was nowhere for it to go but out. "At home, in her room, the yellow room with the crib, in the dresser, the top drawer, I've got lots of baby hats. My Mom has keys. . . ."

The nurse leaned down. "I have to bring you back," she said.

"Please make them give her a nicer hat," I repeated. Stupid, stubborn. She didn't need fashionable headgear, she needed a miracle, and even I could see that.

The nurse bent closer. "Tell me her name," she said. And sure enough, there was a piece of paper taped to one end of the box. "BABY GIRL SHAPIRO," it read.

I opened my mouth, not sure what would happen, but when the word came I knew instantly, in my heart, that it was right.

"Joy," I said. "Her name is Joy."

When I came back to my room Maxi was there. A quartet of candy-stripers clustered at the door of my room, their faces like blossoms, or balloons packed tight together. Maxi pulled a white curtain close around my bed, shutting them out. She was dressed more soberly than I'd ever seen her—black jeans, black sneakers, a hooded sweatshirt—and she was carrying roses, a ridiculous armload of roses, the kind of garland you'd drape around a prizewinning horse's neck. Or lay across a casket, I thought grimly.

"I came as soon as I heard," she said, her face drawn. "Your mother and sister are outside. They'll only let one of us in at a time."

She sat beside me and held my hand, the one with the tube in it, and didn't seem alarmed when I didn't look at her, or even squeeze back. "Poor Cannie," she said. "Have you seen the baby?"

I nodded, brushing tears from my cheeks. "She's very small," I managed, and started to sob.

Maxi winced, looking helpless, and dismayed at being helpless.

"Bruce came," I said, weeping.

"I hope you told him to go to hell," said Maxi.

"Something like that," I said. I wiped my non-needled hand across my face and wished for Kleenex. "This is disgusting," I said, and hiccoughed a sob. "This is really pathetic and disgusting."

Maxi leaned close, cradling my head in her arm. "Oh, Cannie," she said sadly. I closed my eyes. There was nothing left for me to ask, nothing else to say.

After Maxi left I slept for a while, curled up on my side. If I had any dreams, I didn't remember them. And when I woke up Bruce was standing in the doorway.

I blinked and stared at him.

"Can I do anything?" he asked. I just stared, saying nothing. "Cannie?" he asked uneasily.

"Come closer," I beckoned. "I don't bite. Or push," I added meanly. Bruce walked toward my bed. He looked pale, edgy, twitchy in his own skin, or maybe just unhappy to be near me again. I could see a sprinkling of blackheads on his nose, standing out in sharp relief, and I could tell from his posture, from the way his hands were crammed in his pockets and how his eyes never left the linoleum, that this was killing him, that he wanted to be anywhere but here. *Good,* I thought, feeling rage bubble up in my chest. Good. Let him hurt.

He settled himself on the chair next to my bed, looking at me in quick little peeks—the drainage tubes snaking out from beneath my sheet, the I.V. bag hanging beside me. I hoped that he was sickened by it. I hoped that he was scared.

"I can tell you exactly how many days it's been since we talked," I said.

Bruce closed his eyes.

"I can tell you exactly what your bedroom looks like, exactly what you said the last time we were together."

He grabbed for me, clutching blindly. "Cannie, please," he said. "Please. I'm sorry." Words I once thought I would have given anything to hear. He started crying. "I never wanted . . . I never meant for this to happen. . . ."

I looked at him. I didn't feel love, or hate. I didn't feel anything but a bone-deep weariness. Like I was suddenly a hundred years old, and I knew at that moment I would have to live a hundred more years, carrying my grief around like a backpack full of stones.

I closed my eyes, knowing that it was too late for us. Too much had happened, and none of it was good. A body in motion stays in motion. I'd started the whole thing by telling him I'd wanted to take a break. Or maybe he'd started it by asking me out in the first place. What did it matter anymore?

I turned my face to the wall. After a while, Bruce stopped crying. And a while after that, I heard him leave.

I woke up the next morning with sunlight spilling across my face. Instantly my mother hurried through the door and pulled a chair up

beside my bed. She looked uncomfortable—she was good about cracking jokes, laughing things off, keeping a stiff upper lip and soldiering
on, but she wasn't any good with tears.

"How are you doing?" she asked.

"I'm shitty!" I shrieked, and my mother pulled back so fast that her
wheeled chair scooted halfway across the room. I didn't even wait for
her to pull herself back toward me before continuing my tirade. "How
do you think I am? I gave birth to something that looks like a junior-
high science experiment, and I'm all cut open and I h-h-hurt . . ."

I put my face in my hands and sobbed for a minute. "There's
something wrong with me," I wept. "I'm defective. You should have
let me die. . . ."

"Oh, Cannie," my mother said, "Cannie, don't talk that way."

"Nobody loves me," I cried. "Dad didn't, Bruce didn't . . ."

My mother patted my hair. "Don't talk that way," she repeated.
"You have a beautiful baby. A little on the petite side, for the time
being, but very beautiful." She cleared her throat, got to her feet, and
started pacing—typical Mom behavior when there was something
painful coming.

"Sit down," I told her wearily, and she did, but I could see one of
her feet jiggling anxiously.

"I had a talk with Bruce," she said.

I exhaled sharply. I didn't even want to hear his name. My mother
could tell this from my face, but she kept talking.

"With Bruce," she continued, "and his new girlfriend."

"The Pusher?" I asked, my voice high and sharp and hysterical.
"You saw her?"

"Cannie, she feels just awful. They both do."

"They should," I said angrily. "Bruce never even called me, the
whole time I was pregnant, then the Pusher does her thing . . ."

My mother looked shaken by my tone. "The doctors aren't sure
that's what caused you to . . ."

"It doesn't matter," I said querulously. "I believe that's what did it,
and I hope that dumb bitch does, too."

My mother was shocked. "Cannie . . ."

"Cannie what? You think I'm going to forgive them? I'll never forgive them. My baby almost died, I almost died, I'll never have another baby, and now just because they're sorry, it's all supposed to be okay? I'll never forgive them. Never."

My mother sighed. "Cannie," she said gently.

"I can't believe you're taking their side!" I yelled.

"I'm not taking their side, Cannie, of course I'm not," she said. "I'm taking your side. I just don't think it's healthy for you to be so angry."

"Joy almost died," I said.

"But she didn't," said my mother. "She didn't die. She's going to be fine. . . ."

"You don't know that," I said furiously.

"Cannie," said my mother. "She's a little underweight, and her lungs are a little underdeveloped . . ."

"She was deprived of oxygen! Didn't you hear them! Deprived of oxygen! There could be all kinds of things wrong!"

"She looks just the way you did when you were a baby," my mother said impatiently. "She's going to be fine. I just know it."

"You didn't even know you were gay until you were fifty-six!" I shouted. "How am I supposed to believe you about anything!"

I pointed toward the door. "Go away," I said, and started to cry.

My mother shook her head. "I'm not going," she said. "Talk to me."

"What do you want to hear about?" I said, trying to wipe my face off, trying to sound normal. "My my asshole ex-boyfriend's idiot new girlfriend pushed me, and my baby almost died. . . ."

But what was really wrong—the part that I didn't think I'd be able to bring myself to say—was that I had failed Joy. I'd failed to be good enough, pretty enough, thin enough, lovable enough, to keep my father in my life. Or to keep Bruce. And now, I'd failed at keeping my baby safe.

My mother wheeled in close again and wrapped her arms around me.

"I didn't deserve her," I wept. "I couldn't keep her safe, I let her get hurt . . ."

"What gave you that idea?" she whispered into my hair. "Cannie, it was an accident. It wasn't your fault. You're going to be a wonderful mother."

"If I'm so great, why didn't he love me?" I wept, and I wasn't even sure who I was talking about—Bruce? My father? "What's wrong with me?"

My mother stood up. I followed her eyes to the clock on the wall. She watched me watching, and bit her lip. "I'm sorry," she said softly, "but I have to run out for a few minutes."

I wiped my eyes, buying time, trying to process what she'd told me. "You have to . . ."

"I have to pick up Tanya at her continuing education class."

"What, Tanya forgot how to drive?"

"Her car's in the shop."

"And what is she studying today? Which facet of herself is she addressing?" I inquired. "Codependent granddaughters of emotionally distant grandparents?"

"Give it a rest, Cannie," my mother snapped, and I was so stunned that I couldn't even think to start crying again. "I know you don't like her, and I'm sick of hearing about it."

"Oh, and now is the time you decided to bring it up? You couldn't wait until maybe your granddaughter makes it out of intensive care?"

My mother pursed her lips. "I'll talk to you later," she said, and walked out the door. With her hand on the doorknob, she turned to face me one more time. "I know you don't believe it, but you're going to be fine. You have everything you need. You just have to know it in your own heart."

I scowled. *Know it in my own heart.* It sounded like New Age crap, like something she'd pirated from one of Tanya's stupid *Healing Your Hurt* workbooks.

"Sure," I called after her. "Go! I'm good at being left. I'm used to it."

She didn't turn around. I sighed, staring at my blanket and hoping none of the nurses had heard me spouting third-rate soap opera dialogue. I felt absolutely wretched. I felt hollow, like my insides had been scooped out and all that was left was echoing emptiness, vacant black holes. How was I going to figure out how to be a decent parent, given the choices my own parents had made?

You have everything you need, she'd told me. But I couldn't see what she meant. I considered my life and saw only what was missing—no father, no boyfriend, no promise of health or comfort for my daughter. Everything I need, I thought ruefully, and closed my eyes, hoping that I'd dream again of my bed, or of the water.

When the door opened again an hour later I didn't even look up. "Tell it to Tanya," I said, with my eyes still shut. "'Cause I don't want to hear it."

"Well, I would," said a familiar deep voice, "but I don't think she has much use for my kind . . . and also, we haven't really been introduced."

I looked up. Dr. K. was standing there, with a white bakery box in one hand and a black duffel bag in the other. And the duffel bag appeared to be wriggling.

"I came as soon as I heard," he began, folding himself into the seat my mother had recently occupied, setting the box on my nightstand and the duffel bag on his lap. "How are you feeling?"

"Okay," I said. He looked at me carefully. "Well, actually lousy."

"I can believe it, after what you've been through. How is . . ."

"Joy," I said. Using her name felt strange . . . presumptuous somehow, as if I was testing fate by saying it out loud. "She's small, and her lungs are a little underdeveloped, and she's breathing with a ventilator . . ." I paused and swiped a hand across my eyes. "Also, I had a hysterectomy, and I seem to be crying all the time."

He cleared his throat.

"Was that too much information?" I asked through my tears.

He shook his head. "Not at all," he told me. "You can talk to me about anything you want to."

The black duffel bag practically lurched off his lap. It looked so funny I almost smiled, but it felt as if my face had forgotten how. "Is that a perpetual motion machine in your bag, or are you just glad to see me?"

Dr. K. glanced over his shoulder at the closed door. Then he leaned close to me. "This was kind of a risk," he whispered, "but I thought . . ."

He lifted the bag onto the bed and eased the zipper open. Nifkin's nose popped out, followed by the tips of his oversized ears, and then, in short order, his entire body.

"Nifkin!" I said, as Nifkin scrambled onto my chest and proceeded to give my entire face a tongue-bath. Dr. K held him, lifting him clear of my various tubes and attachments, as Nifkin licked away. "How did you . . . where was he?"

"With your friend Samantha," he explained. "She's outside."

"Thank you," I said, knowing that the words couldn't begin to express how happy he'd made me. "Thank you so much."

"No problem," said the doctor. "Here . . . look. We've been practicing." He lifted Nifkin and set him on the floor. "Can you see?"

I propped myself up on my elbows and nodded.

"Nifkin . . . SIT!" said Dr. K., in a voice every bit as deep and authoritative as James Earl Jones's telling the world that this . . . is CNN. Nifkin's butt hit the linoleum at lightning speed, his tail wagging triple-time. "Nifkin . . . DOWN!" And down went Nifkin, flat on his belly, looking up at Dr. K. with his eyes sparkling and his pink tongue curled as he panted. "And now, for our final act . . . PLAY DEAD!" And Nifkin collapsed onto his side as if he'd been shot.

"Unbelievable," I said. It really was.

"He's a fast learner," said Dr. K., loading the now-squirming terrier back into the duffel bag. He bent back to me. "Feel better, Cannie," he said, and rested one of his hands on top of mine.

He walked out and Samantha walked in, hurrying over to my bed. She was in full lawyer garb—a sleek black suit, high-heeled boots, a caramel-colored leather attaché case in one hand and her sunglasses and car keys in the other. "Cannie," she said, "I came . . ."

". . . as soon as you heard," I supplied.

"How do you feel?" asked Sam. "How's the baby?"

"I feel okay, and the baby . . . well, she's in the baby intensive-care place. They have to wait and see."

Samantha sighed. I closed my eyes. I suddenly felt completely exhausted. And hungry.

I sat up, tucking another pillow behind my back. "Hey, what time is it? When's dinner? You don't have, like, a banana in your purse or something?"

Samantha rose to her feet, grateful, I thought, to have something to do. "I'll go check . . . hey, what's this?"

She pointed at the bakery box that Dr. K. had left behind.

"Don't know," I said. "Dr. K. brought it. Take a look."

Sam ripped through the string and opened the box, and there, inside, was an éclair from the Pink Rose Pastry Shop, a wedge of chocolate bread pudding from Silk City, a brownie still in its Le Bus wrapping paper, and a pint of fresh raspberries.

"Unbelievable," I murmured.

"Yum!" said Samantha. "How does he know what you like?"

"I told him," I said, touched that he'd remember. "For Fat Class, we had to write down what our favorite foods were." Sam cut me a sliver of éclair, but it tasted like dust and stones in my mouth. I swallowed to be polite, sipped some water, then told her that I was tired, that I wanted to sleep.

I stayed in the hospital another week, healing, while Joy got bigger and stronger.

Maxi showed up every morning for a week and sat beside me and read from *People, In Style,* and *Entertainment Weekly* magazines, embroidering each story from her own personal stash of anecdotes. My mother and sister stayed with me in the daytime, making conversation, trying not to linger too long at the pauses that came where I would normally be saying something smart-ass. Samantha came every night after work and regaled me with Philadelphia gossip, about the antiquated former stars Gabby had interviewed and the how Nifkin had taken to stopping, mid-walk, and planting himself in front of my apartment building and refusing to budge. Andy came with his wife and a box of Famous Fourth Street chocolate chip cookies and a card that everyone in the newsroom had signed. "Get Well Soon," it read.

I didn't think that would be happening, but I didn't tell him that.

"They're worried about you," Lucy whispered when my mother was in the hall, talking about something with the nurses.

I looked at her and shrugged.

"They want you to talk to a psychiatrist."

I said nothing. Lucy looked very serious. "It's Dr. Melburne," she said. "I had her for a while. She's horrible. You better cheer up and start talking more, or else she's going to ask you about your childhood."

"Cannie doesn't have to talk if she doesn't want to," said my mother, pouring a cup of ginger ale that nobody would drink. She straightened my flowers, plumped my pillows for the fourteenth time, sat down, then got up again, looking for something else to do. "Cannie can just rest."

Three days later, Joy took her first breaths without the ventilator.

Not out of the woods yet, the doctors warned me. Have to wait and see. She could be fine, or things could go wrong, but probably she'll be okay.

And they let me hold her, finally, lifting up her four-pound-six-ounce body and cradling her close, running my fingertips over each of her hands, each fingernail impossibly small and perfect. She clutched at my finger fiercely with her own tiny ones. I could feel the bones, the push of her blood beneath her skin. *Hang on,* I thought to her. *Hang in there, little one. The world is hard a lot of the time, but there're good things here, too. And I love you. Your mother loves you, baby Joy.*

I sat with her for hours until they made me go back to bed, and before I left I filled out her birth certificate, and my handwriting was clear and firm. Joy Leah Shapiro. The Leah was for Leonard, Bruce's father's middle name. Leah, the second sister, the one Jacob didn't want to marry. Leah, the trick bride, the one her father sent down the aisle in disguise.

I bet Leah had a more interesting life anyhow, I whispered to my baby, holding her hand, with me in my wheelchair and her in her glass box that I forced myself not to see as a coffin. I bet Leah went on hiking trips with her girlfriends and had popcorn and Margaritas for dinner, if that's what she wanted. I'll bet she went swimming naked and slept under the stars. Rachel probably bought Celine Dion CDs and those Franklin Mint collectible plates. She was probably boring, even to herself. She never went on an adventure, never took a chance. But you and me, baby, we're going to go on adventures. I will teach you how to swim, and how to sail, and how to build a fire . . . everything my mother taught me, and everything else I've learned. Just make it out of here, I thought, as hard as I could. Come home, Joy, and we'll both be fine.

Two days later, I got part of my wish. They sent me home, but decided to keep Joy. "Just for another few weeks," said the doctor, in what I'm sure he imagined was a comforting tone. "We want to make sure that her lungs are mature . . . and that she's gained enough weight."

I burst into bitter laughter at that one. "If she takes after her mother," I announced, "that shouldn't be a problem. She'll gain weight like a champ."

The doctor gave me what he no doubt believed was a comforting pat on the shoulder. "Don't worry," he said. "Things should be fine."

I limped out of the hospital, blinking, in the warm May sunshine, and eased myself into my mother's car, sitting quietly as we drove back home. I saw the leaves, the fresh green grass, the St. Peter's schoolgirls in crisp plaid jumpers. I saw, but didn't see. To me, the whole world looked gray. It was as if there was no room inside of me for anything except fury and fear.

My mother and Lucy unloaded my bags from the trunk and walked me to my building. Lucy carried my bags. My mother walked slowly beside me, and Tanya huffed behind us. My leg muscles felt wobbly and underused. My stitches ached, my ankle itched in its walking cast. It turned out that I'd only sprained my ankle when I'd fallen, but nobody had thought to look at my legs until days later, so the foot had stayed bent, and the tendons stayed torn, which meant a walking cast for six weeks: small potatoes, in relation to everything else I was dealing with.

I fumbled through my purse. My wallet, the half-empty pack of chewing gum, a Chap Stick and a book of matches from the Star Bar looked like relics from another life. I was groping for my keys when Lucy put her key into the first-floor door.

"I don't live here," I said.

"You do now," said Lucy. She was beaming at me. My mother and Tanya were, too.

I limped across the threshold, my cast thumping on the hardwood floors, and stepped inside, blinking.

The apartment—a twin of mine up on the third floor, all dark wood and circa 1970s fixtures—had been transformed.

Sunlight streamed in from windows that hadn't been there before, sparkling on the pristine, polished maple floors that had been neither pristine nor polished nor maple when I'd last seen the place.

I walked slowly into the kitchen, moving as if I were underwater. New cabinets stained the color of clover honey. In the living room were a new couch and love seat, overstuffed and comfortable, upholstered in buttery yellow denim—pretty, but sturdy, I remember telling Maxi, as I pointed out things I coveted in the latest issue of *Martha Stewart Living* one lazy afternoon. A beautiful woven rug in garnet and dark blue and gold covered the floor. There was a flat-screen TV and a brand new stereo in the corner, stacks of brand-new baby books on the shelves.

Lucy was practically dancing, beside herself with joy. "Can you believe it, Cannie? Isn't it amazing?"

"I don't know what to say," I told her, moving down the hall. The bathroom was unrecognizable. The Carter administration-era pastel wallpaper, the ugly dark wood vanity, the cheap stainless steel fixtures, and the cracked toilet bowl—all gone. Everything was white tile, with gold and navy accents. The tub was a whirlpool bath, with two showerheads, in case, I guessed, I wanted to bathe with a partner. There were new glass-fronted cabinets, fresh lilies in a vase, a profusion of the thickest towels I ever felt stacked on a brand-new shelf. A tiny white tub for giving the baby a bath sat on one counter, along with an assortment of bath toys, little sponges cut into the shapes of animals, and a family of rubber duckies.

"Wait until you see the baby's room!" Lucy crowed.

The walls were painted Lemonade Stand yellow, just the way I'd done them upstairs, and I recognized the crib that Dr. K. had put together. But the rest of the furniture was new. I saw an ornate changing table, a dresser, a white wood rocking chair. "Antiques," Tanya breathed, running one thick fingertip along the curved whitewashed wood that was tinged very faintly pink. There were framed pictures on the walls—a mermaid swimming in the ocean, a sailboat, elephants marching two by two. And in the corner was what looked like the world's smallest branch of Toys "R" Us. There was every toy I'd ever seen, plus a few I hadn't. A set of building blocks. Rattles. Balls. Toys that talked, or barked, or cried, when you squeezed them, or pulled their strings. The exact same rocking horse I'd admired in a shop in Santa Monica two months ago. Everything.

I sank slowly down into the yellow denim love seat, underneath the hanging mobile of delicate stars and clouds and crescent moons, next to a three-foot-high Paddington Bear.

"There's more," said Lucy.

"You won't even believe it," said my mother.

I wandered back to the bedroom. My plain metal bedframe had been replaced with a magnificent wrought-iron canopy bed. My pink sheets had been swapped for something gorgeous—rich stripes of white and gold, tiny pink flowers.

"That's two-hundred-thread-count cotton," Lucy boasted, ticking off the merits of my new linens, pointing out the pillow shams and dust ruffle, the hand-knotted carpet (yellow, with a border of pink roses) on the floor, opening the closet to show off yet more of the pinkish-whitewashed antique furniture—a nine-drawer dresser, a bedside table topped with a gorgeous spray of daffodils in a blue ginger jar.

"Open the blinds," said Lucy.

I did. There was a new deck outside the bedroom window. There was a big clay pot of geraniums and petunias, benches and a picnic table, a gas grill the size of a Volkswagen Bug in the corner.

I sat down—collapsed, really—onto the bed. There was a tiny

card on the pillow, the kind you'd get with a bouquet of flowers. I slid it open with my thumbnail.

"Welcome home," it read on one side. "From your friends," said the other.

My mother and Lucy and Tanya stood in a line, regarding me, waiting to hear my approval.

"Who . . . ," I started. "How . . ."

"Your friends," said Lucy impatiently.

"Maxi?"

The three of them exchanged a sneaky look.

"Come on, you guys. It's not like I've got other friends who could afford all this."

"We couldn't stop her!" Lucy said.

"Really, Cannie, that's true," said my mother. "She wasn't taking no for an answer. She knows all of these contractors . . . she hired a decorator to find you all these things . . . there were people working in here, like, around the clock . . . "

"My neighbors must have loved that," I said.

"Do you like it?" asked Lucy.

"It's . . ." I lifted my hands, and let them sink into my lap. My heart was beating too fast, pushing pain into every part of my body that hurt. I thought of the word that I needed. "It's amazing," I finally said.

"So what do you want to do?" asked Lucy. "We could go to Dmitri's for dinner . . ."

"There's a documentary about lesbians of size at the Ritz," rasped Tanya.

"Shopping?" asked my mother. "Maybe you want to stock up on groceries while we're here to help you carry things."

I got to my feet. "I think I'd like to go for a walk," I said.

My mother and Lucy and Tanya looked at me curiously.

"A walk?" my mother repeated.

"Cannie," my sister pointed out, "your foot's still in a cast."

"It's a walking cast, isn't it?" I snapped. "And I feel like walking."

I got to my feet. I wanted to exult in this. I wanted to feel happy. I was surrounded by the people I loved; I had a beautiful place to live. But I felt like I was looking at my new apartment through a dirty mirror, like I was feeling the crisp cottons and plush carpets through thick rubber gloves. It was Joy—not having Joy. None of this would feel right until my baby came home, I thought, and I was suddenly so angry that my arms and legs felt weak with the force of it, and my fists and feet tingled with the desire to hit and kick. Bruce, I thought, Bruce and the goddamn fucking Pusher. This should be my triumph, goddammit, except how can I be happy with my baby still in the hospital, when Bruce and his new girlfriend were the ones who put her there?

"Fine," said my mother uneasily. "So we'll walk."

"No," I said. "By myself. I want to be by myself right now."

They all looked puzzled, even worried, as they filed out the door.

"Call me," said my mother. "Let me know when you're ready for Nifkin to come back."

"I will," I lied. I wanted them out already, out of my house, my hair, my life. I felt like I was burning up, like I had to move or explode. I stared out the window until they'd all piled in the car and driven off. Then I pulled on a jogging bra, a ratty T-shirt, a pair of shorts, a single sneaker, and thumped out of the house and onto the hot sidewalks, determined not to think about my father, about Bruce, about my baby, about anything. I would just walk. And then, maybe, I'd be able to sleep again.

May drifted into June, and all of my days were built around Joy. I'd go to the hospital first thing in the morning, walking the thirty blocks to the Children's Hospital of Philadelphia as the sun came up. Robed and masked and gloved, I'd sit beside her on a sterile rocking chair in the NICU, holding her tiny hand, brushing her lips with my fingertips, singing her the songs we'd danced to months before. Those were the only moments I didn't feel the rage consuming me; the only times I could breathe.

And when I felt the anger coming back, when I'd feel my chest tightening and my hands wanting to hit something, I'd leave her. I'd go home to pace the floors and pump my breasts, to clean and scrub floors and counters that I'd cleaned and scrubbed the day before. And I'd take long, furious walks through the city, with my ankle in the increasingly filthy walking cast, charging through yellow lights and shooting evil glances at any car that dared inch toward the intersection.

I got used to the little voice in my head, the one from the airport, the one that had floated up to the ceiling and watched me rage at Bruce while mourning quietly that he wasn't the one. I got used to the voice asking *Why?* every morning, when I laced up my sneakers and yanked a succession of nondescript shirts over my head . . . and asking *Why?* again at night, when I'd play my messages back—ten, fifteen messages from my mother, my sister, from Maxi, and Peter Krushelevansky, from all of my friends—and then erase each one without ever calling back, until the day I started erasing them without even listening. *You're too sad,* the voice would murmur, as I stomped up Walnut Street. *Take it easy,* said the voice, as I gulped scalding black coffee, cup after cup, for breakfast. *Talk to someone,* said the voice. *Let them help.* I ignored it. Who could help me now? What was there left for me but the streets and the hospital, my silent apartment, and my empty bed?

I let the voice mail keep taking my calls. I instructed the post office that I would be out of town for an indefinite period and to please hold my mail. I let my computer gather dust. I stopped checking my e-mail. And on one of my walks I dropped my pager into the Delaware River without missing a single step. The cast came off, and I started going on even longer walks—four hours, six hours, meandering loops through the city's worst neighborhoods, past crack dealers, hookers of the male and female variety, dead pigeons in gutters, the burned-out skeletons of cars, without seeing any of it, and without being afraid. How could any of this hurt me, after what I'd already lost? When I ran into Samantha on the street, I told her I was too busy to hang out, shifting from foot to foot with my eyes on the horizon so I wouldn't have to see her worried face. Getting things ready, I explained, waiting to be off again. The baby's coming home soon.

"Can I see her?" Sam asked.

Instantly, I shook my head. "I'm not ready . . . I mean, she's not ready."

"What do you mean, Cannie?" asked Sam.

"She's medically fragile," I said, trying out the term I'd heard over and over in the baby intensive care ward.

"So I'll stand outside and look at her through the window," said Sam, looking perplexed. "And then we'll go have breakfast. Remember breakfast? It used to be one of your favorite meals."

"I've got to go," I said brusquely, trying to edge my way around her. Samantha didn't budge.

"Cannie, what is going on with you, really?"

"Nothing," I said, shoving past her, my feet already moving, my eyes fixed far ahead. "Nothing, nothing, everything is fine."

NINETEEN

I walked and walked, and it was as if God had fitted me with special glasses, where I could only see the bad things, the sad things, the pain and misery of life in the city, the trash kicked into corners instead of the flowers planted in window boxes. I could see husbands and wives fighting, but not kissing or holding hands. I could see little kids careering through the streets on stolen bicycles, screaming insults and curses, and grown men who sounded like they were breakfasting on their own mucus, leering at women with unashamed, lecherous eyes. I could smell the stink of the city in summer: horse piss and hot tar and the grayish, sick exhaust the buses spewed. The manhole covers leaked steam, the sidewalks belched heat from the subways churning below.

Everywhere I looked, I just saw emptiness, loneliness, buildings with broken windows, shambling addicts with outstretched hands and dead eyes, sorrow and filth and rot.

I thought that time would heal me and that the miles would soothe my pain. I waited for a morning where I woke up and didn't instantly imagine Bruce and the Pusher dying horrible gruesome deaths . . . or, worse yet, losing my baby, losing Joy.

I would walk to the hospital at the break of dawn and sometimes before, and walk laps around the parking lot until I felt calm enough to walk inside. I would sit in the cafeteria gulping cup after cup of water, trying to smile and look normal, but inside, my head was spinning furiously, thinking knives? guns? car accident? I would smile and say hello, but really, in my head I was plotting revenge.

I imagined calling the university where Bruce had taught freshman English and telling them how he'd only passed his drug test by ingesting quarts and quarts of warm water spiked with goldenseal that he bought from a 1-800 line in the back pages of *High Times*. Urine Luck, the stuff was called. I could tell them he was showing up stoned at work—he used to do it, probably he still was doing it, and if they watched him long enough they'd see. I could call his mother, call the police in his town, have him arrested, taken away.

I imagined writing to *Moxie*, including a picture of Joy in the NICU, growing bigger, growing stronger, but still a pathetic sight, run through with tubes, breathing on a ventilator more often than not, with who knew what horrors strewn in her future—cerebral palsy, learning disabilities, blind, deaf, retarded, a menu of disasters that the doctors hadn't mentioned. I'd gone online, to sites with names like preemie.com, reading first-person stories from parents whose children had survived, horribly damaged; who'd come home on oxygen or sleep apnea monitors or with holes cut in their throats so they could breathe. I read about kids who grew up with seizure disorders, learning disabilities, who never quite caught up, never quite got right. And I read stories about the babies who died: at birth, in the NICU, at home. "Our Precious Angel," they'd be headlined. "Our Darling Daughter."

I wanted to copy these stories and e-mail them to the Pusher, along with a photograph of Joy. I wanted to send her a picture of my daughter—no letter, no words, just Joy's picture, sent to her house, sent to her school, sent to her boss, to her parents if I could find them, to show them all what she'd done, what she'd been responsible for. I found myself planning walking routes that would bring me by gun shops. I found myself looking in their windows. I didn't go inside yet, but I knew that was next. And then what?

I didn't let myself answer the question. I didn't let myself think beyond the image, the picture that I treasured: Bruce's face when he opened his door and saw me standing there with a gun in my hand; Bruce's face when I said, "I'll show you sorry."

Then one morning I was burning past a newsstand and I saw the new issue of *Moxie*, the August issue, even though it was only just July, and so hot that the air shimmered and the streets turned sticky in the sun. I yanked a copy off the rack.

"Miss, you gonna pay for that?"

"No," I snarled, "I'm going to rob you." I tossed two bucks and change on the counter and started flipping furiously through the pages, wondering what the headline would be. "My Daughter the Vegetable?" "How to Really, Really Screw Up Your Ex's Life?"

Instead I saw a single word, big black letters, a somber incongruity in *Moxie*'s light-hearted, pastel-heavy lineup. "Complications," it said.

"Pregnant," says the letter, and I can't read any more. It's as if the very word has poleaxed me and left me paralyzed, save for the icy crawling along the back of my neck, the beginning of dread.

"I don't know an easy way to say this," she has written, "so I'll just say it. I am pregnant."

I remember sixteen years ago standing on the bimah in my synagogue in Short Hills, looking over the crowd of friends and relatives and mouthing those time-honored words, "Today I am a man." Now, feeling this rush of ice to my stomach, feeling my palms start to sweat, I know the truth: Today, I am a man. For real, this time.

"Not quite," I said, so loudly that the homeless people loping along the sidewalks stopped and stared. Not hardly. A man. A man would have called me. At least sent a postcard! I turned my attention back to the page.

But I'm not a man. As it turns out, what I am is a coward. I tuck the letter in a notebook, stuff the notebook in a desk drawer, lock the drawer, and accidentally on purpose, lose the key.

They say—they being the great philosophers, or possibly the cast of *Seinfeld*—that breaking up is like pushing over a Coke machine. You can't just do it, you have to set the thing in motion, rock it back and forth a few times. For C. and me it wasn't like that. It was a clean, swift break—a thunderclap. Intense and awful and over in seconds.

Liar, I thought. Oh, you liar. It wasn't a thunderclap, it wasn't even a breakup, I just told you I wanted some time!

Then, less than three months later, my father died.

I went back and forth with the telephone in my hand, her number still first on my speed-dial. Call her? Don't call her? Was she my ex or my friend?

In the end I opted for her friendship. And later, when a houseful of mourners picked over deli trays in my mother's kitchen, I opted for more

And now, three months later, I am still mourning my father, but I'm feeling as if I'm over C., truly and completely. I know what real sadness is now. I can explore it every night like a kid who's lost a tooth and can't stop tonguing the pulpy, wounded, empty space where the tooth once was.

Except now she's pregnant.

And I don't know whether she's set out to trick me or trap me, whether I'm even the father, whether she's pregnant at all.

"Oh, this is unbelievable," I announced to Broad Street at large. "This is fucking unbelievable!"

And, the thing is, I'm too chicken to ask.

It's your choice, I imagine I say with my silence. Your call, your game, your move. I manage to silence the part of me that wonders, that wants to know how she chose: whether she went to the clinic on Locust Street and marched past the protestors with their pictures of bloody dead babies; whether she did it in a doctors' office, whether she went with a friend, or a new lover, or alone. Or whether she's marching around her hometown right now with a belly as big as a beachball and books full of baby names.

I don't ask, or call. I don't send a check, or a letter, or even a card. I'm done, empty, dried out and cried out. There's nothing left for her or for a baby if there is one.

When I let myself think about it I get furious at myself (how could I have been so dumb?) and furious at her (how could she have let me?). But I try not to let myself think of it too much. I wake up, work out, go to the office, and go through the motions, try to keep the tip of my tongue away from that hole in my smile. But deep down I know that I can only postpone this so long, that even my cowardice can't stave off the inevitable. Somewhere in my desk, tucked in a notebook and locked in a drawer, there's a letter with my name on it.

"You're late!" the head nurse scolded, and smiled at me to show she didn't mean it. I had the copy of *Moxie* curled up like I meant to smack a dog with it. "Here," I said, handing it off. She barely spared it a glance. "I don't read this stuff," she said. "It's worthless."

"I agree," I said, heading toward the nursery.

"There's someone here to see you," she said.

I walked to the nursery and sure enough, there was a woman standing at my window, the window in front of Joy's Isolette. I could see short, impeccably coiffed gray hair, an elegant black pantsuit, a platinum diamond tennis bracelet around one wrist. A light whiff of Allure was in the air, her freshly polished fingernails glittered under the fluorescent lights. The Ever-Tasteful Audrey had put together just the right ensemble for going to visit her son's illegitimate premature firstborn.

"What are you doing here?" I demanded.

Audrey gasped and took two giant steps backward. Her face went two shades paler than her Estée Lauder foundation.

"Cannie!" she said, and pressed one hand against her chest. "I . . . you scared me."

I stared at her, saying nothing, as her eyes moved over me, unbelieving.

"You're so thin," she finally said.

I looked down and observed with not much interest that this was true. All that walking, all that plotting, my only food a snatched bite of bagel or banana and cup after cup of bitter black coffee, because the taste matched the way I felt inside. My refrigerator held bottles of breast milk and nothing else. I couldn't remember the last time I sat down and ate a meal. I could see the bones in my face, the jut of my hipbones. In profile, I was Jessica Rabbit: nonexistent butt, flat belly, improbable bosom, thanks to the milk. If you didn't get close enough to notice that my hair was dirty and matted, that I had giant black circles under my eyes and that, most likely, I smelled bad, I was an actual babe.

The irony had not been lost on me: After a lifetime of obsession, of calorie counting, Weight Watching, and StairMastering, I'd found a way to shed those unwanted pounds forever! To free myself of flab and cellulite! To get the body I'd always wanted! I should market this, I thought hysterically. The Placenta Abruptio Emergency Hysterectomy Premature and Possibly Brain-Damaged Baby Diet. I'd make a fortune.

Audrey fingered her bracelet nervously. "I guess you're wondering . . . ," she began. I said nothing, knowing exactly how hard this was for her. Knowing, and not giving a damn. A part of me wanted to see her twist in the wind like this, to struggle for the words. A part of me wanted her to suffer.

"Bruce says you won't speak to him."

"Bruce had a chance to speak to me," I told her. "I wrote and told him I was pregnant. He never called."

Her lips trembled. "He never told me," she whispered, half to herself. "Cannie, he is so sorry about what happened."

I snorted, so loud I was afraid I'd bother the babies. "Bruce is a day late and a dollar short."

She bit her lip, twirling the bracelet. "He wants to do the right thing."

"Which would be what?" I asked. "Having his girlfriend refrain from any more attempts on my baby's life?"

"He said that was an accident," she whispered.

I rolled my eyes.

"He wants to do the right thing," she repeated. "He wants to help out. . . ."

"I don't need money," I said, deliberately crude, spelling it out. "Not his or yours, either. I sold my screenplay."

Her face lit up, so glad that we were on a happy subject. "Honey, that's wonderful!"

I said nothing, hoping she'd fall apart in the face of my silence. But Audrey was braver than I'd given her credit for.

"Could I see the baby?" she asked.

I shrugged and stabbed one finger at the window. Joy was in the center of the nursery. She looked less like an angry grapefruit; more like a cantaloupe, perhaps, but still tiny, still frail, still with the science-fiction-looking ventilator attached to her face more often than not. The chart at the end of her glass crib read "Joy Leah Shapiro." She was wearing just a diaper, plus pink and white striped socks and a little pink hat with a pompom on top. I'd brought the nurses my stash, and every morning they made sure that Joy got a different hat. She was far and away the best chapeau'd baby in all of the NICU.

"Joy Leah," whispered Audrey. "Is she . . . did you name her after my husband?"

I nodded once, swallowing hard around the lump in my throat. I can give her this much, I thought. After all, she wasn't the one who ignored me, who didn't call me, who had caused me to fall into a sink and almost lose my baby.

"Will she be all right?"

"I don't know," I said. "Probably. They say probably. She's still small, and she has to get bigger, her lungs have to grow until she can breathe on her own. Then she'll come home."

Audrey wiped her eyes with the Kleenex she extracted from her purse. "And you'll stay here? You'll raise her in Philadelphia?"

"I don't know," I told her. Honest to a fault. "I don't know if I want to go back to the paper, or maybe back out to California. I have friends there." But even as I said it, I wondered if it was true. After dashing off a perfunctory thank-you note that couldn't begin to express the gratitude I should have felt for everything she'd done for me, I'd been giving Maxi the same silent treatment as all of my friends. Who knew what she was thinking, or whether she even thought she was my friend still?

Audrey straightened her shoulders. "I would like to be a grand-mother to her," she said carefully. "No matter what happened between you and Bruce. . . ."

"What happened," I repeated. "Did Bruce tell you I had a hys-terectomy? That I'll never have another baby? Did he happen to men-tion that?"

"I'm sorry, Cannie," she said again, sounding shrill and helpless and even a little scared. I shut my eyes, slumping against the glass wall.

"Just go," I told her. "Please. We can talk about this some other time, but not right now. I'm too tired."

She put her hand on my shoulder. "Let me help you," she said. "Can I get you something? Some water?"

I shook my head, shook her hand off, turned my face away. "Please," I said. "Just go." And I stood there, turned away from her, with my eyes shut tight, until I heard her soles slap-slapping back down the hallway. That was where the nurse found me, leaning against the wall and crying, with my hands curled into fists.

"Are you okay?" she asked, and touched my shoulder. I nodded, and turned toward the door.

"I'll be back later," I told her. "I'm going for a walk."

That afternoon, I walked for hours, until the streets, the sidewalks, the buildings turned into a grayish blur. I remember that I bought a

Snapple lemonade somewhere, and a few hours later I stopped at a bus station to pee, and I remember that at one point the ankle I'd had the cast on started throbbing. I ignored it. I kept walking. I walked south, then east, through strange neighborhoods, over trolley tracks, past burned-out drug houses, abandoned factories, the slow, brackish twist of the Schuylkill. I thought maybe, somehow, I would walk all the way to New Jersey. *Look,* I would say, standing in the lobby of Bruce's high-rise apartment building like a ghost, like a guilty thought, like a wound you'd thought had scabbed over that had suddenly started to bleed. *Look at what's become of me.*

I walked and walked until I felt something strange, an unfamiliar sensation. A pain in my foot. I looked down, lifting my left foot, and watched in dumb confusion as the sole slowly peeled off the bottom of my filthy sneaker and flopped onto the street.

A guy sitting on a stoop across the street whooped laughter. "Hey!" he shouted, as I stared stupidly from shoe to sole and back again, trying to make sense of it. "Baby needs a new pair of shoes!"

My baby needs a new pair of lungs, I thought, limping and looking around. Where am I? The neighborhood wasn't familiar. None of the street names rang any bells. And it was dark. I looked at my watch. 8:30, it said, and for a minute I didn't know whether it was morning or night. I was sweaty and grimy and exhausted . . . and lost.

I dug in my pockets, looking for answers, or at least cab fare. I found a five-dollar bill, a fistful of change, and some assorted lint.

I looked for landmarks, for a pay phone, for something.

"Hey," I called to the guy on the stoop. "Hey, where am I?"

He cackled laughter, rocking back on his heels. "Powelton Village! You in Powelton Village, baby!"

Okay, then. That was a start.

"Which way's University City?" I called.

He shook his head. "Girl, you lost! You all turned around!" His voice was deep and resonant, and sounded Southern. He lifted himself off his stoop and walked over to me—a middle-aged black man in a white undershirt and khakis. He peered closely at my face. "You sick?" he finally asked.

I shook my head. "Just lost," I said.

"You go to the college?" he continued, and I shook my head again, and he moved even closer, his expression growing more concerned.

"Are you drunk?" he asked, and I had to smile.

"No, really," I said. "I just went for a walk and got lost."

"Well, you better get found," he said. For one sick, terrifying moment I was absolutely certain he was going to start talking to me about Jesus. But he didn't. Instead, he took a long, careful inventory of me, from my falling-apart sneakers, up my scabby, bruised shins, to the shorts that I'd folded over twice at the waistband so they wouldn't slide down off my hips, and the T-shirt I'd been wearing for five days running, and my hair that had grown past my shoulders for the first time in more than a decade, and was doing a sort of impromptu dreadlock thing in the absence of being washed and brushed.

"You need help," he finally said.

I bowed my head and nodded. Help. This was true. I needed help.

"You got people?"

"I do," I told him. "I have a baby," I began, and then my throat closed up.

He raised his arm and pointed. "University City that way," he said. "You go to the corner of 45th Street, the bus take you straight there." He dug in his pocket, found a slightly tattered bus transfer pass, and pressed it into my hand. Then he bent and looked at my shoe. "Stay here," he said. I stood, stock-still, afraid to move so much as a muscle. Afraid of what, exactly, I wasn't sure.

The man came out of his house with a silver roll of duct tape in his hand. I lifted my foot, and he wrapped tape around and around it, holding the sole in place.

"Be careful," he said. *Keffel,* the word sounded like. "You a mother now, you need to be careful."

"I will," I said. I started limping off toward the corner he'd pointed at.

As filthy as I was, with duct-taped shoes and tears cutting slow tracks through the grime on my cheeks, nobody spared me so much as a glance on the bus. Everyone was too wrapped up in their own private coming-home-from-work thoughts—dinner, children, what was on TV, the minutiae of normal lives. The bus heaved and groaned its way across town. Things started looking familiar again. I saw the stadium, the skyscrapers, the far-off glimmering white tower of the *Examiner* building. And then I saw the University of Philadelphia's Weight and Eating Disorders office, where I'd gone a million years ago. When the only thing I thought I had to worry about was not being thin.

Get found, I thought, and pulled the "Stop Requested" cord so hard I thought for a moment I'd yanked it off. I took an elevator up to the seventh floor, thinking that I'd find all the lights out and the doors locked, wondering why I was even bothering.

But his light was on, and his door was open.

"Cannie!" said Dr. K., beaming. Beaming until he stood up, came around the desk, and got a good whiff of me. And a good look.

"I'm a success story," I said, and tried to smile. "Look at me! Forty pounds of ugly flab gone in just months!" I swiped one hand across my eyes. "I'm thin," I said, and started crying. "Yay, me."

"Sit down," he said, and closed the door. He put his arm around my shoulders and eased me toward his couch, where I sat, sniffling and pathetic.

"Cannie, my God, what happened to you?"

"I went for a walk," I began. My tongue felt thick and furry, and my lips felt cracked. "I got lost," I said. My voice had gone strange and croaky. "I went for a walk, and I got all turned around. I got lost, but now I'm trying to be found."

He put his hand on my head, stroking gently. "Let me take you home."

I let him lead me to the elevator, out the door, into his car. On the way out, he stopped at a soda machine and bought a cold can of Coke. I grabbed it without asking and guzzled the whole thing down. He didn't say a word, not even when I burped hugely. He pulled into a convenience store and came out with a quart of water and an orange Popsicle.

"Thanks," I rasped, "that's very nice of you." I drank the water, sucked on the Popsicle.

"I've been trying to call you," he said. "At work and at home."

"I'm very busy," I recited.

"Is Joy home yet?"

I shook my head.

He looked at me. "Are you okay?"

"Busy," I croaked again. My breasts were aching. I looked down and was unsurprised to see two circular stains beneath the V of sweat from my collarbone down.

"Busy with what?" he asked.

I shut my mouth. I hadn't really planned any dialogue beyond "busy."

At a stoplight, he looked over at me, staring at my face. "Are you okay?"

I shrugged. The car behind us honked, but he didn't move. "Cannie," he said kindly. A single tear trickled down my cheek. He reached out to brush it away. I jerked back as if I'd been burned.

"No!" I shrieked. "Don't touch me!"

"Cannie, my God, what's the matter?"

I shook my head, stared at my lap, where the ruins of the Popsicle were melting. We drove in silence for a while, the car purring beneath us, cool air whispering from the air conditioner over my knees and my shoulders.

At another traffic light, he started to talk again. "How's Nifkin? Did he remember anything I taught him?" He glanced at me quickly. "You remember when we visited you, right?"

I nodded. "I'm not crazy," I said. But even as I said it, I wasn't sure whether it was true. Did crazy people know they were crazy? Or did they think they were perfectly normal, all the while doing crazy things, wandering around filthy and with their shoes falling apart and their heads so full of rage it felt as if they'd explode?

We drove for a few more blocks in silence. I couldn't think of what to say, what to do next. I knew that there were questions I should ask him, points that I should make, but it felt as if my head was full of buzzing static.

"Where are we going?" I finally managed. "I should go home. Or to the hospital. I should go back there."

We pulled up at a red light. "Are you working?" he asked me. "I haven't seen your byline. . . ."

It had been so long since I'd had this kind of normal cocktail-party conversation with anyone, it took me a while to get the words sorted out right. "I'm on leave."

"Are you eating right?" He squinted sideways at me in the dark. "Or maybe I should ask, are you eating anything?"

I shrugged. "It's hard. With the baby. With Joy. I go to the hospital to see her twice a day, and I'm getting things ready at home. . . . I walk a lot," I finished up.

"I can see that," he said.

Another few blocks of silence, another red light. "I've been thinking about you," he said. "I was hoping you'd stop by, or call. . . ."

"Well, I did, didn't I?"

"I thought maybe we could see a movie. Or go to that diner again."

It sounded so bizarre I almost laughed. Was there a time I'd gone to dinner, to movies, when my every thought hadn't been about my baby and my rage?

"Where were you going, when you got lost?"

"For a walk," I said in a small voice. "Just for a walk."

He shook his head but didn't question me. "Why don't you let me take you to my place? I'll make you dinner."

I considered this. "Do you live near the hospital?"

"Even closer than you. I'll take you as soon as you like."

I nodded once, giving in.

I was quiet on the elevator ride to the sixteenth floor, quiet as he unlocked his door, apologizing for the mess, asking if I still liked chicken and did I want to use the phone? I nodded for chicken, shook my head for phone, and walked through his living room slowly, running my hands along the spines of his books, considering the framed family pictures, seeing but not really seeing. He disappeared into the kitchen, then emerged with a stack of folded things: a fluffy white towel, a pair of sweatpants and a T-shirt, miniature bars of soap and bottles of shampoo from a hotel in New York City.

"Would you like to freshen up?" he offered.

The bathroom was big and clean. I stripped off my shirt, then my shorts, halfheartedly trying to remember when they'd been clean. From the look and smell, I surmised that it had been a while. I folded them, then folded them again, then decided the hell with it and tossed them in the trash. I stood under the water for a long time, with my eyes closed, and thought of nothing but the feeling of the water on my face. *Found,* I told myself. *Try to get found.*

When I come out of the shower, dressed, with my hair toweled dry, he was putting food on the table.

"Welcome back," he said, smiling at me. "Is this okay?"

There was a tossed salad, a small roast chicken, a platter of potato pancakes, which I hadn't seen anyone serve outside of Chanukah in years. I sat down. The food actually smelled good—the first time anything had smelled good to me in a while.

"Thank you," I said.

He piled my plate high, and didn't talk while I ate, although he watched me carefully. Every once in a while I'd look up and see him . . . not staring, exactly. Just watching me.

Finally, I pushed my plate away. "Thank you," I said again. "That was really good."

He led me over to the couch and handed me a ceramic bowl full of chocolate ice cream and mango sorbet.

"Ben and Jerry's," he said. I stared at him, my head still staticky, remembering that he'd brought me dessert once before, when I was in the hospital. "Remember when we talked about ice cream in class?"

I looked at him blankly.

"When we were talking about trigger foods?" he prompted. And I remembered then, sitting around the table a million years ago, talking about things I liked to eat. It felt unbelievable that I had ever liked anything . . . that I'd enjoyed regular stuff. Food, and friends, and going for walks and to movies. Could I ever have a life like that again? I wondered. I wasn't sure . . . but I thought that maybe I could try.

"Do you remember all of your patients' favorite foods?" I asked.

"Only my favorite patients," he said. He sat in the armchair across from me while I ate it, slowly, savoring each mouthful. I sighed when I was finished. It had been so long since I'd eaten this well; so long since anything had tasted good.

He cleared his throat. I figured that was my cue to go. He probably had plans for the night. He possibly even had a date. I racked my brain and tried to remember. What day was it? Was it the weekend?

I yawned, and Dr. K. smiled at me. "You look so tired," he said. "Why don't you rest for a while?"

His voice was so warm, so soothing. "You like tea, not coffee, right?" I nodded. "I'll be right back," he said.

He went to the kitchen and I stretched out my legs on the couch, and by the time he came back I was half asleep. My eyelids felt so heavy. I yawned, and tried to sit up, as he handed me a mug.

"Where were you going today?" he asked.

I turned my head away, reaching for the blanket that was draped over the back of the couch. "I just went for a walk. I guess I got kind of lost or something. I'm fine, though. You shouldn't worry. I'm fine."

"You're not," he said, sounding almost angry. "You're very obviously not fine. You're half-starved, you're stomping around the city, you quit your job . . ."

"Leave of absence," I corrected. "I'm on a compassionate leave of absence."

"You don't have to be ashamed to ask for help."

"I don't need help," I told him, reflexively. Because that was my reflex, ingrained as a teenager, honed over the years. *I'm okay. I can handle it. I'm fine.* "I've got everything under control. I'm fine. We're fine. Me and the baby. We're fine."

He shook his head. "How are you fine? You're not happy. . . ."

"Why should I be happy?" I shot back. "What's to be happy about?"

"You have a beautiful baby. . . ."

"Yeah, no thanks to anyone else."

He stared at me. I stared back, furious. Then I put down my tea and got to my feet.

"I should go."

"Cannie . . ."

I looked for my socks and my duct-taped shoes. "Could you take me home?"

He looked distressed. "I'm sorry . . . I didn't mean to upset you."

"You haven't upset me. I'm not upset. But I want to go home."

He sighed, and looked down at his feet. "I thought . . ." he mumbled.

"Thought what?"

"Nothing."

"Thought what?" I repeated, more insistently.

"It was a bad idea."

"Thought what," I said again, in a tone that wasn't taking no for an answer.

"I thought that if you came here, you'd relax." He shook his head, seeming stunned by his own hopes, his own presumptions. "I thought maybe you'd want to talk about things. . . ."

"There's really nothing to talk about," I said. But I said it more gently. He had given me dinner, clean clothes, an orange Popsicle, a ride. "I'm okay. Really. I am."

We stood for a minute, and something passed between us, some small easing of the tension. I could feel the blisters on both feet, and how my cheeks felt tight and painful with sunburn. I could feel the cool thin cotton of his T-shirt on my back, and how nice it was, and my belly full of good food, and how nice that was. And I could feel my breasts, which ached dully.

"Hey, you wouldn't happen to have a breast pump in here?" I asked. My first attempt at a joke since I'd woken up in the hospital.

He shook his head. "Would ice help?" he asked. I nodded, and sat back down on the couch, where he brought me ice wrapped in a towel. I turned my back to him and tucked the ice under my shirt.

"How's Nifkin?" he asked again.

I shut my eyes. "With my mom," I muttered. "I sent him to stay with her for a while."

"Well, don't let him stay away too long. He'll forget his tricks." He took a sip of his tea. "I was going to teach him how to speak, if we'd had a little more time together."

I nodded. My eyelids were feeling heavy again.

"Maybe some other time," he said. He kept his eyes politely averted as I shifted the ice around. "I'd like to see Nifkin again," he said. He paused and cleared his throat. "I'd like to see you, too, Cannie."

I looked at him. "Why?" A rude question, I knew, but I felt like I was past the point of good manners . . . of any manners, really. "Why me?"

"Because I care about you."

"Why?" I asked again.

"Because you're . . ." He let the last word hang there. When I looked at him he was waving his hands in the air, like he was trying to sculpt phrases out of the air. "You're special."

I shook my head.

"You are."

Special, I thought. I didn't feel special. I felt ridiculous, really. I felt like a spectacle of a woman, a sob story, a freak. How must I look, really? I imagined myself on the street that night, my shoe falling apart, sweaty and filthy, my breasts leaking. They should take a picture, put my poster up in every junior high school, staple it in bookstores next to the Harlequin novels and the self-help books about finding your soulmate, your life partner, your one true love. I could be a warning; I could turn girls away from my fate.

I must have dozed off then, because when I came awake with a start, with my cheek against the blanket and the towel full of ice melting in my lap, he was sitting right across from me.

He'd taken his glasses off, and his eyes were gentle.

"Here," he said. He had something in his arms, cradled like a baby. Pillows. Blankets. "I made up the guest bedroom for you."

I walked there in a daze, aching from exhaustion. The sheets were cool and crisp, the pillows like an embrace. I let him draw back the covers, help me onto the bed, tuck them up over me, smooth the blanket over my shoulders. His face seemed so much softer without his glasses, in the dark.

He sat on the edge of the bed. "Will you tell me why you're so angry?" he asked.

I was so tired, and my tongue felt heavy and slow in my mouth. It was like being drugged, or hypnotized; like dreaming underwater. Or maybe I would have told anyone, if I'd let anyone get close enough to ask. "I'm mad at Bruce. I'm mad that his girlfriend pushed me, and I'm mad that he doesn't love me. I'm mad at my father, I guess."

He raised an eyebrow.

"I saw him . . . in California. . . ." I paused to yawn, to fight the words out. "He didn't want to know me." I passed my hands over my belly, or where my belly had been. "The baby . . . ," I said. My eyelids felt freighted, so heavy I could barely keep them open. "He didn't want to know."

He brushed the back of his hand against my cheek, and I leaned into his touch like a cat, unthinking. "I'm so sorry," he said. "You've had a lot of sadness in your life."

I breathed in, then out, pondering the truth of this. "That's not exactly a news flash," I said.

He smiled. "I just wanted you to know," he said, "I wanted to see you, so I could tell you . . ."

I stared at him, wide-eyed in the dark.

"You don't have to do everything alone," he said. "There are people who care about you. You just have to let them help."

I sat up then. The sheets and blankets fell around my waist. "No," I told him, "that's wrong."

"What do you mean?" he asked.

I shook my head, once, impatiently. "Do you know what love is?"

He considered the question. "I think I heard a song about it once."

"Love," I said, "is the rug they pull out from under you. Love is Lucy always lifting the football at the last second so that Charlie Brown falls on his ass. Love is something that every time you believe in it, it goes away. Love is for suckers, and I'm not going to be a sucker ever again." When I closed my eyes I could see myself as I was, months ago, lying on the bathroom floor, highlights in my hair and makeup on my face, the expensive shoes and fancy clothes and diamond earrings that couldn't keep me safe, couldn't keep the wolf from my door.

"I want a house with hardwood floors," I said, "and I don't want anyone else to come inside."

He was touching my hair, saying something. "Cannie," he repeated. I opened my eyes.

"It doesn't have to be that way."

I stared at him in the dark. "How else could it be?" I asked, quite reasonably.

He leaned forward and kissed me.

He kissed me, and at first I was too shocked to do anything, too shocked to move, too shocked to do anything but sit there, perfectly still, as his lips touched mine.

He pulled his head back. "I'm sorry," he said.

I leaned toward him. "Hardwood floors," I whispered, and I realized I was teasing him, and that I was smiling, and it had been so long since I had smiled.

"I will give you whatever I can," he said, looking at me in a way that made it clear that he was, somehow, oh miracle of miracles, taking this all seriously. And then he kissed me again, pulled the sheets up to my chin, pressed his warm hand on top of my head, and walked out of the room.

I listened as the door closed and as he settled his long body onto the couch. I listened until he'd clicked the lights off and his breathing became deep and regular. I listened, holding the blankets tight around me, holding that feeling of being safe, of being tucked in and taken care of, around me. And I thought clearly then, for the first time since Joy had been born. I decided, right there in that strange bed in the dark, that I could go on being scared forever, that I could keep walking, that I could carry my rage around, hot and heavy in my chest forever. But maybe there was another way. *You have everything you need,* my mother had told me. And maybe all I needed was the courage to admit that what I needed was someone to lean on. And then I could do it—could be a good daughter, and a good mother. Maybe I could even be happy. Maybe I could.

I slipped out of bed. The floor was cool on my bare feet. I moved stealthily through the darkness, out of the room, easing the door shut behind me. I went to him there on the couch, where he'd fallen asleep with a book falling from his fingers. I sat on the floor beside him and leaned so close that my lips practically touched his forehead. Then I closed my eyes and took a deep breath and jumped into the water. "Help," I whispered.

His eyes opened instantly, as if he hadn't been sleeping, but waiting, and he reached out one hand and cupped my cheek.

"Help," I said again, as if I were a baby, as if this was a word I'd just learned and could not stop repeating. "Help me. Help."

Two weeks later Joy came home. She was eight weeks old, and she'd topped seven pounds and was finally breathing on her own. "You'll be fine," the nurses told me. Except I decided that I wasn't ready to be by myself yet. I was still too hurt inside, still too sad.

Samantha offered to let us stay with her. She'd take leave from work, she said, she had weeks built up, she'd do whatever it took to get her house ready. Maxi volunteered to fly in or, alternately, to fly us both up to Utah, where she was shooting a cowgirl epic with the unwieldy title *Buffalo Girls 2000*. Peter, of course, was first in line to tell us that we could stay with him or that, if I wanted, he could stay at my place with us.

"Forget it," I told him. "I've learned my lesson about giving men the milk for free and then expecting them to buy the cow."

He turned a gratifying shade of crimson. "Cannie," he began, "I didn't mean . . ."

And I laughed, then. It was still feeling good to laugh. I'd gone too long without it. "Kidding," I said, and looked at myself ruefully. "Believe me, I'm in no shape to think about that for a while."

In the end, I decided to go home—home to my mother and horrible Tanya, who'd agreed to put her loom in storage for the duration and give me and Joy back the Room Formerly Known as Mine. Actually, they were both glad to have us. "It's so nice to hold a baby again!" said my mother, considerately ignoring the fact that tiny, bristly, sickly Joy, with her sleep apnea monitor and myriad health concerns, was not exactly the sort of baby a grandmother would dream about.

I thought it would be for a week or two—just a chance for me to regroup, to rest, to get used to taking care of a baby. In the end, we stayed for three months, me in the bed that had been mine when I was a girl, and Joy in a crib beside me.

My mother and Tanya let me be. They brought trays of food to my door and cups of tea to my bedside. They retrieved my CDs and a half-dozen books from my apartment, and Tanya presented me with an afghan in purple and green. "For you," she said shyly. "I'm sorry about what happened." And she was, I realized. She was sorry, and she was trying—she'd even managed to quit smoking. For the baby, my mother had told me. That was nice.

"Thanks," I said, and wrapped it around me. She smiled like the sun coming out.

"You're welcome," she said.

Samantha came a few times a week, bringing me treats from the city—grilled grape leaves from the Vietnamese food stall in the Reading Terminal, fresh plums from a farm in New Jersey. Peter visited, too, bringing books, newspapers, magazines (never *Moxie*, I was pleased to note), and little gifts for Joy, including a tiny T-shirt that read "Girl Power."

"That is so great," I said.

Peter smiled, and reached into his briefcase. "I got you one, too," he said.

"Thanks," I said.

Joy stirred in her sleep. Peter looked at her, then at me. "So how are you really?"

I stretched my arms over my head. I was very very tan, from all that time walking in the sun, but things had started to change. I was taking showers, for one thing. I was eating, for another. My hips and breasts were coming back, and I felt okay with it . . . like I recognized myself again. Like I was reclaiming not only my body, but the life I'd left behind. And all things considered, it hadn't been such a bad life. There were things that I had lost, true, and people who wouldn't ever love me again, but there was also . . . potential, I thought, and I smiled at Peter. "Better," I told him. "I guess I'm doing better now."

* * *

Then one morning in September, I woke up and felt like walking again.

"Do you want some company?" Tanya rasped.

I shook my head. My mother watched me lace up my sneakers, her brow furrowed. "Do you want to take the baby?" she asked.

I stared at Joy. I hadn't even considered it.

"She might like some fresh air," said my mother.

"I don't think so," I said slowly.

"She won't break," said my mother.

"She might," I replied, feeling my eyes fill. "She almost did before."

"Babies are stronger than you give them credit for," she said. "Joy's going to be okay . . . and you can't keep her inside forever."

"Not even if I home-school?" I asked. My mother grinned and handed me the Snugli baby carrier. Awkwardly, I strapped it over my chest, and lifted Joy inside.

She was so small, still, so small, she felt like an autumn leaf against me. Nifkin looked at me and pawed my leg, whining softly. So I hitched him to his leash and took him, too. We walked slowly, down to the edge of the driveway, then out onto the street, moving at a pace that would have made an arthritic snail look speedy. It was the first time I'd been out on the street since I'd arrived, and I felt terrified—of the cars, of the people, of everything, I thought ruefully. Joy nestled against me with her eyes closed. Nifkin marched beside me, growling at cars that went by. "Look, baby," I whispered against Joy's downy head. "Look at the world."

When we got back from our morning walk Peter's car was parked in the driveway. Inside, my mother and Tanya and Peter were sitting around the kitchen table.

"Cannie!" said my mother.

"Hello," said Peter.

"We were just talking about you," Tanya said. Even after close to a month smoke-free, she still sounded like Marge Simpson's sisters.

"Hey," I said to Peter, pleased to see him. I gave a genial wave, then unstrapped Joy, wrapped her in a blanket, and sat down with her in my lap. My mother poured me tea as Joy stared at Peter, wide-eyed. He'd been over before, of course, but she'd always been asleep. So this was their first real meeting.

"Hello, baby," Peter said solemnly. Joy screwed up her face and started to cry. Peter looked distressed.

"Oh, I'm sorry," he began.

"Don't worry about it," I told him, turning Joy so that she faced me, and rocking her until her sobs subsided into whimpers, then hiccoughs, then quiet.

"She isn't used to men," said Tanya. I thought of at least six snappy comebacks to that, but prudently kept my mouth shut.

"I think babies are scared of me," Peter said, sounding mournful. "I think it's my voice."

"Joy's heard all kinds of voices," I said tartly. My mother shot me an evil look. Tanya didn't seem to notice.

"She's not scared," I said. She was, in fact, asleep, her lips slightly parted and her eyelashes long and dark against her rosy cheeks where there were still tears drying. "Here," I said, "see?"

I wiped her face and tilted Joy toward him so he could see. He leaned down, looking at her. "Wow," he said reverently. He reached out one long, slender finger and gently touched her cheek. I beamed down at Joy, who promptly woke up, took one look at Peter, and started bawling again.

"She'll get over it," I said. "Rude baby!" I whispered in her ear.

"Maybe she's hungry," said Tanya.

"Wet diaper," suggested my Mom.

"Disappointed with ABC's prime-time lineup," I said.

Peter cracked up.

"Well, she's a very discerning viewer," I said, bouncing Joy against my shoulder. "She really liked *Sports Night.*" Once she'd settled down, I helped myself to tea, and to a fistful of the chocolate-chip cookies in the center of the table. I added an apple from the fruit bowl and went to work.

Peter looked at me approvingly. "You look much better," he pronounced.

"You say that every time you see me," I told him.

"You do," he insisted. "Much healthier."

And it was true. With three meals a day, plus snacks, I was quickly regaining my old prediet Anna Nicole Smith proportions. And I continued to welcome the changes. I could see it all differently now. My legs were sturdy and strong, not fat or ungainly. My breasts now had a purpose besides stretching out my sweaters and making it hard to find a non-beige bra. Even my waist and hips, riddled with silvery stretch marks, suggested strength, and told a story. I might be a big girl, I reasoned, but it wasn't the worst thing in the world. I was a safe harbor and a soft place to rest. Built for comfort, not for speed, I thought, and giggled at myself. Peter smiled at me. "Much healthier," he said again.

"They'll kick you out of the weight-loss center if it gets out about your telling me that," I said.

He shrugged as if it didn't matter. "I think you look fine. I always did," he said. My mother was beaming. I shot her a mind-your-own-business look and settled Joy in my lap.

"So," I said, "what brings you to these parts?"

"Actually," he said, "I was wondering if you and Joy would like to go for a ride."

I felt my chest tighten again. Joy and I hadn't gone anywhere in the car since her arrival, except for checkups at the hospital. "Where to?" I asked, trying to sound casual.

"Down the shore," he said, using the typical Philadelphia construction. "Just for a little drive."

It sounded nice. It also sounded absolutely terrifying. "I'm not sure," I said regretfully. "I'm not sure she's ready."

"She's not ready, or you're not ready?" asked my helpful mother. I sent her an even more intense mind-your-own-business look.

"I'll be there," Peter said. "So you'll have medical assistance, if you need it."

"Go on, Cannie," said my mother.

"It'll be good for you," urged Tanya.

I stared at him. He smiled at me. I sighed, knowing I was defeated. "Just a short ride," I said, and he nodded, eager as a schoolboy, and stood up to help me.

*   *   *

Of course, it took a while—forty-five minutes, to be precise, and three bags full of diapers, hats, socks, sweaters, stroller, bottles, blankets, and assorted baby paraphernalia, all shoved in the trunk—before we were ready to leave. Then Joy got stowed in the infant seat, I sat on the passenger's side, Peter took the wheel, and we headed down to the Jersey shore.

Peter and I talked a little at first—about his job, about Lucy and Maxi and how Andy'd actually gotten a death threat after savaging one of Philadelphia's famous old fish-houses that had been coasting on its reputation and so-so snapper soup for decades. Then, when we turned on to the Atlantic City Expressway, he smiled at me and touched a button on the dashboard, and the roof over our heads slid away.

"A moon roof!" I said, impressed.

"Thought you'd like it!" he shouted back.

I looked back at Joy, tucked snug in her infant seat, wondering if the wind would be too much. But she actually looked like she was enjoying it. The little pink ribbon I'd tied in her hair, so that everyone would know she was a girl, was bobbing in the breeze, and her eyes were wide open.

We drove to Ventnor and parked in a lot two blocks from the beach. Peter unfolded Joy's complicated carriage while I got her out of the car, wrapped her in more blankets than the warm September day merited, and set her into the carriage. We walked slowly down to the water, me pushing, Peter walking beside me. The sunshine felt wonderful, thick as honey on my shoulders, making my hair glow.

"Thank you," I said. He shrugged and looked embarrassed.

"I'm glad you like it," he said.

We walked on the boardwalk—up for twenty minutes, back for another twenty, because I'd decided I didn't want Joy outside for more than an hour. Except the salt air didn't seem to be bothering her. She'd fallen fast asleep, her little rosebud mouth slack, her pink ribbon coming unfurled, and her fine brown hair curling around her cheeks. I leaned close to hear her breathing, and to check her diaper. She was fine.

Peter returned to my side with a blanket in his arms. "Want to sit on the beach?" he asked.

I nodded. He unfolded the blanket, I unstrapped Joy, and we walked down close to the water and sat there, watching the waves break. I worked my toes into the warm sand, and stared at the white foam, the blue-green depths, the black edge of the ocean against the horizon, and thought of all the things I couldn't see: sharks and bluefish and starfish, whales singing to each other, secret lives that I would never know.

Peter draped another blanket over my shoulders, and let his hands linger there for a few seconds.

"Cannie," he began. "I want to tell you something."

I gave him what I hoped was an encouraging smile.

"That day on Kelly Drive, when you and Samantha were walking," he said, and cleared his throat.

"Right," I said. "Go on."

"Well," he said. "I, um . . . I'm not actually a jogger."

I looked at him, confused.

"I just . . . well, I remember how in class you used to say you went on bike rides there, and you'd go for walks, and I didn't feel that I could call you . . ."

"So you started jogging?"

"Every day," he confessed. "Morning and night, and sometimes on my lunch hour. Until I saw you."

I sat back, surprised by the extent of his dedication, knowing that if it were me, no matter how much I felt that I wanted to see the other person, it probably wouldn't be enough to get me to jog. "I, um, have shinsplints now," he mumbled, and I burst out laughing.

"It serves you right!" I said. "You could've just called me . . ."

"But I couldn't," he said. "First of all, you were a patient . . ."

"Was a patient," I said.

"And you were, um . . ."

"Pregnant with another man's child," I supplied.

"You were oblivious!" he exclaimed. "Completely oblivious! That was the worst part! There I was, mooning after you, giving myself shinsplints . . ."

I giggled some more.

"And first you were sad about Bruce, who even I could tell wasn't right for you . . ."

"You were hardly objective," I told him, but he wasn't through.

"And then you were in California, and that wasn't right for you, either. . . ."

"California's very nice," I said, in California's defense.

He sat down next to me and wrapped his arms around my shoulders, pulling me and Joy tightly against him. "I thought you were never coming home," he said. "I couldn't stand it. I thought I'd never see you again, and I didn't know what to do with myself."

I smiled at him, turning so I could look him in the eye. The sun was setting over us, and seagulls swooped and squawked above the waves.

"But I did come home," I said. "See? No shinsplints necessary."

"I'm glad," he said, and I leaned against him, letting him support me, with the setting sun glowing in his hair and the warm sand cradling my feet, and my baby, my Joy, safe in my arms.

"So I guess the question is," I began, in his car on the way home, "what do I do with my life now?"

He smiled at me quickly before turning his eyes back to the road. "I was actually thinking more along the lines of whether you wanted to stop for dinner."

"Sure," I said. Joy was asleep in her infant seat. We'd lost her pink ribbon somewhere, but I could see sand glittering on her bare feet. "So now that we've got that settled . . ."

"Do you want to go back to work?" he asked me.

I thought about it. "I think so," I said. "Eventually. I miss it," I said. Knowing, as soon as I said it, that it was the truth. "I don't think I've ever gone this long without writing something. God help me, I even miss my brides."

"So what do you want to write?" he asked. "What do you want to write about?"

I considered the question.

"Newspaper articles?" he prompted. "Another screenplay? A book?"

"A book," I scoffed. "As if!"

"It could happen," he said.

"I don't think I've got a book in me," I said.

"If you did," he said seriously, "I'd devote all of my medical training to getting it out."

I laughed. Joy woke up and made a questioning noise. I looked back and waved at her. She stared at me, then yawned and went back to sleep.

"Maybe not a book," I said, "but I would like to write something about this."

"Magazine article?" he suggested.

"Maybe," I said.

"Good," he said, sounding like it had been settled once and for all. "I can't wait to see it."

The next morning, after I'd walked with Joy, had breakfast with Tanya, talked to Samantha on the phone, and made plans to see Peter the next night, I went down to the basement and fetched the dusty little Apple that had gotten me through four years of Princeton. I wasn't expecting much, but when I plugged it in it chugged and bleeped and lit up obligingly. And even though the keyboard felt strange under my hands, I took a deep breath, wiped the dust from the screen, and started writing.

Loving a Larger Woman

by Candace Shapiro

When I was five I learned to read. Books were a miracle to me—white pages, black ink, and new worlds and different friends in each one. To this day, I relish the feeling of cracking a binding for the first time, the anticipation of where I'll go and whom I'll meet inside.

When I was eight I learned to ride a bike. And this, too, opened my eyes to a new world that I could explore on my own—the brook that burbled through a vacant lot two streets over, the ice-cream store that sold homemade cones for a dollar, the orchard that bordered a golf course and that smelled tangy, like cider, from the apples that rolled to the ground in the fall.

When I was twelve I learned that I was fat. My father told me, pointing at the insides of my thighs and the undersides of my arms with the handle of his tennis racquet. We'd been playing, I remember, and I was flushed and sweaty, glowing with the joy of movement. You'll need to watch that, he told me, poking me with the handle so that the extra flesh jiggled. Men don't like fat women.

And even though this would turn out not to be absolutely true—there would be men who would love me, and there would be people who'd respect me—I carried his words into my adulthood like a prophecy, viewing the world through the prism of my body, and my father's prediction.

I learned how to diet—and, of course, how to cheat on diets. I learned how to feel miserable and ashamed, how to cringe away from mirrors and men's glances, how to tense myself for the insults that I always thought were coming: the Girl Scout troop leader who'd offer me carrot sticks while the other girls got milk and cookies; the well-meaning teacher who'd ask if I'd thought about aerobics. I learned a dozen tricks for making myself invisible—how to keep a towel wrapped around my midsection at the beach (but never swim), how to fade to the back row of any group photograph (and never smile), how to dress in shades of gray, black, and brown, how to avoid seeing my own reflection in windows or in mirrors, how to think of myself exclusively as a body—more than that, as a body that had fallen short of the mark, that had become something horrifying, unlovely, unlovable.

There were a thousand words that could have described me—smart, funny, kind, generous. But the word I picked—

the word that I believed the world had picked for me—was
fat.

When I was twenty-two I went out into the world in a suit
of invisible armor, fully expecting to be shot at, but determined that I wouldn't get shot down. I got a wonderful job,
and eventually fell in love with a man I thought would love
me for the rest of my life. He didn't. And then—by accident—I got pregnant. And when my daughter was born
almost two months too soon I learned that there are worse
things than not liking your thighs or your butt. There are
more terryifing things than trying on bathing suits in front of
three-way department-store mirrors. There is the fear of
watching your child struggling for breath, in the center of a
glass crib where you can't touch her. There is the terror of
imagining a future where she won't be healthy or strong.

And, ultimately, I learned, there is comfort. Comfort in
reaching out to the people who love you, comfort in asking for
help, and in realizing, finally, that I am valued, treasured,
loved, even if I am never going to be smaller than a size sixteen, even if my story doesn't have the Hollywood-perfect
happy ending where I lose sixty pounds and Prince Charming
decides that he loves me after all.

The truth is this—I'm all right the way I am. I was all
right, all along. I will never be thin, but I will be happy. I will
love myself, and my body, for what it can do—because it is
strong enough to lift, to walk, to ride a bicycle up a hill, to
embrace the people I love and hold them fully, and to nurture
a new life. I will love myself because I am sturdy. Because I did
not—will not—break.

I will savor the taste of my food and I will savor my life, and
if Prince Charming never shows up—or, worse yet, if he drives
by, casts a cool and appraising glance at me, and tells me I've
got a beautiful face and have I ever considered Optifast?—I
will make my peace with that.

And most importantly, I will love my daughter whether she's

big or little. I will tell her that she's beautiful. I will teach her to
swim and read and ride a bike. And I will tell her that whether
she's a size eight or a size eighteen, that she can be happy, and
strong, and secure that she will find friends, and success, and
even love. I will whisper it in her ear when she's sleeping. I will
say, Our lives—your life—will be extraordinary.

I read through it twice, cleaning up the punctuation, fixing the
numerous typos. Then I stood up and stretched, placing my palms flat
against the small of my back. I looked at my baby, who was beginning
to resemble an actual infant of the human species, rather than some
miniaturized, prickly fruit-human hybrid. And I looked at myself:
hips, breasts, butt, belly, all of the problem areas I'd once despaired of,
the body that had caused me such shame, and smiled. In spite of
everything, I was going to be fine.

"We both are," I said to Joy, who did not stir.

I called information, then dialed the number in New York. "Hello;
Moxie," said a chirpy subteen-sounding secretary. My voice didn't
tremble even slightly when I asked for the managing editor.

"May I ask what this is in reference to?" the secretary singsonged.

"My name is Candace Shapiro," I began. "I'm the ex-girlfriend of
your 'Good in Bed' columnist."

I heard a sharp intake of breath on the other end of the line.
"You're C.?" she gasped.

"Cannie," I corrected.

"Ohmygod! You're, like, real!"

"Very much so," I said. This was turning out to be very amusing.

"Did you have the baby?" asked the girl.

"I did," I said. "She's right here, sleeping."

"Oh. Oh, wow," she said. "You know, we were wondering how
that turned out."

"Well, that's why I'm calling," I said.

TWENTY

The good thing about naming ceremonies for Jewish baby girls is that they're not tied to a specific time. With a boy, you've got to do the bris within seven days. A girl, you can do it in six weeks, three months, whenever. It's a newer service, a little bit free-form, and the rabbis who do namings tend to be accommodating, New Age-ish types.

Joy's naming was on December 31, on a crisp, perfect winter morning in Philadelphia. Eleven o'clock in the morning, with brunch to follow.

My mother was among the first wave of arrivals. "Who's my big girl?" she cooed, lifting Joy from her crib. "Who's my bundle of joy?" Joy chuckled and waved her arms. My beautiful daughter, I thought, feeling my throat catch at the sight of her. She was almost eight months old, and still it felt like every time I saw her she was a miracle.

And even strangers said she was a miraculously beautiful baby, with peachy skin, wide eyes, sturdy limbs pillowed with cushiony rolls of fat, and a wonderfully happy way about her. I'd named her perfectly. Unless she was hungry, or her diaper was wet, Joy was always smiling, always laughing, observing the world closely through her wide, watchful eyes. She was the happiest baby I knew.

My mother handed her over, then impulsively reached and hugged us both. "I am so proud of you," she said.

I hugged her hard. "Thank you," I whispered, wishing that I could tell her what I really wanted to, that I could thank her for loving me when I was a girl, and for letting me go now that I was a woman. "Thank you," I said again. My mother gave me a final squeeze, and kissed Joy on top of her head.

I filled Joy's white tub with warm water and gave her a bath. She cooed and clucked as I poured the water over her, washing her legs, her feet, her fingers, her sweet little baby behind. I rubbed on lotion, dusted her with powder, snapped her into a white knitted dress and put a white hat with roses embroidered around the edges on her head. "Baby," I whispered in her ear, "baby Joy." Joy waved her fists in the air like the world's tiniest triumphant athlete and gurgled a liquid string of syllables, like she was having a conversation in a language none of us had learned.

"Can you say mama?" I asked.

"Ahh!" Joy announced.

"Not even close," I said.

"Oo," she said, looking at me with her big, clear eyes, as if she understood every word.

Then I handed her off to Lucy and went to take my own shower, to do my hair and face, to practice the speech I'd been writing for days.

I could hear the doorbell chiming, the door opening and closing, people coming inside. The caterers had come first, and Peter had come second, with two boxes wrapped in silver paper and a bouquet of roses. "For you," he'd said, and put the flowers in a vase. Then he took Nifkin for a walk and emptied the dishwasher while I finished getting things in order.

"What a sweetheart," said one of the caterer's assistants. "I don't think my husband even knows where the dishwasher is."

I smiled my thanks without bothering to correct her. It was all too confusing to explain to strangers . . . like telling them I'd gone through the day with all my clothes on backward. First comes love, then comes marriage, then comes baby in a baby carriage. Even little kids knew how it was supposed to go. But what could I do? I reasoned. What happened happened. I couldn't undo my history. And if it had given me Joy, there was no way I would want to.

I walked into the living room with Joy in my arms. Maxi was there, and she smiled at me, giving me the tiniest of waves. Samantha was next to her, and next to Sam were my mother and Tanya, Lucy and Josh, Betsy and Andy and Andy's wife, Ellen, and two of the nurses from the hospital who'd taken care of Joy. And, in one corner, was Audrey, impeccably turned out in crisp cream-colored linen. Peter was standing beside her. All my friends. I bit my lip and looked down to keep from crying. The rabbi asked for silence, then asked for four people to come forward to hold the posts of the huppah. It was my grandmother's, I saw, recognizing the fine old lace from my cousins' weddings. It was the huppah I would have been married under, had I gotten things in the right order. At naming ceremonies the huppah is meant to shelter the baby and the husband and wife. But I'd made prior arrangements, and at the rabbi's request everyone crowded under the huppah with me. My baby would get her name surrounded by all of the people who'd loved and sustained us, I decided, and the rabbi had said that it sounded fine to her.

Joy was awake and alert, taking it all in, beaming as if she knew she was the center of attention, as if there was no doubt that it was exactly where she was meant to be. Nifkin sat politely by my feet.

"Shall we begin?" asked the rabbi. She gave a short speech about Israel and Jewish tradition, and how Joy was being welcomed into the religion handed down from Abraham, Isaac, and Jacob, and also Sarah, Rebecca, and Leah. She chanted a blessing, said prayers over bread and wine, daubed a cloth in Manischevitz and pressed it against Joy's lips. "Ooh!" Joy chortled, and everybody laughed. "And now," said the rabbi, "Joy's mother, Candace, will tell how she chose the name."

I took a deep breath. Joy looked at me with her wide eyes. Nifkin was very still against my leg. I pulled a notecard out of my pocket.

"I've learned a lot this year," I began. I took a deep quavering breath. *Don't cry,* I told myself. "I learned that things don't always turn out the way you planned, or the way you think they should. And I've learned that there are things that go wrong that don't always get fixed or get put back together the way they were before. I've learned that some broken things stay broken, and I've learned that you can get through bad times and keep looking for better ones, as long as you have people who love you." I stopped and swiped my hand across my eyes. "I named my baby Joy because she is my joy," I said, "and she's named Leah after her father's father. His middle name was Leonard, and he was a wonderful man. He loved his wife, and his son, and I know that he would have loved Joy, too."

And that was all. I was crying, Audrey was crying, my mother and Tanya were holding each other, and even Lucy, who tended to go non-reactive at sad occasions ("It's the Prozac," she'd explain), was wiping away tears. The rabbi observed this all, a bemused look on her face. "Well," she finally said, "shall we eat?"

After the bagels and whitefish salad, after butter cookies and apple cake and mimosas, after Nifkin had devoured a quarter pound of Nova lox and been sick behind the toilet, after we'd opened the gifts and I'd spent fifteen minutes telling Maxi that Joy, wonderful baby that she was, was really not going to be needing a strand of cultured pearls until at least her eighteenth birthday, after we'd cleared away the wrapping paper and put away the leftovers and the baby and I had taken a nap, Peter and Joy and I walked down to the river to wait for the century's end.

I was feeling good about things, I thought, as I bundled Joy into her stroller. Preproduction on my movie was beginning. My version of "Loving a Larger Woman" had come out at the end of November, replacing Bruce's column. The response, the managing editor told me, had been overwhelming, with every woman who'd ever felt too big, too little, too ugly or strange to fit in or be worthy of love writing in to praise my courage, to decry B's selfishness, to share their own stories about being big and female in America, and to offer best wishes to baby Joy.

"I've never seen anything like this," the managing editor had said, describing the piles of mail, baby blankets, baby books, teddy bears, and assorted religious and secular good-luck icons that had filled the

Moxie mailroom. "Would you consider writing for us regularly?" She had it all figured out—I'd do monthly dispatches from the single-mom front, ongoing updates on my life and Joy's. "I want you to tell us what it's like to live your life, in your body—to work, to date, to balance your single friends with your obligations as a mother," she said.

"What about Bruce?" I asked. I was thrilled with the chance to write for *Moxie* (and even more thrilled once they'd told me what it paid), but I was less than enamoured with the thought of seeing my articles appear next to Bruce's every month, watching him tell readers about his sex life while I filled them in on spit-up and poopy diapers and how I could never find a bathing suit that fit.

"Bruce's contract hasn't been renewed," she said crisply. Which was just fine with me, I said, and happily agreed to her terms.

I spent December settling back into my new apartment, and my life. I kept things easy. I'd wake up in the mornings and get dressed and dress the baby, put Nifkin on his leash, push Joy in the stroller, walk to the park, sit in the sun. Nifkin would fetch his ball, the neighbors would fuss over Joy. After, I'd meet Samantha for coffee, and practice being out in public, around cars and buses and strangers and the hundred thousand other things I'd learned to be afraid of after Joy came into the world so abruptly.

Along those lines, I found a therapist, too: a warm woman about my mother's age with a comforting way about her, plus an endless supply of Kleenex, who did not seem at all alarmed when I spent the first two sessions crying nonstop, and the third one telling the once-upon-a-time story of how much my father had loved me and how it had hurt me when he'd left, rather than addressing what surely seemed like the more pertinent issues at hand.

I called Betsy, my editor, and made arrangements to come back part-time, to pitch in on some big projects, to work from home if I was needed. I called my mother and made a standing date: Every Friday night, dinner at her house, and Joy and I would sleep over so we could go to Wee Ones swimming class at the Jewish Center the next morning. Joy took to the water like a little duck. "I've never seen anything like it," Tanya would growl, as Joy paddled her arms, looking adorable in a small pink bathing suit with ruffles all over the bottom. "She's going to swim like a fish!"

I called Audrey and apologized . . . well, I did whatever apologizing I could, in between her nonstop apologies for Bruce. She was sorry for how he'd behaved, sorry he hadn't been there for me, sorriest of all that she hadn't known so she could have made him do the right thing. Which, of course, wasn't possible. You can't make grownups do what they don't want to do. But I didn't say any of that.

I told her I'd be honored if she would have a role in Joy's life. She asked, very nervously, if I had any intention of letting Bruce have a role in Joy's life. I told her that I didn't . . . but I told her that things change. A year ago I couldn't have imagined myself with a baby. So who knows? Next year maybe Bruce will come over for brunch or a bike ride, and Joy will call him Daddy. Anything's possible, right?

I didn't call Bruce. I thought about it and thought about it, turned it over and over in my mind, and looked at it from every angle I could think of, and in the end I decided that I couldn't. I'd been able to let go of a lot of the anger . . . but not all of it. Maybe that too would come in time.

"So you haven't talked to him at all?" Peter asked, as he walked alongside me, balancing one hand beside mine on Joy's stroller.

"Not once."

"You don't hear from him?"

"I hear . . . things about him. It's this very Byzantine system. Audrey tells my mother, who tells Tanya, who tells everyone she knows, including Lucy, who usually tells me."

"How do you feel about that?"

I smiled at him, beneath the sky, which had finally gone completely black. "You sound like my shrink." I took a deep breath and huffed it out, watching it turn into a silver cloud and blow away. "It was awful at first, and it still is sometimes."

His voice was very gentle. "But only sometimes?"

I smiled at him. "Hardly ever," I said. "Hardly every anymore." I reached for his hand and he squeezed my fingers. "Things happen, you know? That's my one big lesson from therapy. Things happen, and you can't make them un-happen. You don't get do-overs, you can't roll back the clock, and the only thing you can change, and the only thing it does any good to worry about, is how you let them affect you."

"So how are you letting this affect you?"

I smiled sideways at him. "You're very persistent."

He looked at me seriously. "I have ulterior motives."

"Oh?"

Peter cleared his throat. "I wonder if you'd . . . consider me."

I tilted my head. "For the position of in-house diet counselor?"

"In-house something," he muttered.

"How old are you, anyway?" I teased. It was the one topic we'd never quite gotten around to during our trips to bookstores and the beach and to the park with Joy.

"How old do you think I am?"

I took my honest guess and revised it five years downward. "Forty?"

He sighed. "I'm thirty-seven."

I was so startled at that there was no way to even try to hide it. "Really?"

His voice, usually slow and deep and self-assured, sounded higher, hesitant, as he explained. "It's just that I'm so tall, I think . . . and my hair started going gray when I was eighteen . . . and, you know, being a professor, I think everyone just makes certain assumptions. . . ."

"You're thirty-seven?"

"Do you want to see my driver's license?"

"No," I said, "no, I believe you."

"I know," he began, "I know I'm still probably too old for you, and I'm probably not exactly what you had in mind."

"Don't be silly . . ."

"I'm not glamorous or quick on my feet." He looked down at his feet and sighed. "I'm kind of a plodder, I guess."

"Plotter? Like, *Murder, She Wrote?*"

A faint twitch of a smile lifted his lips. "Plodder. Like, one foot in front of the other."

"Especially now with the shinsplints," I murmured.

"And I . . . I mean, I really . . ."

"Have we come to the emotional part of the presentation?" I asked, still teasing. "You don't mind that I'm a larger woman?"

He wrapped his long fingers around my wrist. "I think you look like a queen," he said with such intensity that I was startled . . . and tremendously pleased. "I think you're the most amazing, exciting woman I've ever met. I think you're smart, and funny, and you have the most wonderful heart . . ." He paused, swallowing hard. "Cannie." And then he stopped.

I smiled—a private, contented smile—as he sat there, holding my wrist, waiting for my answer. And I knew what it was, I thought, looking at him looking at me. The answer was that I loved him . . . that he was as kind and considerate and loving a man as I could ever hope for. That he was warm-hearted, and decent, and sweet, and that we could have adventures together . . . me, and Peter, and Joy.

"Would you like to be the first man I kiss this millennium?" I inquired.

Peter leaned close. I could feel his warm breath on my cheek. "I would like to be the only man you kiss this millennium," he said emphatically. And he brushed my neck with his lips . . . then my ear . . . then my cheek. I giggled until he kissed my lips to quiet me. Snuggled against my chest, squeezed between us, Joy gave a little shout and waved one fist in the air.

"Cannie?" Peter whispered, his voice pitched low, for my ears only, and one hand in his jacket pocket. "I want to ask you something."

"Shh," I said, knowing in my heart what his question was, and what my answer would be. *I do,* I thought. *I will.* "Shh," I said, "they're starting."

Above our heads, fireworks burst, in great blooms of color and light. Silver sparks showered down, racing toward the river, and the night was full of explosions and the whistling shrieks as the spent fire-crackers hurtled through the night and into the water. I looked down. Joy's face was rapt, her eyes wide, both her arms extended, as if she wanted to embrace what she was seeing. I smiled at Peter, holding up one finger, asking him with my eyes to wait. Then I unstrapped Joy from her carryall, putting my hands under her armpits, holding her in front of me as I scrambled to my feet. Ignoring the good-natured shouts of "Down in front!" and, "Hey, lady, be careful!" I stood on the ledge, letting the cold and the light pour down over my hair, my face, and my daughter. I raised my arms over my head and lifted Joy up toward the light.

In Her Shoes

For Molly Beth

PART ONE

In Her Shoes

ONE

"Baby," groaned the guy—Ted? Tad?—something like that—and crushed his lips against the side of her neck, shoving her face against the wall of the toilet stall.

This is ridiculous, Maggie thought, as she felt him bunching her dress up around her hips. But she'd had five vodka-and-tonics over the course of the last hour and a half, and at this point was not in much of a position to call anything ridiculous. She wasn't even sure she could pronounce the word.

"You're so hot!" Ted or Tad exclaimed, discovering the thong that Maggie had purchased for the occasion.

"I want the thong. In red," she'd said.

"Flame," the salesgirl at Victoria's Secret had replied.

"Whatever," said Maggie. "Small," she added, "extra small if you have it." She gave the girl a quick scornful look to let her know that while she might not know red from flame, she, Maggie Feller, was not worried. She might not have finished college. She might not have a great job—or, okay, after last Thursday, any job at all. The sum total of her big-screen experience might be the three seconds that a sliver of her left hip was visible in Will Smith's second-to-last video. And she might be just barely bumping along while some people, like namely her sister, Rose, went whizzing through

Ivy League colleges and straight into law schools, then into law firms and luxury apartments on Rittenhouse Square like they'd been shot down the water slide of life, but still, she, Maggie, had something of worth, something rare and precious, possessed by few, coveted by many—a terrific body. One hundred and six pounds stretched over five feet and six inches, all of it tanning-bed basted, toned, plucked, waxed, moisturized, deodorized, perfumed, *perfect.*

She had a tattoo of a daisy on the small of her back, the words "BORN TO BE BAD" tattooed around her left ankle, and a plump, pierced red heart reading "MOTHER" on her right bicep. (She'd thought about adding the date of her mother's death, but for some reason that tattoo had hurt more than the other two put together.) Maggie also had D-cup tits. Said tits had been a gift from a married boyfriend and were made of saline and plastic, but this didn't matter. "They're an investment in my future," Maggie had said, even as her father looked hurt and bewildered, and Sydelle the Stepmonster flared her nostrils, and her big sister, Rose, had asked, "Precisely what kind of future are you planning?" in that snotty voice of hers that made her sound like she was seventy. Maggie didn't listen. Maggie didn't care. She was twenty-eight years old now, at her tenth high school reunion, and she was the best-looking girl in the room.

All eyes had been on her as she strolled into the Cherry Hill Hilton in her clinging black spaghetti-strap cocktail dress and the Christian Louboutin stilettos she'd swiped from her sister's closet the weekend before. Rose might have let herself turn into a fat load—a big sister in more ways than one—but at least their feet were still the same size. Maggie could feel the heat of the gazes as she smiled, sashaying over to the bar, hips swaying like music, bangles chiming on her wrists, letting her former classmates get a good look at what they'd missed—the girl they'd ignored, or mocked and called retarded, the one who'd shuffled down the high school hallways swimming in her father's oversized army jacket, cringing against the lockers. Well, Maggie had blossomed. Let them see, let them drool. Marissa Nussbaum and Kim Pratt and especially that bitch Samantha Bailey with her dishwater-blond hair and the fifteen pounds she'd packed on her hips since high school. All the cheerleaders, the ones who'd scorned her or looked right past her. Looked right through her. Let them just feast their eyes on her now . . . or, better yet, let their wimpy, receding-hairlined husbands do the feasting.

"Oh, God!" moaned Ted the Tadpole, unbuckling his pants.

In the next stall, a toilet flushed.

Maggie wobbled on her heels as Ted-slash-Tad aimed and missed and aimed again, jabbing at her thighs and backside. It was like being bludgeoned with a blind snake, she thought, and snorted to herself, a noise that Ted evidently mistook for a groan of passion. "Oh, yeah, baby! You like that, huh?" he demanded, and started poking her even harder. Maggie stifled a yawn and looked down at herself, noting with pleasure that her thighs—firmed from hours on the treadmill, smooth as plastic from a recent waxing—did not so much as quiver, no matter how violent Ted's thrusts got. And her pedicure was perfect. She hadn't been sure about this particular shade of red—not quite dark enough, she'd worried—but it was the right choice, she thought, as she looked down at her toes, gleaming back up at her.

"Jesus CHRIST!" yelled Ted. His tone was one of commingled ecstasy and frustration, like a man who's seen a holy vision and isn't quite sure what it means. Maggie had met him at the bar, maybe half an hour after she'd arrived, and he was just what she had in mind—tall, blond, built, not fat and balding like all the guys who'd been football gods and prom kings in high school. Smooth, too. He'd tipped the bartender five dollars for each round, even though it was an open bar, even though he didn't have to, and he'd told her what she wanted to hear.

"What do you do?" he'd asked, and she'd smiled at him. "I am a performer," she said. Which was true. For the past six months, she'd been a backup singer for a band called Whiskered Biscuit that did thrash-metal covers of 1970s disco classics. So far, they'd booked precisely one gig, as the market for thrash-metal renditions of "MacArthur Park" was not overwhelming, and Maggie knew that she was in the band only because the lead singer was hoping she'd sleep with him. But it was something—a tiny toehold on her dream of being famous, of being a star.

"You weren't in any of my classes," he'd said, tracing his forefinger around and around her wrist. "I would have remembered you for sure." Maggie looked down, toying with one of her auburn ringlets, debating whether she should slide her sandal along his calf, or unpin her hair, letting her curls cascade down her back. No, she hadn't been in his classes. She'd been in the "special" classes, the "remedial" classes, the classes with the scrubs and the burnouts and the big-print textbooks that were a different shape—slightly longer and thinner—than any of the books the other kids carried. You could tuck those books under brown paper covers and shove them in your backpack, but the other kids always knew. Well, fuck them. Fuck all of them. Fuck all the pretty cheerleaders and the guys who'd been happy to fool around with her in the passenger seat of their parents' cars but wouldn't even say "Hi" to her in the halls the next Monday.

"Christ!" yelled Ted again. Maggie opened her mouth to tell him to keep it down, and threw up all over the floor—a clear spill of vodka and tonic, she noted as if from a great distance, plus a few decomposing noodles. She'd had pasta—when? Last night? She was trying to remember her last meal when he grabbed her hips and swung her around roughly so that she was facing the front of the stall, banging her hip against the toilet-paper dispenser in the process. "AGHH!" Ted announced, and came all over her back.

Maggie whirled to face him, moving as quickly as she could through the sloshing vodka/noodle mess on the floor. "Not the dress!" she said. And Ted stood there, blinking, his pants puddled around his knees, his hand still on his dick. He grinned foolishly at her. "That was great!" he said, and squinted at her face. "What was your name again?"

• • •

Fifteen miles away, Rose Feller had a secret—a secret currently splayed flat on his back and snoring, a secret who had somehow managed to dislodge her fitted sheet and kick three pillows to the floor.

Rose propped herself up on her elbow and considered her lover by the glow of the streetlights that filtered through her blinds, smiling a sweet, secret smile, a smile none of her colleagues at the law firm of Lewis, Dommel, and Fenick would have recognized. This was what she had always wanted, what she'd spent her whole life secretly dreaming of—a man who looked at her like she was the only woman in the room, in the world, the only woman who'd ever existed. And he was so handsome, even better looking without his clothes than in them. She wondered if she could take a picture. But the noise would wake him up. And who could she show it to?

Instead, Rose let her eyes take a tour of his body—his strong legs, his broad shoulders, his mouth, half-open, the better to snore with. Rose turned on her side, away from him, drew up the blanket tight under her chin, and smiled, remembering.

They'd been working late on the Veeder matter, which was so boring that Rose could have wept, except the partner on the case was Jim Danvers, and she was so in love with him that she would have spent a week reviewing documents if it meant she'd be close enough to him to smell the good wool of his suit, the scent of his cologne. It got to be eight o'clock, and then it got to be nine, and finally they sealed the last of the pages into the messenger's pouch and he looked at her with his movie-star smile and said, "Do you want to get a bite to eat?"

They went to the bar in the basement of Le Bec-Fin, where a glass of wine turned into a bottle, where the crowd dwindled and the candles burned down until it was midnight and they were alone and the conversation stuttered to a stop. While Rose was trying to figure out what to say next—something about sports maybe?—Jim reached for her hand and murmured, "Do you have any idea how beautiful you are?" Rose shook her head because, really, she had no idea. Nobody had ever told her she was beautiful, except her father, once, and that didn't really count. When she looked in the mirror, she saw nothing but an ordinary girl, a plain Jane, a grown-up bookworm with a decent wardrobe—size fourteen, brown hair and brown eyes, thick, straight eyebrows, and a chin that jutted forward slightly as if to say, *You and what army?*

Except she'd always harbored the secret hope that someday, somebody would tell her that she was beautiful, a man who'd slide her hair out of its ponytail, slip her glasses off her face, and look at her like she was Helen of Troy. It was one of the main reasons she'd never gotten contacts. And so she'd leaned forward, every fiber of her being quivering, staring at Jim, waiting for more of the words she'd always wanted to hear. But Jim Danvers just grabbed her hand, paid the bill, and whisked her out the door, up to her apartment, where he'd pulled off her shoes, shucked her skirt, kissed his way from her neck down her belly, and spent forty-five minutes doing things to her that she'd only dreamed of (and seen once on *Sex and the City*).

She shivered deliciously, pulling the comforter up to her chin, reminding herself that this could be trouble. Sleeping with a colleague went against her personal code of ethics (an easy code to maintain, she admitted, because she'd never had a colleague who'd wanted to sleep with her). More problematic, though—relationships between partners and associates were explicitly forbidden by firm rules. Both of them could be disciplined if anyone found out. He'd get in trouble. She'd probably be asked to leave. And she'd have to find another job, start all over again—another round of interviews, boring half-days spent reciting the same answers to the same questions: *Have you always wanted to be a lawyer? What areas of the law appeal to you the most? What kind of practice do you see yourself developing? How would you fit in with this firm?*

Jim hadn't been like that. He interviewed her when she came to Lewis, Dommel, and Fenick. It was a beautiful September afternoon three months ago when she walked into the conference room, in her navy blue interview suit, with the folder full of firm PR clutched to her chest. After five years at Dillert McKeen she'd been looking for a change—a slightly smaller firm that would give her more responsibilities. This was her third interview of the week, and her feet, in navy Ferragamo pumps, were killing her, but one look at Jim Danvers had banished all thoughts of aching feet and other firms. She'd been expecting a standard-issue partner—fortyish, balding, bespectacled, carefully avuncular with potential female colleagues. And there was Jim, standing at the window, and when he turned to greet her, the late-afternoon light turned his blond hair into a golden crown. Not standard issue at all, and not fortyish, either— maybe thirty-five, Rose thought, a baby partner, five years older than she was, and so handsome. That jaw! Those eyes! The tantalizing whiff of aftershave he left in his wake! He was the kind of guy who'd always been strictly off-limits to Rose as she'd toiled through high school, college, and law school, keeping her nose to the grindstone and her grades in the stratosphere. But when he'd smiled, she'd caught a glint of silver against his teeth. A retainer, she saw, her heart lifting, blossoming inside of her chest. So maybe he wasn't perfect. Maybe there was hope.

"Ms. Feller?" he asked, and she nodded, not trusting her voice. He smiled at her, crossed the room in three long steps, and took her hand in his.

It had started, for her, at that moment—the sun behind him, his hand wrapped around hers, sending bolts of electricity shooting straight between her legs. She'd felt something she'd only read about, something she wasn't even sure that she believed in—passion. Passion as hot and steamy as anything from her Harlequin romances, passion that stole the breath right out of her throat. She looked at the smooth skin of Jim Danvers's neck and wanted to lick it, right there in the conference room.

"I'm Jim Danvers," he said.

She cleared her throat. Her voice was breathy, husky, a wanton rasp. "I'm Rose." Shit. What was her last name again? "Feller. Rose Feller. Hi."

It had started so slowly between them—the glance held a beat too long while waiting for the elevator, a hand that would linger at the small of her back, the way his eyes would seek her out in a crowd whenever the associates and partners wound up in a meeting together. Meanwhile, she gleaned whatever gossip she could. "Single," said her secretary. "Extremely single," said a paralegal. "Serial heartbreaker," whispered a first-year associate as she reapplied her lipstick in the ladies' room mirror. "And I hear he's good." Rose had blushed, washed her hands, and fled. She didn't want Jim to have a reputation. She didn't want him discussed in bathrooms. She wanted him to be hers alone. She wanted him to tell her she was beautiful, again and again.

In the apartment upstairs, a toilet flushed. Jim grunted in his sleep. When he rolled over, she felt his foot brush against her shin. Oh, dear. Rose ran an experimental toe up the length of her calf. The news was not good. She'd been meaning to shave her legs, had been meaning to shave them for some time, kept promising she'd shave them before she went to her aerobic class, but she'd last attended class three weeks ago, and she'd been wearing tights to work every day, and . . .

Jim rolled over again, pushing Rose to the absolute edge of the mattress. She stared unhappily at her living room, which might as well have borne a sign: Single Girl, Lonely, Late '90s. A trail of his-and-hers clothing lay on the floor beside five-pound bright yellow dumbbells propped up next to a Tae Bo tape that was still in its original plastic shrink-wrap. The treadmill she'd bought to fulfill a get-in-shape New Year's Resolution three New Years ago was draped with her dry cleaning. There was a half-empty Passionberry Punch wine cooler on the coffee table, four shoe boxes from Saks piled by the closet, and a half-dozen romance novels beside her bed. Disaster, Rose thought, wondering what she could do before dawn to give her apartment the appearance of being inhabited by someone with an interesting life. Was there an all-night emporium that sold throw pillows and bookcases? And was it too late to do something about her legs?

As quietly as she could, she reached for the portable phone and crept into the bathroom. Amy answered on the first ring. "Wassup?" she asked. In the background, Rose could hear Whitney Houston wailing, which meant that her best friend was watching *Waiting to Exhale* for the hundredth time. Amy wasn't black, but that didn't stop her from trying.

"You won't believe it," Rose whispered.

"Did you get laid?"

"Amy!"

"Well, did you? I mean, why else would you be ringing me now?"

"Actually," said Rose, flicking on the light and studying her glowing face in the mirror, "actually, I did. And it was . . ." She paused, and gave a little hop in the air. "It was so good!"

Amy whooped. "Way to go, girlfriend! So who's the lucky guy?"

"Jim," Rose breathed. Amy whooped even louder.

"And it was unbelievable!" said Rose. "It was . . . I mean, he's so . . ."

Her call waiting beeped. Rose stared at the phone unbelievingly.

"Ooh, popular girl," Amy said. "Call me back!"

Rose clicked over, glancing at her watch. Who'd be calling her at almost one in the morning? "Hello?" She could hear loud music, voices—a bar, a party. She slumped against the bathroom door. Maggie. Big surprise.

The voice on the other end was young, male, and unfamiliar. "Is this Rose Feller?"

"Yes. Who's this, please?"

"Um . . . well, my name's Todd."

"Todd," Rose repeated.

"Yeah. And, um . . . well, I'm here with your sister, I guess. Maggie, right?"

In the background, Rose could hear her sister's drunken shout.

"Little sister!" Rose scowled, grabbing a bottle of shampoo—"specially formulated for thin, limp, lifeless hair"—and tossed it under the sink, reasoning that if Jim stayed for a shower, he didn't need to be confronted with evidence of her problem locks.

"She's . . . um. Sick, I think. She had a lot to drink," Todd continued, "and she was . . . well . . . I don't know what else she was doing, really, but I found her in the bathroom and we were kind of hanging out for a while, and then she kind of passed out, and now she's, um, getting kind of loud. She told me to call you first, though," he added. "Before she passed out."

Rose could hear her sister shouting, "I'm King of the World!" "How nice of her," she said, throwing her prescription zit cream and a box of pantyliners in after the shampoo. "Why don't you just take her home?"

"I don't want to really get involved. . . ."

"Tell me, Todd," Rose began pleasantly, in the voice she'd practiced in law school, the one she imagined using to sucker witnesses into telling her what she needed to know. "When you and my sister were hanging out in the bathroom, what exactly was going on?"

There was silence on the other end.

"Now, I don't need to know specifics," said Rose, "but I'm inferring that you and my sister are already, to use your word, 'involved.' So why don't you be a stand-up guy about it and take her home?"

"Look, I think she needs help, and I've really got to go. . . . I borrowed my brother's car, I've got to get it back . . ."

"Todd . . ."

"Well, is there someone else I should call?" he asked. "Your parents? Your mother or something?"

Rose felt her heart stop. She closed her eyes. "Where are you?"

"The Cherry Hill Hilton. The high school reunion." Click. Todd was no more.

Rose leaned against the bathroom door. Here it was—her real

life, the truth of who she was, barreling down on her like a bus with bad brakes. Here was the truth—she wasn't the kind of person Jim could fall in love with. She wasn't what she'd made herself out to be—a cheerful, uncomplicated girl, a normal girl with a happy, orderly life, a girl who wore pretty shoes and had nothing more pressing on her mind than whether *ER* was a rerun this week. The truth was in the exercise tape she didn't have time to unwrap, let alone exercise to; the truth was her hairy legs and ugly underwear. Most of all, the truth was her sister, her gorgeous, messed-up, fantastically unhappy and astonishingly irresponsible sister. Only why tonight? Why couldn't Maggie have let her enjoy this one night?

"Fuck," she groaned softly. "Fuck, fuck, fuck." And then Rose padded back into her bedroom, groping for her glasses, sweatpants, boots, and car keys. She scribbled a quick note for Jim ("Family emergency, be back soon") and hurried to the elevator, steeling herself to drive off into the night and pull her sister's chestnuts out of the fire yet again.

The hotel had a "Welcome! Class of '89" banner still drooping from the front door. Rose stomped through the lobby—all faux marble and crimson carpet—and into the deserted lounge, which smelled of cigarette smoke and beer. There were tables covered in cheap red-and-white paper tablecloths with plastic pom-poms as centerpieces. In the corner, a guy and a girl were making out, leaning drunkenly against the wall. Rose squinted toward them. Not Maggie. She walked to the bar, where a man in a stained white shirt was putting away glasses and where her sister, in a tiny dress that was inappropriate for November—or, really, for any appearance in public—was slumped on a barstool.

Rose paused for a minute, considering her strategy. From a distance, Maggie looked just fine. You didn't notice the smeared makeup, the reek of booze and barf that surrounded her like a thick cloud, until you got up close.

The bartender gave Rose a sympathetic look. "She's been here for half an hour," he said. "I've been watching out for her. She's just had water to drink."

Terrific, Rose thought. *Where were you when she was probably getting gang-banged in the bathroom?*

"Thanks," she said instead, and shook her sister's shoulder. Not gently. "Maggie?"

Maggie opened one eye and scowled. "Leame lone," she said.

Rose gathered the straps of her sister's black dress and lifted. Maggie's butt rose six inches off the seat. "Party's over."

Maggie tottered to her feet and kicked Rose sharply in the shin with one silver sandal. Make that one Christian Louboutin silver stiletto sandal, Rose noticed as she looked down, one silver sandal coveted for three months, purchased just two weeks ago, and, she'd thought, still snug in its shoe box. One silver sandal now stained and splotched with the sticky residue of she didn't want to know what.

"Hey, those are mine!" Rose said, shaking her sister by her dress. *Maggie,* she thought, feeling the familiar fury coursing through her veins. Maggie takes *everything.*

"Fuck youuuu!" Maggie brayed, and twisted her body from side to side, trying to free herself from Rose's grasp.

"I can't believe you!" Rose hissed, hanging on to the straps as Maggie thrashed, and the toes of Maggie's shoes—*her* shoes— kicked at her shins. *Insult to injury,* she thought, imagining the bruises she'd find in the morning. "I haven't even worn them yet!"

"Easy there," the bartender called, clearly hoping that this was going to turn into a sister-on-sister catfight.

Rose ignored him and half dragged, half carried her sister out of the bar and deposited Maggie in her passenger seat.

"If you're going to throw up," Rose advised, yanking the seat belt around her sister, "give me a little advance warning."

"I'll send a telegram," Maggie muttered, reaching into her purse for her lighter.

"Oh, no," said Rose, "don't even think about smoking in here." She flicked on the lights, wrenched the steering wheel to the right, and started driving out of the deserted parking lot and onto the highway, heading toward the Ben Franklin Bridge and Bella Vista, where Maggie had the most recent in her extended series of apartments.

"Not this way," said Maggie.

"Okay," said Rose. Her hands tightened on the wheel in frustration. "So where are we going?"

"Take me to Sydelle's," Maggie mumbled.

"Why?"

"Just take me, okay? Jesus. I don't need to play twenty questions."

"Of course not," Rose said tightly. "I'm just your personal taxi driver. No need to give me an explanation. Just call my number and I'll show up."

"Bitch," Maggie said thickly. Her head lolled against the back of the seat, rolling back and forth each time Rose yanked on the wheel.

"You know," Rose said, in her most reasonable tone, "it is possible to attend one's high school reunion and not wind up drinking so much vodka that you don't even notice that you've passed out in the ladies' room."

"Whaddare you, a DARE officer?" asked Maggie.

"It's possible," Rose continued, "to simply attend, to reacquaint yourself with old friends, to dance, to dine, to drink responsibly, to wear clothes that you've bought for yourself instead of the ones you've taken from my closet . . ."

Maggie opened her eyes and stared at her sister, noting the large white plastic hair clip. "Hey, 1994 called," she said. "It wants its hairstyle back."

"What?"

"Don't you know that nobody wears those anymore?"

"So why don't you tell me what the really fashionable girls are wearing when they have to go pick up their drunk sisters in the middle of the night," said Rose. "I'd love to know. Have Nicky and Paris Hilton launched a line for us yet?"

"Whatever," Maggie mumbled, staring out the window.

"Are you happy this way?" Rose continued. "Drinking every night, running around with God knows who . . ."

Maggie rolled down the window and ignored her.

"You could go back to school," said Rose. "You could get a better job."

"And be just like you," Maggie said. "Wouldn't that be fun? No sex in, what's it been, Rose, three years? Four? When was the last time a guy looked at you?"

"I could have plenty of guys looking at me if I wore your clothes," Rose said.

"Like they'd fit," said Maggie. "Your *leg* wouldn't fit into this dress."

"Oh, right," said Rose. "I forgot that being a size zero is the most important thing in the world. Because it's obviously made you so successful and happy." She honked the horn longer than was necessary to get the car in front of her to move. "You've got problems," Rose said. "You need help."

Maggie threw back her head, cackling. "And you're just perfect, right?"

Rose shook her head, thinking of what she could say to shut her sister up, but by the time she'd formulated her line of attack, Maggie's head was resting on the window, her eyes shut tight.

Chanel, the golden retriever—Sydelle the Stepmonster's dog—turned in wild circles up and down the length of the yard as Rose drove up the driveway. A light went on in an upstairs bedroom, and another light appeared in the downstairs hall as Rose grabbed Maggie by her straps and hauled her onto her feet.

"Get up," she ordered.

Maggie stumbled in her sister's grasp, weaving up the driveway until she arrived at the front door of the oddly shaped modern house that their father and stepmother called home. The hedges were pruned into tortured curlicues, per Sydelle's instructions, and the doormat read, "Welcome Friends!" Rose had always figured the mat had come with the house, as their stepmother was neither particularly welcoming nor especially friendly. Maggie staggered up the path and bent over. Rose thought she was throwing up until she saw Maggie flip over one of the flagstones and fish out a key.

"You can go now," said Maggie, leaning against the door and fumbling with the lock. She waved good-bye without turning around. "Thanks for the ride; now, get lost."

The front door flew open as Sydelle Levine Feller stepped out into the night, lips pursed, bathrobe belted tightly around her five foot figure, face gleaming with skin cream. In spite of hours of exercise and thousands of dollars' worth of Botox shots and the recent addition of tattooed eyeliner, Sydelle Levine Feller was not a pretty woman. For one thing, she had tiny, dull brown eyes. For another, she had enormous, flaring nostrils—the kind of thing Rose always figured that the surgeons couldn't correct, because surely Sydelle had to have noticed that she could easily fit a Hebrew National salami up each one.

"She's drunk," Sydelle said, her nostrils flaring. "What a surprise." As always, she addressed her most hurtful remarks to the air three inches to the left of the recipient's face, as if she were directing her observation to some invisible onlooker who would undoubtedly see her side of things. Rose could remember dozens— no, hundreds—of those catty observations zinging past her own left ear . . . and Maggie's. *Maggie, you need to apply yourself to your schoolwork. Rose, I don't think you need a second helping.*

"Can't get anything by you, can I, Sydelle?" asked Maggie. Rose snorted in spite of herself, and for a moment, the two of them were a team again, united against a common, formidable enemy.

"Sydelle, I need to talk to my father," said Rose.

"And I," Maggie announced, "need to use the facilities."

Rose looked up and saw the glint of her father's glasses through the bedroom window. His tall, thin, slightly stooped frame was floating in pajama bottoms and an old T-shirt, and his fine gray hair drifted up around his bald spot. *When did he get so old?* Rose thought. He looked like a ghost. In the years since they'd been married, Sydelle had gotten more vivid—her lipstick increasingly brighter, her highlights ever more golden—and her father had faded, like a photograph left in the sun. "Hey, Dad!" she called. Her father turned toward her voice and started to open the window.

"Darling, I'll take care of this," Sydelle called up toward the bedroom window. Her words were sweet. Her tone was icy. Michael Feller paused with his hands at the bottom of the window, and Rose could imagine his face crumpling into its familiar expression of sadness and defeat. An instant later, the light flicked off, and her father vanished from view. "Shit," Rose muttered, although she wasn't surprised. "Dad!" she yelled again, helplessly.

Sydelle shook her head. "No," she said. "No, no, no."

"This episode brought to you by the word *No*," said Maggie, and Rose laughed, then returned her attention to her stepmother. She remembered the first day Sydelle had showed up at their apartment. Their father had been dating her for two months and had gotten dressed up for this occasion. Rose recalled him tugging at the sleeves of his sport jacket, readjusting the knot of his tie. "She's very excited about meeting both of you," he told Rose, who was then twelve, and Maggie, who was ten. Rose remembered thinking that Sydelle was the most glamorous woman she'd ever seen. She'd worn gold bracelets and gold earrings and shiny gold sandals. Her hair was streaked with ash and copper, her eyebrows were plucked to thin golden parentheses. Even her lipstick had a golden tinge. Rose was dazzled. It wasn't until later that she noticed Sydelle's less-lovely features—the way that her mouth fell naturally into a frown, how her eyes were the color of a muddy puddle, the nostrils that loomed like twin Lincoln Tunnels in the center of her face.

At dinner, Sydelle slid the bread basket out of her reach. "None for us!" she'd simpered, with what Rose thought was supposed to be a conspiratorial wink. "We girls need to watch our figures!" She pulled the same trick with the butter. When Rose made the mistake of reaching for a second helping of potatoes, Sydelle pursed her lips. "It takes the stomach twenty minutes to send a message to the brain that it is full," she lectured. "Why don't you wait a while and see if you really want those?" Her father and Maggie got ice cream for dessert. Rose got a dish of grapes. Sydelle had nothing. "I don't care for sweets," she said. The whole performance made Rose feel like throwing up . . . throwing up, and then sneaking back to the refrigerator for a belated bowl of ice cream. Which, if she remembered correctly, was exactly what she'd done.

Now she stared at Sydelle, imploring, wanting desperately to be done with this task, to drop Maggie off and hurry back to Jim . . . if he was even still there.

"I'm very sorry," Sydelle said, in a tone indicating that she was really anything but sorry. "If she's been drinking, she can't come in."

"Well, I haven't been drinking. Let me talk to my father."

Sydelle shook her head again. "Maggie is not your responsibility," she recited, parroting the speech she'd no doubt memorized from a Tough Love book. Or, more likely, a Tough Love pamphlet. Sydelle wasn't much of a reader.

"Let me talk to him," Rose said again, knowing it was hopeless.

Sydelle turned her body so that she was blocking the doorway, as if Rose and Maggie might try to sneak in past her. And Maggie wasn't improving the situation.

"Hey, Sydelle!" she cawed, shoving her sister aside. "You look great!" She squinted at her stepmother's face. "You did something new, right? Chin lift? Cheek implant? Li'l Botox? What's your secret?"

"Maggie," Rose whispered, grabbing her sister's shoulders and telepathically begging her to shut up. Which Maggie didn't do.

"Way to spend our inheritance!" she howled.

Sydelle finally looked right at them, instead of at the space between the two girls. Rose could practically hear what she was thinking, which was that her daughter, the much-vaunted Marcia, would never behave in such a fashion. Marcia—or My Marcia, as she was commonly called—was eighteen and a freshman at Syracuse by the time Sydelle and her father had wed. My Marcia, as Sydelle never tired of reminding Rose and Maggie, wore a perfect size six. My Marcia had been a member of the National Honor Society and the homecoming court. My Marcia had joined the best sorority at Syracuse, had graduated with honors, had worked for three years as an assistant to one of the top interior decorators in New York City before marrying a dot-com gazillionaire and gracefully retreating into motherhood and a seven-bedroom showplace in Short Hills.

"You both need to leave," said Sydelle, and closed the door, leaving Maggie and Rose out in the cold.

Maggie stared up at the bedroom window, perhaps hoping that their father would toss his wallet down. Finally, she turned and headed to the driveway, pausing only to yank one of Sydelle's curlicued hedges out of the ground and throw it at the doorstep, where it landed in a rattling shower of dirt. As Rose watched, Maggie pulled off the purloined high heels and hurled them at her sister on the lawn. "Here you go," she said.

Rose's hands curled into fists. She should have been in her apartment, in bed with Jim. Instead, here she was, in the middle of the night, in the middle of a frozen lawn in New Jersey, trying to help her sister, who didn't even want to be helped.

Maggie crossed the lawn on her bare feet and began limping down the road. "Where do you think you're going?" Rose called.

"Somewhere. Anywhere." Maggie said. "Don't worry about me, I'll be okay." She'd made it almost to the corner before Rose caught up.

"Let's go," Rose said roughly. "You can stay with me." Even as the words were exiting her lips, her internal alarms were sounding shrieking whoops of warning. Inviting Maggie to stay was like offering to host a hurricane, which she'd learned the hard way five years ago when Maggie had moved in with her for three horrible weeks. Maggie in your house meant that money would go missing along with your best lipstick, favorite pair of earrings, and costliest shoes.

Your car would vanish for days at a time and reappear with an empty gas tank and brimming ashtrays. Your house keys would disappear, and your clothes would waltz off their hangers, never to be seen again. Maggie in residence meant mess and confusion, dramatic scenes, tears and fights and hurt feelings. It meant the end of any peace and quiet she might have been foolish enough to hope for. Quite possibly, she thought with a shudder, it meant the end of Jim.

"Come on," Rose said again.

Maggie shook her head back and forth, a child's exaggerated no.

Rose sighed. "It'll only be for the night," she said. But at the touch of Rose's hand on her shoulder, Maggie whirled around. "No it won't," she said.

"What?"

"Because I got evicted again, all right?"

"What happened?" asked Rose, and restrained herself from adding, "this time."

"I got mixed up," Maggie muttered.

Mixed up, Rose had long ago learned, was Maggie's shorthand for the ways the world confounded her, the ways that her learning disabilities had her hamstrung and crippled. Numbers tripped her up, fractions and directions and balancing a checkbook were absolute impossibilities. Tell her to double a recipe and she couldn't. Ask her to find her way from Point A to Point B and Maggie would usually wind up at Point K, where she'd unfailingly locate a bar and have a few guys clustered around her by the time Rose showed up to retrieve her.

"Fine," said Rose. "We'll figure it out in the morning."

Maggie wrapped her arms around herself, and stood, skinny and shivering. She really should have been an actress, Rose thought. It was a shame all of this dramatic ability never got put to better use than extracting cash, shoes, and temporary housing from her family.

"I'll be fine," said Maggie. "I'll just stay here until it gets light, and then . . ." She sniffled. Goose bumps dotted her arms and shoulders. "I'll find somewhere to go."

"Come on," said Rose.

"You don't want me," Maggie repeated sadly. "Nobody does."

"Just get in the car." Rose turned and started walking toward the driveway, and she wasn't a bit surprised when, after a moment, Maggie followed. There were some things in life you could always count on, and Maggie needing help, Maggie needing money, Maggie just plain *needing* was one of them.

Maggie was quiet during the twenty-minute ride to Philadelphia, while Rose tried to decide how she was going to keep her sister from noticing that there was a pantsless partner in her bed. "You take the couch," she whispered once they were in her apartment, hurrying to snatch Jim's suit off the floor. Maggie didn't miss a thing.

"My, my," she drawled. "What have we here?" Her hand darted into the bundle of clothing in Rose's arms and emerged, seconds later, triumphantly clutching Jim's wallet. Rose grabbed for it, but Maggie jerked it away. *So it begins,* thought Rose.

"Give that back," she whispered. Maggie flipped the wallet open.

"James R. Danvers," she recited loudly. "Society Hill Towers, Philadelphia, Pee-Aye. Very nice."

"Shh!" Rose whispered, casting an alarmed glance at the wall behind which James R. Danvers presumably slumbered.

"Nineteen sixty-four," Maggie read in a stentorian voice. Rose could practically hear the gears turning as Maggie struggled to do the math. "He's thirty-five?" she finally asked. Rose grabbed the wallet from Maggie's hand.

"Go to sleep," she hissed.

Maggie selected a T-shirt from the clothes draped over Rose's treadmill and pulled her dress over her head. "Don't say it," she warned.

"You're too thin," Rose blurted, shocked by the sight of the prominent sweep of Maggie's collarbone and the individual bumps of her vertebra, made all the more pathetic by her ridiculous store-bought breasts.

"And you haven't been using the Ab Master I bought you," Maggie retorted, yanking the shirt over her head and snuggling into the couch.

Rose opened her mouth, then shut it. *Just get her to sleep,* she told herself.

"Your boyfriend looks cute, though," Maggie said, and yawned. "Could you bring me a glass of water and two Advils, please?"

Rose ground her teeth, but fetched the medication and the water, and watched Maggie gulp the pills, chug the water, and close her eyes without so much as a "thank you." In her bedroom, Jim still lay on his side, snoring softly. She rested one hand lightly on his arm.

"Jim?" she whispered. He didn't move. Rose contemplated crawling into bed with him, dragging the blankets up over her head and handling the morning in the morning. She glanced back at the door, looked down at Jim, and realized that she couldn't. She couldn't sleep with a naked man with her sister in the next room. Her job was, and had always been, to set an example for Maggie. Shacking up with a man who was sort of her boss didn't qualify. And what if he wanted sex again? Maggie would overhear, or worse, walk in, and stare. And laugh.

Instead, Rose pulled an extra blanket from the foot of the bed, grabbed a pillow from the floor, tiptoed back into the living room, and arranged herself on the armchair, thinking that in the annals of romantic history, this was probably the worst way a night like hers could end. She shut her eyes and listened for Maggie's breathing, the way she always had through all the years they'd shared a bedroom. Then she rolled over, trying to stretch out as much as she could. Why didn't she at least get the couch? Why had she invited Maggie over at all? Just then, Maggie started talking.

"Remember Honey Bun?"

Rose closed her eyes in the darkness. "Yes," she said. "I remember."

Honey Bun had come to them in the spring, when Rose was eight and Maggie was six. Their mother, Caroline, had woken them up early on a Thursday morning. "Shh, don't tell!" she'd whispered, hurrying them both into their best party dresses, then having them put on sweaters and coats on top. "It's a special surprise!" They'd called good-bye to their father, still lingering over coffee and the business section, hustled past the kitchen where the countertops were crammed with boxes of chocolate and the sink was filled with dirty dishes, and climbed into the station wagon. Instead of turning into the school entrance, the way she did most mornings, Caroline steered right past it, and kept going.

"Mom, you missed the turn!" called Rose.

"No school today, honey," their mother singsonged over her shoulder. "Today's a special day!"

"Yay!" said Maggie, who'd gotten the coveted front seat.

"Why?" asked Rose, who'd been looking forward to the day at school because it was Library Day and she'd get to pick out more books.

"Because something very exciting has happened," their mother said. Rose could remember exactly how her mother looked that day, the way her brown eyes glowed, and the gauzy turquoise scarf she'd wrapped around her neck. Caroline started talking very quickly, her words tumbling over each other, looking over her shoulder to tell Rose the big news. "It's candy," she said. "Fudge, really. Well, different than fudge. Better than fudge. Like divinity. Have you girls ever had that?"

Rose and Maggie shook their heads.

"I was reading in *Newsweek* about this woman who made cheesecakes," Caroline rambled, speeding around a curve and lurching to a stop at a traffic light. "And all of her friends raved about the cheesecakes, and first she got one supermarket in her neighborhood to carry them, and then she got a distributor, and now her cheesecakes are carried in eleven states. Eleven!"

A chorus of honks came from behind them. "Mom," said Rose. "Green light."

"Oh, right, right," said Caroline, stepping on the gas. "So last night I was thinking, well, I can't make cheesecake, but I can make fudge. My mother made the best fudge in the world, with walnuts and marshmallows, so I called her for the recipe and I was up all night, making batches and batches, had to go to the supermarket twice for ingredients, but here!" And she jerked the wheel sideways, pulling into a gas station. Rose noticed that her mother's fingernails were broken and sooty brown, as if she'd been digging through dirt. "Here! Try!" She reached into her purse and came up with two wax-paper-wrapped squares. "R and M Fudge," they read, in what looked to Rose like eyeliner.

"I had to improvise, of course, the packaging will change, but taste it and tell me whether that's not the best fudge you've ever had in your life!"

Rose and Maggie unwrapped the fudge. "Delicious!" said Maggie, with her mouth full.

"Ooh, yum," said Rose, struggling to swallow the lump of fudge, which was sticking in her throat.

"R and M for Rose and Maggie!" said their mother, starting to drive again.

"Why can't it be M and R?" asked Maggie.

"Where are we going?" asked Rose.

"To Lord and Taylor," their mother said gaily. "I thought about supermarkets, of course, but what I decided is that this is really a gourmet product, not a grocery item, and it should be sold in boutiques and department stores."

"Does Dad know about this?" asked Rose.

"We're going to surprise him," said Caroline. "Take off those sweaters and make sure your faces are clean. We're making a sales call, girls!"

Rose turned on her side, remembering the rest of the day—the manager's polite smile when her mother had upended her handbag on the costume jewelry counter and dumped out two dozen squares of wax-paper-wrapped R and M fudge (and two squares reading "M and R," which Maggie had changed in the car). How their mother had whisked them up to the girls' department and bought them matching rabbit-fur muffs. How they'd had lunch in the Lord and Taylor tearoom, cream-cheese-and-olive sandwiches with the crusts cut off, tiny pickles barely longer than Rose's baby finger, slices of angel food cake with strawberries and whipped cream. How beautiful their mother looked, her cheeks flaring pink, her eyes sparkling, her hands fluttering like birds, ignoring her own lunch as she described her sales ideas, her marketing plans, how R and M Fudge would be as popular as Keebler or Nabisco. "We're starting small, girls, but everyone has to start somewhere," she'd said. Maggie nodded and told Caroline how good the fudge was and asked for seconds on sandwiches and cake, and Rose sat there, trying to force down a few bites of her lunch and wondering whether she'd been the only one to notice the manager's raised eyebrows and overly polite smile when all that candy came cascading onto the countertop.

After lunch they went walking through the mall. "Each of you can get one present," their mother said. "Anything you want. Anything at all!" Rose asked for a Nancy Drew book. Maggie wanted a puppy. Their mother didn't hesitate.

"Of course a puppy!" she'd said, her voice rising. Rose noticed other shoppers staring at the three of them—two little girls in party dresses, one woman in a skirt printed with red poppies and a turquoise scarf, tall and beautiful, carrying six shopping bags and talking way too loud. "We should have gotten a puppy a long time ago!"

"Dad's allergic," Rose said. Her mother either didn't hear, or decided to ignore her. She grabbed her daughters by their hands and hurried them over to the pet shop, where Maggie picked out a small tan cocker spaniel puppy and named it Honey Bun.

"Mom was nuts, but she was fun, wasn't she?" Maggie asked in her underwater voice.

"Yeah, she was," said Rose, remembering how they'd come home, laden with shopping bags and Honey Bun's cardboard carrying case, to their father sitting on the couch, still in his suit and tie from work, waiting.

"Girls, go to your room," he'd said, taking Caroline by the hand and leading her to the kitchen. Rose and Maggie, carrying Honey Bun in her box, walked quietly upstairs, but even through the closed bedroom door, they could hear their mother's voice rising to a shriek. *Michael, it was a good idea, it was a legitimate business idea, there's no reason it won't work, and I just bought the girls a few treats, I'm their mother, I can do what I want, I can take them out of school once in a while, it doesn't matter, we had a nice day, Michael, a special day, a day they'll always remember, and I'm sorry I forgot to call the school, but you shouldn't have worried, they were with me and I'M THEIR MOTHER I'M THEIR MOTHER I AM THEIR MOTHER. . . .*

"Oh, no," Maggie whispered, as the puppy started to whine. "Are they fighting? Is it our fault?"

"Shh," said Rose. She gathered the puppy into her arms. Maggie's thumb crept into her mouth as she leaned against her sister, and they listened to their mother's screams, now punctuated with the sound of things being thrown and things breaking, and their father's murmur, which seemed to consist of a single word: *Please.*

"How long did we have Honey Bun?" asked Maggie. Rose twisted in the armchair and struggled to remember.

"A day, I think," she said. It was coming back to her now. The next morning, she'd gotten up early to walk the dog. The hallway was dark; their parents' bedroom door was closed. Their father was sitting at the kitchen table alone.

"Your mother's resting," he said. "Can you take care of the dog? Can you get breakfast for yourself and Maggie?"

"Sure," said Rose. She gave her father a long look. "Is Mom . . . is she okay?"

Her father sighed, and restacked the newspaper. "She's just tired, Rose. She's resting. Try to keep quiet, and let her rest. Take care of your sister."

"I will," Rose promised. When she came home from school that afternoon, the dog was gone. Her parents' bedroom door was still closed. And here she was, twenty-two years later, still keeping that promise, still taking care of her sister.

"It was really good fudge, wasn't it?" asked Maggie. In the dark, she sounded like her six-year-old self—happy and hopeful, a merry little girl who wanted to believe everything her mother told her.

"It was delicious," said Rose. "Good night, Maggie," she said, in a tone she hoped would make it clear that she wasn't interested in any more discussion.

When Jim Danvers opened his eyes the next morning, he was alone in the bed. He stretched, scratched himself, then got to his feet, wrapped a towel around his waist, and went in search of Rose.

The bathroom door was locked, and he could hear water running behind it. He knocked gently, sweetly, seductively, even, imagining Rose in the shower, Rose's skin flushed and steamy, Rose's bare chest beaded with water . . .

The door swung open, and a girl who was not Rose stalked out.

"Hlgho," said Jim, struggling for some combination of "hello" and "who are you?"

The strange girl was slender, with long reddish-brown hair piled on top of her head, a delicate heart-shaped face, and full pink lips. She had painted toenails, tanned legs that stretched toward her chin, and hard nipples (he couldn't help but notice) poking against the threadbare front of her T-shirt. She scowled at him sleepily. "Was that even English?" she asked. Her eyes were wide and brown and rimmed with layers of liner and sleep-smeared mascara—hard, watchful eyes, the color of Rose's eyes, but somehow very different.

Jim tried it again. "Hello," he said. "Is, um, Rose around?"

The strange girl cocked her thumb toward the kitchen. "In there," she said. She leaned against the wall. Jim became aware that a towel was all he was wearing. The girl cocked one leg behind her, resting her foot flat against the wall, and eyed him slowly, up and down.

"You're Rose's roommate?" he guessed, unable to remember whether Rose had mentioned a roommate.

The girl shook her head, just as Rose rounded the corner, fully clothed, shoes and lipstick on, with two cups of coffee in her hands.

"Oh!" she said, and stopped so quickly that coffee sloshed backward, splashing her wrists and the front of her blouse. "Oh. You guys have met?"

Mutely, Jim shook his head. The girl said nothing . . . just kept staring at him with a small, sphinxlike grin.

"Maggie, this is Jim," Rose said. "Jim, this is Maggie Feller. My sister."

"Hello," said Jim, and bobbed his head, clutching his towel tightly.

Maggie gave a short nod. They stood there for an instant, the three of them, Jim feeling ridiculous in his towel, Rose, with coffee dripping from her sleeves, and Maggie staring back and forth between them.

"She came last night," said Rose. "She was at her high-school reunion, and . . ."

"I don't think he needs details," said Maggie. "He can wait for the *E! True Hollywood Story* like everyone else."

"Sorry," said Rose.

Maggie sniffed, turned on her heel, and stalked back to the living room. Rose sighed. "Sorry," she said again. "It's always a production with her."

Jim nodded. "Hey," he said quietly, "I want to hear all about it. Just give me a minute . . ." he said, nodding toward the bathroom.

"Oh!" said Rose, "oh, I'm sorry."

"Don't worry," he said, whispering, nuzzling her cheek and the soft flesh of her neck with his stubble. She trembled, and the remaining coffee quivered in the cups.

When Jim and Rose left a half-hour later, Maggie had returned to the couch. One bare foot and smooth, naked calf poked out from the blankets. Rose was sure she wasn't sleeping. She was certain

that this—the tanned curve of her sister's leg, the scarlet toenails—
was a calculated display. She hustled Jim out the door, thinking
that this had been what she'd wanted—to perform the classic kit-
tenish Hollywood wake-up, all smudgy and glamorous and gorgeous, with the slow fluttering of eyelashes, the contented smile.
And now Maggie got to be the smudgy, sexy, glamorous one, while
she was bustling around like Betty Crocker, offering people coffee.

"Are you working today?" he asked. She nodded.

"Work on the weekends," he mused. "I'd forgotten what being
an associate was like." He kissed her good-bye at her front door—a
brisk, businesslike peck—and looked in his wallet for his parking
stub. "Huh," he said, frowning, "I could've sworn there was a hundred bucks in here."

Maggie, Rose thought to herself, even as she reached into her wallet for a twenty. Maggie, Maggie, Maggie, who always makes me pay.

TWO

Morning. Ella Hirsch lay alone in the center of her bed and assessed her various aches, pains, and maladies. She began with her cranky left ankle, progressed to her throbbing right hip, paused at her intestines, which felt both empty and knotted at the same time, and moved steadily upward, past the breasts that were shrinking each year, up over her eyes (the cataract surgery last month had been a success), and on to the hair that she wore unfashionably long and dyed a warm auburn—her one vanity.

Not bad, not bad, thought Ella, as she swung first her left leg, then her right one, out of the bed, resting her feet lightly on the cool tiled floor. Ira, her husband, had never wanted tiles—"Too hard!" he'd said, "Too cold!" And so they'd had wall-to-wall carpeting. Beige. The day shiva was over, Ella had been on the phone, and two weeks later, the carpet was gone and she had her tile—a creamy white marble that felt smooth under her feet.

Ella put her hands on top of her thighs, rocked back and then forth, once and then twice, and struggled, groaning slightly, out of the queen-sized bed—her second apres-Ira purchase. It was the Monday after Thanksgiving, and Golden Acres, "a retirement community for active seniors," was unusually quiet, because most of those active seniors had spent the holiday with their children and grandchildren. Ella, too, had celebrated, in her own little way. She'd had a turkey sandwich for dinner.

She smoothed out her quilt and considered the day—breakfast, and the poem she had to finish, then she'd take the trolley to the bus stop and take the bus to her weekly volunteer session at the pet shelter. Then she'd come home for lunch and a nap, and maybe she'd read for an hour or two—she was halfway through taping a book of Margaret Atwood short stories for the vision impaired. Dinner was early—"Four o'clock's the late seating here," she'd heard somebody joking, and it was funny because it was true—and then the Clubhouse had Movie Night. Another empty day, stuffed as full as she could manage.

She'd made a mistake, moving here. Florida had been Ira's idea. "A new start," he'd said, fanning the brochures out over the kitchen table, with the lights glinting off his bald spot, his gold watch and wedding ring. Ella had barely glanced at the glossy photographs of sandy beaches, surf and palm trees, white buildings with elevators and wheelchair ramps and showers with built-in stainless steel grab bars. She'd thought only that Golden Acres, or any of the dozen communities just like it, would be a good place to hide. No more former friends and neighbors to stop her at the post office or the grocery store, to place well-meaning hands on her forearm and say, *How are you two holding up? How long has it been now?* She'd been almost happy, almost hopeful, packing up their house in Michigan.

She hadn't known, couldn't have guessed, could never have figured that the whole point of a retirement community was children. They hadn't showed that in the brochures, she thought bitterly— how every living room she'd visit would have every available surface crammed with pictures of children, grandchildren, great-grandchildren. How every conversation would eventually make its way back to that most precious commodity. *My daughter loved that movie. My son bought a car just like that. My granddaughter's applying to college. My grandson said that senator's a crook.*

Ella kept herself apart from the other women. She stayed busy. Pet shelter, hospital, Meals on Wheels, shelving books at the library, pricing goods at the thrift store, the column she wrote for the Acres's weekly newspaper.

On that morning, she sat at her kitchen table, a cup of hot tea in front of her, with sunshine gleaming on her tiled floor, and took out her notebook and pen. She was going to finish the poem she'd started last week. Not that she was much of a poet, but Lewis Feldman, the editor of the *Golden Acres Gazette,* had come to her in desperation after the regular poet had broken her hip. The deadline was Wednesday, and she wanted to have Tuesday free for revisions.

"Just Because I'm Old," was the title she'd come up with. "Just because I'm old," the poem began, "because my step's a little slow, because my hair has gotten gray, because I nap most ev'ry day . . ."

And that was as far as she'd gotten. She sipped her tea, considering. Just because she was old . . . well, what?

"I AM NOT INVISIBLE," she wrote, in big bold capital letters. Then she crossed it out. It wasn't true. She did feel she'd turned sixty and been erased, somehow, and had been invisible for the last eighteen years. Real people—young people—looked right through her. But "invisible" would be a very hard word to rhyme.

She decided to come back to 'invisible' and wrote, beneath it, "I matter." *Matter* should be easier . . . but then, what could she rhyme that with? "I can make a good cake batter?" "I can hear the trolley's clatter?" "Even though I've gotten fatter?"

Yes! *Fatter* was good. People at Golden Acres would identify. Especially, she thought with a smile, her almost-friend Dora, who volunteered at the thrift shop with her. Dora wore elastic-waist everything, and always ordered whipped cream with dessert. "I spent seventy years watching what I ate," she'd say, spooning a mouthful of hot fudge or cheesecake. "My Mortie's gone now, so why should I worry?"

"I matter. Even thought I've gotten fatter, I'm still here," Ella wrote. "I have ears to hear the sounds of life around me . . ."

Which was true, she mused. Except the sounds of life at Golden Acres were, if she was perfectly honest, the constant drone of traffic, the occasional wail of the ambulance siren, and people picking fights with each other because they'd left their clothes in the communal dryer at the end of the hall, or put plastic bottles into the "glass only" recycling bin. Not exactly the stuff of poetry.

"The ocean's gentle thunder," she wrote instead. "The sound of children laughing. The music of sun and smiles."

There. That was good. The ocean part was even possible— Golden Acres was a mile away from the shore. The trolley went there. And "the music of sun and smiles." Lewis would like that. In his life before Golden Acres, Lewis had run a chain of hardware stores in Utica, New York. He liked editing—"newspapering," he called it—a lot better. Every time she saw him, he had a red grease pencil tucked behind his ear, as if he might be called upon at any minute to dash off a headline, or edit some copy.

Ella closed her notebook and took a sip of her tea. Eight-thirty, and it was already getting hot. She rose from her seat thinking only of the full day she had before her, the full week after that. Only, as she walked, she could hear the very thing she'd written about—the sound of children's laughter. Boys, from the sound of it. She could hear their shouts, and their sandals slapping as they ran back and forth along the corridor outside of her door, chasing the tiny, darting chameleons who sunned themselves on the ledge, most likely. They were Mavis Gold's grandsons, she thought. Mavis had mentioned she was getting ready for a visit.

"I got one! I got one!" called one of the boys, his voice full of excitement. Ella closed her eyes. She should go outside and tell them not to be afraid, that the chameleons had more to fear from their clumsy, sweaty boy-palms and boy-fingers than the boys had to fear from the chameleons. She should go and tell them to stop shouting before Mr. Boehr in 6-B came out and started yelling about his insomnia.

Instead, she turned her face from the window before she let herself open the blinds and look at the boys. Children hurt . . . even though it had been more than fifty years since her daughter had been a child, and more than twenty years since she'd last seen her granddaughters.

Ella set her lips in a tight line and walked resolutely toward the bathroom. She wouldn't go down that road today. She wouldn't think about the daughter-who-was-gone, or the grandchildren she would never get to know, about the life that was snatched away from her, excised as cleanly and completely as a tumor, leaving not even a scar for her to cherish, to remember it by.

THREE

More and more, Rose Feller was starting to think that her boss had lost his mind.

Sure, she knew that everyone thought his or her boss was crazy. All of her friends—well, Amy—had the usual spate of complaints: the unreasonable demands, the inconsiderate treatment, the drunken ass-patting at the company picnic.

But now, filing into the conference room for the pep rally that Don Dommel had instituted as a Friday afternoon ritual, Rose was once again faced with the possibility that one of her firm's founding partners wasn't just eccentric or odd, or any of those polite adjectives reserved for powerful men, but he was actually honest-to-God nuts.

"People!" the man of the hour bellowed, thwacking a PowerPoint chart of the firm's billable hours with his fist. "We have GOT to do BETTER than THIS! THIS," he continued, "is GOOD, but not GREAT. And with the talent we've got, even GREAT is NOT GOOD ENOUGH! We have to GRIND DOWN the handrail of mediocrity and OLLIE OVER to excellence!"

"Huh?" muttered the associate on Rose's right. He had frizzy gingery hair and his skin, pale as skim milk, was a badge of honor in this place, the sure sign that he was making his minimum billable hours and, hence, not getting out much. Simon Something, Rose thought.

Rose shrugged at him, and slumped in her seat. How many law firms had pep rallies, anyhow? she thought. How many associates had received custom-made skateboards with the words "DOMMEL LAW" painted on the top, instead of the customary cash, for their holiday bonuses last year? How many managing partners delivered weekly speeches couched almost exclusively in sports metaphors, followed by an overamplified rendition of "I Believe I Can Fly"? How many law firms had theme music at all? Not many, Rose thought sourly.

"Is an Ollie a person or a thing?" Simon Something persisted. Rose gave another shrug, hoping, as she did each week, that Dommel's Xtreme gaze wouldn't fall on her. Don Dommel had always been a jock, Rose knew. He'd jogged through the seventies, felt the burn during the eighties, even finished a few triathalons before plunging headlong into the brave new world of extreme sports and taking his law firm along with him. At some point past his fiftieth birthday he'd decided that conventional exercise, no matter how strenuous, just wasn't enough. Don Dommel didn't just want to be fit, he wanted to be edgy and hip, radical and cool. Don Dommel wanted to be a fifty-three-year-old lawyer on a skateboard. Don Dommel, apparently, saw no contradiction between those two things.

He bought two specially-made skateboards and found a semi-homeless kid who seemed to live in Love Park to coach him (technically, the kid worked in the mail room, but nobody'd ever seen so much as the tip of his dreadlocks down there). He constructed a wooden ramp inside of the law firm's parking garage, spent every lunch hour on it, even after he'd broken his wrist, bruised his tailbone, and developed a limp that had him lurching through the firm's halls like an imperfectly rehearsed drag queen.

And it wasn't enough that he himself wanted to become an urban warrior. Don Dommel had to extend his vision to the entirety of the firm. One Friday, Rose had come into work and found a nylon jersey shoved into her mail slot, with her last name on the back above the words *I Can Fly!* "Please," Rose had said to her secretary. "I can barely walk before I've had my coffee." But the jerseys weren't optional. A firm-wide e-mail said that all associates should wear them every Friday. The week after that, once she'd reluctantly tugged the jersey over her shoulders, Rose had put her mug under the coffee dispenser only to find that it, plus all of the firm's water-coolers and soda machines, were dispensing only Gatorade. Which, the last time Rose had checked, wasn't caffeinated. Which meant it was going to do her no good at all.

So now she sat miserably in a seat in the center of the third row with her fly jersey pulled over her suit jacket, sipping warm sports beverage and wishing desperately that she had coffee. "This is getting ridiculous," she murmured to herself, as Dommel once again dispensed with the afternoon's advertised topic ("Effective Depositions," Rose remembered) in favor of a video of Tony Hawk highlights.

"Psst," said Simon, out of the corner of his mouth, as Dommel tore into a cringing first-year. ("YOU! DO YOU BELIEVE YOU CAN SOAR?")

Rose glanced at him. "Psst? Did you actually just say 'psst'? Are we in a detective novel?"

Simon raised his eyebrows in an exaggerated sneaky manner and opened a brown paper bag. Rose's nose twitched at the scent of coffee. Her mouth watered. "Want some?" he whispered.

She hesitated, looked around, considered the breaches of etiquette involved in sipping someone else's coffee, then decided that if she didn't get some caffeine, she'd be a jittery, worthless mess for the rest of the day. She ducked her head and gulped.

"Thanks," she whispered. He nodded, just as Don Dommel's white-hot gaze fell upon him.

"YOU!" roared Dommel. "WHAT'S YOUR DREAM?"

"To be six foot ten," Simon answered without hesitation. A ripple of laughter started in the back of the room. "And to play for the

Sixers." The laughter swelled. Don Dommel stood on the stage looking bewildered, as if his audience of loyal associates had suddenly turned into donkeys. "Maybe not as a center. I'd be happy to play guard," Simon continued. "But if that's not going to happen . . ." He paused, and looked up at Don Dommel. "I'd settle for being a good lawyer."

Rose giggled. Don Dommel opened his mouth, then shut it, then lurched across the stage. "THAT!" he finally announced, "THAT is the SPIRIT I'm looking for. I want EACH and EVERY ONE OF YOU to go BACK and THINK about that kind of WINNING ATTITUDE!" Dommel concluded. Rose had pulled her jersey off over her suit jacket and wadded it into her purse before his mouth was shut.

"Here," Simon said, offering her his cup of coffee. "I've got more in my office, if you want this one."

"Oh, thanks," Rose said, taking the cup, still scanning the sea of departing bodies for Jim's. She caught up with him by the receptionist's desk.

"What in God's name was that about?" she asked.

"Why don't you come into my office, and we can discuss it," he said, for the benefit of anyone within earshot, smiling a wicked smile, for her benefit alone. He closed the door and whirled her into his arms.

"Umm, do I detect dark roast?" he asked, kissing her.

"Don't rat me out," said Rose, kissing him back.

"Never," he growled, lifting her hips (*Oh, God,* thought Rose, *don't let him hurt himself!*) and settling her on his desk. "Your secrets," he said, kissing her neck, "are safe," and now his lips were sliding down her cleavage and his hands were busy with her buttons, "with me."

FOUR

At eleven o'clock the following Monday morning, Maggie Feller
opened her eyes and stretched her arms over her head. Rose was
gone. Maggie walked to the bathroom, where she drank thirty-two
ounces of water and continued with her in-depth examination of
her habitat, starting with the medicine cabinet, where the shelves
were so well-stocked it seemed as if her sister expected a dire medical emergency to befall Philadelphia, and that she alone would be
called upon to play Florence Nightingale to the city's entire population.

There were bottles of painkillers, boxes of antacids, a jumbo-
sized jug of Pepto-Bismol, a family-sized box of Band-Aid bandages, and a Red Cross–approved first-aid kit. There was Midol and
Advil and Nuprin, NyQuil and DayQuil, cough syrup and cold
tablets and tampons. Here was a girl who made good use of the
coupons at CVS, Maggie thought, as she sorted through Ace bandages and multivitamins, calcium tablets and dental floss, rubbing
alcohol and hydrogen peroxide, prescription-strength benzoyl peroxide and four unopened toothbrushes. Where was the eyeliner?
Where were the blush and the concealer that her sister so desperately needed? Maggie hadn't found anything cosmetic except for a
single half-used lipstick. There was makeup remover—a tub of

Pond's cold cream—but no makeup. What did Rose think? That somebody was going to sneak into her apartment in the dead of night, tie her up, put makeup on her face, and then leave?

Plus, there wasn't so much as a single condom or tube of spermicide, although there was an unopened package of Monistat—so just in case her celibate sister somehow managed to get a yeast infection from a toilet seat or something, she'd be ready. It was probably on sale, Maggie snorted, helping herself to a bottle of Midol.

The bathroom was also minus a scale. Which wasn't a surprise, given Rose's history with bathroom scales. When they were teenagers, Sydelle had taped a laminated chart on the girls' bathroom wall. Each Saturday morning, Rose would stand on the scale, her eyes shut and her face impassive, as Sydelle recorded the number and then sat on the toilet seat, quizzing Rose about what she'd eaten during the week. Even now, Maggie could hear her stepmother's too-sweet voice. *You had a salad? Well, what kind of dressing was on it? Was it fat free? Are you sure? Rose, I'm only doing this to help you. I've got your best interests at heart.*

Yeah, right, Maggie thought. As if Sydelle was ever interested in anyone but herself, and her own daughter. In the bedroom, Maggie pulled on a pair of her sister's sweatpants and continued her inventory, gathering what she called Information.

"You're a very smart girl," her old teacher Mrs. Fried used to tell her, back in elementary school. Mrs. Fried, with her gray curls and impressive shelf of a bosom, with her beaded eyeglass chain and knitted sweater vests, had taught Maggie what was euphemistically called "enrichment" (and what was known to the students as "special ed") from second grade through sixth. She was a kind, grandmotherly woman who'd become Maggie's ally, especially during her first months in a new school, in a new state. "Part of what makes you so smart is that you can always think of another way to get the job done. So if you don't know what a word means, what do you do?"

"Guess?" guessed Maggie.

Mrs. Fried smiled. "Figure it out through context, is how I'd

put it. It's all about finding solutions. Solutions that work for you."
Maggie had nodded, feeling pleased and flattered, which were not
normally ways she felt during class. "So imagine you are on your
way to the Vet, for a concert, but there's a big traffic jam. Would
you go home? Skip the concert? No," Mrs. Fried had said, before
Maggie'd had a chance to ask her who was playing at this theoretical concert so she could figure out how much effort it was worth.
"You'd just find another way to get there. And you're smart enough
to do it really well." In addition to figuring out a word's meaning
from context, Mrs. Fried's alternative strategies taught Maggie to
add numbers if she couldn't multiply them, to chart out a paragraph's meaning, circling the subject, underlining the verbs. In the
years since school, Maggie had come up with a few new strategies of
her own, like Information, which could be defined as knowing
things about people that they didn't want or expect you to know.
Information was always useful, and it was usually easy to come by.
Through the years Maggie secretly perused credit-card bills and
diaries, bank statements and old photographs. In high school, she'd
located a battered copy of *Forever* between Rose's mattress and box
spring. Rose had turned over her allowance for almost an entire
school year before deciding that she didn't care if Maggie told her
father how she'd dog-eared the pages with sex scenes.

Maggie snooped over to her sister's desk. There were gas bill,
electric bill, phone bill, and cable bill, all neatly paper-clipped
together, the return envelopes already bearing stamps and address
labels. Here was a receipt from Tower Records, which told her that
Rose had purchased (and worse, paid full price for) a copy of George
Michael's greatest hits. Maggie pocketed it, sure that it would be
useful, even if she wasn't sure how. A receipt from Saks for a pair of
shoes. Three hundred and twelve dollars. Very nice. A schedule of
classes at the gym, six months out of date. No surprise there.
Maggie closed the drawer and moved on to what was sure to be the
depressing terrain of Rose's closet.

She flipped through the hangers, shaking her head at the

clothes that ranged in shade from black to brown, with the occasional gray sweater thrown in for fun. Drab, drab, drab. Boring suits all in a row, and dowdy sweater sets, a half-dozen skirts designed to hit Rose in the dead center of her calves, as if she'd picked them out to give her legs the illusion of maximum thickness. Maggie could have helped her. But Rose didn't want help. Rose thought her life was fine. Rose thought it was everyone else who had the problems.

There was a time, when they were little girls, that people thought they were twins, with their matching pigtails and identical brown eyes and the defiant way their jaws poked forward. Well, not anymore. Rose was maybe an inch or two taller, and at least fifty pounds heavier, maybe more—Maggie could make out a faint slackening under her jawline, the beginning of the dread double chin. She had shirts in her closet from Lane Bryant, which Maggie didn't even want to touch, although she knew that fat wasn't contagious. And Rose just didn't care. Her hair, shoulder-length, was usually shoved into an untidy bun or ponytail or, worse, done up in one of those plastic clips that everyone else in the world had tacitly agreed to stop wearing five years ago. Maggie wasn't even sure where Rose was still finding them—dollar stores, probably—but somehow she had an endless supply, even though Maggie made it a point to toss a few in the trash whenever she visited.

Maggie took a deep breath, pushing the last jacket aside, and began with the thing she'd been saving for dessert—her sister's shoes. As always, what she saw dazzled her and made her feel sick, like a little kid who'd gorged on too much Halloween candy. Rose, fat, lazy, unfashionable Rose, Rose who couldn't be bothered to exfoliate or moisturize or polish her fingernails, had somehow managed to acquire dozens of pairs of the absolutely most perfect shoes in the world. There were flats and stilettos and high-heeled Mary Janes, suede loafers so buttery soft you wanted to rub them against your cheek, a pair of Chanel sandals that were little more than a slim leather sole and wisps of gold wire and ribbon. There were knee-high Gucci boots in glossy black, ankle-high Stephane Kelian boots in cinnamon, a pair of crimson cowgirl boots with hand-stitched jalapeño peppers winding up the sides. There were lace-up Hush Puppies in raspberry and lime; there were Sigerson Morrison flats and Manolo Blahnik mules. There were Steve Madden loafers and, still in their Saks box, a pair of Prada kitten heels, white, with white-and-yellow daisies appliquéd over the toes. Maggie held her breath and eased them on. As always—as all of Rose's shoes did—they fit her perfectly.

It wasn't fair, she thought, stalking into the kitchen in the Pradas. Where was Rose going to wear a pair of shoes like these, anyhow? What was the point? She scowled and opened a cabinet. Whole Wheat Total. All-Bran. Golden raisins and brown rice. Jesus Christ, she thought, wrinkling her nose. Was it National Healthy Colon week? And there were no Fritos, no Cheetos, no Doritos . . . nothing at all from the all-important Ito food group. She rummaged through the freezer, past the veggie burgers and pints of whole fruit all-natural sorbet sitting in a row until she hit pay dirt—a pint of Ben and Jerry's New York Superfudge Chunk, still in its brown paper bag. Ice cream had always been her sister's go-to comfort food, Maggie thought, grabbing a spoon and proceeding back to the couch, where a section of newspaper sat at the center of the coffee table, with a red pen laid beside it. Maggie picked it up. Today's classified ads, thoughtfully provided by big sister Rose. Of course.

Well, she thought, this was a pretty pass. That was one of the things Mrs. Fried used to say. Whenever something would go wrong in the classroom—a spilled can of paint, a lost book—Mrs. Fried would clasp her hands across her chest and shake her head until her eyeglass chain rattled and say, "Well, this is a pretty pass!"

But even Mrs. Fried couldn't have predicted this, thought Maggie, eating ice cream with one hand and circling classified ads with the other. Not even Mrs. Fried could have seen Maggie Feller's downfall coming as swiftly as it had, so that Maggie still felt as if somewhere between the ages of fourteen and sixteen she'd walked off the edge of a cliff and had been falling ever since.

Elementary school and junior high had been fine, she remembered, spooning the cool creaminess even faster past her lips (and not noticing when she accidentally dropped a chocolate-covered walnut on the shoe). She'd had to go to "enrichment" during recess three days a week, but not even that had mattered much, because she was still the prettiest, most fun girl in her class, the girl with the cutest outfits, the best Halloween costumes that she'd make herself, the most interesting ideas of what to do during recess. And after her mother died and they'd moved to New Jersey, when her father would be at work in the afternoons and Sydelle would be off at some volunteer committee thing and Rose, of course, would be busy with the chess club or debate team, she'd been the girl with access to an empty house and an unlocked liquor cabinet. She'd been popular. It was Rose who'd been the nerd, the geek, the loser, Rose who'd skulked around with her thick glasses hiding half her face and dandruff silting her shoulders, Rose who'd been the one the girls had laughed at.

She could close her eyes and still remember one afternoon at recess. She'd been in fourth grade and Rose was in sixth. Maggie was heading to play hopscotch with Marissa Nussbaum and Kim Pratt when Rose had strolled right through a game of dodgeball, oblivious, holding a book up to her eyes.

"Hey, move it!" one of the older boys, a sixth-grader, shouted, and Rose raised her head and looked puzzled. *Move, Rose,* Maggie thought as hard as she could, as Kim and Marissa tittered. Rose kept walking, not picking up the pace, when another one of the big boys picked up the ball and threw it at her, as hard as he could, grunting with the effort. He'd been aiming for her body, but his aim wasn't good, and he hit Rose in the back of her head. Rose's glasses went flying. Her books flew out of her arms as she staggered forward, got her feet tangled, and fell flat on her face.

Maggie's heart stopped beating. She stood as if she'd been

frozen, stood as still as the circle of sixth-grade boys, who'd looked at each other uneasily, as if they were trying to decide whether this was still funny, or whether they'd really hurt this girl and could get in trouble. And then one of them—Sean Perigini, most likely, the tallest boy in sixth grade—started laughing. And then they were all laughing, all the sixth-grade boys, and then all the kids who'd been watching, as Rose, of course, started to cry, and then wiped the snot off her face with a palm that was bleeding from her fall and started groping around for her glasses.

Maggie had stood there, part of her knowing she shouldn't let them do that, and part of her thinking, cruelly, *Let Rose figure it out. She's the one who's such a loser. She brought this on herself.* Plus, Maggie wasn't the one who fixed things. Rose was. So she'd stood, watching, for what felt like an unbearably long time, until Rose found her glasses. One of the lenses was cracked, Maggie saw, as Rose lurched to her feet, gathering her books, and . . . oh, no. Her sister's pants had split right down the back and Maggie and everyone else could see her underwear, her Holly Hobbie underwear, which raised the pointing and laughing to a hysterical pitch. *Oh, God,* thought Maggie, feeling sick, *why did Rose have to wear those today?*

"You're going to have to pay!" Rose was shouting at Sean Perigini, holding her broken glasses and probably with no idea that everyone could see her underwear. The laughter built. Rose's eyes swept the playground, past the kickball game, past the kids on the swing sets and jungle gym, through the big kids, the fifth and sixth graders shrieking and clutching each other as they laughed at her, until finally she caught sight of Maggie, standing between Kim and Marissa on the little section of grass beside the flower bed that was, by unspoken consent, reserved for the most popular girls. Rose squinted at Maggie, and Maggie could read the hatred and misery in her sister's eyes as clearly as if Rose had walked over and shouted in her face.

I should help, a voice inside of her whispered again. But Maggie just stood there, watching, listening to the other kids laugh, thinking that this was somehow some dark part of the bargain that had made her the pretty one.

She was safe, Maggie thought fiercely, as Rose wiped her face, gathered her books, and, ignoring the taunts and laughter and the singsonged catcalls of "Hol-ly! Hob-bie!" that a few of the fifth-grade girls had already taken up, walked slowly back into the school. Maggie'd never make the mistake of wandering through a dodgeball game and she'd certainly never wear cartoon-character underwear. She was safe, she thought, as Rose pushed through the double glass doors and headed inside—to the principal's office, no doubt. "Do you think she's okay?" Kim had asked, and Maggie had tossed her head scornfully. "I think she's adopted," she'd said, and Kim and Marissa had giggled, and Maggie had laughed, too, even though the laughter felt like gravel in her chest.

And then, as fast as a dodgeball flying through the air to whack her unsuspecting head, everything changed. When, exactly? Her fourteenth year, at the tail end of eighth grade, in the gap between junior high, where she'd ruled, and high school, where everything had fallen apart.

It had started with the standardized assessment test. "Nothing to worry about!" Mrs. Fried's junior-high replacement had said in a falsely cheerful voice. The new "enrichment" teacher was ugly, with caked-on makeup and a wart next to her nose. She'd told Maggie that she could take an untimed version of the test. "You'll do fine!" But Maggie stared at the page of blank bubbles that she was supposed to fill in with her number two pencil, feeling her heart sink, knowing that it wasn't going to be fine. *You're a smart girl,* Mrs. Fried had told her a dozen times. But Mrs. Fried was gone, back in the elementary school. High school was going to be different. And that test—"just for our records! Results kept confidential!"—had somehow tripped her up and ruined everything. She wasn't supposed to have seen her scores, but her teacher had left a copy on the desk, and Maggie had peeked, first trying to read the words upside down and then just grabbing the thing and flipping it around so that she could read it. The words hit her like a hammer. "Dyslexic," it said. "Learning disabled." It might as well have read, "You're dead," Maggie thought, because that was what those words really meant.

"Now, Maggie, let's not get hysterical," Sydelle had said that night, after the teacher had called to share the "confidential" results. "We'll get you a tutor!"

"I don't need a tutor," Maggie had said furiously, feeling tears scalding her throat.

Rose, sitting in the corner of Sydelle's white-on-white living room, had looked up from *Watership Down.* "It might help, you know."

"Shut up!" Maggie had said, the forbidden words flying out of her mouth. "I'm not stupid, Rose, so just shut up!"

"Maggie," their father had said, "nobody's saying you're stupid. . . ."

"That test said I was stupid," said Maggie. "And you know what? I don't even care. And why'd you have to tell her?" she demanded, pointing her finger at Sydelle. "And her?" Maggie continued, pointing at Rose. "It's none of her business!"

"We all want to help," Michael Feller had said, and Maggie had ranted that she didn't need help, she didn't care what the dumb test said, she was smart just like Mrs. Fried had always said. No, she didn't need a tutor, no she didn't want to go to private school, she had friends, unlike some people she could name, she had friends and she wasn't stupid no matter what the test said, and plus even if she was stupid, she'd rather be stupid than ugly like four-eyes in the corner, even if she was stupid, that was okay, it was no biggie, she'd be fine.

But she wasn't fine. When she started high school, her friends were placed in the honors-level courses, and Maggie had been sent to the remedial classes, with no friendly Mrs. Fried to tell her that she wasn't a dummy or a retard, that her brain just worked a little differently, and that they'd figure out tricks to get her through. She got stuck with the indifferent teachers—the burned-out older ones who just wanted to be left alone, like Mrs. Cavetti, who wore cock-eyed wigs and too much perfume, or Mrs. Learey, who'd give them in-class reading assignments and then spend the entire period filling photo albums with endless pictures of her grandchildren.

Maggie figured it out fast—the worst teachers got the worst kids as punishment, for being bad teachers. The worst kids got the worst teachers as punishment for being poor—or dumb. Which in this fancy town were often interpreted as the same thing. Well, Maggie figured, if she was someone's punishment, she'd act like punishment. She stopped bringing her books to class and started toting a toolbox-sized makeup kit instead. She'd take polish off her nails during the lectures, reapply a different shade during the pop quiz, after she'd answered all of the questions with the same letter—*A* for one class, *B* for the next. Multiple-choice quizzes were all these teachers ever came up with. "Maggie, please come to the blackboard," one of the crappy teachers would drone. Maggie would shake her head without lifting her eyes from her makeup mirror. "Sorry, can't help," she'd call, fluttering her fingertips. "I'm drying."

She should have flunked everything, should have been left back in every grade. But the teachers kept passing her—probably because they didn't want to see her again the next year. And her friends moved farther and farther away from her with each new school year. She tried for a while, and Kim and Marissa tried, too, but eventually the gap got too wide. They were playing field hockey, they were joining student council, they were taking SAT prep courses and visiting colleges, and she'd been left behind.

By sophomore year, Maggie decided that if the girls were going to ignore her, the guys certainly wouldn't. She started wearing her hair piled high and her cleavage leveraged higher by lace underwire bras that peeked through her shirts. She'd arrived for the first day of school in low-slung jeans that barely clung to the ridge of her hips, high-heeled black leather boots, and a consignment-store lace bustier beneath the army jacket she'd swiped from her father.

Lipstick, nail polish, enough eye shadow to paint a small wall with, an armful of black rubber bracelets, and big, floppy fabric bows in her hair. She took her cues from Madonna, whom she idolized, Madonna, who was just starting to have her videos played on MTV. Maggie devoured every scrap of information about the singer she could find—every magazine interview, every newspaper profile— and marveled at the similarities. They both had dead mothers. They were both beautiful, both talented dancers who'd studied tap and jazz since they were little girls. They were both street-smart, with sex appeal to spare. Boys buzzed around Maggie like flies, buying her packs of cigarettes, inviting her to parties where no parents were present, keeping her cup filled, holding her hand, walking her into an unused bedroom or the backseat of a car when it got late.

It took a while for Maggie to notice that they weren't calling, or asking her to dances, or even saying hello to her in the halls. She'd cried about it—late at night, when Rose was asleep, when nobody could hear her—and then she'd decided not to cry. None of them were worth her tears. And they'd all be sorry, ten years down the road, when she was famous and they were nothings, stranded in this shitty little town, fat and ugly and unfamous, not special at all.

So that was high school. Cringing around the edges of the popular crowd like some kicked dog still holding on to the memories of the days when they'd petted and praised her. Parties on weekends at the house of whoever's parents were away. Beer and wine, joints or pills, and they'd be drunk and, eventually, she figured it was easier if she was drunk, too, if things were a little blurry around the edges and she could imagine seeing what she wanted in their eyes.

And Rose . . . well, Rose hadn't gone through the kind of John Hughes metamorphosis where she shed her glasses, got a good haircut, and the football captain fell in love with her at the prom. But she did change in smaller ways. She stopped having dandruff, for one thing, thanks to Maggie's not-so-subtle trick of leaving large bottles of Head and Shoulders in the shower. She still wore glasses, still dressed like a geek, but somewhere along the line she'd acquired a friend—Amy, who was, in Maggie's opinion, just as weird as Rose was—and didn't seem bothered by the fact that the pretty girls still laughed at her, or ignored her, and still occasionally referred to her as Holly Hobbie. Rose was in the honors classes, Rose got straight A's. Maggie would have dismissed all of those things as further signs of her sister's social hopelessness except that those accomplishments had started to matter.

"Princeton!" Sydelle had said, over and over, when Rose was a senior and her acceptance letter had come in the mail. "Well, Rose, this is quite an achievement!" She'd actually cooked Rose's favorite foods for dinner—fried chicken and biscuits and honey—and she hadn't said a word when Rose reached for seconds. "Maggie, you must be very proud of your sister!" she'd said. Maggie had just rolled her eyes in an unspoken "whatever." Like Princeton was such a big deal. Like Rose was the only person who'd ever succeeded in spite of a dead mother. Well, Maggie had a dead mother, too, but did she get extra points for that? No, she did not. She just got questions. From neighbors. From teachers. From everyone who knew her sister. "Can we expect great things from you?" Well, obviously, they couldn't, Maggie thought, inking an emphatic red circle around an ad for waitresses at a "busy, successful Center City restaurant." She'd got the body, Rose had gotten the brains, and now it was looking like brains might count for more.

So Rose graduated from Princeton while Maggie put in a few half-hearted semesters at the local community college. Rose had gone to law school, and Maggie had waitressed at a pizza parlor, done baby-sitting and housecleaning, dropped out of bartending school when the instructor tried to stick his tongue in her ear after the lesson on martinis. Rose was plain, and fat, and frumpy, and up until this morning Maggie had never known her to have a boyfriend except for, like, ten minutes in law school. Yet somehow she was the one with the great apartment (well, the apartment that could have been great if Maggie had decorated it), and with money and friends, the one people looked at with respect. And this guy,

Jim Whatever, was cute in a semi-nerdy way, and Maggie just bet that he was rich, too.

It wasn't fair, thought Maggie, stalking back to the kitchen. It wasn't fair their mother had died. It wasn't fair that she'd somehow used up her handful of good years by junior high and was now living in her sister's shadow, doomed to watch Rose get everything she wanted, while she got nothing at all. She crumpled up the empty container of ice cream, gathered the newspaper, and was getting ready to toss them both when something in the paper caught her eye. It was the magic word: *auditions*. Maggie dropped the ice-cream carton and turned her full attention to the newspaper. "MTV Announces Auditions for VJs," she read. Excitement rose within her like a balloon, along with panic—what if she'd missed it? She scanned the story as rapidly as she could. *December 1. Open call. In New York.* She could be there! She'd tell Rose she had a job interview, which was technically sort of the truth, and she'd get Rose to lend her money for a bus ticket, and clothes. She'd need an outfit. She'd have to buy something new; she could see that instantly; nothing she had was even remotely right. Maggie folded the newspaper carefully and hurried to her sister's closet to see which shoes she'd wear to the Big Apple.

FIVE

Lewis Feldman ushered Mrs. Sobel into his office—a converted closet with the words *Golden Acres Gazette* stenciled on the glass—and closed the door behind them.

"Thank you for coming," he said, pulling the red grease copyediting pencil from behind his ear and setting it on his desk. Mrs. Sobel perched on a chair, crossed her ankles, and clasped her hands in her lap. She was a tiny woman with blue hair and a blue wool cardigan sweater and blue veins pulsing in her hands. He gave her what he hoped was a reassuring smile. She gave him a tentative nod.

"Let me just begin by saying how grateful I am for your help," he said. "We were really in a pinch." Which was true—ever since the *Gazette*'s previous food critic, the Noshing Gourmet, had suffered a heart attack that had landed him facedown in a western omelet, Lewis had been stuck recycling old reviews, and the natives had been getting restless, not to mention tired of reading about the Rascal House yet again.

"This was a very fine first effort," he said, spreading the tear sheet on his desk, so Mrs. Sobel could see what her review looked like, laid out on the page. "Italian Restaurant Tempts Tastebuds," read the headline, beneath a drawing of a winking little bird—the Early Bird, of course—with a cartoon worm clutched in its beak. "I had just a few suggestions," said Lewis, as Mrs. Sobel gave another trembly little nod. He braced himself—running hardware stores hadn't been nearly as tough as taking the fragile egos of retired women in his hands on a biweekly basis—and began to read.

" 'Mangiamo's Italian Restaurant is located in the shopping mall on Powerline Road, next to where the Marshall's used to be, and across from the frozen yogurt shop. It looks like it should be easy to get to, but my husband, Irving, had a very difficult time making the left-hand turn.' "

Mrs. Sobel gave another nod, this one slightly more assertive. Lewis kept reading.

" 'The restaurant has red carpet, white tablecloths with small candles on them. The air conditioner is turned up very high, so you should bring a sweater if you go to Mangiamo's. The minestrone soup was not the way I make it. It had kidney beans, which neither I nor Irving enjoy. The Caesar salad was good, but it is made with anchovies, so if you are allergic to fish, you should get the house salad instead.' " And now Mrs. Sobel was leaning forward eagerly, nodding along, repeating the words in a low, breathless whisper.

" 'For entrees, Irving wanted the chicken parmesan, even though cheese does not agree with him. I had the spaghetti and meatballs, because I thought Irving would eat that. Sure enough, the chicken was hard for him to chew, so he had my meatballs, which were soft.' " Lewis looked at Mrs. Sobel, who was leaning forward, eyes bright.

"See, here's the thing," he said, wondering whether Ben Bradlee and William Shawn had ever had problems like this. "What we're trying to do is be objective."

"Objective," Mrs. Sobel repeated.

"We're trying to give a snapshot of what it's like to eat at Mangiamo's."

She nodded again, confusion replacing the eagerness in her eyes.

"So when you talk about the left-hand turn, and how it was difficult to make, or how the way they make their soup isn't the way you make yours . . ." *Be careful,* Lewis, he told himself, picking up his pencil and tucking it securely behind his ear again. "Well, those are interesting things, and very nicely written, but they might not be exactly helpful to other people who are going to be reading this and using it to decide whether they want to go there."

Now Mrs. Sobel drew herself up straight, a trembling reed of indignation. "But those things are true!" she said.

"Of course they're true," Lewis soothed her. "I'm just wondering whether they're useful. Like, the air-conditioning, and telling people to bring a sweater. That's a very, very useful detail. But the section on the soup . . . not every reader needs to see the restaurant's soup placed in the context of your soup." And then he smiled, and hoped the smile would work. He thought it probably would. His wife, Sharla—Sharla of blessed memory, dead for two years—had always told him he could get away with anything because of his smile. He wasn't a handsome man, he knew. He had a mirror, and while his eyes weren't so great anymore, he could still tell that he was much more Walter Matthau than Paul Newman. Even his ear-lobes had wrinkles. But the smile was still working. "I'm sure that any soup would suffer, being compared to your soup."

Mrs. Sobel sniffed. But she was looking decidedly less offended.

"Why don't you take this home with you, take another look at it, and try to ask yourself, with everything you're writing, whether it's going to help"—he thought for a minute, then pulled a name out of the air—"Mr. and Mrs. Rabinowitz decide whether to go there for dinner."

"Oh, the Rabinowitzes would never go there," said Mrs. Sobel. "He's very cheap." And then, when Lewis was still sitting behind his desk, utterly nonplussed, she gathered her purse and cardigan and the copy of her story and marched grandly out the door, past Ella Hirsch, who was on her way in.

Ella, Lewis noticed with great relief, neither trembled or nodded. She wasn't nearly as ancient, or fragile, as Mrs. Sobel. She had clear brown eyes and reddish hair that she wore pulled back in a twist, and he'd never once seen her in polyester pants, which were preferred by most of the Acres's female residents.

"How are you?" she asked.

Lewis shook his head. "Honestly, I'm not quite sure," he told her.

"That doesn't sound good," she said, handing him her neatly typed poem. Would he have had a little bit of a crush on Ella even if she wasn't the best writer at the *Golden Acres Gazette?* Probably, Lewis decided. Except he didn't think she was interested. The times he'd invited her for coffee to talk about story ideas, she'd seemed happy to come along, and just as happy when the coffee was gone and she could tell him good-bye.

"Thanks," he said, setting her papers in his in box. "So what are you up to this weekend?" he asked, trying to sound casual.

"I'm at the soup kitchen tomorrow night, and then I've got two books for the blind to read," she said. It was polite, Lewis thought, but it was still a refusal. Had she read that book that all the women were passing around the pool a couple years ago, the one that talked about playing hard to get and had caused eighty-six-year-old Mrs. Asher to hang up on him, mid-edit, after declaring that she was a creature unlike any other and that, as such, it was incumbent upon her to end all phone calls with men?

"Well, thanks for the poem. You're the only one who made your deadline. As usual," Lewis said. Ella gave him a faint smile and headed for the door. Maybe it was his looks, he thought glumly. Sharla had bought him a bulldog calendar for one of the anniversaries they'd celebrated together in Florida, and he'd accused her of trying to tell him something. She'd given him a resounding kiss on his cheek and told him that while his modeling career was probably dead in the water, she loved him anyhow.

Lewis shook his head, hoping to clear away the memories, and picked up Ella's poem. "Just Because I'm Old," he read, and smiled at the line that read "I AM NOT INVISIBLE," and decided that Ella was worth yet another try.

SIX

Rose Feller leaned across the table. "The usual stipulations, counselor?" she asked. The opposing counsel—a whey-faced man in an unfortunate greenish gray suit—nodded, even though Rose would have bet that he didn't know what "the usual stipulations" actually were any more than she did. But every deposition she'd ever attended had started out with the lawyer in charge saying "the usual stipulations," and so she said it, too.

"Okay, if everyone's ready, we'll begin," she said, with a confidence that was more feigned than felt, as if she'd done hundreds of depositions by herself, instead of just two. "My name is Rose Feller, and I am an attorney at Lewis, Dommel, and Fenick. Today I'm representing the Veeder Trucking Company and Stanley Willet, the comptroller of Veeder, who's present and sitting to my left. This is the deposition of Wayne LeGros—" She paused and glanced across the table at the witness, hoping for confirmation that she was pronouncing his last name correctly. Wayne LeGros refused to meet her eyes. "Wayne LeGros," she continued, deciding that if she was saying it wrong he'd speak up, "the president of Majestic Construction. Mr. LeGros, could you begin by giving us your name and address?"

Wayne LeGros, who was short, fiftyish, with iron-gray hair in a buzz cut and a heavy class ring on one thick finger, swallowed hard.

"Wayne LeGros," he said loudly. "I live at five-thirteen Tasker Street. In Philadelphia."

"Thank you," Rose said. In truth, she sort of felt sorry for the guy. She'd never been deposed, except in law school, in mock trial, but she was sure it wasn't fun. "Can you tell us your job title?"

"President. Majestic," said loquacious Mr. LeGros.

"Thank you," Rose said again. "Now, as I'm sure your counsel has explained, we're here today to gather information. My client is contending that you owe them . . ." she glanced down fast at her notes. "Eight thousand dollars, for the lease of equipment."

"Dump trucks," LeGros offered.

"That's right," said Rose. "Can you tell us how many trucks were leased?"

LeGros shut his eyes. "Three."

Rose slid a piece of paper across the table. "This is a copy of the lease agreement you signed with Veeder. I've already had the court reporter mark it as Plaintiff's Exhibit fifteen-A." The court reporter nodded. "Could I ask you to read the parts I've highlighted?"

LeGros took a deep breath and squinted at the page. "It says Majestic agrees to pay Veeder two thousand dollars a week for three dump trucks."

"Is that your signature?"

LeGros took a minute to study the photocopy. "Yep," he finally said. "It's mine." A note of petulance had crept into his voice, and he'd pulled the class ring off his finger and was spinning it on the conference table.

"Thank you," said Rose. "Now, was this project in Ryland completed?"

"The school? Yeah."

"And was Majestic Construction paid for its work?"

LeGros nodded. His attorney raised his eyebrows at him. "Yeah," LeGros said.

Rose slid another sheet of paper across the table. "This is

Plaintiff's sixteen-A—a copy of your invoice to the Ryland School Board, marked 'paid in full.' Was that account paid?"

"Yeah."

"So you were paid for the work you did on the project?"

Another nod. Another dirty look from his attorney. Another "yeah." For the next half-hour, Rose painstakingly led LeGros through a stack of stamped invoices and notices from a collection agency. It wasn't the stuff of Grisham thrillers, she thought as she slogged onward, but if she was lucky it would get the job done.

"So the job in Ryland was completed, and you paid your subcontractors?" Rose summarized.

"Yeah."

"Except not Veeder."

"They got theirs," he mumbled. "They got paid for other things."

"Pardon me?" Rose asked politely.

"Other things," LeGros repeated. He ducked his head. Spun his ring. "Things they owed other companies. Things they owed my dispatcher," he said, biting off each syllable. "Why don't you ask him about my dispatcher?"

"I certainly will," Rose promised. "But right now, it's your deposition. It's your turn to tell your story."

LeGros stared down again, at the ring, at his hands.

"Tell me your dispatcher's name," she prodded gently.

"Lori Kimmel," LeGros muttered.

"And where does she live?"

He stared down sullenly. "Same place I do. Fifth and Tasker."

Rose felt her pulse spike. "She's your . . ."

"My lady friend," said LeGros, with a look on his face that said, *Want to make something of it?* "Ask him," he said, sticking a thumb toward Stanley Willet. "Ask him," he repeated. "He knows all about her."

LeGros's lawyer laid a hand on his forearm, but LeGros would not be stopped.

"Ask him about the overtime she worked! Ask him about how

she never got paid! Ask him about how when she left the company, he said he'd pay her vacation and sick days, and never did!"

"Could we take a break?" LeGros's attorney. Rose nodded. The court reporter raised her eyebrows. "Sure," said Rose. "Fifteen minutes." She ushered Willet into her office as LeGros and his attorney huddled in the hall.

"What's this about?"

Willet shrugged. "The name sounds familiar. I could make a few calls . . ."

Rose nodded toward her telephone. "Hit nine," she said. "I'll be back in a minute." She hurried to the bathroom. Depositions made her nervous, and being nervous made her have to pee, and . . .

"Ms. Feller?" It was LeGros's attorney. "Can I speak to you for a minute?" He pulled her into the conference room. "Look," he said. "We'd like to settle."

"What happened?"

The lawyer shook his head. "You can probably fill in the blanks. His girlfriend used to work for your guy. As best I can tell, she left without giving notice and figured she was entitled to all of her vacation and sick pay. Veeder told her to forget about it, and I think that my guy figured he could just bill Veeder for what she said she was owed."

"You didn't know that?"

The lawyer shrugged. "I just got this case two weeks ago."

"So he'll . . ." Rose let her voice trail off suggestively.

"Pay it back. All of it."

"Plus interest. This has gone on for three years," said Rose.

LeGros's lawyer winced. "One year's interest," he said. "We'll write you a check right now."

"Let me run it by my client," said Rose. "I'll recommend that he accept." Her heart was racing, her blood pounding in her veins. Victory! She felt like doing a dance. Instead she returned to Stan Willet, who was staring at her diplomas.

"They want to settle," she said.

"Good," he said, without turning toward her. Rose swallowed her disappointment. Of course he wasn't going to be as excited as she was. To him eight thousand dollars was pocket change. But still! She couldn't wait to tell Jim how well she'd done! She ran through the terms. "They're willing to write us a check today, which means you won't waste time chasing after the money. My recommendation is that we accept."

"Fine," he said, his eyes still on the glass frames and Latin writing of her diplomas. "Write it up, send it over." Finally, he turned toward her. "Good stuff in there." He cracked a thin smile. "Bury them in paper, right?"

"Right," Rose agreed, feeling her heart sink. She'd been brilliant! Well, maybe not brilliant in a flashy way, but competent. Extremely competent. Goddamnit, she'd hunted down every last little memo, every single bill, every solitary scrap of paper that proved her client's case! She walked Stan Willet to the elevator, hurried back to her office, and dialed Jim's extension.

"They settled," she said happily. "Eight thousand plus a year's interest."

"Nice job," he said, sounding pleased. Pleased, and distracted. She could hear the click of his mouse in the background. "Can you write me up a memo?"

Rose felt as though he'd dumped ice water on her head. "Sure," she said. "I'll have it done this afternoon."

Jim's voice softened. "Congratulations," he said. "I'm sure you were great."

"I buried them in paper," said Rose. She could hear Jim breathing, and the sound of other voices in the background.

"What was that?"

"Nothing." She set down the phone without saying good-bye. Instantly, a message popped up on her screen. From Jim. She clicked it open.

"Sorry I couldn't talk more," it read, then—her heart lifted as she read the words—"can I stop by tonight?"

She typed her response. "YES!" And then she sat back in her chair, beaming, feeling pleased, thinking that everything was finally right in her world. She was a professional success. It was Friday night, and she wouldn't be alone. She had a man who loved her. True, she also had her little sister camping out on her couch, but that wouldn't last forever, she thought, and started typing up the memo.

Euphoria lasted until four in the afternoon; happiness until six; and by the time nine o'clock rolled around and Jim still hadn't put in an appearance, Rose's mood was dipping toward miserable. She headed to the bathroom, where her ever-helpful little sister had left an article from *Allure* taped to the mirror. "This Season's Best Brows!" read the headline. And there were tweezers on the sink.

"Okay," Rose said to herself. "I can take a hint." At least this way, if—when—Jim came, he'd find her waiting with perfectly plucked brows. Rose peered at herself in the mirror and decided that her life would be easier if she'd just been born a different kind of girl. Not really different, but a better, prettier, more polished, slightly thinner version of the person she already was. The thing was, of course, she had no idea, really, of how to be anything other than what she was. And it wasn't for lack of trying.

When she was thirteen years old, Rose and Maggie Feller moved into Sydelle's house. "It just makes sense!" Sydelle said sweetly. "I've got plenty of room." The house was a four-bedroom modern monstrosity painted a flat, brilliant white, and looked out of place on a street full of Colonials, like a spaceship that had crash-landed in the cul-de-sac. Sydelle's house—and Rose never thought of it any other way—had huge windows and odd angles and strangely-shaped rooms (a dining room that was almost a rectangle, a bedroom that was not quite a square). The rooms were full of glass tables, glass-and-metal furniture with pointed edges, and mirrors everywhere, including a mirrored wall in the kitchen that showed every stray fingerprint, every deep breath—and every bite or nibble that everyone in the kitchen ever took. Plus, there were digital scales in every bath-

room, including the downstairs powder room, and a variety of mag-
nets with diet-related slogans on the refrigerator. The one Rose
remembered best had a picture of a cow contentedly munching grass
beneath the legend "Holy Cow! Are you eating again?" Every glittering, reflective surface, every magnet and every scale seemed to
conspire with Sydelle to send the message that Rose was inadequate,
unfeminine, not pretty enough, and way too big.

The week they'd moved in, Rose had asked her father for money.
"Is there something special you need?" he asked, staring at her
with concern. Rose never asked him for money above the five dollars in allowance she got each week. Maggie was the one who regularly hit him up—she wanted Barbie dolls, a new lunch box,
scented Magic Markers and glittery stickers, and a poster of Rick
Springfield for her wall.

"School supplies," Rose said. He gave her a ten-dollar bill. She
walked to the drugstore and purchased a small notebook with a
purple cover. For the rest of the school year she'd used it to write
down her careful notations of what women did. It was her secret
project. Sydelle, she knew, would be happy to tell her what women
did and did not do, say, wear, and, most important, eat, but Rose
wanted to figure it out for herself. Looking back, she figured she
must have had some dim idea that she was supposed to have magically absorbed the pertinent information at some point in her girlhood . . . and the fact that she hadn't, and that Sydelle felt she had
room to issue proclamations on skin care and calorie counting, was
an indictment of her dead mother. Which, of course, made Rose all
the more determined to puzzle it out on her own.

"Nails curved, not straight!" she would write . . . or "no dumb
jokes!" She convinced her father to buy her a yearlong subscription
to *Seventeen* and *Young Miss* magazines, and she'd saved up her
allowance to buy herself a copy of a paperback called *How to Be
Popular!* that she'd seen advertised in the back of both magazines.
She had studied those pages as carefully as any Talmudic scholar
had ever pored over the sacred texts. She would watch her teachers,

neighbors, her sister, even the hair-netted ladies in the cafeteria, and try to figure out how girls and women were supposed to be. It was like a math problem, she told herself, and once she solved it, once she'd figured out the equation of shoes plus clothes plus hairdo plus the right kind of personality (and, of course, once she'd figured out how to approximate the right kind of personality), she'd get people to like her. She'd be popular, like Maggie.

Of course it had been a disaster, she thought, wiping her breath off the mirror and leaning in close with the tweezers. All of her planning and note taking had been for nothing. Popularity was a code she couldn't crack. No matter how many pages she'd filled, no matter how often she'd imagined sitting with Missy Fox and Gail Wylie in the high-school cafeteria, her purse slung over the back of her chair, her Diet Coke and Baggies of carrots before her, it had never worked out right.

By high school, she'd given up on clothes and makeup, on hair and nails. She quit reading the advice columns and the stories in her magazines that dictated everything from how to talk to a guy to the precise angle of an eyebrow's arch. She abandoned the hope that she'd ever be pretty or popular, and kept what was left of her fashion focus on shoes. Shoes, she reasoned, could not be worn incorrectly. There were no variables with shoes, no collars to turn up or down, no cuffs to roll or leave unrolled, no piece of jewelry or hairdo that would make or break (in Rose's case, mostly break) the outfit. Shoes were shoes were shoes, and even if she wore them with the wrong things, she couldn't wear them the wrong way. Her feet would always look right. She'd look the popular-girl part, from the ankles down, even if from the ankles up she was still a loser.

It was only natural that she'd be thirty years old and clueless about almost anything style-related except for the relative merits of nubuck versus suede or the shape of this season's heels. Rose sighed and squinted at herself. Crooked. "Shit," she said, and raised the tweezers. The doorbell chimed.

"Coming!" Maggie sang.

"Oh, no," said Rose. She hurried out of the bathroom, shoving past her sister, who shoved her right back.

"Jesus, what is your problem!" Maggie demanded, rubbing her shoulder.

"Just move!" said Rose, groping for her wallet, extracting a wad of bills, and shoving them toward Maggie. "Go away! Go see a movie!"

"It's almost ten," Maggie pointed out.

"Find a late show!" said Rose, and flung open the door. And there was Jim, smelling faintly of cologne and more strongly of scotch, with a dozen red roses in his arms. "Hello, ladies," he said.

"Ooh, pretty!" said Maggie, taking the flowers. "Rose, put these in a vase," she said, handing them off to her sister. "May I take your coat?" she asked Jim.

Jesus! Rose gritted her teeth and walked to the kitchen. When she got to the living room, Maggie and Jim were sitting side by side on the couch. Maggie showed no signs of leaving . . . and, Rose noticed, the money she'd given her had magically disappeared. "So Jim!" Maggie said brightly, leaning toward him, her bountiful cleavage on display, "how have you been?"

"Maggie," said Rose, balancing herself on the arm of the couch, which was the only available seating, "don't you have plans?"

Her sister gave her an evil smile. "Not at all, Rose," she said. "I'm in for the night."

SEVEN

On Monday morning, Maggie Feller hopped off the bus, slung her backpack over her shoulder, and wove deftly through Port Authority. It was nine-thirty, and the auditions started at nine, and she would have been earlier, except she hadn't been able to decide between the caramel leather Nine West boots (with boot-cut jeans) or the Stuart Weitzman Mary Janes (with pencil skirt and fishnet stockings).

She turned the corner at Forty-second Street and her heart sank. There had to be a thousand people out in front of the MTV studio windows, jamming every inch of the sidewalk, crowding the little strip of grass in the center of Broadway.

Maggie stopped a girl in a cowboy hat. "Are you here for the auditions?"

The girl made a sour face. "I was. But they took the first three thousand people, and told the rest of us to go home."

Maggie's heart sank even further. This would not do. This would not do at all! She hurried through the crowd as fast as her high heels would carry her, finally locating a harried-looking woman with a walkie-talkie and a jacket with a yellow "MTV" logo on the back. *Confidence,* Maggie told herself, and tapped the woman on her shoulder.

"I'm here for the audition," she announced.

The woman shook her head. "Sorry, hon," she said, without looking up from her clipboard. "Doors are closed."

Maggie reached into her backpack, grabbed her purloined bottle of Midol, and rattled it in the woman's face. "I have a medical condition," she said.

The woman looked up and cocked her eyebrow. Maggie wrapped her fingers around the label, but not fast enough. "Midol?"

"I have debilitating cramps," Maggie announced. "And I'm sure that you're familiar with the Americans with Disabilities Act."

Now the woman was staring at her curiously.

"You can't discriminate against me just because of my troubled uterus," Maggie said.

"Are you serious?" the woman grumbled . . . but Maggie could see that she was more amused than irritated.

"Look, just give me a chance," she pleaded. "I came all the way from Philadelphia!"

"There are people here who came all the way from Idaho."

Maggie rolled her eyes. "Idaho! Do they even have cable there? Look," she continued, "I went through extensive preparations to be here."

The woman raised her eyebrows.

"Would it interest you to know," Maggie continued, "that I've had a very personal portion of my anatomy waxed into the MTV logo?"

For one dizzying instant, Maggie thought the woman was actually going to ask to see. Instead, she laughed, scribbled something on her clipboard, and beckoned to Maggie. "I'm Robin. Follow me," she said. Once she'd turned, Maggie jumped into the air, clicked her heels together, and gave a little shriek of glee. She'd made it! Well, she'd made it part of the way, she thought, hurrying after Robin. Now it was just a question of wowing the judges, and she'd be home free.

• • •

Inside, the corridors were even more jammed than the sidewalks had been. There were guys with cornrows and bandanas and jeans that drooped toward the floor rapping softly to themselves, gorgeous girls in miniskirts and low-cut tops preening into hand-held mirrors. Maggie quickly deduced that most of them were in their early twenties, and subtracted five years from her age on the form Robin gave her to fill out.

"Where are you from?" asked the girl in front of her, a tall, skinny girl who'd done herself up like Ginger Spice.

"Philadelphia," said Maggie, figuring that she had nothing to lose by being gracious. "I'm Maggie."

"I'm Kristy. Are you nervous?" asked the girl.

Maggie signed her form with a flourish. "Not really. I don't even know what they want us to do."

"Talk into the camera for thirty seconds," said Kristy, and sighed. "I wish they'd have us perform or something. I've taken dance classes since I was four. I can do tap and jazz, I can sing, I've got a monologue memorized . . ."

Maggie gulped. She'd taken dance classes, too—twelve years' worth—but no acting, and the only thing she'd memorized for the occasion was Rose's address, so MTV would know where to send flowers after she'd won. Kristy ran her fingers through her hair. "I don't know," she murmured, piling her hair on top of her head, then letting it tumble back down toward her shoulders. "Up or down?"

Maggie studied Kristy. "How about a French twist? Here," she said, digging in her backpack for her hairbrush, hairspray, bobby pins, and elastics. The line inched forward. By the time Maggie made it to the front, three hours had flown by, and she'd done Kristy's hair and redone her makeup, smoothed glittery gold eyeshadow onto an eighteen-year-old named Kara, and lent Latisha, who'd been behind her in the line, Rose's Nine West boots.

"Next!" called the bored-looking guy behind the camera.

She took a deep breath, feeling no nerves at all, feeling nothing but a supreme confidence, a blazing joy as she stepped into the tiny blue-carpeted cubicle beneath the circle of burning-hot light. Behind the cameraman, Robin grinned and gave her a thumbs-up.

"Tell us your name, please," she said.

Maggie smiled. "I'm Maggie May Feller," she said, her voice low and clear. God, she could see herself on the monitor hanging overhead! She sneaked a quick peek, and there she was! On TV! Looking terrific!

"Maggie May?" asked Robin.

"My mother named me after the song," said Maggie. "I think she always knew that I was destined for musical greatness."

Robin scanned Maggie's form. "It says here you used to be a waitress."

"That's right," said Maggie, licking her lips. "And I think that's given me the perfect experience to work with rock stars."

"What do you mean?" Robin asked.

"Well, once you've handled frat boys having waffle fights, you can handle anything," Maggie said. "And when you're a waitress, you see all kinds of people. You've got your girls on diets who have all kinds of weird allergies." She raised her voice to a snotty soprano. " 'Are there peanuts in this?' Which is fine, except they ask it about everything. Including iced tea. You've got picky vegetarians, vegans, the Zone dieters, diabetics, macrobiotics, macrobiotic Zone diabetics with high blood pressure who can't have salt . . ." And now she was off and running, ignoring the lights, ignoring the competition, ignoring even Robin and the guy in the baseball cap. It was just her and the camera, the way it was always meant to be. "And if you've ever had to dump iced coffee in some guy's lap because he was trying to leave his tip in your cleavage, well, you're not going to be afraid of Kid Rock."

"What kind of music do you like?" asked Robin.

"All kinds," said Maggie. She licked her lips and tossed her hair. "Madonna's my idol. Except for the whole yoga thing. I just can't get into that. Of course, I'm a singer, too, in a band called Whiskered Biscuit . . ."

The guy behind the camera started laughing.

"Perhaps you're familiar with our soon-to-be hit single, 'Lick Me Where I'm Pink'?" Maggie asked.

"Could you sing us a little bit?" asked the cameraman.

Maggie beamed. This, finally, was what she'd been waiting for. She pulled her hairbrush out of her backpack and used it as a microphone, tossing her hair and wailing, "Lick me where I'm pink! Pour yourself a drink! Don't wanna hear your problems, what am I, your fucking shrink?" She wondered, fleetingly, whether it was okay to say "fuck" on MTV, and then figured that the damage was done.

"Anything else we should know about you, Maggie?" Robin asked.

"Only that I'm ready for prime time," Maggie said. "And if Carson Daly's ever single again, you've got my number." She blew the camera a kiss, then stuck out her tongue, mockingly, flashing her piercing at the camera.

"Way to go!" Kristy whispered. And Latisha was applauding, and Kara gave her a thumbs-up, and Robin hurried out of the booth into the line, tapped Maggie on her shoulder, grinned, and pulled her down a corridor to where a group of a dozen other people were waiting. "Congratulations," she whispered. "You've made the callbacks."

"You're where?" Rose demanded.

"I'm in New York!" Maggie yelled into her cell phone. "MTV's having auditions for VJs, and guess who got a callback!"

There was silence on the other end of the line. "You told me you had a job interview," Rose finally said.

Maggie's face flushed. "What do you think this is?"

"A wild-goose chase," Rose said.

"God, can't you even be happy for me?" The girl next to her, a six-foot-tall amazon in a leather catsuit, scowled at her. Maggie scowled back and moved to a corner of the waiting room.

"I'd be happy if you got a job."

"I'm going to get a job!"

"Oh, you know for sure that MTV's going to hire you? And what are they paying?"

"A lot," said Maggie sullenly. In truth, she wasn't sure what the job paid . . . but it had to be a lot. It was on television, right? "More than what you're making. You know what I think? I think you're jealous."

Rose sighed. "I'm not jealous. I just want you to give up this whole crazy fame thing and get a job, instead of wasting your money going to New York."

"And be just like you," Maggie said. "No thanks." She slipped the phone into her purse, and stared furiously at the ground. Fucking Rose! Why had she thought that her sister would be happy for her, or impressed with hearing how she'd talked her way into the auditions and wowed everyone? Well, she thought, reaching into her purse for her lipstick, she'd just show Big Sistershit. She'd ace the audition, she'd get the job, and the next time Rose saw her she'd be on TV, larger than life and twice as lovely.

"Maggie Feller?"

Maggie took a deep breath, gave her mouth a final touch of lipstick, and headed back to capture her dream. This time, they led her to a larger room where three blinding-bright lights perched high on stainless-steel scaffolds shone down on her. Robin smiled at Maggie from over her clipboard and pointed toward a television set.

"Have you ever read off a TelePrompTer?" Robin asked.

Maggie shook her head.

"Well, it's easy," she said, demonstrating. She walked over a masking-tape X on the floor and faced the screen. "Coming up next!" she read, her voice loud and enthusiastic. "We've got the hot new debut from the Spice Girls! And don't touch that remote, 'cause you'll see Britney Spears within the hour!"

Maggie stood, staring at the television set. The words rolled down the screen, then reversed themselves and zipped back up so fast that Maggie felt instantly queasy. She could read. She could read just fine. Just not as fast as other people. And not while the words were moving around like this!

She realized that Robin was staring at her. "Okay?"

"Oh, sure!" said Maggie. She walked to the taped X on shaking legs. "Coming up next," she whispered to herself. She shook her hair, licked her lips. The lights shone down on her, as merciless as fire. She felt sweat form at her hairline. "Whenever you're ready," called the cameraman.

"Coming up next," Maggie began with a confidence she didn't feel. The words started to roll down the screen. "We've got . . ." She stared at the screen. The words wiggled some more. "The debutt video from the Spice Girls! And . . ." Oh, shit. "Debut," she whispered. "Debut!" she said, out loud, and wondered for perhaps the millionth time in her life why words weren't spelled the way they were pronounced. The cameraman was laughing, only not in a nice way. She peered at the screen, praying with all of her heart, *please just let me be able to read this okay*. A B. Something with a B and a Y. What? "Boyz II Men?" she guessed. "Yes, Motown Philly's back again! And . . ."

The cameraman was staring at her curiously. So was Robin. "Are you okay?" she asked. "Can you see the screen all right? Do you want to try again?"

"Coming up next!" Maggie said, much too loudly. *Please, God,* she thought, as hard as she could. *I'll never ask you for anything else again, only just let me be able to do this.* She stared at the screen, trying as hard as she could, as the *b*'s flipped into *d*'s and the *w*'s turned upside down. "We've got a lot of great music, right after this next commercial here . . ." And now the words had dissolved into incomprehensible hieroglyphics, and Robin and the cameraman were both staring at her with expressions she could read just fine. Pity.

"Coming up next, we've got the same crap we played for you yesterday," Maggie snarled as she turned on her heel—make that

Rose's heel—and blundered toward the door, swiping at her eyes. She ran through the waiting room, almost knocking over Ms. Catsuit, and had shoved her way into the hall, but not before she heard Robin's voice for the last time, saying, "Next!" and, "Let's hurry up, people; we've got a lot of you left to get through."

EIGHT

Lewis Feldman stood on the landing, a bouquet of tulips in one hand, a box of chocolates in the other, and a sense of trepidation as heavy as a winter coat hanging on his shoulders. Did this ever get any easier? he wondered, taking a deep breath and staring up at Ella Hirsch's door.

"The worst thing she can say is no," he reminded himself. He shifted the tulips to his left hand and the chocolates to his right, and stared down at his pants, which, in spite of his best efforts in the laundry room, were wrinkled and had a suspicious stain below one of the pockets, as if a pen had exploded—which, Lewis thought glumly, was probably exactly what had happened.

A no wouldn't kill him, he reminded himself. If the small heart attack he'd had three years ago hadn't killed him, certainly Ella Hirsch's rejection wouldn't, either. And there were other fish in the sea, fish who'd flopped right out of the water and into his boat before he'd even thought to bait a hook. But he hadn't been interested in Lois Ziff, who'd dropped by two weeks after Sharla's funeral with a kugel and her blouse undone an extra button's worth, exposing a bonus three inches of wrinkled cleavage. He hadn't been interested in Bonnie Begelman, who'd slipped an envelope through his door last month with two movie tickets and a note saying she'd be happy to join him "when you're ready." In the days after Sharla's death, in the weeks when he endured daily visits from what he'd come to think of as the Casserole Brigade, dozens of women with concerned faces and Tupperware, he hadn't thought he'd ever be ready, even though she'd given him her blessing.

"Find someone," she'd told him. She was in the hospital for the last time, and they both knew it, even though that truth remained unspoken between them. He was holding her hand, the one without the IV needles in it, and he'd leaned forward to brush her thin hair off her forehead.

"Sharla, let's not talk about this," he'd said. She'd shaken her head and stared at him, her blue eyes lit with a familiar spark—a spark he hadn't seen much of since the day he'd come home to find her sitting quietly on the couch. He'd looked at her and known, even before she raised her head, even before he'd she'd told him, *It's back. The cancer came back.*

"I don't want you to be alone," she said. "I don't want you turning into one of those unpleasant widowers. You'll eat too much sodium."

"Is that all you're worried about?" he teased her. "My sodium?"

"Those men get nasty," she said. Her eyes were slipping shut. He held her straw to her lips so she could sip. "Self-righteous and crotchety. I don't want it happening to you." Her voice was fading. "I want you to find someone."

"Do you have anyone in mind?" he asked. "Anyone special you've noticed?"

She didn't answer. He thought she was asleep—eyelids slipped shut, thin chest rising and falling slowly beneath the fresh bandages—but she said something else to him. "I want you to be happy," she said, each word coming in a separate puff of breath. He'd bowed his head, afraid that if he looked at her, his wife, the woman he'd loved and lived with for fifty-three years, he'd start crying and wouldn't be able to stop. So he sat by her bed and held her hand and whispered into her ear how much he loved her. He thought, when she'd died, that he'd never even want to look at another woman again, and the neighbor ladies, with their kugels and their cleavage, didn't appeal. Nobody had until now.

It wasn't that Ella reminded him of Sharla—at least, not physically. Sharla had been small, and with age she'd only gotten smaller. She'd had round blue eyes and bobbed blond hair, a too-big nose and a too-big bottom that she'd despaired of, and she'd loved coral lipstick and costume jewelry: necklaces of painted glass beads, dangly earrings that flashed and glittered when she moved. She'd reminded him of some tiny, exotic bird with iridescent plumage and a high, sweet song. Ella was different. She was taller, with fine features—a sharp nose, a firm jawline—and the long auburn locks she kept twined around her head, even though all of the other ladies at Golden Acres had short hair. Ella reminded him a little bit of Katharine Hepburn—a Jewish Katharine Hepburn, not quite so regal, or terrifying, a Hepburn steeped in some secret melancholy.

"Hepburn," he muttered. He shook his head at his own foolishness and started up the steps. He wished his shirt weren't wrinkled. He wished he had a hat.

"Well, hello!"

Lewis was so startled he actually jumped a little bit, and stared at a woman whose face he didn't recognize.

"Mavis Gold," the woman supplied. "And where are you off to, all dressed up?"

"Oh . . . just . . ."

Mavis Gold clapped her hands, causing her tanned upper arms to jiggle in a celebratory fashion. "Ella!" she whispered—a whisper so loud that cars on the Causeway probably heard it, Lewis thought. She ran one fingertip appreciatively over the top of a tulip. "They're beautiful. You're such a gentleman." Mavis beamed at him, kissed his cheek, and thumbed away the lipstick she'd left. "Good luck!"

He nodded, took a deep breath, repositioned his gifts for the last time, and turned the doorbell's crank. He listened for a radio, a television set, and heard nothing but Ella's feet padding quickly across the floor.

She opened the door and looked at him with a puzzled expression. "Lewis?"

He nodded, suddenly tongue-tied. She was wearing blue jeans, the kind that came only as far as the middle of her calves, and a loose white shirt and no shoes. Her feet were bare, long, and pale, beautifully shaped, with a polish the color of mother-of-pearl on the nails. Her feet made him want to kiss her. Instead, he swallowed hard.

"Hello," he said. There. That was a start.

A furrow appeared between Ella's eyebrows. "Was the poem too long?"

"No, no, the poem was fine. I'm here because . . . well, I was wondering if . . ." *Come on, old man!* he told himself. He'd been in a war; he'd buried a wife; he'd watched his son become a Republican with a Rush Limbaugh bumper sticker on the back of his minivan. He'd survived worse things than this. "Would you like to have dinner with me?"

He could see her getting ready to shake her head even before it happened. "I . . . I don't think so."

"Why not?" It came out louder than he'd intended.

Ella sighed. Lewis took advantage of her momentary silence. "Okay if I come in?" he asked.

She looked reluctant as she opened the door and ushered him inside. Her apartment wasn't cluttered, as so many of the smallish rooms at Golden Acres tended to become, when tenants tried to cram a lifetime's worth of possessions into space that was never meant to hold very much. Ella's apartment had tiled floors, cream-colored walls, the kind of white sofa that, in Lewis's experience, was much better in theory than in practice, especially if you had grandchildren, and the grandchildren liked grape juice.

He sat at one end of the couch. Ella sat at the other, looking flustered as she tucked her bare feet underneath her.

"Lewis," she began.

He got to his feet.

"Please don't leave. Let me explain," she said.

"I'm not leaving, I'm finding a vase," he told her.

"Wait," she said, sounding alarmed at the thought of him going through her things. "I'll do it." She hurried into the kitchen and produced a vase from a cabinet. Lewis filled it with water, put the tulips inside, came back to the living room, and set it in the center of her coffee table.

"There," he said. "Now, if you're going to say no, you'll have to look at those tulips every day and feel guilty," he said.

She looked, for an instant, as if she might be getting ready to smile . . . then the look was gone, as if he'd imagined it.

"The thing of it is," she started.

"Hold on," he said. He opened the box of candy. "You go first," he said.

She waved the box away. "Really, I can't . . ."

He put on his glasses and unfolded the candy map. "The dark chocolate hearts have cherry cordial inside," he reported. "And those roundish ones are nougat."

"Lewis," she said firmly. "You're a wonderful person, and . . ."

"But," he said. "I hear a *but* coming." He got up again, went to her kitchen, put water on to boil. "Where's your good china?" he called.

"Oh," she said, hurrying after him.

"Don't worry," he said. "I'm just making us a cup of tea."

Ella looked at him, then at the kettle. "Okay," she said, and pulled two mugs advertising the Broward County Public Library from a shelf. Lewis dropped tea bags into the mugs, located her sugar bowl (filled with packets of Sweet 'n Low), and set it on the table, alongside a pint of lactose-free milk.

"Are you always this handy?" she asked.

"I wasn't always," he said. He opened the refrigerator, found a lemon in back of her vegetable crisper, and sliced it as he talked.

"Then my wife got sick, and she knew . . . well. She knew. So she gave me lessons."

"Do you miss her?" Ella asked.

"Every day," he said. "I miss her every day." He set her cup on a saucer and carried it over to the table. "How about you?"

"Well, I never met your wife, so I can't say that I miss her . . ."

"A joke!" He applauded, and sat down beside her and studied the table. "I think it still needs something," he said. He opened Ella's freezer. "May I?"

She nodded, looking slightly dazed. He dug around until he found a familiar-shaped object that he instantly recognized as frozen Sara Lee pound cake. It had been a favorite of Sharla's. More than once he'd woken up in the middle of the night to find her in front of the television set, watching infomercials and munching on a hunk of thawed pound cake. Usually those nights signaled the conclusion of one of her twice-yearly grapefruit-and-tuna-fish diets, and she'd come back to bed with a guilty smile and a mouth that tasted like butter. *Kiss me,* she'd whisper, sliding her nightgown over her shoulders. *Let's burn off some of those bad old calories.*

He handed the cake to Ella. "Okay?"

She nodded, and put the cake into the microwave. Lewis sipped his tea and watched her move. Her hips looked original, he thought, and laughed at himself for noticing something like that. Adam, one of his grandsons, had told him during his last visit that he could tell just by looking whether a woman's chest was real or not, and Lewis had decided that he had the same talent for hip joints.

"What are you smiling about?"

He gave a small shrug. "My grandson."

Her face crumpled like a paper bag. She quickly smoothed it back again, so fast he wasn't sure he'd seen what he'd seen, which was despair. He wanted to reach over and hold her hands, hold her hands and ask her to tell him what was wrong, what hurt enough to make her look that way. He actually started to move his hands across the table when he noticed she was staring down as if a roach had just crawled out of the pound cake.

"What?"

She pointed at the cuffs of his shirt. Lewis looked down. One cuff was missing a button, and the other one was badly frayed and slightly browned.

"Did you burn that?" Ella asked.

"I guess I must have," Lewis said. "I'm not so great with the iron."

"Oh," said Ella. "I could . . ." She closed her mouth abruptly and smoothed her hair, looking flustered. Lewis saw his chance, an inflatable raft bobbing in the waves, and grabbed for it with all his might.

"Give me some lessons?" he asked humbly. *Forgive me, Sharla,* he thought, imagining he'd have to hide all the notes she'd left him, the boxes and bottles carefully labeled "for colors" and "for whites."

Ella was wavering. "Well," she said. The microwave chirped. Lewis fetched the cake. He served Ella a slice, then cut one for himself.

"I know it's an imposition," he said, "and I know how busy you are. But since my wife died, I'm kind of at loose ends. Last week I actually tried to figure out whether it would be easier to just buy new clothes every month or so . . ."

"Oh, don't do that!" said Ella. "I'll help you." He could tell that her assent had come at a cost, that there was a battle going on behind her eyes, her sense of obligation and sympathy warring with her fierce desire to be alone. "Just let me get my book."

Her book turned out to be a four-inch-thick marvel of scheduling, a half-illegible maze of scribbles and arrows and phone numbers and Post-it notes. "Let's see," said Ella, scrutinizing each page. "Wednesday I'm at the hospital . . ."

"What's wrong?"

"I rock babies," Ella said. "Thursday's the soup kitchen, then the hospice, Friday is Meals on Wheels . . ."

"Saturday?" Lewis asked. "Not to frighten you, but I'm almost out of underwear."

Ella made a noise in the back of her throat that sounded almost like laughter. "Saturday," she agreed.

"Good," he told her. "Five o'clock? I'll take you to dinner once we're done."

He was out the door before she could think to say anything to him, and as he whistled his way down the hall, he was unsurprised to see Mavis Gold, who claimed that she was on her way to the laundry room, in spite of the visible absence of her laundry.

"How'd it go?" she whispered. He gave her a thumbs-up and smiled as she clapped her hands. Then he hurried home to spill ink on his pants and pull a few buttons off his favorite shirt.

NINE

"Okay," Rose called from her seat in front of her computer. "Name, got that. Address, you can use mine." Her fingers flew over the keyboard. "Objective?"

"To get a job," said Maggie, who was sprawled on the couch with her face buried under half an inch of what she'd informed her sister was a pore-reducing clay mask.

"How about if we say 'a position in retail'?" asked Rose.

"Whatever," said Maggie, flicking on the TV. It was Saturday morning, five days after her ignominious audition, and MTV was introducing the winner of the VJ contest—a pretty, bubbly brunette with a pierced eyebrow. "Coming up next, we'll have the debut of the Spice Girls's latest video!" the girl burbled. Maggie flipped quickly away.

"Listen," said Rose. "I'm trying to help you. Could you please pay attention?"

Maggie made a huffing noise and clicked the TV off.

"Employment history," Rose prompted.

"Huh?"

"You know, your other jobs. Maggie, haven't you ever done a résumé before?"

"Oh, sure," said Maggie. "All the time. You know, just like you go to the gym."

"Other jobs," Rose repeated.

Maggie stared longingly at the cigarettes in her purse, but she knew that lighting up would result in either Rose's lung-cancer lecture or her my-house-my-rules rap. "Okay," she said, and closed her eyes. "T.J.Maxx," she began. "For six weeks. October through right before Thanksgiving." She sighed. She'd actually liked that job. She'd been good at it, too. When she worked the dressing room, she wouldn't just give her customers the plastic tag and point them toward the dressing room. She'd take the clothes, lead them in, open a cubicle, and hang each garment neatly, the way they did it at the fancy department stores and boutiques down-town. And when the women came out to spin and squint in front of the three-way mirror, tightening a belt or untucking a shirt, Maggie would be there, offering suggestions, telling them hon-estly (but carefully) when an outfit didn't flatter, hurrying back to the racks to find another size or another color, or something else entirely, something totally different, something they'd never even imagined themselves wearing, but something that Maggie could see. "You're a jewel!" she could remember one of her ladies saying, a tall, sleek, black-haired woman who would have looked great in anything, but looked especially great in the outfit Maggie'd put together—a little black dress with the perfect black leather bag and black slingback pumps, plus a belt of gold links that she'd res-cued from the clearance bin. "I'm going to tell the manager how much help you've been!"

"What happened?" asked Rose.

Maggie kept her eyes shut. "I quit," she mumbled. In fact, what had happened was what usually happened with her jobs—things would be going fine until she ran up against something. There was always something. In this case, it was the cash register. She'd scanned a coupon for ten percent off, and it hadn't gone through. "Well, can't you just do it manually?" the customer had demanded.

Maggie had scowled at her, and stared at the total. One hundred and forty-two dollars. So ten percent was . . . She bit her lip. "Fourteen dollars!" said the woman. "Come on!" At which point Maggie had straightened up slowly, paged the manager, and turned to the next customer in line with a sweet smile.

"Can I help you?"

"Hey!" the ten-percent woman had said. "You didn't finish me!"

Maggie ignored her as the next customer in line piled her sweaters and jeans onto the belt and Maggie flicked open a plastic bag. She knew what was going to happen. The woman was going to call her stupid. And there was no way Maggie was going to stand for that. She didn't even want to be here. Her talents were wasted on the cash register, her time was better spent in the dressing room, where she could actually help people instead of just work the scanner like a robot.

The supervisor came hurrying over, register keys jingling against her chest. "What's the problem?"

The ten-percent woman pointed a finger at Maggie. "She couldn't ring up my coupon."

"Maggie, what's the problem?"

"It wouldn't go through," Maggie had muttered.

"Well, ten percent," said the supervisor. "Fourteen dollars!"

"Sorry," Maggie muttered, staring at the floor, as the customer had rolled her eyes. At the end of her shift, when the supervisor had started to say something about how there was a calculator available or how she could always ask for help, Maggie had taken off her polyester pinny, dropped her name tag onto the floor, and walked out the door.

"Okay," said Rose. "But if they ask, tell them you didn't find it challenging enough."

"Fine," said Maggie, and stared at the ceiling as if the highlights of her employment history were inscribed there, a retail-and-fast-food version of the Sistine Chapel. "Before T.J.Maxx, I was at the Gap, and before that I was at Pomodoro Pizza, and before that

was the Starbucks on Walnut Street, and then I was at the
Limited—no, wait, that's wrong. I was at Urban Outfitters first,
and the Limited before that, and . . ."

Rose was typing madly.

"Banana Republic," Maggie continued. "Macy's accessories,
Macy's fragrance, Cinnabon, Chik-fil-A, Baskin-Robbins . . ."

"What about that restaurant? The Canal House?"

Maggie winced. She'd been doing fine at the Canal House until
Conrad, the Sunday manager, had gotten all over her case.
MargarET, the salt shakers aren't full. MargarET, I need you to give
the busboy a hand. She'd told him over and over that her name
wasn't even Margaret—just Maggie—but he'd ignored her for an
entire month until she'd conceived of her revenge. Late one night in
May, she and her then-sort-of-boyfriend had scaled the roof and
wrenched the *C* free from the restaurant's sign. Which meant that
dozens of women in corsages had shown up for Mother's Day
brunch at the Anal House.

"I quit," said Maggie. *Before they could fire me,* she thought.

"Fine," said Rose, staring at the screen. "We're going to have to
edit."

"Whatever," said Maggie, and stomped into the bathroom,
where she washed the clay off her face. So her work history wasn't
the greatest, she thought furiously. It didn't mean she wasn't a hard
worker! It didn't mean she didn't try!

Her sister banged on the door. "Maggie, are you almost done in
there? I need to take a shower."

Maggie wiped off her face and went back to the living room,
flicked the television set back on, before sitting down in front of
the computer. While Rose took a shower, Maggie stored her
résumé, opened a new window, and started typing a list for Rose.
Exercise regularly (aerobics and weights), she typed. *Get regular
facials. Join Jenny Craig (they are running a special!)* She typed,
grinning, and then added a helpful link to an article about Carnie
Wilson's weight-loss surgery. She shoved a cigarette between her

lips and tripped out the door, leaving the printed-out list on Rose's seat and the article ("Star Sheds Half Her Body Weight!") on Rose's screen, so that it would be the first thing her sister saw when she came home from work.

"Lock the door behind you!" Rose called from her bedroom. Maggie ignored her. If she was so smart, let her lock her own door, she thought, and headed out into the hall.

"A lawyer?" The guy with the beard squinted at Rose. "Hey, what do you call six lawyers at the bottom of the ocean?"

Rose gave a small shrug and looked longingly toward Amy's front door, hoping that Jim would soon come through it.

"A good start!" the bearded guy bellowed.

Rose blinked at him. "I don't get it," she said.

He stared, unsure if she was kidding.

"I don't understand. I mean, why are the lawyers at the bottom of the ocean? Are they snorkeling or something?"

Now the guy was looking decidedly uncomfortable. Rose furrowed her forehead. "Wait . . . are they at the bottom of the ocean because they drowned?"

"Well, yeah," said the guy, using one fingernail to pry the label off his beer.

"Okay," said Rose slowly. "So there's six dead, drowned lawyers at the bottom of the ocean . . ." She paused and looked at the guy expectantly.

"It was just a joke," he said.

"But I don't understand why it's funny," she said.

The guy took two steps backward.

"Wait," said Rose. "Wait! You have to finish explaining this to me!"

"I'll be . . . um," said the guy. He sidled off toward the bar. Amy shot her a dirty look across the room and shook her head. *Bad girl,* Amy mouthed, wagging her index finger. Rose shrugged. She wasn't normally so mean, but Jim's tardiness—combined with Maggie's three-weeks-and-counting residence—had put her in a foul mood.

Rose stared at her best friend, thinking that at least one of them had changed since the misery of junior high. By ninth grade, Amy had grown to six feet tall, weighing in at perhaps a hundred and ten pounds, and the boys in the class called her Ichabod Crane—just Ick for short. But she'd gotten comfortable with her gangly frame. Now she wore her knobby wrists like expensive bracelets and wielded the fine bones of her face and hips like unusual pieces of art. She'd had dreadlocks in college, but after graduation she hacked her hair off and dyed it a dark red. She wore tight black tops and long black boot-cut jeans, and she looked fabulous. Exotic, and mysterious, and sexy, even when she opened her mouth and her thick, unreconstructed Jersey-girl accent came out. Amy always had at least half a dozen boyfriends, former boyfriends, and would-be boyfriends lining up for the privi lege of buying her deep-dish pizza and listening to her dissect the state of hip-hop music in America.

Plus, Amy was a chemical engineer—an occupation that typi-cally garnered at least a few interested questions from strangers she'd meet at parties—while Rose was a lawyer, which usually drew one of two responses: the first, typified by Mr. Lawyer Joke, and the second, Rose was pretty sure, soon to be elucidated by the tall, pale fellow in glasses who'd parked himself on the couch beside her, interrupting her special private time with the bowl of cheese curls.

"Amy tells me you're a lawyer," he began. "You know, I'm hav-ing a bit of a legal problem myself."

Of course you are, Rose thought, her smile spackled to her face. She glanced at the clock. Almost eleven. Where was Jim?

"There's this tree," the guy said. "It's growing on my property, see? But the leaves fall mostly into my neighbor's yard . . ."

Yeah, yeah, yeah, Rose thought. And you're both too lazy to rake the goddamn leaves. Or he chopped the tree down without your permission. And instead of just talking about the tree like normal people, or, God forbid, actually hiring a lawyer of your own, you want to unload on me.

"Excuse me," Rose murmured, cutting the guy off midway

through his saga, made her escape, and twisting through the crowd
until she found Amy in the kitchen, leaning against the refrigerator, twirling a glass of wine in her fingers, head tilted back, laughing at whatever the guy in front of her was saying.

"Hey, Dan," Amy drawled. "This is my friend Rose."

Dan was tall, dark, and gorgeous. "Pleased to meet you," he said.
Rose gave him a weak smile, clutching her purse—and within it, her
cell phone—tightly to her side. She needed to talk to Jim. He was
the only person that could soothe her and make her smile and convince her that life wasn't pointless and that the world wasn't full of
joke-spouting idiots and litigious tree owners. Where was he?

She eased herself away from Dan and reached into her purse, but
Amy was right behind her.

"Forget it," she said sternly. "Don't chase. It's not ladylike.
Remember? Men like to be the hunters, not the prey." Amy took
the cell phone from Rose's hand and replaced it with a slotted
spoon. "Dumplings," she said, pointing Rose toward the stove, and
a pot of steaming water.

"What have you got against Jim, anyhow?" Rose asked.

Amy gazed at the ceiling, then leveled her eyes at Rose. "It's
not him, it's you. I'm worried about you."

"Why?"

"I'm worried that you're more into it than he is. I don't want
you to get hurt."

Rose opened her mouth, then shut it fast. How could she convince Amy that Jim was just as into it as she was when he wasn't
even here? And there was something else, something catching at
the corner of her mind, something about the night he'd showed up
late, with his arms full of flowers, and how he'd smelled of scotch,
and rose blossoms, and, faintly, of something else. Perfume? she'd
thought, and then stopped the thought in its tracks and built a
wall around it, a wall composed largely of the word *no*.

"And isn't he your boss?"

"Not exactly," Rose said. Jim wasn't her boss any more than any other partner was her boss. Which was to say, he was at least somewhat her boss. Rose swallowed hard, shoved that thought to its accustomed hiding place in the back of her head, and steamed a batch of shrimp dumplings. When Amy's back was turned, she grabbed her purse again, hurried down a hallway lined with African masks, ducked into Amy's downstairs bathroom, and dialed Jim's work number. No answer. She dialed her own number. Maybe he'd misunderstood her and stopped by her house instead of heading straight to Amy's.

"Hello?"

Drat. Maggie. "Hi," said Rose. "It's me. Did Jim call?"

"Nuh-uh," said Maggie.

"Well, if he calls tell him . . . tell him I'll see him later."

"I probably won't be here. I'm on my way out," said Maggie.

"Oh," Rose said. There were a dozen things she wanted to ask: Going where? With what friends? With what money? She bit down hard. Asking Maggie would only infuriate her, and sending an angry Maggie out on the town was a little like handing a loaded gun to a two-year-old.

"Lock the door behind you," she said.

"I will."

"And please take off my shoes," Rose said.

There was a pause. "I'm not wearing your shoes," said Maggie.

Sure, because you just took them off, thought Rose. "Have fun," she said instead. Maggie promised that she would. Rose splashed cool water on her cheeks and wrists and stared at herself in the mirror. She'd smeared her mascara. Her lipstick had evaporated. And she was stuck at a party, steaming dumplings, alone. Where was he?

Rose opened the door and tried to edge past Amy, who was standing in the doorway with her long arms crossed on her bony chest. "Did you call him?" she demanded.

"Call who?" asked Rose.

Amy laughed. "You are just as crummy a liar as you were when you had a crush on Hal Lindquist." She took a cocktail napkin and wiped mascara from underneath Rose's eyes.

"I did not have a crush on Hal Lindquist!"

"Oh, sure. You just wrote down exactly what he was wearing every day in your math binder because you wanted future generations to have a record of what Hal Lindquist wore in 1984."

Rose smiled at herself. "So which one of these guys is your date?" Amy made a face. "Don't ask. It was supposed to be Trevor."

Rose struggled to remember what Amy had told her about Trevor. "Is he here?"

"Indeed he is not," said Amy. "Check this out—we're at dinner."

"Where?" Rose asked dutifully.

"Tangerine. Very nice. And we're sitting there, and the lights are low, and the candles are flickering, and I haven't spilled any couscous on myself, and he tells me why he broke up with his last girlfriend. Evidently he'd developed certain interests."

"What interests?"

"Shit," said Amy, with an absolutely straight face.

"What?"

"You heard me. Consenting acts of defecation."

"You're kidding," Rose gasped.

"I shit you not," Amy deadpanned. "And so I'm sitting there, absolutely horrified. Needless to say, I couldn't eat another bite, plus I had to spend the rest of the meal making sure I didn't fart, because he'd think I was flirting . . ."

Rose started laughing.

"Come along," said Amy, pocketing the napkin and thrusting a beer into Rose's hand. "Join the party."

Rose went back to the kitchen, heated up artichoke dip, replenished the cracker basket, made conversation with another one of Amy's wannabes, although at the end of it she couldn't remember a word of what either one of them had said. She longed for Jim— who, based on the available evidence, was not longing for her.

TEN

Jim Danvers opened his eyes and thought the same thing that he thought every morning: today I will be good. *Lead me not into temptation,* he recited, dragging his razor over his jaw, staring at himself sternly in his bathroom mirror. *Get thee behind me, Satan,* he said, pulling on his pants.

The trouble was, Satan was everywhere. Temptation lurked around every corner. Here it was, leaning against a building, waiting for the bus. Jim slowed his Lexus and grabbed an eyeful of the blond in tight jeans, wondering what her body looked like beneath her bulky winter coat, wondering how she'd move in bed, how she'd smell, how she'd sound, and what it would take to find out.

Stop, he ordered himself, just stop, and punched the radio into life. Howard Stern filled the front seat, his tone leering, wise, and knowing. "Are those real, honey?" he inquired of the morning's starlet. "Real silicone," she giggled. Jim swallowed hard and switched to the classical station. It was so unfair. Ever since a wet dream on the third night of a Boy Scout camping trip at age twelve had heralded the advent of puberty, he'd dreamed of women with a concentrated fierceness, the abstract longing of a starving man stuck on an island with back issues of *Bon Appetit*. Blondes, brunettes, and redheads, small-breasted willowy girls and short bouncy curvy ones, black, Hispanic, Asian, white, young, old, and in between, and even, God help him, a cute girl in leg braces he'd glimpsed on the Jerry Lewis telethon—in his fantasy world, Jim Danvers was an equal opportunity employer.

And he'd never been able to have them. Not at age twelve, when he was short and pudgy and frequently out of breath. Not at fourteen, when he was still short and no longer pudgy but fat, and his face was riddled with what Dr. Guberman swore was the worst case of cystic acne he'd ever seen. At sixteen he shot up six inches, but the damage was done, and the nickname Fudgie the Whale unfortunately followed him to college. What followed was the classic vicious circle—he was miserable because of his weight. He ate to stanch his misery, feeding his pain with pizza and beer, which only made him bigger, which only pushed the women further away. He'd lost his virginity senior year to a prostitute who'd looked him up and down, cracking her gum in a meditative fashion before insisting that she be on top. "Not to criticize, hon," she'd said, "but I think what we've got here is a liability issue."

Law school could have been different, he thought to the soothing strains of Bach. He'd gotten even taller, and after the embarrassing ten minutes with the prostitute he'd taken up jogging, tracing Rocky's route through the Philadelphia streets (although he was pretty sure that even initially Rocky could make it farther than three blocks without having to stop and catch his breath). The weight came off. His skin cleared up, leaving behind only a fading webwork of interesting scars, and he'd gotten his teeth fixed. What remained was a crippling shyness, a paralytic lack of self-esteem. All through his twenties, through his years rising steadily through the ranks at Lewis, Dommel, and Fenick, whenever he'd heard women laughing he'd assumed they were laughing at, or about, him.

And then, somehow, everything had changed. He remembered the night he'd made partner, how he'd joined three of his recently elevated colleagues at an Irish bar on Walnut Street. "It's Nanny

Night," one of them had said, giving Jim a meaningful wink. Jim didn't know what he meant, but he soon found out. The bar was packed with Irish lasses, blue-eyed Swedes, Finnish girls with French braids. A half-dozen lilting accents chimed over the brass-and-mahogany bar. Jim was stunned into speechlessness and immobility. He stood frozen in a corner and downed champagne and stout and lager long after his colleagues went home, staring helplessly as the girls giggled and complained about their charges. On his way to the men's room, he'd bumped into a red-haired freckled girl with twinkling blue eyes. "Steady there!" she'd said, laughing as he mumbled an apology. Her name was Maeve, he'd learned, as she led him back to her table. "A partner!" she'd cooed, as her friends looked on approvingly. "Congratulations!" And somehow he'd wound up in her bed, spending a joyful six hours tasting her freckles, filling his hands with the crackling fire of her hair.

Since then he'd turned into a slut. There really was no other word for it. He wasn't a Don Juan or a Romeo; he wasn't a stud or a cocksman. He was a slut, living out every one of the fantasies of his frustrated adolescence in a city that suddenly seemed full of good-natured girls in their twenties, all of them just as eager for a no-strings-attached romp as he was. He'd turned some kind of magical corner where what he was (and what he earned) had some-how trumped the way he looked. Or his looks had improved. Or, to women, the words "I'm a partner" sounded exactly like "take off your panties." He couldn't explain it, but suddenly there were nan-nies and students and secretaries, bartenders and baby-sitters and waitresses, and he didn't even need to go to bars to find them. Why, right in the office there was a certain paralegal who'd be happy to stay late, to lock his office door behind her and take off everything except a lilac brassiere and a certain pair of sandals she had that laced around her calves, and . . .

Stop, Jim told himself. It was unseemly. It was embarrassing. It had to stop. He was thirty-five and a partner. He'd gorged himself at the all-you-can-eat flesh banquet for the past year and a half, and it should have been enough. Think of the risks, he instructed himself. Disease! Heartbreak! Angry fathers and boyfriends! The three guys who'd made partner when he had were already married, and two of them were fathers, and although nothing explicit had ever been said, it was clear that they'd chosen the kind of lifestyles the firm's powers approved of. Home and hearth, with possibly a discrete diversion on the side, that was the way to go, not these wild weekends of girls whose last names he didn't always catch. His colleagues' attitudes had already started to shift from awe to awed amusement. Soon they'd be looking at him with just amusement. And after that would come amused disgust.

And there was Rose. Jim felt himself soften as he thought of her. Rose wasn't the prettiest girl he'd ever been with, not the sexiest. She tended to dress like a repressed librarian, and her idea of sexy lingerie was when her cotton panties matched her cotton bra, but still, there was something about her that bypassed the hot wiring below his belt and grabbed directly at his heart. The way she looked at him! Like he was one of the coverboys from her romance novels come to life, like he'd left his white steed at a parking meter and had charged through a thicket of thorns to rescue her. He was surprised that the whole firm hadn't figured out what was going on between them, in spite of the rules about partners dating associates. Then again, maybe he was being blind. Maybe everyone had figured it out already. And here he was, tempted a hundred times a day to break her heart.

Sweet Rose. She deserved better than him, Jim thought, piloting his Lexus into the law firm's garage. And for her, he'd try to be as good as he could be. Already he'd swapped his hot secretary for a sixtysomething motherly type who smelled of lemon Luden's cough drops, and he'd stayed out of the bars for an unprecedented three weeks running. She was good for him, he told himself, stepping into the elevator that would take him to his office. She was sharp and smart and kindhearted; she was the kind of girl he could see growing old with, spending the rest of his life with. And for Rose he'd walk the straight and narrow, he vowed, looking over the trio of chattering secretaries who'd entered the elevator beside him before taking one last whiff of their mingled perfume, swallowing hard, and looking away.

ELEVEN

"Why do we have to do this again?" asked Maggie as she flung herself into the passenger's seat. It was the same question she asked as they set out for every home football game. They'd been going once a year for almost twenty years, Rose thought, and the answer never changed.

"Because our father is a very limited man," she said, and started driving toward the Vet. "Are you going to be warm enough? You remember we're playing Tampa, not going there." Maggie had dressed for the football game in a black catsuit, black boots with chunky heels, and a cropped leather jacket with a fake fur collar. Rose, on the other hand, had on jeans and a sweater, plus a hat, a scarf, mittens, and an oversized yellow down coat.

Maggie peered at Rose's jacket. "You look like a mattress that someone peed on," she said.

"Thanks for sharing," said Rose. "Fasten your seat belt."

"Fine," Maggie replied, pulling a flask out of one of the jacket's minuscule pockets. She took a swig and tilted it toward her sister. "Apricot brandy," she said.

"I'm driving," said Rose, her mouth set in a tight line.

"And I'm drinking," said Maggie, and giggled. The sound of her sister's laughter reminded Rose of every other football game they'd attended since her father, in a slightly misguided act of involved parenting, had bought the first set of season tickets in 1981.

"We hate football," Maggie had informed him with the absolute conviction of being ten years old and right about everything. Michael Feller's face had gotten pale.

"We do not!" Rose had said, and she'd given her sister a fast upper-arm pinch.

"Ow!" said Maggie.

"Really?" asked their father.

"Well, we don't like watching it on TV so much," said Rose, "but we'd love to see a real game!" She'd given her sister an insurance pinch to make sure she wouldn't say otherwise. And that was that. Every year, the three of them—eventually the four of them, once Sydelle appeared on the scene—would go to Eagles home games together. Maggie used to lay out her outfits days in advance, mittens trimmed with fake fur and hats with fluffy pom-poms, and once, if Rose remembered right, a miniature pair of tasseled cheerleader's boots. Rose would make peanut butter and jelly sandwiches, and she'd put them in a lunch box, along with a thermos of hot chocolate. They'd bring blankets on the coldest days, and the three of them would huddle together, licking peanut butter off of their numb fingers, as their father would curse at every sack and fumble, then look guiltily at the girls and say, "Pardon my French."

"Pardon my French," Rose murmured. Maggie looked at her curiously, then took another slip of her brandy and hunched herself lower into the seat.

Their father and Sydelle were waiting for them by the ticket window. Michael Feller was dressed in jeans, an Eagles sweatshirt, and a down coat in the team colors of silver and green. Sydelle wore her customary look of icy discontent, a face full of makeup, and an ankle-length mink coat.

"Maggie! Rose!" their father called out, handing them their tickets.

"Girls," said Sydelle, kissing the air three inches to the right of their cheeks, then reapplying her lipstick. Rose followed her stepmother up toward their seats. Listening to the click of Sydelle's heels echo on the concrete, Rose wondered—and not for the first time—why in the world this woman had ever married her father. Sydelle Levine had been a divorcée in her mid-forties whose stockbroker husband had had the bad manners to leave her for his secretary. *Très* cliché, but Sydelle had survived the indignity, perhaps buoyed by the ample alimony payments her husband had eagerly agreed to (Rose imagined him thinking that even a million dollars a year was a small price to pay for years of Sydelle-free bliss). Michael Feller was eight years younger, a middle manager at a medium-sized bank. He'd be comfortable, but never rich. Plus, he had baggage—the dead wife, the daughters.

What could the attraction have been? Rose had spent hours of her adolescence trying to puzzle it out in the years after Michael Feller and Sydelle Levine met in the Beth Shalom lobby (Sydelle had been on her way in for a five-hundred-dollar-a-plate fund-raiser, and Michael had been on his way out of a Parents Without Partners meeting).

"Sex!" Maggie had said, cackling. And it was true that, objectively speaking, their father was a handsome man. But Rose wasn't sure. She thought that Sydelle had seen her father not just as handsome, or a good catch, but as her true love, her second chance. Rose always believed that Sydelle had really loved him—at least at the beginning. And she'd bet that her father hadn't been looking for anything more than a traveling companion—and, of course, a surrogate mother for Maggie and Rose, given Sydelle's success with My Marcia. Michael Feller had already found the love of his life, and buried her back in Connecticut. And every week that went by, Sydelle grew a little more aware of that truth, and became a little more disappointed—and a little meaner to Michael Feller's daughters.

It was sad, thought Rose, sitting down, pulling her hat over

her ears, and wrapping her scarf tightly around her neck. Sad, and
unlikely to change. Sydelle and her father were in it for the long
haul.

"Want some?"

Startled, Rose jumped a little in her seat, and turned to face her
sister, who'd flung her legs over the seat in front of her and was
waggling her little flask of apricot brandy. "No thanks," said Rose,
and turned to her father. "How have you been?" she asked.

"Oh, you know," he said. "Work's keeping me busy. My Vanguard
500 fund had a terrible quarter. I—RUN YOU BASTARD!"

Rose leaned past her sister to talk to Sydelle. "And what's new
with you?" she asked, making her regular game-day effort to be nice
to her stepmother.

Sydelle fluffed her mink. "My Marcia's redecorating."

"That's exciting," said Rose, trying to sound enthusiastic.

Sydelle nodded. "We're going to a spa," she continued. "In
February," she said, and cast a meaningful glance toward Rose's
midriff. "You know that when she got married, My Marcia bought
a size six Vera Wang, and . . ."

". . . had it taken in," Rose recited silently to herself, just as
Maggie said the same words, only out loud.

Sydelle narrowed her eyes. "I don't know why you feel com-
pelled to be so rude."

Maggie ignored her and held out her hand for her father's
binoculars as the cheerleaders took the field. "Fat, fat, old, fat," she
recited, making her way down the line. "Bad dye job; ooh! bad
boob job, old, fat, old. . . ."

Michael Feller waved at the beer vendor. Sydelle grabbed his
hand, and put it back in his lap. "Ornish!" she hissed.

"Pardon me?" said Rose.

"Ornish," said Sydelle. "We're doing the Dean Ornish diet.
Plant-based." She gave another sideways glance, this time at Rose's
thighs. "You might want to try it."

I'm in hell, thought Rose bleakly. *Hell is an Eagles game, where the bleachers are always freezing, and the team is always losing, and my family is insane.*

Her father patted her shoulder and flipped open his wallet. "Want to get us hot chocolate?" he asked.

Maggie leaned over. "Can I have money, too?" she asked. Then she squinted at the wallet. "Who's that?"

"Oh," their father said, looking embarrassed, "it's just this article I cut out. I was meaning to give it to Rose . . ."

"Dad," said Rose. "That's Lou Dobbs."

"Right," said her father.

"You're carrying a picture of Lou Dobbs around in your wallet?"

"Not his picture," Michael Feller said. "This article. About preparing for retirement. It's very good."

"Do you have pictures of us in there?" Maggie demanded, grabbing for the wallet. "Or just Lou Whoever?" She flipped through the pictures. Rose looked, too. There were school pictures of her and Maggie that dated from sixth and fourth grade, respectively. A picture of Michael and Caroline, on their wedding day—a candid shot, with Caroline puffing out her lower lip to blow her veil off her forehead, and with Michael gazing at her. There was not, Rose noted, a shot of Michael and Sydelle. She wondered if Sydelle had noticed. Judging from her icy expression, the way her tiny eyes were fixed straight ahead, Rose guessed that the answer was yes.

"Go Birds!" the guy in the row behind them blatted into Rose's ear, and then belched as a finale. Rose got to her feet and headed into the echoing, windswept concourse, where she bought herself a cup of watery hot chocolate and a hot dog in a squishy white bun, which she devoured in four gigantic bites. Then she leaned against the railing, picking bits of relish off of her scarf, counting the minutes until eight o'clock when she was going to meet Jim for dinner. *Hold on,* she told herself. She bought three more cups of hot chocolate and carried them carefully back to the seats.

TWELVE

"Mrs. Lefkowitz?" Ella rapped hard on the aluminum door, balancing a lunch tray on her hip. "Hello?"

"Go to hell!" came the slurred voice from inside. Ella sighed and kept knocking.

"Lunchtime!" she called out, as cheerfully as she could.

"Fuck off!" yelled Mrs. Lefkowitz. Mrs. Lefkowitz had suffered a stroke, and her recuperation had unfortunately coincided with the week that Golden Acres had been getting free HBO. The free HBO had included a Margaret Cho stand-up special. Mrs. Lefkowitz had been calling Ella "Ass Master" ever since, and laughing uproariously each time she said it.

"I've got soup," Ella called.

There was a pause from the other side of the door. "Cream of mushroom?" Mrs. Lefkowitz asked hopefully.

"Split pea," Ella confessed.

Another pause, and then the door was flung open, and there was Mrs. Lefkowitz, four feet eleven inches, white hair rumpled and wild. She wore a pink sweatshirt and matching sweatpants and knitted pink-and-white booties—the kind of outfit you'd give a newborn, Ella thought, and tried not to smile, as her final Meals on Wheels client for the day glared at her furiously.

"Split pea sucks," said Mrs. Lefkowitz. The left corner of her mouth drooped slightly, and she held her left arm bent at an odd angle tightly against her side. She looked at Ella hopefully. "Maybe you could make cream of mushroom?"

"Do you have any?" asked Ella.

"Sure, sure," said Mrs. Lefkowitz, shuffling toward the kitchen, her tiny form swimming in all that pink yarn. Ella followed along, setting the tray down on the kitchen table. "Sorry I yelled at you. I thought you were someone else."

Who? Ella wanted to ask. As far as she could tell, she was the only one who ever saw Mrs. Lefkowitz, outside of her doctors and the home-care health aide who came three times a week.

"My son," Mrs. Lefkowitz supplied. She turned toward Ella with a can of Campbell's in her right hand.

"You tell your son to"— Ella couldn't bring herself to repeat it—"eff off?"

"Kids today," said Mrs. Lefkowitz complacently.

"Well, it's nice that he's visiting," said Ella, dumping the congealed grayish mass into a saucepan.

"I told him not to come," said Mrs. Lefkowitz. "But he said, 'Ma, you were on the verge of death.' I said, 'I'm eighty-seven years of age. What did you think I was on the verge of? Club Med?'"

"Well, that's lovely that he's visiting."

"Bullshit," said Mrs. Lefkowitz. "He just wants to get some sun. I'm convenient," she said, her drooping lip quivering. "Guess where he is right now. On the beach. Probably staring at the girls in the bikinis, and drinking a beer. Hah. He couldn't wait to get out of here."

"The beach sounds nice," Ella said as she stirred.

Mrs. Lefkowitz pulled a chair away from the table, carefully seated herself upon it, and waited until Ella pushed her chair close to the table's edge. "I guess," she said. Ella set the bowl in front of her. Mrs. Lefkowitz dipped her spoon and raised it toward her lips. Her wrist trembled, and half the soup wound up on the front of her sweatshirt. "Shit," she said, and her voice was small and wavering and defeated.

"Do you have plans for dinner?" asked Ella, handing Mrs. Lefkowitz a napkin and tipping the soup into a coffee mug.

"I told him I'd cook," she said. "Turkey. He likes turkey."

"I could help you," said Ella. "Maybe we could make a platter of different deli sandwiches. Easy to eat." She stood up, looking for a pen and a pad of paper so she could make a list. "We can go buy some brisket, and turkey and corned beef . . . cole slaw and potato salad, if he likes that . . ."

Mrs. Lefkowitz smiled with half of her mouth. "I used to buy it with caraway seeds, and at the end of dinner I'd find a little pile of caraway seeds on the side of his plate. He'd never complain . . . he'd just pick them all out and leave them there."

"My daughter was like that with raisins. She'd pick them out of anything," said Ella. Mrs. Lefkowitz looked at her sharply. Ella let her voice trail off.

Mrs. Lefkowitz maneuvered a spoonful of soup to her mouth and appeared not to notice Ella's silence. "So we'll go shopping?" she said.

"Sure," said Ella, bending to put the dishes in the dishwasher, turning her back to Mrs. Lefkowitz. Lewis was coming to pick her up tonight. They were going to a movie. And how soon before his questions came? *Do you have children? Do you have grandkids? Where are they? What happened? You don't see them? Well, why not?* "Sure."

THIRTEEN

"You're home!" said Maggie.

Rose entered the apartment warily. It had been a terrible day. She'd been at work for thirteen hours, and Jim's office door had been closed for all of them, and she was in no mood for Maggie's nonsense.

In the apartment's small living room, all the lights were blazing, something smelled like it was burning in the kitchen, and Maggie, dressed in ruffled red pajama shorts and a red T-shirt that read "SEX KITTEN" in silver letters, was perched on the couch, channel surfing. A bowl of singed-looking microwaved popcorn sat in the center of the table next to a bowl of reheated frozen corn, two celery sticks, and a jar of peanut butter. This, in Maggie's world, passed for a balanced meal.

"How's the job search going?" asked Rose, hanging up her coat and heading into the bedroom, where her bed was strewn with what appeared to be the entire contents of her closet. "What's this? What happened?"

Maggie plopped herself on top of the heap. "I decided to sort out your clothes."

Rose stared at the tangle of blouses and jackets and pants, now just as much a mess as Maggie's baggage out in the living room. "Why are you doing this?" she said. "Don't touch my things!"

"Rose, I'm trying to help you," said Maggie, sounding affronted. "I figure it's the least I can do, since you've been so generous." She stared at the floor. "Sorry I upset you," she said. "I just wanted to help."

Rose opened her mouth, then closed it. This was part of her sister's particular genius—just at the moment when you were ready to kill her, to throw her out on the street, to demand that she pay back your money and return your clothes and your shoes, she'd say something that would catch in your heart like a fishhook.

"Fine," she muttered. "Just put everything back when you're done."

"You're supposed to go through all of your stuff every six months," said Maggie. "I read it in *Vogue*. And you, obviously, have fallen behind. I found acid-wash jeans," she added with a shudder. "But not to worry. I threw them away."

"You should have taken them to Goodwill."

"Just because someone is poor," declared Maggie, "does not mean they must be unfashionable." She extended the bowl of corn toward her sister. "Niblet?"

Rose grabbed a spoon and helped herself. "How do you know what I'm wearing and what I'm not?"

Maggie shrugged. "Well, some of it's obvious. Like those size twelve pants from Ann Taylor?"

Rose knew the ones. She'd bought them on sale, and squeezed into them once four years ago after a week's worth of nothing but black coffee and Slim-Fast. They'd been hanging in her closet ever since, a silent reproach, a reminder of what was possible if she'd buckle down and stop eating french fries and pizza and . . . well, pretty much everything else she liked. "They're all yours," she said.

"They're way too big. But maybe I could have them taken in," Maggie said, and turned her attention to the television set.

"When are you going to put everything back?" asked Rose, imagining trying to sleep atop the litter of her wardrobe.

"Shh!" said Maggie, lifting one finger, and pointed toward the

TV, where a small, wheeled hunk of red-painted metal was menacing a bluish object that had a rotating blade protruding from its center.

"What is this?"

"Television," Maggie replied, stretching one leg out in front of her, and turning it this way and that, inspecting her calf. "It's this box, with pictures, and the pictures tell a delightful story!"

Rose thought about reaching for her wallet. *This is a paycheck,* she'd say, holding the object in question out for her sister's inspection. *It represents money, which you earn by holding a job.* Maggie took a swallow from the open bottle of champagne by her side. Rose opened her mouth to ask where she'd gotten champagne, then realized it was the bottle someone had given her when she'd passed the bar that had been reposing in a back corner of her refrigerator ever since.

"How's that champagne?" Rose asked.

Maggie took another gulp. "Delicious," she said. "Now, pay attention. Watch and learn. On this show, *BattleBots,* there are these guys who build robots . . ."

"That's a nice hobby," said Rose, who tried whenever she could to encourage Maggie in the pursuit of acceptable men.

Maggie waved a dismissive hand. "They're geeks. They build these robots, and the robots fight each other, and the winner gets . . . something. I'm not sure what. Look, look, there's my favorite," she said, pointing at what looked like a miniature trash truck with a spike welded to its middle. "That's the Philiminator," she said.

"Huh?" asked Rose.

"The guy who made it, his name is Phil, so it's the Philiminator." Sure enough, the camera had panned to a pale, lanky guy in a baseball cap reading "Philiminator." "He's undefeated in three rounds," Maggie said, as a second robot rolled into view. This one was a shiny green and looked like a souped-up Dustbuster. "Grendel," said the announcer.

"Okay," said Maggie. "You root for Grendel."

"Why?" asked Rose, but by then the match was starting. The two robots started off after each other, zipping around the concrete floor like small, crazed dogs.

"Go, Philiminator!" Maggie hollered, waving the champagne bottle exuberantly. She looked at her sister.

"Yay, Grendel," said Rose. Maggie's robot zipped in close. The spike from its center rose, and rose, and came crashing down like a guillotine, spearing Grendel through its center, as Maggie clapped and shouted her encouragement.

"Whew! Close one," said Maggie.

The robots wheeled around to face each other again.

"Come on, Philiminator. FUCK HIM UP!" Maggie bellowed.

Rose burst out laughing, as a spiked wheel on the front of Grendel started whirring. "Ooh, look out . . . here I come!"

Now Grendel advanced on his opponent. The Philiminator lifted its spike and speared its opponent through its center.

"Yeah!" Maggie cheered.

The two robots were locked together now, joined by the spike. Grendel twisted this way and that, unable to get free. "Come on . . . come on . . ." Rose muttered. Grendel's wheel whirred, striking sparks off the floor. The Philiminator raised its spike for the death blow, and Grendel zipped away.

"GO GRENDEL!" Rose hollered, and jumped to her feet. "Yes! YES!" Maggie sulked as Grendel charged at its opponent, wedged its nose underneath the much taller Philiminator, and flipped it on its back.

"Noooo," wailed Maggie as Rose's robot ran over hers once, and then again, until the thing was no more than a collection of crushed parts and broken pieces.

"Oh, yes. OH YES!" said Rose, pumping her fist in the air. "That's what I'm talking about!" she shouted, just the way she'd heard guys in the row behind her at Eagles games holler after particularly crucial touchdowns. Then she turned toward her sister, sure that Maggie would be smirking at her, doing a poor job of showing how pathetic she found Rose's excitement. Except Maggie wasn't smirking. Maggie, her cheeks flushed, was beaming at her sister, holding out her hand for a high five, laughing as she offered her sister the bottle of champagne. Rose hesitated, then took a swallow.

"Want to order a pizza?" Rose offered. She could envision the rest of the night—pizza and pajamas and fresh popcorn, the two of them on the couch beneath the blanket, watching TV.

Maggie did smirk then . . . but only a little. And her voice was almost kind. "You're really living now, aren't you?" she asked. "You should get out more."

"I get out enough," said Rose. "You should stay in more."

"I stay in plenty," said Maggie, rising gracefully to her feet. She padded into the bedroom, returning minutes later dressed in skintight faded jeans, slung low around her hips, a red top that left one shoulder and arm completely bare, and Rose's jalapeño leather cowboy boots. Rose's hand-stitched red leather cowboy boots, bought on a weekend in New Mexico, where Rose had gone once for a seminar about insurance law. "You don't mind, do you?" said Maggie, gathering her purse and her keys. "I found them in your closet. They looked lonely."

"Sure," said Rose. She stared at her sister and wondered what it must be to move through life being so thin and so pretty; what it would be like to have men look at you with unconditional approval, unmitigated desire. "Have fun."

"I always do," said Maggie, and breezed out the door, leaving Rose with the popcorn, the flat champagne, the ruin of clothes strewn across her bed. She flicked the television set into its customary silence, and started to clean up the mess.

FOURTEEN

"Can I help you?" asked Ella. It was Ella's afternoon at the thrift shop, where she passed a few pleasant, mostly uninterrupted hours sorting bags of clothing and putting price tags on furniture and dishes. A young woman in bright orange leggings and a stained T-shirt edged down the aisle that was decorated with fake pine swags and gold and silver tinsel, in preparation for the holidays.

"Sheets," the woman said, biting her lip nervously. Ella could see the faint remnant of a bruise high on her cheek. "I'm looking for sheets."

"Well, it's your lucky day," said Ella. "It just so happens we got a shipment in from Bullock's. Irregulars, of course, but I don't see a thing wrong with them, except the colors are a little . . . well, you'll see."

She started off down the aisle, walking briskly in her black pants and white blouse with her name tag clipped to the front. "Right here," said Ella, pointing to where the sheets were—a few dozen packets in all, some for queen-sized beds, some for twins. They were turquoise and hot pink, but they were new. "Now, they're five dollars each. How many will you need?"

"Um, two twins." The woman picked up the plastic-wrapped packages, turning them over in her hands. "Are the pillowcases extra?"

"Oh! Actually, no," said Ella. "It's five dollars for the set."

The woman looked relieved as she picked up a pair of pillow-cases and walked to the cash register. She pulled a five-dollar bill out of her pocket, and three crumpled singles. When she started rooting around for change, lining pennies up carefully on the counter, Ella slipped her sheets into a bag.

"That's fine," she said.

The woman looked up at her. "Are you sure?"

"It's fine," Ella repeated. "Take care of yourself, and come back . . . we're getting new stuff in all the time."

The woman smiled—politely, Ella thought—and walked out, her flip-flops slapping on the sidewalk. Ella stared at her back, wishing she'd found a way to slip some towels into the woman's bag along with the sheets. She sighed, and felt frustrated. It had been like that with Caroline—Ella always wanting to do more, to fix things for her daughter, to chase after her, with calls, with cards, with letters, with money, dangling the promise of vacations and trips, saying the same thing a dozen different ways: *Let me help you.* But Caroline hadn't wanted to be helped, because accepting help meant admitting that she couldn't do it herself. And look how that had turned out.

The door swung open again and Lewis walked into the thrift store with a bundle of newspapers under his arm.

"Hot off the presses!" he said. Ella tried for a smile and looked at her poem. "I AM NOT INVISIBLE," she read. Not invisible, she thought sadly. Just doomed.

Lewis was looking at her closely. "Still want lunch?" he asked, and when she nodded and closed the cash register, he offered her his arm. She walked out into the steamy sunshine, still wishing she'd done things differently. She wished she'd been able to start a con-versation, to maybe ask if the woman needed help, and then figured out how to help her. And, she thought, she wished that Lewis would never find out what kind of a person she really was. She hadn't brought up children and, so far, he hadn't asked . . . but someday soon he would, and what then? What would she say? What could she say, really, except that she used to be a mother, that she wasn't a mother anymore, and that it was her fault? And he'd stare at her, unable to make sense of it, and she wouldn't be able to explain it properly, even though she knew that it was true, and it was the stone she couldn't swallow, the river she couldn't cross. Her fault. And no matter how she tried to make up for it, what small acts of goodness she attempted, she would carry that around with her until the day she died.

FIFTEEN

"There's someone to see you," said Rose's secretary. Rose looked up from her computer and saw her sister, resplendent in black boot-cut leather pants, a cropped denim jacket, and the red cowboy boots, waltz into her office.

"Good news!" Maggie said, beaming.

Please let it be a job, Rose prayed. "What is it?"

"I had a job interview! At this great new bar!"

"Terrific!" said Rose, trying to match her enthusiasm to Maggie's. "That's great! When do you think they'll let you know?"

"I'm not sure," said Maggie, who was lifting and replacing books and folders from Rose's bookcase. "Maybe after the holidays."

"But wouldn't the holidays be their busy time?"

"Jesus, Rose, I don't know!" Maggie picked up the small plastic replica of Xena, Warrior Princess—one of Amy's birthday gifts— and stood it on its head. "Do you think you could maybe try to be happy for me?"

"Sure," said Rose. "And have you made any progress on putting my clothes back?" For the past several nights, the pile of clothing had shifted from her bed to the floor, but had not yet made it to the closet.

"I started," said Maggie, flopping into the seat across from Rose's desk. "I'll take care of it! It's not such a big deal."

"Sure, for you it isn't," said Rose.

"What is that supposed to mean?"

Rose got to her feet. "I mean, you're living with me rent-free, you haven't found a job . . ."

"I told you, I had an interview!"

"I don't think you're trying very hard."

"I am!" Maggie shouted. "What do you know about it?"

"Shh!"

Maggie slammed the door and glared at her sister.

"I know that it can't be that hard to find a job! " Rose said. "I see help-wanted signs all over the place! Every store, every restaurant . . ."

"I don't want to work in another store. I don't want to waitress."

"So what do you want to do?" Rose demanded. "Sit around like a princess, waiting for MTV to call?"

Maggie's face reddened as if she'd been slapped. "Why are you so mean?"

Rose bit her lip. They'd done this dance before, or, rather, Maggie had . . . with her father, with well-meaning boyfriends, the occasional concerned teacher or boss. Different partners, same steps. She could gauge the precise instant when Rose was going to apologize. And a heartbeat before Rose opened her mouth, the instant she began to inhale the air that would form the words *I'm sorry,* Maggie started talking again.

"I'm trying," she said, swiping at her eyes. "I'm trying very hard. It's not easy for me, Rose, you know? It's not easy for everyone the way it's easy for you."

"I know," Rose said gently. "I know you're trying."

"I try. Every day," said Maggie. "I'm not a freeloader. I don't sit around and feel sorry for myself. I go out and I look for a job . . . every . . . day. And I know I'm never going to be a lawyer like you . . ."

Rose made a protesting noise. Maggie cried a little louder. ". . . but that doesn't mean I just sit around and do nothing. I'm trying, Rose, I'm trying so h-h-h-hard . . ."

Rose crossed the room to hug her. Maggie shrugged away.

"Okay," said Rose. "Okay, don't worry about it. You'll find a job . . ."

"I always do," said Maggie, segueing seamlessly from her weepy Renee Zellweger into strength-through-adversity Sally Field. She wiped her eyes, blew her nose, straightened her back, and looked at her sister.

"I'm sorry," Rose said. "I'm really, really sorry." Wondering, even as she said the words, precisely what she was apologizing for. It had been over a month now. Maggie showed no signs of leaving. Her clothes and toiletries, compact disc cases and cigarette lighters, were still tossed all over Rose's apartment, which was feeling smaller by the day, and the night before Rose had burned her finger after dipping it in a saucepan that she thought held hot caramel sauce, which turned out to be Maggie's eyebrow wax. "Look," she said helplessly, "have you had dinner yet? We can go out, maybe see a movie . . ."

Maggie wiped her eyes again and squinted at her sister. "You know what we should do? We should go out. Like, really out. To a club or something."

"I don't know," said Rose. "You always have to wait to get into those places. And they're so smoky and loud . . ."

"Come on. Just once. I'll help you pick out an outfit . . ."

"Oh, fine," said Rose reluctantly. "I think there's some law firm thing going on at one of those places on Delaware Avenue."

"What kind of thing?" asked Maggie.

Rose rifled through her mail until she found the invitation. " 'A holiday cocktail party,' " she read. " 'Finger food, free games.' Maybe we can go there."

"To start with," said Maggie. She opened the door and bounced out of the office. "Let's go!"

Back at Rose's apartment, Maggie pulled a blue sweater and a black skirt from the pile beside the bed. "Go take a shower," she said, "and be sure to moisturize!"

When Rose got out of the shower, Maggie's multitiered makeup case was open, and she had a row of products lined up on the counter. Two kinds of foundation, three different concealers, a half-dozen discs of eye shadow and blush, brushes for eyes, for cheeks, for lips. . . . Rose sat on the toilet and stared, feeling dizzy.

"Where did all of this stuff come from?" she asked.

"Here and there," said Maggie, sharpening a gray eye pencil.

Rose studied the case again. "And how much do you think it all cost?"

"Dunno," said Maggie, smoothing lotion onto her sister's cheeks with quick, sure strokes. "But whatever it was, it was worth it. Just wait!"

Rose sat there, still as a mannequin, for the fifteen ticklish minutes Maggie spent on her eyelids alone. She got fidgety as Maggie blended foundation on the back of her hand, and brushed it on, then stood back, considering, then came forward again to brush on powder and blush, and she was downright bored by the time Maggie brought out the eyelash curler and the lip pencil, but she had to admit that the cumulative effect was . . . well, stunning.

"Is that me?" she asked, staring at herself in the mirror, at the new hollows underneath her cheekbones, and the way her eyes looked smoky and mysterious beneath the gold and cream eyeshadow Maggie had applied.

"Isn't it great? I'd do your makeup for you every day," Maggie said. "You'd have to start a serious skin-care regimen first, though. You *need* to exfoliate," she said, in the same tone another woman would have said, "You *need* to leave that burning building." She held up a black skirt and the blue top in one hand, a pair of thin-strapped high-heeled blue sandals in the other. "Here, try this."

Rose wriggled into the skirt and the low-cut top. Both of them were tighter than the things she normally wore, and together . . .

"I don't know," she said, forcing herself to stare at her body and not be distracted by her face. "Don't you think I look kind of . . ." The word *cheap* teetered on her lips. Her legs looked long and sleek in the blue shoes, and she had a veritable Grand Canyon of cleavage going on. Maggie approved.

"You look great!" she said, and spritzed her sister from her treasured bottle of Coco. Twenty minutes later, Rose's hair was up, her earrings were in place, and they were out the door.

"This party sucks," said Maggie, slurping her dirty martini.

Rose tugged at her top, squinting at the crowd. She couldn't see without her glasses, but of course Maggie wouldn't let her wear them. "Guys don't make passes at girls who wear glasses!" she'd singsonged, then spent five minutes pestering her sister about why she didn't just get the laser treatments already, like the newscasters and supermodels did.

They were at Dave and Buster's, a glorified arcade for grownups perched on the less-than-scenic bank of the Delaware River, where the law firm was, indeed, having its semi-annual Young Associates Social. Rose's name tag, perched next to her brand-new astonishing cleavage, read, "I AM Rose Feller," and then she'd added, in parentheses, "Litigation." Maggie's original name tag had read, "I AM drinking," until Rose made her take it off. Now it read, "I AM Monique," at which Rose had rolled her eyes but decided wasn't worth a fight.

The place was lousy with young lawyers, networking and sipping microbrewed beer, watching Don Dommel and his dreadlocked protégé show off their tricks on the Virtual Vert Ramp. There was a buffet laid out against one wall—Rose could make out what looked like a tray of vegetables and dips, and a stainless-steel pan of small fried chunks of something—but Maggie had pulled her away. "Mingle!" she'd said.

Now Maggie nudged her sister and pointed at a man-shaped blob standing by the foosball table. "Who's that?" she demanded.

Rose squinted. All she could make out was blond hair and broad shoulders. "Not sure," she said.

Maggie tossed her hair. Maggie, of course, looked unbelievable.

Maggie was wearing pink sandals and black leather pants that Rose knew for a fact cost two hundred dollars because she'd found the receipt on the kitchen counter, paired with a small, sparkly, silvery halter top that tied around her neck and left her entire back bare. She'd blown her hair out straight—a process that took the better part of an hour—and adorned her slender arms with rows of silver bangles. Maggie had done her lips in pale pink, loaded on the mascara, and rimmed her eyes in silvery pencil. She looked like a visitor from the future, or possibly from a television show.

"Well, I'm going to talk to him," she announced. She ran her fingers through her hair, which hung in a perfectly straight sheet of shimmering auburn, grimaced at Rose, asked whether she had lipstick on her teeth, and stalked into the crowd. Rose gave her top a final yank. Her feet hurt, but Maggie hadn't budged on the question of Rose's shoes.

"One must suffer to be beautiful," she had intoned, taking two steps back and surveying her sister carefully before wondering aloud whether Rose didn't have a pair of control-top panty hose that would offer a bit more control.

Rose peered across the room to see her sister assailing the unsuspecting barrister with the double whammy of her hair toss and bangle shake. Then she sidled toward the buffet table, glanced once, guiltily, over her shoulder, and loaded a small plate with dip, crackers, baby carrots, chunks of cheese, and a scoop of fried whatever-it-was. She found a table in the corner, kicked off her shoes, and started eating.

Another man-shaped blob—this one was short and pale, with tightly curled gingery hair—approached her. "Rose Feller?" he inquired.

Rose swallowed and nodded, peering at his name tag.

"Simon Stein," said the guy. "We were sitting next to each other at the pep rally."

"Ah," said Rose, and tried to nod in a manner that would give the impression that she recognized him.

"I gave you coffee," he said.

"Oh, right!" said Rose, remembering. "You saved my life! Thank you!"

Simon gave a modest nod. "So we're going to be travel buddies," he said.

Rose stared at him. The only travel she had planned was a recruiting trip to the University of Chicago Law School on Monday. Just her, and Jim.

"I'm subbing for Jim Danvers," Simon said. Rose felt her heart sink.

"Oh," she said.

"He got busy, so they asked me if I wanted to go."

"Oh," Rose said again.

"So, listen, do you live in Center City? I'll give you a ride to the airport."

"Oh," said Rose for the third time, and added another word just to change things up. "Sure."

Simon leaned closer to her. "Listen," he said, "you don't by any chance play softball, do you?"

Rose shook her head. Her one experience with the game had come during gym class her junior year of high school, when she'd failed to connect even once during the six-week session and dozens of at-bats, and she'd gotten hit in the chest with a foul ball. And there'd been nothing soft about it.

"We've got a team, you know. Motion Denied," said Simon, as if he hadn't noticed her head shake. "Co-ed. Only we don't have enough women on the roster. We'll have to forfeit if we can't find some more."

"Alas," said Rose.

"It's an easy game," said Simon. Rose figured he was probably a litigator. The men among them tended toward a terrierlike persistence. "Good exercise, fresh air . . ."

"Do I look like I need exercise and fresh air?" she asked, then looked down at herself ruefully. "Don't answer that."

Simon Stein continued his pitch. "It's fun. You'll meet lots of people."

She shook her head. "Really, you don't want me. I'm hopeless."

A woman came over and hooked one of her arms through Simon's. "Honey, come play pool with me!" she cooed. Rose winced. This was the girl she privately called Ninety-five, 1995 being the year she graduated from Harvard, a fact that she'd managed to drop into every single conversation Rose had ever had with her.

"Rose, this is Felice Russo," said Simon.

"We've actually met," Rose said. Felice reached up to smooth Simon's hair, which was not, in Rose's opinion, going to be improved by any amount of smoothing. Just then Maggie returned, with her cheeks flushed and a lit cigarette in her hand.

"This party still sucks," she announced, and looked around. "Introduce me."

"Maggie, this is Simon and Felice," said Rose. "We work together."

"Oh," said Maggie, taking a deep drag. "Great."

"What a beautiful bracelet," said Felice, pointing at one of Maggie's bangles. "It is indigenous?"

Maggie stared at her. "Huh? I got it on South Street."

"Oh," said Felice. "It's just that there was this little boutique in Boston that sold stuff like that, and I bought a few pieces there in college."

Here it comes, thought Rose.

"I went to Boston once," said Maggie. "I had a friend at Northeastern."

Three . . . two . . . one . . .

"Oh, really?" said Felice. "What year? I was at Harvard. . . ."

Rose grinned. And did she imagine it, or was Simon Stein smiling, too?

"Let's sit down," he said, and the four of them relocated to a spindly-legged cocktail table. Felice was still yammering about Cambridge in the wintertime. Maggie gulped her martini. Rose thought longingly of a return trip to the buffet.

"So you'll think about softball?" asked Simon.

"Oh, um . . . sure," she said.

"It's really fun," he said.

"Isn't it?" said Felice. "In college, I used to play intramural squash. Of course, not many schools have that, but luckily Harvard does."

And now she wasn't imagining it. Simon Stein had definitely rolled his eyes.

"We have happy hours, too," he said.

"Really?" asked Rose, just to be polite. "Where?"

While Simon was running through the roster of bars that Motion Denied had visited, Maggie and Felice had somehow gotten onto the topic of television.

"Oh, *The Simpsons*. I love *The Simpsons*! Do you know," Felice asked, leaning forward as if imparting some valuable secret, "in the episode about Homer's mother, where she has a fake driver's license?"

"No," said Simon.

"No," said Rose.

"I don't like cartoons," said Maggie.

Felice ignored them. "The address on the license was forty-four Bow Street, which is the actual address of *The Harvard Lampoon*!"

Maggie stared at Felice for a minute, then leaned toward her sister. "You know," she stage-whispered, "I think Felice went to Harvard."

Simon started coughing and took a large gulp of his beer. "Excuse us," Rose murmured, giving Maggie a swift kick, then dragging her toward the door.

"Not nice," Rose said.

"Oh, please," said Maggie. "Like she was such a treat."

"Not really," said Rose. "She's horrid."

"Horrid!" Maggie hooted. She tugged her sister toward the exit sign. "Come on, let's go away from all this horridness."

"Home?" Rose asked hopefully.

Maggie shook her head. "Somewhere much better than that."

• • •

Later—much, much later—the sisters sat across from each other in a booth at the International House of Pancakes.

They'd been to a club. Then an after-hours club. Then an after-party. And then, unless Rose was desperately mistaken, or enduring some sort of vodka-fueled hallucination, there'd been karaoke. She shook her head to clear it, but the memory remained—standing on stage, her shoes kicked off, a crowd chanting her name as she wailed a not-quite-on-key rendition of "Midnight Train to Georgia" while Maggie cavorted behind her, her own personal Pips.

"He's leaving . . ." Rose sang experimentally.

"All aboard! All aboard! All aboard!" Maggie chanted.

Oh, God, Rose thought, slumping in the booth. So it was true. *No more vodka,* she told herself sternly, and bit her lip, remembering what had caused her to get so drunk in the first place. Jim, canceling on their trip to Chicago, leaving her with Simon Stein. "I think you're more into this than he is," Amy had said, and the evidence was certainly suggesting that Amy was right. What had she done wrong? How could she win him back?

"You ladies ready?" asked the bored-looking waitress, pen poised over her pad.

Rose ran her fingertips over the menu as if it were braille. "Pancakes," she finally said.

"What kind?" asked the waitress.

"She'll have the buttermilk pancakes," said Maggie, taking the menu out of Rose's hands. "I'll have the same thing. And we'd like two large orange juices, and a pitcher of coffee, please."

The waitress walked away.

"I didn't know you could sing!" Maggie said as Rose began to hiccup.

"I don't sing," Rose said, "I litigate."

Maggie dumped four packets of Sweet'n Low into the cup of coffee that the waitress had set before her. "Wasn't that fun?"

"Fun," Rose repeated. She hiccupped again. The eyeliner and

mascara that Maggie had carefully applied the night before had run and smeared. She looked like a raccoon. "So what are you gonna do?" she asked.

"About what?" asked Maggie.

"About your life," said Rose.

Maggie scowled. "Now I remember why we never go out together. You have half of a wine cooler and decide to come up with a ten-step plan to improve me."

"I just wanna help," Rose said. "You need to have a goal."

The waitress arrived, dropped off the plates and a pitcher of hot maple syrup.

"Wait," asked Rose. She squinted tipsily at the waitress. "Are you guys hiring?"

"I think so," said the waitress. "I'll bring an application by with your check."

"Don't you think you're a little overqualified?" asked Maggie. "I mean, college, law degree . . . do you really just want to serve pancakes?"

"Not for me, for you," said Rose.

"Oh, you want me to serve pancakes," said Maggie.

"I want you to do something," said Rose, gesturing with drunken grandeur. "I want you to pay for your phone bill. And maybe gimme some money for groceries."

"I don't eat anything!" said Maggie, which was not quite true. She didn't eat much—an English muffin here, some milk and cereal there. It wouldn't add up to much. And it wasn't like Rose didn't have the money for it, either. She'd seen her sister's bank statements, which were kept in chronological order in a manila folder labeled "Bank Statements." Still, she could imagine Rose walking through the kitchen with a yellow legal pad, taking notes. *One Lean Cuisine Oriental Chicken dinner! One-half cup orange juice! Two packets microwave popcorn! Three teaspoons salt!*

Maggie felt her face heating up. "I'll give you some money," she said, biting off each syllable furiously.

"You don't have any money," said Rose.

"So I'll get some," Maggie said.

"When?" asked Rose. "When might this blessed event occur?"

"I've got an interview."

"Which is great, but it isn't a job."

"Fuck you. I'm leaving," Maggie said, throwing down her napkin.

"Sit down," said Rose wearily. "Eat your breakfast. I'm going to the bathroom."

Rose left the table. Maggie sat down, stabbed at her food, and didn't eat it. When the waitress came with the job application, Maggie filched a pen from her sister's purse, plus twenty dollars from her wallet, and filled the thing out with Rose's name, checking every possible "time available" slot and adding "I'll Do Anything!" in the comment section. Then she gave the application to the waitress, dumped boysenberry syrup on her sister's pancakes, knowing that Rose did not like colored syrups, and stomped out of the restaurant.

Rose came back to the table and gave a puzzled look at the ruin of her breakfast.

"Your friend left," said the waitress.

Rose shook her head slowly. "She's not my friend, she's my sister," she said. She paid the bill, pulled on her jacket, wincing at her blistered feet, and limped out the door.

SIXTEEN

"No more," said Ella, and passed her hand over the top of her wine-glass. It was their first dinner out, their first official dinner-date, which she'd finally consented to after weeks of effort on Lewis's part, and she'd agreed to share a bottle of wine with him, which was a mistake. It had been years—maybe even as long as a decade—since she'd had wine, and it had, predictably, gone straight to her head.

Lewis set the bottle down, and wiped his mouth. "I hate the holidays," he said, as casually as if he'd been telling her that he'd never liked artichokes.

"What?" she'd said.

"The holidays," he continued. "Can't stand them. Haven't been able to for years."

"Why?"

He poured himself another half-glass of wine. "Because my son doesn't come to visit me," he said shortly. "Which makes me the same as the rest of the yentas."

"He doesn't come ever?" Ella asked hesitantly. "Are you . . . Is there . . ."

"He spends the holidays with his in-laws," said Lewis, and from the halting way he spoke, Ella could tell that this was a painful topic. "They see me in February, when the kids have vacation from school."

"Well, that must be nice," said Ella.

"It's very nice," said Lewis. "I spoil them rotten. And I look forward to it, but the holidays are still not that great." He shrugged a little, as if to say that it wasn't the worst thing in the world, but Ella knew it had to be hard, being alone.

"So how about you?" Lewis asked, the way she knew he would, because as nice as he was and as well as they were getting along, she couldn't avoid this question forever. "Tell me about your family."

Ella forced herself to relax, reminding herself not to tense her shoulders or clench her hands into fists. She'd known that this was coming. It was only natural. "Well," she began. "My husband, Ira, was a college professor. The history of economics, that was his specialty. We lived in Michigan. He died fifteen years ago. Stroke." This was the acceptable Acres shorthand for a dead spouse: name, rank, how long they'd been gone, and what had carried them off, in generic terms (the ladies would, for example, not hesitate to whisper "cancer," but nothing could drag the prefix "prostate" from their lips)

"Was it a good marriage?" asked Lewis. "I know that it's none of my business . . ." And he trailed off and looked at Ella hopefully.

"It was . . ." she began, toying with her butter knife. "It was a marriage of the time, I suppose. He worked, and I ran the house. Cooked, cleaned, did the entertaining . . ."

"What was Ira like? What did he like to do?"

The funny thing was, Ella could barely remember. And what rose in her mind finally was the word *enough*. Ira had been nice enough, smart enough, had made enough money, had cared for her and for Caroline enough. He'd been a little cheap (frugal was how he'd put it), and more than a little vain (Ella couldn't help but cringe as she remembered the comb-over he'd maintained well past the point of plausibility), but for the most part he'd been . . . enough.

"He was fine," she said, knowing it was, at best, a tepid endorsement. "He was a good provider," she added, aware of how old-fashioned that sounded. "He was a good father," she concluded, although it hadn't been quite true. Ira, with his economics textbooks and smell of chalk dust, had been mostly bewildered by Caroline—beautiful, fragile, strange, furious Caroline, who'd insisted on wearing her tutu on the first day of kindergarten and had announced, at age eight, that she wouldn't answer to anything but Princess Maple Magnolia. Ira took her fishing and to ball games, and probably, secretly, wished that their one child had been a son, or at least a more normal sort of girl.

"So you have children?" Lewis asked.

Ella took a deep breath. "I had a daughter, Caroline. She died." She'd broken with protocol here. There was a name and the fact of a death, but nothing else: what Caroline had been, when she'd died, and what had killed her.

Lewis laid his hand on hers gently. "I'm sorry," he said. "I can't imagine what that must have been like."

Ella said nothing, because there were no words for what it was like. Being the mother of a dead child was worse than all of the clichés said it was. It was the worst thing. It was so bad she could only think of Caroline's death in snatches and snapshots, and not even many of those, a handful of memories, each one more painful than the last. She remembered the sleek mahogany stretch of the coffin, cool and solid under her hand. She could see the faces of Caroline's girls in their navy dresses, dark-brown hair swept into identical ponytails, and how the older girl had held the younger one's hand as they approached the coffin, and how the younger one was crying and the older one was not. "Say good-bye to Mommy," Ella remembered the older sister saying in her husky voice, and the little sister just shook her head and cried. She could remember standing there, feeling utterly empty, as if a giant hand had scooped out everything inside of her—her guts, her heart— and left her looking the same, but not being the same at all. She could remember Ira leading her around as if she were crippled, or blind, his hand on her elbow, helping her into the car, out of the car, up the funeral parlor steps past Maggie and Rose. They don't have a mother, she'd thought, and the thought had hit her like a bomb going off in her brain. She'd lost her daughter, which was a terrible thing and a tragedy, but these girls had lost a mother. And surely that was worse.

"We should move here," she'd told Ira that night, after he'd guided her into the chair in their hotel room. "We'll sell the house, rent an apartment . . ."

He'd stood beside the bed, polishing his glasses with the end of his tie, and looked at her with pity in his eyes. "Don't you think that would be locking the barn door after the horse has already gotten out?"

"Barn!" she'd screamed. "Horse! Ira, our daughter is dead! Our granddaughters have no mother! We have to help! We have to be here!"

He'd stared at her . . . and then, with the only piece of prescience she'd ever seen from him in almost thirty years of marriage, he'd said, "Maybe Michael doesn't want us here."

"Ella?" Lewis asked.

She swallowed hard, remembering how it had been raining the night she got the phone call, and how, days later, back at home, she'd dismantled the telephone: unscrewing the mouthpiece, detaching the coiled cord that joined the receiver to the phone itself, prying off the dial, unscrewing the bottom, and pulling out the telephone's wires and circuits, breaking the telephone that had brought her such horrible news into its component parts, and then staring at it, breathing hard, thinking, irrationally, *Can't hurt me now, can't hurt me now.* She could tell him how this had soothed her for about five minutes, until she'd found herself at Ira's dusty worktable in the basement, his hammer in her hand, smashing each of the pieces into a thousand shiny shards, and how she'd wanted to smash her own hands as punishment for believing what she'd wanted to believe—that Caroline was telling her the truth, that she was taking her medication, that everything was fine.

Lewis was looking at her. "You okay?"

Ella took a deep breath. "Fine," she said faintly. "Just fine."

Lewis studied her, then got to his feet, and helped Ella up. Once she'd risen, he kept one hand warm upon her elbow, steering her toward the door. "Let's go for a walk," he said.

SEVENTEEN

Maggie Feller spent Sunday afternoon in Sydelle's all-white fortress, playing Information.

She had woken up with the phone shrilling through her hangover. "Rose, the phone!" she'd moaned, except Rose wasn't answering. And Sydelle the Terrible kept calling until Maggie finally picked up and agreed to come over and get her things out of her bedroom. "We need the space," Sydelle said.

Stick it up your nose, Maggie thought. *There's plenty of room there.* "Well, where am I supposed to put everything?" she asked instead.

Sydelle had sighed. Maggie could practically see her stepmother—thin lips compressed to the width of a paper cut, nostrils flaring, strands of freshly colored ash-blond hair wagging stiffly as she shook her head. "You can move your things to the basement, I suppose," said Sydelle, her tone indicating that this was a concession akin to letting her wayward stepdaughter set up a roller coaster on the front lawn.

"That's very generous of you," Maggie said sarcastically. "I'll be over this afternoon."

"We'll be at a workshop," Sydelle had said. "Macrobiotic cooking." As if Maggie had asked. Maggie took a hot shower, helped herself to Rose's car keys, and made the drive to New Jersey. The house was empty, except for the idiot dog Chanel (whom Rose had nicknamed Knockoff), who, as usual, howled as if she were a burglar, then tried to hump her leg. Maggie shoved the dog outside and spent half an hour hauling boxes to the basement, which left her a whole hour for Information.

She started with Sydelle's desk, but didn't find anything interesting—some bills, stacks of stationery, a sheet of wallet-sized pictures of My Marcia in her wedding gown, a framed eight-by-ten of My Marcia's twins, Jason and Alexander—so she'd moved to the more fruitful hunting ground of the master bedroom's walk-in closet, which had previously yielded one of her prize finds—a jewelry box made of carved wood. The box was empty except for a pair of gold hoop earrings and a bracelet of narrow gold links that rattled inside it. Her mother's? Maybe, thought Maggie. It couldn't be Sydelle's because she knew where Sydelle kept her stuff. She'd considered pocketing the bracelets, but had decided not to. Maybe her father looked at these things, and would notice if they were gone, and Maggie didn't like the thought of him reaching for the jewelry box and finding nothing there.

She started at the first shelf. There was a rubber-banded stack of old tax returns that she picked up, flipped through, and replaced. My Marcia's cheerleading trophies, Sydelle's sweaters. Maggie stood on her tiptoes, reaching over rows of her father's summer shirts and brushing her fingertips along the top of the shelf until they stopped at what felt like a shoe box.

Maggie pulled the box off the shelf—it was pink, old-looking, crumpled around the corners. She brushed dust off the cover, carried it out of the closet, and sat down on the bed. It wasn't Sydelle's because Sydelle labeled her shoe boxes with a description of the shoes they contained (most of them very expensive, with painfully pointed toes). Plus, Sydelle wore a six narrow, and this box, according to the label, had once held a pair of pink Capezio ballet flats, girls' size four. Little kids' shoes. Maggie opened the box.

Letters. It was full of letters, at least two dozen of them. Cards, really, in colored envelopes, and the first one she pulled out was addressed to her, Miss Maggie Feller, at their old apartment, the two-bedroom place they'd lived in until her father had moved them all into Sydelle's house. The postmark read August 4, 1980, so it had been sent right around her eighth birthday (which, if she remembered right, had been a very glamorous affair at the local bowling alley, with pizza and ice cream afterward). There was a return-address sticker in the upper-left-hand corner. It said that the card came from someone named Ella Hirsch.

Hirsch, thought Maggie, feeling her heart beat faster at the prospect of this mystery. Hirsch had been their mother's maiden name.

She eased one edge of the envelope open. After almost twenty years, the glue let go easily. It was a birthday card, a little-kid's card with a pink frosted birthday cake and yellow candles on the front. "HAPPY BIRTHDAY!" it read. And inside, beneath the preprinted "WISHING YOU A VERY HAPPY DAY!" she read, "Dear Maggie, I hope you're well. I miss you very much and would love to hear from you." Then a telephone number and a signature that said "Grandma," with the words *Ella Hirsch* written in parenthesis beneath it. And a ten-dollar bill, which Maggie shoved in her pocket.

Interesting, Maggie thought, getting to her feet and walking to the bedroom window, checking out the street for signs of Sydelle's car. Maggie knew she had a grandmother; she had vague memories of sitting on someone's lap, smelling flowery perfume, and feeling a smooth cheek against her own while her mother took her picture. She vaguely remembered the same woman, this grandmother, at her mother's funeral. What had happened to the photograph was no mystery—after they moved in with Sydelle, all public evidence of their mother had disappeared. But what had happened to the grandmother? She remembered, years ago, on her first birthday in New Jersey, asking her father. "Where's Grandma Ella? Did she send me something?" A shadow had crossed her father's face. "I'm sorry," he'd said—or at least, that's what Maggie'd thought he'd said. "She can't come." And then, the next year, she remembered asking the same question and getting a different answer. "Grandma Ella's in a home."

"Well, so are we," said Maggie, who didn't understand what the big deal was.

But Rose knew. "Not this kind of home," she said, looking at her father, who gave her a nod. "In a home for old people." And that had been the end of that. But still, home or not, their grandmother had sent these cards. So why hadn't Maggie and Rose ever received them?

She wondered whether the cards were all the same, and selected another one from the stack, this one from 1982, addressed to Miss Rose Feller. This one wished Rose a happy Chanukah, and was signed the same way—"I love you, I miss you, I hope you're well, love, Grandma (Ella)." And another bill, a twenty, this time, which joined the ten in Maggie's pocket.

Grandma. Ella, she thought to herself. What had happened? Her mother had died, and there'd been a funeral. The grandmother would have been there for sure. Then they'd moved, from Connecticut to New Jersey, within a month of their mother's death, and as carefully as Maggie searched her memory, she couldn't remember seeing or hearing from the grandmother ever again.

Her eyes were still closed when she heard the garage-door opener churn into life, followed by car doors slamming. She added the Rose card to the money in her pocket and jumped to her feet.

"Maggie?" called Sydelle, her heels clicking on the kitchen floor.

"Almost done," Maggie yelled. She put the box back on the shelf and walked downstairs, where her father and Sydelle were unloading grocery bags full of various sprouts and whole grains.

"Stay for dinner," her father offered, kissing her cheek as she shrugged on her coat. "We're making . . ." He paused and squinted at one of the bags.

"Quinoa," said Sydelle, pronouncing the word with faux-Latino verve—*keen-wah!*

"No thanks," said Maggie, doing the buttons slowly, watching her father put groceries away. Hard to believe he'd once been handsome. But she'd seen pictures of him when he was younger, before his hairline had relocated to the center of his scalp and his face had sagged into a mass of wrinkles and resignation. And sometimes, from behind, or when he moved a certain way, she could look at the set of his shoulders and the shape of his face and see someone who'd been good-looking enough for a woman as beautiful as her mother to love. She wanted to ask her father about the cards, only not in front of Sydelle, because she knew that Sydelle would manage to change the subject from the mysterious grandmother to exactly what Maggie was doing going through their closet in the first place.

"Hey, Dad," she began. Sydelle zipped by her, heading toward the pantry with cans of the same brand of ultrabland, all-natural, salt-and-taste-free soup she'd found in Rose's kitchen. "Do you want to have lunch with me one day this week?"

"Sure," said her father—at the same instant when Sydelle asked, "How's that job hunt going, Maggie?"

"Fine!" she said brightly. *Bitch,* she thought.

Sydelle arranged her coral-painted lips into a bright, fake smile. "Glad to hear it," she said, turning her back on Maggie, heading back toward the pantry. "You know that we only want the best for you, Maggie, and we've been concerned . . ."

Maggie grabbed her purse. "Gotta go," she said. "Places to go, people to do!"

"Call me!" said her father. Maggie gave a brief, distracted wave and got into Rose's car, where she pulled out the card and the money and studied them to make sure that they were still there, that she hadn't made them up, that they'd said what she thought they'd said. *Grandma.* Rose would know what to do about it. Except when Maggie got home, Rose was packing. "I'm going to the office to finish up a brief. I'll be home late, and I'm leaving early in the morning. Business trip," she'd said, in her bossy, self-important way, rushing around with her suits and her laptop. Well, when Rose came home, they'd put their heads together and figure out the Mystery of the Missing Grandmother.

EIGHTEEN

On Monday morning, Simon Stein stood in the lobby of Rose's apartment building, wearing khaki pants and loafers, a Lewis, Dommel, and Fenick polo shirt with the firm's logo embossed on its chest, and a Lewis, Dommel, and Fenick baseball cap on his head. Rose hurried out of the elevator and walked right past him.

"Hey!" Simon said, waving.

"Oh," said Rose, running her hands through her wet hair. "Hi." The morning had gotten off to a terrible start. When she'd reached under the bathroom sink for her tampons, she'd found an empty box, bearing only plastic wrappers and the rattling remnants of a single tampon applicator. "Maggie!" she'd yelled. And Maggie, who'd been asleep, had rummaged through her purse and tossed Rose a single Slender Regular by way of consolation. "Where did all my Supers go?" Rose had demanded. Maggie had just shrugged. Rose would have to buy more at the airport, assuming she could shake Simon Stein for long enough, and . . .

". . . forward to this," Simon was saying, merging onto the highway.

"I'm sorry?"

"I said, I'm really looking forward to this," he said. "Aren't you?"

"Oh, I guess," said Rose. In fact, she wasn't looking forward to it at all. She'd spent weeks dreaming about being alone with Jim, in a city where nobody knew them, away from everyone at the firm. They'd have a wonderful romantic dinner somewhere . . . or maybe they'd just order room service. Stay in. Get reacquainted. And now she was stuck with Simon Stein, Boy Wonder.

"Do you think they picked us because we're good examples of young associates, or because they want to get rid of us?" she asked.

"Oh," said Simon, steering the car into the long-term parking lot, "me they picked because I'm a good example. You, they're just trying to get rid of."

"What?"

"Just kidding," he said, and gave her an impish smile. Revolting, thought Rose. Grown men should not look impish.

They got to the gate a full forty-five minutes before boarding would commence. *Perfect*, thought Rose, and dropped her stuff on a chair. "Listen, I'm just going to run to the newsstand," she said, and was relieved when Simon nodded and opened up a copy of *ESPN: The Magazine*. It was ridiculous, she knew, but she'd never been one of those women who could simply plop a box of Kotex Super Plus on top of her lettuce and turkey breast at the grocery store and stand, unflinching, as some teenage guy scanned her groceries. No indeed. Her tampons had to be purchased at the same CVS, and she'd lurk in the aisles until she could be guaranteed no line and a female clerk. It was no big deal, she knew (and certainly Amy and Maggie had told her), but for some reason she was always embarrassed buying them. Probably because when she got her period, her father had been so completely freaked out he'd left her in the bathroom, bleeding onto wadded-up toilet paper, for three hours, until Sydelle returned from her Jazzercise class with a box of sanitary napkins. Maggie, she remembered, had waited patiently on the other side of the door, pumping Rose for information.

"What's going on in there?" she'd asked.

"I've become a woman," Rose had replied from her perch on the edge of the bathtub. "Yay me."

"Oh," Maggie said. "Well, congratulations." And, Rose remembered, Maggie had tried to shove a *People* magazine underneath the door and had actually baked her a cake, thick with chocolate frosting, with "Congradulations Rose" written on top. True, their father had been too mortified to eat a bite, and Sydelle had made unpleasant noises about the fat grams and the misspelling, but it had been nice.

On the airplane, she shoved her bag into the overhead compartment, fastened her seat belt, and stared out the window, nibbling at her mixed nuts, trying to ignore her growling stomach, thinking that if she hadn't been so busy trying to make her brief as Jim-pressive as possible, or running around playing Guess What Maggie's Taken Now, she'd have had time to buy a bagel. Simon, meanwhile, had reached under his seat and retrieved a small box-shaped nylon pouch. He unzipped it with a flourish.

"Here," he said.

Rose glanced to her left and saw that he was holding a seed-studded roll.

"Nine-grain," he said. "From Le Bus. I've got an eleven-grain one."

"In case nine grains aren't enough?" Rose asked. She stared at him curiously, then accepted the roll, which was still warm and, all things considered, delicious. A minute later, he tapped her arm and offered her a wedge of cheese.

"What is this?" she finally asked. "Did your Mom pack you lunch?"

Simon shook his head. "My mother's lunches were nothing like this. She's not a morning person. So every morning, she'd, like, stagger down the stairs . . ."

"Stagger?" asked Rose, readying herself to produce the necessary sympathy if Simon started in on some dreary tale about his mother's drinking problem.

"She's not really graceful under the best circumstances, and especially not when she's half asleep. So she'd stagger downstairs and grab the economy-size loaf of generic white Wonder bread, and whatever lunch meat had been on sale, and a five-pound tub of margarine." Rose could almost picture his mother, in a ratty nightgown and bare feet, standing in front of the kitchen counter, performing this detested chore. "So she'd slap down the bread, and then she'd spread the margarine, or try to, but the margarine was cold, so usually it wasn't very spreadable, and the bread would rip, and you'd get these sandwiches with, like, lumps of margarine in them, and then she'd slap down a wad of lunch meat"—Simon performed the slapping motion—"and she'd put the other slice of bread on top, and shove the sandwich in a Baggie, and put it in a brown paper bag with some bruised fruit and a handful of peanuts in shells. And that was lunch. And that," he concluded, pulling a brownie from his bag and offering Rose half of it, "explains me."

"How does it explain you?"

"You grow up in a house where nobody cares about food, and you either end up not caring about food yourself, or probably caring too much." He gave his belly an affectionate pat. "Guess which one I am. How were your school lunches?"

"It would depend," Rose said.

"On what?"

Rose bit her lip. School lunches, for her, had fallen into three categories. Her mother's happy lunches were beautiful affairs—the sandwiches with crusts neatly cut off, the carrots peeled and cut into sticks of equal length, the apple washed, a paper napkin folded at the bottom of the bag, sometimes containing fifty cents for an ice-cream sandwich and a note reading "Have a treat on me." Then there were the deteriorating lunches. The crusts would stay on the bread. The carrots wouldn't be peeled—one time, her mother had put a whole carrot into her lunch bag, with the green fronds still on top. She'd forget napkins, forget milk money, sometimes forget the sandwich altogether. Once, Rose remembered, Maggie had caught her at her locker, looking dismayed. "Look," she'd said, and showed Rose that her lunch bag contained nothing except, inexplicably, her mother's checkbook. Rose had looked inside her own bag and found a crumpled leather glove.

"We got hot lunch, mostly," she told Simon. Which was true.

She'd had two years of her mother's lunches, good and bad, followed by the third category—ten years of steam-table pizza and mystery meat and Sydelle's offers of Lean Cuisine and chopped salad, which Rose usually turned down.

Simon sighed. "I would have killed for hot lunch. Anyhow," he said, his face brightening, "do you think this will be fun?"

"Do you remember what you were like as a first-year law student?"

Simon considered. "Insufferable," he said.

"Right. Me, too. So I think we can safely assume that the vast majority of these kids are going to be just as obnoxious as we were."

"Ah." said Simon. He reached into his briefcase and pulled out a handful of magazines. "Reading material?"

Rose considered a copy of *Cook's Illustrated,* then picked up something called *The Green Bag.* "What's this?"

"A fun legal journal," said Simon.

"As if," Rose said. She turned back toward the window, closed her eyes hoping that Simon would leave her alone, and feeling relieved when he did.

The first candidate blinked at Rose and Simon, repeating Simon's last question. "My goals?" she asked. She was disgustingly young and fresh-faced in her black suit as she stared at Rose and Simon in a way that was probably meant to be assertive but instead just made her look nearsighted. "I want to be sitting where you are five years from now."

Only with better feminine protection, Rose thought. For the past ten minutes she'd had the distinct feeling that the airport tampon wasn't getting the job done.

"Tell us why you're interested in Lewis, Dommel, and Fenick," Simon prompted.

"Well," she began confidently, "I'm very impressed by your firm's commitment to pro bono work . . ."

Simon glanced at Rose and made a check mark on the piece of paper they were using to keep score.

". . . and I respect the partners' understanding that there should be balance between work and family commitments . . ."

Simon made a second check mark.

"And," the young woman concluded, "I think Boston would be a wonderful city to work in."

Rose and Simon stared at each other, mid-check-mark. *Boston?*

The candidate stared at them uncertainly. "There's so much to do there! So much history!"

"True," said Simon, "but we're actually located in Philadelphia."

The young woman gulped. "Oh," she said.

"There's lots to do in Philadelphia, too," said Rose, thinking that this was something she would have done as a law student— scheduled so many interviews that all of the firms would have run together in one great big, family-friendly, committed-to-pro-bono blur.

"Tell us about yourself," Rose prompted the red-haired guy sitting across from her.

He sighed. "Well," he began, "I got married last year."

"That's great," said Simon.

"Yeah," the guy said bitterly, "except she told me last night that she's leaving me for our Criminal Law professor."

"Oh, dear," Rose murmured.

" 'He's advising me on my paper,' she told me. Okay, I wasn't suspicious. Would you have been suspicious?" he demanded, glaring at Simon and Rose.

"Um," said Simon. "Well, I'm not married."

The law student slumped in his suit. "Look, you've got my résumé," he said. "If you're interested, you know where to find me."

"Yeah," whispered Simon, as the guy left the room and the next candidate entered, "in the bushes outside the professor's apartment building with night-vision goggles and a mayonnaise jar to pee in."

• • •

"I began my legal career out of disgust," began the thin-lipped brunette. "Do you remember the case of the hot McNugget?"

"No," said Rose.

"Not really," said Simon.

The law student shook her head and stared at them scornfully. "A woman, through the drive-through of McDonald's, orders McNuggets. The McNuggets arrive, fresh from the fryer. They're hot. The woman bites into a McNugget, burns her lip, sues McDonald's for failing to inform her that the McNuggets would be dangerously hot, and wins hundreds of thousands of dollars. I was disgusted." She glared at them both to highlight her disgust. "Rewards like that create the cancer of litigiousness that's infecting America."

"You know, my uncle had that," Simon said sadly. "Cancer of litigiousness. Nothing much you can do for it, either."

The woman glared at them. "I'm serious!" she said. "Frivolous lawsuits are a terrible problem for the legal profession." Simon nodded attentively, and Rose stifled a yawn as the woman spent fifteen minutes giving them pertinent examples, cases, decisions, and footnotes, until she stood up abruptly, smoothing her skirt.

"Good day," she said, and marched out the door.

Rose and Simon stared at each other, then burst out laughing.

"Oh, dear," said Rose.

"I believe we have a winner," said Simon. "The Hot McNugget. That's what we're calling her. Agreed?"

"I don't know," said Rose. "What about the guy who spit when he talked? Or Miss Boston?"

"I was dying to tell her that she wouldn't like Boston, because it's not much of a college town, but she didn't look like someone who enjoyed *Spinal Tap*," he said. "And now I'm feeling somewhat remiss, because we didn't ask any of them how they feel about alternative sports." He shook his head in mock despair. "I don't think we can go back to Philadelphia."

"The guy with the ex-wife looked like he's got a snowboard in his garage."

"Yeah," said Simon, "right next to his crossbow. And how about that blonde?"

Rose bit her lip. "That blonde" had been their second-to-last applicant. Mediocre grades and no experience to speak of, but she was gorgeous.

"I think some of the partners would have appreciated her," Simon said dryly. Rose winced. Did he mean Jim?

"Anyhow," said Simon, gathering his papers into the inevitable Lewis, Dommel, and Fenick folder. "What do you feel like for dinner?"

"Room service," said Rose, getting to her feet.

Simon looked dismayed. "Oh, no, no, we have to go out to eat somewhere! Chicago's got great restaurants!"

Rose gave him what she hoped was a kind look. "I'm really tired," she said, which was true. Also, she had cramps. And she wanted to be in her hotel room for Jim, who, in lieu of his presence, had offered her the consolation prize of a phone call. Was phone sex hard to do, she wondered? Could she pull it off, without sounding like one of those sleazy ads on late-night cable, or, alternately, like she was reading from the Clinton/Lewinsky depositions?

"Your loss," said Simon. He raised his hand in a salute, pushed his folder into a Lewis, Dommel, and Fenick tote bag (grown men, Rose thought, should not carry tote bags), and was gone, as Rose hurried off to the hotel room, and the telephone, and Jim.

NINETEEN

Maggie made a bet with herself that she could get a job before Rose came back from Chicago. If she had a job, she figured, Rose would be pleased with her, and willing to apply herself to the Case of the Missing Grandmother. So she gave up on the bartending gig and set out with her stack of résumés. Within a day she'd landed a job at the Elegant Paw, a chichi pet-grooming establishment around the corner from Rose's apartment, on a block that boasted two French bistros, a cigar bar, a women's clothing boutique, and a cosmetic store called Kiss and Make Up.

"You like dogs?" asked Bea, the manager, who was wearing overalls and smoking an unfiltered Marlboro as she worked on a shih tzu with a blow dryer.

"Absolutely," Maggie had said.

"And I can see that you like grooming," said Bea, taking in Maggie's tight jeans and tighter sweater. "You'll do fine. You wash the dogs, clip their nails and whiskers, condition their fur, blow them dry. It's eight bucks an hour," she added, picking the shih tzu up by its tail and its collar and depositing it into a plastic pet crate.

"Fine," said Maggie.

Bea handed her an apron, and a bottle of Johnson's baby shampoo, and nodded toward a small and dingy-looking poodle. "You know about the anal glands?"

Maggie stared at her, hoping she'd heard wrong. "Excuse me?"

Bea smiled. "Anal glands," she repeated. "Let me show you." Maggie had watched, revolted, as Bea lifted the dog's tail. "See here?" She pointed at the pertinent area. "Squeeze." She demonstrated. The smell was revolting. Maggie felt like throwing up. Even the poodle looked ashamed of itself.

"Do I have to do this for every dog?" she'd asked.

"Just the ones that need it," said Bea. Like that was some big consolation.

"And how do I tell which ones need it?" Maggie persisted.

Bea laughed. "Check to see if they're swollen," she said. Maggie shuddered, but swallowed hard and tentatively approached her first dog, who looked just as dubious about the whole enterprise as she was.

After eight hours, Maggie had washed sixteen dogs and had sixteen different kinds of dog fur clinging to her sweater.

"Good work," said Bea, nodding her approval as she tied a candy-cane-striped bandana around a sheltie's collar. "Next time wear better shoes. Flats, sneakers. You got shoes like that?"

Well, she didn't, but Rose did. Maggie limped onto the street, shoving her pruney hands into her pocket, glad that at least she'd have the place to herself for the night. She could make a bowl of popcorn and a drink, and there'd be no sister to complain that she was playing the music too loud or wearing too much perfume, or to ask pesky questions about where she was going, and when she'd be back.

Maggie squinted at the space on the street where Rose's car had been . . . a space that was presently occupied by only an iced-over puddle and a few dead leaves.

Okay, maybe it wasn't this space precisely, Maggie thought, trying to calm herself even as her heart started hammering in her chest. Pine Street. It had definitely been Pine Street. She walked to the stop sign by one of the French bistros, crossed at the corner, walked back down the length of the street, past the cigar bar and

Kiss and Make Up, which were both closed for the night, moving from streetlight to streetlight, from lamplit glow to absolute darkness, and still, no car.

She walked to the corner, then back again, underneath the streetlamps decorated with gold tinsel Christmas wreaths, feeling the icy air biting at her neck. It had been Pine Street, she was sure of it . . . except, what if she was wrong? That would be it for Rose, Maggie realized, imagining her sister coming home from Chicago to learn that her car had disappeared. She'd have Maggie out the door and on her way back to Sydelle's house before Maggie could even start explaining. And wasn't this the way her life always worked? One step forward, two steps back. Get an audition at MTV and get tripped up by the TelePrompTer. Get a job and find out that the car's been stolen. Get your foot in the door and have the thing swing shut on your toes. Fuck, she thought, turning in a circle. Fuck, fuck, fuck!

"They get you, too?" A man in a leather jacket was walking toward her. He cocked his thumb at the sign Maggie hadn't noticed until then. "Street cleaning," he said, and shook his head. "They used to just give tickets, but everyone ignored them, so they started towing last week."

Shit. "Where do they take the cars?"

"Impound lot," he said, shrugging. "I'd give you a ride, but . . ." And he looked at the space where his car had presumably been parked with such a mournful expression that Maggie had to laugh. "Come with me," he said. She looked at him, trying to puzzle out his features, but it was dark and he had the hood of his coat pulled up. "I'm just going to grab a quick beer while I wait for my buddy, and then he can run us over there. You got your checkbook?"

"Um . . ." said Maggie. "Will they take a credit card?"

The guy shrugged. "Guess we'll find out," he said.

The guy's name was Grant, and Tim was his buddy, and one beer was actually more like three, plus an Irish coffee that Maggie sipped slowly as she rocked her shoulders to the music and tried not to keep looking at the time while she performed the necessary motions. Cross your legs, lick your lips, twirl a lock of your hair around one finger. Look fascinated, yet somewhat mysterious. Look up from underneath your eyelashes, as if the guy is the most interesting guy you've ever seen, as if what he's saying is the most amazing thing you've ever heard. Pout like a model in an ad for panty hose or push-up bras. Toy with your swizzle stick. Stare at them, then drop your eyes shyly. Maggie could have done it in her sleep. And the guys, of course, had no clue. The guys never did.

"Hey, Monique, you want to come to a party with us once we get the cars back?"

She gave a rote nod, a tiny shrug, and crossed her legs again. Grant laid his hand on her knee, edging it up toward her thigh. "You're so soft," he said. She leaned into him for a second, then edged away. Forward, then back.

"Let's get the cars first. Then we'll see," she said, knowing that as soon as she got the car, she was going straight home. She was tired, and she just wanted to get the car, take a shower, collapse into the comfort of her sister's bed.

It was after ten o'clock when they finally stood up and shrugged into their coats. Grant held out his arm for her. Maggie breathed a quiet sigh of relief and smiled prettily as she let him help her off her barstool and up into Tim's truck. They were on the highway, then off, then on again, somewhere in South Philadelphia, Maggie thought. She thought she could see the Delaware River glimmering in the dark. Finally Tim turned onto a long, twisting road with no lights. Maggie felt an icy fingertip poke her in the chest as the men laughed and sang along to the radio and passed a bottle back and forth over her head. This could get bad, she thought. Where was she? Who were these guys? How could she have been so dumb?

She was trying to form a plan when Tim jerked the truck into a hard right turn, and they bounced alongside a lot full of cars, surrounded by a ghostly pale fence.

"Here we are," he said. Maggie peered into the darkness. There were cars upon cars upon cars . . . dozens of rows of them, burnt-out junkers and shiny new models, and there, right in front, was Rose's little silver Honda. And, at the far end, the dim shapes of guard dogs—German shepherds, Maggie thought—moving slowly along the fence.

Tim opened his door, crunching what sounded like half a roll of breath mints between his teeth. "Office is this way," he said, pointing to a cinderblock shack where light shone through the window. "You two coming?"

Maggie took another look. The gate was open. She could just walk to the car, get in, drive it right through the gate. She slid off the truck seat and onto the ground. "I'm going to get my car," she announced.

"Well, sure. That's what we brought you here for," said Tim.

Maggie bit her lip. The truth was, her license had expired six months ago, and she'd meant to get it renewed, but she kept forgetting. And of course the car was registered in Rose's name, not hers. Chances were, even if they did take her credit card they might not let her leave with the car. She'd have to think of something else.

She rocked her hips, settling her feet into the ground. It was so cold that her cheeks hurt, so cold that the inside of her nose was freezing, and every inch of her body was covered in goose bumps. And then she started walking, like she was walking on hot coals. Not too slow and not too fast.

"Hey!" said Grant, "hey!" She felt, rather then saw, him start to move, and she could see what he had in mind as if a movie screen had suddenly lowered before her eyes. First they'd get the cars, then go back to the bar, where one drink would become three or four or five. Then they'd tell her she couldn't drive, why didn't she come back to their apartment, sit for a while, have some coffee? And the apartment would smell like dirty laundry and underarms, and there'd be pizza boxes on the counter and dishes in the sink. Want to watch a movie? they'd ask, and it would be a naked-girl porno movie, and there'd be a bottle of something, and one of them would look at her with slow glazed eyes, *Hey sweetheart,* he'd say, grinning a slow glazed grin, *Hey, sweetheart, hey, baby, why don't you get comfortable? Why don't you come over here?*

Which was when Maggie started to run.

"Hey!" Grant yelled one more time, sounding seriously pissed. She could hear him panting behind her as her feet beat a swift tattoo on the frozen ground. She remembered a story, the story of Atalanta who did not want to be married, Atalanta who the gods let race for the golden apple, Atalanta who ran faster than all the men, who would have won the race, except she'd gotten tricked. Well, no one would trick her.

A-ta-lan-ta, A-ta-lan-ta, her feet pounded, and her breath came in silvery gasps. She was almost there, was almost there, was so close that if she'd stretched out her fingertips, she could have brushed the driver's side door handle, when Grant grabbed her around the waist and lifted her off of her feet.

"Where you going," he panted into her ear, his breath sour and moist, "where you going so fast?" He slipped one hand up her sweater.

"Hey!" she screamed, flailing her legs, as he held her away from him and laughed, hearing a dog howl in the distance. Tim was running toward them. "C'mon, man, put her down," he said.

"Put me down!" Maggie shrieked.

"Not yet," said Grant, his hand crawling over her chest. "Don't you want to have some fun with us before you go?"

Oh, God, Maggie thought. *Oh, no.* She remembered a night like this from long ago, a night in high school, a party in someone's big backyard. She'd had some beer, and then she'd had some pot, and then someone had given her a cup of sticky brown liquor, and she'd downed that, too, and things had started to get fuzzy. She'd hooked up with a guy, and they'd been lying on the grass, behind a tree, his pants unzipped, her sweater shoved up around her neck, and she'd looked up and there'd been two other guys standing there, staring down at them, holding cans of beer. Standing there, waiting their turns. And at that moment, Maggie had had a sense of how slippery a thing her own power was, how fast it could turn in her hands, like a knife in the sink, slick with soap, how quickly and deeply the blade could cut her. She'd staggered to her feet, making convincing gagging noises. "Sick," she'd gasped, and run into the house with her fingers laced over her mouth, and hidden in the bathroom until four in the morning, when everyone had passed out or gone home. But what would she do now, when there was no bathroom to run to, no party to disappear into, and no one around to save her?

Maggie kicked out as hard as she could and felt her heel connect with the soft muscle of Grant's thigh. He sucked in his breath, and she wriggled out of his arms.

"What the fuck!" she shouted, as Grant glared at her, looking sullen, and Tim stared at the ground. "What the FUCK?!?!" she repeated.

"Cocktease," Grant said.

"Asshole," Maggie jeered. Her hands were shaking so badly that she dropped the keys twice before she managed to get the car door unlocked.

"You've got to pay for that," said Tim, walking toward her slowly with his hands held open, palms up. "They've got your plate numbers . . . They'll send you a ticket in the mail, they'll make you pay all kinds of fines . . ."

"Fuck you," said Maggie. "Stay away from me. My sister's a lawyer. She'll sue you for assault."

"Look," said Tim, "I'm sorry. He had too much to drink . . ."

"Fuck you," said Maggie. She started the car and flicked on the high beams. Grant threw his arms over his eyes. Maggie revved the engine and thought for a minute about how it would feel to just stomp on the gas and squash him like a squirrel. Instead, she took a deep breath, tried to steady her hands on the wheel, and drove out of the gate.

TWENTY

If Maggie had been a regular roommate, the telephone bill would have been the beginning and the end of it, the straw that broke the camel's back. But Maggie was no regular roommate, Rose reminded herself. Maggie was her sister. But when she'd gotten home after two days in Chicago (the flight had been late, her luggage had been lost, the airport overheated and jammed with Christmas travelers) and found the phone bill sitting on the counter, she was astonished to see that it was more than three hundred dollars, a significant increase over her normal forty-dollar bill. The culprit: a two hundred and twenty-seven dollar phone call to New Mexico.

She vowed she wouldn't confront her sister with it as soon as Maggie walked in the door. She'd let Maggie hang her coat up, take her shoes off, and then she'd casually mention that the phone bill had come, and had Maggie made a new friend in Albuquerque? Except that when she went to the bedroom to put her things away she saw that her entire wardrobe was still in a pile on the floor, and that her sheets and pillows had been tossed on top of Mount Fashion. Which meant that Maggie had been sleeping in her bed. And wearing her shoes, Rose thought. And eating her porridge if she'd had porridge to eat.

Rose sat on the couch, fuming, until after midnight, when Maggie sauntered in, smelling like a barroom floor, with something wriggling stuck in her coat.

"You're here!" Maggie said.

"Yes, I am," said Rose. "And so is the phone bill," she said, as Maggie kicked her shoes into the corner and dropped her purse on the couch.

"I brought you something!" Maggie said. Her color was high and her pupils were enormous, and she smelled like whiskey. "Two things, actually," she said, holding two fingers up in the air and opening her coat with a flourish. "Honey Bun Two!" she announced, as a small, crumpet-shaped brown dog dropped to the floor. It had moist brown eyes and a brown leather collar and a face that looked as though somebody had smashed it in with a frying pan.

Rose stared. "Maggie . . . what is that?"

"Honey Bun Two," Maggie repeated, heading to the kitchen. "My gift to you!"

"I can't have dogs in here!" Rose shouted. Meanwhile, the little brown dog had taken a fast tour of Rose's apartment and was now standing in front of her coffee table, looking like a dowager who was displeased with her hotel room.

"You'll have to take it back," said Rose.

"Fine, fine," said Maggie, sauntering back into the living room. "She's just visiting, anyhow."

"Visiting from where?"

"My new job," said Maggie. "I'm now a dog groomer at the Elegant Paw." She sneered at her sister. "I'm employed. I've been working for two days. Are you happy?"

"We need to talk about the phone bill," said Rose, forgetting her plan to be calm and reasonable. "Did you make a phone call to New Mexico?"

Maggie shook her head. "Don't think so."

Rose shoved the bill toward her sister. Maggie stared at it. "Oh, yeah."

"Oh, yeah what?"

"I got my tarot cards read. But God, it was only like half an hour! I didn't think it would cost that much."

"Your tarot cards," Rose repeated.

"It was right before my audition," Maggie mumbled. "I had to find out whether it was an auspicious day for a new job."

"Unbelievable," Rose said to the ceiling.

"Rose, do we have to talk about this right now?" Maggie asked. "I'm really tired. I had a really hard night."

"Oh, sure," said Rose. "After two whole days of work, you must be exhausted."

"Whatever," Maggie said. "And I'll pay you back for the phone bill."

The little dog took one more look at her, then gave a dismissive snort and heaved itself onto the couch, where it began pawing at the pillow, scratching at it with its nails. "Cut that out!" Rose called. The dog ignored her, pawing and poking at the pillow until it was arranged to its satisfaction, then curling up on top of it and falling instantly asleep.

"Maggie!" Rose yelled. There was no answer. The bathroom door stayed closed, and she could hear the shower running and the little dog snoring. "What's the other surprise?" Rose asked. No answer. She stood outside the bathroom door, the phone bill clutched in her hand, before turning away in disgust. Tomorrow morning, she promised herself.

Except the next morning began with what had become a routine event at Rose's apartment—a call from a bill collector.

"Hello, may I speak to Maggie Feller?" the calls would begin. "This is Lisa calling from Lord and Taylor." Or Karen from Macy's, or Elaine from Victoria's Secret. Today, it was Bill from the Gap. At night, Rose would come home and find the answering machine crammed with messages: Strawbridge, Bloomingdale's, Citibank, American Express.

"Maggie!" Rose called. Her sister was curled up on the sofa, and the dog was curled up on a pillow on the floor—a pillow that Rose saw was now brocaded with drool. "Telephone!"

Maggie didn't turn over or open her eyes—she just extended one arm toward the phone. Rose shoved it into her hand and headed to the bathroom, closing the door on Maggie's irate voice spiraling higher and higher, saying, "Yes," and "No," and "I already sent you a check!" When she got out of the shower Maggie was still on the phone, and the dog was gnawing on what Rose was pretty sure was one of her red cowboy boots. "Jesus!" she hissed, and slammed the door as hard as she could.

Rose took the elevator to the lobby and crossed the street, hoping that her car would be in the same general area where she'd left it before her Chicago trip. And there it was, almost exactly where she'd left it. Thank God for small favors, she thought, sliding behind the wheel, when an old man tapped on the glass, startling her so badly that she let out a little scream.

"I wouldn't do that," he said.

"Huh?" said Rose.

"Booted," he said. "Take a look."

Rose got out of the car and walked around to the passenger's side. Sure enough, a bright yellow metal boot had been attached to the front wheel, along with a bright orange notice. "Delinquent?" Rose read. *Maggie,* she thought. *This is Maggie's fault.* She glanced at her watch, figuring she had enough time to run back up to the apartment and get some answers from Miss Maggie. She stormed back through the lobby ("Forget something?" the doorman called at her back), punched the button for the elevator, stared furiously at the mirrored ceiling as the elevator rose, and half-ran down the hall back to her apartment. "Maggie!" she called. No answer. The shower was running. "Maggie!" Rose yelled, pounding on the bathroom door. No answer. Rose turned the doorknob. It was unlocked. She stormed into the bathroom, intending to rip open the shower curtain, never mind that her sister was naked, and get some answers about what the hell was going on. She took one step into the steamy bathroom and stopped. She could make out her sister's silhouette through the plastic of the shower curtain. Her back was to the door, and her forehead was pressed against the tiled wall. More than that—worse than that—she could hear what Maggie was saying. One word, over and over.

"Stupid . . . stupid . . . stupid . . . stupid . . ."

Rose froze in her tracks. Maggie reminded her of a pigeon she'd once seen. She'd been walking to the Wawa on the corner and almost tripped over the pigeon, and instead of looking scared, the bird had glared at Rose with its tiny, hate-filled red eyes. She'd stumbled, almost falling, and when she started walking again, she saw the problem. One of the pigeon's feet was horribly mangled. It was hopping on its one good foot, with the injured one curled up tight against its body.

Rose had thought for a moment that she should try to help it. "Oh," she'd said, and reached out her hand, thinking . . . thinking what? That she'd scoop the filthy thing up, rush it to a vet? The bird had simply glared at her some more before hopping off with a terrible, pathetic wounded dignity.

Maggie was just like that, Rose thought. She was hurt, too, but you couldn't point that out, couldn't offer to help, couldn't say anything that would hint that you knew that Maggie was hurt or flawed or broken, that there were things she couldn't figure out, or fix on her own.

Rose backed out of the bathroom quietly, easing the door shut. *Maggie,* she thought, feeling the familiar mixture of pity and fury tangling in her heart. She walked back to the elevator, through the lobby, out into the sunshine, and caught a cab on the corner. The car, she thought. The phone bill. The bill collectors. The dog. The clothes on the floor, the cosmetics crowding her counter, the "Final Notice" envelopes jammed in her mailbox. Rose closed her eyes. This would have to end. But how?

TWENTY-ONE

Ella had sand in her shoes. She eased them off and rubbed the sole of her foot carefully against the floor of the car, trying to dislodge the grains before putting her shoes back on.

Lewis looked over at her when they pulled up to a red light. "Okay?" he asked.

"Yes," said Ella, and smiled to prove it. They'd gone for a late dinner (late in that it was after seven o'clock), and then they'd gone to a concert—and not one at the Acres Clubhouse, either, but at an honest-to-goodness club, in Miami, with Lewis driving his big car slowly through the steamy, sweet-smelling night.

Now, as Lewis pulled through the residents' gate at Golden Acres, Ella wondered what would happen. If she'd been a younger woman, she'd probably have counted their dates (six so far), calculated how long they'd been seeing each other, and come to the conclusion that Lewis probably wanted Something. Sixty years ago and she'd have been bracing herself for a half-hour of sweaty grappling and fumbling before curfew ended their fun. But what could happen, at her age? After what she'd been through? She'd thought her heart was dead; a withered stump of a thing, incapable of feeling anything, incapable of flowering. At least that was what she'd believed for the years after Caroline's death. But now . . .

Lewis pulled into a parking spot in front of his building. "Would you like to come up? Have some coffee?"

"Oh, I'll be up all night," she said, and giggled like a silly schoolgirl. They rode together in the elevator in silence. Ella thought that maybe she'd been misreading things. Maybe he just wanted to take her up to offer her tea and torment her with pictures of his grandchildren. Or, more likely, he was just looking for a friend, a sympathetic ear, someone who'd listen to stories about his dead wife. Sex was out of the question. He was probably on medication, like everyone else Ella knew. Only what if he had Viagra? Ella bit her lip. She was probably being silly. She was seventy-eight years old. Who'd be in a big hurry to take her to bed, all droopy and wrinkled and age-spotted the way she was?

Lewis was staring at her curiously as he unlocked his door. "You look like you're a million miles away," he said.

"Oh, I . . ." Ella began, unsure of exactly what she intended to say as she followed him inside. His apartment, she could tell, was much bigger than hers, and while hers overlooked the parking lot and the interstate highway beyond it, his faced the ocean.

"Have a seat," he said. Ella planted herself on the couch and felt a trilling note of—of what? Fear? Excitement? He hadn't turned on any lights.

He came back and sat beside her, pressed a warm mug of tea into her hands. Then he got up again and raised the blinds, and Ella saw the water shining in the moonlight. She could see the waves rolling up onto the pale sand. And the windows were so big, and she felt so close to the water, it was like . . .

"It's like being on a ship!" she said. And it was. Even though she hadn't been on a ship in years and years, this was what it had been like. She could almost feel motion, the rocking of the waves, taking her out to sea, far away from what she knew, far away from herself. And when Lewis took her hand, it felt as right as anything she could remember, as right and as natural as the motion of the water coming up onto the sand.

TWENTY-TWO

"She has to get out of my house," Rose said to Amy. They were sitting in a corner of Amy's favorite cafe, sipping iced tea and waiting for their lunches to arrive. Rose had taken a cab to work and spent most of her morning on the phone with the Philadelphia Parking Authority, trying to find out what had happened to her car and how much Maggie's latest stunt would cost her. Then she'd glanced at the clock, groaned, realized that she hadn't gotten any work done yet, and called her apartment. Maggie hadn't picked up. Rose had left a terse message— "Maggie, call me at the office when you get this." By one o'clock there'd been no response, and Rose had met Amy for salads and strategy.

"Remember when she stayed with me for three weeks that time? Remember how I thought that was a living hell? Remember how I swore never again?"

Amy gave a sympathetic nod. "I remember."

Rose winced. She remembered, too, how Amy had stopped by to watch a movie during the week of Maggie's visit, and had discovered the next day that two lipsticks and forty bucks were missing from her purse.

"Look," Amy said, "you've been a good sister to her. You've been more than patient. Has she found a job?"

"She says she has."

"She says," Amy repeated. "And is she giving you money for rent? For groceries? For anything?"

Rose shook her head. The tall, black, gorgeous waitress sauntered over with their plates, dropped them on the table, and sashayed away without appearing to notice Rose's empty water glass.

"Why do we keep coming here?" Rose asked, picking up her fork. "The service is horrible."

"I like to keep my money in the community," said Amy.

"Amy," Rose said patiently, "you aren't in the community." She ate a few bites of her salad, then pushed her plate away. "What am I going to do about Maggie?"

"Kick her to the curb," said Amy, through a mouthful of spinach. "Tell her she gots to get."

"And where's she going to go?"

"Not your problem," Amy said. "Look, I know that sounds cold, but Maggie's not going to starve on the street. And she's not your responsibility. You're her sister, not her mom."

Rose bit her lip. Amy sighed. "I'm sorry," she said. "I'm sorry Maggie's such a wreck. I'm sorry Sydelle's such a nightmare. I'm sorry about your mom. But, Rose, what you're trying to do here . . . it's not going to work. You can't be her mother."

"I know," Rose mumbled. "I just don't know what to do. I mean, I know what I'm supposed to do, I just don't know how to do it."

"Repeat after me: 'Maggie, you need to leave,'" Amy said. "Seriously. She'll go to your father and Sydelle's, and if that doesn't convince her to straighten up and fly right until she's got enough money for a place on her own, nothing will. You can even give her some money—and notice that I'm saying 'give' and not 'lend.' I'll help you, if you want."

"Thanks," said Rose, and got to her feet. "I've got to go."

"And so does Maggie," Amy said. "You need to take care of yourself here." Rose nodded miserably. "Call me if you need help. Call me if you need anything. Let me know what happens."

Rose promised that she would, and headed back to her office.

She checked her messages. Nothing from Maggie, but there was something from Sydelle. "Rose, please call us. Immediately."

So maybe that was where her sister had gone. Rose took a deep breath and dialed. "It's Rose," she said.

"You need to do something about your sister," said Sydelle, proceeding to launch into a recitation of the most recent and egregious of Maggie's abuses. "Do you know we've got bill collectors calling our house at eight in the morning?"

"Me, too," said Rose.

"Well, can't you do something?" Sydelle demanded. "You're a lawyer, can't you tell them it's illegal to call here? Honey, it's no good for your father . . ."

Rose wanted to say that it was no good for her, either—that nothing Maggie ever did was good for anyone but Maggie—but she kept her mouth shut and said she'd do what she could. She hung up the phone and called home again. Still no answer. Now she was getting worried. Maybe Maggie was at work. Sure, she thought sourly. And maybe the judges would be stopping by shortly to crown her Miss America. Rose logged on to her computer and checked her e-mail. Something from a partner asking, quite tersely, when Rose would be done with the draft of her brief. A group e-mail from Simon Stein entitled "Softball Pre-Season Meeting" that Rose deleted without reading.

She got to her feet and began pacing the length of her office. She needed to see Jim, she decided. She needed to see him now. She needed to see him whether he wanted to see her or not. She looked down and noticed with dismay that she was wearing two completely different black loafers—a natural consequence of having her sister dump every shoe she owned onto the floor. *Maggie!* she thought furiously, and, hurrying down the hallway, blew past Jim's secretary ("Hey! He's on a phone call, Rose!") and right into his office.

"Rose? What's going on?" he asked, hanging up the phone and closing the door behind her.

Rose stared down at her mismatched shoes. What was going on was that her apartment was a mess, her life was falling apart, she owed the Parking Authority two hundred dollars, there was a dog living illegally in her living room, and, evidently, she couldn't even dress herself anymore. She needed him to hold her, to cradle her head in his hands and tell her that the two of them were just starting out, and that it might have been a rocky start because of Maggie's omnipresence, but that soon they'd be together again.

"Hey," said Jim, leading her to the leather seat in front of his desk, the one for clients, the sloping Eames chair that canted their butts back and away from his own, assuring that he'd always be taller than they were, no matter what.

Rose stood instead, and took a deep breath. *Summarize,* she told herself. "I miss you," she said.

Jim looked rueful. "I'm sorry, Rose," he said, "but it's been just crazy around here."

Rose felt as if she were on a roller coaster that had just crested a hill that she hadn't seen coming, and now the bottom of her world was falling away. Couldn't he see that she needed him?

He wrapped his arms around her shoulders, but kept her body at a distance. "How can I help?" he murmured. "What can I do?"

"Come over tonight," she said, pressing her lips against his neck, knowing that she was doing the very thing that women were never ever under any circumstances supposed to do—namely, begging. "I need to see you. Please!"

"It might be late," he said. "Like, ten or so."

"It's okay if you're late. I'll wait for you." *I'll wait forever,* she thought, and let herself out of the office. His secretary glared at her.

"You can't just walk right *in,*" said the secretary. "You have to be *announced.*"

"I'm sorry," said Rose, feeling as though she'd done nothing but apologize all day long. "I am. I'm sorry."

TWENTY-THREE

Rose's phone was ringing again. Maggie ignored it. She dropped her towel on the living room floor and walked into the shower. It was her third shower of the morning. Maggie had taken lots of showers in the day following her up-close and personal encounter with the dynamic duo of Grant and Tim, spending ten, twenty, thirty minutes scrubbing herself with her loofah, washing her hair until it squeaked. And she still felt dirty. Dirty and furious. All these weeks on Rose's couch, and what did she have to show for herself? No money. No man. No head shots. Nothing, nothing, nothing. Just assholes who'd grab her in parking lots like she was nothing. Like she wasn't even real.

She heard her sister's voice blatting from the answering machine. "Maggie, are you there? Pick up if you're there. I really need to talk to you. Maggie . . ."

She wrapped herself in a towel, palmed the condensation off the mirror, ignoring her sister's voice on the answering machine, and looked at herself. Weapon One, as always, was her body, and it was finer than a gun, sharper than a knife. She'd find those guys again. She'd haunt the city until she found them, at a bar or on the bus. Somewhere. She'd walk over to them, head held high, chest thrust out, and smile. The smile would be the hardest part, but she was sure that she could manage it. She was an actress. She was a star. She would smile and lay her hand between Tim's shoulder blades, ask how he was doing. She'd sip her drink, leaving lipstick half-kisses on the rim, and brush her knee against his. She'd lean close and whisper that she'd had a great time that night, that she was sorry she'd run away, and could they maybe do it again? Were they free tonight? And they'd bring her back to the apartment. And then it would be Weapon Two. Maybe a knife. A gun, if she could find one. Something that would cause them permanent damage, something that would show them that she was not a girl to be fucked with.

The phone rang again. "Maggie, I know you're there. Would you please pick up the phone? I just got off the phone with the parking people again, and they say the car was taken out of an impound lot and there's a bunch of fines . . ."

Maggie ignored the phone and cranked up the stereo—Axl Rose wailing "Welcome to the Jungle." "Do you know where you are?" he squealed. She shoved her feet into Rose's newest acquisition, a pair of knee-high black leather boots that hugged her calves. Two hundred and sixty-eight dollar boots, and her sister could buy them without a second thought, because nothing ever went wrong for Rose. Oh, no. Rose wouldn't get tripped up by a TelePrompTer, Rose would never park on the wrong side of the street, Rose wouldn't have assholes groping at her in parking lots, and Rose certainly never would have to take a job that involved squeezing dogs' asses just to make ends meet. Rose had everything, and Maggie had nothing. Nothing at all, except for the little dog who'd been dumped at the Elegant Paw for months until Maggie had rescued her and taken her home.

Naked except for the boots, she paced back and forth from the bedroom to the living room to the kitchen and back again, hearing the squeak of the soles against the hardwood floors, smelling the leather and the soap and sweat from her body, seeing a red fog. Seeing the knife. Seeing herself flashing in the mirror as she stalked past the bathroom, flushed and wet and lovely—a clever disguise, a flower with creamy petals on long-stemmed legs. Nobody looking at her would ever suspect what she really was.

The intercom buzzed. The dog whined. "Don't worry," Maggie said, and yanked a T-shirt over her head. She thought about panties for a minute, then figured, why bother? It was eight o'clock—too early for Rose to be home and start lecturing her again. It was probably only the asshole next door telling her to turn her music down.

She turned out the lights and flung the door open, eyes blazing, prepared to give someone a piece of her mind, and saw Rose's boyfriend standing before her.

"Rose?" he said, squinting at her through the darkness. And Maggie laughed—a brief giggle at first, but the laughter kept rolling up her throat like poison, like throwing up in reverse. She wasn't Rose. She would never be Rose. She lacked her sister's abilities, her sister's easy successes. She'd never be the one to offer advice, to poke and prod and scold and lay down rules and offer cheesy sympathy laced with impatience. Rose. Hah! She threw back her head and let the laughter come. "Not hardly," she finally said.

He looked her up and down, his eyes lingering on her boots, on the span of bare thigh, on her breasts. "Is Rose home?" he asked.

Maggie shook her head and gave him a slow, saucy smile. A plan was forming in her brain. Revenge, she thought, the blood pounding in her temples. *Revenge.* "Would you like to come in and wait for her?" she asked. Jim stared at her, his eyes licking her up and down, and Maggie could practically read his mind. She was Rose, only improved, amplified, digitally perfected; Rose, only a thousand times better.

He shook his head. Maggie leaned against the doorframe insolently.

"Let me guess," she said in a rich, taunting voice. "You're looking to upgrade from ground chuck to filet."

Jim shook his head again, still staring at her.

"Or maybe," Maggie continued, "you want both of us. Is that it? A sister sandwich?"

He stared at her, trying to look outraged, but she could tell from the expression that had flickered across his face just how appealing he found that idea.

"Well, you'll have to wait," said Maggie. "Nobody home but little old me." She reached down, grabbed the hem of her T-shirt, pulled it up over her head, arching her back so that her breasts almost brushed his chest. He groaned. She took a short step forward, closing the distance between them. His hands closed over her breasts, and she was sucking at his neck with her hot, avid mouth.

"No," he whispered, even as his arms were wrapping around her.

"Don't," she said, and wrapped one naked leg around him, pressing herself against him.

"Don't what?"

And now she lifted her other leg so that she was twined around him like a snake, and he moaned as he lifted her and carried her inside. "Don't tell me no."

By the time she made it back to her apartment building, it was almost nine o'clock, and the elevator was crowded. Rose wedged herself into the last available bit of space and tried to ignore the suffocating perfume of the woman next to her.

"I swear, either I'm going crazy, or there's a dog in this building," the woman announced to the elevator at large.

Rose stared at her feet.

"I don't know who'd be inconsiderate enough to have a pet here," the woman continued. "There are people with terrible allergies."

Rose glanced up desperately at the floor indicator. Third floor. Thirteen to go.

"People are unbelievable," the woman continued. "They just don't care! Tell them what the rules are, and they say, 'Oh, well, those are rules for other people. Not for me. Because I'm *special.*'"

Finally, the scent-drenched lady got off the elevator, and Rose arrived at her floor. Walking down the hallway, she hoped that her sister would be home, and began rehearsing her speech. *Maggie, we*

*need to discuss things. The dog has to go. The calls have to stop. I need my
apartment back. I need my shoes back. I need my life back.*

She turned her key, opened the door, and walked into pitch
darkness. She heard voices, a giggle, the little dog's whine.

"Maggie?" she called. There was a tie flung over the sofa. Oh,
great, she thought bleakly. Now she's bringing guys home to my
apartment. And doing God knows what with them on my bed.
"Maggie!" she yelled, and walked into the bedroom. And there was
her sister, on the bed, absolutely naked except for Rose's new Via
Spiga boots, below a naked Jim Danvers.

"Oh, no," said Rose. She stood, staring, trying to make sense of
what she was seeing. "No," she whispered. Maggie rolled out from
beneath Jim and stretched languidly, giving her sister a long look
at her slender back, her perfect little butt, her long, smooth legs rising from the black leather boots, before plucking Jim's T-shirt off
the floor, pulling it over her head, and strutting out of the room,
into the hall, as if it were a catwalk, as if there were an audience of
thousands, with flashbulbs and notepads, all of them waiting for
her. Jim shot Rose a desperately shamed look and yanked up the
blankets.

Rose clapped her hand over her mouth, turned and ran to the
bathroom, where she threw up into the sink. She ran water until
she'd washed the remains of her lunch down the drain. Then she
splashed her face, scrubbed her hair back with wet, shaking hands,
and went back to the bedroom. Jim had his boxer shorts on, and
was scrambling to pull on the rest of his clothes. Rose saw his
retainer glinting on her bedside table.

"Get out," she said.

"Rose," he said, and reached for her hands.

"Get out and take her with you. I don't want to see either one of
you ever again."

"Rose," he said.

"Get out! Get out! Get out!" She could hear her voice, spiraling
up into a shriek. She reached for something to throw at him—a

lamp, a candle, a book. Her hand wrapped around a bottle of massage oil, scented with sandalwood. Open. Capless. Recently used, no doubt, and bought with Maggie's credit card, another bill her sister would never pay. She threw it as hard as she could, wishing that it were glass, that it would break up and cut him. Instead, it bounced harmlessly off his shoulder and rolled on the floor, dribbling oil as it rolled beneath her bed.

"I'm sorry," Jim muttered, without meeting her eyes.

"I'm SAW-REE," Rose parroted. "Oh, you're sorry, huh? And so that makes it okay?" She stared at him, shaking. "How could you? How could you?"

She ran through the living room, where Maggie sat on the couch, channel surfing, and into the kitchen. She pulled out a trash bag and started filling it with everything she could find that belonged to either one of them. She snatched Maggie's lighter and cigarettes from the coffee table and threw them in. She picked up Jim's briefcase and hurled it against the wall as hard as she could, hearing a satisfying crack as something inside of it broke. She went to the bathroom and gathered up Maggie's stockings and bras, wisps of black and cream-colored synthetic satin, lined up on the shower curtain rack, and shoved them into the garbage bag, too. Back in the bedroom, Jim was pulling on his pants. Rose ignored him, grabbing Maggie's *Fifty Great Résumés* workbook. Maggie's nail polish and nail polish remover, her tubes and tins and pots of blush, foundation, mascara, hair mousse, her tiny tank tops and skintight jeans and knockoff Doc Martens from Payless. "Get out, get out, get out," she muttered under her breath, dragging the garbage bag behind her.

"Talking to yourself, Rosie Posey?" Maggie called. The words were ice-cold, but Maggie's voice was shaking. "You shouldn't do that. It makes you sound crazy."

Rose picked up a sneaker and threw it at her sister's head. Maggie ducked. The shoe bounced off the wall. "Get out of my house," Rose said. "You aren't welcome."

Maggie hooted. "Not welcome? Well, isn't that too bad."

She strolled into the bathroom. Breathing hard, sweating, Rose pulled the bag into her bedroom. Jim had gotten into his clothes, but his feet were still bare.

"I don't suppose it would do any good to say that I am sorry." He had gone from looking stricken to just plain sheepish.

"Save it for someone who cares," Rose snarled.

"Well, I want to say it anyhow." He cleared his throat. "I'm sorry, Rose. You deserve better."

"Asshole," she said, in a dead voice that surprised her, and scared her, and reminded her of someone else, from years and years ago. She felt as if this were all happening at a great distance, or to somebody else. "With my sister," she said. "My sister."

"I'm sorry," Jim said again. Maggie, who was now standing hip-sprung in the hallway, and who'd gotten herself dressed in painted-on jeans and spaghetti-strapped top, said nothing.

"You know the really pathetic part? I could have loved you. And Maggie won't even remember your name," she said to Jim. She felt the words, hateful forbidden words, words she'd never spoken before, bubbling up in her chest. She thought that maybe she should try to stop them, and then she thought, why? Had the two of them tried to stop themselves? "See, Maggie's very pretty, but she's not very bright." She turned, slowly, tucking her hair behind her ears. "In fact, Jim, if I were a betting woman, I'd say that she can't even spell it right now. Three letters long," she said, stabbing three fingers into the air. "And she can't do it. Want to ask her? Huh? Hey, Maggie, you want to give it a try?"

From behind her, she heard Maggie gasp.

"You're an asshole," she continued steadily, turning back to Jim, pinning him with her eyes. "And you," she said, turning to face her sister. Maggie's face was pale, her eyes were enormous. "I always knew you didn't have a brain. Now I know you don't have a heart."

"Fat pig," Maggie muttered.

Rose laughed. She dropped the bag and laughed. She rocked

back on her heels and laughed until tears spurted out of the corners of her eyes.

"She's crazy," Maggie said loudly.

"Fat . . . pig . . ." Rose gasped. "My God," she said, pointing at Jim. "You're a cheater, and you . . ." She pointed at Maggie, groping for the right word. "You're my sister," she finally said. "My *sister.* And the worst thing you can say about me is 'fat pig'?"

She lifted the bag, twirled it, tied the top into a knot, and heaved it as hard as she could at the door. "Get out," she said. "I never want to see either one of you again."

Rose spent most of the night on her hands and knees, scrubbing, trying to remove every trace of Maggie and Jim from her apartment. She yanked the sheets and pillowcases and comforters off her bed, dragged them to the laundry room, and doused them in two cups of detergent. She washed her kitchen and bathroom floors with Pine-Sol and warm water. She mopped the hardwood floors in her living room and bedroom and hall. She scrubbed the bathtub with Lysol, then scrubbed the tile shower walls with an antibacterial antimildew spray. The little dog watched for a while, following her from room to room, as if Rose were the new cleaning lady and the dog were a distrustful matron, then yawned and resumed its nap on the sofa. By four in the morning, Rose's mind was still whirling, and the one thing she could see clearly when she closed her eyes was a picture of her sister, in Rose's own new boots, churning her body up and down above Jim, who lay in the bed with a glazed, blissful look in his eyes.

She pulled on a clean nightgown, got into bed, and yanked the clean sheets up to her chin with an angry jerk of her wrists. Then she shut her eyes, breathing hard. She thought that she'd managed to tire herself out. She thought she might sleep.

Instead, she closed her eyes and fell headlong into the memory she knew was there, hiding, crouched and waiting for her. The memory of the worst night of her life, which had also starred Maggie.

• • •

It was an early day, a teachers' in-service, and it was just after noon on a late-May day when school let out. Rose had collected her books from her locker and met Maggie outside the first-grade classroom, checking to make sure that her sister had her own backpack. Maggie did. She also had a familiar-looking piece of pink paper in one hand.

"Again?" asked Rose, and held out her hand for the note from Maggie's teacher. She read it while Maggie walked ahead of her, toward the path behind the elementary school that would lead them home.

"Maggie, you can't bite people," Rose said.

"She started it," her sister called back sullenly.

"It doesn't matter," said Rose. "Remember what Mom said? You have to learn to use your words."

She hurried to catch up with her sister, huffing slightly beneath the weight of her backpack. "Did it bleed?" she asked Maggie.

Maggie nodded. "I could have bitten it off," she bragged, "if Miss Burdick wasn't looking."

"Why would you want to bite off someone's nose?"

Maggie pursed her lips even tighter. "She made me mad."

Rose shook her head. "Maggie, Maggie, Maggie," she said, the way she'd heard her mother saying it. "What are we going to do with you?"

Maggie rolled her eyes, then looked at her sister. "Will I be on punishment?" she asked.

"I don't know," said Rose.

Maggie pursed her lips. "It's Megan Sullivan's sleep-over party."

Rose shrugged. She knew all about the sleep-over party. Maggie had had her pink Barbie suitcase packed for days.

"Did you get any library books?" Rose asked, and Maggie nodded, and pulled *Goodnight Moon* from her backpack.

"That's a little kid book," Rose said.

Maggie glared at her sister. It was true, but she didn't care.

"Good night, mittens on the chair. Good night, people, every-where," she whispered, and started skipping down the path.

The path ended behind the McIlheneys' yard. Rose and Maggie skirted the swimming pool and the deck, crossed the McIlheneys' front yard, then crossed the street to their house, which was a twin of the McIlheneys'—a twin, really, of every house on the street. Two stories, three bedrooms, red brick, and black shutters, and square green lawns, like houses in a little kid's coloring book.

"Wait up!" Rose yelled, as Maggie skipped across the street and dashed up their gravel driveway toward the front door. "You're not supposed to cross the street yourself! You're supposed to hold my hand!"

Maggie ignored her, hurrying ahead, pretending she couldn't hear. "Mom!" she called, setting her key down on the counter and sniffing to see what was for lunch. "Hey, Mom! We're home!"

Rose walked through the front door and set the backpack down. The house was silent, and she could tell even before Maggie told her that their mother wasn't home.

"Her car's not here!" Maggie reported breathlessly. "And I looked under the apple magnet, and there's no note."

"Maybe she forgot it was an early day," Rose said. Except she'd reminded her mother that morning, sneaking into the gloomy bed-room, whispering *Mom? Hey, Mom?* Her mother had nodded when Rose said they'd be home early, but she hadn't opened her eyes. *Be a good girl, Rose,* she'd said. *Take care of your sister.* It was the same thing she said every morning—when she said anything at all.

"Don't worry," said Rose. "She'll be back by three." Maggie looked worried. Rose took her hand. "Come on," she said. "I'll make you lunch."

Rose made eggs, which was nice, even though she wasn't supposed to, because they weren't allowed to turn on the stove. "Don't worry," Rose told Maggie. "You can double check me to make sure I turned it off."

Then it was one-thirty. Maggie wanted to cut through the backyard to play at her friend Natalie's house, but Rose thought it would be better if they stayed and waited for their Mom to come home. So they sat in front of the television and watched Heckle and Jeckle cartoons for half an hour (Maggie's choice), then educational *Sesame Street* (Rose's).

At three o'clock their mother still hadn't come home. "She probably just forgot," said Rose, but now she was starting to worry, too. The day before she'd heard her mother on the telephone. "Yes!" she was shouting at someone. "Yes!" Rose had edged right up to the closed bedroom door and pressed her ear against it. It had been months since she'd heard her mother speak in anything more than a drowsy, distracted mumble. But now she was yelling, each word hard and distinct as a pane of glass. "I. Am. Taking. My. Medication," her mother said. "For God's sake, let it go! Let me be! I'm fine! Fine!"

Rose closed her eyes. Her mother wasn't fine. She knew it, and her father did, too, and probably whoever her mother was screaming at knew it, too.

"It's okay," she told her sister again. "Can you find Mom's red phone book? We have to call Dad."

"Why?"

"Just find it, okay?"

Maggie came running with the book. Rose found her father's office number and dialed carefully. "Yes, may I speak to Mr. Feller, please?" she asked, in a voice at least an octave higher than her normal husky one. "This is his daughter Rose Feller calling." She waited, her face still, the telephone pressed to her ear, her little sister standing beside her. "Oh. I see. All right. No. Just tell him we'll see him later. Thank you. Okay. Good-bye."

She set the phone down.

"What?" asked Maggie. "What?"

"He's out," Rose said. "The lady she didn't know when he'd be back."

"But he'll be home for dinner. Right?" asked Maggie, her voice spiraling higher and higher and ending in a squeak. Her face was pale, her eyes were enormous, as if the prospect of having both parents go missing was more than she could take. "Right?"

"Of course," said Rose, and then did something that let Maggie know that there was really, actually something to be afraid of—she handed her sister the remote control and walked out of the room.

Maggie trailed her.

"Go away," said Rose. "I have to think."

"I can think, too," said Maggie. "I can help you think."

Rose took off her glasses and polished them on the edge of her shirt. "Maybe we should see if there's anything missing."

"Like a suitcase?"

Rose nodded. "Like that."

The girls hurried upstairs, opening their parents' bedroom door, and looking inside. Rose braced herself for the usual wreckage—tangled sheets, pillows on the floor, a collection of half-empty glasses and half-eaten pieces of toast on the bedside table. But the bed was neatly made. The dresser drawers were all closed. On the bedside table, Rose found a pair of earrings, a bracelet, a watch, and a plain gold band. She shuddered, then slipped the ring in her pocket before Maggie could see, and could start asking questions about why their mother had cleaned her room and taken off her wedding ring.

"Suitcase is here!" said Maggie, bounding happily out of the closet.

"Good," said Rose, through lips that felt frozen. She'd have to try calling her father again and telling him what she'd found, as soon as she could get her sister busy doing something else. "Come on," she said, and led Maggie out of the bedroom and back down the stairs.

Maggie worked the rolling pin back and forth over the plastic bag full of potato chips. Rose looked up at the clock for the third time in less than a minute. It was six o'clock. Rose was trying to pretend that everything was all right, even though nothing was all right at all. She hadn't been able to get her father on the phone, and their mother still wasn't home. Even if she'd forgotten about the early dismissal, she should have been home by three-thirty.

Think! Rose thought to herself, as her sister ground the potato chips into shards, then into dust. She had already pretty much decided that their mother had gone AWAY again. She and Maggie weren't supposed to know about AWAY—about where it was, about that her mother had been there. But Rose knew. Last summer, after their mother had come back from AWAY, Maggie had come to her with a crumpled brochure.

"What's this say?" she asked.

Rose read it carefully. " 'Institute of Living'," she said, staring at the drawing—a cupped palm holding the faces of a woman, a man, and a child.

"What's it mean?"

"I don't know," said Rose. "Where did you find it?"

"In Mom's suitcase."

Rose hadn't even asked what Maggie was doing looking in their mother's suitcase—even at six, Maggie was a notorious snoop. A few weeks later, Rose had been driving home from a Hebrew school field trip with the Schoens when they'd passed a bunch of buildings with a sign in front, and the sign had had the exact same picture on it as the brochure—same faces, same cupped hands.

"What's that?" she'd asked, trying to be casual, because the car had sped past the sign too fast for her to try to puzzle out.

Steven Schoen had snickered. "The loony bin," he'd said, and his mother had whirled around so fast her hair whipped against her cheeks, and Rose could smell Aqua Net. "Steven!" she'd scolded, and then turned to Rose, her voice soft and syrupy sweet. "That's a place called the Institute of Living," she'd explained. "It's a special kind of hospital for people who need help with their feelings."

So. That was AWAY. Rose wasn't too surprised, because anyone could tell that their mom had needed some kind of help. But where was she now? Had she gone back there?

Rose looked at the clock again. Five minutes past six. She called her father's office again, but the phone just rang and rang. She set the receiver down and walked into the family room, where Maggie was now sitting on the couch, looking out the window. She sat down next to her sister.

"Is it my fault?" Maggie whispered.

"What?"

"Is it my fault she went away? Did she get mad at me because I get in trouble at school?"

"No, no," Rose said. "It's not your fault. She's not away. She probably just got confused or something, or maybe she had car trouble. There's lots of things it could be!" But even as she reassured Maggie, Rose slipped her hand into her pocket and felt the cold gold ring. "Don't worry," she said.

"I'm scared," Maggie whispered.

"I know," said Rose. "Me, too." They sat on the couch, side by side, as the sun went down, waiting.

Michael Feller pulled into the driveway at just after seven o'clock, and Rose and Maggie hurried out the door to meet him.

"Daddy, Daddy!" Maggie said, catapulting herself toward her father's legs. "Mom's not here! She's gone! She didn't come back!"

Michael turned to his oldest daughter. "Rose? What's going on?"

"We got home from school early . . . it's a teachers in-service day, I brought home the notice about it last week . . ."

"She didn't leave a note?" asked their father, hurrying to the kitchen, so fast that Rose and Maggie had to run to keep up.

"No," said Rose.

"Where is she?" asked Maggie. "Do you know?"

Their father shook his head and reached for the red address book and the telephone. "Don't worry. I'm sure it's nothing to worry about."

Midnight. Rose had made Maggie eat some of the tuna noodle casserole, and tried to make their father eat some, too, but he'd

waved her away, sitting hunched by the phone, making call after
call after call. At ten, he'd noticed that they were still awake and
he'd hurried them into their nightgowns and into their beds, forgetting to make them wash their faces or brush their teeth. "Go to
sleep," he said. For the last two hours they'd been lying side by side
in Rose's bed with their eyes wide open in the darkness. Rose had
told Maggie stories—"Cinderella" and "Little Red Riding Hood,"
the story of the princess and the enchanted slippers who danced and
danced and danced.

The doorbell rang. Rose and Maggie sat straight up at the exact
same instant.

"We should get that," said Maggie.

"It might be her," said Rose.

They held hands as they ran down the stairs in bare feet. Their
father was at the door already, and Rose could tell without even
hearing a word that was said, that something very bad was happening, that their mother was not okay, that nothing would ever be
okay again.

A tall man was at the door, a man in a green uniform and a
broad-brimmed brown hat. "Mr. Feller?" he was asking. "Is this the
residence of Caroline Feller?"

Her father swallowed hard and nodded. The tall man's hat
dripped rainwater onto the floor. "I'm afraid I have some bad news,
sir," he said.

"Did you find our mother?" Maggie asked in a tiny gasping
voice.

The trooper looked at them sadly. His leather belt creaked as he
reached to put his hand on their father's shoulder. Raindrops fell on
Maggie's and Rose's bare feet. He looked down at them, then back
up at their father.

"I think we should talk privately, sir," he said. And Michael
Feller, shoulder slumped, face broken, led him away.

And after that . . .

After that was their father with his Stonehenge face. After that was "car accident," and packing up the house in Connecticut, leaving their school, their house, their friends, their familiar street. Their father piled their mother's things in boxes destined for Goodwill, and Rose and Maggie and their father got in a U-Haul truck and drove to New Jersey. "To start over," their father had said. Like that could ever happen. Like the past was something you could leave behind like a candy bar wrapper or a pair of shoes you'd outgrown.

In her bed in Philadelphia, Rose sat up in the darkness, knowing that she wouldn't be doing any sleeping that night. She remembered the funeral. She remembered the navy blue dress she'd worn, purchased for the first day of school, nine months before, and how it was already too short, and the elastic of the puffed sleeves had left red welts on her arms. She remembered her father's face over the grave, remote and distant, and an older woman with auburn hair, sitting in the back of the funeral parlor crying softly into a handkerchief. Her grandmother. Where had she gone? Rose didn't know. After the funeral, they'd rarely talked about their grandmother, or their mother. They lived far away from the policeman in the hat full of rain, and the driveway he'd parked his cruiser in, with the blue lights still flashing mutely through the darkness, and the road that had brought him to their house. The slick, wet road with its treacherous curves, a ribbon of black, like a lying tongue. They'd gone far away from the road, and the house, and the cemetery where their mother was buried, beneath a blanket of raw-looking sod and a headstone that had her name, the years of her birth and her death, and the words *Wife and Loving Mother* chiseled into it. And Rose had never once been back.

PART TWO

Continuing
Education

TWENTY-FOUR

What she needed, thought Maggie Feller, was a plan.

She sat on a bench inside Thirtieth Street Station, a grand, cavernous room littered with old newspapers and fast-food wrappers, smelling of grease and sweat and winter coats. It was almost midnight. Harried-looking mothers dragged their children along by their arms. Homeless people slept splayed out on the carved wooden benches. I could be one of them, thought Maggie, panic rising inside of her.

Think, she told herself. She had a garbage bag full of stuff, plus her purse, her backpack, and two hundred dollars, two crisp hundred-dollar bills Jim had given her before dropping her off. *Can I help you?* he'd asked, not unkindly, and she'd held out her hand without meeting his eyes. "I want two hundred dollars," she told him. "That's the going rate." He'd dug the money out of his wallet without a word of protest. "I'm sorry," he'd said . . . but sorry about what? And whom was he apologizing to? Not her. Maggie was sure of that. What she needed now was somewhere to stay . . . and then a job again, eventually.

Rose was out of the question. So was her father. Maggie shuddered, imagined herself dragging her bags across the lawn as the idiot dog howled, imagined the look of fake-o sympathy and barely disguised disgust as Sydelle opened the door, and how her eyes would say, *This is just what we expected of you,* even if her mouth was saying something else. Sydelle would want details, would want to know what had happened with Rose and with her job. Sydelle would needle her with dozens of questions, and her father would sit there, his eyes soft and defeated, not asking anything at all.

Where did that leave her? Maggie couldn't see herself in a homeless shelter. All those women, all those failed lives. She wasn't that way. She hadn't failed. Not like that. She was a star, if only someone could see it!

You're not a star, whispered a voice in her head, and the voice sounded like Rose's voice, only colder than Rose could ever sound. *You're not a star, you're a slut, a stupid slut. You can't even work the cash register! You can't balance your checkbook! Evicted! Practically homeless! And you slept with my boyfriend!*

Think, thought Maggie fiercely, trying to drown out the voice. What did she have? Her body. There was that. Jim had turned over the two hundred dollars easily enough. There were men who would pay her to sleep with them, certainly, and men who would pay to watch her dance with her clothes off. At least that was entertaining, performing. And plenty of the rising stars who'd gone before her had done it as a last-ditch measure, a stopgap thing.

So fine, Maggie thought, tightening her grip on her garbage bag as the homeless man two benches back moaned in his sleep. Stripping. Fine. It wasn't the end of the world. But that didn't solve the problem of where she'd stay. It was January, the cold, dead heart of winter. She'd planned on catching a SEPTA train to Trenton, then taking another train into New York City. But she wouldn't get there until two in the morning, and then what would she do? Where would she go?

She got to her feet, clutching her backpack tightly in one hand and her garbage bag in the other, and squinted at the New Jersey Transit board and the names of the towns the trains went to: Rahway. Westfield. Matawan. Metuchen. Red Bank. Little Silver.

That one sounded nice, but what if it wasn't? Newark. Too big. Elizabeth. The butt of Jersey jokes. Brick. Ugh. Princeton.

She'd visited Rose at Princeton a few times, when she was sixteen and seventeen. She could picture it if she closed her eyes— buildings made of carved gray stone, covered in ivy, with gargoyles leering from the ledges. She remembered dorm rooms with fireplaces in them, and wooden window seats that opened up to hold extra blankets and winter coats, and the many-paned leaded-glass windows. She remembered huge classrooms, sloping floors full of hard-edged wooden chairs with desks attached, and a party in a basement, with a keg of beer in the corner, and how vast the library had seemed—three floors up, and three floors down, each one long as a football field. The smell of burning wood and fall leaves, a borrowed red wool scarf warm around her neck, heading down one of the gray slate paths toward a party, knowing she'd never be able to find her way back by herself, because there were so many paths and all the buildings looked almost the same. "It's easy to get lost here," Rose had told her, so she wouldn't feel bad. "It happened to me all the time my freshman year."

Maybe she could get lost there now. She could take a train to Trenton, catch New Jersey Transit to Princeton, and stay there for a few days and regroup. Everyone always told her she looked younger than she was, and she had a backpack, the universal sign of students everywhere. "Princeton," she said out loud, and walked to the ticket window, where she paid seven dollars for a one-way ticket. She'd always meant to go back to college, she thought, heading up the ramp toward the trains. So what if this wasn't the most normal way to do it? When had she, Maggie Feller, ever been the most normal girl?

At two in the morning Maggie made her way across the darkened Princeton University campus. Her shoulder muscles were cramping from the weight of her backpack, and her hands were numb from towing the trash bag full of clothes, but she tried to walk briskly as she joined the crowds of students moving along the sidewalk, with her shoulders back and her head up, as if she knew exactly where she was going.

She'd gotten off the train at Princeton Junction in the middle of a vast parking lot, halogen lamps gleaming coldly in the dark. In an instant of panic, she turned around and sure enough, there were students—or at least people who looked like students—streaming across the platform, down into a tunnel below them. She followed them under the train tracks and then up the other side, where another, much smaller train waited. She bought a ticket on the train, and two minutes later arrived at the campus.

As she walked up the hill, Maggie made a quick but careful study of her fellow travelers—kids coming back from Christmas break, she figured, judging from the conversations and the amounts of luggage. Evidently, she decided, grooming was not a priority for these women, while purchasing the fashions of Abercrombie & Fitch was. None wore much more than lip gloss, and they were arrayed in some version of washed-out jeans, sweaters or sweat-shirts, camel-colored overcoats, plus layers upon layers of hats, scarves, mittens, and winter boots. Well, that explains Rose, she thought and began mentally editing her wardrobe. Little halter top, no. Leather pants, probably not. Cashmere sweater set? Sure, if only she had one, she thought, and shivered as the icy wind bit at her bare neck. She'd need a scarf. Also, she needed a cigarette, though it seemed that none of the girls were smoking. Maybe because it was too cold, but probably because they just didn't. Probably because none of the girls in the Abercrombie & Fitch ads were smokers. Maggie sighed, and edged up as close as she could to a pack of chattering girls, looking for more information.

"I don't know," one of them said, giggling, as they walked past bulletin boards covered with fliers advertising everything from movies and concerts to used guitars for sale. "I think he likes me, and I gave him my number, but so far, nothing."

Then he doesn't like you, dummy, Maggie thought. If they liked

you, they called. It was as simple as that. And these were supposed
to be the smart girls?

"Maybe you should call him," one of her friends suggested. *Sure,*
thought Maggie, who hadn't telephoned a man since she gave up
crank calls at age thirteen. *And maybe you should wave a flag in front of
his room, too, in case he misses the point.*

The pack pulled up in front of a four-story stone building with
a heavy wood door. One of the girls pulled off her mittens and
punched a code into the doorknob. The door swung open, and
Maggie followed them inside.

She was in some kind of common area. There were half a dozen
couches covered in an indestructible industrial blue fabric, a few
scarred coffee tables scattered with newspapers and magazines, a
television set showing *It's a Wonderful Life*—which it wasn't, as far
as Maggie was concerned. Beyond them was a staircase that led,
presumably, to individual dorm rooms . . . and, from the sound of
it, there were parties going on. Maggie set down her bags, and her
fingers tingled as the blood started to come back. *I'm in,* she
thought, feeling triumph mixed with anxiety at what it would take
to pull off her next move.

The pack of girls tromped up the stairs, as graceful as a herd of
elephants in their heavy boots. Maggie followed them into the
bathroom ("So if I call him, what do I say?" the girl who hadn't gotten a phone call was asking plaintively). She waited until they'd
left, then she splashed warm water on her face and wiped off what
was left of her makeup. She tied her hair into a Rose-like ponytail
(the preferred Princeton hairdo, from what she'd seen so far), reapplied deodorant and a quick spritz of perfume, and rinsed her
mouth with water from the sink. For the next part of her plan to
work, she had to look her best, or as close to it as she could come
after what she'd been through.

Then she made her way back into the common room and scouted
it out. If she left the trash bags behind the couch, would anyone steal
them? No. Everyone here already had all of the clothes they could

want, Maggie figured, tucking herself into an armchair in the corner, where she wrapped her arms around her knees and watched, and waited.

She didn't have to wait long. A pack of guys—four, or maybe five of them, in sweatshirts and khakis, talking loud and smelling of beer—jostled their way past the guard at front, past Maggie, and headed toward the stairs. Maggie sidled behind them.

"Well, hey," said one of the guys, peering at her as if she was at the far end of a telescope. "Where are you going?"

Maggie smiled. "The party," she said, as if it were obvious. And he'd grinned at her blearily, one hand on the wall for balance, telling her that it must be his lucky day.

The party—and, of course, there was a party, because even though it was Ivy League, it was still a college, which meant that there would always be a party—was up four flights of stairs, in what Maggie took to be a suite. There was a living room with a couch and a stereo, two bedrooms with two bunk beds apiece, and, in between them, a tub full of ice and the inevitable keg resting atop it. "Get you a drink?" offered one of the stair guys—maybe the one who'd said it was his lucky day, maybe one of his friends. In the dim light, with all the noise and the press of bodies, she couldn't be sure, but she'd nodded just the same, leaning in close and letting her lips just brush his ear as she murmured, "Thanks."

By the time he wove his way back to her, sloshing half the beer on the floor as he progressed, she'd perched herself on a corner of the couch, long legs crossed.

"What's your name?" he asked. He was short and fine-boned with blond curls that would have been more fitting on one of those six-year-old beauty queens than on a college guy, and a watchful, foxy face.

She was ready for the question. "M," she said. She'd decided on the train not to be Maggie anymore. She had failed as a Maggie, had failed to find fame or fortune. From now on, she would just be M.

The guy squinted at her. "Em? Like Auntie Em?"

Maggie frowned. Did she have an Auntie Em? Did he? "It's just M," she said.

"Whatever," the guy said, giving her a shrug. "I haven't seen you around. What's your major?"

"Subterfuge," said Maggie.

The guy nodded as if he understood. Well, thought Maggie, maybe subterfuge was an actual major at this place. She'd have to check. "I'm poli sci," said the guy, and burped hugely. " 'Scuse me."

"No problem," said Maggie, as if she found intestinal gas the most fascinating and charming thing in the world. "What's your name?"

"Josh," said the guy.

"Josh," Maggie repeated, as if this, too, was fascinating.

"Wanna dance?" Josh asked. Maggie took a ladylike sip of her beer, and handed him the cup, which he drained obligingly. They stood, face to face, and danced . . . or, rather, Josh jerked back and forth as if his body was taking a low-grade electrical charge, while Maggie slowly ground her hips against him.

"Wow," he said appreciatively. He slid his hands around her waist and pressed her against the bulge in the front of his khakis. "You're a great dancer."

Maggie almost laughed. Twelve years of lessons, ballet and jazz and tap, and this was what passed for great dancing. Asshole. Instead, she tilted her head up to him, aiming her lips and warm breath toward his ear once more, letting her lips barely skim his neck. "Can we go somewhere quiet?" she asked. The words took a minute to register, but when they did, his eyes lit up.

"Sure!" he said. "I've got a single."

Bingo, thought Maggie. "One more beer first?" she asked, in a little-girl voice. He returned with two, and wound up drinking all of his own and almost all of Maggie's, too, before he wrapped his arm around her waist again, slung her backpack over his shoulder and led her back to the stairs and to the bliss he thought awaited back at his single in a dormitory called Blair. *Blair,* Maggie recited to herself, as she walked and he lurched. She'd have to start keeping a list—the names of places, the names of men. She'd have to be careful. She'd have to be smart. Smarter than Rose, even. Surviving a place like this when you were supposed to be here was one thing, but surviving here when you weren't would be a challenge worthy of all of her cunning, all of her skill, all of the intelligence that Mrs. Fried had promised her, long ago, that she had, no matter what the tests said.

Josh flung open the door like an emperor revealing the cedar walls and golden floors of his palace, and Maggie realized that this was where it could get tricky. She'd have to prepare herself for the possibility of actually having sex with this guy. Two guys in one night, she thought bleakly. Not a statistic she'd set out to achieve.

The dorm room was a tiny rectangle, littered with books and sneakers and tufts of unfolded laundry, smelling like sweat socks and old pizza. "Be it ever so humble," Josh said, giving her a sharp, appraising look, and flung himself onto the bed, shoving a chemistry book, a water bottle, a ten-pound barbell, and what Maggie thought was a fossilized half-eaten hoagie, to the floor. He spread his arms wide and gave her the cold smirk of a boy who's gotten every toy he's ever wanted and broken them just for spite. "Come to papa," he said.

Maggie instead gave him a slow, saucy smile and stood her ground at the foot of the bed. She traced one coy fingertip along her neckline. "Got anything to drink?" she whispered. Josh pointed. "On the desk," he said. Maggie found a flat brown bottle. Peach schnapps. Ugh. She took a swig, trying not to wince as the cloying taste of peaches filled her mouth, and tilted her head at Josh, daring him with her eyes. He was next to her in an instant, his lips cool and faintly repulsive against hers. She darted her tongue into his mouth to the beat of Cyndi Lauper's "Girls Just Want to Have Fun," which she played for herself in her head, and she let the heavy liquid slide from her mouth to his.

"When the work-ing day is done," she heard Cyndi wail in her head, as Josh gazed at her with a new drunken appreciation, clearly believing that he'd died and gone to heaven, or at least to the X-rated section of his internal video store.

She set one of her small hands in the center of his chest and pushed gently. He fell back on the bed like a tree. She took another gulp of schnapps and straddled him, grinding her crotch against him, smiling. *Courage,* she thought to herself. She leaned back on her haunches and pulled her top up over her head. Josh's eyes widened at the sight of her breasts in the faint glow from the lamps outside that filtered in through his window. She tried to put herself in his place, imagining what he saw—a lithe, half-naked girl, the spill of her hair over her shoulders, her white skin and slender midriff and hard brown nipples shining at him.

He reached for her. *Now,* she thought, and tilted the bottle of schnapps so that liquor flowed down her breasts, making a sticky trail toward the waistband of her jeans. "Oh, my God!" Josh groaned, "you are so hot!"

He was huffing and puffing, panting words she couldn't make out, as he snuffled at her skin and the schnapps, and his hands were fumbling uselessly at the waistband on her jeans. She'd counted on him being too drunk to operate a button fly, and it looked as though she'd guessed right.

"Wait," she whispered, flipping herself off of him and coming to lie by his side. "Let me take care of you."

"You're incredible," he said, and lay still with his eyes closed. Maggie leaned close and kissed his neck. He sighed. She planted a trail of tiny kisses from his earlobe to his collarbone, moving a little more slowly with each kiss. He sighed again, reaching down the front of his boxers. Maggie began trailing her tongue toward his chest. Slowly, she told herself, timing each lick and kiss to the beat of her heart. Slowly . . .

Each kiss was lighter than the one before it. Each one took longer to come. She held herself in check, and held her breath, tense beside him, until she heard his breathing slow to a regular rhythm, until she heard the first clotted rattle of a snore. She raised her head an inch and peeked at his face to make sure. His eyes were closed, his mouth was open, a bubble of spit expanded and retracted between his lips. Josh was asleep.

Asleep or passed out. She wasn't sure which, and it didn't matter. Her plan had worked so far. She eased one hand down into his pocket and came up with a plastic card. His student ID. Perfect. Then she crept out of his bed, located her tank top, and pulled it back on as Josh snored. She found a towel on the floor—it smelled sour and felt crusty, but no use looking for clean laundry in here, she thought, grabbing a plastic bucket that contained soap and shampoo.

His wallet was on the desk. She looked at it, considering, then picked it up and flipped it open. There were a half-dozen credit cards, a decent-sized wad of cash. She'd look through it later, she decided, and shoved the whole thing in her pocket before turning to the closet. Did she dare? She inched across the floor, and eased the door open by millimeters. Josh had not one but two leather jackets, plus all manner of shirts, sweaters, and khaki pants, sneakers and hiking boots, jeans and polo shirts, windbreakers, winter coats, and even a tuxedo wrapped in dry-cleaner's plastic. Maggie took two of the sweaters, and then looked in the corner. Bonus! There was a goosedown sleeping bag tucked neatly into a stuff sack, and an electric camping lantern next to it. He'd never miss them, and if he did, she was sure that whoever'd bought him all of his other stuff would just send a check for more.

Josh groaned thickly and rolled over, flinging one arm across the pillow where Maggie's head had been. Maggie felt her heart stop. She forced herself to count to a hundred before moving again, then gathered her spoils, cramming the sleeping bag and lantern into her backpack. She eased the door open, and headed into the hallway. It was four in the morning. Maggie could still hear stereos blaring, and the drunken whoops and shouts of people coming back from parties.

The bathrooms were at the end of the hall, and they had locks that required codes but, luckily, the ladies' room door was propped open by the prone body of a passed-out coed who'd succumbed half in and half out of one of the stalls. Maggie stepped over her legs and stripped, hanging her clothes neatly on one of the hooks, hanging the towel on top of them.

She stepped under the warm water and closed her eyes. Okay, she thought to herself. Okay. Next would come food and a place to regroup. She was thinking of the library, thinking how at every college she'd ever attended or visited the security guards never looked too closely at identification cards. If you looked like you belonged, they just waved you in. So first she'd get her clothes from behind the couch in the first dorm, and then she'd use his ID to sneak into a dining hall for some food, and then . . . .

Maggie looked down and saw a white plastic hair clip sitting in the soap dish. . . . the same kind of ugly thing that her sister used to shove her hair back off her face. *Rose,* she thought, and was suddenly caught in such a drowning wave of regret that her breath caught in her throat. *Rose,* she thought, *I'm sorry.* And in that instant, naked and alone, Maggie felt as wretched as she ever had in her life.

TWENTY FIVE

Maybe this is what it feels like to go crazy, Rose thought, and rolled over and gave herself to sleep again.

In her dream, she was lost in a cave, and the cave kept getting smaller and smaller, the ceiling pressing lower and lower until she could feel the stalactites—or possibly the stalagmites, Rose had always gotten them confused—pushing wet against her face.

She woke up. The dog that Maggie had left behind was perched on a pillow beside her, licking her cheeks.

"Ugh," said Rose, burying her face in a pillow and rolling away. For a minute she didn't remember anything. Then it all came crashing back—Jim and Maggie. In bed. Together. "Oh, God," she groaned. The dog put its paw on top of her forehead, as if it were taking her temperature, and gave an inquisitive-sounding whine.

"Go away," Rose said. Instead, the dog turned in three circles on top of the pillow, curled itself into a graham-cracker-colored bundle and started to snore. Rose closed her eyes and followed the dog back into sleep.

When she woke up again, it was after eleven o'clock in the morning. She staggered to her feet and almost slipped in the warm, wet puddle outside of the bathroom. She stared at her wet foot dumbly, then back at the dog, still perched on the bed.

"Did you do this?" she asked. The dog just stared. Rose sighed, then dug out the Pine-Sol and a roll of paper towels and dealt with the mess. She couldn't blame the dog, she supposed . . . the poor thing hadn't been walked since yesterday.

She plodded to the kitchen, put on a pot of coffee, poured herself a bowl of bran flakes, and moved her spoon through them, back and forth. She didn't want bran flakes, she realized. She didn't want anything. She couldn't imagine ever feeling hungry again.

She stared at the telephone. What day was it? Saturday. Which gave her the weekend to get herself together. Or maybe she should just go ahead and call in sick right now, leave someone a message saying she wouldn't be in this week. But who? If Maggie were here, she'd know what to say. Maggie was the queen of white lies, half-truths, and mental-health days, which she felt completely justified in taking. Maggie.

"Oh, God," Rose groaned again. Maggie was back at her father's house, or lurking in the bushes or on a bench outside, certain that the morning would make Rose change her mind. Well, fat chance of that, she thought fiercely, giving up on breakfast and setting her bowl next to the sink.

The dog, evidently, did not share her black mood or lack of appetite. It had materialized by her feet and was staring at her cereal bowl with wet and avid eyes. Rose realized she had no idea what Maggie had fed the thing. She hadn't noticed any dog food around. Not that she'd been noticing much of anything. Except Jim. Or lack thereof. Tentatively, she lowered her cereal bowl to the floor. The dog sniffed it, lowered her nose, took a small lick of the milk, then snorted once, dismissively, and stared up at Rose.

"No good?" asked Rose. She rummaged through her cabinets. Pea soup. Probably not. Black beans . . . she didn't think so. Tuna fish! Or was that for cats? She decided to give it a go, mixing it with mayonnaise and setting it in front of the dog, along with a cup of water. The dog wolfed it down, making little grunts of happiness and nosing the bowl across the entire length of the kitchen floor, attempting to remove every last morsel of mayonnaise and flake of fish.

"Okay," said Rose. It was now the unimaginable hour of one in the afternoon. Her apartment was spotless, thanks to last night's cleaning. She wandered into the bathroom and stared at herself for a long moment. She was an ordinary girl, with ordinary hair and ordinary brown eyes. She had lips and cheeks and eyebrows, and there was nothing remarkable about any of them.

"What's wrong with me?" she asked the face in the mirror. The dog sat at the bathroom door, staring. Rose brushed her teeth, washed her face, made the bed, moving through the room on heavy, leaden legs. Go out? Stay in? Go back to sleep?

The dog was scratching at the front door.

"Hey, stop that!" She looked around, wondering whether Maggie had left a leash, then she pulled out a scarf she'd bought once during a single misguided afternoon when she'd thought she might actually become a scarf-wearing sort of person—the kind of woman who accessorized, instead of the kind of woman whose scarves inevitably wound up either slammed in the car door or trailing in her soup.

She knelt down and threaded the scarf through the dog's collar. The dog looked unhappy and put-upon, as if it—she?—realized that the scarf was polyester, not real silk. "A thousand pardons," Rose said sarcastically, finding her keys and sunglasses and mittens and a twenty-dollar bill to tuck into her pocket so that she could buy pet food. Then she headed to the elevator, scooped the dog up under her coat, slid past the doorman and headed out the door. There was, if she remembered right, a strip of grass at the corner of her street. The dog could do its business there, and then she'd cross the street to the Wawa, tie the dog to a parking meter the way she'd seen other people do, and buy dog food, and a doughnut, Rose decided. A jelly doughnut. Possibly two jelly doughnuts, and coffee with cream and three packets of sugar. She'd gain weight . . . but that didn't matter. Who'd be seeing her naked now? Who'd care? She could gain weight; she could let her leg hair grow until it was long enough for French braids; she could wear every single frayed, dingy, snapped-elastic pair of panties she had. None of it mattered anymore.

The dog shot Rose a grateful look as soon as they'd made it out of her building, trotted to the gutter, and squatted there, peeing for what felt like a very long time.

"Sorry about making you wait," Rose said. The dog snorted. Rose wasn't sure what that was supposed to mean. The dog certainly snorted a lot. Maybe it was just a . . . a breed thing. Maybe this was a particularly snorty breed of dog. Rose had no idea. After Honey Bun, their dog for a day, she and Maggie had never had so much as a goldfish. Too much extra responsibility for their father, who clearly found the two girls burden enough. And then after she and Maggie had left the house, Sydelle purchased her designer dog, a dog with a pedigree, and papers to prove it. "I'm allergic," her father had said. "Don't be silly," Sydelle had replied. And that was the end of that. Chanel the idiot golden retriever stayed. Her father suffered.

"What a cute little pug!" said a dark-haired woman, kneeling to let the dog sniff her hand. Pug, Rose said to herself. Okay, so the dog was a pug. That was a start.

"Come," Rose said, wrapping the scarf around her hand, and the dog walked sedately by her left heel as they made their way to the convenience store. "Stay," said Rose, and tied her scarf around a meter. The dog—the pug—looked up at her like a dinner guest waiting for the soup course. "I'll be back," said Rose. She went inside and spent ten minutes staring at the bewildering array of pet food before purchasing a bag of kibble for small adult dogs. She also bought a plastic bowl to pour the food into, two jelly doughnuts, coffee, two pints of ice cream, and a bag of cheese curls she'd grabbed from a display promising that they'd be the most CheeseRageous thing she'd ever eaten. The cashier raised his eyebrows at her haul. Rose came in here a lot, but all she ever purchased were newspapers, black coffee, and the occasional can of Slim-Fast.

"I'm on vacation," she explained, wondering why she felt the need to explain anything to a guy who worked the cash register at the Wawa. But he gave her a nice smile, and snuck a square of Bazooka gum into her bag, along with her receipt.

"Enjoy," he said. Rose returned his smile weakly, and went outside, where the dog was still sitting, tethered to its parking meter.

"What's your name?" Rose wondered out loud.

The dog just stared.

"I'm Rose," said Rose. "I'm a lawyer." The dog walked beside her. There was something in the set of her head, the way her ears were cocked, that suggested she might actually be listening. "I'm thirty years old. I graduated summa cum laude from Princeton, then I went to the University of Pennsylvania law school, where I was a *Law Review* editor, and . . ."

Why was she giving the dog her résumé? This was silly. The dog wasn't going to hire her. Probably neither was anyone else. Word would get out about her and Jim. It had probably started already, Rose realized bleakly. It was probably going on while she was at the firm and she was too dumb and doped up with love to see it.

"I was having an affair," said Rose, as she and the dog paused for a red light. The teenage girl with the gold hoop through her lip standing next to her on the sidewalk stared at Rose curiously, then started walking faster. "There was this guy." She paused. "Well, isn't there always. He was kind of my boss, actually, and he turned out to be . . ." She swallowed hard. "Bad. Very, very bad."

The dog gave a single sharp bark—of despair? Affirmation? Rose wasn't sure. She wanted to call Amy, but she didn't think she could cope with the sting of having to tell her best friend that she'd been right, that Jim had been as big a jerk as Amy had imagined . . . and that Maggie, her sister, who she'd opened her house to, her sister who she'd tried to help, had been worse still. The light turned green. The dog barked again, and tugged gently against the scarf. "It's over," said Rose—just to say something, just to end the story somehow, even if she was just talking to a dog, and the dog wasn't listening. "Over," she repeated, and crossed the street. The dog looked at her, then looked back down.

"So the girl who was taking care of you. That was Maggie. My sister," she continued, as they walked closer to her apartment building. "We'll have to feed you, and get you a leash, and figure out where you came from. Have to take you back." She stopped at a corner and considered the dog again—small, coffee-colored, harmless, she supposed. The dog looked up at her, then gave a brisk and, Rose thought, dismissive snort. "Fine," she said, "don't be grateful." She crossed the street and walked herself home.

TWENTY-SIX

Who ever told the truth about a marriage? Certainly Ella never had. She and her friends would talk about their husbands like they were children, or pets—some strange species responsible for bad smells and strange noises and messes they'd have to clean up. They turned their husbands into punch lines. They spoke of them in shorthand, a code of rolled eyes and pronouns. He. Him. *He doesn't eat green vegetables, so how am I supposed to make the kids do it? I'd love to go on that cruise, but of course I'll have to ask him.*

Ella used to contribute from her own small stock of anecdotes, the stories that would make Ira appear as simple as a child's cartoon drawn in broad lines. She'd have the ladies howling around the bridge table with stories of how he wouldn't go on a trip longer than twenty miles without a mayonnaise jar in case he didn't like the looks of the gas station rest rooms, or the eighty dollars he'd spent on a do-it-yourself yogurt-making kit. Not ice cream, not beer, she'd say, as the ladies laughed so hard they had to wipe tears from their cheeks, not something you'd actually want, but yogurt. Ira the yogurt king.

Those were the stories she told, but she never told the truth about her marriage. Never told the ladies how it felt to live with someone who'd become more like a roommate than a husband, like someone who'd been assigned to share your living quarters for the duration of a trip. Never told them about the bruising politeness, the way Ira would thank her when she poured his coffee, or the way he'd take her arm when they were out in public, at weddings or his company's Christmas party, how he'd hold her arm and guide her from the car out to the sidewalk, as if she were made of glass. As if she were a stranger. And she'd certainly never mentioned the way they'd quietly moved into separate beds after Caroline started school, and how Ira had relocated to the guest room the week their daughter had gone off to college. Things like that were never spoken of, and Ella wouldn't have even known how to begin the conversation.

The sound of banging startled her from her reverie. Mrs. Lefkowitz was pounding at the door. "Ass Master? You in there?" Ella hurried to let her in, hoping that none of her neighbors had overheard. Mrs. Lefkowitz shuffled into Ella's kitchen, reaching into her oversized pink crocheted purse and setting a glass bottle on the countertop.

"Pickles," she announced. Ella stifled a smile and emptied the jar of Claussen's finest into a serving dish, as her guest peered into her living room and sniffed. "He's not here yet?"

"Not yet," Ella called, peering into the oven. She'd never figured out Florida cuisine, if there was such a thing, and on the infrequent occasions when she had to cook for someone other than herself, she found herself relying on the same handful of company meals she'd cooked during her years of marriage. Tonight she'd be serving a brisket, potato pancakes, a tsimmes of carrots and prunes, with challah from the bakery, and Mrs. Lefkowitz's pickles, and two kinds of cake and a pie. Too much food, she thought, too much for just the three of them, and too heavy for these hot Florida nights, but when she'd been running to the grocery store or bustling around in her too-small kitchen, the work had kept her mind off how nervous she was.

"I'd like to meet your friends," Lewis had said, and how could Ella tell him that she didn't really have friends here? He'd think that she was crazy, or that there was something wrong with her.

And Mrs. Lefkowitz had been, if anything, even more insistent. "A gentleman caller!" she'd cackled, after Ella had made the mistake of letting Lewis drop her off for Meals on Wheels duty, and she'd followed Ella around the kitchen, thumping the floors with her cane. "Is he handsome? Good income? A widower, or divorced? Toupee? Pacemaker? Does he drive? Does he drive at night?"

"Enough!" Ella had said, laughing, with her hands in the air in the universal gesture of surrender.

"Then it's settled," said Mrs. Lefkowitz, with a crooked grin that made her look like a lopsided Cheshire cat.

"What's settled?" Ella asked.

"You'll have me over for dinner. It'll be good for me to get out," Mrs. Lefkowitz said airily. "My doctor says so." She picked up what she'd told Ella was a PalmPilot from the coffee table. "Should we say five o'clock?"

That had been three days ago. Ella glanced at her watch. It was five after five. "Late!" Mrs. Lefkowitz observed helpfully from the living room couch. Lewis knocked on the door.

"Hello, ladies," he said. He had an armful of tulips, a bottle of wine, and something in a square cardboard box tucked underneath his arm. "Smells delicious!"

"I made too much," Ella said weakly.

"So you'll have leftovers," he said, and held out his hands to Mrs. Lefkowitz, who, Ella saw, had applied a fresh streak of geranium pink lipstick.

"Hello, hello!" she cooed, looking him over as he helped her to her feet.

"You must be Mrs. Lefkowitz," he said. In the kitchen, Ella held her breath, hoping that she'd finally learn Mrs. Lefkowitz's first name. Instead, Mrs. Lefkowitz gave a coquettish giggle and allowed Lewis to walk her to the table.

After dinner and dessert and coffee in the living room, Mrs. Lefkowitz gave a contented sigh and a small burp. "My trolley's coming," she announced, and limped out into the night. Lewis and Ella exchanged a smile.

"I brought you something," Lewis said.

"Oh, you shouldn't have," Ella said reflexively, as Lewis retrieved his cardboard box. She felt her heart contract into an icy ball as she saw what he'd brought. A photo album.

"I was telling you about my family the other night, so I thought maybe you'd want to see some pictures," Lewis said, settling himself on her couch as if this wasn't unusual or terrifying at all. As if anyone could do this—open a photo album, look the past right in the face. Ella's face felt frozen, but she made herself smile, and sit next to him.

Lewis flipped his album open. There were pictures of his parents, first, standing stiffly in their old-fashioned clothes, and Lewis and his brothers. And here was Sharla, wearing orange or bright pink or turquoise (and, sometimes, all three together), and their son. There were shots of Lewis and Sharla's house in Utica, a ranch with pots of roses beside the front door. "That was John's high-school graduation, or was it college? . . . there we are at the Grand Canyon, which you probably could recognize without me. . . . That was my retirement dinner." Wedding pictures, bar mitzvah parties, the beach, the mountains; the babies. Ella endured them all, smiling and nodding and saying the right things until finally, blessedly, Lewis closed the book.

"How about you?"

"How about me what?" she asked.

"Could I see pictures of you?"

She shook her head. "I don't have many," she told him. And it was the truth. When she and Ira had sold their house in Michigan and moved down here, they'd put all kinds of things into storage—furniture and winter coats, boxes and boxes of books. And all of their pictures. It hurt too much to see them. But maybe . . .

"Wait here," Ella said. She went to the closet in the back bedroom and reached past the boxes of clothes and extra towels, and felt for an old purse that contained a plain white envelope, with a handful of snapshots inside. She came back to the couch and showed Lewis the first in the stack, a shot of her and Ira, standing in the spray of Niagara Falls on their honeymoon.

Lewis studied the photograph carefully, tilting it from side to side beneath the lamp on the side table.

"You look worried," he finally said.

"Maybe I was," said Ella, shuffling through the snapshots. There was Ira, posing beside a "Sold" sign in front of their house in Michigan, Ira behind the wheel of their first new car. And finally, at the bottom of the stack, was a shot of Ella and Caroline.

"Here," she said, and passed Lewis the picture. Their next-door neighbor had taken it the day they'd come home from the hospital. Ella was in the background, with her small suitcase, and Ira was by the door, with Caroline, three days old, wrapped in a pink blanket, peering out suspiciously from his arms. "My daughter," she said, steeling herself for what was coming next. "Caroline."

"She was a beautiful baby," said Lewis.

"She had black hair. A head full of black hair," Ella remembered. "And she cried for what felt like a year, nonstop."

She flipped to the last two pictures. Caroline and her father, posing in a rowboat, wearing matching caps and fisherman's vests. And finally, Caroline on her wedding day, with Ella standing above her, arranging the folds of her veil.

"What a beautiful girl," said Lewis. Ella said nothing. There was silence. "I didn't want to talk about Sharla for months," Lewis said. "So I'll understand if you don't. But sometimes it's nice just to talk. To remember the good times."

Had there been good times with Caroline? It felt as if all she could remember was the heartache and endless nights of worry, waiting wide-eyed in the dark listening for the door (or the window, if Caroline had been grounded) to creak open. She remembered sitting on the gold velvet love seat in the living room, a tiny coffin too narrow to lie down in, waiting for her daughter to come home.

"She was," Ella began. "She was so beautiful. Tall, with brown hair, lovely skin, and she was . . . lively. Funny." *Crazy,* her mind whispered. "Mentally ill," she said instead. "She was manic-depressive. Bipolar, they call it now. We found out when she was in high school. She'd been having . . . episodes." Ella shut her eyes, remembering how Caroline had barricaded herself in her bedroom for three days, refusing to eat, screaming through the door that there were ants in her hair and she could feel them when she slept.

Lewis made a sympathetic noise. Ella kept talking, the words spilling out over each other like she'd kept them dammed up too long.

"We saw doctors. All kinds of doctors. And they gave her medicine, and it made her better in some ways, but it slowed her down, too. It was hard for her to think, she said." Ella could remember Caroline on lithium, how her face had bloated into a pale circle, and how her hands had swollen like cartoon mittens, how she'd yawned all day long. "She'd take it sometimes, and stop taking it, and tell us she was taking it. She went to college, and did all right for a while, and then . . ." Ella drew a shuddering breath. "She got married, and seemed to be doing well. She had two daughters. And she died when she was twenty-nine."

Lewis's voice was gentle. "What happened?"

"Car accident," said Ella. Which was the truth. Or a truth. Caroline was in a car. The car had crashed. She had died. But what had happened before that was also the truth, which was that Ella hadn't stepped in when she should have. She had given in to her daughter's repeated pleas to be left alone, to live her life, feeling resignation and sadness and also a great, shameful relief that she couldn't ever talk about—not to Ira, not to anyone. She'd called Caroline every week, but she'd visited only twice a year, for weekends. In the place of facts, she'd created fiction—the Daughter, to go along with the Husband. She'd display her snapshots like a winning poker hand—Caroline and her husband, Caroline and Rose, Caroline and Maggie. Her lady friends would ooh and aah, and all along, Ella knew the truth—the pictures were pretty, but the reality of Caroline's life was something else. It was jagged rocks hiding beneath the pretty curls of the waves, it was black ice on the pavement.

"Car accident," she said again, as if Lewis had questioned her, because "car accident" was enough of the truth, and never mind the letter that had come in the mail the day after the funeral, the letter sent from Hartford the day Caroline had died, the letter that was two lines long, written on a wide-ruled page ripped out of a schoolgirl's notebook in faint, wavering letters. "I Can't Anymore. Take Care of my Girls."

"And the granddaughters?" he asked gently.

Ella pressed her hands against her eyes. "I don't know them," she said.

Lewis's hand moved in warm circles on her back. "We don't have to talk about it anymore," he said. Oh, but he didn't know, and she couldn't explain it. How could he ever understand Caroline's dying wish, and how over the years avoidance became easier and easier. Caroline said, "Leave me alone," so she'd left her alone, and Michael Feller had said, "We're better off without you," and Ella had let him push her away, feeling sadness mixed with that secret, shameful relief. And now she'd never know her own granddaughters. And it was exactly what she deserved.

TWENTY-SEVEN

Rose woke up on Monday morning, then on Tuesday, and on Wednesday and Thursday, too, thinking that this would be the day— the day she took a shower, brushed her teeth, snuck the dog out the front door for her walk, came back home, then donned her suit and panty hose, pulled her briefcase out of the hall closet, and went to work like the rest of the world.

Every morning she'd wake up, full of good intentions and high energy. She'd lecture herself in the shower about how the Chinese symbol for crisis was the same as the one for opportunity. She'd walk the dog to Rittenhouse Square, and she'd look to the south, to where the gleaming glass face of the high-rise that housed Dommel, Lewis, and Fenick stood like a fifty-two story reproach, and her heart would sink. Really, everything would sink—all of her internal organs, kidney and liver and whatever else was down there, all of it joining in a universal cringe, all of it thinking, "No" and "Can't" and "Not today."

So she'd go home and call Lisa, her secretary, and explain that she was still sick. "I think it's the flu," she'd croaked on Monday.

"No prob," Lisa had said—Lisa, who never wasted an entire word on Rose when a portion of a word would do. But by the end of the week Lisa wasn't sounding quite so tolerant, and had actually granted Rose a full sentence. "You'll be back Monday, right?"

"Right," Rose had said, trying to sound crisp and competent and sure of herself. "Certainly," she said. "Of course." Then she'd plopped down on the couch and watched *A Wedding Story*. In her week away from work, Rose had become completely addicted to the show. *A Wedding Story* lasted half an hour and was as carefully structured as a sonnet, or a geometry proof. First segment: Meet the Bride and Groom (yesterday the bride had been Fern, a clerk at a drugstore, and the groom had been Dave, a heavily bearded long-distance trucker twenty years her senior). Second segment: How They Met ("I walked in for Pepto-Bismol," Dave had rumbled, "and there she was, behind the counter. Prettiest girl I'd ever seen.") Part Three: Wedding Plans (Fern and Dave were getting hitched at the Radisson. Dinner and dancing to follow, with Dave's two sons from two previous marriages serving as best men.) Final segment: The Big Day. (Fern walked down the aisle, a vision in off-white. Dave had cried. Rose had, too).

It had been like that for four days running. She'd eat doughnuts and cry at every bride, every groom, every dress, every mother and mother-in-law, every first kiss and first dance; at dumpy social workers from Alabama, schoolteachers from New Jersey, tech-support assistants from San Jose with actual, visible mustaches, girls with bad skin and bad perms and bad grammar. Everyone else in the world can do this, she'd think, as the dog wedged herself onto her lap and licked at her tears. Everyone but me.

On Saturday morning the telephone started ringing. Rose ignored it, hitching the dog to the leash she'd finally purchased and hurrying out the door before noticing she was still in her slippers. Her fuzzy bunny slippers. Oh, well. A homeless guy eyed her appreciatively. "You looking good, baby!" he yelled. Well, that was encouraging, Rose thought. "You heavy-set, but you still looking good!" Okay, she amended, maybe not so encouraging. She spent twenty minutes letting the dog sniff hedges, hydrants, the bases of parking meters and other dogs' butts, and when she came home, the phone was still ringing, as if it hadn't ever stopped. The phone rang while she stood like a lump of lead in the shower, letting the water thunder down on her head, trying to muster the energy to wash her hair. At five o'clock, Rose finally yanked it to her ear.

"What?" she said.

"Where the hell have you been?" Amy demanded. "I left you fourteen voice-mail messages at work; I sent you six e-mails; I stopped by the other night . . ." Her voice trailed off.

Rose vaguely remembered knocking, and how she'd pulled her pillow over her head until it stopped.

"Your secretary says you're sick, and my friend Karen saw you wandering around Rittenhouse Square in your pajamas and slippers."

"I was not wandering. And I wasn't wearing pajamas," Rose said haughtily, ignoring the matter of the slippers for the time being. "They were sweatpants."

"Whatever," said Amy. "What's going on? Are you sick?"

Rose glanced longingly at the television set, then forced herself to look away. "I need to talk to you," she finally said.

"Meet me at La Cigale in fifteen minutes," said Amy. "No, half an hour. You'll need to find some regular clothes. I don't think you'd be welcome in your jammies."

"They weren't pajamas!" Rose repeated, but Amy had hung up. She set the phone back on the counter and set off to find some shoes.

"Okay," said Amy, who'd already ordered coffee and a pair of scones as big as baseball mitts. "What'd he do?"

"Huh?" Rose asked.

"Jim," Amy said impatiently. "I know this is all that son of a bitch's fault. Tell me what he did, and we'll figure out what to do to repay him."

Rose smiled a tiny smile. Amy had honed her philosophy of failed relationships, and how to behave in their wake, over years of bad boyfriends. Step one: Mourn for a month (two weeks if the relationship hadn't involved sex). Step two: If you'd been dumped or cheated on, permit yourself one scandalous act of revenge (her last boyfriend, a hard-core vegan, had doubtlessly been shocked and horrified to find himself enrolled in the Organ Meat of the Month Club). Step three: Get over it. No regrets, no moping, no late-night drive-bys or dialing while drunk. Just on to the next adventure.

"So what did he do?"

"He cheated on me," Rose said.

Amy shook her head. "I knew it." She narrowed her eyes. "Now, how are we going to make him pay? Professional humiliation? Anonymous letter to the law firm? Something disgusting left in his car?"

"Like what?" Rose asked.

"Anchovy paste," Amy said. "A few squirts inside the glove compartment, and his Lexus will never be the same."

"Well, it wasn't just him," said Rose.

"What do you mean?"

"It was Maggie," said Rose.

Amy spat out a chunk of her scone. "What?"

"Maggie," Rose repeated. "I walked in on them." She'd said it so many times in her head, and to the little dog, that when she finally gave voice to the story, she felt as if she were reciting a poem she'd memorized years ago. "I walked in and they were in bed. And she had my new boots on."

"The Via Spigas?" Amy was sounding more horrified by the minute. "Oh, Rose. I am so sorry."

But not surprised, thought Rose.

"Oh, God," said Amy, looking stricken. "That little bitch."

Rose nodded.

"How could she?"

Rose shrugged.

"After you gave her a place to live, and probably money, and tried to help her . . ." Amy rolled her eyes toward the ceiling. "What are we going to do?"

"Never see her again," Rose said.

"Yeah," said Amy, "I imagine this might make Thanksgivings pretty awkward. So where is Little Miss Hot Pants?"

"I don't know," Rose said dully. "With my father and Sydelle, I guess."

"Well, then she's already suffering," said Amy. "Now, how about you?"

"Oh, I'm suffering plenty," Rose said, and sighed, and poked at her scone.

"What can I do?" Amy asked.

Rose shrugged. "Nothing to give it but time, I guess," she said.

"And retail therapy," said Amy, pulling Rose to her feet. "The mall beckons. It'll cheer you up. Come along."

All afternoon, Amy and Rose walked through the King of Prussia Mall. Rose eventually managed to fill three shopping bags with things she didn't need, with anything that caught her eye and gave her even a second's hope that her life—that she herself—could be repaired. She bought exfoliating scrubs and moisturizing creams. She bought candles scented with lavender and a beef-basted rawhide bone and a two-hundred-dollar beaded evening bag. She bought lipsticks and lip glosses and lip liners, three pairs of shoes, and a red cashmere ankle-length skirt that she couldn't imagine ever actually wearing. Finally, she headed to the bookstore.

"Self-help?" Amy asked. *"Better Sex through Yoga? How to Snare Mr. Fabulous in Ten Sneaky Steps?"* Rose laughed a little, shook her head, and located Current Fiction. Ten minutes later she'd amassed a stack of ten glossy paperbacks about women who found love, lost love, and then found it again.

"Just remember, I've still got that anchovy paste, in case you change your mind," Amy said as they walked through the parking lot. "And if you want an impartial third party to give Miss Maggie May a talking-to."

"You aren't impartial," said Rose.

"Well, no," said Amy. "But I play impartial on TV." She looked at her watch. "Do you want me to come home with you? Or do you want to come with me? I'm going to my mom's house for dinner . . ."

Rose shook her head. "I'm okay," she said, thinking she could do without a night at Amy's mom's house—the inevitable pasta supper, followed by a few hours indulging Amy's mom's passion for the posable dolls and jewelry from QVC.

"Call me," said Amy. "I'm serious."

Rose said she would. As her first step toward normal living, she presented the pug with the rawhide bone and forced herself to listen to all forty-three of her voice-mail messages. Sixteen from Amy, a dozen from work, three from her father, a handful from telemarketers, a half-dozen from bill collectors, and a single inexplicable call from a manager at the International House of Pancakes telling Rose to come in for an interview whenever she liked. She left her father a message saying she was alive and well, deleted the rest, and slept for eighteen hours straight. On Sunday morning—the day she had decided would be her absolute final day of moping—she called Amy to let her know that she was still alive, if not well. She put on lipstick and the red cashmere skirt, tucked one of the books into her pocket, leashed the little dog, and walked to her customary bench in the park. It was time for a decision.

"Pro," she whispered to herself. "I'm a lawyer, and it's a good job. Con," she said, as the dog snuffled at her feet. "It makes me sick to even think of going there."

She opened her book, pulled a pen out of her pocket, and started writing next to the breathless quotes that decorated the first few pages of all the books she'd purchased ("A witty, sexy romp!"). "Pro," she wrote on the book's inside cover, "if I go to work I'll have money. Con . . ." The little dog at her feet gave a short bark. Rose looked at her side and saw that a second dog, a strange, spotted, quivery-looking thing the size of a cat, had hopped on the bench and was now sitting beside her, regarding her with fearless black eyes.

"Hello," she said, and allowed the dog to sniff her mitten.

"Who are you?" She squinted at the tag around the dog's neck and wondered what kind of name Nifkin was. Foreign, probably. "Go home," she urged the spotted dog, whose whiskers trembled with each breath. "Go find your people." The dog merely stared at Rose and showed no signs of moving. Rose decided to ignore it.

"Con," she continued. She closed her eyes again and felt a wave of sickness wash over her as she imagined walking into the lobby, getting onto the elevator, and stepping onto the floor and walking the hallways where she'd fallen in love with Jim and imagined that he was in love with her.

"Con," she repeated, and opened her eyes. Nifkin was still sitting next to her on the bench, and now there was a little girl in a red coat standing in front of her. She had on red mittens and red rubber boots, and hair the color of maple syrup pulled into a thin carrot-shaped ponytail. Jesus, Rose thought, what am I? Snow friggin' White?

"Dog!" the girl announced, and waved one mittened fist.

"That's right," said Rose, as the pug gave a small, excited snort.

The girl bent down and stroked the pug's head. The pug wriggled in pleasure. Meanwhile, quivery little Nifkin had hopped off the bench and was sitting next to the little girl, so both of them were staring up at Rose. "I'm Joy," the little girl announced.

"Hi!" said Rose in a loud, cheerful voice. "This is . . ." Oh, dear. She still had no idea what the dog's name was. "This is the dog I walk!"

The little girl nodded as if this made perfect sense, pulled on Nifkin's leash, and toddled across the park. Meanwhile, a white-haired woman in sunglasses was looking at them. "Petunia?" she called. "Is that Petunia?"

Petunia, Rose thought. The pug looked back at her. Rose thought she could detect a hint of embarrassment on her squashed features.

"Hi, Petunia!" the woman said, as Petunia gave a regal snort.

"So is Shirley back from Europe already?" the woman asked.

"Um," said Rose weakly. She hadn't counted on running into any of the dog's intimates.

"I thought she was boarding her until next month," the woman continued.

Rose saw a lifeline, and seized it with all her might.

"That's right," she said. "This is actually a new service . . . a daily walk. So the dogs can, you know, get some fresh air, visit their neighborhoods, see their friends . . ."

"What a great idea!" said the woman, as two other dogs—a large chocolate-colored dog with a broad, snaky tail, and a prancing black poodle with its red tongue lolling—came over to them. "So you work for the kennel?"

"Actually, I'm . . . freelance," said Rose. She remembered reading a fairy tale where a princess was cursed, and every time she opened her mouth, frogs and toads would leap out. Rose decided that she had been similarly afflicted—when she opened her mouth, out came not warty amphibians, but lies. "I walk dogs for the kennel, but I also do, you know, house calls for individual pets . . ."

"Do you have a card?" asked an old guy at the end of the poodle's leash.

Rose made a show of groping in her pockets and coming up empty-handed. "I'm sorry," she said. "I seem to have left them at home . . ."

The guy pulled a pen and paper out of his pocket, and Rose scribbled her home telephone number, then added the words *Rose Feller, Dog Care* beneath them. And soon she was standing at the center of a mad Maypole of leashes and fur and fast-talking owners, all, it seemed, in search of responsible pet care.

Yes, Rose told them, she'd watch cats, too. No, she said, she didn't do obedience training, but she'd be more than happy to escort dogs to classes.

"Pet sitter!" called a woman in a droopy green sweater. Her dog was as low to the ground as Petunia, but perhaps twice her size, with a deeply wrinkled face and drool dripping from his ponderous jowls. "Memorial Day weekend?" she said.

"I'll be here," Rose said. Petunia and the wrinkly dog gave each other grave and solemn sniffs, as if they were members of the same club and giving each other the secret handshake.

"Are you licensed?" the woman asked, in the quick staccato rhythms of a former drill sergeant. "Licensed? Bonded? Insurance?"

"Um . . ." said Rose. The crowd held its breath. "Just finishing the paperwork. By next week I'll be good to go," she concluded, making a mental note to figure out what it would take to get licensed and insured as a pet walker.

"And your rates?"

Rates, thought Rose. "Um . . . ten dollars per walk, twenty-five dollars for a full day's care." From the look on the pet owners' faces, Rose determined that she'd offered them a bargain. "It's my new customer special," she added. "And of course, if you'd rather your dog stayed in the kennel, I can pick them up there and take them for a walk in the park every day. Kind of the best of both worlds. Just give me a call!" She gave a jaunty wave and hurried out of the park. "Who's Shirley?" she asked the pug, who made no reply. "Is your name really Petunia?" she inquired. The pug continued to ignore her as Rose made her way toward the Elegant Paw. The bells jangled as she pushed the door open, and the woman behind the desk leapt to her feet.

"Petunia!" she cried, stubbing out her cigarette. Petunia barked once and began wagging not just her tail but her entire backside. "Oh, thank God! We've been going crazy!"

"Hi," said Rose, as the woman rushed around the counter, knelt on the floor, and rubbed Petunia from head to tail.

"Where'd you find her?" asked the woman. "God, we've been frantic! Her owner isn't due back for three weeks, but we didn't want to call her . . . I mean, can you imagine? You drop your dog off at the kennel and fly to Europe, and you get a call saying that the dog's been lost?" The woman straightened up, smoothing her denim overalls, and stared at Rose through her tangle of frizzy gray curls. "So where'd you find her?" she repeated.

"In the park," said Rose, who decided that she'd do all of her lying for the month—for the year, even—in this single day. "She didn't look lost or anything, but I know her . . . I mean, I don't know her, but I've seen her in the park before, and I figured that maybe you knew her, too . . ."

"Thank God," the woman said again, and scooped Petunia into her arms. "We were really worried. Pugs are very delicate, you know . . . they get all kinds of colds, respiratory infections, anything going around . . . I don't know who's been taking care of her for the last few weeks, but it looks like they've done a good job." She turned her eyes back to Rose. "There's a reward, of course . . ."

"No, no," said Rose, "I'm just happy she's back where she belongs . . ."

"I insist," said the woman, scooting back around the counter and opening the cash register. "So what's your name? Do you live around here?"

"I, um," said Rose. "I do, actually. I live in the Dorchester, and I'm an associate at Lewis, Dommel, and Fenick. But here's the thing. I'm starting a new business. A dog-walking company."

"Well, there's a bunch of those in town already," said the woman, tossing Petunia a biscuit, which she caught on the fly and munched noisily.

"I know," said Rose. "But here's the difference. I'll walk dogs who are being boarded. So they can get some fresh air and exercise."

Now the woman was looking mildly interested. "How much?"

"I'm going to charge ten dollars a walk," she said. And, just as the woman's face started to draw itself into a frown, she said, "which I'd split with you. Because it would be good for new business."

"So they'd pay ten dollars for a walk, and you'd give me five?"

"That's right," said Rose. "For the first month's worth of business. Then we'll see where I am." She was already starting to do the math, running calculations through her head—five dollars a walk times, maybe, ten dogs a day at the kennel, plus perhaps another three or four at ten dollars per walk . . .

"I do errands for the owners, too," said Rose, thinking quickly of all the things she'd always meant to make time for in her previous life as a lawyer. "Dry cleaning, groceries, making doctor's and dentist appointments, picking up gifts . . . If you want to try me out, I'll walk Petunia for free."

"Tell you what," said the woman. "I'll give it a try, as long as we keep Petunia's little adventure just between us."

"Deal," said Rose, and the woman came out from behind the register to shake her hand.

"I'm Bea Maddox."

"I'm Rose Feller."

The woman squinted at her. "Any relation to Maggie?"

Rose felt her smile freeze on her face. "Maggie's my sister. But I'm not like her," she said. She could feel Bea's eyes on her. Rose drew herself up straight and squared her shoulders and tried to look responsible, dependable, mature—in short, un-Maggie-like.

"You know, she's still got my keys," Bea said.

"I don't know where she is right now," said Rose. "I'll pay you back for them, though."

The woman stared at her, then shrugged. "I guess we could give it a try. It doesn't look like I've got anything to lose. And you did find this one." She gave Rose her card and directed Rose to the copy shop on the corner to make up a few signs with her name and her rates and the services she offered.

Rose went to the copy shop, dropped a freshly printed flyer at the Elegant Paw, then hurried home, where she changed her outgoing voice mail message to say, "You've reached Rose Feller at Rose's Pet Care. Please leave me a message, including your name, number, pet's name, and the dates you'll require service, and I will get back to you as soon as possible." *Taking a break,* she told herself, listening to the message again. She felt as though her life had turned into a movie, with a stranger playing the part of her. Taking a break, she repeated sternly. She'd never taken off more than a week at a time. She'd gone straight from college to law school with barely time to do her laundry in between. She was due, she decided.

Next stop, the law firm. First thing Monday morning, Rose sat on the couch, took a deep breath, and dialed not Lisa but Don Dommel himself. His secretary put her right through. Rose wasn't sure whether that was a good sign or a very bad one. She braced herself for his bluster, for the suggestions he was bound to have: Drink wheat grass! Toss a medicine ball around! Take up BMX biking!

"Rose!" said Don heartily. "How are you feeling?"

"Actually, much better," she said. She sat on the couch, pushing the stack of *Dog Fancy* magazine and *Dogs for Dummies* aside and realizing how empty the apartment felt without Petunia. "Listen, I'm wondering . . . I'm going through some personal difficulties right now . . ."

"Would you like to take a leave of absence?" Don asked, so hastily that Rose was sure he'd been thinking about it since the first day when Jim had shown up for work and she hadn't. "The firm's got a very flexible policy . . . unpaid leave, of course, but you'll keep all of your benefits, and you'll be free to pick up right where you left off. When you feel ready, of course. Or if not . . ." His voice trailed off. Rose could read volumes into the short silence that ensued. *Go away,* Don Dommel was thinking, so hard she could practically hear the words. *You're a problem, you're a scandal, you're a piece of juicy gossip, you're egg yolk on our collective tie. Go away and don't come back.*

"Six months?" she asked, figuring that in six months she'd have her head on straight, and she'd be ready to pick up where she'd left off.

"Excellent!" Don agreed. "Now, you should certainly feel free to get in touch should you need references . . ."

"Of course," said Rose. She was astonished at how easy this was, how easy it was to let go once she'd made up her mind. All the work she'd been obsessed with . . . reassigned, she supposed, to some other hungry young associate. It was completely unfair. Jim was as much to blame as she was. She knew that. But Jim would stay; he'd get his equity, his raises, his holiday bonus, his corner office with a view of City Hall. And she would get unpaid leave and pro forma letters of recommendation. Whatever, she thought. Fine. She'd be fine. Somehow, she would.

". . . happens," said Don, who was, evidently, not through with her.

"I'm sorry?" said Rose.

"It happens," said Don, and now he'd dropped the bluster and bombast of the pep rallies, and his voice was actually kind. "Not every firm is a perfect fit."

"That's very true," Rose said gravely.

"Keep in touch," said Don. Rose promised she would, and hung up the phone. Then she sat back and considered. No more law, she thought. "At least for now," she said out loud, and found that the words didn't even cause her a momentary pang of unhappiness. "Pets," she said, and laughed a little, because it was strange to think of herself this way—Rose Feller, a creature of pure ambition, Rose Feller, the eternal striver, bypassing the fast track for a pooper-scooper. "I'm just taking a break," she told herself. Then she put on a pot of water for tea, settled herself on the couch, closed her eyes, and wondered what on earth she'd done.

TWENTY·EIGHT

Maggie remembered once overhearing her sister on the telephone when she'd come back from college for Thanksgiving. "I live at the library," she'd declared melodramatically. Well, Rose should get a look at her little sister now.

For her first week at Princeton, Maggie slept in different places—snatching a few hours' shut-eye on a couch in a dorm's common room, a bench in a basement laundry room—while carefully casing the lower levels of Firestone Library, looking for more permanent accommodations. She found them on C floor, the third level down, in the far southeast corner, a place Maggie came to think of as the Hurt Book Room. These were books with torn pages and broken bindings, books whose spines had snapped and whose glue had given way, a stack of ancient *National Geographic*s in one corner, a pile of books written in some curlicued alphabet she'd never seen before, and three chemistry textbooks in which the tables appeared to be missing a few of the more recently discovered elements. Over an afternoon, Maggie watched the door carefully. As far as she could tell, no book ever left the Hurt Book Room . . . and no new books came in. Even better, there was a hardly used ladies' room right around the corner, which boasted not only toilets and sinks, but a shower. The marble tiles were coated in dust, but when Maggie eased the taps open, the water ran clear.

And so, on her seventh day on campus, in the windowless room of forgotten books, Maggie set up her base camp. She hid in the bathroom's handicapped stall until the last student had been shooed out of the library, and the doors were locked behind them. Then she crept into the room, spread her sleeping bag between two tall shelves of dusty old books, flicked on the stolen lantern, and lay down on top of the bag. There. Cozy. And safe, too, with the door locked, and with all of her stuff stowed neatly under one of the bookshelves. Casual passers-by wouldn't even know that anyone was there, unless they knew exactly where to look, and what to look for. It was exactly the effect that Maggie was seeking for herself. To be there, but not really there, to be present but invisible at the same time.

She reached into the pocket of the jeans she'd been wearing since she arrived. There was the wad of bills, the three different student IDs she'd acquired during her days of sticky-fingered scavenging in the library. There were Josh's credit cards, and one of Rose's, too, a key she'd found and kept even though she'd probably never know what door it unlocked. And an old birthday card. *Wishing you a very happy day,* she read, and then she set the card on a shelf where she'd be able to see it.

She crossed her arms over her chest, and breathed in the darkness. It was quiet down there, three floors below the ground, beneath the weight of thousands of books, quiet as she imagined a tomb would be. She could hear every click of her tongue against her teeth, the rustle of the sleeping bag every time she moved.

Well, she thought, at least she'd be able to sleep. But she wasn't tired yet. She rifled through her backpack until she found the paperback she'd picked up after someone had left it unfolded across an armchair. *Their Eyes Were Watching God,* it said, but the drawing on the cover didn't make it look like a religious book. It was a picture of a black woman (actually, she was sort of purplish on the cover, but Maggie assumed she was meant to be black), and she was lying on her back under a green tree, looking up at it with a pleased, dreamy expression. Not as good as *People,* she figured, but certainly better than those legal magazines Rose had lying around, or the antiquated medical textbooks on the shelf closest to her sleeping bag. Maggie opened the book up and started to read.

TWENTY-NINE

"Ella?" Lewis asked. "Are you okay?"

"Sure," she said, and nodded for emphasis.

"You got kind of quiet," he said.

"I'm fine," she said, and smiled at him. They were sitting together on Ella's screened-in porch, listening to the crickets chirp and the frogs croak and Mavis Gold discussing last night's episode of *Everybody Loves Raymond.*

"So tell me this," Lewis began. "What do you regret?"

"That's a strange question," said Ella.

"That's not an answer," Lewis replied.

Ella thought about it. Where could she start? Not with the real regrets, she decided. "You know what I regret? I've never been swimming in the ocean."

"Really? Never?"

"Not since I've moved here. Not since I was a little girl. I went one day, I had my towel and my bathing cap and everything, but it just seemed too . . ." It had taken her half an hour just to find a parking space, and the beach had been crowded with girls in shockingly small bikinis and boys in brightly colored bathing trunks. There'd been a dozen different songs blaring from a dozen different radios, and the air was full with loud teenager voices, and the sun seemed too bright, and the ocean seemed too big, and she'd turned around and gotten back in her car before even setting foot on the sand. "I think I'm too old," she said.

He got to his feet, shaking his head. "No such thing. Let's go."

"Lewis! Now? But it's so late!"

"I don't think the beach has hours," he said.

She'd stared up at him, a million reasons why not to go running through her head. It was late, she had an early-morning appointment, it was dark, and who knew who they'd find out there? Midnight drives to the beach were something for teenagers or newlyweds, not senior citizens with arthritis and hearing aids.

"Come on," he said, tugging at her hands. "You'll like it."

"I don't think so," she said. "Another time, maybe." But somehow she was on her feet, and out the door, and the two of them were tiptoeing past Mavis Gold's quiet apartment like coconspirators, or kids on a dare.

The beach was just ten minutes away. Lewis pulled into a spot right by the sandy edge, held her door, and helped her out of the car. "Leave your shoes," he said.

And there it was, the water that she'd seen a hundred times, from her car, from his high windows, from the postcards and the glossy brochures that had lured her to Golden Acres in the first place. There it was, moving restlessly, with waves swelling and foaming and running up onto the sand, close enough to tickle her bare feet.

"Oh!" she said, and jumped a little. "It's cold!"

Lewis bent down and rolled up his cuffs, and then rolled hers. He held her hand and they waded out until the water was past their ankles, almost at their knees. Ella held still, feeling the pull and suck of the water as the waves rearranged the sand. She could hear the roar of the waves, and she could smell smoke from a fisherman's bonfire, far off down the beach. She let go of Lewis's hand.

"Ella?" he asked.

She waded out further, two steps, then three, and the water was past her knees, past her thighs. Her loose cotton shirt floated out around her, billowing each time the waves rolled in. The water was shockingly cold, colder than the lakes of her girlhood, and her teeth chattered until her body adjusted to the temperature.

"Hey, be careful!" he called.

"I will," she called back. Suddenly, she was afraid. Did she even remember how to swim? Was it the kind of thing you could forget? Oh, she should have waited until daytime, or at least brought a towel . . .

No more, she thought. No more. She'd been afraid for twenty years—longer even, if you counted all of those terrible nights when Caroline was out and she didn't know where—but she didn't want to be afraid here. Not now. And swimming had been her favorite thing for years of her girlhood, her young-woman-hood. She'd felt invincible in the water, and free, as if she could do anything, as if she could go forever, could swim to China. *No more,* she thought again, and pushed off with her feet, propelling herself forward. A wave hit her full in the face. She spluttered, spat out salt water, and moved through it, her hands reaching through the dark water, feet churning unsteadily before finding their rhythm. And there it was. The water held her, and she was swimming again.

"Hey!" Lewis called. Ella half expected to turn around and see her little sister, Emily, standing at the edge of the water, pale and goose-pimpled, crying, "Ella! You're out too far! Ella, come back!"

She turned, and almost laughed to see Lewis paddling after her, his teeth clenched and head held high (to protect his hearing aid, she figured). She floated on her back, her hair streaming out with each wave until he'd caught up with her, and then she'd reached for him, brushing his hand with her fingertips and setting her feet back on the sand.

"If I'd known we were going to be swimming," he panted, "I would have worn my trunks."

"I didn't know!" she said. "It was an impulse!"

"Well, have you had enough?"

She lifted her feet, tucked her legs against her chest, and let the water hold her. She felt like an egg in a pot of warm water, buoyed and surrounded entirely. "Yes," she finally said, and paddled with her arms until she'd turned around, and by Lewis's side she paddled back toward the shore.

Later, sitting on top of a picnic table on the beach, wrapped in a musty blanket Lewis had unearthed from the trunk of his car, she said, "You asked me before what I regret."

"This was before our dip?" he asked, as if the salt water had obliterated his memory.

"Yes," said Ella. "Before. But I want to tell you the truth now." She breathed deeply, remembering the feeling of the water all around her, holding her up, making her brave. She remembered being a little girl and swimming out farther then any of the other kids, farther than any of the grownups, so far that Emily would later swear that she was barely a speck in the water. "I regret that my granddaughters are lost to me."

"Lost to you," Lewis repeated. "Why?"

"When Caroline died, their father took them away. He moved them to New Jersey, and he didn't want me to keep in touch. He was very angry . . . at me, at Ira, at everyone. Angry at Caroline, too, but she wasn't there to be angry at, and we were. I was." She wrapped the blanket around her more tightly. "I don't blame him for that." She looked down at her hands. "There was a part of me that was . . ." She breathed again. "Relieved, I guess. Caroline was so hard to deal with, and Michael was so angry, and it just felt safer not to have to deal with any of them. So I took the easy way out. I stopped trying. Now they're lost."

"Maybe you should try again," said Lewis. "Maybe they'd be glad to hear from you. How old are they?"

Ella didn't respond, even though she knew the answer. Maggie would be twenty-eight, and Rose would be thirty. They could both be married, with husbands and children and different last names and no use for an old woman, a stranger, barging in with a heart full of sad memories, and their dead mother's name on her lips. "Maybe," she repeated, because Lewis was looking at her, sitting cross-legged on top of the picnic bench with his hair still damp from the water. And Lewis had nodded, and smiled at her, and she knew she wouldn't have to answer any other questions that night.

THIRTY

Princeton was not going to be a problem. But money was. Maggie realized that her math skills weren't the greatest, but two hundred bucks, minus the twenty or so she'd spent on food at the Wawa during the days she hadn't been able to sneak into a dining hall or a study break offering free pizza or Thomas Sweet ice cream, plus stolen credit cards that she was too afraid to use, did not equal enough to fund a new life. It wouldn't even be enough for a plane ticket to California, let alone a deposit on an apartment, and head shots.

There must be more money, Maggie whispered to herself. It was a line from a short story she'd read in another abandoned book, a story about a little boy who could ride a rocking horse and see the winners of real horse races; and the more urgently he rode, the louder his house seemed to whisper. *There must be more money.*

She considered her options as she sat inside the Student Center, nursing a ninety-cent cup of tea. She needed a job that paid cash, and the only possibility she'd seen was printed on a flier that she'd pulled down from the library wall. She set her mug aside and carefully unfolded the sheet of yellowing paper. "Housekeeper Needed," it read. "Light cleaning, some errands, once a week." Then there was a telephone number starting with 609.

Maggie pulled out her cell phone—the one her father had bought her, the one where the bills for the charges went directly to his office—and dialed. Yes, an old-woman-sounding voice informed her, the job was still open. Once a week, easy work, but if Maggie was interested, she'd have to provide her own transportation. "You could take the bus," she said. "Right from Nassau Street."

"Would you mind paying me in cash?" asked Maggie. "It's just that I haven't gotten my checking account set up here. I've got an account at home . . ." She let her voice trail off.

"Cash will be fine," the woman said crisply. "Assuming you work out."

So Thursday morning Maggie got up extra early, creeping like a mouse through the silence of the library before any of the lights came on, making sure her things were tucked out of sight. She hid in the first-floor bathroom and listened to the security guards unlock the front doors. Ten minutes after the library opened for business, she walked out the door, and was on her way to Nassau Street.

"Hello there," called the woman on the porch. She was short and thin with white hair flowing past her shoulders, and she wore what looked like a man's oxford shirt with a pair of leggings underneath it, and sunglasses, even though it was cloudy outside.

"You must be Maggie," she said, tilting her head in Maggie's direction. She put one hand on the railing for balance and held out the other one for Maggie to shake. Blind, Maggie realized, and shook the woman's hand carefully. "I'm Corinne. Come on in," she said, leading the way into a large Victorian house that already seemed scrupulously clean, and precisely organized. In the entryway hall, there was a stark wooden bench to the right and a series of cubbyholes hanging above it and a pair of shoes in each cubbyhole. A raincoat and a winter coat hung on adjoining hooks; an umbrella and hat and mittens were laid neatly on a shelf above them. And next to the empty coat rack was a white cane.

"I don't think you'll find the work too difficult," said Corinne, taking careful birdlike sips from a cup of coffee in a lemon-yellow mug. "The floors need to be swept and mopped," she began, ticking off the tasks on her fingers. "I'd like you to organize the recycling, the glass and paper in particular. The laundry should be sorted, the dishwasher needs to be emptied, and . . ."

Maggie waited. "Yes?" she finally asked.

"Flowers," said Corinne, and tilted her chin up defiantly. "I'd like you to buy some flowers."

"Okay," said Maggie.

"I'm sure you're wondering why I want them," said Corinne.

Maggie, who hadn't been wondering, said nothing.

"Because I can't see them," said Corinne. "But I know what flowers look like. And I can smell them, too."

"Oh," said Maggie. And then, because "Oh" seemed somehow insufficient, "Wow."

"The last girl said she brought flowers," said Corinne, pursing her lips. "But they weren't real ones." Her lip curled. "Plastic. She thought it wouldn't matter."

"I'll find some real flowers," said Maggie.

Corinne nodded. "I would appreciate that," she said.

It took Maggie less than four hours to do everything Corinne had asked. She wasn't an experienced housekeeper, because Sydelle had never trusted the girls to do anything right and had employed an anonymous army of housekeepers to maintain the pristine state of her glass-and-metal-filled rooms. But Maggie did a good job, sweeping every mote of dust from the floors, then folding the laundry and returning dishes and silverware to their shelves and drawers.

"My parents left me this house," Corinne said while Maggie worked. "It's the house I grew up in."

"It's beautiful," said Maggie, which was true. But it was also sad. Six bedrooms, three bathrooms, a vast staircase that curved through the center of the house, and the only resident a blind woman who slept in a single narrow bed with a single flat pillow, who would never appreciate all of the space or how the sun looked as it spilled through the wide windows and pooled on the hardwood floors.

"Are you ready to go to the market?" Corinne asked.

Maggie nodded, then remembered that nodding would do her no good. "All set," she said.

Corinne used her fingertips to extract a single bill from her wallet. "This is twenty dollars?" she asked.

Maggie inspected the bill and said that yes, it was a twenty.

"That's all the money machine gives out," said Corinne. *Then why are you asking me?* thought Maggie. Then she realized that it was possibly a test. And, for once, she'd managed to pass on her first try. "You can go to Davidson's market. It's right up the street."

"Do you want a flower with a smell?" asked Maggie. "Like lilacs or something?"

Corinne shook her head. "No smell will be necessary," she said. "Use your discretion."

"Do you need anything else while I'm there?"

Corinne seemed to consider this. "Yes. You can surprise me," she said.

Maggie walked to the market, thinking of what she might buy. Daisies, for starters, and she was lucky to find bunches of them clustered in a green plastic tub out front. She wandered the aisles, considering and rejecting plums, a pint of strawberries, a bundle of green-smelling spinach, a half-gallon of milk in a heavy glass bottle. What would Corinne like? Something that smelled seemed too obvious, especially since she'd been so quick to reject scented flowers, but Maggie wanted something . . . She groped for the word, and grinned when she found it—*sensual.* Something that had a feel to it, a weight, a heft, like the glass milk bottle, or the satiny feel of the daisy's petals. And suddenly, there it was, right in front of her, another glass jar, only this one glowing amber. Honey. "Orange Blossom Honey. Locally Produced," read the label. And even though it was $6.99 for even the smallest jar, Maggie added it to her basket, along with a bumpy-looking loaf of twelve-grain bread. Later, back in the large, clean house, when Corinne sat across from Maggie at the kitchen table, slowly munching a slice of the toasted bread spread thick with honey and then pronouncing it perfect, Maggie knew that she wasn't just paying her an empty compliment. She'd passed her second test of the day by finding exactly the right thing.

THIRTY-ONE

"I'm worried about your sister," Michael Feller said without preamble. Rose sighed and stared at her cup of coffee, as if Maggie's face might appear inside of it. So what else was new?

"It's been eight weeks," her father continued, as if Rose had somehow lost track of time. His face looked as pale and vulnerable as a peeled hard-boiled egg, all high, wide forehead and sad little eyes above his standard-issue gray banker's suit and subdued maroon tie. "We haven't heard from her. You haven't heard from her," he said, his voice rising at the end of the sentence, turning it into a question.

"No, Dad, I haven't," said Rose.

Her father sighed—a typical Michael Feller sigh—and poked at his dish of melting ice cream. "Well, what do you think we should do?"

Meaning, what do you think I should do, thought Rose. "Did you try all of her ex-boyfriends? That should have taken you a week or two," she said. Her father was silent, but Rose could hear reproach in what he wasn't saying.

"Did you call her cell phone?" she asked.

"Of course," said Michael. "Her voice mail's working. I leave messages, but she doesn't call back."

Rose rolled her eyes. Her father pretended not to notice.

"I'm really worried," Michael continued. "This is a long time for us not to hear anything. I wonder . . ." His voice trailed off.

"If she's dead?" Rose supplied. "I don't think we're going to get that lucky."

"Rose!"

"Sorry," she said, not very sincerely. She didn't care if Maggie was dead. Well . . . Rose pulled a handful of napkins out of the dispensers. That wasn't true. She didn't want her awful little sister to be dead, but she thought she'd be perfectly happy if she never saw or heard from her again.

"And, Rose, I'm worried about you, too."

"Nothing to worry about," Rose said, and started to fold one of the napkins into a pleated fan. "Everything's fine."

Her father's voice was dubious as he raised his gray eyebrows. "Are you sure? You're okay? You're not having . . ."

"Having what?"

Her father paused. Rose waited. "Having what?" she asked again.

"Some kind of trouble? You don't want to, um, talk to someone or something?"

"I'm not nuts," Rose said bluntly. "You don't have to worry about that."

Her father raised his hands, looking helpless and upset. "Rose, that wasn't what I meant . . ."

But of course, Rose thought, it was exactly what he meant. Their father never talked about it, but she knew it had been on his mind as he'd watched his daughters—especially Maggie—make their way toward womanhood. *Are you cracking up, are you losing your mind, are those bad strands of DNA starting to speak up, are you looking into taking a short fast drive around a tight, slippery curve?* "I'm fine," Rose said. "I just wasn't happy at that particular law firm, so I'm taking some time to figure out what I want to do next. Lots of people do it. It's very common."

"Well, if you're sure," her father said, and turned his attention back to his ice cream—a special treat, Rose knew, as Sydelle hadn't allowed anything more caloric than ice milk and Tofutti into their house since the early 1990s.

"I'm fine," said Rose. "You don't have to worry about me." With heavy emphasis on the *me,* to make it clear who her father did have to worry about.

"Could you call her?" Michael asked.

"And say what?"

"She won't talk to me," he said sadly. "Maybe she'll talk to you."

"I don't have anything to say to her."

"Rose. Please?"

"Fine," Rose grumbled. That night, she set her alarm for one in the morning, and when it went off she groped through the darkness for her telephone and punched in Maggie's cell phone number.

One ring. Two. And then her sister's voice, loud and cheerful. "Hello?"

Jesus! Rose made a disgusted noise. She could hear party sounds in the background—music, other voices. "Hel-lo!" Maggie trilled. "Who's this?"

Rose hung up. Her sister was like a fucking Weeble, she thought. She'd wobble, she'd screw up, she'd steal your shoes and your cash and your guy, but she'd absolutely never fall down.

The next morning, after her first round of dog walks, she called her father at his office. "She's alive," she reported.

"Oh, thank goodness!" her father said, sounding absurdly relieved. "Where is she? What did she say?"

"I didn't speak to her," Rose said. "I just heard her voice. The prodigal daughter is alive and well, and has lived to party another day."

Her father was silent. "We should try to find her," he said.

"Feel free," said Rose. "And give her my best when you do." She hung up the phone. Let her father try to track down his wayward daughter. Let Michael and Sydelle try to sucker her into coming home. Let Maggie Feller be someone else's problem for once.

She walked out the door and into a world she'd only discovered since defecting from full-time employment and spending her days traversing the city's streets, often with a bouquet of leashes in her hands. The city from nine to five was hardly the ghost world she'd been imagining. There was an entirely different population, a secret city of mothers and babies, shift workers, students and deliverymen, the retired and unemployed, moving through streets and corners of the city that she'd never even known about, in spite of her years at law school and her years at the firm. Why would an unmarried, childless lawyer have known about Three Bears Park, a tiny pocket of a playground between Spruce and Pine Streets? Would a woman who took the same route to work every day have known that on the five hundred block of Delancey every house flew a different flag? How could she have suspected that the shops and grocery stores would be bustling at one in the afternoon, filled with people in khakis and sweaters instead of business suits and briefcases? Who knew that she could easily fill her hours with the stuff she used to cram into mere minutes of spare time?

Her days began with dogs. She had her own key to the Elegant Paw, and each morning at the time she'd normally be buying her large black coffee and heading to the office, she'd be unlocking the door to the kennel, leashing two or three or four dogs, stuffing her pockets with biscuits and plastic poop bags, and heading toward Rittenhouse Square. She'd spend forty-five minutes there, in the square of the park, surrounded by dress shops and bookstores and fancy restaurants and high-rise apartment buildings, letting her charges sniff at bushes and hedges and other dogs. Then she'd spend her morning running errands. Drop-offs at the drugstore, pickups at the dry cleaners, zipping along sidewalks and side streets with her pockets heavy with keys, opening up doors for decorators, landscapers, exterminators, personal chefs, even chimney sweeps.

In the afternoons, she'd go on another round of walks, heading back to Rittenhouse Square for her daily date with the little girl, the spotted dog, and the woman who was with them.

Over her eight weeks as a dog-walker she'd become fascinated with the little girl, Joy, the dog Nifkin, and the woman she guessed was the girl's mother. They came to the park between four and four-thirty every afternoon. Rose would spend an hour tossing the tennis ball for her afternoon dogs and inventing a life for the woman and the girl and the dog. She imagined a husband, handsome in a regular-guy kind of way. She gave them a big house with fireplaces and bright woven rugs, a wooden chest full of every kind of toy and stuffed animal for the little girl. She sent them on family trips to the shore, hiking in the Poconos. She imagined them getting off an airplane—the father pulling a big wheeled suitcase, the mother pulling a medium one, the little girl with an appropriately small bag. Papa Bear, Mama Bear, Baby Bear, and the dog trotting jauntily behind them. In her mind, she gave them a quiet, happy life—good jobs, enough money, dinners at home on weeknights, just the three of them, the parents urging the little girl to drink her milk, the little girl surreptitiously sneaking her vegetables to the dog named Nifkin.

She'd already progressed from nodding hello to waving hello to actually saying "Hi." Given enough time, Rose thought, things might blossom into actual conversation. She sat and watched as the little girl chased the spotted dog toward the fountain, and the mother, who was tall, broad-shouldered, and heavy hipped, talked on her cell phone.

"No, I don't like liverwurst," she overheard the woman saying. "That's Lucy. Remember? The other daughter?" She rolled her eyes at Rose and mouthed *My mother*. Rose gave what she hoped was an understanding nod and a little wave. "No, I don't think Joy likes liverwurst either, Ma." She paused, listening, then shook her head. "No, Peter does not like liverwurst. In fact, I don't think anyone really likes liverwurst. I don't even know why they make it anymore." Rose laughed. The woman smiled at her, still listening. "Nifkin likes liverwurst," she said. "We can give it to him!" Another pause. "Well, I don't know what you should do with it. That was my one suggestion. Put it on crackers or something. Tell your book club it's paté. Okay. Right. We'll see you then. Okay. Bye."

She hung up the phone and put it in her pocket. "My mother thinks I'm unemployed," she began.

"Oh," said Rose, and cursed her rusty conversational skills.

"I'm not," said the woman. "But I work at home. Which, to my mother, seems to mean that I don't work at all, so she can call me whenever she wants to and ask me about liverwurst."

Rose laughed. "I'm Rose Feller," she said.

The woman extended her hand. "I'm Candace Shapiro. Cannie."

"Mom!" The little girl had suddenly reappeared, holding Nifkin's leash.

Cannie laughed. "Excuse me," she said. "I'm Candace Shapiro soon-to-be Krushelevansky." She made a funny face. "Try fitting that on a business card."

"So you're married?" asked Rose. She winced, shut her mouth, and wondered what had happened to her. Two months out of the office, two months with mostly dogs and deliverymen, and she'd forgotten how to talk to people.

But Cannie didn't act as though she'd noticed anything strange. "Engaged," she said. "We're doing the deed in June."

Huh, Rose thought. Well, if Hollywood stars could have babies before they got married, she supposed regular Philadelphians could, too. "Are you having a big wedding?"

Cannie shook her head. "Nope. Small. In our living room. Rabbi, family, a few friends, my mother, her life partner, their softball team. Nifkin's going to be the ring dog, and Joy will be the best baby."

"Oh," said Rose. "Um . . ." That didn't sound like any of the nuptials she'd seen on TV. "How," Rose began, and then stopped, unsure of herself, before starting again with the most banal of cocktail-party questions. "How did you meet your husband-to-be?"

Cannie laughed and flipped her hair over her shoulders. "Now that," she said, "is a long and involved story. It started with a diet."

Rose snuck a glance at Cannie and decided that it couldn't have been a very successful diet.

"I actually met Peter when I was pregnant with Joy, but I didn't know I was pregnant yet. He was running this weight-loss study, and I thought that if I lost weight this guy who I'd broken up with would want me back." She smiled at Rose. "But you know how it goes. You chase after the wrong guy until the final reel and then find out the right one was there waiting all along. Love works in mysterious ways. Or is that the Lord? I can never remember."

"The Lord, I think," said Rose.

"If you say so," said Cannie. "So how about you? Are you married?"

"No!" said Rose emphatically. "I mean, no," she said, in a more modulated tone. "It's just that . . . well, I just ended a relationship. Well, I didn't end it exactly. My sister . . . anyhow. Long story." She looked down at her hands, then at Petunia, curled at her feet, then over at Joy and Nifkin, who were playing fetch with a red mitten, then over at half a dozen dogs standing in the middle of a triangle of grass. "I guess I'm trying to figure out what's next."

"Do you like what you're doing now?" Cannie asked.

Rose looked at Petunia, at the other dogs in the park, at the grayish tennis ball in her hand, and the bunch of plastic poop bags beside her. "Yes," she said. It was true. She liked all of her dogs— the disdainful, snorty Petunia; the golden retriever who was always so glad to see her that he whirled in circles of joy when he heard her key in the door; the grave bulldogs; the fractious schnauzers; the narcoleptic cocker spaniel named Sport who'd occasionally fall asleep at red lights.

"And what else do you like?" Cannie prompted.

Rose shook her head, smiling ruefully. She knew what made her sister happy—size two leather pants, sixty-dollar French skin cream, men telling her she was beautiful. She knew what made her father happy—a bear market, dividend checks, a crisp new copy of *The Wall Street Journal,* the infrequent occasions when Maggie'd managed to hold a job. And what made Amy happy—Jill Scott records, Sean Jean pants, and the movie *Fear of a Black Hat.* She knew what Sydelle Feller loved—My Marcia, organic grains, Botox shots, and feeding fourteen-year-old Rose dietetic Jell-O for dessert while everyone else got ice cream. Once upon a time, she'd even known the things that made her mother happy, like clean sheets and bright red lipstick, and the costume-jewelry pins that she and Maggie would pick out for her birthday. But what did Rose herself like, besides shoes, and Jim, and foods that were bad for her?

Cannie smiled at Rose, and got to her feet. "You'll figure it out," she said cheerfully. She whistled for Nifkin, and the dog came running, with Joy trailing behind him, her cheeks pink and her hair coming loose from its ponytail. "Will we see you tomorrow?"

"Sure," said Rose. She pocketed the tennis ball and began gathering her charges, holding five leashes in her left hand and the leash of a single renegade greyhound in her right. She dropped dogs off until she was left with just Petunia. The pug trotted a few steps ahead of her like a plump croissant with legs. Petunia made her happy, even though she'd had to relinquish Petunia to her owner, Shirley, a no-nonsense seventy-two-year-old woman who lived downtown and who luckily consented to let Rose walk the pug every day. What else? Not clothes, really. Not money, because all she'd ever done with her exorbitant six-figure salary was pay her rent and her student loans, sock away a prudent percentage for her retirement, and let the rest gather interest in a money market account, per Michael Feller's explicit instructions.

So what?

"Yo!" called a bicycle messenger. Rose scooped Petunia into her arms and jumped aside as the bike whizzed past them. Its rider had a bag slung over his shoulder and a walkie-talkie, bleating static, on his hip. Rose watched him pedal off down the street, remembering that she'd had a bike, when she was a girl. A blue Schwinn, with a blue-and-white seat and a white straw basket and pink and white plastic tassels on the handlebars. There had been a bike path that ran behind her parents' house in Connecticut, a trail that led to the town golf course and soccer fields. It also wove through a crab apple orchard, and in the fall, Rose used to ride her bike there, her wheels crunching through the fallen crab apples, whispering over the red and gold leaves. Sometimes her mother would come with her, on her own bike, which was the grown-up version of Rose's, a Schwinn three-speed with a baby seat over the rear wheel, a seat that had once held Rose and Maggie.

What had happened to her bike? Rose tried to remember. When they'd moved to New Jersey, they'd lived in a rented condominium just off the highway, which meant parking lots and roads with no sidewalks or shoulders. She'd probably outgrown the bike while they'd lived there, and when they'd moved to Sydelle's, she'd never gotten a new one. She'd gotten her driver's license instead, three days after she turned sixteen, and she'd been excited, at first, about the prospect of freedom, until she realized that most of her driving would consist of dropping her sister off at parties, picking her up after dance lessons, and going grocery shopping.

She dropped Petunia off in Shirley's apartment and decided that over the weekend she'd buy herself a bike—a used one, to start with, so she could see if she liked it. She'd buy one, and maybe put a Petunia-sized basket on the handlebars, and she'd ride it . . . somewhere. She'd heard that there were bike trails in Fairmount Park and a towpath that ran all the way from the art museum out to Valley Forge. She'd buy a bike, she thought, smiling now and walking with a bounce to her step. She'd buy a bike, she'd get a map, she'd pack a picnic of bread and cheese and grapes and brownies and a can of gourmet dog food for Petunia. She'd have an adventure.

THIRTY-TWO

Mrs. Lefkowitz hadn't wanted to go for their weekly walk. "I can get my exercise in here," she'd told Ella, waving her cane at the ten-by-sixteen-foot expanse of her living room, into which she had crammed a couch, two love seats, an armchair with doilies decorating the arms, and an enormous wide-screen TV.

"Not the way you need to," Ella had said patiently.

"*The View* is on," she said, gesturing at the television set, where four women on the television screen were yelling at each other. "Don't you like *The View?*"

"You mean the ocean?" Ella asked innocently. "I love the view of the ocean. Let's go outside and have a look."

"Also, I've got a proposal for you," said Mrs. Lefkowitz, playing what was clearly her last card. "I've been thinking about you. Your predicament."

"Later," Ella said firmly.

"Agh, I give up," Mrs. Lefkowitz said. She put on gigantic square-lensed sunglasses, smeared zinc over her nose, and knotted the laces of her Nikes. "Come on, Bruce Jenner. Let's get this over with."

They walked down the drive toward the tennis courts, where, last month, someone had hit *Drive* instead of *Reverse* and plowed right through the fence, right through the net, and right into an unfortunate woman named Frieda Mandell, who'd been playing a desultory game of doubles and ended up splayed on the hood of a Cadillac, with her racquet still in hand. This, Mrs. Lefkowitz had announced mordantly, was clear evidence that sports and exercise—tennis in particular—could kill you if you weren't careful.

But her doctor had insisted she walk, and so every Tuesday at ten, Ella and her charge walked slowly to the clubhouse, had lunch, and took the trolley back home. Somewhere along the line, Ella had even started to enjoy the older woman's company.

Mrs. Lefkowitz's walk had a rhythm. She'd plant the cane, sigh, step forward with her right foot, then drag her left foot behind it. Plant, sigh, stomp, shuffle. It was soothing, really, Ella thought.

"So what's new?" asked Mrs. Lefkowitz. "You still seeing that one?"

"Lewis," said Ella.

Mrs. Lefkowitz nodded. "He's a good one. Reminds me of my first husband."

Ella was puzzled. "Your first husband? Did you have two?"

Plant, sigh, stomp, shuffle. "Oh, no. I just call Leonard my first husband. It makes me sound more worldly."

Ella bit back her laughter and kept a light hand on Mrs. Lefkowitz's elbow as she negotiated a crack in the sidewalk.

"Does Lewis have a good income?"

"Fine, I think," said Ella.

"You think? You think?" Mrs. Lefkowitz demanded. "Don't think. Find out! You could be left with nothing! Like that Charles Kuralt!"

Ella was confused. "He was left with nothing?"

"No, no, no. Not him. But he had, remember, the other girl-friend. And she was left with nothing."

"Not even the Winnebago?"

"Sure. Laugh," said Mrs. Lefkowitz darkly. "You won't be laughing when you're eating the cheese the government gives out."

"Keep walking," said Ella.

"And his children," Ella said. "Do they know about you?"

"I think so," said Ella.

"Make sure," said Mrs. Lefkowitz. "You know about Florence Goodstein, right?'

Ella shook her head.

"Well," Mrs. Lefkowitz began, "she and Abe Meltzer were keeping company. They'd go to movies, and dinner, and Flo would drive Abe to his doctors' appointments. One day his kids called her to check up on their father, see how he was doing, and Flo happened to mention that she was tired. Well, they heard 'tired' and thought she didn't want to take care of him anymore. And the very next day," said Mrs. Lefkowitz, pausing as the story reached its crescendo, "they flew down here, packed up his apartment, and moved him to assisted living in New York."

"Oh, my," said Ella.

"Flo was beside herself," said Mrs. Lefkowitz. "It was like the raid on Entebbe."

"I'm sorry for her. Keep walking," Ella said.

Mrs. Lefkowitz lifted her sunglasses and peered at Ella. "Are you ready to hear my proposal?"

"Sure," said Ella. "What's it about?"

"Your granddaughters," said Mrs. Lefkowitz, and resumed her shuffling walk.

Ella groaned inwardly. She couldn't believe she'd told Mrs. Lefkowitz about her lost granddaughters. Then again, a year ago she'd never have believed she'd be able to tell the story to anyone. Now, it seemed, she couldn't keep her mouth shut.

"Do they have the Emil?" Mrs. Lefkowitz asked.

"Emil?" Ella repeated.

"Emil, Emil," said Mrs. Lefkowitz impatiently. "On the computer."

"Oh, e-mail," said Ella.

"What I said," said Mrs. Lefkowitz, with a long-suffering sigh.

"I don't know."

"Well, we could find out. On the Internet. We could find out all kinds of things about them."

Ella's heart lurched. "Do you have a computer?" she asked, barely daring to hope.

Mrs. Lefkowitz gave a dismissive wave with her good hand. "Sure, who doesn't?" she asked. "My son got me an iMac for my birthday. Tangerine. Guilt," she said, apparently in response to Ella's unspoken questions of *What color?* and *Why?* "He doesn't visit too much, so he sends the computer, e-mails me pictures of my grandbabies. You want we should go back and look up your granddaughters?" she asked hopefully.

Ella bit her lip. She could hear the voice inside of her crying, *Look them up!* at war with the much more familiar, much more insistent voice that said, *Let them go,* could feel anticipation and fragile hope shot through with pure terror. "Let me think about it," she finally said.

"Don't think," said Mrs. Lefkowitz, drawing herself up to her four feet eleven inches and whacking at the ground with her cane, narrowly missing Ella's left foot. "There is no think, only do."

"What?"

"Yoda," said Mrs. Lefkowitz, and began the laborious process of turning herself around. "Let's go."

THIRTY-THREE

"Step out the front door like a ghost into the fog," said a guy in a rumpled white linen shirt, as Maggie walked through Firestone Library's doors at ten o'clock on a not-at-all foggy morning.

Maggie looked at him as he fell into step beside her, his own backpack slung loosely—slung stylishly, somehow—over his shoulders. He had a long, pale face, brown hair curling past his ears, and what he wore—the linen shirt with pressed oatmeal-colored linen pants—was a significant deviation from the unofficial campus uniform of jeans and a T-shirt.

"It's not foggy out," she said. "And isn't that from a song?"

"Notwithstanding," he said. He pointed at the copy of *My Antonia* that Maggie had tucked under her arm. "Women in Literature?"

Maggie gave a shrug that could have been either a yes or a no, figuring the less she said, the better. In her weeks on campus, excepting her first night at the party, she hadn't been saying much more than "Thank you" or "Excuse me" to the other students. Which was fine, Maggie thought. She had Corinne to talk to. She had books. She had a comfortable chair in the library's sunny reading room staked out, a favorite little table in the Student Center when she felt like a change of scenery. She'd finished the Zora Neale

Hurston, finished *Great Expectations,* and was now working her way through *A Tale of Two Cities,* rereading *My Antonia,* and plowing through *Romeo and Juliet,* which was much harder going than the Baz Luhrmann movie had made it out to be. Conversation with students could only lead to questions, and questions could only lead to trouble.

"I'll walk you," said the guy.

"That's okay," said Maggie, and tried to edge away.

"Not a problem," the guy said cheerfully. "It's in McCosh, right?"

Maggie had no idea where Women in Literature met or where McCosh might be located, but she nodded again, and picked up her pace. The guy kept up with her easily. Long legs, Maggie observed with dismay.

"I'm Charles," said the guy.

"I'm sorry," she finally said, "I'm not interested, okay?"

Charles stopped and smiled at her. He looked a little bit like a picture of Lord Byron that Maggie'd seen in one of her purloined books—a long blade of a nose, an amused curl to his lips. No six-pack, she was sure, no biceps to hang on to. Not her type. "You haven't even heard my pitch yet," he said.

"There's a pitch?" asked Maggie unhappily.

"Absolutely," said Charles. "I. Um. This is awkward. But it happens that I have need of a woman."

"Don't you all," said Maggie, slowing her pace so that her feet were practically dragging, figuring that if she couldn't run away from him, she could perhaps make him hurry away from her and off to his own class.

"No, no, not like that," he said, smiling and matching her pace again. "I'm in a playwriting class, and we have to present scenes, and I need a woman—an ingenue type—to do my scene for me."

Maggie looked at him. "You mean acting?" She stopped walking and stared up at him. He was tall, she saw. With nice gray eyes, too.

Charles nodded. "The very thing. I'm hoping," he said, as he and Maggie continued toward McCosh Hall, "to do a one-act at

Theatre Intime in the spring." He pronounced it *Ohn-Team*, and for a moment Maggie wasn't sure what he meant. She'd walked by that building a hundred times and she'd always figured it sounded like it was spelled: *In Time*. Which scared her—how many other things had she been getting wrong, even if she was only getting them wrong in the privacy of her own head? "So if the scene goes well, it'll be, you know, a good first step. So," he concluded, "want to help a brother out?"

"You're not my brother," said Maggie. "And how do you even know that I can act?"

"You can, though, can't you?" asked Charles. "You have that look."

"What look is that?"

"Dramatic," he said promptly. "But I'm getting ahead of myself. I don't even know your name."

"It's Maggie," said Maggie, momentarily forgetting her desire to be known as M.

"I'm Charles Vilinch. And I'm right, aren't I?" asked the guy. "You're an actress, right?"

Maggie simply nodded, hoping he wouldn't ask for specifics, as she didn't think that either her stint singing backup for Whiskered Biscuit or her hip's appearance in the Will Smith video would impress him much. "Look, I'd like to help you, but . . . well, I don't think I can," said Maggie, with real regret, because starring in a play—even if it was just some lousy student one-act—was extremely appealing. It could, she thought, be a start. Princeton wasn't that far from New York. Maybe word of the play, and its star, would reach the city. Maybe a casting agent or director would take a train down for a look. Maybe . . .

"Why don't you take today to think about it?" said Charles. "I'll call you tonight."

"No," said Maggie, thinking quickly. "No, um, my phone's not working."

"Then meet me for coffee," he said easily.

"I can't . . ."

"Decaffeinated tea, then," said Charles. "Nine o'clock in the Student Center. I'll see you there." And he loped off, leaving Maggie at the entrance to the lecture hall, where students—women, mostly, with a few holding her very same *My Antonia*—were streaming through the doors. Maggie stood for a minute, thinking *Why not?* as the bodies poured around her. It would be more trouble to turn around than to simply follow the crowd inside. She'd sit in the back, she figured. Nobody would notice. Plus, she was curious as to what the professor would say about the book. Maybe she'd even learn something.

THIRTY·FOUR

"Are you doing okay?" Amy had asked Rose one morning over blueberry pancakes at the Morning Glory Diner. Amy, in fitted black pants and a midnight-blue blouse, was on her way to the airport and a business trip that would take her to rural Georgia and deepest Kentucky, where she'd be lecturing at waste-water treatment facilities ("which smell," she'd told Rose, "about how you'd imagine they would"). Rose, in her now-customary loose-fitting Army-Navy surplus khaki pants, was on her way to take ten recently read romances to the Book Trader, in exchange for ten more, and then walk a schipperke named Skip.

Rose chewed and thought about it. "I'm good," she answered slowly, as Amy's spidery fingers snagged a piece of bacon off her plate.

"You don't miss work?"

"I miss Maggie," Rose mumbled into a mouthful of pancake. It was the truth. The Morning Glory was in Maggie's old neighborhood, right around the corner from the apartment she'd been kicked out of just before she'd moved in with Rose. While Rose was in college, and then in law school, Maggie would come to stay for a weekend once or twice a semester, and then, once Rose started working, she'd come to South Philadelphia and meet Maggie for brunch, or drinks, or pick her sister up for a trip to the King of Prussia Mall. Rose had fond memories of Maggie's series of apartments. No matter where she was living, the walls would wind up painted pink, and Maggie would park her antique hair dryer in the corner, set up a makeshift bar somewhere, with a thrift-shop martini shaker standing perpetually at the ready.

"So where is she?" asked Amy, wiping a butter knife with a napkin and using it to inspect her lipstick.

Rose shook her head, feeling the familiar Maggie-induced sensations of anger, frustration, fury, and sympathy rising up in her throat. "I don't know," she said. "I don't know if I want to know."

"Well, knowing Maggie, she'll turn up," said Amy. "She'll need money, or a car, or a car full of money. Your phone will ring and there she'll be."

"I know," said Rose, and sighed. She did miss her sister . . . except *miss* wasn't quite the right word. Sure, she missed having a companion, having someone to share breakfasts and pedicures and trips to the mall with. She even found that she missed Maggie's noise, Maggie's clutter, the way she'd turned the thermostat up to eighty degrees, until her apartment felt like a trip to the tropics, and how, in Maggie's hands, even the most mundane story would turn into a three-act adventure. She remembered Maggie trying to flush a wad of makeup-caked Kleenex down Rose's recalcitrant toilet, yelling, "Take it all, bitch!" at the bowl; Maggie throwing a fit in the Shampoo and Soap aisle of the drugstore because they were out of her particular-colored-hair-specific brand of conditioner; the flicking, go-away motion she'd make with her fingertips when she wanted Rose to give her more room on the couch; the song her sister would sing in the shower. "It had to be me . . . it had to be me . . ."

Amy drummed her knife impatiently on the edge of her plate. "Earth to Rose."

"Right here," said Rose, and waved weakly. Later that morning, she pulled her bike up to a pay phone, dug a fistful of change out of her pocket, and dialed her sister's cell phone again. One ring, then two. "Hello?" Maggie demanded, her voice brash and bossy. "Hello, who's this?"

Rose hung up, wondering if Maggie would see the 215 area code and wonder if it was her, and if she'd care.

THIRTY⚡FIVE

If Maggie Feller had learned one thing in her fourteen years of deal-ing with members of the opposite sex, it was this: your bad hookups will always come back to haunt you. There could be a guy you'd never seen before in your life, and all you had to do in order to guarantee that you'd be seeing him everywhere was spend a few quality minutes alone with him in the backseat, the bedroom, or behind a locked bathroom door. Then he'd be popping up in the cafeteria, in the halls, sitting behind the counter of the diner where you'd just started work, and holding some other girl's hand at the next Friday night party. It was the Murphy's Law of relationships— the guy you never want to see again was the guy you'd never be able to avoid. And Josh, from her first night on campus, was, unfortu-nately, no exception.

She wasn't sure he'd even recognize her—he'd been so com-pletely drunk, and it had been late, and she'd been fresh off the train, without a chance to perfect her Princeton camouflage. But Josh was everywhere, looking as if he was just on the verge of attaching her face to his missing money, sleeping bag, camping lantern, and clothes.

She'd look up from her book in the library and catch a glimpse of his sweatshirt, and the side of his face. She'd be refilling her mug with coffee in the dining hall and he'd be standing behind the salad bar, studying her. He actually started talking to her the Saturday night she dragged a stolen pillowcase full of her laundry into the laundry room, operating under the mistaken assumption that absolutely nobody would be doing their laundry on a Saturday night.

"Hey," he said casually, while peering at her bras and panties as she stuffed them into the machine.

"Hi," she said, keeping her head down.

"What's going on?" he asked. Maggie gave a small shrug, dumping detergent on top of the laundry from one of those little cardboard packets she'd bought from the vending machine.

"You want some fabric softener?" He lofted his jug at her, and smiled. But his eyes weren't smiling. His eyes were taking a careful inventory of her face, her hair, her body, measuring what he saw against what he remembered from that one night in his bed.

"No thanks. I'm fine," she said. She pushed her quarters into the slot. Just then, her cell phone rang. Her father, she figured— he'd called before, and she'd never answered, but now she grabbed at the phone as if it were a life buoy and she was drowning. "Hello!" she said cheerfully, turning her face and her body away from Josh's scrutiny.

There was no answer, just breathing. "Hello!" Maggie said again, hurrying up the stairs, past a group of students who were passing around a bottle of champagne and singing some kind of football fight song. "Who's this?" No answer. Just a click, then silence. She shrugged, put the phone in her pocket, and hurried out into the cool spring air. There were lamps illuminating the path at regular intervals, and there were carved wooden benches along the path and alongside the buildings. Maggie selected a bench away from the light, and sat down in a corner. Time to go, she was thinking. It's not a big campus, and you're seeing that guy everywhere, and it's only a matter of time before he figures out who you are and what you did, if he hasn't figured it out already. Time to cash in your chips, time to put the cards down, time to get on the next bus to somewhere.

Except, the weird thing was, she didn't want to leave. She was having . . . what? Maggie tucked her legs up against her chest and stared up at the tree branches, heavy with tight green buds, and the starry night sky. Fun. Well, not fun exactly, not fun like a party was fun, not fun like getting dressed up and looking great and feeling people's jealous eyes moving over her was fun. It was a challenge— the kind of challenge that her series of dead-end minimum-wage jobs never gave her. It was like being the star of her own detective show.

And it wasn't just a question of not letting anyone notice. These were the smart kids, the honors-course kids, the National Merit Finalist kids, the cream of the crop, the pick of the litter. If Maggie could move invisibly among them, didn't it prove what Mrs. Fried had always told her? If she could survive Princeton, if she could sit in the back row of a dozen different classes and actually follow what was being taught, didn't it mean that she was smart, too?

Maggie brushed dew off the seat of her jeans and got to her feet. Plus, there was Charles's play, his directorial debut, a Beckett one-act at Theatre Intime. And she was the star. She'd been meeting with him every few days for rehearsal, running her lines in the Student Center, or in an empty classroom in the arts building down on Nassau Street.

"I'm over in Lockhart," he'd told her the last time they'd met, walking her back from 185 Nassau. "I stay up late. I've got two roommates," he added, before Maggie had a chance to lift an eyebrow. "I guarantee that your virtue is safe with me."

Well, it was late now. She wondered if he'd be up. She wondered, wrapping her arms around herself, if he'd possibly be willing to lend her a sweatshirt. She hurried across the campus. Lockhart, if she remembered right, was right next to the University Store. Charles's room was on the first floor, and when Maggie tapped on the window, he pulled back the shade and smiled, and hurried around to let her in.

Charles's room was like nothing she could have imagined. It was like walking into another country. Every inch of wall space, and the ceiling, too, was covered with Indian-print tapestries and dozens of silver-framed mirrors. An Oriental rug, crimson and gold and blue, covered the floor, and instead of a coffee table in the center, there was an old, battered trunk—a treasure chest, Maggie thought. He and his roommates had pushed their desks against the walls and surrounded the chest with piles of cushions—red with gold fringe, purple with red fringe, a sage-green one embroidered with gold thread and beads.

"Have a seat," said Charles, indicating the cushions. "Do you want something to drink?" There was a tiny refrigerator in the corner, a cappuccino machine on top of it.

"Wow," said Maggie. "Are you running a harem?"

Charles laughed and shook his head. "Nah," he said. "We just like to play around. Last semester Jasper went to Africa, and we had kind of a safari theme going, but the animal heads on the walls freaked me out. This is better."

"Very nice," said Maggie, walking a slow circle of the room, checking it out. There was a small, fancy-looking stereo in the corner, with compact discs organized by genre—jazz, rock, world beat, classical—and then alphabetically. In another corner there was a small, high table stacked with travel books—Tibet, Senegal, Machu Picchu. When she breathed deeply, she could catch the scent of incense and cologne and cigarettes. The half-sized refrigerator contained bottled water, lemons, apples, and apricot jam. Not a single beer or bottle of condiment.

Gay, Maggie decided, closing the refrigerator door. Gay, she thought, with a certain degree of relief. Gay without a doubt. She picked up a framed photograph from Charles's desk. It was him, with his arm slung over the shoulders of a laughing girl.

"Your sister?" she asked.

"Ex-girlfriend," he said. *Huh,* Maggie thought.

"I'm not gay," Charles said. Then he laughed a little apologetically. "It's just that everyone who comes over here thinks that. And then I have to spend three months acting as heterosexual as possible."

"So what, you have to scratch yourself every five minutes instead of every ten? That's not hard work," said Maggie, plopping herself back onto the cushions, and flipping through a book about Mexico. Whitewashed houses stark against that piercing blue sky, weeping Madonnas in tiled courtyards, white-tipped waves curling onto golden sand. She was disappointed. She'd only known three kinds of guys in her entire life—those who were gay, those who were old, and the third category, a hundred times larger than the first two, those who wanted her. If Charles wasn't gay, and he certainly wasn't old, then he probably wanted her. Which made Maggie feel sad, and a little cheated. She'd never had a guy who was just a friend before, and she'd spent enough time with Charles that he liked her for her brains and her quickness, her resourcefulness, instead of the one thing that every other guy in the world usually liked her for.

"Well, I'm glad we got that cleared up. And I'm glad you're here. I've got a poem for you."

"For me? Did you write it?"

"No. We had it last week in my History of Poetry class." He flipped open a *Norton Anthology* and began to read:

> " 'Márgarét, áre you gríeving
> Over Goldengrove unleaving?
> Leáves, líke the things of man, you
> With your fresh thoughts care for, can you?
> Áh! ás the heart grows older
> It will come to such sights colder
> By and by, nor spare a sigh
> Though worlds of wanwood leafmeal lie;

And yet you *will* weep and know why.
Now no matter, child, the name:
Sórrow's spríngs áre the same.
Nor mouth had, no nor mind, expressed
What heart heard of, ghost guessed:
It ís the blight man was born for,
It is Margaret you mourn for.' "

He closed the book. Maggie took a deep breath. Her arms had bro-ken out into goose bumps. "Whoa," she said. "Dark. But I'm not Margaret."

"Oh, no?"

"No," she said. "I'm just Maggie. Maggie May, actually." She gave an embarrassed laugh. "From the noted poet, Rod Stewart. My mother liked the song."

"What's your mother like?" Charles asked.

Maggie looked at him, then away. Usually, at this moment of the back-and-forth with her guy of the hour, this would be the point where Maggie would produce her own version of the tragic tale of her mother's death, and lay it in the guy's lap like a gaily wrapped package. Sometimes she'd have her mother dying of breast cancer, and sometimes she'd stick to car wreck, but always she'd lavish the story with detail and drama. The chemotherapy! The cop at the door! The funeral, with the two little girls crying over the coffin! But she didn't feel like telling Charles that version of the story. She felt like telling him something closer to the truth, which scared her, because if she told him the truth about this, what else would she be tempted to blurt out?

"Not much to tell," she said lightly.

"Oh, I know that's not true," he said. She felt his eyes on her. She knew what was coming. *Why don't you come a little closer? Or, Can I pour you a drink?* And soon she'd feel his lips on her neck or his arm around her shoulders, with his hand edging toward her breast. It was a dance she'd done too many times.

Except the words never came, and his lips never came. Instead, Charles stayed just where he was. "Fine. Hold out on me," he said, and smiled at her—a friendly smile, she thought, and felt relieved. Maggie glanced at the antique-looking clock on his desk. It was after one. "I should go," she said. "Got to get my laundry."

"I'll walk you," said Charles.

"No, that's okay."

But he was shaking his head and picking up his backpack. "It isn't safe to walk around by yourself."

Maggie almost laughed at him. Princeton was the safest place she'd ever been. It was safer than a kiddie pool, safer than a child's car seat. The only thing she'd ever seen go wrong was when somebody dropped their tray in the dining hall.

"No, really. I'm actually hungry. Have you ever been to P.J.'s?"

Maggie shook her head. Charles affected a look of absolute horror. "It's a Princeton tradition. Excellent chocolate chip pancakes. Come on," he said, holding the door for her, "my treat."

THIRTY-SIX

Rose Feller figured that the day would come.

After three months of dog-walking and dry-cleaning pickups, trips to the drugstore and the grocery store and the video store, she figured she was overdue to run into some of the familiar faces from her less-than-halcyon days at Lewis, Dommel, and Fenick. So on a sunny, sixty-degree day in April, when Shirley, Petunia's owner, handed her an envelope with the familiar address printed on the outside and said, like it was no big deal, "Could you drop this off at my attorney's office?" Rose had just swallowed hard, tucked the envelope into her shoulder bag, and got on her bike, pedaling toward Arch Street and the tall, gleaming tower where she'd once worked.

It could be, she reasoned as she rode, that nobody would even recognize her. She'd spent her days at Lewis, Dommel, and Fenick in pantsuits and heels (*and in love*, her tattletale brain insisted on reminding her). Today she was wearing shorts, a pair of ankle-high socks decorated with skillets, fried eggs, and coffee cups (a little something Maggie had left behind), and hard-soled bicycling shoes. Her hair had grown out past her shoulders and was braided in two pigtails—Rose had learned through trial and error that it was one of the only styles that worked underneath a bicycle helmet. And although she hadn't lost any weight since her untoward departure from the world of litigation, her body looked different. Days of biking and walking had given her muscles in her arms and legs, and her office-drone pallor had been replaced by a tan. Her cheeks glowed pink, her hair, bound in its pigtails, was shiny. So she had that going for her, at least. *Get through it,* she told herself, as she walked off the elevator and over to the reception desk, her bare brown calves flashing, her shoes clattering on the tiled floor. *Get through it.* It wouldn't be hard. She'd drop off the package, get a signature, and . . .

"Rose?"

She held her breath, half hoping that what she'd heard had issued from her imagination rather than from an office across the lobby. She turned, and standing there was Simon Stein, instigator of intramural softball, his gingery hair garish under the overhead lights, and his muted red-and-gold tie highlighting the gentle swell of his belly.

"Rose Feller?"

Well, she thought, giving him a half-smile and a quick wave, it could be worse. It could be Jim. Now, if she could just dump her envelope and get out of here . . .

"How are you?" asked Simon, who'd hustled across the lobby and was now standing right beside her, looking her up and down as if she'd mutated into some previously unknown species. Maybe she had, she thought grimly. The Former Lawyer. How many of those had Simon Stein ever seen?

"I'm fine," she said quietly, and handed the envelope to the receptionist, who was looking at Rose with undisguised curiosity, trying to match the tanned girl in shorts with the sober young woman in suits.

"They told us you were on leave," said Simon.

"I am," she said shortly, collecting the signed receipt from the receptionist and turning toward the door. Simon followed after her, even as Rose willed him to go away.

"Hey," he said, "have you had lunch?"

"I should really get going," she said, as one of the elevators opened and a crowd of partners came pouring out. Rose peeked up surreptitiously, looking for Jim's face, and didn't start breathing again until she didn't see it.

"Free food," said Simon Stein, and gave her a charming grin. "Come on. You've got to eat anyhow. We'll go somewhere fancy and pretend that we're important."

Rose laughed. "Not with me dressed like this, we can't."

"Nobody's going to say anything," said Simon, and followed Rose onto the elevator as if he was one of the dogs she walked each day. "It's going to be fine."

Ten minutes later, they were sitting at a table for two at the Sansom Street Oyster House, where, just as Rose had feared, she was the only woman who wasn't wearing hose and heels. "Two iced teas," said Simon Stein, loosening his tie and rolling his sleeves up over his freckled forearms. "Do you like clam chowder? Do you eat fried food?"

"Sure and sometimes," said Rose, who'd unfastened her pigtails and was trying to casually rearrange her hair.

"Two bowls of New England clam chowder, and the mixed seafood platter," he said to the waitress, who nodded approvingly.

"Do you always order for strangers?" asked Rose, who'd decided that her hair was a lost cause and was now trying to tug her shorts down over the scabs on her right knee.

Simon Stein nodded and looked pleased with himself. "Whenever I can," he said. "Did you ever get food envy?"

"What's that?" asked Rose.

"When you go to a restaurant and order something, and then you'll see them bring someone else's food and it'll look, like, ten times better than what you ordered?"

Rose nodded. "Of course. Happens all the time."

Simon looked smug. Actually, given his curly red hair and his grin, he looked sort of like Ronald McDonald. "Well, it never happens to me," he said.

Rose stared at him. "Never?"

"Well, hardly ever," said Simon. "I'm an expert orderer. A master of the menu."

"A master of the menu," Rose repeated. "You should be on TV. Cable, at least."

"I know it sounds crazy," said Simon, "but it's true. Ask anyone I've ever been out with. I'm never wrong."

"Okay," said Rose, rising to the challenge, and thinking of the best restaurant she'd been to recently, with 'recently' defined as six months ago, when she'd gone with Jim late one night after work, when they were both certain they wouldn't see anyone he knew. "London."

"The city or the restaurant?"

Rose resisted the urge to roll her eyes. "The restaurant. It's in the art museum neighborhood."

"Of course," said Simon. "You'd get the salt and pepper squid, roast duck with sweet ginger, and the white chocolate cheesecake for dessert."

"That's amazing," Rose said, only half-sarcastically.

Simon shrugged his shoulders and raised his small hands to the heavens. "Look, lady, it's not my fault if all you ever eat is a baked potato and broiled fish."

"How do you know that?" asked Rose, who had, if she remembered it right, ordered the broiled salmon at London.

"Lucky guess," said Simon. "Also, that's all most women ever eat. Which is a pity. Try me again."

"Brunch at Striped Bass," said Rose, naming one of the best restaurants in town. Her father had taken her and Maggie as a special treat. Rose had gotten the turbot. Maggie, she remembered, had gotten three rum and Cokes and, eventually, the sommelier's phone number.

Simon Stein closed his eyes. "Do they have the eggs Benedict with poached lobster on the menu?"

"I don't know. I've never actually been for brunch."

"We should go," said Simon.

We? thought Rose.

"Because that's what you get," he continued. "You start with the oysters, if you like oysters . . . you do like oysters, don't you?"

"Sure," said Rose, who'd never had oysters.

"And then you get the eggs Benedict with poached lobster. It's really good." He smiled at her. "Next?"

"Penang," said Rose. Penang was the new, hot, Malaysian fusion spot that had just opened in Chinatown. She'd only read about it, but Simon Stein didn't know that.

"Coconut sticky rice, roast chicken wings, beef rendang, and those summer rolls with the fresh shrimp."

"Wow," said Rose, as the waitress set their soup in front of them. She dipped her spoon in, tasted, and closed her eyes as her mouth filled with the texture of heavy cream and the faint salty tang of the ocean, of fresh, sweet clams and potatoes cooked until they dissolved on her tongue. "My fat grams for the week," she said once she'd recovered.

"It doesn't count if someone else is paying," said Simon Stein, offering Rose the oyster crackers. "Try some of these."

Rose ate half her cup of soup before it occurred to her to speak again. "This is delicious," she said.

Simon nodded, as if he expected nothing else but her praise for the soup. "So can you tell me a little bit more about this leave?"

Rose swallowed hard against a lump of clam and potato. "It . . . um . . ."

Simon Stein was looking at her quizzically. "Are you sick?" he asked. "Because that was one of the rumors."

"One of the rumors?" Rose repeated.

Simon nodded, and pushed his own empty soup cup aside. "Rumor one was mysterious illness. Rumor two was that you'd been head-hunted by Pepper, Hamilton. Rumor three . . ."

Just then the waitress reappeared with a platter heaping with golden-brown strips and filets. Simon busied himself squeezing lemon over everything and giving the french fries a judicious sprinkle of salt.

"What was Rumor Three?" Rose demanded.

Simon Stein stuffed two fried scallops into his mouth, and looked at her with wide blue eyes, guileless beneath his curly, strawberry-blond lashes. "Mmhph oo er narphing mm mhmphair."

"What?" said Rose.

Simon swallowed. "That you were having an affair," he said. "With one of the partners."

Rose's mouth fell open. "I . . ."

Simon raised one hand. "You don't have to say anything. I shouldn't have even brought it up."

"Does everyone think that?" Rose said, trying not to sound shocked.

Simon helped himself to tartar sauce and shook his head. "No. Most people are betting on either lupus or lower back trouble."

Rose ate a few clam strips and tried to look nonchalant, and feel like she wasn't ridiculous. But she was ridiculous, of course. She'd ditched her job, her boyfriend had ditched her, she was dressed like an overgrown schoolgirl, and now a guy who was practically a stranger was salting her fries. Worst of all, everyone knew about her and Jim. And she'd thought it was a secret. How dumb could you get? "Was there a specific partner's name attached to this rumor?" she asked, trying to sound as if it didn't even matter, dipping a shrimp into the tartar sauce and hoping against hope that at least part of her secret was still safe.

Simon Stein shrugged. "I didn't listen," he said. "It was just gossip, that's all. You know how lawyers are. They've got to have answers for everything, so when someone just disappears, you know, they want an explanation."

"I didn't disappear. I'm on leave. As you know," Rose said stubbornly, and ate a piece of flounder, which was, all things considered, very tasty. She swallowed and cleared her throat. "So. Um. What else is going on at the firm. How are you?"

He shrugged. "The same. I've got a case of my own now. Unfortunately, it's the Stupid Bentley Case."

Rose gave him a sympathetic nod. The Stupid Bentley Case involved a client who'd inherited his father's millions and, apparently, none of his father's brains. The client had bought a used Bentley, then had spent the two years subsequent to the purchase trying to get his money back from the dealership. His contention was that the car had produced a cloud of oily black smoke since the first time he'd taken it on the highway. The dealership's belief—which was, unfortunately for the client, supported by the client's now ex-wife—was that the smoke was the result of the client driving the Bentley with its emergency brakes on. As Simon told some of the details, Rose could hear him trying to sound bored and cynical—disgusted that the firm's client was such a boob, disgusted with a process that had allowed the case to go as far in the system as it had—but the boredom and cynicism were a thin and easily cracked patina over Simon Stein's obvious enthusiasm for his work. Sure, it was a small case, and sure, the client was an ass, and no, his sparkling eyes and waving hands said, this case wasn't going to set legal precedent, but still, she could tell that he was having fun as he described the depositions, the discovery, the subpoenaing of the subliterate mechanic named Vitale. Rose sighed, listening, wishing she still felt that way about the legal life, and wondering if, really, she ever had.

"But enough about the Bentley," Simon concluded, popping the second-to-last fried shrimp into his mouth and tossing the last one to Rose. "You look terrific, by the way. Very rested."

Rose looked down at herself ruefully, from her slightly sweaty T-shirt down to the calves that were tattooed with grease from her bicycle chain. "You're too kind."

"Would you like to have dinner with me on Friday?" asked Simon. Rose stared.

"I know that was kind of abrupt," said Simon. "It's the result of billing by the hour, I think. You just blurt out what you have to say, because the meter's running."

"Don't you have a girlfriend?" asked Rose. "And didn't she go to Harvard?"

"Gone," said Simon. "It wasn't working out."

"Why not?"

Simon thought it over. "She didn't have much of a sense of humor, and the Harvard stuff . . . well, I guess I just couldn't see spending my future with a woman who referred to her period as the Crimson Tide."

Rose snorted. The waitress took their plates and put dessert menus in front of them. He barely spared it a glance. "Hot apple cobbler," he said. "Want to split it?"

He smiled at her, and she saw that even though he was shortish, and vaguely egg-shaped, and about as far from Jim looks-wise as Saks Fifth Avenue was from Kmart, she had to admit that he was funny. Nice, too. Sort of appealing. Not to her, of course, she thought hastily, but still . . .

Simon, meanwhile, was staring at her expectantly, and humming the chorus of what Rose recognized as "Lawyers In Love." "So are we on for dinner?"

"Why not?" said Rose.

"I was hoping for a more enthusiastic response than that," Simon Stein said dryly.

Rose smiled at him. "Yes, then."

"She smiles!" said Simon; and when the waitress brought the cobbler, he said, "Let's put some ice cream on top of that. We're celebrating."

Ella sat in front of the keyboard at Mrs. Lefkowitz's computer, took a deep breath, and stared at the blank screen. "I don't think I can do this," she said.

"What?" Mrs. Lefkowitz called from the kitchen. "Did it freeze up again? Just restart the computer. You'll be fine."

Ella shook her head. She didn't think that she would be fine at all. She was in Mrs. Lefkowitz's spare bedroom, which served as a sort of office-cum-storage area, with the tangerine iMac perched on top of a ponderous claw-footed walnut desk, aside a red velvet couch with the stuffing leaking out, beneath a stuffed elk's head, flanked by a copper-and-bamboo umbrella stand, which housed Mrs. Lefkowitz's cane. "I don't think I can do this," Ella said again . . . but nobody heard her. Lewis and Mrs. Lefkowitz were in the kitchen, slicing up muffins and fresh fruit, and in the living room the television set was blaring *Days of Our Lives.*

Ella squeezed her eyes shut, typed in "ROSE FELLER" and hit the "enter" key before she lost her nerve.

When she opened her eyes, Mrs. Lefkowitz and Lewis were standing behind her, and the screen was full of words.

"Wow," Lewis said.

"Popular name," observed Mrs. Lefkowitz.

"How do I know which one's her?" Ella asked.

"Just try one," said Lewis. Ella clicked one of the links, and discovered that the words "Rose" and "Feller" had brought her to Feller Florals in Tucscon, Arizona. She sighed, returned to the search page, and clicked another link. This one was a record of marriage licenses from Wellville, New York, for a Rose Feller born in 1957. Not her Rose. She backed up, clicked once more, and finally, her granddaughter's face, twenty-two years older than when Ella had seen it last, filled the screen.

"Oh!" she gasped, and read through each word on the page as fast as she could. "She's a lawyer," she said, in a voice that didn't sound like it belonged to her.

"Well, that's not the worst thing she could be," said Mrs. Lefkowitz, and cackled. "At least she's not in jail!"

Ella stared. It was Rose. It had to be. She had the same eyes, the same serious expression, the same eyebrows that followed a straight line across her forehead that Ella remembered from when she'd been a little girl. Ella got up and collapsed on Mrs. Lefkowitz's loveseat. Lewis took her place and starting scrolling through the text. "Princeton University . . . University of Pennsylvania law school . . . specialty in commercial litigation . . . lives in Philadelphia . . ."

"She was so smart," Ella murmured.

"You can e-mail her," said Lewis.

Ella buried her face in her hands. "I can't," she said. "Not yet. I'm not ready. What would I say?"

"You'd start with 'hello,' " said Mrs. Lefkowitz, and laughed at her own wit.

"Where's her sister?" Ella managed to ask. "Where's Maggie?"

Lewis gave her a reassuring look that felt like his hand, warm on her shoulder. "I'm looking," he said. "Haven't found anything yet."

But he would, Ella knew. The girls were out there, living lives she couldn't imagine. And they were grown-ups now. They could make their own decisions about whether to let her into their lives or not. She could write to them. She could call. But what would she say?

Mrs. Lefkowitz plopped down beside her. "You can do it!" she said. "Come on, Ella. What do you have to lose?"

Nothing, Ella thought. *Everything.* She shook her head and shut her eyes. "Not today," she said. "Not yet."

THIRTY-EIGHT

Much to her surprise, Maggie Feller found that she was actually getting a strange sort of education at Princeton.

She'd certainly never planned on it, she thought as she walked across campus with an armload of books. But the truth was, that first class had hooked her. And Charles had hooked her, too, with his books of monologues, his conversations about things no guy had ever wanted to discuss with her—character arcs, moods and motivation, books and real life and how they were the same and how they were different. Even the one fly in her ointment, Josh, the unfortunate and suddenly ubiquitous hookup, felt like a distraction instead of a real danger. She liked being a student, she thought ruefully. She should have given it more of a chance ten years ago.

Take poetry. For Maggie, reading anything from the simplest sentence on up involved a sort of detective work. First, she'd have to sound out and decipher each individual letter of every single word. Once she had them individually, she'd have to string them together, nouns and verbs and the gaudy baubles of adjectives, and read it over and over and over again before she could extract the meaning, like a chunk of walnut tucked into a gnarled shell.

She knew this wasn't how it worked for most people. She knew that Rose could glance at a paragraph or a page and know what it meant as if she'd soaked the knowledge of it in through her skin, which was why she could devour thick romance novels, while Maggie stuck to magazines. But poetry, Maggie had found, was the great equalizer, because poetry wasn't made to be obvious on its surface, and every reader, whether they were Princeton smarties or community-college dropouts, had to go through the process of deciphering the words, then the sentences, then the stanzas, pulling the poem apart and putting it back together before it would yield its meaning.

Three and a half months into her campus camp-out, Maggie walked into "her" Modern Poets class and settled herself in the back row, making sure to leave an empty seat on either side of her. Most of the students clustered near the front, hanging breathlessly on Professor Clapham's every word, practically dislocating their shoulders when they threw their hands into the air to volunteer an answer, which meant that Maggie was fine in the back. She sat, opened her notebook, and copied the day's poem from the blackboard, whispering each word to herself as she wrote it.

One Art

The art of losing isn't hard to master;
so many things seem filled with the intent
to be lost that their loss is no disaster.

Lose something every day. Accept the fluster
of lost door keys, the hour badly spent.
The art of losing isn't hard to master.

Then practice losing farther, losing faster:
places, and names, and where it was you meant
to travel. None of these will bring disaster.

I lost my mother's watch. And look! my last, or
next-to-last, of three loved houses went.
The art of losing isn't hard to master.

I lost two cities, lovely ones. And, vaster,
some realms I owned, two rivers, a continent.
I miss them, but it wasn't a disaster.

—Even losing you (the joking voice, a gesture
I love) I shan't have lied. It's evident
the art of losing's not too hard to master
though it may look like *(Write* it!) like disaster.

"I lost my mother's watch," Maggie whispered as she scribbled down the poem. The art of losing. She could write a book about that. The things she found in the school's various lost-and-found boxes continued to boggle her mind—and keep her very well outfitted. With her textbooks and sweatshirts, hats and mittens from J.Crew or the Gap, she looked the part of a Princetonian. And she was starting to believe her own fiction. The semester was drawing to a close, and Maggie felt like she was close to becoming an actual, honest-to-God student. Except the summer was coming. And what did students do during the summer? They went home. And she couldn't. Not yet.

"The art of losing's not too hard to master," she wrote, as Professor Clapham, blond, in her late thirties, and enormously pregnant, waddled to the front of the room.

"This is a villanelle," she said, settling her books on the desk and herself, gingerly, into a chair, and flicking her laser pointer on. "One of the most demanding rhyme schemes. Why do you think Elizabeth Bishop matched this particular form to her subject matter? Why was this a good fit?"

Silence. Professor Clapham heaved a sigh. "Okay," she said, not unkindly, "let's start at the very beginning. Who can tell me what this poem's about?"

Hands shot up. "Loss?" offered a sleek blond girl in the front row. *Duh,* thought Maggie.

"Of course," said the professor, in a tone only marginally kinder than Maggie's mental *Duh* had been. "But the loss of what, exactly?"

"Losing love," ventured a boy with bare, hairy legs exposed by his shorts, and a sweatshirt bearing the bleach stains of someone not yet used to managing his own laundry.

"Whose love?" Professor Clapham demanded. She put her hands at the small of her back and stretched as if her back hurt or, maybe, as if her students' ignorance was causing her physical pain. "And is the love lost already, or does the poet place that loss, out of all the others, in the realm of the theoretical? Is she talking about this loss as a possibility? A probability?"

Blank stares and bowed heads.

"A probability," Maggie blurted, and then sat, crimson, as embarrassed as if she'd farted.

But the professor gave her an encouraging look. "Why?"

Maggie's hands and knees were trembling. "Ummm," she said, in a faint and fading voice. And then she thought of Mrs. Fried, bending over her, her glasses swinging on a beaded chain, whispering, *Just try, Maggie. It doesn't matter if you're wrong. Just try.*

"Well," Maggie began, "at the beginning of the poem, she's talking about real things, stuff that everybody loses, like keys, or people's names."

"And then what happens?" the professor prompted. Maggie got it, almost as if she'd plucked a kite out of the sky.

"It shifts from the tangible to the intangible," she said, the long words rolling off her lips as if she'd been saying them all her life. "And then the poet starts getting . . ." Shit. There was a word for this. What was the word for this? "Grandiose," Maggie finally managed. "Like, she lost a house—okay, lots of people move; but then she says she's lost a whole continent . . ."

"Which, we can assume, would not be hers to lose," Professor Clapham said dryly. "So we see another shift."

"Right," Maggie agreed, her words coming faster, tumbling over one another. "And the way she writes about it, like it doesn't even matter that much . . ."

"You're talking about Bishop's tone," the professor said. "Would you call it ironic? Detached?"

Maggie thought about it as two girls in the front row raised their hands. Professor Clapham ignored them. "I think," Maggie said slowly, staring at the words on the page, "I think she wants to sound detached. Like it doesn't matter to her, right? Like the words she's using. *Fluster*. A fluster isn't a big deal. Or even the line that repeats, about how the art of losing isn't hard to master. It's like she's making fun of herself by even calling it an art." In fact, the tone's poem reminded Maggie of the way her sister talked about herself. She remembered watching the Miss America Pageant with Rose, asking Rose what her talent would be, and how Rose had thought about it and then said, very thoughtfully, "Parallel parking." "So she's trying to, like, turn it into a joke. But then, by the end . . ."

"Let's consider the structure again," the professor said, and while her words were intended for the rest of the class, her eyes were still on Maggie's. "A B A. A B A. Stanzas of three lines, until we reach the end, the final quatrain, and what happens?" She nodded at Maggie.

"Well, it's four lines, not three, so it's different. And there's that interruption—'write it!'—it's like she wants to be distant, she wants to be apart from it, but she's thinking of what's going to happen when she loses . . ."

"Loses what?" Professor Clapham asked. "Or loses who? Is this a poem about a lover, do you think? Who is the 'you' of this poem?"

Maggie bit her lip. "I don't think so," she said. "But I don't know why. I think that it's more a poem about losing . . ." *A sister,* she thought. *A mother.* "A friend, maybe," she said out loud.

"Very good," said the professor, as Maggie flushed crimson again, this time in pleasure, rather than shame. "Very good,"

Professor Clapham repeated, and then she turned back to the board, back to the class, back to the rhyme scheme and the formal demands of a villanelle. Maggie barely heard a word of it. She was still blushing. She, who never blushed, not even when she'd had to dress up like a gorilla for the three-day stint as a singing telegram girl, had turned the rich ripe red of a Jersey tomato.

That night, she curled up on top of her sleeping bag, thinking about her sister, wondering if Rose had taken that particular poetry class and had read that particular poem, and whether Rose would ever believe that it was Maggie, Maggie above all of the other students, who'd understood the poem best. She wondered when she'd get to tell Rose about it, and turned restlessly in the dark, trying to puzzle out what she'd have to do in order to get her sister to even speak to her again; what she'd have to do to get Rose to forgive her.

By the next morning, riding the bus to Corinne's through the bright spring sunshine, she was starting to feel regret. The whole point of being at Princeton was try to be . . . what was the word? . . . *interstitial*. It wasn't a word she'd learned on campus, it was a word she'd gotten from Rose. She could close her eyes and see Rose pointing out the commercials crammed onto half of the TV screen while the credits for the show that had just ended ran beside them. *Interstitial* meant, basically, the thing between the thing—the stuff that happened alongside the main event, while you were paying attention to something else.

And now she'd gone and shouted out answers in class. What was she thinking? Someone was going to notice her. Someone was going to remember. Someone was going to start wondering exactly where she lived, what her major was, what year she was, and what she was doing there.

Swirling the mop over Corinne's already gleaming floors, she wondered if maybe she wanted to be discovered, if she was tired of being invisible. She was doing something . . . well, not important, exactly, but something that required a certain level of daring, and cunning, and skill, and she wanted to be acknowledged for it. She

wanted to tell Charles, or Rose, or someone, everything she'd figured out. How she'd learned to be careful never to fall into regular,
detectable patterns. How she'd figured out no fewer than six different places to take showers (Dillon gym, the basement shower in the
library, and four dormitories where the locks were reliably broken),
how she knew the only washing machine that would run without
quarters and the single soda machine that would routinely disgorge
a free can of Coke if you hit it just right.

She wanted to tell them how she'd figured out the dining
halls—how, if you sneaked in through the steamy dish room in the
early morning hours, dressed as if you were working there, in
grungy sneakers and jeans and a sweatshirt, everyone assumed that
you were one of the student employees, just grabbing a bite before
taking your place behind the steam tables or on the dish line. She
wanted to explain how easy it was to slip food into her backpack—
peanut butter sandwiches, pieces of fruit, layered between napkins.

She wanted to tell them about Thursday lunches at the
International Student Center, where for two dollars she could get a
giant plate heaping with rice and stir-fried vegetables and chicken
curried in coconut milk—the best food she'd ever had, she thought
sometimes—with the tea they served that tasted like cinnamon,
how she'd drink cup after cup with teaspoonfuls of honey, and it
would chase the heat of the food out of her mouth, and how nobody
ever asked her anything because most of the other lunchgoers were
graduate students and new to English, so the most she ever got was
a shy smile, and a nod, and change for her five-dollar bill.

She used Windex to clean Corinne's glass cabinets and imagined introducing Rose to Charles and seeing her sister nod her
approval. "I'm fine," she imagined telling her sister; "you shouldn't
have been so worried about me, because I'm fine." And then she
would say that she was sorry . . . and, well, after that, who knew?
Maybe Rose could find a way for Maggie to get credit for the classes
she'd listened in on. Maybe Maggie could even get a degree some
day, if she kept plugging away, because she'd found that if she took

her time, even the thickest books weren't so awful. And she'd star in all of Charles's plays, and give her sister tickets to the premiere, and also something great to wear, because Lord knew that if left to her own devices Rose would just show up in something frumpy, like one of her shoulder-padded sweaters that made her look like small bear, and . . .

"Hello?" Corinne said. Maggie jumped and practically fell off the step stool.

"Hi," she said. "I'm up here. I didn't hear you come in."

"I move on little cat feet. Like the fog."

"Carl Sandburg," said Maggie.

"Very good!" said Corinne. She ran her fingertips along the countertops, then eased herself into a seat at the dining room table that Maggie had wiped clean. "How's school?"

"It's very good," said Maggie. She hopped off the step stool, folded it up, and stowed it on its hook inside the closet. And it was good. Except for the fact that she didn't really belong here. Except for the fact of Rose, the terrible thing she'd done to her, and her sense that nothing she'd learned in college would help her figure out how to make that right again.

THIRTY-NINE

In the week since her walk with Mrs. Lefkowitz, Ella had managed to learn a great deal about her granddaughter Rose, and almost nothing about Maggie.

"This one, this Rose," Mrs. Lefkowitz had said. "She's everywhere!"

Indeed, cyberspace was littered with references to Rose, from the directory of her high school's National Honor Society to an article in the *Daily Princetonian* about on-campus recruiting. Ella learned where Rose had gone to school, what area of law she was practicing, even extrapolated her telephone number from an on-line search engine.

"She's done all right for herself," said Mrs. Lefkowitz, as they plodded past the tennis courts.

"It said she's on indefinite leave," Ella noted, remembering her granddaughter's stern face flickering on the computer screen. "That doesn't sound good."

"Feh," said Mrs. Lefkowitz. "She's probably on vacation."

Maggie, meanwhile, proved much harder to pin down. Mrs. Lefkowitz, Ella, and Lewis had tried every possible combination of MAGGIE FELLER and MAGGIE MAY FELLER and even MARGARET FELLER, even though it wasn't right, and found not a single reference to her younger granddaughter, not so much as a mention, not even a telephone number. "It's like she doesn't exist," Ella had said, frowning. "Maybe . . ." She let her voice trail off, unwilling to give voice to the horrible thought that had seized her.

Mrs. Lefkowitz shook her head. "If she was dead, there'd be an obituary."

"Are you sure?" asked Ella.

"How do you think I keep up with my friends?" Mrs. Lefkowitz asked. She reached into her pink fanny pack and pulled out an orange cell phone. "Here. You should call the Rose one. Quick, before you lose your nerve."

Ella shook her head, thinking of her granddaughter's face. "I don't know," she said. "I want to, but . . . I have to think about it. I want to do it just right."

"Think, think," said Mrs. Lefkowitz. "You're taking too long. Just do it! Some of us are not planning to live forever."

Ella stayed awake all night, lying alone on top of her comforter as the frogs croaked and the horns honked and the sky finally got light. When she pushed herself out of bed, she made herself say it out loud. "Today," she announced to her empty apartment. "I'm going to call her today."

That morning, at the hospital, Ella set a sleeping baby back into its Isolette and hurried down the hall. There was a bank of pay phones right across from the surgical lounge. Ella stationed herself in front of the phone the farthest from the doors and fumbled for her calling card. She poked at the keyboard, punched in her calling card number, then Rose's law-firm number. Voice mail, she thought—she, who hadn't prayed since the last night her daughter had gone missing, had suddenly become God's intimate companion. Please, Lord, let it be voice mail.

And it was . . . but it wasn't what she'd expected to hear. "You have reached a nonworking number at Lewis, Dommel, and Fenick," said the disembodied computerized voice. "Please press zero to be connected with an operator." Ella pressed zero, and after a minute a receptionist said, "It's an outrageous day at Lewis, Dommel, and Fenick!"

"Excuse me?" said Ella.

"They make us say that instead of 'hello,' " said the receptionist in a hushed whisper. "How can I help you?"

"I'm trying to reach Rose Feller," said Ella.

"I'll connect you," the receptionist singsonged. Ella's heart leapt in her chest . . . but the woman who answered the phone wasn't Rose, just a bored-sounding woman who identified herself as Lisa, Rose's former assistant.

"She's on leave," Lisa said.

"I know," said Ella, "but I was wondering if I could leave her a message? This is her grandmother," she said, feeling herself swell with fear, and pride, the instant she'd spoken the words *her grandmother.*

"Sorry," said Lisa. "She doesn't call in for her messages. She hasn't been here in months."

"Oh," said Ella. "Well, I've got her home number, so I'll try her there."

"Fine," said Lisa.

"Thank you," said Ella. She hung up the phone and sank into a chair outside the lounge, feeling exhilarated and terrified at the same time. She'd taken the first step, and what was the corny thing that Ira, of all people, used to say? *The greatest journey begins with a single step.* True, he'd usually say it before starting on a fresh batch of yogurt, but still, Ella thought. It was true, and she'd done it. She hadn't chickened out, she thought, reaching for the telephone again, hurrying to call Lewis and give him the amazing news. She'd jumped into the water. She'd begun.

FORTY

Rose had to give Simon Stein this—he was nothing if not persistent.

The day after they'd had lunch, a dozen red roses had arrived at her apartment, with a card saying, "Looking forward to seeing you again. PS: Don't eat a big lunch." She'd rolled her eyes at that, hoping he wasn't getting the wrong idea, as she loaded the roses into an inadequate vase and set them on her kitchen counter, where they promptly began making the rest of her belongings look shabby and unromantic in comparison. He was a nice enough guy, certainly, but nobody she'd ever be attracted to. Besides, she thought later, swinging one leg over her bicycle and heading down Pine Street to begin her morning rounds, she was through with love, and it would take more than a man who styled himself a walking Zagat's guide to change her mind.

"I'm on hiatus from romance," she told Petunia, as they strolled through the morning sunshine on their daily walk. Rose had to admit that while she liked all of the dogs she cared for, she'd always have a soft spot for the scowling little pug.

Petunia squatted, peed briefly into the gutter, snorted a few times, and began her pursuit of street sushi—pizza crusts, puddle beer, discarded chicken bones. "I think it's a good idea to take a break every once in a while," Rose said. "So I'm taking a little break."

That evening, Rose shaved her legs carefully, toweled herself off, and surveyed the outfits she'd laid out on her bed. Of course, none of them looked right. The red skirt that had looked adorable in the mall bunched up oddly around her hips. The green sundress was hopelessly wrinkled, the denim skirt was missing a button, and the long black skirt made her look as if either she'd come straight from the office or she was in mourning, or as if she'd been in mourning at the office. God, where was Maggie when she needed her?

"Shit!" Rose said. She was sweating, in spite of her freshly applied deodorant, and already five minutes late. "Shit, shit, shit!" She pulled on the red skirt, yanked a white T-shirt over her head, and reached into her closet for her snakeskin slides, figuring that even if the outfit was a near-disaster, her shoes would be, as always, without fault.

She groped along the shelf. Boots, boots, loafers, heels, pink slides, black slides, the ill-advised pair of Tevas she'd purchased the week she thought she might become one of those fresh-faced, rosy-cheeked L.L. Bean girls who hiked the Appalachian Trail during spring break . . . where the hell was the pair she was looking for?

"Maggie," she moaned, with her hands still rooting through the tangle of straps and buckles. "Maggie, if you took my shoes, I swear to God . . ." And then, before she could decide what she was vowing to do to her sister, if she ever saw her sister again, Rose's fingertips brushed the tops of the slides in question. She snatched them off the shelf, shoved her bare feet inside of them, grabbed her purse, and headed for the door. She stabbed the elevator button, then rocked from leg to leg, making sure her keys were in her purse, trying to avoid her reflection in the elevator doors, certain that she wouldn't like what she'd see. The Former Lawyer, she thought, glancing ruefully at her legs, freshly shaved but still scabby.

Simon Stein was waiting outside her building, wearing a button-down blue shirt, khakis, and brown loafers, the uniform at

Lewis, Dommel, and Fenick on the days that didn't require a team jersey. Unfortunately, he hadn't grown eight inches and become handsome and broad-shouldered since she'd seen him last. But he was holding open a cab door in a very polite manner. "Hi," he said, and looked her over approvingly. "Pretty dress."

"It's a skirt," said Rose. "Where are we off to?"

"Surprise," said Simon, and gave her a confident nod. A practiced, lawyerly, brisk little *everything's fine* nod. A nod that Rose herself had once deployed to great effect. "Don't worry. I'm not going to kidnap you or anything."

"Or anything," Rose repeated, still shocked at the sight of seeing her nod performed by Simon Stein. The cab pulled to the curb on a suspect-looking block of South Street. There was a chain-link fence holding back an overgrown tangle of weeds and grass on one side of the street, a burned-looking house with boarded-up windows on the other, and at the corner, a little concrete storefront, painted green, with the words *Jerk Hut* in neon over the window.

"So this is where all my boyfriends have been coming from!" said Rose. Simon Stein, to his credit, gave a Petunia-ish snort, and held the door open for Rose to climb out, his blue eyes alight with amusement—or maybe just excitement about dinner, Rose thought. He had a brown paper bag tucked under one arm, Rose noticed. She glanced around uneasily, noticing a cluster of men leaning against the boarded-up building, passing a bottle back and forth, and the litter of broken glass on the sidewalk.

"Not to fear," said Simon, holding her elbow and steering her toward the storefront . . . then past it, where there was a painted wooden door, standing in the center of the sidewalk, with nothing on either side of it but the ratty-looking tangle of green. He put his hand on the door and looked at Rose. "Do you like Jamaican food?"

"Do I have a choice?" asked Rose, glancing back over her shoulder at the men as their cab pulled away.

If it wasn't for the square glittering mica-flecked gray stones that formed a path through the tangle of city growth—empty bottles, half-rotted newspaper, something that looked a lot like a used condom—Rose would have been certain they were wandering toward another vacant lot. The grass was knee-high, seemingly untended, and she could hear what sounded like steel drums in the distance.

Then they rounded a corner, and Rose could see a multilayered deck behind the tiny storefront, a deck tented in orange cloth, and lined with tiny white lights like stars. The edges of the deck were ringed with lit torches, and there was a three-piece band on one of the platforms. She could smell cloves and chilies and wood smoke curling from the grill, and above her head, even on this lousy block of South Street, the sky was full of stars.

Simon led Rose to a wooden table on the deck and pulled out Rose's chair. "Isn't this great?" he asked, looking pleased with himself. "You'd never know it was back here."

"How'd you find it?" asked Rose faintly. She was still looking at the sky.

"Instinct," Simon said. "And it was reviewed in the paper." He pulled a six-pack out of the brown paper bag and peppered her with questions. Did she like spicy food? Was she allergic to nuts or shellfish? Did she have any philosophical or gustatory objection to eating goat? It was like giving a medical history, centered solely on food, Rose thought, smiling and telling him that yes, she liked spicy, no, she wasn't allergic, and that she supposed she could taste the goat.

"Good," said Simon, closing the menu. Rose felt relieved, as if she'd passed some kind of test. Which was ridiculous, she thought. Who was Simon Stein to be giving her tests, and what did it matter whether she passed them?

After the curried goat and the spicy shrimp, after the beef patties and jerk chicken wings and coconut rice, and after Rose had an unprecedented three beers, plus a swallow of a fourth, Simon asked Rose a question.

"Tell me something you like," he said.

Rose hiccupped. "A person?" she asked coyly, "or a thing?" She was thinking that he would say, "a person," and she would say, "you," at which point, she figured, he would decide that it was okay to kiss her. She'd played the kissing-Simon scenario in her mind somewhere after the third beer, and had decided that if the night ended with her being kissed by Simon Stein, it would be okay. There were worse things, she reasoned, than sitting underneath the stars on a warm spring Saturday night, being kissed by a man, even if the man was a good three inches shorter than she was, and obsessed with food and the law firm's softball team. He was nice. Really nice. So she'd kiss him.

But Simon Stein surprised her. "A thing," he said. "A thing you like."

Rose considered her options. Your smile? This place? The beer? Instead she fished in her purse and produced her key chain, her new key chain that she purchased at the dollar store on Chestnut Street after she started acquiring people's keys. "I like this," she said, and showed him that at the end of the key chain there was a tiny flashlight, no bigger than a wine cork. It took her a few tries, because her fingers were thick and somewhat clumsy from the beer, but she managed to turn it on and flash it at his face. "This cost a dollar."

"A bargain," said Simon Stein. Rose frowned. Was he making fun of her? She took another swallow of beer and tossed her hair.

"Sometimes," she said, "I think about getting on my bike and riding across the country."

"By yourself?"

Rose nodded. She could picture, it, too—getting a set of panniers to clip over her back wheel, and one of those little trailers that long-distance cyclists tow behind their bikes, getting a one-person tent and a sleeping bag, and sticking Petunia in the trailer and . . . going. Riding in the morning, stopping for lunch at a diner or café, pedaling a few more hours, then setting her tent up by a stream, writing in a journal (in this fantasy, she kept a journal, though she didn't in real life), reading one of her romance novels, and falling asleep under the stars.

It was like the fantasy she'd had in the years after her mother had died, of getting a motor home, one of those Winnebagos a lane and a half wide with all of the modern conveniences built right in. She must have seen a picture somewhere, or maybe even been inside of one. She remembered how they were like little self-contained worlds, with the beds that folded out of the walls, and the tiny two-burner stoves, the shower stalls barely big enough to fit into, TV sets hidden in the ceilings. Her dream had been to get her father and Maggie and just drive away. They'd leave their place in New Jersey and go somewhere warmer, somewhere where there was no wet road, no gray headstone, no trooper at the door. Phoenix, Arizona; San Diego, California; Albuquerque, New Mexico. Someplace sunny, where it was always summer, where it smelled like oranges.

She'd lie awake in bed and roll those names on her tongue, imagining the trailer, imagining Maggie tucked tight into the bottom bunk bed, imagining herself brave enough to sleep on top, and their father at the wheel, his face handsome and happy in the light of the dashboard. They'd get their dog, Honey Bun, back, and their father would stop being allergic, and Honey Bun would sleep on a pillow in the passenger's seat, and their father wouldn't cry anymore. They'd drive and drive until they were far away, until they'd outrun the memory of her mother, and the kids who'd tormented her on the playground and the teachers who shook their heads at Maggie. Then they'd find somewhere to stay by the ocean. She and Maggie would be best friends. They'd swim every day, and cook their food on a campfire, and sleep snug in the mobile home every night.

"Thank you," her father would say. "This was such a good idea, Rose. You saved us." Rose would feel the truth of it, like sunshine, like the feel of her own skin, the weight of her own bones. She would save all three of them, she'd think, and finally fall asleep, dreaming of bunk beds and turning wheels and the ocean she'd never seen.

"Would you be lonely?" asked Simon.

"Lonely?" Rose repeated. For a moment, she wasn't sure what

he was talking about. She was still lost in the fantasy of the mobile home, which she'd embroidered and amplified over the years, even when she realized it would never come true. The one time she'd come across an ad for a used Winnebago in the neighborhood shopping circular and hesitantly pointed it out to her father, he'd squinted at her as if she'd started speaking Martian, then said, kindly, "I don't think so."

"Don't you think you'd miss people?" asked Simon.

Rose shook her head instantly. "I don't need . . ." She took a deep breath, stopping herself before she said it. Suddenly she felt hot, unbearably hot and uncomfortable. The music was too loud, and her face was flushed, and the spicy food was forming an excruciating knot in her stomach. She gulped at her glass of water and started again. "I'm very independent," she said. "I like being alone."

"What's wrong?" he asked. "Are you okay? Do you want some ginger ale? They make their own here; it's great if your stomach's upset. . . ."

Rose waved him away, then buried her face in her hands. With her eyes closed she could still see the Winnebago the way she'd imagined it, the three of them beneath an awning that would extend from the wall, holding hot dogs over a campfire on a beach, sitting up in their sleeping bags, safe and snug in their perfect little home like caterpillars in a cocoon. She'd wanted so badly for it to be true, and instead she'd lost her father to Sydelle, and to a world of box scores and stock tickers, where the only subjects he could safely discuss were free-throw percentages and the stability of the bond market, where the only things he let himself feel were excitement when the Eagles won and disappointment when his investments lost. And Maggie . . .

"Oh," she moaned, aware that she was probably scaring Simon Stein, but unable to help herself. Maggie. She thought she'd be able to save Maggie. And look how that had turned out. She didn't even know where her sister, her own sister, was living.

"Oh," she said again, softly, and now Simon Stein's arm was wrapped around her shoulder.

"What is it?" he asked. "Do you think you've got food poisoning?" He sounded so solicitous that Rose started to laugh. "Can you drink some water?" He reached for his pocket. "I've got Pepcid, Alka-Seltzer . . ."

Rose raised her head. "Does this happen a lot to you on dates?"

Simon Stein pursed his lips. "I wouldn't say it happens frequently," he finally said. "But maybe on occasion." He looked at her carefully. "Are you okay?"

"Insofar as I don't have food poisoning, I'm fine," said Rose.

"Then what is it?" he asked.

"I just . . . I was thinking of someone."

"Who?"

And Rose blurted the first thing that came into her head. "Petunia. This dog that I take care of." And Simon Stein, to his eternal credit, did not laugh or so much as snicker, or look at her like she was crazy. He simply stood up, folded his napkin, left a ten-dollar tip on the table, and said, "So let's go get her."

"This is crazy," Rose whispered.

"Shh," said Simon Stein.

"We could get in trouble," Rose insisted.

"Why?" Simon asked. "You're supposed to walk the dog on Saturday. Well, it's Saturday."

"It's Friday night."

"It is," said Simon, consulting his watch, "five minutes after midnight."

Rose rolled her eyes. They were in the elevator of Petunia's apartment building, which was empty except for the two of them. "Do you always have to be right?"

"I prefer it," Simon said, and this struck Rose as hysterically funny. She started laughing. Simon put his hand over her mouth.

"Shh," he whispered. Rose fumbled with her flashlight key chain, found the key whose masking-tape label read, "Petunia," and handed it to Simon.

"Okay," said Simon, "here's how we're going to pull this off. I'll unlock the door. You turn off the alarm. I'll grab the dog. Where do you think she'll be?"

Rose considered this. Her brain felt fogged. After all of the beers at the Jerk Hut, they'd gone to a bar to perfect Operation Petunia; there had been some vodka involved. "I don't know," she finally answered. "When I come get her, she's usually on the couch, but I don't know where she sleeps when her people are home."

"Well, leave that to me," he said. Rose was inclined to do just that. She hadn't been keeping score, but she was almost positive that he hadn't had as much vodka as she'd had.

"Leash?" asked Simon, and Rose reached into her pocket and pulled out the two shoelaces that they'd pulled out of Simon's shoes and tied together at the bar. "Treat?" Rose fished in her purse and came up with a napkin-wrapped beef patty, the grease staining the napkin. "Note?" Rose produced another napkin. After three drafts, they'd decided that "Dear Shirley, I was in the neighborhood and thought I'd give Petunia an early walk," sounded the most plausible.

"Are you ready?" asked Simon, grasping Rose by the shoulders and looking deeply into her eyes, smiling at her. "Are you set?" asked Simon, and Rose nodded again. Simon leaned forward and gave her a kiss on the lips. "Let's do it," he said, only Rose was so shocked by the intensity of the kiss that she stood there, frozen, as Simon unlocked the door and the alarm started howling into the night.

"Rose!" he hissed. She rushed into the apartment, stabbing at the alarm keypad, as Petunia scuttled into the living room, barking frantically before she slid to a stop on the hardwood floors and started wagging her tail.

Shirley hurried behind the dog, portable phone at the ready. "Oh," she said, peering at the two of them. "Simon. You don't knock anymore?"

Rose gaped, staring from Simon to Shirley to Petunia, who was currently trying to launch herself into Simon's arms. And Simon was smiling at her. "Rose," he said, "this is my grandmother. Nanna, you know Rose, right?"

"Of course I know Rose," Shirley said impatiently. "Petunia, cut that out!" A chastened Petunia stopped jumping and sat on the floor, her stump of a tail moving in frantic circles, her pink tongue lolling. Rose stood as if she'd been frozen, staring and trying to make sense of it, but sense was not forthcoming.

"So . . . you know Petunia?" she finally asked.

Simon nodded. "I've known Petunia since she was this big," he said, holding his hands in the shape of a teacup.

"And you know Simon," said Shirley.

"We used to work together," said Rose.

"Great," said Shirley. "So now that everyone knows everyone, can I go to sleep?"

Simon walked over and kissed his grandmother's forehead. "Thanks, Nanna," he said sweetly. "Sorry we woke you up."

Shirley nodded, said something that Rose couldn't quite hear, and left them alone in the hallway. Petunia, still on her haunches, still with her tail wagging happily, looked from Simon's face to Rose's face and back again.

"What did she say?" Rose asked faintly.

Simon smiled at her. "I think she said, 'It took you long enough.' "

"What did . . . How did . . ."

Simon pulled Petunia's leash out of the drawer where Shirley kept it, and smiled at Rose. "Let's go for a walk," he said. He held Petunia's leash in one hand, and Rose's hand in the other, and led them up to his apartment, where Petunia curled up at the foot of the bed, and Rose and Simon lay together on top of his blue comforter, whispering and kissing and sometimes laughing so hard that Petunia woke up and snorted at them, until the sun came up.

FORTY-ONE

Maggie stepped out of the shower, dried off quickly, and pulled on her clean clothes as fast as she could. She brushed her hair into a ponytail, took one last look behind her, then eased the door shut, moving fast, before she could lose her nerve. She was going to tell Charles her story. She'd pitch it as a play she was thinking about writing. *Once upon a time, a girl ran away to college.* She'd hear what he said, she'd watch his face as she told him, and if he seemed receptive, she'd tell him that it was true. She pushed the door open and ran into a man. Josh. Josh from her first night at Princeton, who was standing there in the darkness, glaring at her, with her backpack dangling from his hands.

Her breath froze in her throat as she reeled backward against a wall. Josh didn't look drunk or dazed or flirtatious and besotted. He looked like he wanted to kill her, and that he might be convinced to settle for hurting her instead. *Bad hookups always come back,* Maggie thought, and inched backward, wondering what he wanted, wondering how he'd even gotten in here, because the library was closed. He must have waited for her, which meant that they were alone in the library basement together . . .

Oh, God, thought Maggie, inching backward, trying to melt into the wall. This was going to be bad. This was going to be so bad.

"Well, hello," he said softly, and rubbed his thumb over her tattoo, the one that said "Mother," the one she figured he'd finally remembered from that one night in his bed. "Little M. You owe me something, I think."

"I'll give the money back," Maggie whispered, as he pressed so close to her that his nose brushed hers. "It's in my bag; I never even spent it; I'll give it back to you right now . . ." She shuddered as he held her, and bit back hard against a scream. *Disaster,* she thought bleakly. Just like the poem said. *Like disaster.* She squirmed against him, thinking that she could run, that maybe she'd have a chance then, but he was holding on too tightly, and kept whispering horrible things at her.

"What are you doing here?" he asked her. "You don't belong. You're not supposed to be here. So what's your story?"

"I'll give you your money. Just let me go," said Maggie, and tried to wriggle away, but he had her cornered, pushed up against the icy granite of the library wall. He kept talking to her—talking at her, really, pushing words into her face as she twisted. His voice was constant, but as he talked, his tone shifted from hectoring and accusatory to an oily wheedle.

"Maybe I should let you make it up to me some other way," he said, running his eyes over her body in a way that made her feel like he'd just dumped acid down her shirt. "I don't remember exactly what happened that night, but I don't think we finished what we started. And we're all alone here. We could finish up now."

Maggie moaned and writhed desperately. "Let me go," she begged.

"Why should I?" asked Josh. His pale face was flushed. His blond hair hung over his forehead, and he sprayed her with spit as he talked. "You're in trouble. A lot of trouble. I went through your backpack. Three IDs. Very nice. My credit cards, of course, and plenty of cash. Who's that from? How many other guys? And are you living down here? Do you have any idea what would happen if I told campus security? Or the cops?"

Maggie turned her face down and started to cry silently. She couldn't help it. In a way, this talking, his hands binding her wrists, was every bit as bad as it had been when the guys had grabbed at her in the impound lot . . . and she was as frightened as she'd been there. It was the shame of it, his words raining down on her like a hailstorm, scalding her skin. And it was so unfair. What was her crime? What had she taken? Some food, when there was plenty to go around. Some books, which their owners were stupid or lazy or rich enough to just leave lying around, unattended. Some clothes from lost-and-found baskets, some empty seats in lecture halls where the professors were going to talk anyhow.

Maggie lifted her chin and widened her eyes. "Okay," she said. "That's enough." She forced herself to smile, forced herself to pull her hair free from her ponytail and flick it over her shoulders. "You got me," she murmured. "You got me right where you want me." She summoned every ounce of charm she had, all of the sex appeal she'd kept buried under sweatshirts for the semester, and gave him a smile as rich and inviting as a dollop of caramel on a scoop of vanilla ice cream. "Want to go exploring?" she asked, hearing the quiver in her voice and praying that he missed it, praying that her body would be a sufficient distraction.

Josh wiped his hands on his jeans. It was all the opening Maggie needed. She grabbed her backpack by a strap and whirled it at him, whacking him on the side of his face. He stumbled backward. She kicked him in the shin as hard as she could. He gasped and doubled over, and Maggie took off.

She bolted up three flights of stairs, pushed through the heavy glass doors, hearing alarms blaring behind her, as she sprinted across the courtyard, holding her backpack by the strap that had broken when he grabbed her, her mind blank, her feet flying, her blood singing with adrenaline. It was a gorgeous spring night. Students in shorts and T-shirts drifted along the walkways, lounged under the weeping willows, called each other's names through open windows. Maggie felt as if she were naked, or wearing a sign that read, "I DON'T BELONG HERE." She ran faster and faster, a cramp stabbing at her rib cage, out of the campus, onto the sidewalk, over to the bus station on Nassau Street. *Please God please God please,* she prayed, and a bus rolled into view. She jumped on board, grabbed change from her pocket and shoved it in the till, then sat down, wrapping her arms around her backpack. Her heart was still thundering in her chest.

Get to Corinne's, she thought. Get to Corinne's and think of something that will make her let me in, even though it's the middle of the night and I'm not supposed to be there until the morning. She sat back in the seat and squeezed her eyes shut, thinking that she was in a box, another box, same as when she'd started out here, and she'd have to think her way out of it, same as she had before. Then she pulled her cell phone out of her pocket, swallowed hard, and dialed her sister's number. It was late. It was a school night. Rose would be home. She'd know what to do.

Except Rose wasn't home. "Hello, you've reached Rose Feller, and Feller Pet Care," said the machine. What? "Please leave me a message with your name, number, the name of your pet, and the dates you require service, and I will return your call as soon as possible." Wrong number, Maggie thought. It had to be. She dialed again and got the same thing, only this time after the beep she opened her mouth. "Rose," she croaked. "I'm . . ." I'm what? I'm in trouble—again? I need you to bail me out—again? Maggie closed her eyes and her telephone. She'd figure it out herself.

"Maggie?" asked Corinne, looking off-balance as she stood at her door. "What time is it? What are you doing here?"

"It's late," said Maggie. "There's been . . . I have . . ." She took a deep breath. "I was wondering if I could stay for a few days. I'll pay you rent, or I'll clean for you for free . . ."

Corinne held the door open with her hip. "What happened?"

Maggie ran through the possibilities. Could she tell Corinne she'd had a fight with a roommate? Had she told Corinne that she had roommates? She couldn't remember. And what if the terrible boy had followed her here? If he knew she was staying in the library, maybe he knew she was working here, too.

"Maggie?" Corinne's forehead was wrinkled. She didn't have her sunglasses on, and Maggie could see her blue eyes darting back and forth like lost fish.

"Something happened," Maggie said.

"I think we've established that," said Corinne, letting Maggie in and walking toward the kitchen with her fingertips brushing along the wall. Maggie sat at the table while Corinne filled the kettle, flicked on the gas, took two mugs and two tea bags down from the shelf beside the stove. "Can you tell me what?"

Maggie bowed her head. "Not really," she whispered.

"Is it drugs?" Corinne asked sharply, and Maggie was so startled that she laughed.

"No," she said. "Not drugs. I just need to lay low for a while." Which, she realized, made her sound like a complete criminal, but it was all she could think of on short notice. "I'm just kind of stressed," she added lamely. "And it's so peaceful here."

Clearly, she'd said the magic words. Corinne beamed. She spooned sugar into the tea and brought the cups to the table. "Finals are hard, aren't they?" she said. "I remember trying to study for mine. The dorms were so noisy, and the library got so crowded! Don't worry," she told Maggie. "You can stay in any of the rooms on the third floor. They're all clean, right?"

"Right," said Maggie. She'd cleaned them herself. She sipped her tea and tried to stop her heart from racing. Plan. Plan. She needed another plan. She'd stay here a few days. She'd have to buy herself some new things; she had a change of clothes and some underwear in her backpack, but the rest of her stuff was in the library and she couldn't go get it. And then where? Could she go back to her father, back to Rose? Would they take her back? Would she want to go?

She closed her eyes and saw herself sitting in the back row of the poetry class, telling the professor what "One Art" meant. She saw Charles's face, his hair falling over his forehead as he talked about Shakespeare and Strindberg and how he'd seen John Malkovich on stage once. Nobody at Princeton had known she was a failure or a fuckup, her family's shame, the black mark on their report card. Nobody at Princeton knew she was any different than they were. Until the boy in the library. Until now.

She blinked hard. She wouldn't cry. She'd figure this out. Lay low, she thought. Then get out. She couldn't stay here while that guy was still on campus, and after the students went home, she wouldn't be able to stay, because there'd be no one left for her to blend in with. So then what?

"Maggie?" Corinne asked. Maggie stared at her. "Do you have family? Is there someone I should call?"

Maggie sniffed and bit her lip. She wanted to cry, but what good would crying do? "No," she said. Her voice was wobbly. "I don't. I don't have anyone."

Corinne cocked her head. "Are you sure?"

Maggie thought of her backpack, the money she kept wrapped in a rubber band, snug in one of the inside zippered pockets. She heard Josh's voice. *I went through your backpack.* She grabbed for it, yanking it open. The money was gone. Her IDs and credit cards were gone. There was nothing except clothes, and books, and . . . Her fingers brushed the softened paper of the birthday card. She pulled it out, opened it up, reading it for the hundredth time, the birthday greetings, and the signature, and the phone number.

"A grandmother," she said, in a quivery voice. "I have a grandmother."

Corinne gave a well-that's-settled nod. "Go to sleep," she said. "Take whichever bedroom you want. You can call her in the morning."

And so, the next morning, Maggie stood in the center of Corinne's sun-washed kitchen, with her cell phone in her hand, and dialed the number that the grandmother had written on the card almost twenty years before. The phone rang and rang. Maggie crossed the fingers of both hands. *Please,* she thought, unsure of what she wishing for, except for someone to answer.

And somebody did.

Rose Feller woke up at five in the morning in a strange bed with her heart pounding. *Maggie,* she thought. She'd been dreaming of Maggie.

"Maggie," she said out loud, but even as she was saying it, even as she was swimming up through sleep toward wakefulness, she wasn't sure that it was Maggie she'd seen. A woman running through a forest. That had been all. A woman with terrified eyes, her mouth stretched into a scream, running through green branches that reached out like arms to trap her.

"Maggie," she said again. Petunia stared up at Rose, before deciding that there was neither an emergency nor food at hand, and closed her eyes again. Rose swung her legs out of the bed. Simon put his hand on her hip.

"Shh," he said, pulling her back toward him, curling his body around hers and kissing the back of her neck. "What's wrong?" He nuzzled her, and she felt the crisp curls of his hair brush against her neck. "Did you have a bad dream?"

"I dreamed about my mother," said Rose, in a low voice, slower and deeper than her own, an underwater sleeping voice. But was that right, either? Her mother. Maggie. Or maybe it was here, running through those trees, tripping over roots, falling down on her knees and splayed hands, then getting up, running some more. But running from whom? And toward what? "My mother's dead, you know. Did I tell you that? I can't remember. She died when I was little."

"I'll be right back," Simon whispered, and got up from the bed. She heard him padding through the kitchen, returning in his silly striped pajamas a minute later with a glass of water in his hand. She drank it gratefully as he got back into bed and turned off the lights. Then he curled around her again, with one hand snug across her forehead and the other cupping the base of her head as if she were something delicate and rare.

"I'm sorry about your mom," he said. "Do you want to talk about it?"

Rose shook her head.

"You can tell me anything," said Simon. "I'll take care of you. I promise." But Rose told him nothing that night. She just closed her eyes, let herself lean against him, and let herself fall into asleep.

Ella was sitting at her table, staring at her notebook, working on compiling a list of free health screenings for the upcoming week's *Golden Acres Gazette* when the telephone rang.

"Hello?" she said.

No answer . . . just breathing.

"Hello," she repeated. "Mrs. Lefkowitz, is that you? Are you all right?"

A young woman's voice answered her question. "Is this Ella Hirsch?"

Telemarketer, thought Ella. "Yes, it is."

The voice paused. "Did you have a daughter named Caroline?"

Ella drew a breath. "I do," she said without thinking. "That is, I did."

"Well," said the young woman. "You don't know me. My name is Maggie Feller."

"Maggie," Ella said instantly, feeling the familiar mixture of hope and relief and exhilaration and terror flooding through her as she said her granddaughter's name again. "Maggie. I called. That is, I called your sister . . . did she get my message? Did she tell you?"

"No," said Maggie, and paused. "Look," she started again. "You don't know me, and you don't have any reason to help me out, but I'm in trouble right now, I'm in a lot of trouble . . ."

"I'll help you," Ella answered immediately, and squeezed her eyes shut, hoping fiercely as Maggie told her how.

PART THREE

I Carry Your Heart

FORTY-TWO

Rose Feller had never wished for a mother as much as she did during her engagement to Simon Stein. Their first date had been in April. By May they were seeing each other four and five days a week. By July Simon had all but moved into Rose's apartment. And in September he'd taken her back to the Jerk Hut, ducked under the table, ostensibly to retrieve a dropped napkin, and reappeared with a black velvet box in his hand. "It's too soon," Rose had said, still not quite believing that this was happening, and Simon had looked at her steadily and said, "I'm sure about you."

The wedding was set for May, and it was already October, which meant, as the salesladies this afternoon had been quick to point out, that Rose was late in selecting a wedding dress. "Do you know how long it takes for the dresses to arrive?" the woman at the first shop had asked. Rose had thought of retorting, "Do you know how long it took me to find a guy to marry?" but decided to keep her mouth shut.

"This is torture," she said, struggling to haul up the panty hose that had developed an inch-thick run the instant she'd poked one foot inside.

"Shall I call Amnesty International?" Amy asked. Rose shook her head and tossed her sneakers into a corner of the peach-painted, lace-curtained dressing room of a bridal shop (or "shoppe," as Rose had learned to think of them), where the air smelled like lavender potpourri and the Muzak played only love songs. She was strapped into a bustier that hoisted her breasts to practically chin level and, as she would later discover, left nasty welts in her side, plus a girdle that the saleslady had tried to tell her was really a "shaper brief," except Rose knew a girdle when she saw one—and when she felt one cutting off her air supply. But the saleslady had insisted. "The proper foundation garments are crucial," she'd said, looking at Rose as if to say, *and the rest of my brides-to-be have already figured that out.*

"You don't know what I'm going through," Rose moaned. The saleslady bundled a dress in her arms and held it open for Rose. "Dive," she ordered. Rose tucked her arms by her sides, bent at the waist, wincing at the pinch of her double-barreled girdle, and shoved her head through the opening, groping. The dress's full skirt fell down to her ankles as Rose poked her arms through the sleeves and the saleslady started attempting to work the zipper up her back.

"What are you going through?" asked Amy.

Rose closed her eyes and uttered the name that had haunted her during the two months of her engagement, and who would, she felt certain, continue to bedevil her as the wedding date drew closer. "Sydelle," she said.

"Oy," said Amy.

"Oy is not the half of it," said Rose. "My wicked stepmother has now decided that she wants to be my best friend." And it was true. When she and Simon had driven to New Jersey to tell Michael Feller and his wife the good news, Michael had hugged his daughter and clapped Simon on the back, while Sydelle sat on the couch looking stricken. "How wonderful," she finally managed, the words squeezing through her thin, perfectly-painted lips while her jumbo nostrils flared as if she was trying to inhale the coffee table. "How wonderful for you both!" And the very next day she'd called Rose at home to insist that they have tea to celebrate, and to offer her services as a wedding planner. "Not to toot my own horn, dear, but people are still talking about My Marcia's wedding," she'd said. Rose thought that was understandable, given Sydelle's penchant for mentioning Marcia's wedding in every conversation, but she was caught so completely off guard by Sydelle's doing something that didn't involve criticism of her clothes, hair, or diet, that she agreed. With her brand-new ring still feeling strange on her finger, she'd gone off to the Ritz-Carlton to meet Sydelle for tea.

"It was wretched," she remembered as Amy nodded and smoothed the elbow-length lace gloves she'd tried on. Rose had spotted her stepmother instantly. Sydelle sat alone at a table set with a teapot and two gold-rimmed cups. She looked as formidable as always. Her hair was blow-dried into immobility, and her skin looked as shiny and taut as shrink-wrap. She wore immaculate makeup, imposing gold accessories, and the brown leather jacket that Rose had ogled in the window of Joan Shepp on her way to the hotel.

"Rose," she'd cooed, "you look marvelous." The glance she gave to Rose's khaki skirt and ponytail suggested otherwise. "Now," she said, once they'd made a few minutes of small talk, "let's get to the details. Do you have a color scheme in mind?"

"Um," said Rose. Which was all the opening that Sydelle Feller required.

"Navy," she decreed. "Navy's the latest. Very, very chic. Very now. I'm seeing . . ." And she closed her eyes, allowing Rose a moment to marvel at the shades of brown, taupe, and putty eyeshadow cleverly blended on her lids. ". . . bridesmaids in simple navy sheaths . . ."

"I'm not having bridesmaids. Just Amy. She'll be my maid of honor," said Rose. Sydelle raised one perfectly plucked eyebrow.

"What about Maggie?"

Rose stared at the pink linen tablecloth. She'd gotten a very strange message from Maggie months before. A one-word message, consisting of only Rose's name, and the word *I'm.* No word since then, although every few weeks Rose would call the cell phone and hang up after her sister had said "Hello." "I'm not sure," she said.

Sydelle sighed. "Let's talk tables," she said. "I'm seeing navy tablecloths with white napkins, very nautical, very crisp, and we'll want delphiniums, of course, and those gorgeous gerbera daisies . . . or, no. No," said Sydelle, shaking her head once, as if Rose had contradicted to her. "Pink roses. Can you see it? Masses and masses of pink roses, overflowing from silver bowls!" She smiled, looking pleased with herself. "Roses for Rose! Of course!"

"Sounds beautiful!" said Rose. And it did, she guessed. "But, um, with the bridesmaids . . ."

"And of course," Sydelle continued, as if Rose hadn't spoken, "you'll want My Marcia, too."

Rose gulped. She didn't want My Marcia. At all.

"I know she'd be honored," Sydelle said sweetly.

Rose bit her lip. "Um," she began. "I really . . . I think . . ." *Come on!* she urged herself. "Just Amy, really. That's all I want."

Sydelle pursed her lips and flared her nostrils.

"Maybe Marcia could do a reading," Rose said, groping desperately for a bone to throw her stepmother.

"Whatever you like, dear," Sydelle said icily. "It's your wedding, of course." Which was the line Rose had repeated to Simon that night.

"It's our wedding. Of course," she said, and buried her head in her hands. "I just have this horrible feeling that I'm going to wind up with My Marcia and five of her best friends in matching navy sheaths walking me down the aisle."

"You don't want My Marcia?" Simon asked innocently. "But she's so classy! You know, I heard that when she was married, she bought a size six Vera Wang and had it taken in."

"I've heard that rumor, too," Rose muttered.

Simon took her hands. "My beloved," he said, "it's our wedding. It will be just the way we want it. As many bridesmaids as you want. Or none at all."

That night, Rose and Simon wrote out the short list of what

they wanted (great food, a kick-ass band), and what they didn't ("Celebration," a garter toss, My Marcia).

"And no chicken dance!" Simon said the next morning.

"We're having roses!" Rose yelled toward his departing blue-suited back. "Silver bowls overflowing with pink roses! Doesn't that sound beautiful!"

Simon shouted a word that sounded alarmingly like "allergic" over his shoulder, and hurried toward the bus. Rose sighed, and went inside to call Sydelle. By the end of their conversation, she'd agreed to outfit her wedding party in navy, to dress the tables in white, to let My Marcia read a poem of her choosing, and to meet with Sydelle's preferred florist the following week.

"What kind of women talk about 'my florist'?" Rose asked Amy, as Amy cruised the glass case full of headpieces, finally selecting a pearl-studded pouf and plopping it on her own head.

"Pretentious ones," Amy said, affixing an ankle-length veil shimmering with tiny crystals to Rose's head. "Ooh, pretty!" She found a matching veil and put it on her own head. "Come along," she said, and tugged Rose toward a mirror.

Rose looked at herself in the seventh and final dress she'd selected. Yards of lace swirled around her legs. A glittering bodice, stiff with sparkling crystals, encased approximately two-thirds of her midriff and gaped open in back. Stiff embroidered sleeves choked her arms. Rose stared at herself miserably. "Oh, God," she said, "I'm a Mardi Gras float!"

Amy burst out laughing. The saleslady stared at both of them. "Would shoes help?" she asked.

"I think a lighter would help," Amy murmured.

"I think," Rose began. God, she needed a mother. A mother would be able to take the situation in hand, to look at the dress and dismiss it with a brief but undeniable shake of her head. A mother would say, "My daughter likes things that are simple," or, "I see her in an A-line"—or a ballgown, a basque waist, one of those bewildering types of dresses. Even after weeks of study, Rose hadn't been able to puzzle out the differences between them, let alone figure out which one would look best on her. A mother would get her out of this itchy tornado of a dress, out of the iron-lung girdle, out of the showers and teas and cocktail parties and dinners that Rose could no more navigate than she could paddle single-handed up the Schuylkill. And surely a mother would know how to politely tell Sydelle Feller to take her two dozen suggestions and shove them up her tiny, tight ass.

"It's awful," Rose finally blurted.

"Well, I'm sorry," said the saleslady, whose feelings Rose had obviously hurt.

"Maybe something a little less fussy?" Amy suggested. The saleslady pursed her lips and disappeared into the store's back room. Rose slumped into a chair, hearing a sighing noise as the dress deflated around her.

"We should elope," she said.

"Well, I have always loved you, but not in that way," said Amy. "And there's no way I'm letting you elope. You'd deprive me of my butt bow." The day after Rose had told her best friend that she was getting married—before Sydelle had issued her edict on navy— Amy had made a pilgrimage to Philadelphia's premiere thrift shop and procured a frothy salmon-colored frock with tiered layers of tulle, oversized rhinestone buckles at the shoulder, and a butt bow as wide as a city bus, plus, as an engagement gift, a six-inch-thick ivory candle studded with fake plastic pearls and the words *Today I Marry My Best Friend* curling around the sides in gold gilt. "You're not serious," Rose had said, and Amy had shrugged and said that she understood her role as maid of honor, that it was the bride's day to shine, and that if she bought this dress (with shoes dyed salmon to match), she'd be the shoo-in victor at Philadelphia's annual Bridesmaids' Ball, where the women competed to see who had the worst dress. "Plus, as it happens," she'd said, "I look *fierce* in a butt bow."

Now she wrapped her arms around Rose's shoulders. "Don't

worry," she said. "We'll find it. We're just getting started! If it was supposed to be easy, do you think they'd publish thirty million magazines about how to find the dress?"

Rose sighed and got to her feet. Out of the corner of her eye she saw the saleslady approaching, her arms overflowing with silk and satin. "Maybe this dress isn't so bad," she muttered.

"No," said Amy, looking her up and down, "no, it is indeed awful."

"In here, please," the saleslady said curtly, and Rose picked up her skirt and dragged her train in behind her.

FORTY‑THREE

Ella Hirsh had endured almost an entire summer of her grand-daughter's silence before deciding that she wouldn't take one moment more.

Maggie had arrived in May, the day after that first tortured, stop-and-start conversation, during which Ella had to keep asking her to repeat herself to make sure that she understood what her long-lost granddaughter was telling her, that this was Maggie, not Rose, and that she was at Princeton, but not really there. Yes, said Maggie, Rose and her father were fine, but she couldn't call them. No, she wasn't hurt, or sick, but she needed a place to go. She didn't have a job at the moment, but she was a hard worker, and she'd find something. Ella wouldn't have to worry about supporting her. There were a thousand things more that Ella wanted to ask her, but she stuck to the basics, the who and what and where, and the mechanics of how to get Maggie from the New Jersey supermarket parking lot down to Florida. "Can you get to Newark?" she asked, somehow extracting the name of New Jersey's major airport from her head. "Call me when you get there. I'll call the airlines, figure out who's got a direct flight, and there'll be a ticket waiting for you at the gate."

Eight hours later, Ella and Lewis had driven to the Fort Lauderdale airport, and there, clutching a backpack and looking weary and bedraggled and scared, was Caroline.

Ella had gasped and squeezed her eyes shut, and when she'd opened them, she saw that she was wrong. This girl wasn't Caroline, not really. Ella saw that as soon as she blinked . . . but the resemblance was very strong. This girl's brown eyes, the way her hair fell over her forehead, her cheeks and her hands and even, somehow, her collarbones, were all Caroline's. But the determined look on her face, the pugnacious set of her chin, the way her eyes had moved over them quickly, sizing them up, told a different story, and certainly forecast a different ending than the one her own daughter had come to. This girl, Ella saw, would not succumb to the lure of a rain-slicked road. This girl would keep her hands on the wheel.

There was an early awkward moment—would they hug?—which Maggie had solved by shifting her backpack into her arms and holding it like a baby, as Ella stumbled through the introductions. Maggie hadn't said much on the way out to short-term parking. She'd refused Ella's offer of the front seat, and sat up straight in the backseat as Lewis drove and Ella tried hard not to pester her with too many questions. Still, she had to know, for her own safety, her own peace of mind, if nothing else. "If you'll tell me what kind of trouble you're in, I'm sure we can figure it out," said Ella.

Maggie had sighed. "I was . . ." She paused. Ella stared at her in the rearview mirror as Maggie groped for the name of her transgression. "I was living with Rose, and it didn't work out, and I've been staying on campus for a few months . . ."

"Staying with friends?" Lewis guessed.

"Staying in the library," said Maggie. "Living there. I was . . ." She stared out the window. "I was like a stowaway. Stowaway," she repeated, which made her sound like she'd been having a grand adventure on the high seas. "Only there was someone watching me, and he was going to get me in a lot of trouble. So I had to leave."

"Do you want to go back to Philadelphia?" asked Ella. "Back to Rose?"

"No!" said Maggie, so vehemently that Ella jumped a little in her seat, and Lewis accidentally hit the horn. "No," she repeated. "I don't know where I want to go. I don't really have a place in Philadelphia. I was in an apartment, but I got evicted from there, and I can't go back with my father, because his wife hates me, and I can't go back with Rose . . ." And she'd sighed a piteous sigh and wrapped her arms around her knees, throwing in a small shiver for dramatic effect. "I guess maybe I could go to New York. I'll get a job and save up my money, and I'll go New York. Find a roommate or . . . something," she'd concluded.

"You can stay with me as long as you need to," said Ella. The words were out of her mouth before she'd considered them, before she'd thought to wonder whether it was a good idea or not. Judging from the look on Lewis's face, the answer was probably "not." Maggie had been evicted. Then she'd been living with her sister, which, for some reason, hadn't worked out. She didn't feel welcome at her father's house. She was stowing away—whatever that meant—in a school where she wasn't enrolled, living in the library. How could that add up to anything but trouble?

As Lewis steered them through the airport traffic, back toward Golden Acres, Maggie had sighed, cupped her chin in her palm, staring out the window as the palm trees and traffic rolled by. "Florida," she said. "I've never been here before."

"How is . . ." Ella began. "Can you tell me about your sister?"

Maggie was quiet. Ella pressed on. "I looked Rose up on the Internet, at her law firm . . ."

Maggie shook her head, staring out the window, as if envisioning her sister's face reflected in the glass. "Is that, like, the worst picture in the world? I kept telling her to make them take another one, and she kept saying, 'It doesn't matter, Maggie. Don't be so superficial.' And I said, 'That picture's out there for the whole world to see, and it isn't superficial to want to look your best,' but of course she didn't listen. She never listens to me," said Maggie, and then closed her mouth as if worried that she'd said too much. "Where are we going, exactly? Where do you live?"

"We live in a place called Golden Acres. It's . . ."

". . . a retirement community for active seniors," she and Lewis recited together.

In the rearview mirror, Maggie's eyes widened in alarm. "A nursing home?"

"No, no," said Lewis. "Don't worry. It's just a place for older people."

"Condominiums," added Ella. "And there are stores, and a clubhouse, and a trolley that runs for people who don't drive anymore . . ."

"Sounds great," said Maggie, obviously not meaning it. "So what do you do all day?"

"I volunteer," said Ella.

"Where?"

"Oh, all over. The hospital, the pet shelter, the thrift store, Meals on Wheels, and there's this woman I'm helping, she had a stroke last year. . . . I keep busy."

"Do you think I could find a job here?"

"What kind of job?" asked Ella.

"I've done everything," said Maggie. "Waitressing, dog grooming, hostessing . . ."

Hostessing? Ella wondered what that meant.

"Barista, bartender," Maggie continued, "baby-sitting, working in an ice-cream shop, working at a fried-dough stand . . ."

"Wow," said Ella. Maggie wasn't through.

"I sang in a band for a while." Maggie thought better of telling the grandmother the name of the band, on the off chance that she'd know what a whiskered biscuit even was. "Telemarketing, spraying people with perfume, T.J.Maxx, the Gap, the Limited . . ." Maggie paused and yawned hugely. "And at Princeton I helped out this blind lady. I cleaned her house. I brought her things."

"That's . . ." Again, Ella was out of words.

"So I guess this will be okay," Maggie said. She yawned, redid her ponytail, then curled up on the backseat and fell instantly asleep. At the next red light, Lewis looked over at Ella.

"Okay?" he asked.

Ella gave him a small shrug, then a smile. Maggie was here, and no matter what the truth turned out to be, that was something.

When Lewis pulled into his parking space, Maggie was still asleep in the backseat, with a lock of brown hair stuck to her sweaty cheek. Her bitten fingernails were so precisely like Caroline's fingers that Ella felt her heart lurch hard against her rib cage. Maggie opened her eyes, stretched, grabbed her backpack, and stepped out of the car, blinking. Ella followed her gaze. There was Irene Siegel, pushing her walker across the parking lot, and Albert Gantz, slowly unloading an oxygen tank from his trunk.

"It is the blight man was born for," Maggie said in a low, resigned voice.

"What was that, dear?" asked Lewis.

"Nothing," Maggie said. She shouldered her backpack and followed Ella inside.

True to her word, Maggie got a job at a bagel shop half a mile from Golden Acres. She'd work the early shift, creeping out of the apartment at five in the morning, working through breakfast and lunch. And then what? Ella had asked, because Maggie rarely reappeared at the apartment before eight or nine. Her granddaughter had shrugged. "I go to the beach," she said. "Or the movies. Or the library." For weeks, Ella had offered dinner. Each time, Maggie refused. "I already ate," she'd say—although, skinny as she was, Ella sometimes wondered whether Maggie ate anything at all. She'd decline Ella's offers to watch TV, to go to a movie, to join her at the Clubhouse for a bingo game. The only thing that had gotten even a flicker of interest was Ella's offer of a library card. Maggie had accompanied her grandmother to the small, one-story library, filled out her forms with Ella's address, then disappeared into the Fiction and Literature shelves, emerging an hour later with her arms full of poetry books.

And that was thàt. For May. For June. For July and August. At night, Maggie would come home, nod hello, and disappear. She'd emerge for a shower, then slip silently into the back bedroom, easing the door closed behind her, carrying her single towel, her shampoo, her toothbrush and toothpaste, with her as if she were an overnight guest, even though Ella had told her that she was welcome to leave her things wherever she wanted. There was a small television set in Maggie's bedroom, but Ella never heard it go on. There was a telephone, too, but Maggie never called anyone. She read, Ella knew—every three or four days she'd notice a new library book in Maggie's bag, thick novels, biographies, books of poetry, the kind of odd, fragmented, non-rhyming poems that never made sense to Ella—but Maggie never seemed to talk to anyone, and Ella was starting to worry that she never would.

"I don't know what I'm going to do," she said. It was eight in the morning, almost eighty-five degrees, and she'd fled to Lewis's apartment after Maggie had glided past her and out the door again.

"About the weather? Just wait. It can't last."

"About her," said Ella. "Maggie. She doesn't talk to me! She doesn't even look at me. She pads around on her bare feet . . . I never hear her coming. . . . She's out until all hours, she's gone when I wake up. . . ." Ella paused, took a deep breath, and shook her head.

"Well, normally I'd say to give her time . . ."

"Lewis, it's been months, and I don't even know the story with her sister, or her father. I don't even know what she likes for dinner! You've got grandchildren . . ."

"Grandsons," Lewis said. "But I think you're right. This calls for drastic measures." He nodded, and got to his feet. "We need to call in the big guns."

Luckily, Mrs. Lefkowitz was home. "Let's start out with a few questions," she said, moving back and forth across her cluttered living room in her familiar plant, sigh, shuffle, stomp. "Do you have prunes in your refrigerator?"

Ella stared at her.

"Prunes," Mrs. Lefkowitz prompted.

"Yes," said Ella.

Mrs. Lefkowitz nodded. "You got Metamucil on the kitchen counter?"

Ella nodded. Didn't everyone?

"What magazines do you subscribe to?"

Ella thought. "*Prevention*, the thing the AARP sends . . ."

"Do you get the HBO and the MTV?"

Ella shook her head. "I don't have cable."

Mrs. Lefkowitz rolled her eyes and plopped down on an over-stuffed armchair, on top of a needlepoint pillow that announced, "I'm the Princess." "Young people have their own things. Their own music, their own TV programs, their own . . ."

"Culture?" Lewis supplied.

Mrs. Lefkowitz nodded. "There's nobody here for her," she said. "Nobody her own age. How'd you like to be twenty-eight and stuck in a place like this?"

"She didn't have anywhere else to go," said Ella.

"Neither do prisoners," said Mrs. Lefkowitz. "It doesn't mean they have to like being in jail."

"So what should we do?" Ella asked.

Mrs. Lefkowitz struggled to her feet. "You got money?" she demanded.

Ella nodded.

"Then let's go," she said. "You drive," she said, pointing her chin at Lewis. "We're going shopping."

• • •

Coaxing Maggie out of her room proved to be a costly proposition. First, there were the magazines, almost fifty dollars' worth, each one fatter and glossier and more crammed with perfume samples and subscription-card come-ons than the last. "How do you know about all of this?" Ella asked, as Mrs. Lefkowitz stacked an issue of *Movieline* on top of the latest *Vanity Fair.* Her friend waved her good arm carelessly. "What's to know?" she asked.

Their next stop was a gigantic electronics store. "Flat screen, flat screen," Mrs. Lefkowitz recited as she zipped down the aisles in the motorized scooter she used for her shopping expeditions. Two hours and several thousand dollars later, Lewis's car was packed with a flat-screen TV, a DVD player, and a dozen videos, including the first season of *Sex and the City,* which Mrs. Lefkowitz guaranteed that all the young women were raving about. "I read about it in *Time,*" she boasted, lifting herself into the passenger's seat. "Turn left up here," she told Lewis. "We're going to the supermarket and liquor store," she said, and smiled to herself. "We're going to have a party." At the liquor store, she accosted the pimply-faced clerk in a polyester pinny. "Do you know how to make a cosmopolitan?" she demanded.

"Cointreau . . ." the clerk ventured.

Mrs. Lefkowitz pointed at Lewis. "You heard the man!" she said.

Later, their arms laden with cointreau and vodka, cheese puffs and corn chips, miniature hot dogs and frozen egg rolls, plus two bottles of nail polish (one red, one pink), and cardboard boxes full of electronics. Ella and Lewis and Mrs. Lefkowitz piled into the elevator up to Ella's apartment.

"Do you really think this will work?" she asked, as Lewis put the frozen foods in her freezer.

Mrs. Lefkowitz pulled up a seat at the kitchen table and shook her head. "No guarantees," she said, pulling a hot-pink piece of paper out of her purse. "You're Invited!" it read in silver letters across the top.

"Where's that from?" Ella asked, peering over her shoulder.

"My computer," said Mrs. Lefkowitz, tilting the invitation so that Ella could read that Miss Maggie Feller was invited to a *Sex and the City* party on Friday night at Ella's house. "I can do anything. Invitations, calendars, parking permits . . ."

"What's that?" asked Lewis, who'd been putting snack foods away.

Mrs. Lefkowitz suddenly became very interested in the contents of her purse. "Oh, nothing. Never mind."

Lewis stared at her. "You know, one of my reporters told me that there were people printing up fake parking permits. He wants to do an investigative series."

Mrs. Lefkowitz lifted her chin defiantly. "You're not going to turn me in, are you?"

"Not if this works, I won't," he promised.

Mrs. Lefkowitz nodded, then handed Ella the invitation. "Slip it under her door when she's gone."

"But, if it's a party . . . who's coming?"

Mrs. Lefkowitz stared at her. "Well, your friends, of course."

Ella looked helplessly at Lewis. Mrs. Lefkowitz squinted at her. "You do have friends here, don't you?"

"I—" Ella began. "I have coworkers."

"Coworkers," Mrs. Lefkowitz said to the ceiling. "Well, never mind. It'll just be the three of us, then." She pushed herself up from the table. "See you Friday!" she said, and thumped her way out the door.

"I feel like the witch in 'Hansel and Gretel,' " Ella said, sliding a tray of miniature egg rolls into the oven. It was Friday night, after nine, which meant that Maggie could appear at any moment—if she came home at all. "Did you get your invitation?" Ella had called toward the closing door as Maggie left for work in the morning. The girl had responded with a vaguely affirmative-sounding grunt as the door had closed behind her.

"Why?" Lewis asked. Ella pointed at the lures—the piles of

magazines, the bowls of chips and dips, the platters of deviled eggs and chicken wings and half a dozen other treats that she knew would give her devastating heartburn if she risked more than a bite.

Mrs. Lefkowitz tugged at her sleeve. "One more thing," she said. "The secret weapon."

"What?" Ella asked, glancing at her watch.

"Your daughter," said Mrs. Lefkowitz.

Ella stared. "What?"

"Your daughter. Caroline, right?" Mrs. Lefkowitz said. "All of this"—she swept her hand toward Ella's living room, where Lewis was fiddling with the DVD player and contentedly eating his way through a platter of spinach puffs—"will probably work. But if it doesn't, what's the one thing you've got that Maggie wants?"

"Money?" Ella guessed.

"Well, that, maybe," said Mrs. Lefkowitz. "But there's lots of places she can get money. How many places can she get the story of her mother?"

The story of her mother, Ella thought to herself, wishing with all her heart that it was a longer, happier tale.

"Information," Mrs. Lefkowitz said. "That's what we have that the young people want. Information." She considered. "And some Microsoft stock, in my case. But for you, information ought to be enough." She nodded as Maggie's key turned in the lock. "Showtime!" she whispered. Ella held her breath. Maggie walked into the apartment as if she had blinders on, looking not to the left, and the kitchen stocked with tempting goodies, nor to the right, with the new television set on which a woman was talking about . . . no. She must be hearing it wrong, Ella thought, as the actress burbled, "I don't want to be the up-the-butt girl!" and Mrs. Lefkowitz laughed into her cosmopolitan. Halfway down the hall, Maggie paused.

"Maggie?" Ella called. She could almost feel how torn her grand-daughter was—wanting to stay, wanting to go. *Please don't let me mess this up,* Ella prayed. Maggie turned around. "Do you want . . ." What? What could she offer this wary girl with her watchful brown eyes, so similar to and so different from her own lost daughter's eyes? She held out her hand, and the drink she was holding. "It's a cosmopolitan. It has vodka and cranberry juice . . ."

"I know," Maggie said scornfully, "what's in a cosmopolitan." It was one of the longer sentences Ella had gotten out of her granddaughter. Maggie took the drink and swallowed half of it in one mouthful. "Not bad," she said, turned on her heel and strode into the living room. Mrs. Lefkowitz handed her the bowl of Fritos. Maggie plopped herself on the couch, swallowed the remaining half of her drink, and picked up a copy of *Entertainment Weekly.* "I've seen this episode," she said.

"Oh," said Ella. On the one hand, that was bad news. On the other hand, it was a second unsolicited sentence from her granddaughter. And Maggie was there, wasn't she? That was something, right?

"But it's a good one," said Maggie. She flipped the magazine back onto the coffee table and looked around. Ella glanced desperately at Lewis, who hurried out of the kitchen with the pitcher full of drinks. He refilled Maggie's glass. Maggie daintily selected a chicken wing from the platter and sat back with her eyes on the screen. Ella felt herself relax in increments. It wasn't a victory, she told herself, through four straight episodes of women saying things that would have gotten her mouth washed out with soap sixty years ago. But it was a start. She glanced over at her granddaughter. Maggie's eyes had slipped shut. Her eyelashes lay like a spiky fringe on top of her cheek. There was a dusting of Cheetos debris on her chin. And her lips were pursed, as if she were awaiting a kiss in her dreams.

After four cosmopolitans, three chicken wings, and a fistful of Fritos, Maggie had bid Ella and Company good night. She lay on the thin mattress of the pullout couch and closed her eyes, thinking that she might have to reconsider her plan for handling Florida.

Initially, she'd decided to simply watch, wait, stay out of the way, until she could figure things out. That might take some time, Maggie'd acknowledged. Everything she knew about old people she'd learned from TV, from commercials, mostly, which told her that they had high blood sugar and overactive bladders, and were in need of panic buttons to press when they'd fallen and couldn't get up. She'd sit back and focus on the grandmother, who clearly had money. And guilt. Whatever Ella Hirsch had done or hadn't done, she clearly felt beyond awful about it. Which meant that if Maggie was patient, she'd be able to convert those awful feelings into cash—cash she could add to the pile growing slowly in the box beneath her bed. She was earning just minimum wage at Bagel Bay, but Maggie figured that with a few tearful scenes, a few sad stories about how much she missed her mother and how much she would have welcomed the love of a grandmother, or any woman, really, in her short but troubled life, she'd be waltzing out of death's waiting room—aka Golden Acres—with enough money to buy whatever she wanted.

The problem was that getting things from Ella would be almost too easy. It wasn't enough of a challenge, after all of the challenges Maggie had been through. It felt . . . disappointing, somehow. Like gearing up to power your fist through a cinderblock wall and winding up punching a marshmallow instead. The grandmother was so absolutely pathetic that Maggie, who didn't feel bad about much, felt the tiniest bit lousy about planning to separate her from her money. She ate up scraps of Maggie's company, her attention, every word she said, as if she'd been starving in the desert and Maggie were a dish of good ice cream. Now there was the new television set, the DVD player, all of the food, in addition to Ella's constant offers of dinner, movies, day trips to Miami or the beach. Ella was trying so hard that it made Maggie's stomach twist. And the only thing she'd asked for was that Maggie call her father and tell him that she was all right. There'd been no mention made of rent, or of giving Ella money for gas or car insurance, or groceries, or anything at all. So why should she be in a hurry to leave?

Watch and wait, she thought, tucking the pillow more firmly under her cheek. Maybe she'd get Ella to take her to Disney World. Ride the teacups. Send home a postcard. *Wish you were here.*

FORTY-FOUR

"Tell me why we're doing this again?" Rose whispered.

"Because generally, when two people decide to get married, it's traditional for their parents to meet," Simon whispered back "And it's going to be fine," he said. "My parents love you, and I'm sure they'll like your father, and as for Sydelle . . . what's the worst that could happen here?"

In the kitchen, Simon's mother, Elizabeth, was scowling at a cookbook. She was a short, plump woman with silvery-blond hair and the same milky skin as her son. Dressed in a long, flower-patterned skirt, a ruffled white blouse, and a yellow apron whose wide pockets were accented with fabric roses, she looked sort of like a domestic, Jewish Tammy Faye Bakker, minus the eyelashes. In her case, though, looks were deceiving. She taught philosophy at Bryn Mawr in the same flowery skirts and cashmere cardigans that she wore around the house. She was sweet, and funny, and easygoing . . . but wherever Simon had gotten his talents for cooking, and food appreciation, it hadn't been from her. "Shallot," she murmured. "I don't think I have that. In fact," she said, smiling as her son walked in and kissed her cheek, "I'm not sure I know what it is."

"It's sort of a cross between an onion and a clove of garlic," said Simon. "Why? Was it in your crossword puzzle?"

"Simon, I'm cooking," she said firmly. "I can, you know," she added, sounding mildly offended. "I'm a very fine cook, when I do it. It's just that I usually don't."

"And you decided to give it a go tonight?"

"It's the least I can do to welcome the *mishpochah*," she said, beaming at Rose, who smiled back and relaxed, leaning against a counter. Simon, meanwhile, was sniffing the air suspiciously.

"What are you making?"

She tilted the cookbook so he could read it.

"Roast chicken with wild rice and apricot stuffing," said Simon, looking impressed. "Did you remember to clean the chickens?"

"They're from the organic grocery store," she said. "I'm sure they're fine."

"Yeah, but did you take out the innards? The neck and the liver and all? The stuff that they put inside the cavity? Wrapped in plastic?"

Now Rose sniffed, too . . . and noticed that the kitchen smelled a great deal like burning plastic. Mrs. Stein looked worried. "They felt kind of crowded when I was stuffing them," she said, bending to open the oven.

"Nothing to worry about," said Simon, deftly extracting the pan of smoking, raw-looking chicken.

"Towel's on fire," Simon's father remarked, strolling into the kitchen.

"What?" asked Simon, whose attention was focused on the chicken. Tall and thin, with tufts of the same gingery hair that Simon had, Mr. Stein calmly swallowed the mouthful of cheese and crackers he'd been eating and pointed to a dish towel on top of the stove that had indeed burst into flames.

"Towel," he said. "Fire." He walked to the stove, flicked the flaming towel neatly into the sink, where it hissed and smoked, and gave his wife a squeeze. "Calamity Jane," he said affectionately. She swatted at him, still studying her cookbook.

"You're not eating up all the cheese and crackers, are you?"

"Not at all," said Mr. Stein, "I've moved on to the cashews." He turned to Rose, offering the plate of cheese and crackers. "My advice," he said, his voice low and his tone conspiratorial, "fill up on this."

Rose smiled at him. "Thanks," she said.

Simon's mother rolled her eyes and wiped her hands. "So is your, um, Sydelle a good cook?"

"She's usually got my father on some kind of weird diet," said Rose. "High-carb, low-fat, high-protein, vegetarian . . ."

"Oh," said Elizabeth, frowning, "do you think this will be okay? I probably should have asked . . ."

"This will be fine," said Rose, knowing that as soon as Sydelle arrived, food would be the last thing on her mind. The Steins, as it turned out, lived in a large, sprawling, somewhat messy mansion set on two acres of shaggy green grass on a street full of similarly impressive domiciles. Mr. Stein was an engineer who invented parts for airplanes. He'd patented two of them years ago, Simon had told her, which was where a lot of the money came from. Now he was almost seventy, semiretired, and he spent a lot of his time at home looking for his glasses, the cordless telephone, the remote control, and his car keys. Which was probably because Mrs. Stein seemed to spend a lot of her time at home moving things from one pile of stuff to another. That, and working in her overgrown vegetable garden and reading the kind of bodice-ripping novels that Rose had always read in secret, books that always had three words in their titles. *Her Forbidden Desire* was currently perched on top of the microwave, and Rose had also glimpsed *Passion's Tawny Flame* facedown on the living room sofa. Simon told Rose that in high school he'd given his mother a fake gift certificate for a nonexistent book he'd entitled *Love's Moist Panties*. "Was she mad?" Rose had asked. Simon thought about it. "I think she was actually disappointed that the book didn't exist."

Now Simon sniffed the air again, looking worried. "Ma, the walnuts," he said.

"They're fine," said Elizabeth Stein serenely, and shook dinner rolls out of a paper bag and into a napkin-lined basket that looked as if it had been kicked in on one side. "Oh, dear," she murmured. "Lopsided."

This, too, was typical. Simon's parents tended to be unconcerned with formality when it came to tableware. Rose wasn't surprised to see the table covered with a handmade linen tablecloth, set with mismatched plates. She counted three plates from the Steins' set of good china, rimmed with gold, and three from their everyday plates, bought in bulk from Ikea. There were four water glasses and two coffee mugs for drinking water, three wineglasses, two brandy snifters, and a single champagne flute for wine, and a different paper napkin, one of which read, "HAPPY ANNIVERSARY," at each of the plates. Sydelle was going to shit, Rose decided, and smiled to herself, thinking that it suited her just fine.

Simon walked up behind her, carrying a pitcher full of ice water and two bottles of wine. "My advice to you," he said, handing her a glass, "is start drinking heavily."

A car turned into the driveway. Rose glimpsed her father's face, his familiar high forehead and bald spot, and Sydelle sitting beside him, resplendent in lipstick and pearls. She grabbed her fiancé's hand. "I love you," she whispered.

Simon stared at her curiously. "I know."

The car doors slammed. Rose listened to the sounds of polite "hellos" and the sound of Sydelle's heels tap-tapping on the Steins' scuffed hardwood floors. Family, she thought. She swallowed hard, squeezed Simon's hand, wishing for something she couldn't name, for ease and comfort, for a fast joke and a breezy manner, for the absolute right outfit. In other words, for Maggie. To be Maggie for one night, or at least have the benefit of her sister's advice and presence. This was her family, old and new, and Maggie should be here.

Simon stared at her curiously. "You okay?"

Rose poured herself a half-glass of red wine and drank it quickly. "Fine," she said, and followed him into the kitchen. "Fine."

FORTY-FIVE

"Rosenfarb!" Maggie shouted at the guard. The guard nodded slowly (no surprise—Maggie had quickly figured out that everyone at Golden Acres did everything slowly), and she stomped on the gas as the parking gate wavered up into the sky. In the months she'd been at Golden Acres, Maggie had privately been conducting an experiment to see whether simply shouting any Jewish-sounding last name at the security guards would be enough to gain admittance. So far, she'd run through *Rosen, Rosenstein, Rosenblum, Rosenfeld, Rosenbluth,* and, once, late at night, *Rosenpenis,* in her personal homage to *Fletch.* The guards (if you could call antiques in old polyester uniforms guards at all) had not so much as batted a gray eyelash as they waved her through.

Maggie piloted Lewis's school-bus-sized Lincoln toward her grandmother's apartment building, parked it in the designated slot, and climbed up the stairs, heading for her bedroom, a room with blank walls and a beige pullout couch that could have been the little sister of the one Maggie remembered from Rose's apartment. The room was so spare and so clean that Maggie wondered whether Ella had ever used it, whether she'd ever had anyone stay overnight.

It was three in the afternoon. She figured that she'd go upstairs, grab the bathing suit she'd found in Ella's closet, go to the beach, kill some time before dinner. Maybe she'd eat with Ella. Maybe they'd pop in another one of the DVDs that Ella had come home with the week before. Except when she opened the door, she was surprised to see her grandmother sitting at the kitchen table, hands folded in front of her, like she'd been waiting.

"Hi," said Maggie. "Aren't you supposed to be at the hospital? Or the hospice? Or someplace that starts with 'hosp'?"

Ella shook her head, smiling faintly. In black slacks and a white blouse, her hair twined around her head as usual, her grandmother looked shabby and small, a monochrome mouse crumpled in a corner.

"We need to talk," Ella said.

Oh boy, thought Maggie. *Here it comes.* She'd gotten this speech, or a version of it, from roommates and boyfriends—and, of course, from Sydelle. *Maggie, you're taking advantage. Maggie, you need to contribute. Maggie, your father shouldn't have to take care of you his whole life.*

But Ella had a different speech in mind. "I owe you an explanation. I've been meaning to talk to you for a long time, but . . ." Her voice trailed off. "I know you're probably wondering where I was, all those years. . . ."

Ah, Maggie thought. So this was what Ella was getting at. Not Maggie's dependence, but Ella's own guilt. "You sent cards," she said.

"That's right," said Ella, nodding. "And I called, too. You never knew?" She asked the question, even though she knew the answer. "Your father was very angry at us. At me and my husband. Then, after Ira died, just at me."

Maggie pulled up a chair and sat down at the table. "Why angry?" she asked.

"He thought I did a terrible thing to him," the grandmother said. "He thought that I—well, my husband and I—should have told him more about Caroline. Your mother."

"I know what her name is," Maggie said irritably. The subject of her mother—her mother's name in this old woman's mouth—

flared like an old wound. She wasn't ready for this. She didn't want to hear about her mother; she didn't want to think about her mother; she didn't want to know the truth, or whatever the grandmother's version of the truth was. Her mother was dead, the first of her life's losses, and that was more truth than any daughter should have to handle.

Ella kept talking. "I should have told your father that she was . . ." Ella stumbled over the words. "Mentally ill . . ."

"You're lying," said Maggie sharply. "She wasn't crazy, she was fine, I remember."

"But she wasn't always fine, right?" asked Ella. Maggie closed her eyes, hearing only snatches of what her grandmother was saying: *manic episodes* and *clinical depression, medication,* and *shock treatment.*

"So if she was crazy like that, why'd you let her get married?" Maggie demanded. "Why'd you let her have kids?"

Ella sighed. "We couldn't stop her," she said. "Whatever her problems were, Caroline was a grown woman. She made her own decisions."

"You were probably glad to get rid of her," Maggie muttered, voicing one of her own worst fears, because it was easy for her to imagine how happy her father and Sydelle and Rose, and her father too, would be to get rid of her, to foist her off on some unsuspecting love-struck guy so that she'd be his problem, not theirs.

Ella looked shocked. "Of course not! I was never glad to get rid of her! And when I lost her . . ." She swallowed hard. "It was the worst thing I could imagine. Because I lost her, and I lost you and Rose, too." She looked down at her hands, folded on the table. "I lost everything," she said. And she lifted her tear-filled eyes and stared at Maggie. "But now you're here. And I hope . . ."

She reached down next to the table. "Here," she said, and pushed a box across the table. "These were in Michigan, in storage. I sent for them. I thought maybe you'd like to see."

Maggie reached inside the box. It was full of photo albums, old ones. She opened the one on top, and there she was—Caroline.

Caroline as a teenager, in a tight black sweater and lots of black eyeliner. Caroline on her wedding day, in a fitted lace dress and a long
sweep of veil. Caroline on the beach in a blue bathing suit, squinting in the sunshine, with Rose clutching her leg and baby Maggie
in her arms.

Maggie flipped through the pages faster and faster, watching
her mother get older, watching herself grow up, knowing that the
pictures would stop, that her mother never got older than thirty,
that in this world she and Rose would be forever frozen as little
girls. *The art of losing isn't hard to master.* Her grandmother was staring at her, her old eyes full of hope. *No,* Maggie thought. *Not this.*
She couldn't stand this. She didn't want to be anyone's hope. She
didn't want to stand in for anyone's dead daughter. She didn't want
anything, she told herself sternly, not anything, not anything at all
except some money and a plane ticket out of this place. She didn't
want to see the grandmother as anything but a means to an end, a
pocketbook and a sad story. She didn't want sympathy extended
toward her, and she sure as hell didn't want to feel sorry for anyone
else.

She closed the book with a snap, rubbing her palms against her
shorts as if they were dirty. "I'm going for a walk," she said, shoving past Ella's chair, heading for the bedroom, grabbing the old-
lady bathing suit she'd found in the back bedroom's closet, her
towel and sunblock, and an empty notebook and hurrying out the
door.

"Maggie, wait," Ella called. Maggie didn't break stride.
"Maggie, please!" Ella called, but Maggie was already gone.

Maggie walked through Golden Acres, past Crestwood and
Farmington and Lawndale, past all the streets with made-up
English-village-sounding names and the buildings that looked
exactly identical to the ones standing next to them. *Make her pay,*
she whispered to herself.

People owed her—everyone who'd mocked her in high school,

everyone who'd made her less than she was, who'd conspired to keep her invisible, undiscovered. She was almost thirty, for chrissake, and still without a part to her credit, and the closest she'd come to a 90210 address was when she'd watched reruns on TV.

Make her pay, she told herself. She got to the swimming pool, which was deserted except for a handful of old people sunning themselves, reading, playing quiet games of cards. Maggie put on the old-lady swimsuit in the bathroom, then dragged one of the lounge chairs into prime tanning position, spread her towel on the chair, spread herself on top of the towel, and stared at her notebook. How much money would it take to get her out of here? Five hundred dollars for plane fare, she wrote. Another two thousand for security deposit, first and last month's rent. That was more than she'd saved right there. Maggie groaned to herself, tore out the page, crumpled it, and laid it by the side of the chair.

"Hey!" called an old man in a shirt unbuttoned to display a bathmat's worth of frothing white chest hair, "no littering!"

Maggie glared at him, shoved the crumpled piece of paper under her shorts, and resumed writing.

"Head shots," she wrote. How much would those cost?

"Miss!" called a strange voice. "Oh, miss!"

Maggie looked up. This time, it was an old woman in a fringed pink bathing cap.

"I'm sorry to bother you," she said, edging toward Maggie. The loose flesh of her thighs and upper arms wobbled with each step. "But you're going to get a very bad sunburn unless you wear sunblock."

Maggie silently brandished her tube of Bain de Soleil at the old woman, who did not appear to be at all deterred. And was it her imagination, or were the other old people moving toward her, inching their chairs closer each time she closed her eyes, like some kind of senior-citizen *Dawn of the Dead?* "Oh, I see, I see," said the woman, "SPF fifteen, that's good, very good, of course thirty would be better, or even forty-five, and it should be waterproof, really. . . ."

She paused, waiting for a response. Maggie ignored her. The woman kept talking. "And I notice that you haven't put any on your back. Do you need some help?" she inquired, leaning toward Maggie. The thought of having some strange old saggy creature actually touching her caused Maggie to recoil, shaking her head and saying, "No, thank you, but I'll be fine."

"Well, if you need me," the old woman said cheerfully, wobbling back toward her chair, "I'm right here. My name's Dora," she said, in answer to the question that Maggie hadn't asked. "What's your name, dear?"

Maggie sighed. "Maggie," she said, figuring that a fake name might be too much trouble to remember. Back to Maggie, she thought grimly, and returned to her notebook, underlining the words "head shots." She would explain to the grandmother what they were and why she needed them, how much she wanted to be an actress, how she'd always wanted to be an actress, and how, without a loving mother to make those dreams come true, she'd been forced to rely on her wits and her luck, only now . . .

"Excuse me!"

Oh, for chrissake, Maggie thought, and squinted through the sunlight at a pair of old guys in shorts. With sandals. And socks.

"We were hoping you could help us settle a dispute," the leader of the pair began. He was a tall, skinny, bald man, sunburned to the color of a salmon.

"I'm kind of busy," said Maggie, indicating her notebook, hoping that they'd leave her alone.

"Don't bother the girl, Jack," said the other man—he was short and barrel-shaped, with a fringe of white hair and atrocious black-and-red plaid shorts.

"It's just a quick question," said the man who was probably Jack. "I was just wondering—well, we were just discussing . . ." Maggie stared at him impatiently. "You look so familiar," he said. "Are you an actress?"

Maggie tossed her hair over her shoulders and favored the

geezers with her most dazzling smile. "I was in a music video," she said. "Will Smith."

The tall man stared at her, eyes wide. "Really? Did you meet him?"

"Well, not exactly," Maggie said, propping herself up on her elbows. "But I saw him at lunch. At craft services," she said, tossing out the terminology and shaking her auburn curls. And suddenly there were four old people gathered around her, Jack and his friend, the blabbering woman Dora, and the guy who'd yelled at her about the trash. Maggie saw liver spots and sunblock, mothball-smelling shorts, wrinkles and whiskers and flyaway white hair.

"An actress. My goodness," said Jack.

"Wow," echoed the barrel-shaped guy.

"Who do you belong to?" burbled Dora, who'd reappeared. "Oh, your grandparents must be so proud of you!"

"Do you live in Hollywood?"

"Do you have an agent?"

"When you got that tattoo," rasped Jack's barrel-shaped friend, "did it hurt?"

Dora shot him a sharp look. "Herman, who cares?"

"I care," said Herman, looking truculent.

Jack jiggled the edge of Maggie's chair impatiently and said what to Maggie were the magic words. "Tell us all about yourself," he said. "We want to hear everything."

FORTY-SIX

Simon set his briefcase on the floor of Rose's apartment and held his arms open. "Bride-elect!" he called. He'd come across the term in a small-town newspaper when he had to drive out to central Pennsylvania for a deposition, and had been using it on Rose ever since.

"Just a minute!" called Rose from the kitchen, where she was sitting at the table flipping through the folders from three different catering companies that had arrived in the mail that day. Simon wrapped his arms around her. "How serious are you about baby lamb chops?" she murmured into his neck. "Because I have to tell you, they're expensive."

"Money is no object," Simon declared grandly. "Our love must be celebrated with all the proper pomp and circumstance. And lamb chops."

Rose set a gift-wrapped box in front of him. "This came today, and I can't figure out what it is."

"An engagement gift!" said Simon, rubbing his hands together and reading the return address. "From Aunt Melissa and Uncle Steve!" He opened the box, and together they stared at the gift inside. After a minute, Simon glanced at Rose, and cleared his throat. "I think it's a candleholder."

Rose pulled the block of glass out of its nest of tissue paper and held it up toward the light. "There's no candle."

"Well, but there's a place for a candle," said Simon, pointing out the shallow indentation on one of its sides.

"I don't think that's deep enough for a candle," said Rose. "And if it was a candleholder, wouldn't they have sent it with a candle? So we'd know?"

"It has to be a candleholder," said Simon, without conviction. "What else could it be?"

Rose stared at the glass block some more. "I was thinking maybe a serving piece?"

"For very small meals?" asked Simon.

"No, no, for, like, nuts or candy or something."

"The hole's not big enough for nuts or candy."

"Oh, but it's big enough for a candle?"

They stared at each other for a minute. Then Simon picked up a thank-you note and started writing. "Dear Aunt Melissa and Uncle Steve. Thank you for the lovely gift. It will look . . ." He paused, staring at the ceiling. "Lovely?"

"You just said lovely," said Rose.

"Wonderful!" Simon amended. "It will look wonderful in our home, and will provide hours of entertainment for years to come as we try to figure out what in God's name it is. Thank you for thinking of us, and we look forward to seeing you soon." Simon signed their names, capped the pen, and turned to Rose, beaming. "There!"

"You didn't really write that," said Rose.

"No," said Simon. "I didn't. How many left?"

Rose consulted the list. "Fifty-one."

"Are you kidding?"

"It's your fault," Rose said. "I blame you."

"Just because my family buys us gifts . . ."

"Just because my family's not ridiculously enormous . . ."

Simon stood up, grabbed Rose around the waist, and blew a

raspberry against the side of her neck. "Take it back," he said. "Ridiculously enormous!"

"Take it back," he whispered into her ear, "or I will force you to do my every bidding."

Rose twisted around to face him. "I am not," she said breathlessly, "writing those thank-you notes myself!"

Simon pulled her close and kissed her, running his hands through her hair. "The notes can wait," he said.

Later, lying in bed, warm and naked beneath the down comforter, Rose rolled onto her side and finally started talking about the thing she'd been holding off on from the moment he'd come home. "There's something else," she said. "My father called today. About Maggie."

Simon's face was neutral. "Oh?" he asked.

Rose flipped onto her back and stared at the ceiling. "She's resurfaced," she said. "All my father would tell me over the phone was that she's fine. He wants to see me, he says. To tell me the rest."

"Okay," said Simon.

Rose shut her eyes and shook her head. "I'm not sure I want to know the rest. Whatever the rest is. I just don't . . ." Her voice trailed off. "The thing about Maggie is, she's horrible."

"What do you mean?" Simon asked.

"She's . . . I mean, she . . ." Rose grimaced. How was she supposed to explain to the man she loved about her sister? Her sister, who stole money and stole shoes and even stole boyfriends, and then went missing for months on end? "Just take my word for it. She's very bad news. She has learning disabilities . . ." And then she stopped. The learning disabilities, really, were just the tip of the Maggie iceberg. And wasn't it just like her sister to reappear as soon as Rose got engaged, as soon as there was a chance that she'd be the center of attention, for a change? "She's going to ruin our wedding," she said.

"I thought Sydelle was going to ruin our wedding," said Simon.

Rose smiled in spite of herself. "Well, Maggie's going to ruin it more." God, she thought. Things had been so calm with Maggie gone off to who-knows-where. No bill collectors blasting at the morning's silence with their phone calls, no former or potential boyfriends disrupting Rose and Simon's sleep. Things stayed where Rose put them. None of her shoes, or her clothes, or her cash, ever went wandering. The car stayed where she parked it. "I'll tell you one thing," Rose continued. "She's not going to be a bridesmaid. She'll be lucky if she gets an invitation."

"Okay," said Simon.

"She'll be lucky if she gets dinner," said Rose.

"More food for me," said Simon.

Rose stared at the ceiling some more. "I still think that glass thing was some kind of serving dish."

"I already licked the envelope," said Simon. "Let it go."

"Agh," said Rose. She closed her eyes and wished for a normal family, like Simon's. No dead mother, no vanished little sister, no father who reserved most of his passion for the morning market reports, and certainly no Sydelle. She rested her face against the cool cotton of the pillowcase for a minute, then got up and went to the living room and picked up a thank-you note—a card of heavy cream paper that had their names, *Rose* and *Simon,* set on either side of a gigantic *S,* to stand for *Stein,* which was not going to be Rose's last name. But even though she'd pointed that out to the Stepmonster, Sydelle had gone ahead and ordered them mono-grammed thank-you cards that suggested that Rose was going to be Rose Stein, like it or not.

Dear Maggie, thought Rose. *How could you do what you did to me? And when are you coming home?*

FORTY-SEVEN

Ella walked up to the fence surrounding the swimming pool and pressed her face against it. "There," she said, giving the single word all of the sadness and disappointment she felt. "There she is."

Lewis stepped next to her, and Mrs. Lefkowitz zipped up in her new scooter. Together, the three of them stood at the fence, looking through the diamond-shaped holes. Looking at Maggie.

Her granddaughter lay on a chaise lounge beside the deep end, resplendent in a brand-new pink bikini, with a silver chain, thin as a filament of hair, clinging to her belly. Her skin shone with suntan lotion. Her hair was arranged in a soft pile of loose curls on top of her head, and her eyes were hidden behind small round sunglasses. And around her were four people—an old woman in a faded pink rubber bathing cap, and three old men in shorts. As Ella watched, one of the old men leaned forward, toward Maggie, as if he was asking her a question. Her granddaughter propped herself up on one elbow, looking thoughtful. When her lips moved, her audience burst into laughter.

"Oh," said Lewis. "It looks like she's made some new friends."

Ella felt her heart give a painful twist, as Maggie continued to amuse her new acquaintances, looking more relaxed and at ease than Ella had ever seen her, as the Water Babies aerobics class splashed energetically to a wavery tape recording of "Runaround Sue." Every day for the past week—every day since Ella had tried to tell Maggie about her mother—this had been her granddaughter's routine. Maggie would come home from work, dash into the back bedroom, swap her Bagel Bay uniform for her bathing suit and shorts, and come here. "I'm going swimming," she'd say. Ella was never invited. And Ella could see where this was going. Maggie would move out—into an apartment of her own, or maybe in with one of her new friends, some pleasant old woman who'd offer all of the benefits of being a grandmother with none of the messy complications or painful history. Oh, she thought, it wasn't fair! She'd waited for so long, she'd hoped for so much, and now, to see Maggie slipping away from her like this!

"What should I do?" she whispered.

Mrs. Lefkowitz backed up her scooter and drove it, full speed ahead, toward the entrance to the pool.

"Wait!" Ella cried. "Where are you going?"

Mrs. Lefkowitz didn't turn, didn't stop, and didn't answer. Ella shot a helpless glance at Lewis.

"I'll go . . ." he began.

"We better . . ." she said.

Ella's pulse beat in her throat as she hurried after Mrs. Lefkowitz, who was speeding through the gates, straight toward Maggie, and didn't show any signs of slowing down.

"Hey!" one of the old guys called as Mrs. Lefkowitz zipped past him, bumping into the table on which he'd spread a hand of cards. She ignored him and pulled her scooter up to Maggie's lounge chair. Maggie lowered her sunglasses and stared. Breathing hard, Ella and Lewis hurried after Mrs. Lefkowitz, and for one bizarre moment Ella was reminded of a dozen spaghetti westerns and the scene each one of them had, where the good guys made their stand against the enemy on a conveniently deserted street or in the middle of an empty corral. All the scene needed, she thought, was for some tumbleweed to blow past Mrs. Lefkowitz's scooter. Even the

Water Babies had ceased their splashing and stood quietly in the shallow end, water dripping from their tanned, wrinkled arms, watching to see what would happen next.

Maggie stared at Mrs. Lefkowitz, and Maggie's new friends eyeballed Ella and Lewis, and Ella made a careful study of the cracked concrete beneath her feet, wishing for a cowboy hat and, even more desperately, for a script. Was she the good guy or the bad guy here? Was she the hero, come to rescue the damsel in distress, or the villain, come to lash her to the train tracks?

Hero, she decided, just as Mrs. Lefkowitz rolled the scooter forward another six inches, nudging the edge of Maggie's lounge. Ella was reminded of a puppy pushing its nose against a closed door.

"Maggie, dear," Mrs. Lefkowitz said, "there's something that maybe you can help me with."

Maggie raised her eyebrows as one of the old men glared at Mrs. Lefkowitz.

"She's tired," he said belligerently, gripping his cane with two hands. "She had a very long day. And she was just getting ready to tell us about how she almost got a job at MTV."

Mrs. Lefkowitz wasn't moving. "So go ahead. Tell."

Maggie looked over Mrs. Lefkowitz's head and addressed herself to Ella. "What do you want?"

The words rose up, unbidden, to Ella's mouth and threatened to spill over. *I want you to love me. I want you to like me. I want you to stop running away.* "I . . ." she managed.

"She's busy," the short, round, barrel-shaped man said, stepping in front of Maggie's lounge chair protectively.

"Are you Maggie's grandmother?" asked the woman in the pink bathing cap. "Oh, you must be so proud of her! Such a beautiful girl, and so accomplished . . ."

Maggie bit her lip, and the old man with the cane made an unpleasant noise as Lewis quietly pulled two chairs over to Maggie's circle and motioned for Ella to sit.

"MTV?" Mrs. Lefkowitz asked, nodding knowledgeably, as if

she'd invented the station. "Were you going to be a contestant on one of their game shows?"

"On-air talent," Maggie muttered.

"Like the Carson Daly," said Mrs. Lefkowitz, crossing her hands over her lumpy waist and tilting her square sunglasses toward the sun. "So handsome, that one."

The two groups arranged themselves in an uneasy half-circle around Maggie's lounge chair. Ella and Lewis and Mrs. Lefkowitz were on one side, Maggie's new friends on the other. Maggie stared at one group, then the other. Then she gave an almost invisible shrug, reached into her backpack, and pulled out a notebook. Ella felt herself relax the tiniest bit. It wasn't progress, exactly, but at least Maggie hadn't bolted, or asked them to leave.

"It's Jack, isn't it?" Lewis asked the man who'd been gripping the cane. The man—Jack—gave an affirmative grunt. Lewis offered him his hand. The talkative woman began quizzing Mrs. Lefkowitz about her scooter. The two other men went back to their game of cards. Ella closed her eyes, and breathed quietly, and hoped.

In her lounge chair, Maggie also had her eyes closed, thinking about what to do and how to make things right, even when part of her protested that it wasn't her job to fix things. Except nobody in Florida knew what was her job and what wasn't. Nobody here knew what a mess she'd made of her life. Nobody here knew Rose, and how she was the one who took care of things, the same way they didn't know that Maggie was always the one who needed saving, or fixing, or help. She had a job, a place to live, people who cared about her. Now it was time for her to start repairing the damage, starting with the one she'd hurt the worst—starting with Rose.

She squeezed her eyes shut, feeling afraid, part of her wanting to jump to her feet, hurry through the gate, jump behind the wheel of Lewis's long car, and drive off someplace where nobody knew her, where nobody knew who she was, or what she'd done, or where she'd come from. But she'd already run to Princeton, and then she'd run here. She didn't want to run anymore.

In the shallow end, the Water Babies began their cool-down. In the chair beside her, her grandmother cleared her throat. "I bet you miss people your age," Ella said. "It must be hard for you, being the only young person here."

"I'm okay," said Maggie.

"She's fine," growled Jack.

Maggie opened her eyes, then opened her notebook. "*Dear Rose,*" she wrote. Ella looked at the page, then very quickly looked away. Dora, the woman in the pink bathing cap, had no such compunctions.

"Who's Rose?" she asked.

"My sister," said Maggie.

"You've got a sister? What's she like?" Jack put down his cards, and Herman set aside his *Mother Jones.* "She's got a sister!"

"She's a lawyer in Philadelphia," said Ella, and then closed her mouth and looked at Maggie for help. Maggie ignored her, closing her notebook, getting up and walking through the gauntlet of senior citizens to the edge of the pool, where she dangled her legs in the water.

"Is she married?" asked Dora.

"What kind of law?" asked Jack. "Does she do wills, by any chance?"

"Is she coming to visit?" demanded Herman. "Does she look like you? Does she have any tattoos?"

"She's not married," said Maggie. "She has a boyfriend . . ." *Or at least, she used to have a boyfriend, until I fucked that up that for her.* Maggie stared unhappily into the chlorinated depths of the deep end.

"Tell us more!" urged Dora.

"Does she have anything pierced?" asked Herman.

Maggie smiled and shook her head. "She doesn't look like me. Well, a little bit, maybe. We have the same color eyes and hair, but

she's bigger than I am. And no tattoos, either. She's very conservative. She wears her hair twisted up all the time."

"Like you!" Ella said.

Maggie started to protest, then touched her ponytail and realized that it was true. She hopped into the water, flipped onto her
back, and floated.

"Rose can be funny," she said. Ella hurried to the edge of the
pool to listen. The rest of Maggie's pool friends followed after her,
jostling for prime position along the deep end's ledge. "And mean,
sometimes. When we were girls, we had to share a room. We had
twin beds, and there was a space in between them, and she'd lie
there, reading, and I used to jump over her." Maggie started to
smile as she remembered. "She'd be lying there, and I'd jump back
and forth, from one bed to the other, and I'd say, 'The quick brown
fox jumped over the lazy dog!'"

"So you were the quick brown fox," said Ella.

Maggie gave her a "duh" look that was quickly repeated by
Jack, Dora, and Herman. "I'd do it until she hit me," she said.

"She hit you?" asked Ella.

"I'd jump back and forth, and I could see that she was getting
really irritated, but I'd keep doing it until she'd stick her arm up in
the air and bat me down when I was jumping." Maggie nodded and
pulled herself out of the water, looking strangely pleased with the
memory of being hit by her sister, mid-leap.

"Tell us more about Rose," Dora said, as Jack handed her a
towel and her tube of Bain de Soleil.

"She doesn't care that much about looks. And stuff," said
Maggie, resuming her sprawling position on her lounge chair,
remembering Rose squinting at herself in the mirror, or Rose
clumping mascara onto her lids, then heading out the door with
half-moons of black on her cheeks.

"Oh, I'd like to meet her," said Dora.

"Invite her for a visit," said Jack, cutting his eyes toward Ella.
"I'm sure your grandmother would love to have both of you."

Maggie knew that he was right. Ella would love to meet Rose. What grandmother wouldn't? A smart, successful granddaughter with a law degree. But Maggie wasn't sure whether she was ready to see Rose again, even if Rose was willing to forgive her. Things were going better for her than they ever had, ever since she'd left Philadelphia that terrible night. For once in her life, she wasn't in Rose's shadow, she wasn't the second sister, the one who wasn't as smart, wasn't as successful, the one who was just pretty in a time when pretty felt as if it mattered less and less. Corinne and Charles hadn't known about her history, her struggles, the remedial classes, all the jobs she'd quit or been fired from, all the girls who used to be her friends. Dora and Jack and Herman didn't think she was stupid or a slut. They liked her. They admired her. They listened to what she had to say. And Rose would show up and ruin everything. "A bagel shop?" she'd ask, in a tone suggesting that a bagel shop was the best Maggie could hope for—a bagel shop, a spare bedroom, a borrowed car, the kindness of strangers.

Maggie opened her notebook again. "Dear Rose," she wrote once more, and then stopped. She couldn't think of how to do this, of what she was going to say next.

"This is Maggie, in case you can't tell from the handwriting," she wrote. "I am in Florida with our grandmother. Her name is Ella Hirsch, and she was . . ." Agh. This was so hard. There was a word for what she wanted to say here. Maggie could almost catch it, could practically taste it on her tongue, and the feeling caused her heart to quicken, the way it had during the classes at Princeton, when she'd sat in the back with the right answers waiting to burst from her mouth. "What's the word that means that someone wants to be with someone else, but they're not, because of a fight or something?" she called.

"The Yiddish word?" asked Jack.

"Who's she gonna write to in Yiddish?" asked Herman, returning his attention to *Mother Jones*.

"Not Yiddish," said Maggie. "The word for where there's two

relatives, or something, but other people in the family are angry at each other about stuff, so the relatives never meet."

"*Estranged,*" said Lewis. Jack glared at him. Maggie appeared not to notice.

"Thanks," she said.

"Glad to be of use in my golden years," said Lewis.

"Her name is Ella Hirsch, and she was estranged from us," Maggie wrote, and stared at the page. This was the hard part . . . but she'd had practice at Princeton, working with words, picking out the best ones the way a careful cook chooses the best apples from the basket, the plumpest chicken from the butcher's case.

"I'm sorry for what happened last winter," she wrote, deciding that this was probably the best way to handle it—flat out, in the open. "I am sorry I hurt you. I want . . ." And she paused again, aware that everyone was staring at her, as if she were some rare aquatic creature recently brought into captivity, some animal at the zoo who'd just learned an amusing new trick.

"What's the word for when you want to make something right?"

"*Reconciliation,*" Ella said quietly, and spelled it, and Maggie wrote it twice, just to be sure she got it right.

FORTY EIGHT

"Okay," said Rose, as she got into the passenger's seat of her car, "okay, so you swear and affirm under penalty of perjury as defined by the Pennsylvania Code that there will be absolutely nobody else from Lewis, Dommel, and Fenick at this wedding?" This was important information. Of all the things she'd covered with Simon—dead mother, vanished sister, unspeakable stepmother—they'd never gotten around to the topic of Mr. Jim Danvers. And Rose was determined not to have to do it at the nuptials of two of Simon's law-school classmates mere months before their own wedding.

"As far as I know," said Simon, straightening his tie and starting the car.

"As far as you know," Rose repeated. She flipped down the mirror, glanced at her makeup, and began swiping at an unblended patch of concealer beneath her right eye. "So I'll just have to keep my eyes open for skateboards."

"I didn't tell you?" Simon asked innocently. "Don Dommel fell off his board and hit his head on a railing and saw God. No more extreme anything. He's into meditation now. There's yoga every afternoon at lunchtime. The whole place smells like incense, and the secretaries have to say *Namaste* when they answer the phone.'"

"Heh," said Rose.

"Rose," said Simon, "it's a wedding, not a mob hit. Calm down."

Rose began rooting in her purse for a lipstick, thinking that it was easy for Simon to say. He wasn't the one who had to explain himself. She was starting to understand why Maggie had been so defensive. Moving through the world with a title—doctor, lawyer, college student—gave you armor. Having to continually try to find a way to tell people who you were—which really meant telling them what you did—was difficult when you didn't fit into one of the world's neat little cubes. *Well, I'm an aspiring actress, but I'm waitressing right now,* or, *I used to be a lawyer, but for the last ten months I've been walking dogs.*

"You'll be fine, Rose," said Simon. "You just have to be happy for my friends, and drink champagne, and dance with me . . ."

"You didn't mention dancing," said Rose, and gazed dismally at her feet, currently cramped in the first pair of high-heeled shoes she'd worn since her defection from big firm life. *Courage,* she told herself. "I'm sure this is going to be great!" She swallowed hard. She was sure it was going to be awful. She didn't do well at large functions, which was one of the reasons she was semi-dreading her own nuptials. She had too many memories of bar and bat mitzvah parties, afternoons like these in synagogues and country-club ballrooms, where she'd always felt like the tallest, ugliest girl, and how she'd station herself in a corner close to the chopped liver and miniature hot dogs in puff pastry, reasoning that if nobody could see her, it wouldn't hurt when nobody asked her to dance, and she'd spend hours alone, eating, and watching Maggie win the limbo contest.

Flash forward eighteen years, add one fiancé, and here she was again, she thought, following Simon through church doors festooned with giant tufts of lilies and white satin ribbons. Except instead of chopped liver and teeny weenies, there'd be crudités and champagne, and there'd be no limbo-ing little sister to distract her. Rose picked up a program. "The bride's name is Penelope?"

"We actually call her Lopey," said Simon.

"Lopey. Right," said Rose.

"I'll introduce you to some people," Simon said. And, in short order, Rose met James, and Aidan, and Leslie, and Heather. James and Aidan were also law-school classmates of Simon's. Leslie worked in publicity; Heather was a buyer at Macy's. Both of them were tiny little things wearing linen sheaths (Heather's was cream, Leslie's was yellow) and cashmere wraps slung loosely over their shoulders. Rose looked around the room, despair welling in her chest as she realized that every single other woman—every single one of them!—was wearing a simply cut dress and a wrap, and delicate little sandals, and here she was, in the wrong outfit, in the wrong color, with pumps, not sandals, and chunky beads, not pearls, and her hair was probably a frizzy mess staging a jailbreak from the tortoiseshell combs she'd carefully positioned an hour ago. Shit. Maggie would have known what she was supposed to wear, Rose thought dismally. Where was her sister when she needed her?

"And what do you do?" asked Heather. Or maybe it was Leslie. They were both blondes; only, one of them had a pageboy and the other had her hair pinned into a graceful chignon; and they both had the kind of translucent skin that comes from excellent breeding and regular exposure to the air inside of Talbots' dressing rooms.

Rose fiddled with her beads, wondering if anyone would notice if she slipped them into her purse during the service. "I'm an attorney."

"Oh!" said Leslie. Or possibly Heather. "So do you work with Simon?"

"I'm . . . I'm actually . . ." Rose shot Simon a desperate look, but he was deep in conversation with the guys. She wiped at her damp forehead, realizing that she'd probably just removed her foundation. "I used to work at Lewis, Dommel, and Fenick, but I'm sort of taking a break for the time being."

"Oh," said Leslie.

"That's nice," said Heather. "And you're getting married, right?"

"Right!" Rose agreed, too loudly, and wrapped her fingers around Simon's forearm, taking care to make sure that her engagement ring was front and center, in case they'd think that she was lying.

"I took three months' leave from work to plan my wedding," said Heather. "Oh, I remember that time. All those meetings . . . the menus, the flowers . . ."

"I just worked part time," chimed in Leslie. "I'd keep busy, of course, with the Junior League, but mostly it was all wedding, all the time."

"Would you excuse me?" Rose murmured, knowing that any minute they were going to start talking dresses, and she'd be forced to reveal the truth, which was that she hadn't been looking since her one disastrous afternoon with Amy. *No dress, no job,* their eyes would say, *and no membership to the Junior League. What kind of a bride are you?*

Rose hurried out into the aisle, back through the foyer, and out onto the brick path, where a tall man in a suit was standing as if he were waiting for her. Rose stopped, and stared up at his crisp white shirt, red-and-gold patterned tie, square jaw, tanned skin, sparkling blue eyes. Jim Danvers.

"Hello, Rose," he said.

He looked exactly the same. But what had she expected? That he'd wither up and die without her? That he'd go bald, that he'd develop adult acne, that hair would sprout out of his ears?

Rose nodded at him, hoping he couldn't tell that her knees were shaking, her hands were trembling, that even her neck was wobbling, too. Come to think of it, she saw, he did have hair coming out of his ears. Not much, really, not the kind of disgusting bristly growth she'd noticed coming out of other men's ears, but still . . . there it was. Ear hair. The incontrovertible evidence that he wasn't perfect. Then again, sleeping with her sister could also be interpreted as evidence of his lack of perfection, but still, she found the ear hair comforting.

"What brings you here?" he asked. His voice sounded higher than she remembered it. Could it be that Jim Danvers was nervous?

Rose tossed her hair. "Oh, Lopey and I go way back. We rode horses together, and then we were in that a capella singing group together in college. We were sorority sisters, we went on double dates . . ."

Jim shook his head. "Lopey's a vegetarian, and I think she believes that riding horses would be exploitative. Also, she was a pretty hard-core lesbian in college, so any double-dating you did would have to be of the all-female variety."

"Ah," said Rose, "I must have been thinking of the groom, then."

Jim gave a short, uncomfortable laugh. "Rose," he began. "I've been meaning to talk to you."

"Lucky me," said Rose.

"I've missed you," he said.

"What's not to miss?" she said. "Come meet my fiancé."

His eyes widened almost imperceptibly. "Take a walk with me first," he said.

"I don't think so."

"Come on. It's a beautiful day."

She shook her head.

"You look so beautiful," he murmured.

She whirled, glaring at him. "Look, Jim. You've had your fun with me, so why don't you give it a rest? I'm sure there's plenty of women here who'd be impressed with your talents."

Now Jim looked distressed. "Rose, I'm sorry. I'm sorry if I offended you."

"You slept with my sister," she said. "I'm a little past offended."

He took her arm and tugged her toward a wooden bench, sat down beside her, and looked earnestly into her eyes. "I've been wanting to talk to you for a while. The way it ended . . . What I did . . ." He clutched her hands. "I wanted to be good for you," he said in a choked voice. "I was weak. I was an idiot. I threw away everything we could have had, and I've felt horrible about myself for months . . ."

"Please," she said. "I've felt horrible about myself for practically my entire life. You think I'm going to feel sorry for you?"

"I want to make it up to you," he said. "I want to make it right."

"Forget it," she said. "It's over. I've moved on. I'm engaged now. . . ."

"Congratulations," he said sadly.

"Oh, come on," she said. "Don't tell me you even thought for a minute that you and I were . . . that we would . . ."

He blinked. And were those tears in his eyes? *Amazing*, thought Rose, who felt as if she were observing a specimen on a slide through a microscope. I wonder if he can make himself cry whenever he wants to?

Now he was taking her hands, and she could predict every single one of his moves, every word that he'd say.

"Rose, I'm sorry," he began, and she nodded, because she'd figured that would be his lead-in. "What I did was unforgivable," he said, "and if there was any way to make it up to you . . ."

She shook her head and got to her feet. "There's not," she said. "You're sorry for what happened. I'm sorry, too. Not only because you're the kind of guy you turned out to be, but . . ." And suddenly her throat felt thick, as if she were trying to swallow a sweat sock. "Because you ruined . . ." *My life?* she thought. No, that wasn't true. Her life was fine, or it would probably be fine, once she got the whole career thing back on track, and she was with Simon now, Simon who was so kind, who called forth all of the goodness in her own heart, who made her laugh. The short, spectacularly failed romance she'd had with Jim felt like nothing more than a far-off bad dream. He hadn't ruined her, but he'd damaged something else, hurt it possibly beyond repair. "Because of Maggie," she finally said.

And now he was pulling her back to the bench, and he was talking about her future, how terrible he'd felt when she'd left Lewis, Dommel, and Fenick, and how that had been unnecessary—he was a cad, yes, he'd admit to that, but at least he was discreet, and nothing would have happened to her at work—and where had

she landed? Did she need help? Because he could help her, it was
the least he could do in light of what had happened, and . . .

"Stop! Please!" said Rose. She could hear the strains of a string
quartet filtering through the garden, and the church doors creaking
shut. "We need to get back."

"I'm sorry," he said.

"I accept your apology," Rose said formally. And then, because
he looked so sad—and because, in spite of her absent sister, wicked
stepmother, and lack of a legal career, she was so happy—she leaned
close to him and kissed his cheek lightly. "It's okay," she said. "I
hope you'll be happy."

"Oh, Rose," he groaned, and wrapped his arms around her.

And suddenly, there was Simon, his eyes wide and shocked.
"They're starting," he said quietly. "We should go."

Rose looked at him. His pale face was even paler than it usually
was. "Simon," she said. Oh, God.

"Come on," he said, in a soft, toneless voice, and he walked her
up toward the wedding, where the flower girls had already started
their trip down the aisle, strewing pale-peach rose petals as they
went.

Simon sat quietly through the service. He was silent during dinner.
When the band started to play, he made a beeline for the bar, and
stood there, drinking beer, until Rose finally convinced him that
they should talk, and they should do it in private. He held the car
door open for her—a gesture that had always seemed kind, but now
seemed ironic, even cruel. "Well," he began. "Interesting afternoon." His eyes were straight ahead, and there were splotches of
hectic red high on his pale cheeks.

"Simon, I'm sorry you saw that," Rose said.

"Sorry that it happened, or sorry that I saw?" Simon asked.

"Let me explain," she said. "I've been meaning to tell you about
this. . . ."

"You kissed him," Simon said.

"It was a kiss good-bye," said Rose.

"Good-bye for what?" Simon asked. "What was going on with you two?"

Rose sighed. "We dated."

"A partner dating an associate? How daring," Simon said.

Rose squeezed her eyes shut. "I know. It was really stupid. A big mistake for both of us."

"When did your association begin?"

"Our association?" Rose repeated. "Simon, it wasn't a corporate merger!"

"Not a corporate one, evidently," he said. "Why didn't it work out?"

"Infidelity," Rose said quietly.

"Yours or his?" Simon shot back.

"His! Of course his! Come on, Simon, you know me better than that." Rose took a look at him. He ignored her. "Don't you?"

Simon said nothing. Rose stared out the window, at the blur of trees and buildings, at other cars. How many couples in how many cars were fighting? she wondered. And how many of the women were doing a better job of explaining themselves than she was?

"Look, the important thing is that it's over," she said, as he parked the car in front of their apartment. "It's really, truly, genuinely, absolutely over, and I'm sorry that you saw what you saw, but it doesn't mean anything. Believe me, Jim Danvers is the last thing I want in my life. Which is what I was telling him when you showed up."

Simon exhaled. "I believe you," he said, "but I want to know what happened. I want to understand it."

"Why? I don't want to know about your old girlfriends."

"This is different."

"Why?" Rose followed him into the bedroom, finally pulling her beads over her head.

"Because whatever happened between you two, it was bad

enough to make you never want to see the inside of a law office again."

"Not every law office," Rose said. "It's really that particular one that presented a problem."

"Don't change the subject. You have this . . . this history. And I don't know anything about it."

"Everyone's got a history! You're friends with people named Lopey, which could have been pointed out to me earlier . . ."

"But I don't know any of your history!"

"What do you want to know?" she asked him. "Why is it so important?"

"Because I want to know who you are!"

Rose shook her head. "Simon, it's not like I'm some huge mystery. I had a . . ." she searched for the least offensive word. "A relationship with this guy. It didn't end well. And it's over. And that's all!"

"How did it end?" Simon asked again.

"He did something," Rose began. "Something with someone . . ." She swallowed hard.

"When you're ready to tell me," Simon said coolly, "I'll be happy to listen."

He walked into the bathroom. Rose listened to him slamming the door and starting the shower. She walked back to the living room, bending to scoop up the pile of mail they'd both stepped over when they'd come home. Bill, bill, credit-card offer, actual card with her name on it, her name written in very familiar, large, looping handwriting.

Rose sank onto the couch. Her hands were shaking as she opened the envelope and unfolded the single sheet of notebook paper inside.

Dear Rose, she read. Words jumped out at her. *Grandmother. Sorry. Florida. Ella. Reconciliation.*

"Oh, my God," Rose breathed. She forced herself to read the whole thing twice, then hurried into the bedroom. Simon was standing in front of the bed with a towel wrapped around his waist and a serious look on his face. Wordlessly, Rose handed him the letter.

"My . . . grandmother," she said. The word felt strange in her mouth. "It's from Maggie. She's staying with my grandmother."

Now Simon looked even more upset. "You have a grandmother? You see what I mean, Rose? I didn't even know you had a grandmother!"

"I didn't know either," Rose said. "I mean, I guess I knew I had one, but I don't know anything about her." She felt like she'd suddenly been plunged underwater, like everything was slow and strange. "I have to . . ." she said. "I should call them." She sank onto the bed, feeling dizzy. A grandmother. Her mother's mother. Who, evidently, wasn't living in some old-age home, the way Rose had always believed, unless they were letting twentysomething vagabonds stay in those places, too. "I should call them. I should . . ."

Simon was staring at her. "You really didn't know you had a grandmother?"

"Well, I mean, I knew that my mother came from somewhere. But I thought she was . . . I don't know. Old, or sick. In a home. My father said that she was in a home." Rose stared at the letter, feeling her stomach clench. Her father had lied to her. Why had her father lied about something as important as this?

"Where's the phone?" she asked, jumping to her feet.

"Hey, hold on. Who are you going to call? What are you going to say?"

Rose set down the telephone and picked up her car keys. "I've got to go."

"Go where?"

Rose ignored him, hurrying to the door, running for the elevator, her heart thrumming in her chest as she ran down the street to her car.

Twenty minutes later, Rose found herself in the same place where she and her sister had stood almost a year ago—on Sydelle's doorstep, waiting for admission. She leaned against the doorbell. The dog howled. Finally, the lights flicked on.

"Rose?" Sydelle stood in the front door, blinking at her. "What are you doing here?" Her stepmother's face looked strange somehow beneath the glare of the light. Rose looked carefully before deciding that it was just the usual—another eye lift. She shoved Maggie's letter at her stepmother. "You tell me," she said.

"I don't have my glasses," Sydelle parried, pulling her lace-trimmed bathrobe tightly around her and pursing her lips at the blank spot on her walkway where Maggie had yanked out the shrub back in November.

"Then let me fill you in," said Rose. "This is from Maggie. She moved in with my grandmother. My grandmother who I didn't know was still making sense."

"Oh," said Sydelle. "Oh. Um . . ."

Rose stared. If her stepmother had ever been at a loss for words, she sure couldn't remember it. But there she was, nonplussed and twitching uncomfortably underneath her face cream and stitches.

"Let me in," said Rose.

"Of course!" Sydelle said in a strange, twittery voice, and stepped aside.

Rose strode past her and stood at the foot of the stairs. "Dad!" she yelled.

Sydelle put her hand on Rose's shoulder. Rose jerked away. "This was your idea, wasn't it?" she said, glaring at her stepmother. " 'Oh, Michael, they don't need a grandmother. They've got me!' "

Sydelle stepped back as if Rose had slapped her. "That's not how it happened," she said in a quivering voice. "I never thought I could be a substitute for . . . for everything you'd lost."

"Oh? Then how did it happen?" Rose demanded. She felt as if every cell of her body had been pumped to the bursting point with rage, as if she were going to explode. "Fill me in!"

Michael Feller hurried down the stairs, dressed in sweatpants and a white T-shirt, polishing his glasses with his handkerchief. His

fine hair floating like a mist over his bald head. "Rose? What's
going on?"

"Well, what's going on is that I've got a grandmother, she's not
in a home, Maggie's living with her, and nobody saw fit to mention
any of this to me," Rose said.

"Rose," said Sydelle, reaching toward her.

Rose whirled toward her. "Don't touch me," she said. Sydelle
flinched.

"That's enough!" said Michael.

"No," said Rose. Her hands were shaking, her face was on fire.
"No, it's not enough. It's not even a good start. How could you?"
she yelled, as Sydelle cringed into a corner of her freshly wallpa-
pered foyer. "I know you never liked us. But hiding a grandmother?
Even for you, Sydelle, that's a stretch."

"It wasn't her," said Michael Feller taking Rose by the shoulders. "It wasn't her idea. It was mine."

Rose gaped at him "Bullshit," she said. "You wouldn't . . ." She
stared at her father, his faint gray eyes and high white forehead, her
sad, kind-hearted, lost dog of a father. "You wouldn't . . ."

"Let's sit down," Michael Feller said.

Sydelle looked at Rose. "It wasn't me," she said, in a flat, dull
voice. "And I'm sorry . . ." Her voice trailed off. Rose stared at her
stepmother, who had never looked less monstrous, had never
seemed more pathetic. Her face looked small and vulnerable, in
spite of the tattooed lipstick and taut skin. Rose stared at her, trying to remember whether she'd ever heard those words before,
whether Sydelle had ever been sorry for anything. She decided that
if her stepmother had ever apologized to her, she couldn't remember it.

"You don't know . . ." Sydelle drew a whispery breath. "You
don't know what it was like to live in this house. You don't know
what it was like to spend years never being good enough. Never
being the first choice, never being the one anyone really wanted.
Never being able to put a foot right."

"Gee, I'm sorry," Rose said, in a snotty voice she could have borrowed from her little sister.

Sydelle lifted her eyes and glared at Rose. "Nothing I did was ever what you wanted," she said, and blinked her freshly-stitched eyelashes. "I never had a chance with you or Maggie. Not with any of you."

"Sydelle," Michael said gently.

"Go on," Sydelle said. "You tell her. Tell her the whole thing. It's time she knew."

Rose stared at her stepmother seeing, for the first time, the vulnerability that lay beneath the makeup, the Botox, the diet tips and condescension. She looked and saw a woman who'd left sixty behind her, whose thin body was stringy and unwelcoming, and whose face looked like a cruel caricature, a harshly etched drawing of a woman instead of the real thing. She looked and saw the sadness Sydelle had lived with every day—a husband still in love with his dead first wife, an ex-husband who'd left her, a daughter grown and gone.

"Rose," her father said. Rose followed him into Sydelle's living room. The leather couches had been replaced by slipcovered suede, but they were still a blinding white. She sat down on one end, her father sat on the other.

"I'm sorry about Sydelle," he began, and looked out into the foyer. He was waiting for her, Rose thought. Waiting for her to come and do his dirty work.

"She's going through a really bad time right now," her father said. "Marcia's giving her mother a very hard time."

Rose shrugged, not feeling terribly sympathetic toward either Sydelle or My Marcia, who'd never had much time for or interest in her stepsisters, other than making sure they weren't touching her things while she was off at college.

"She's joined Jews for Jesus," he said, and looked away.

"You can't be serious."

"Well, that's what we thought at first, that she was kidding."

"Oh, God," Rose said, thinking that Sydelle, who had mezuzahs on every door of the house, including the bathrooms, and scowled at every shopping-mall Santa she saw, had to be in agony. "So she's Christian?"

Her father shook his head. "We drove up to visit last weekend and she had a big wreath on the door."

"Ho ho ho," said Rose cheerlessly.

"Rose," her father said, a warning tone in his voice. Rose lifted her head and glared at him.

"Now, moving on to more pertinent topics. My grandmother."

Michael Feller swallowed hard. "She called you? Ella?"

"Maggie wrote to me," said Rose. "She said she's living with this . . . with Ella. So what's the story?"

Her father said nothing.

"Dad?"

"I'm ashamed of myself," Michael finally said. "I should have told you about this—about Ella—a long time ago. He laced his hands around his knees and rocked back and forth, clearly wishing for an annual report or at the very least a *Wall Street Journal* to get him through this. "Your mother's mother," he began. "Ella Hirsch. She moved to Florida a long time ago. After . . ." He paused. "After your mother died."

"You told us she was in a home," Rose prompted.

Michael Feller curled his hands into fists, planted them on his thighs. "She was," he said. "Just not the kind of home you probably thought."

Rose stared at her father. "What do you mean?"

"Well, she was in a home. Her home." He swallowed hard. "With Ira, I guess."

"You lied to us," Rose said flatly.

"It was a lie of omission," her father said. Clearly, this was a line he'd thought of long ago, a line he'd been rehearsing in his head for years. Michael took a deep breath. "After your mother . . ." His voice trailed off.

"Died," Rose supplied.

"Died," said Michael. "After she died I was angry. I felt . . ." He paused, and stared at Sydelle's glass-and-metal coffee table.

"Angry at Mom's parents? Angry at Ella?"

"They tried to tell me about Caroline, but I didn't want to listen. I was so in love with her . . ." Rose winced at the pain in her father's voice. "I was so in love with her. And I was so angry at them. Your mother was on lithium when I met her. She was stable. But she hated the way the medicine made her feel. And I'd try to make her take it, and Ella, her mother, would, too, and for a while she'd be fine, and then . . ." He exhaled, pulling off his glasses as if he couldn't bear their weight on his face. "She loved you. She loved all of us. But she couldn't . . ." Michael's voice caught in his throat. "And it didn't matter. It didn't change how I felt about her."

"What was she like?" asked Rose.

Her father looked surprised. "You don't remember?"

"You didn't exactly keep a shrine to her in our house or anything." She swept her hands around Sydelle's spotless living room— the white walls and white carpet, the bookshelves that had never held books, only glass objets and an eight-by-eleven framed shot of My Marcia's wedding. "There aren't any pictures of her. You never talked about her."

"It hurt." said Michael. "It hurt to remember. It hurt to see her face. I thought it would hurt you and Maggie, too."

"I don't know," said Rose. "I wish . . ." She looked down at her feet in the woven white carpet. "I wish she hadn't been a secret."

Michael was quiet. "I remember the first time I saw her. She was walking across the campus at the University of Michigan, pushing her bike, and she was laughing, and it was like a bell going off in my head. She was the most beautiful thing I'd ever seen. She had a pink scarf tied in her hair . . ." Her father's voice drifted off.

Rose could remember glimpses, snatches, pieces of stories, a sweet, chiming voice, a smooth cheek pressed against hers. *Sweet dreams, dream girl. Sleep tight, honey bun.* And everyone had lied by the things they'd told and the things they'd kept secret. Ella had lied to her father about Caroline—or, rather, she'd told him the truth, but he hadn't wanted to listen. And her father had lied to the girls about Ella—or he'd told them a tiny piece of the truth and left the rest of it unsaid.

She got to her feet, her hands clenched into fists. Lies, lies, lies, and where was the truth in all of this? Her mother had been crazy, then dead. Her father had yoked himself to a wicked witch and had given his daughters over to her care. Her grandmother had vanished down a rabbit hole, and Maggie had gone chasing after her. And Rose didn't know anything, not anything at all.

"You just got rid of her. All the time growing up, I don't remember a single picture of her, or any of her things . . ."

"It hurt too much," Michael said simply. "It was bad enough having to look at the two of you."

"Gee, thanks."

"Oh, no, I didn't mean . . ." He took Rose's hand, a move that shocked her into speechlessness. She couldn't remember her father touching her at all except for the occasional peck on the cheek since that disastrous day when she was twelve and came out of the bathroom and whispered that her period had started. "It was just that you two reminded me of her so much. Everything you did, it was like having to remember Caroline all over again."

"And then you married her," said Rose, nodding toward the foyer where, presumably, her stepmother lingered.

Her father sighed. "Sydelle meant well."

Rose gave a short, barking laugh. "Oh, sure. She's wonderful. She just hated me and Maggie."

"She was jealous," said Michael.

Rose was flabbergasted. "Jealous of what? Jealous of me? You have to be kidding. When My Marcia is superior in every way. And even if she was jealous, she was horrible. And you let her get away with it!"

Her father cringed. "Rose . . ."

"Rose, what?"

"There's something I need to give you. It's too late, but still. . . ."

He hurried upstairs and came down with a shoe box in his hands. "These are from her. Your grandmother," he said. "She's in Florida," he said. "She tried to get in touch with me—with you and Maggie—for years. But I didn't let her." He reached into the box and pulled out a creased and faded envelope with "Miss Rose Feller" written on the outside. "This was the last card she sent."

Rose ran her thumb under the flap, which came loose easily from glue that was fifteen years old. Inside was a card with a bouquet of flowers on the front. The flowers were pink and purple, dusted with gold glitter that sparkled dimly on Rose's fingertips. "HAPPY SWEET SIXTEEN," read the silver script above the flowers. And inside . . . Rose opened the card. A twenty-dollar bill and a photograph fluttered into her lap. "TO MY GRANDDAUGHTER," read the words in slanted script. "I WISH YOU LOVE AND EVERY HAPPINESS ON YOUR SPECIAL DAY." Followed by a signature. Followed by an address. And a telephone number. And a P.S. that read, "Rose, I would love to hear from you. Please call me any time!!!" It was the three exclamation points, Rose thought, that broke her heart the most. She looked at the photograph. It was a picture of a little girl—round-faced, brown-eyed, with bangs and two neat pigtails tied with red yarn ribbon and a serious look on her face, sitting on an older woman's lap. The woman was laughing. The little girl was not. Rose flipped the snapshot over. *Rose and Grandma, 1975,* it read, in the same blue ink, the same slanted script. Nineteen seventy-five. She would have been six.

Rose got to her feet. "I have to go now," she said.

"Rose," her father called, helplessly, toward her back. She ignored him, walking out of the house. Then she sat behind the wheel of her car, with the card still in her hands, and closed her eyes, remembering her mother's voice, her mother's pink-lipsticked smile, a tanned arm reaching out from behind a camera. *Smile, honey! Why such a sourpuss? Smile for me, Rosie Posy. Smile pretty, baby doll.*

FORTY-NINE

"Read more!" Maggie said.

"I can't," Lewis insisted, and gave her an extremely dignified look across Ella's dining room table. "It would be a breach of journalistic ethics."

"Oh, come on," Ella pleaded. "Just the first few sentences. Please?"

"It would be very, very wrong," he said, and shook his head sadly. "Ella, I'm surprised that you'd even want me to do such a thing."

"I'm a bad influence," Maggie said proudly. "At least tell us what Irving ordered."

Lewis threw his hands in the air in mock resignation. "Fine," he said. "But you're sworn to secrecy." He cleared his throat. " 'Irving and I do not care for French food,' " Mrs. Sobel's latest began. " 'The dishes are much too rich for us. We have also found that many French restaurants are noisy and dim, which is supposed to be romantic, but makes it hard to read your menu, let alone see your meal.' "

"Poor Mrs. Sobel," Ella murmured.

Lewis shook his head at her, then kept reading. " 'Most cooks do not know how an omelet should be made. An omelet should be fluffy and light, with the cheese just melted. And I am sorry to report that

Bistro Bleu is no exception. My omelet was overcooked and rubbery. The potatoes were not as hot as they should have been, and they were made with rosemary, which Irving does not care for.' "

"Again with Irving," said Ella.

"Irving's trouble?" asked Maggie.

"Irving's allergic. To everything," Lewis explained. "He's allergic to things I didn't know you could be allergic to. White flour, shellfish, all seeds, all nuts . . . half of that woman's reviews are devoted to how long it took her to find Irving something to eat, and then there's another quarter of the review reserved for the discussion of how whatever Irving ended up eating didn't agree with him . . ."

"This is Irving Sobel?" asked Mrs. Lefkowitz, shuffling toward the table. "Feh. He came to a party I had once and wouldn't eat a bite!"

Maggie rolled her eyes. Mrs. Lefkowitz, their dinner guest, was not in a good mood. She wore a pink sweatshirt, explaining that if she spilled her borscht, it would blend right in, and tan polyester pants. She didn't explain her pants, but Maggie figured that if she spilled anything at all on them, it would only constitute an improvement.

Mrs. Lefkowitz seated herself with a small groan, picked up a kosher dill pickle, and began expounding on the state of the nearby mall. "Hooligans!" she said, through a mouthful of pickle. Maggie relocated her textbooks from the Makeup for Theater class she'd enrolled in at the local community college and set dishes and silverware in their place.

"I think it's called Houlihan's," she said.

"No, no, hooligans," said Mrs. Lefkowitz. "Ruffians! Hoodlums! Teenagers! Everywhere! The mall is full of them, and all of the clothes are these teeny-tiny things with, with ruffled sleeves," she said. "Miniskirts! Shirts that you can see right through! Pants," she continued, glaring at Maggie, "that are made out of leather. Have you ever in your life heard of such a thing?"

"Actually—" Maggie began. Ella bit back a smile. She knew for a fact that Maggie owned a pair of leather pants, and a leather miniskirt, too.

"What's the occasion?" Ella asked instead. "What were you shopping for?"

Mrs. Lefkowitz waved a dismissive hand over the bowls of borscht. "My son. Remember him? The actuary? Mister Excitement? Well, he calls me up and says, 'Ma, I'm getting married.' I say, 'At your age? You need a wife like I need tap-dancing shoes.' He tells me that his mind's made up, and that she's a wonderful girl. I tell him that at fifty-three he's got no business going with girls, and he tells me I've got nothing to worry about, she's thirty-six, but a very mature thirty-six." She glared at Ella and Maggie as if they were responsible for causing her son to fall in love with a very mature thirty-six-year-old. "This I should live to see," she concluded, and helped herself to a piece of rye bread. "So now I need an outfit. Which of course I can't find."

"What are you looking for?" asked Maggie.

Mrs. Lefkowitz cocked a gray eyebrow. "The princess speaks!"

"I talk!" cried Maggie, affronted. "And it just so happens that I am an expert shopper."

"Well, then, what would you suggest for my son's third wedding?"

Maggie considered Mrs. Lefkowitz carefully—her cap of tousled iron-gray curls, her eyes, bright blue and inquisitive, the pink lipstick she applied even to the drooping corner of her lips. She wasn't fat, exactly, but she didn't have much of a shape, either. Her waist had thickened, her breasts had drooped.

"Hmm," Maggie said out loud, considering possibilities.

"Like a science project, she looks at me."

"Shh," said Ella, who'd seen Maggie look this way before, curled on her couch at night, poring over her poetry books in a pool of lamplight with a concentration that almost made it seem as if she were hypnotizing herself.

"What's your favorite thing?" Maggie suddenly asked.

"Hot-fudge sundaes," said Mrs. Lefkowitz promptly. "But I'm not allowed to have them anymore. Only with frozen yogurt," she said, wrinkling her face to demonstrate her feelings about frozen yogurt, "and that fat-free fudge topping, that they aren't even allowed to call fudge, because it's not. Fudge topping," she said again, and shook her head, clearly prepared to deliver a speech on the failings of fake fudge topping. But Maggie stopped her.

"Your favorite thing to wear."

"To wear?" Mrs. Lefkowitz looked down at herself as if she were surprised she was wearing anything at all. "Oh, I like what's comfortable, I guess."

"Your favorite thing ever," said Maggie, twisting her hair into a ponytail. Ella perched on the edge of a dining room chair, eager to see where this was going.

Mrs. Lefkowitz opened her mouth. Maggie raised her hand. "Think about it first," she said. "Think carefully. Think of all the outfits you ever wore, and tell me what you liked the very best."

Mrs. Lefkowitz closed her eyes. "My going-away suit," she said.

"What's that?"

"My going-away suit," she repeated, as if Maggie hadn't heard her.

"Like you'd wear when you were leaving your wedding and going to the airport for your honeymoon," Ella explained.

"Right, right," said Mrs. Lefkowitz, nodding. "It was a black-and-white-checked print, and the skirt was very fitted here," she said, smoothing her hands along her hips. "I had black pumps . . ." She closed her eyes, remembering.

"What was the jacket like?" Maggie prompted.

"Oh, short, I think," said Mrs. Lefkowitz, sounding almost dreamy. "With jet buttons down the front. It was so beautiful. I wonder what became of it?"

"What if . . ." said Maggie. "What if we went shopping together?"

Mrs. Lefkowitz made a face. "That mall again? I don't think I could stand it."

Maggie wasn't sure she'd be able to stand it, either, making her way through the stores at Mrs. Lefkowitz's snail's pace. "Or how about this?" she said. "You tell me your size . . ."

"Oh, now she wants to get personal!"

". . . and you give me your credit card . . ."

Ella could see Mrs. Lefkowitz getting ready to shake her head. She held her breath and hoped.

". . . and I'll find you an outfit. A few outfits, even. I'll give you a choice. We'll have a fashion show here, you'll try them on for us, and you'll pick the one you like the best, and I'll return the rest of them."

Now Mrs. Lefkowitz was looking at Maggie curiously. "Like a personal shopper?"

"Just like that," said Maggie, walking a slow circle around Mrs. Lefkowitz. "Do you have a budget?" she asked.

Mrs. Lefkowitz sighed. "Two hundred dollars, maybe?"

Maggie winced. "I'll try," she said.

FIFTY

Maggie spent two solid days searching for Mrs. Lefkowitz's wedding finery. Which was good, she thought. It kept her from sitting by the telephone, wondering whether Rose had gotten her letter yet, and whether Rose would call.

Mrs. Lefkowitz was a challenge—no doubt about it, Maggie thought. There was no way she could put her in the kind of fitted suit she'd described, but Maggie could, she thought, find something that would make Mrs. Lefkowitz feel like she was wearing that outfit again. A suit would work, and the skirt could even be on the short side—from what she'd seen of them, Mrs. Lefkowitz's legs weren't bad—but a short jacket was out of the question. Something long, maybe, hip-length, but with a trim to make it look dressy, something that suggested those jet-black buttons. Something she'd seen before. Macy's? Saks? She finally remembered that it had been at neither of those places, but in Rose's closet. Rose had a jacket like that.

Maggie swallowed hard and kept shopping, visiting department stores, consignment stores, thrift shops, flea markets, and the community college's costume department, after she'd promised the head of the department that she'd help with the makeup for an upcoming production of *Hedda Gabler*. In the end, she came up with three choices. The first was an outfit she'd found on sale at the Nordstrom's outlet—a knee-length skirt, fitted but not too tight, in pale pink linen, heavily embroidered in hot pink and red thread, along with a modest matching tank top and an embroidered cardigan that went on top of that. Mrs. Lefkowitz fingered the fabric doubtfully. "This doesn't look like my going-away suit," she said. "And a skirt with a sweater? I don't know. I was thinking a dress, maybe."

"It's not the look we're going for," said Maggie. "It's the sensation."

"Sensation?"

"The feeling you had wearing your going-away suit," she said. "You can't wear the suit again, right?"

Mrs. Lefkowitz nodded.

"So what we're going for is an outfit that gives you the same . . ." She struggled for words. ". . . the same sense of yourself that the suit did." She handed Mrs. Lefkowitz the outfit, still on hangers, plus a wide-brimmed pink hat she'd snatched from the college's costume department. "Just try," she said, and ushered Mrs. Lefkowitz back to her bedroom, where she'd set up a full length mirror.

"I feel ridiculous!" Mrs. Lefkowitz called, as Ella and Lewis sat on the love seat, waiting for the fashion show to begin.

"Just let me see it," said Maggie.

"Do I really have to wear the hat?" came the reply.

"Come on out," called Ella.

Slowly, Mrs. Lefkowitz emerged from the bedroom. The skirt was too long. Maggie could see that right away. And the cardigan sleeves fell past Mrs. Lefkowitz's fingertips, and the tank top gaped.

"They're making clothes for giants these days," she complained, and shook one fabric-covered fist at Maggie. "Look at this!"

Maggie stood back, assessing the look. Then she walked to Mrs. Lefkowitz and rolled the waistband up so that the skirt lifted just past Mrs. Lefkowitz's knees. She folded the cardigan's sleeves, pulled and tucked the tank top into some semblance of a proper fit, and plunked the hat on top of Mrs. Lefkowitz's head. "There," she said, and turned her toward the mirror. "Take a look."

Mrs. Lefkowitz opened her mouth to object, to say that the outfit was horrible and that this hadn't been a good idea at all. Then she closed it. "Oh!" she said.

"You see?" asked Maggie.

Slowly, Mrs. Lefkowitz nodded. "The color," she began.

"Right, right!" said Maggie, who was more excited, more animated, more happy than Ella had ever seen her. "It doesn't fit you right, but the color, I thought, with your eyes, and I know you like pink."

"Not bad, not bad," said Mrs. Lefkowitz, and she didn't sound snappish, or crabby, or anything except enraptured with this vision of herself, with her blue eyes sparkling against the pale of the pink. What was she seeing? Maggie wondered. Maybe herself as a young woman, a newlywed, standing on the steps of the synagogue, holding her new husband's hand.

"So that's choice one," said Maggie, gently pulling Mrs. Lefkowitz away from the mirror.

"I'll take it!" she said.

"No, no," said Maggie, laughing, "you have to see what else I found."

"But I want this!" she said, clutching the hat to the top of her head. "I don't want to try anything else, I want this!" She looked at her bare feet. "What shoes do I need? Can you help me find shoes, too? And maybe a necklace." She brushed her hand over her collarbones. "My first husband gave me a strand of pearls once . . ."

"Next outfit," said Maggie, pushing Mrs. Lefkowitz back toward the bedroom. Outfit Two was a long sleeveless tube dress made of some slinky black synthetic, heavy enough to drape gracefully. She'd found it on sale at Marshalls, and paired it with a black-and-silver wrap with a black fringe on the ends.

"Ooh la la!" called Mrs. Lefkowitz, slipping the dress over her head and sauntering out of the bedroom, waggling the ends of the wrap in a vaguely suggestive fashion. "Racy! I feel like a flapper!"

"Hot stuff!" called Ella.

"It's nice," said Maggie, studying her carefully. The dress fell in a single column, suggesting the outlines of waist and hip rather than clinging too tightly, and it gave Mrs. Lefkowitz the appearance of a figure. She'd need heels, for sure, to pull it off, and Maggie wasn't sure that an eighty-seven-year-old woman in heels was a very good idea. Ballet slippers? she wondered.

"What's next?" asked Ella, clapping her hands.

Outfit Three was Maggie's personal favorite, probably because it had been the hardest one to find. She'd found the jacket on a back rack at a consignment store in a too-hip-for-its-own-good neighborhood in South Beach. "Hand sewn," the salesgirl had assured her—which, Maggie supposed, was meant to justify the one-hundred-and-sixty-dollar price tag. At first, it looked like a regular hip-length black jacket—nothing special. But the sleeves were decorated with swirls of black embroidery, and the pockets—embroidered, too—were set into the jacket on an interesting angle, which served to create the illusion of a waist when there wasn't much in the way of an actual waist there. Best of all, the jacket had a fabulous violet-colored lining, so Maggie had paired it with a long violet skirt and a black top.

"Here," she said, presenting the three pieces together on one hanger, so that Mrs. Lefkowitz could get the idea.

But Mrs. Lefkowitz barely spared it a glance, just snatching it out of Maggie's arms and hurrying back to the bedroom . . . and was it Ella's imagination, or was she humming to herself?

When she came out of the bedroom, she was practically skipping—or skipping as much as someone who's recently suffered a stroke can skip. "You did it!" she said, and kissed Maggie carefully on the cheek, and Ella beamed from the love seat. Maggie looked at her. The skirt wasn't great—it didn't hang right and it wasn't quite the same black as the jacket—and the shirt was just okay, nothing more—but the jacket was gorgeous. It made Mrs. Lefkowitz look taller, and curvier, and . . .

"I look wonderful," said Mrs. Lefkowitz, studying herself in the mirror, appearing not to notice the way the left corner of her mouth drooped, or the fact that her left hand was still curved around her body at an awkward angle. She considered her reflection for a moment, then grabbed the pink hat from Outfit One and plunked it on her head again.

"No, no," said Maggie, laughing.

"But it suits me!" said Mrs. Lefkowitz. "I want it. Can I have it?"

"It's from school," said Maggie.

"Oh, school," said Mrs. Lefkowitz, and made such a sad face that Ella started laughing.

"So which one?" asked Maggie. And Mrs. Lefkowitz, still in the hand-embroidered jacket, looked at her as if she were crazy.

"Well, all of them, of course," she said. "I'll wear the pink to the service, and then the long black dress to the reception, and this," she said, looking at herself, "I'm going to wear for my next appointment with Dr. Parese."

Ella burst out laughing. "What?" she demanded. "Why?"

"Because," said Mrs. Lefkowitz, "he's adorable!"

"Is he single?" asked Maggie.

"Oh, he's about twelve," said Mrs. Lefkowitz, waving her hand, then pausing mid-wave to admire the embroidery on her sleeve. "Thank you, Maggie. You did a wonderful job." She walked back to the bedroom to change. Maggie started returning the clothes to their hangers.

Ella studied her for a minute. "I've got an idea," she said. "I think you should do this for other people."

Maggie paused as she was repositioning the pink cardigan. "What do you mean?"

"Well, there's lots old ladies who have a hard time getting

around the malls, and an even worse time finding anything nice once they're there. But everyone has occasions. Weddings, graduations, anniversary parties . . ."

"Well, this was just a favor," Maggie said. "I'm kind of busy with school and the bagel shop and all . . ."

"I bet that people would pay," said Ella.

Maggie paused, mid-fold. "Really?"

"Of course," Ella said. "What, you want to work for free?"

"How much do you think I could charge for this?"

Ella put one finger on her upper lip and gazed at the ceiling. "A percentage of the cost, maybe?" she said.

Maggie frowned. "I'm not so great with percentages," she said.

"Or a flat fee," said Ella. "Which might be better anyhow, because if you charged a percentage of the cost of the outfit, the cheapskates here would think you were trying to get them to buy more expensive things. How long did it take you to get all of these things?"

Maggie bit her lip, looking thoughtful. "Ten hours, maybe?"

"So charge, say, fifteen dollars an hour."

"Really? That's a lot more than what I'm making at the bagel place . . ."

"This is a little harder than slicing and toasting, don't you think?" asked Ella.

"And believe me, the women here can pay," said Mrs. Lefkowitz, who was back in her pink sweatshirt, looking flushed and pleased. "For all the moaning they do about their fixed incomes, for a beautiful outfit like this, they'll pay."

And now Ella saw her granddaughter's eyes light up and saw that Maggie was beaming. "Could I do it?" she asked. "Do you think it would work? I'd have to advertise . . . and I'd need a car of my own . . ."

"Start small," said Ella. "Don't jump in with both feet. Maybe dip one foot in the water, see how you like it."

"I already know I like it!" said Maggie. "I love to shop, I love picking out people's outfits. . . . I just can't believe—Do you really think people would pay me to do this?"

Mrs. Lefkowitz smiled, opened her suitcase-sized purse, produced her checkbook, and, in her labored, shaky script, wrote Maggie Feller a check for the amount of one hundred and fifty dollars. "I think they would," she said.

FIFTY-ONE

In retrospect, thought Rose, the mimosas had been a mistake.

She tried saying as much to Amy, but the words "the mimosas were a mistake" came out as a champagne-sodden mumble. "Mimoshas were a mistake," she said. Amy, who'd evidently understood her perfectly, gave a vigorous nod, and called to the bartender.

"Two more mimosas," she said.

"Right away, ladies," said the bartender. Where had it all gone so wrong? Rose wondered. Probably when she'd gotten the invitation to the shower that Sydelle Feller had decided to host weeks prior to Maggie's letter, the revelation of the grandmother, the invitation printed on heavy, gilt-edged, cream-colored paper, in a calligraphy so ornate that it was practically illegible.

"Who's throwing this thing?" asked Amy. "Lord and Lady Douchebag?"

"I don't even want to go," said Rose. "I want to go to Florida and meet this grandmother already."

"Did you call?" Amy asked.

"Not yet," said Rose. "Still working on the whole what-to-say thing."

"Well, if the grandmother answers, you say, 'Hello,' " said Amy. "And if Maggie answers, tell her that if she ever sleeps with your boyfriend again, you're gonna kick her size-zero ass from here to Elizabeth, New Jersey. Just try not to get the speeches mixed up."

"First shower, then grandmother," Rose said. And on the appointed day, she had gathered her courage, shaved her legs, and gotten herself to the appointed restaurant at the appointed hour, where precisely one of her friends and three dozen of Sydelle's were waiting to toast the bride-to-be.

"Rose," said Sydelle grandly, rising to greet her. Any trace of the vulnerability Rose had glimpsed on her stepmother's face was gone, buried beneath the familiar layers of makeup, Sydelle's familiar disdain, and high fashion.

"Come say hello to my friends," Sydelle said, trotting Rose over to her cronies, all of them, it seemed, with identical highlighted bobs and freshly lifted eyelids. *They must share a surgeon and a hairdresser,* Rose thought, as Sydelle ran through the introductions. "And here's My Marcia," Sydelle announced, leading Rose over to her stepsister, who was sour-faced, stringy-haired, and wearing a gigantic gold-and-diamond cross. Marcia gave Rose a limp wave and went back to quizzing the waitress about whether there was processed sugar in the pancakes, while her four-year-old twins, Jason and Alexander, wrestled underneath the table.

"How are you?" Rose asked politely.

"I'm blessed," My Marcia said. Sydelle winced. Rose gulped her mimosa, accepted a refill, and hurried over to where Amy was sitting. "Save me," she whispered, as Sydelle chattered away ("I would have invited more of Rose's friends," she overheard her stepmother say, "but I guess she doesn't have any!")

Amy handed her another drink. "Smile," she whispered. Rose grinned. Sydelle clutched her wriggling grandsons to her negligible bosom, got to her feet, and proclaimed, "Those of us who know Rose are so thrilled that this day is here!" And, to Rose's horror, there were two waiters wheeling in a television set. "What's going on?" she whispered to Amy, who shrugged. Sydelle gave her a brilliant smile and pointed the remote control at the screen. And there was Rose in sixth grade, scowling at the camera, all greasy hair and glinting braces. Uncomfortable laughter rippled through the room. Rose closed her eyes.

"We had our doubts," Sydelle continued, smiling brightly. "We watched her go through high school and college with her hair in her eyes and her nose buried in a book." She hit the remote again and there was Rose on her first break from college, with her Freshman Fifteen rippling beneath a pair of too-tight jeans.

"Of course, Rose had romances . . ." She hit the remote again, and there was Rose at her high school prom, in an ill-advised pink lace sheath, and a long-forgotten junior with a gummy smile gripping her waist. "But for reasons we could never understand, nothing ever seemed to work out." Another click. There was Rose at someone's bar mitzvah, shoving a miniature éclair into her mouth. Rose with hamburger juice dripping down her arms. Rose in profile, in late 1980s shoulder pads, looking roughly the size of an NFL linebacker. Rose at Halloween, dressed as a Vulcan, fingers splayed in Mr. Spock's salute.

"Oh, God," Rose whispered. "My 'before' pictures."

"What?" Amy whispered back.

Rose felt hysterical laughter bubbling in her chest. "I think Sydelle's been spending years collecting 'before' pictures, so if I ever went on a diet and got really thin, she'd have plenty of compare-and-contrast photos."

"I can't believe she's doing this!" Amy said, as Sydelle flicked through a series of shots of Rose looking dumpy, Rose looking sulky, Rose with a particularly splendid zit on the tip of her nose.

"Mommy, what's wrong with that lady?" Jason or Alexander demanded, as Marcia shushed him.

"Kill me now," Rose begged her best friend.

"How 'bout I just knock you unconscious for a few hours?" Amy whispered back.

"So let's all raise our glasses and toast the miracle of love!" Sydelle concluded.

More uncomfortable laughter, followed by halfhearted applause. Rose gazed at the stack of gifts, desperately hoping that one of them contained the knife set Simon had registered for, so she could kill herself in the ladies' room.

"Rose?" Sydelle asked, her smile still in place. Rose got to her feet and positioned herself in front of the stack of gifts, where she spent the next hour trying to act excited about salad bowls and Mixmasters, china and wineglasses, a state-of-the-art food scale from Sydelle with a note reading, "We hope you find this useful," with the word *useful* underlined twice.

"Tupperware!" said Rose, in a tone suggesting that she'd waited her whole life for someone to give her fifteen pieces of lidded plastic. "That's wonderful!"

"So convenient!" said Sydelle, smiling and handing Rose another box.

"A salad spinner!" Rose cried, smiling so hard that her face hurt. *I am not going to survive this,* she thought.

"Salad spinner," Amy repeated, writing down the gift and its giver, and stuck the bow through a paper plate for the bow bonnet Rose had already decided she didn't want to wear.

"How lovely!" said Sydelle. Another sharp glance, another gift-wrapped box. Rose swallowed hard and kept unwrapping. After half an hour she'd amassed three cake pans, a cutting board, five place settings, two crystal vases, and had told six different women on six separate occasions that she and Simon weren't planning to have babies any time in the immediate future.

Finally, the last gift was unwrapped, the last bow was affixed to the plate, and the whole arrangement was tied on top of Rose's head.

Amy ducked into the bathroom, and came back to the table looking as if she'd seen a ghost in one of the stalls.

"What?" Rose asked, untangling the bow hat from her hair.

Amy grabbed Rose's sleeve and two fresh mimosas, and dragged her friend into a corner.

"That woman," said Amy, "is breast-feeding."

"Which woman?"

"Marcia!"

Rose looked at Marcia, who'd just returned from the bathroom with Jason and Alexander trailing behind her. "Are you kidding me? They're four."

"I know what I saw," said Amy.

"What, was she squeezing it onto their Frosted Flakes?"

"First of all, I don't think those boys have ever been near a Frosted Flake," said Amy. "Jesus wouldn't approve. And secondly, I know what breast-feeding looks like. Breast. Child. Mouth."

Rose slurped another mouthful of orange juice and champagne. "Well, at least she knows it's organic."

Which was the precise moment that Sydelle Feller swept over.

"Thank you for arranging this," Rose said. Sydelle had wrapped her arms around her, leaning in close.

"You might try being grateful for a change," she hissed.

Rose drew back. "What?" she said.

"I hope you get exactly the wedding you deserve," said Sydelle, turning on her heel and heading for the door. Rose reeled toward her chair, feeling utterly defeated, and the tiniest bit scared. "Oh, my God," she whispered. "She must have heard us talking about Marcia the milk bar."

"Oh, no," said Amy, "I am so sorry."

Rose covered her eyes with her hands. "Boy, that's sure not the kind of thing my *New Jewish Wedding* said people would say to me at my shower."

"Just ignore her," said Amy, picking up the food scale. "Hey," she said, "do you know my thumb weighs four ounces?"

They'd wound up loading a cab with Rose's gifts, piling them in her living room, and heading to a bar down the street, where they drowned their agony in fresh mimosas and speculated on how long Sydelle had been saving up all of those atrocious pictures of her stepdaughter, and whether she might have a similar slide show prepared if Maggie ever got married. Rose came home to an empty apartment. Simon had left a note saying he was out walking Petunia and shopping for dinner. She stood in the center of the kitchen and closed her eyes.

"I miss my mother," she whispered. And it was true, in a non-specific way. It wasn't that she missed her mother; it was that she missed a mother, any mother at all. With a mother around, that fiasco of a shower wouldn't have been nearly so bad. A mother would have enfolded Rose in her arms and sent Sydelle back to whatever sulfur-scented depths had spawned her. A mother would have tapped Rose once on her head with her magic wand, and Rose's drab dress would have been transformed into the perfect wedding gown. A mother would have known how to handle everything.

"I miss my mom," she said again. But saying it out loud, Rose realized that she missed Maggie more. Even if Maggie didn't have a magic wand or a wedding gown, she would have at least been able to make Rose laugh. Rose smiled a little, imagining Maggie making a mimosa-fueled toast, or asking My Marcia whether she could have a little breast milk for her coffee. Maggie would know how to handle this situation. And Maggie, God help her, was all she had.

"I've got to get out of here," she whispered. She pulled her suitcase out of the closet and filled it with stuff she thought she'd need for Florida—shorts and sandals, a bathing suit and a baseball cap, a copy of *Chastity's Voyage* that she'd borrowed from Simon's mother. Ten minutes on the Internet yielded a two-hundred-dollar ticket to Fort Lauderdale. Then she picked up the telephone and punched in the numbers from Maggie's letter—the numbers she hadn't even realized she'd committed to memory. When her sister answered the phone, she forgot the speech that Amy had dictated and simply said, "Maggie? It's me."

FIFTY-TWO

"Okay," said Maggie. "Places, everyone!"

Mrs. Lefkowitz stood to the left of the boarding gate. Lewis stood in the center. Ella was next to him. Maggie rolled back and forth in Mrs. Lefkowitz's motorized scooter, looking them over closely. "Signs!" she said. The three of them lifted their handmade posterboard signs into the air. Mrs. Lefkowitz's read, "Welcome," in pink. Lewis's sign said, "to Florida." Ella's sign, which Maggie had supervised herself, said, "Rose," and Maggie herself carried a poster with a collage of roses on it made of pictures she'd cut from Mrs. Lefkowitz's gardening magazines.

"Now arriving, flight five-twelve from Philadelphia," said the voice on the PA system. Maggie stomped on the brake so hard she almost fell off the scooter.

"You know what?" she said. "I think it would be better if you guys waited by baggage claim."

"What?" asked Ella.

"What'd she say?" asked Mrs. Lefkowitz.

Maggie twisted her sign in her hands and talked fast. "It's just that . . . before I left . . . Rose and I kind of had a fight. And maybe it would be better if I just talked to her first. Alone."

"Okay," said Ella, leading Lewis and Mrs. Lefkowitz off toward baggage claim. Maggie took a deep breath, squaring her shoulders and lifting her sign, scrutinizing the passengers making their way off the plane.

Old lady . . . old lady . . . Mom and toddler, inching down the walkway . . . Where was Rose? Maggie set her sign down, wiped her hands against her shorts. When she stood up, Rose was walking through the door, looking taller than Maggie remembered, and tan, with her hair loose and flowing over her shoulders, held off her face with two cloisonné barrettes. She wore a long-sleeved pink T-shirt and khaki shorts, and Maggie could see muscles moving in her sister's legs as she made her way across the lounge.

"Hey," Rose said. "Nice sign." She peered over her sister's head. "So where's the mysterious grandmother?"

Maggie felt a pang of hurt. Didn't Rose want to know how she was? Didn't she care? "Ella's in baggage claim. Let me take your backpack," she said. "Is that all you brought? You look really good. Have you been working out?"

"Riding a bike," Rose said. She walked down the hall, moving so fast that Maggie had to break into a half-trot to keep up.

"Hey, slow down!"

"I want to see the grandmother," Rose said without looking at her sister.

"She's not going anywhere," Maggie said. She looked down to check out Rose's footwear and saw something glinting on her sister's left hand—a platinum band with a square cut diamond. "Oh, my God. Is that an engagement ring?"

"It is," said Rose, still staring straight ahead.

Maggie felt her heart stop. So much had happened since she'd been gone, and she didn't know about any of it! "Is it . . ."

"Different guy," said Rose. They reached the baggage terminal. Ella and Lewis and Mrs. Lefkowitz stared at Maggie uncertainly. Lewis raised his sign.

"There she is!" Ella called, and she hurried toward her grand-daughters, with Lewis and Mrs. Lefkowitz trailing after her.

Rose stepped forward and nodded, studying Ella's face carefully.
"Hi," she said.

"It's been so long. Too long," said Ella. She stepped forward and
Rose awkwardly allowed herself to be hugged, standing stiffly in
Ella's embrace. "Welcome, dear. I'm so glad you're here!"

Rose nodded. "Thanks. This is all kind of strange . . ."

Ella looked her granddaughter over carefully. Maggie, meanwhile, had resumed her spot on Mrs. Lefkowitz's scooter, and was
driving it in small circles, looking like the world's smallest Shriner
as she peppered her sister with questions and comments. "Who are
you marrying?" she asked. "Where'd you get those barrettes? I like
your hair!" She pulled right up to Rose's feet and looked down at
her sister's sneakers. "Hey," she said, "aren't those mine?"

Rose looked down and smiled faintly. "You left them in the
apartment," she said. "I didn't think you'd need them. And I
wouldn't have known where to send them. And they fit."

"Come on," said Maggie, getting off the scooter and leading her
sister out of the airport. "And tell me what's new. Who's the lucky
guy?"

"His name is Simon Stein," said Rose. She stepped beside
Ella, leaning her head in close, leaving Maggie and Lewis and
Mrs. Lefkowitz following the two of them, trying to overhear
scraps of their conversation. Rose looked so different! She didn't
look pale; she didn't look prissy; she didn't look as if someone
had stuffed a bug up her butt and she was in a hurry to find the
nearest rest room in order to remove it. Her clothes were items
that Maggie might have selected, and her stride was fast but
relaxed. Rose didn't look thinner, but she did look firmer, as if
her mass had been redistributed and rearranged. She seemed
totally at ease in her own body, for perhaps the first time in her
life, and Maggie wondered what had caused such a transformation. Simon Stein, perhaps? The name sounded familiar. Maggie
wracked her brain and finally came up with a picture from their
night at Dave and Buster's, a snapshot of a frizzy-haired guy in a

suit and tie, trying to interest her sister in the firm's softball team.

"Hey, Rose!" she called, catching up. Rose and Ella's heads were close together, and they were talking softly. Maggie felt a fast stab of jealousy. She swallowed hard. "So this guy you're marrying. He's in your law firm, right?"

"My former law firm," said Rose.

"What? Did you change firms?"

"Oh, I changed more than that," said Rose, and then turned her back and walked away, with Ella at her side. Maggie watched them go, feeling sad and frustrated . . . and feeling like this was no more than what she deserved. After what she'd done to Rose, did she really think her sister would come running back, ready to forgive and forget? She sighed, hefted her sister's backpack, and started off down the hall.

FIFTY-THREE

Rose Feller felt the way she imagined an astronaut would feel after crash-landing on a strange new unexplored planet. Planet Grandma, she thought, and swiped at her forehead. It had to be more than ninety degrees out here. How could anyone stand it?

She sighed, readjusted the visor that Ella had lent her, and followed Maggie out the door. "Don't forget your sunblock!" Ella called.

"We won't!" Maggie yelled back, and reached into her pocket to show Rose the tube she was carrying. It was bizarre, Rose thought, as they started off down the baking sidewalk that ran along the perfectly manicured (if somewhat small) green lawns of Golden Acres. But in the months since she'd last seen her, her little sister had somehow transformed herself into a reasonable facsimile of a responsible young adult. And, more mystifying yet, she'd befriended old people. Rose didn't understand that at all. Her own experience with the sixty-five-and-over set was limited to the occasional *Golden Girls* rerun, and her newly found grandmother made her a little uncomfortable, the way she stared, and sniffled, and seemed perpetually on the verge of tears when she wasn't peppering Rose with a million questions about her life. What was her apartment like? How had she and Simon met? What were her favorite foods? Did she like cats, or dogs, or both, or neither? What movies had she enjoyed recently? What books had she read? It was like being on a blind date with no promise of romance, Rose thought. It was exciting, and exhausting, too.

A little old lady on an oversized tricycle pedaled up to them. "Maggie!" she said.

"Hi, Mrs. Norton," said her sister. "How's your hip?"

"Oh, fine, fine," the old woman said. Rose blinked in the sunshine and tried to make sense of what she was hearing and seeing, but the best explanation she could come up with involved her sister being brainwashed, or body-snatched. And how had she managed to survive out here without a steady stream of men who didn't have pacemakers and great-grandchildren? Who was flirting with her, who was buying her drinks and giving her money for her manicures and generally confirming Maggie's own opinion of her worth and beauty? Rose shook her head in disbelief, nodded at Mrs. Norton and her hip, and followed her sister toward the swimming pool. She'd planned on being furious with Maggie, but now she just felt confused, as if the girl she'd been ready to kill didn't even exist anymore.

"Okay, so explain this to me again?" she said.

"These are my pool friends," said Maggie. "Now, Dora's easy, because she's the only woman, and she talks basically nonstop."

"Dora," Rose repeated.

"She was one of my first clients," Maggie continued.

"Clients?" asked Rose. "What are you doing, massage?"

"No, no," said Maggie. "Personal shopping." She dug into her pocket and produced one of the business cards that Mrs. Lefkowitz had whipped up on her computer. "Maggie Feller, Personal Shopper, Your Favorite Things," it read. "That's my catch phrase," said Maggie. "With all of my clients, I ask them what their favorite item of clothing was, and then when I shop for them, I try to reproduce the feeling of whatever that was. Like, if your favorite thing was a blue linen sundress, I don't necessarily buy you a blue linen sundress, but I try to find something that makes you feel the way you felt when you wore it."

"Great," said Rose. And she had to admit that it did sound good. If there was one thing Maggie had always been good at, it was picking out clothes. "So who else are we going to see?"

"Okay, there's Jack, who I think has kind of a crush on Dora, because he insults her all the time. He's the one who used to be the accountant, so he's going to help me with Your Favorite Things. Then there's Herman," Maggie continued. "He doesn't say much, but he's very nice . . . and he's obsessed with tattoos."

"Does he have any?" asked Rose.

"I don't think so," said Maggie. "I haven't exactly made a study. But they know all about you."

Rose wondered exactly what that meant. What would Maggie say about her? "Like what?"

"You know, where you live, what you do. I would have told them you were engaged," she said, "but that was news to me, too. When's the wedding?"

"May," said Rose.

"And how's the planning going? Everything under control?"

Rose felt herself stiffen. "It's fine," she said shortly. Maggie looked hurt, but instead of throwing a tantrum, marching off in a huff, or pouting, she just gave a small shrug.

"Well, if you need any help," she said. "I'm a professional, you know."

"I'll take that under advisement," said Rose. And then they were at the pool, and Jack, who was tall, with a sunburn, was squinting at them, and Dora, who was short and and round and talking a mile a minute, was waving frantically, and Herman was carefully studying Rose's bare arms and legs, no doubt prospecting for body modification. Maggie waved and headed toward them. Rose shook her head in disbelief and spread a towel over one of the creaky metal lounge chairs. Relax, she told herself sternly, arranging her face into a smile and crossing the hot concrete to meet Maggie's new friends.

"Are you two going to be all right in here?" asked Ella. The pull-out couch, which had been sufficient for Maggie, suddenly seemed too small now that two young women would be sharing it.

"We'll be fine," said Rose, flicking a fresh sheet out over the bed. She was still feeling dazed and groggy (and slightly sunburnt) from her first day in Florida. She and Maggie had hung out at the pool, then gone out for an early dinner with Lewis, who was very nice, and Ella, who'd kept staring at Rose in a most disconcerting way. After dinner they'd watched an hour of television, and were now in the small back bedroom. Rose saw that Maggie had taken over, the same way she'd invaded Rose's apartment, transforming both bedroom and porch into a makeshift office-*cum*-boudoir. There was a card table covered with sketches and notebooks and guides to starting and running a small business. There was a dressmaker's dummy that Maggie had bought at a tag sale and had draped with swatches of different fabrics—a length of fringed ivory satin, a piece of plum-colored chiffon. And there were familiar piles of clothes and cosmetics joined by unfamiliar stacks of books. Rose picked one up. *Travels,* by W. S. Merwin. She remembered it from college, and flicked through the dog-eared pages, many of them decorated with Maggie's careless scrawl.

"You're reading poetry?" she asked.

Maggie nodded proudly. "I enjoy it," she said. She pulled a book out of the stack. "This is by Rilkee."

"Rilk*uh*," Rose corrected.

Maggie waved her hand. "Whatever." She cleared her throat. "A good night poem," she said, and began to recite:

"I'd like to sing someone to sleep,
By someone sit, and be still.
I'd like to rock you and murmur a song
Be with you on the fringes of sleep
Be the one and only awake in the house
Who would know that the night is cold.
I'd like to listen both inside and out,
Into you, and the world, and the woods.
The clocks call out with their toiling bells,

And you can see to the bottom of time.
Down in the street a stranger goes by
And bothers a passing dog.
Behind come silence, I've laid my eyes
On you like an open hand,
And they hold you lightly and let you go,
When something moves in the dark."

She nodded, pleased with herself, as Rose stared at her, openmouthed.

"How did you . . . Where did you . . ." She blinked at her sister. *Body-snatched,* she thought again. Somehow, Maggie's greedy, obsessive, shoe-stealing, fame-seeking soul had been sucked out and replaced by Rilke.

"I particularly enjoy the line about the passing dog," Maggie said. "It reminds me of Honey Bun."

"It reminds me of Petunia," said Rose. "That little pug you left in my apartment."

"Oh, right right right," said Maggie. "How is she?"

"She's fine," Rose said shortly, remembering how Maggie had stuck her with the dog, and the mess, and the unerasable mental image of her fornicating with Jim Danvers. She brushed her teeth, washed her face, and got into bed, clinging to the edge of the pull-out mattress, her back to her sister.

"Now don't kick me," Maggie warned. "In fact, try not to make any physical contact with me at all."

"Not a problem." Rose said. "Good night," she said.

"Good night," said Maggie.

Silence, except for the croaking of the frogs. Rose closed her eyes.

"So!" said Maggie cheerfully. "You're marrying Simon Stein!"

Rose groaned. She'd forgotten this about Maggie, how she'd say she was going to sleep, how she'd get into bed, turn out the lights, yawn, stretch, say good night, and give every impression of meaning it, and then, just when you were right about to drop off, start up a conversation.

"Didn't we cover this at dinner?"

Maggie ignored her. "I remember him from that party," she said. "He was cute! Short, but cute. Tell me what kind of wedding you're going to have."

"Small," said Rose, who'd decided that the shorter the answers, the better off she'd be. "Sydelle's helping."

"Oh, no. Disaster waiting to happen. Do you remember My Marcia's wedding?"

"Vaguely," said Rose. "I was only there for the ceremony." Sydelle, considerate as ever, had slated My Marcia's wedding for the weekend of Rose's last law-school finals. She'd stayed for the vows, then ducked back home to study.

"Oh. My. God," Maggie breathed. "It could've been a Fox special. *America's Worst Weddings.*"

"I saw pictures. It looked beautiful." But Rose was starting to get a nagging feeling that there had been some story about My Marcia's nuptials, something her father and Sydelle hadn't wanted to talk about.

"Did you notice," asked Maggie, "that none of the pictures showed anybody's feet?"

Rose couldn't remember.

"Let me tell you why," said Maggie. "The wedding was on the lawn behind this fancy country club, remember?"

"Silver Glen."

"Silver Glen, Silver Lake, Silver Something," Maggie said impatiently. "And it was really pretty—gardens, lawns, all of that—except the automatic sprinklers malfunctioned, and the tent didn't have a floor and there was, like, six inches of muck on the ground. All of the tables started sinking, and it was freezing cold . . ."

"You're kidding," said Rose.

"I'm not!" Maggie said gleefully. "My Marcia was, like, crying her eyes out in the bathroom." Maggie raised her voice to a hysterical warble. "'My special day is ruined! Ruined!'"

"Oh, God," said Rose, who was starting to feel sick—and a certain degree of sympathy for My Marcia.

"Oh, there's more," said Maggie. "Sydelle forgot to get a parking variance, so everyone had to keep running out of the reception to move their cars. Then the sprinklers went off again, in the middle of their first dance, and everyone fled. And," she concluded, "they forgot to assign me a seat, so I had to sit with the band. We had boxed lunches instead of surf and turf."

Rose decided that Maggie's absence from the seating chart was probably not an accident, but decided not to say so.

"It was a horror show," Maggie concluded happily. "But there was an open bar. The one redeeming feature. I enjoyed many cocktails."

"I'm sure," said Rose.

"There was a drink parade with me as grand marshall," Maggie continued.

"Were you even twenty-one then?"

"Not so much," said Maggie. "So what else, what else?"

"Not much," said Rose slowly. It wasn't true, she knew, but why fill Maggie in on her disastrous shower, her fight with her father, running into Jim Danvers? It wasn't time yet. She still had to figure out what was responsible for her sister's miraculous transformation into a responsible, non-attention-seeking, job-holding, senior-citizen-appreciating citizen of Golden Acres.

"Tell me more about the wedding. Are you going to have bridesmaids?"

There was a short, tense silence. "Just Amy, I think," said Rose. "And you, too, I guess. If you want."

"Do you want me to be a bridesmaid?"

"I don't care that much," said Rose. "If you want to be in it, you can."

"Well, it's your wedding," said Maggie. "You should care."

"That's what everyone keeps telling me," said Rose.

"Well," Maggie said stiffly. "Good night, then."

"Good night," said Rose.

"Goodnight," said Maggie. Silence.

"Rose?" Maggie said. "Hey, Rose, could you get me a glass of water with one ice cube, please?"

"Get your own water," said Rose. But even as she was saying it, she swung her legs out of the bed, realizing that she'd forgotten this fact, too: she always got Maggie's water. She'd been bringing it to her since they were little. She'd supplied Maggie with her evening glass almost every night during Maggie's stint in her apartment. And, probably when they were in their eighties, after they'd outlived husbands and left their jobs and moved to whatever the 2060s version of Golden Acres would be, she'd still be fetching her little sister glasses of water with one ice cube.

When Rose got back to the bed, there was something glimmering on her pillow. She looked at it carefully, thinking it could be a bug of some sort. But it wasn't a bug. It was a foil-wrapped square of chocolate. "Just like in the fine hotels," said Maggie.

"Go to sleep," said Rose.

"Fine, fine," said Maggie. But before she finally closed her eyes, she set the chocolate on the bedside table, so that it would be the first thing that her sister saw in the morning.

In her own bedroom, Ella released the breath she hadn't realized she was holding and sank onto her bed. Her brain was spinning with questions. What was the story with Sydelle? Who was My Marcia? Why wasn't Rose really talking to Maggie? Why did Maggie seem so desperate to please her older sister? Would Rose really have a wedding without including Maggie? Would Ella even be invited?

She bit her lip and closed her eyes. There was a story here. Ella was sure of it. There was a reason why Maggie had left Rose's apartment and gone to Princeton, a reason she hadn't talked to her only sister in ten months. Give it time, Lewis had told her. "I'll try," she whispered to herself, and blew two kisses toward her granddaughters' bedroom wall.

FIFTY-FOUR

Rose shoved one gloved hand into a pot filled with boiled turkey legs, extracted one of them, and began pulling the meat off the bone.

"Thank you so much for coming to help," said Ella, who stood beside Rose, peeling carrots, in the synagogue recreation room where they served lunch to the homeless every Friday. "Are you sure you're okay with that?"

"Fine," said Rose. "It's better than the onions, right?"

"Oh, absolutely!" said Ella, wincing at her too-enthusiastic, too-loud tone. She bent back to the carrots, trying hard not to stare at her oldest granddaughter.

Rose had been in Florida for three days, and she was still mostly a mystery to Ella. She answered all of Ella's questions completely and politely, and asked plenty of her own, mostly all of them couched so well that Ella could tell that asking questions was part of what she did for a living. Or part of what she'd done, since Rose explained that she was taking a break from legal life.

"What do you mean, taking a break?" Maggie had asked.

"I meant what I said. Taking a break," Rose had said, without looking at her sister. Something bad had happened between the two of them, Ella knew. But she couldn't guess what it was, and Maggie had been tight-lipped on the subject while she trailed her sister around Golden Acres like a lost puppy dog.

Rose peeled off her gloves, put her hands on her hips, and stretched, rolling her neck. Even in a hairnet, her granddaughter was beautiful, Ella decided. Rose looked the way she'd imagined a biblical heroine to look—tall and strong and stern, somehow, with powerful shoulders and capable-looking hands.

"Are you okay?" she asked.

Rose sighed. "Well, I'm done with the turkey."

"Let's take a break," said Ella. They walked over to a card table in the corner, where Mrs. Lefkowitz sat, reading the latest issue of *Hello!* (because, as she'd said, the gossip from England was always much more interesting).

"The bride-to-be!" she hailed Rose. Rose smiled faintly and sat down in a folding chair.

"So let's hear about the wedding," said Mrs. Lefkowitz. "You got your dress?"

Rose flinched. "The wedding. Um. Well, Sydelle's helping."

"What's a Sydelle?"

"My stepmother," Rose said. "The Cruella De Vil of Cherry Hill." She looked at Ella. "What was my mom's wedding like?"

"It was small," said Ella. "They planned it themselves. They got married in the rabbi's study, on a Thursday afternoon. I wanted to help . . . to make her a wedding . . . but Caroline didn't want much, and your father didn't want anything that Caroline didn't want."

"Sounds familiar," Rose said. "My father's not . . ." Her voice trailed off. "He's not a very strong-willed person."

Except when he's cutting me out of your life, Ella thought. "He loved your mother," she said instead. "Anyone who saw them together knew that. He tried to take care of her, to make her happy."

"I want to talk about your wedding!" said Mrs. Lefkowitz, setting aside her account of Fergie's latest dalliance. "Tell me everything!"

Rose sighed. "Not much to tell, really. It's being planned by a monster, who completely ignores me when I tell her what Simon and I want, and keeps trying to cram her ideas down our throats."

"A lemon," said Mrs. Lefkowitz, and nodded.

"Huh?"

"Think about fruit," she continued. "When you squeeze an orange, what do you get?"

Rose smiled. "Trouble?"

"No, no, Mrs. Smart. You get orange juice. You don't get grapefruit juice, you don't get apple juice, you don't get milk. You get orange juice. Every time. People are like that. They can only give you what they have inside. So if this Sydelle character is giving you so much trouble, it's because she's nothing but trouble on the inside. She's just delivering what's in her heart into the universe." And Mrs. Lefkowitz sat back, looking pleased with herself.

"Where'd you learn that?" asked Ella.

"Dr. Phil," said Mrs. Lefkowitz.

Ella made a mental note to find out who Dr. Phil was.

"So," said Rose, "what kind of fruit is Maggie?"

"A sweet one," said Mrs. Lefkowitz.

Rose laughed. "If that's what you think, then you don't know my sister very well."

"She's not sweet?" asked Ella.

Rose got to her feet. "She takes things," she said. Finally, Ella thought, as Rose started pacing. Finally, we're going to get to the root of this, and find out what went wrong. "She takes everything," Rose continued, her voice cracking. "Haven't you noticed? My sister feels a certain sense of entitlement. Like, she's entitled to anything that's yours. Clothes, shoes, cash, cars . . . other things."

Other things, Ella thought.

"Don't tell me that in all the time she's been with you nothing's ever gone missing."

"I don't think so," Ella said.

"We don't have anything she'd want," said Mrs. Lefkowitz.

Rose shook her head. "Figures," she said, "that once she was done with me, she'd decide to walk the straight and narrow."

Other things, Ella thought again, and she took her best guess at what the heart of the trouble might be. "What did Maggie take?" she asked.

Rose's head whipped around. "Huh?"

Ella repeated the question. "I think she took something that meant a lot to you. What was it?"

"Nothing," Rose said. And now she didn't just sound angry, she sounded furious. At Maggie, Ella thought. And maybe at her, too. "Nothing that meant that much."

"Dear," said Ella, stretching out her hand. Rose ignored her. "I think Maggie's okay," Ella continued, blundering desperately forward. "She's saving her money, I know, and I think her business idea's a good one. She's found outfits for a bunch of people that I know of. Her friend Dora, my neighbor Mavis Gold . . ."

"Just be careful," Rose said. "If she hasn't taken anything of yours yet, it doesn't mean she isn't going to. She might look sweet, but she isn't. Not always." And Ella sat, openmouthed and frozen, as Rose walked out the door.

FIFTY-FIVE

Two days later, Maggie watched Rose as she slept on the lounge chair beside her.

"She's tired," Dora observed.

"Your insights are overwhelming," said Jack.

"She seems nice," said Herman, in one of his rare non-tattoo-related remarks.

"She is nice," said Ella.

Maggie sighed. "I think she's going home," she said. She'd heard Rose on the phone that morning, when she was coming out of the shower, talking quietly to someone who must've been Simon, apologizing quietly, asking him to check flights back to Philadelphia for her.

But Rose couldn't leave. Not like this. Not without Maggie convincing her that she really had changed, that she really was going to be better, and that she really was sorry.

She rolled onto her side, thinking. Rose needed peace and quiet, and Maggie had made sure that she got naps every day, quiet time at the pool, walks at night after dinner. She made sure that Ella had laid in a stock of her sister's favorite foods, including the cheese curls and ice cream that Rose was secretly fond of. She always let her sister have the remote control when they watched TV and didn't complain when Rose went pawing through her library books in search of the poems she'd remembered from college. None of it seemed to be working. Rose stuck close to Ella, asking her questions about their mother, looking at pictures, accompanying her on her rounds. The two of them were thick as thieves, a perfect circle of two. And Rose wasn't inclined to make room for Maggie. Maggie, it was clear, had not yet been forgiven. And Maggie had no idea how to *get* forgiven, except for telling Rose that she was sorry. Which she'd done over and over again, to no avail. There had to be something she could give Rose, some act she could perform to convince her sister that she was sorry and that she'd do better from now on.

Well, she thought, flipping onto her belly, at least Rose had another boyfriend. A husband-to-be. A wedding she was probably planning with all of the ruthless efficiency she'd once brought to bear on her career. Maggie imagined the guest list on a spread sheet. A computer-generated seating chart. A florist cultivating the perfect blooms for her bouquet. But what about wedding dress? Maggie sat up so fast she spilled her water, causing Dora to shriek and Jack to scold and Ella to pass her a towel.

"Hey, Rose!" she called. Rose woke up with a start and stared at her sleepily. "Do you have a wedding dress yet?"

Her sister closed her eyes again. "I'm looking," she said.

"Go back to sleep," said Maggie. It was perfect! If she could find Rose the right wedding dress . . . well, it wouldn't fix everything, but it would be a start. More than a start, it would be a sign—a sign that Maggie was sincere, and that she meant well.

Plus, the more she thought about it, finding the perfect dress for her sister would be symbolic. She remembered that from her class called the Manufacture of Myth, when the professor had talked about sacred quests, how the hero had to go into the world and bring something back—a sword, a chalice, a glass slipper, or enchanted beans. *Gawain and the Green Knight,* the professor had said. "Jack and the Beanstalk." *Lord of the Rings. And what were the objects a symbol for?* the professor had asked. *Knowledge.* Once the hero has acquired this knowledge, he can live happily in the world. Well, Maggie wasn't a hero, and she wasn't sure she quite understood all the stuff about self-knowledge and symbolism, but she was a fabulous shopper. She knew style, and, more, she knew her sister, and she could find Rose a dress.

She flipped open her appointment book. She was pretty busy, what with the Liebermans' fiftieth anniversary party to shop for, and Mrs. Gantz going on her cruise, but she could rearrange her schedule. Where would she start? The bridal department at Saks first, for inspiration. They wouldn't have anything in Rose's size, probably, but at least she could see what they were showing. Then, once she had some idea of what she was looking for, she'd hit her three favorite consignment shops. She'd seen wedding dresses at all of them, had flipped past them casually, hunting for other items, but she knew they were there, and . . .

"Hey," called Maggie, trying to sound casual. "Hey, Rose, how long do you think you'll be staying?"

"Until Monday," said Rose. She got up from the chair, walked slowly to the swimming pool, and dove in. That was four days. Could Maggie find a wedding dress—the right wedding dress—in four days? She wasn't sure. She'd have to start immediately.

"What was your favorite thing?" Maggie asked her sister. "Your favorite thing to wear."

Rose swam to the edge of the pool and hooked her arms over the ledge. "I liked my blue sweatshirt with the hood. Remember that?"

Maggie nodded, her heart sinking. She remembered the blue sweatshirt with the hood very well, because Rose had worn it practically nonstop throughout sixth grade. "I like it," she said stubbornly, when their father tried to get her to take it off so he could wash it.

"You wore that until it fell apart," said Maggie.

Rose nodded. "Old blue," she said affectionately, as if she were talking about a dog or a person instead of a sweatshirt. Maggie felt her heart sinking even further. How on earth was she supposed to figure out a wedding dress from a ratty blue sweatshirt with a zipper running up the front?

She'd have to start from scratch. And, if she only had four days, she'd have to get help. While Rose swam laps Maggie beckoned to Dora and Ella and Lewis. "I need you guys to help me with a project," she whispered.

Dora inched her chair closer, her eyes shining. "Well, that's wonderful news!" she said.

"Don't you even want to know what it is?" Maggie asked.

Dora looked at Lewis. Lewis looked at Ella. The three of them looked at Maggie, and solemnly shook their heads.

"We're bored," said Dora. "Give us something to do."

"Let us help," said Ella.

"Okay, then," said Maggie, flipping to a fresh page in her notebook and mentally mapping out her course of action, "here's how this is going to work."

FIFTY-SIX

"Are you ready?" asked Ella, fussing with her folder full of typed pages. "You might want to sit down."

"I'm old," said Lewis. "I always want to sit down." He pulled up a chair behind his desk in the *Golden Acres Gazette*'s office and stared at Ella expectantly. Ella cleared her throat and glanced at Maggie. Maggie gave her an encouraging smile, and Ella started to read the poem that she and Maggie had written together and called "The Senior Howl."

"I saw the best minds of my generation destroyed by
senior moments, dyspeptic, forgetful, polyester'd
dragging themselves toward the handicapped-parking spaces at
four, looking for an early-bird special."

"Oh, my," said Lewis, trying not to laugh. "I see you two have discovered Allen Ginsberg."

"We have," said Maggie proudly. "Now, I'm going to want a byline, of course."

"Co-byline," said Ella.

"Fine, fine, whatever," Maggie replied.

"How's the top-secret mission coming?" Lewis asked.

Maggie's face fell. "It's harder than I thought," she said. "But I think I'll be okay. You're still going to help, right?"

"Of course," said Lewis. Maggie nodded, hopped off the edge of the desk, and picked up her purse.

"Gotta go," she said. "Mrs. Gantz is waiting for her bathing suits. I'll see you back at the apartment at four."

Ella watched her go, smiling.

"So, my dear," said Lewis. "How goes the grandmothering?"

"Fine," said Ella. "Well, better, anyhow. Maggie's doing terrific. Business is really taking off. She's busy all the time now."

"And Rose?" asked Lewis.

"Well, I think her wedding's making her a little crazy. And I think that Maggie makes her crazy, too. They care about each other, so much. I know that, at least." Ella remembered the way, in the months before Rose's arrival, that Rose would pop up in odd moments of Maggie's conversation—never by name, Ella had noticed, but just as "my sister." As in, "My sister and I used to go to football games with my father." Or, "My sister and I used to share a bedroom, because Sydelle the Terrible made me move out of my bedroom and move in with Rose when she redecorated." Ella treasured every brief mention, every scrap of conversation, every glimpse she got of the two of them as little girls, especially in the early days of Maggie's time in Florida, when Maggie was saying hardly anything at all. Ella could almost see them sometimes, in the room with two twin beds, Rose lying on her belly on the floor, poring over—what? A Nancy Drew book, Ella decided. That seemed about right. And Maggie, a tiny little thing in—what? Red overalls, thought Ella. Maggie would be bouncing back and forth, back and forth, until her red legs and brown hair turned into a blur, shouting, "The quick! Brown! Fox! Jumped over! The lazy dog!"

"I wish," said Ella, then closed her mouth. What did she wish for? What did she want? "I wish I could make everything right between them. I wish I could give Maggie the life she wanted, and tell Rose how to handle her stepmother, and just . . ." She lifted her left hand, waved it as if it were holding a magic wand. "Fix things. Fix everything for them."

"Well, but that's not what grandparents do," said Lewis.

"They don't?" Ella asked morosely.

Lewis shook his head.

"What do grandparents do?" Ella asked plaintively, feeling sorrow for all the years when she was supposed to have learned the answer.

Lewis gazed thoughtfully at the ceiling. "I think you give them unconditional love, and support, and the occasional cash infusion. You give them a place to come, when they need somewhere to go, and you try not to tell them what to do, because they get plenty of that from their parents. And then you let them figure it out for themselves."

Ella closed her eyes. "I wonder if Rose hates me," she said so softly that Lewis almost didn't hear her. She hadn't told him, or Maggie, or anyone, but she'd been both joyful and terrified the first time she'd seen Rose; and how part of her was still waiting for Rose to ask her the questions she couldn't answer.

"How could anyone hate you?" Lewis asked kindly. "You're worrying too much. They're smart girls. They won't blame you for not being there when it wasn't your fault, and they can't expect you to fix everything for them. Nobody could do that."

"Does it make me wrong that I still want to try?" Ella asked.

Lewis smiled at her and took her hand. "No," he said, "it just makes me love you more."

FIFTY-SEVEN

The first problem with trying to find an off-the-rack wedding dress, Maggie learned the next morning, was that they only came in two sizes, neither one of which was the size she thought her sister wore. "Sample sizes," the bored clerk had explained, when Maggie asked to see something that wasn't an eight or a ten. "You'll try 'em on, find what you like, and we'll order it in your size."

"But what if you don't wear an eight or a ten?" she asked.

"We pin 'em if they're too big," said the clerk.

"But what if they're too small?" asked Maggie, fingering the gowns and knowing there was no way they'd fit her sister. The clerk had shrugged and scribbled a name and address on a piece of paper. "They've got larger sizes," she said.

And the next store—a branch of a gigantic bridal-gown chain—did indeed have larger sizes, hanging in its coyly named Diva section. "Do they come with their own entourage?" Ella had asked. Maggie wasn't sure about entourages. But she did know that the dresses were awful.

"I don't know about this," said Ella, showing Maggie the umpteenth empire-waisted A-line dress they'd seen. This one had bunchy silk flowers on the bosom.

"It's okay," said Maggie. "It's adequate, you know? But I want

to find something that's perfect, and I'm not sure this is the place."
She sighed, leaning against a glass case of discounted garters. "I'm
not even sure what the right thing is. I feel like I'll know it when I
see it, but I'm not sure I'm going to see it!"

"Well, what does Rose like?" asked Ella.

"She doesn't know what she likes," said Maggie. "Her favorite
piece of clothing was a blue hooded sweatshirt with a zipper up the
front." She sighed again. "I guess I'd better start talking to dress-
makers." She shook her head. "Maybe we'll get lucky." She gazed
around the store. "Not here, though. Where's Lewis?"

Lewis, as it turned out, was back in the dressing room, offering
helpful critiques to brides-to-be.

"I don't know," said a tiny redhead in a puffy meringue of a
dress, "do you think it's overwhelming me?"

Lewis looked at her carefully. "Put the third one on again, the
one with the low back," he said. "That's still my favorite."

A black girl with shells and beads laced through her braids
tapped his shoulder and twirled around.

"Definitely you," said Lewis, nodding his approval.

"Lewis!" called Maggie. "We're going now!"

A chorus of complaints came from a half-dozen dressing room
stalls. "No! Not yet! Just one more dress!"

Lewis smiled. "It seems like I've got a talent for this. Maggie,
maybe you should put me on retainer."

"Done," said Maggie. "But we've got two days until Rose
leaves, and no dress yet, so we've got to keep shopping. Let's go."

Later that night, Maggie and Ella drove back to Golden Acres through
the night air that was thick with moisture, and the whirring of cicadas,
and disappointment. The dress they'd driven to see had been a disaster—the polyester-satin blend too shiny, the sweetheart neckline too
plunging, the beads around the hem sewn so loosely that a few fell off
to rattle against the fake linoleum of the would-be seller's kitchen floor.
When Maggie said that it wasn't quite right, the woman had told

them they'd be doing her a favor if they just took it with them.

"Was it yours?" asked Maggie.

"It was supposed to be," she said.

So now they were driving back home with the dress swaying from its hook over the backseat like a ghost, and Maggie was feeling pissed-off and panicked.

"What am I going to do?" she asked. And she was surprised when Ella answered.

"You know what I think? I think that this really is a case where it's the thought that counts."

"How's she supposed to wear a thought down the aisle?" Maggie asked.

"Well, she can't, but just that you're doing this, and trying so hard, it shows how much you love her."

"Except she doesn't know that I'm doing this," Maggie said. "And I really want to find her something. It's important. It's really important."

"Well, you don't have to find a dress before Rose leaves. You've got five months. You could always find something you like and order it. Or you could sew her something."

"I can't sew," Maggie said morosely.

"No," said Ella. "But I can. That is, I could. It's been so long, but I used to make all sorts of things. Tablecloths, curtains, dresses for your mother when she was little . . ."

"But a wedding dress . . . well, wouldn't that be hard?"

"Very hard," Ella confirmed. "But we could do it together, once you've figured out what you want."

"I think I know what I want," said Maggie. In fact, after looking at more than a hundred different dresses, and pictures of perhaps five hundred more, she was starting to get a sense of what was going to look perfect on Rose. She just hadn't seen the actual dress outside of her imagination. A ballgown, she was thinking, because Rose had a nice enough shape, and enough of a waist to make it work. A ballgown with maybe a scooped neckline, low but not indecent, maybe with a row of beads or seed pearls along the edge, nothing too flashy, and certainly nothing too itchy. And three-quarter-length sleeves would be the most flattering length, certainly better than the short sleeves, which were somehow matronly, and the sleeveless dresses, which she knew Rose would never wear. And a full skirt, a fairy-tale kind of skirt, a skirt that would sort of remind Rose of Glinda the Good Witch in *The Wizard of Oz*, except not quite that costumey, and definitely a train, although not too much of a train. "And I think Rose would trust me." Which wasn't quite true, Maggie admitted to herself. She hoped Rose would trust her. She *hoped*.

She drove, and thought, picturing the dress in her mind. "When you're sewing," she asked, "do you have to find a pattern of exactly what you want to make?"

"Well, that's the way it's normally done."

"What if you want to sew something different than any patterns you can find?"

"Hmm," said Ella, tapping one fingertip against her lower lip. "Well, I guess what I'd try to do is find parts of patterns and put them all together. It would be tricky. Expensive, too, once you've added up all those yards of fabric."

"Like a few hundred dollars?" Maggie asked in a small voice.

"More than that, I think," said Ella. "But I've got some money."

"No," said Maggie. "No, I want to pay for it. I want it to be from me." She drove through the thick darkness, hearing the far-off rumble of thunder as the skies prepared to deliver Florida's nightly shower. Every old insecurity, every high-school taunt, every boss who'd fired her and landlord who'd evicted her and guy who'd called her stupid rose up in a wave within her. *You can't*, they said. You're dumb. You'll never figure it out.

Her hands tightened on the wheel. But I can! she thought. She remembered the afternoons she'd spent putting her flyers up all over Golden Acres, a drawing of a dress on a hanger and the words *YOUR FAVORITE THINGS*, and *MAGGIE FELLER, PERSONAL*

SHOPPER written on them, and how the phone had rung so constantly for the next two weeks that she'd finally installed her own line. She thought about going over her budget with Jack, how he'd explained it to her over and over again, never once losing his patience, telling her that to save for her own shop she should pretend that her money was a pie, and that she'd need to eat most of the pie to survive—and that was her money for rent and groceries and gas and such—but if she could put away a little piece, even a little tiny sliver every month, that eventually ("Not soon," he'd cautioned, "but eventually") she'd have enough for the big things she wanted. She'd look at the figures again, and carve out a slice for Rose's dress.

And she thought of the little empty store she'd seen, around the corner from the bagel shop, empty for three months, with a sweet green-and-white-striped awning and a storefront of fly-specked glass. She thought of how she'd walk by it on her break and imagine polishing the glass, imagine painting the walls creamy white and dividing the back room into cubicles by hanging lengths of white cotton and gauze. She'd put padded benches in each changing room so the customers could sit, and shelves for them to stick their purses, and she'd find old mirrors at tag sales, and every price would be a round number, tax included. It wouldn't be Hollywood, but it would be what she was good at. What she was best at. Her favorite thing. And she was succeeding at it, which meant there was no reason that she couldn't succeed at this, too. She wouldn't fall down on her face and need to be rescued. She'd be the one who did the rescuing instead.

"Can we try?" she finally asked. The dress in the backseat swayed gently, back and forth, like it was dancing.

"Yes," said Ella. "Yes, dear, of course we can."

FIFTY-EIGHT

"House of Stein, Simon speaking."

"Do they know you answer the phone like that?" asked Rose, rolling over on the bed. It was ten o'clock in the morning. Ella was off holding crack babies at the hospital, and Maggie was on one of her top-secret missions, which meant that Rose had all four rooms of the apartment to herself.

"I knew it was you. Caller ID," said Simon. "How are things? Are you relaxing?"

"Sort of," said Rose.

"Sun and fun, fruity drinks, the occasional cabana boy?"

Rose sighed. Simon was teasing, as usual, and he was funny, as usual, but he didn't sound quite like himself yet. The Jim thing, she thought. And the whole secret-grandmother thing, and Rose's sudden departure for Florida. She'd have to go home soon and start making things right. "The only cabana boys here are eighty years old, with pacemakers."

"Watch out for them," said Simon. "It's the elderly ones who always surprise you. Are you okay?"

"I'm fine. Ella's fine. And Maggie . . ." Rose furrowed her brow. Maggie had changed, and Rose wasn't sure she trusted it. She got out of bed, carrying the phone as she strolled toward Ella's living room. "Maggie's become a businesswoman," she said. "She's a personal shopper, which actually makes a lot of sense. She's got really great taste. She always knows what to wear, and what's going to look best on other people. And the people here, lots of them don't drive anymore, and even the ones who do sometimes have a hard time getting around the malls . . ."

"I have a hard time getting around malls," said Simon. "It's genetic. The last time my mother was at Franklin Mills, she called the police because she thought her car had been stolen, when in reality she'd just forgotten where she'd parked it."

"Oof," said Rose. "So is that why she put twenty stuffed animals in the backseat, and tied all of those ribbons to the antenna?"

"No," said Simon, "she just likes ribbons. And stuffed animals." There was a pause. "I was kind of angry at you when you left, you know."

"About Jim Danvers?" Rose swallowed hard, even though she'd been expecting this.

"Yeah," said Simon. "About that. I'm not upset that it happened. I just want to feel like you can tell me things. Like you can tell me anything. I'm going to be your husband. I want you to lean on me. I want you to say good-bye before you go somewhere." Across the line, Rose heard him swallow hard. "When I came home, and you weren't there . . ."

Rose closed her eyes. She remembered that feeling too well, of what it was like to walk into an empty house and find that the person you loved had disappeared without a word.

"I'm sorry," Rose said. "I'll try." She swallowed hard and walked in front of the bookshelf filled with the pictures of her, and Maggie, and her mother in her wedding dress, smiling a smile that said that she had her whole life in front of her and that it was going to be a life filled with happiness. "I'm sorry about leaving the way I did, and not telling you about Jim. You shouldn't have had to find out that way."

"Probably not," said Simon. "But I was too hard on you about it. I know how stressed out you've been, with all the wedding stuff."

"Well," said Rose, "I'm the one with time for it."

"Oh, along those lines," Simon said. "You got a call last night from a headhunter."

Rose's pulse quickened. When she'd worked at Lewis, Dommel, and Fenick, she'd get calls from headhunters a few times a week, people who'd come across her name and résumé in some legal directory and would call her trying to get her to jump to another firm, where she would undoubtedly wind up working even longer hours. But since she'd taken her leave, the phone had stopped ringing.

"Someone from the Women's Association for Women's Alternatives."

"Really?" Rose was trying to remember whether she'd heard of the group, and what they did. "How'd they get my name?"

"They need a staff attorney," said Simon, sidestepping the question, which gave Rose her answer—Simon had called. "They do advocacy work for low-income women. Custody, child support, visitation, stuff like that. Lots of time in court, I'd bet, and the pay's not great because it would be a part-time position at first, but I thought it might be interesting." He paused. "Of course, if you're not ready yet . . ."

"No! No," said Rose, trying not to shout. "It sounds . . . I mean, I'm very . . . Did they leave a number?"

"They did," said Simon, "but I told them you were on vacation, so no hurry. Go enjoy yourself! Put on your bathing suit, go give some old man a coronary."

"I've got to call Amy first. She's been leaving me messages every day since I've been here, and we keep missing each other."

"Ah," said Simon. "Amy X."

Rose grinned. "You know she only called herself that for three weeks in college."

"I thought she called herself Ashante in college."

"No, Ashante was high school," said Rose, remembering when

her best friend had renounced her "slave name" midway through Mr. Halleck's honors U.S. history class.

"Give her my best," said Simon. "Which will probably not be good enough for her."

"Amy likes you just fine."

"Amy doesn't think anyone's good enough for you," said Simon. "And she's right, but I'm not bad, generally speaking. And you know what?"

"What?"

Simon dropped his voice to a whisper. "I love you very much, my bride-to-be."

"Love you, too," said Rose. She hung up the phone, smiled as she imagined him at his cluttered desk, then dialed her best friend.

"Girl!" shouted Amy, "tell me everything! How's the grandmother? Do you like her?"

"I do," said Rose, surprising herself. "She's sharp, and nice, and . . . happy. I think she was really sad for a long time, and that she's really happy now that Maggie and I are here. The only thing is, she stares at me a lot."

"Why?"

"Oh, you know," said Rose, feeling uncomfortable. "Not seeing me and Maggie grow up. I told her she didn't miss much."

"*Au contraire,* my sister. She missed you winning all those science fairs. She missed you dressing like a Vulcan for three years' worth of Halloween parades. . . ."

Rose cringed.

"She missed us in leg warmers and ripped sweatshirts," said Amy. "Okay, granted, I wish I'd missed that, too."

"We were trendy!" said Rose.

"We were pathetic," Amy corrected her. "Let me talk to the g-mom! I've got stories!"

"Forget it," Rose said, laughing.

"So tell me this . . . is Maggie coming to the wedding?"

"I think so," said Rose.

"Is she going to replace me?" Amy demanded.

"Absolutely not," said Rose. "Your butt-bow is secure."

"Good deal," said Amy. "Go have a piña colada for me."

"And you go keep our drinking water clean," said Rose. She hung up the phone and considered her day. No dogs to be walked, no wedding crisis to resolve. She wandered into her grandmother's living room and picked up a photo album from the top of a stack on the coffee table. "Caroline and Rose" read the label pasted on the front. She opened the book and there she was, a day old, wrapped in a white blanket. Her eyes were squinched shut, and her mother faced the camera, smiling tentatively. God, thought Rose, she was so young! She flipped through the pages. She was a baby, she was a toddler, she was riding a bike with training wheels, her mother behind her, pushing a stroller in which baby Maggie rode in like Cleopatra on her barge. Rose smiled, turning the pages slowly, watching herself and her sister grow up.

FIFTY-NINE

Maggie sat back, gave her ponytail a businesslike tweak, and nodded. "Okay," she announced. "I think that's it." She beckoned Ella and Dora over to her table in the back of the fabric store. "This skirt," she said, showing them the pattern. "This top," she said, laying a second pattern carefully on top of the first. "And these sleeves," she said, displaying yet a third pattern, "only three-quarter-length, not full length."

"We'll make it from muslin first," said Ella. "We'll take our time. We'll be just fine." She gathered up the patterns. "Let's get started first thing in the morning, and we'll see what we shall see."

Maggie sat back and smiled proudly. "It's going to be great," she said.

That night, Maggie came home from her shift at Bagel Bay, and a last-minute stop-off to return three of Mrs. Gantz's rejected bathing suits, and found her sister's bags stacked neatly by the door. Her heart sank. She'd failed. Rose was leaving, and she didn't even know how hard Maggie had been trying to find her a dress. She didn't know how sorry Maggie was. Her sister was still barely talking to her, barely looking at her. It hadn't worked out at all.

Maggie walked toward the back bedroom, hearing Rose's and Ella's voices from the screened-in porch.

"You'd think the little dogs would be the easy ones," Rose was saying. "But really, they're the most stubborn of all. And they bark the loudest, too."

"Did you girls ever have a dog?"

"For a day," said Rose. "Once."

Maggie headed into the kitchen, thinking that she could make dinner for her sister, and at least that would be something, a small but meaningful gesture, an act that would show Rose she cared. She pulled swordfish steaks out of the refrigerator, sliced up purple onions and avocado and teardrop tomatoes for a salad, and set the basket of rolls right by her sister's plate. Rose smiled later when she saw them.

"Carbohydrates!" she said.

"Just for you," said Maggie, and passed her sister the butter.

Ella looked at them curiously. "My stepmonster," said Rose, with her mouth full. She swallowed. "Sydelle. Sydelle hated carbs."

"Except when she went on that sweet-potato diet," Maggie said.

"Right," said Rose, nodding at her sister. "Then she hated red meat. But no matter what diet she was doing, she'd never let me eat bread."

Maggie yanked the bread basket away, and flared her nostrils as wide as she could. "Rose, you'll ruin your appetite!" she said.

Rose shook her head. "Like that was going to happen," she said.

Maggie pulled up her chair and started on her salad. "Remember the traveling turkey?"

Rose closed her eyes and nodded. "How could I ever forget?"

"What is the traveling turkey?" asked Ella.

"Well . . ." said Rose.

"It was one of . . ." Maggie began.

The two of them smiled at each other. "You tell it," said Rose.

Maggie nodded. "Okay," she said. "We were both home for spring break, and Sydelle was on a diet."

"One of many," said Rose.

"Hey. Who's telling the story?" asked Maggie. "So we come home, and what's for dinner? Turkey."

"Turkey with the skin taken off," said Rose.

"Just turkey," said Maggie. "No potatoes. No stuffing. No gravy . . ."

"God forbid!" said Rose.

"Just turkey. We had poached eggs for breakfast, and then it's lunchtime, and out comes the turkey. The same turkey."

"It was," said Rose, "a very big turkey."

"We had it for dinner that night, too. And lunch the next day. And that night we were going to one of Sydelle's friend's houses for dinner, and we were so excited because we thought we'd finally get something that wasn't turkey, except when we got there we found out that Sydelle . . ."

". . . took the turkey with her!" Rose and Maggie concluded together.

"It turns out," said Rose, buttering a roll, "that her friend was on the same diet she was."

"We all had turkey," Maggie said.

"Traveling turkey," said Rose. And Ella sat back, feeling relief wash through her as her granddaughters started to laugh.

That night, for the last time, Maggie and Rose lay side by side on the flimsy pullout mattress, listening to the croaking of the frogs and the warm wind rustling the palm trees, and the occasional squeal of brakes as another resident of Golden Acres made his or her unsteady way home.

"I'm so full," Rose groaned. "Where'd you learn to cook like that?"

"From Ella," said Maggie. "I paid attention. It was good, wasn't it?"

"Delicious," said Rose, and yawned. "So what about you? Do you think you'll stay here?"

"Yes," said Maggie. "I mean, I liked Philadelphia okay. And I still think about California sometimes. But I really like it here. I've got my job, you know. I'm going to grow my business. And Ella needs me."

"For what?"

"Well, maybe she doesn't need me," Maggie conceded. "But I think she likes having me around. And I sort of like being here. I mean, not here here," she said, gesturing to indicate the room, the condominium, the Golden Acres Retirement Community in general, "but Florida. Everyone here is from somewhere else, did you ever notice that?"

"I guess."

"It's good, I think. If everyone went to high school someplace else, it's not like you're always running into people who remember what you were like in high school, or college, or whatever. So you can be different, if you want to."

"You can be different anywhere," said Rose. "Look at me."

Maggie leaned on her elbow and looked at her sister, the familiar face, the hair spilling over the pillow, and saw Rose not as a threat, or a scold, or someone who was always going to tell her that she was doing things the wrong way, but as an ally. A friend.

There was silence for a moment as the sisters lay side by side. In her bedroom, Ella cocked her head and held her breath, listening.

"I'm going to do it, you know," said Maggie. "Your Favorite Things. I'm going to open a store someday. I even know where."

"I'll come down for your grand opening," said Rose.

"And I want to tell you . . ."

"You're sorry," recited Rose. "You've changed."

"No! Well, yes, I mean. It's true."

"I know," said Rose. "I know you have."

"But that's not what I wanted to tell you. What I wanted to tell you is, don't buy a dress."

"What?"

"Don't buy a dress. That's going to be my wedding present to you."

"Oh, Maggie . . . I don't know."

"Trust me," said Maggie.

"You want me to get married in a dress I've never even seen?"

Rose gave a nervous laugh, while picturing the kind of dress Maggie would come up with—cut low, slit high, sleeveless, backless, and fringed.

"Trust me," said Maggie. "I know what you like. I'll show you pictures. I'll let you try it on first. I'll come home. We can do fittings."

"We'll see," said Rose.

"But you'll let me try?" asked Maggie.

Rose sighed. "Fine," she said. "Go for it. Knock yourself out."

Silence again.

"I love you, you know," said one of the girls, and Ella wasn't sure which one. Rose? Maggie?

"Oh, please," said the other sister. "Don't be so sappy."

Ella waited in her bedroom, holding her breath, waiting for more. But there was nothing. And, hours later, moving carefully, when she eased the door open and walked into the bedroom, both of the sisters were sleeping, both curled on their left sides with their left hands tucked under their cheeks. She bent down, hardly daring to breathe, and kissed them each on the forehead. *Luck*, she thought. *Love.* Your heart's every happiness. And, as quietly as she could, she laid two glasses of water, each with a single ice cube, on the bedside table and tiptoed out the door.

SIXTY

"Calm down," said Maggie for the eighteenth time, and leaned close to Rose, who flinched. "If you don't relax, there's no way I'm going to be able to do this."

"I can't relax," said Rose. She was wearing a thick white terry-cloth bathrobe. Her hair, thanks to the hourlong ministrations of Michael from Pileggi, was an elaborate updo of curls, bobby pins, and tiny white blossoms. Her foundation was on, her lips were lined. Amy, resplendent in a simple navy sheath that she'd ornamented with a bed-pillow-sized butt bow, was bustling around looking for the caterers, and the platter of sandwiches they'd promised, and Maggie was currently trying, unsuccessfully, to curl her sister's eyelashes.

"Hello!" Michael Feller, resplendent in a new tuxedo, with his thin hair artfully arranged over his bald spot, stuck his head in the door. "Everything okay in here?" He recoiled as Maggie maneuvered the eyelash curler into place. "What is that?" he asked, sounding scared.

"Eyelash curler," said Maggie. "Rose, I'm not going to hurt you. I promise. Now, just look right at me . . . Don't move your head . . . there! Got 'em!"

"Agh," said Rose, cringing as much as she could with her eyelashes trapped between the metal pincers of the curler. "Ow . . . hurts . . ."

"Don't hurt your sister!" Michael Feller said sternly.

"It . . . does . . . not . . . hurt," said Maggie, easing the curler along the length of Rose's lashes. "There! Perfect! Now I just have to do the other one!"

"God help me," said Rose, and looked at her feet. They looked very nice, she had to admit; she'd been dubious about the whole notion of a pedicure. "I'm not a pedicure kind of person," she'd said. But Maggie, who'd become extremely bossy in the months since Your Favorite Things had been written up in the *Fort Lauderdale Sun-Sentinel,* was not taking no for an answer.

"Nobody's even going to see my feet," Rose had protested, but Maggie had said that Simon was going to see her feet, wasn't he? And so Rose had given in.

Maggie maneuvered the curler toward Eyelash Number Two, curled it carefully, and stepped back to study the effect. "Did you see my date?" she demanded. "I mean, I know this is your special day and all, but . . ." And she paused, looking at her sister.

"Maggie!" Rose exclaimed. "I do believe you're blushing!"

"Am not," said Maggie. "It's just that I know it's a lot of pressure, inviting a guy to a wedding. . . ."

"Charles seems very comfortable," said Rose. In fact, Charles seemed just about perfect, the kind of guy she'd always hoped Maggie would find once she'd gotten over her thing for the semi-employed bass-players-slash-bartenders of the world. He was younger than she was, someone she'd met at Princeton, although Maggie had been evasive about the details. "And he's crazy about you."

"Do you think so?" Maggie asked.

"Definitely," Rose said, just as Amy arrived, brandishing a platter of sandwiches over her head and Maggie ducked through the door.

"I found the food!" she announced.

"Where?" asked Rose, waving at her father as he left.

"With Sydelle, where else?" Amy asked, carefully wrapping half of a turkey sandwich in a napkin and handing it to Rose. "She was scraping mayonnaise off the bread. And My Marcia was asking the rabbi whether she could do the Lord's Prayer."

"You're kidding, right?"

Amy nodded. Rose took a single bite and set the sandwich aside. "Can't eat. Nervous," she said, as Maggie swept back into the room, carrying a large, vaguely dress-shaped bundle wrapped in white plastic.

"Ready for your dress, Cinderella?" she asked.

Rose swallowed hard and nodded. Inside, she was dying. What if the dress wasn't right? She imagined herself walking down the aisle, thread trailing, half-sewn seams gaping open. *Oh, God,* she thought. How stupid had she been to let Maggie take this on?

"Close your eyes," Maggie said.

"No," said Rose.

"Please?"

Rose sighed and gently closed her eyes. Maggie reached over to the zippered plastic bag, gently tugged down the zipper, and eased Rose's dress off the hanger.

"Ta da!" said Maggie, and twirled the dress through the air.

At first all Rose saw was the skirt—layers and layers of tulle. Then, as Maggie held the dress up, she could see how beautiful it really was—the creamy satin bodice dotted with tiny seed pearls, the fitted sleeves, the neckline that she saw was just deep enough. True to her word, Maggie had sent pictures and had flown up to Philadelphia to do a fitting. But the finished product was more beautiful than Rose could ever have hoped for.

"How long did this take you and Ella?" Rose asked, stepping into the skirt.

"Never you mind," said Maggie, fastening the dozens of buttons she'd sewn by hand along the back.

"How much did it cost?" asked Rose.

"Never mind that, either. It's our gift to you," said Maggie, straightening the neckline, and turning her sister toward the mirror.

"Oh," gasped Rose, looking at herself. "Oh, Maggie!"

And then Amy was walking toward them, holding Rose's bouquet of pink roses and white lilies in her hand, and the rabbi was sticking his head around the door, smiling at Rose and telling her that it was time, and Ella hurried in after him, her corsage tilted to one side, a shoe box in her hands.

"You look beautiful," said Ella and Maggie at the exact same time, and Rose was staring at herself, knowing that the dress was the exact thing she was supposed to be wearing, knowing she'd never looked prettier, or happier, than she did at this moment, with her sister on her right side and her grandmother on her left.

"Here," said Ella, opening the shoe box. "These are for you."

"Oh, I've got shoes already. . . ." Rose peeked inside and saw the most perfect pair of shoes—ivory satin, with low heels, and embroidered in the same thread as her dress. "Oh, my God. They're so pretty. Where did you find them?" She stared at Ella and took a guess. "Were they my mom's?"

Maggie looked at Ella and held her breath.

"No," said Ella. "They were mine." She wiped her eyes with a handkerchief. "I know I should probably lend you earrings or a necklace or something, if you still need something borrowed, but . . ."

"They're perfect," said Rose, slipping the shoes on her feet. "And they fit!" she said.

Ella shook her head, and her eyes filled with tears. "I know," she whispered back.

"Don't start crying yet," said Lewis, poking his head through the door. "We haven't even gotten started." He grinned at Rose. "You look lovely. And I think they're ready when you are."

Rose hugged Ella, then reached out for her sister. "Thank you for my dress. It's unbelievable. The most beautiful thing I've ever seen!"

"You're welcome," said Ella.

"Oh, it was nothing," said Maggie.

"You guys ready?" asked Rose, and Maggie and Ella nodded. The caterer threw the doors open, and the guests looked at Rose and smiled. Camera bulbs flashed. Mrs. Lefkowitz sniffled. Michael Feller lifted Rose's veil. "You look so beautiful," he whispered in her ear. "I'm so proud of you."

"I love you," Rose said. She turned. At the end of the aisle, Simon was smiling at her, his warm blue eyes glowing, the yarmulke perched on top of his carefully cropped curls, his parents beaming beside him. Ella grabbed Maggie's hand and squeezed.

"You did it," she whispered, and Maggie nodded happily, and the two of them looked at Rose and caught her eye. *We love you,* Ella thought, and smiled, sending all of her good wishes through the air . . . and, in that instant, Rose looked at them through her veil and smiled back.

"And now," the rabbi intoned, "Maggie Feller, sister of the bride, will read a poem."

Maggie could feel the tension as she stepped forward and smoothed her dress (sage green, sleeveless, and without the slit in the skirt or the plunging neckline she knew her big sister was dreading) and stepped forward. She was certain, she thought, as she cleared her throat, that Sydelle and her father would be expecting her to bust out something that began, "There once was a girl from Nantucket." Well, they were in for a surprise.

"I'm so happy for my sister right now," said Maggie. "When we were growing up, Rose always took care of me. She always stuck up for me, and wanted what was best for me. And I'm so happy because I know that Simon will do the same things for her, and that we'll always be a part of each other's lives. We'll always love each other, because that's what sisters do. That's what sisters are." She gave Rose a smile. "So, Rose, this is for you."

Maggie took a deep breath and, even though she'd practiced the poem a dozen times on the plane, had long since committed it to memory, she felt a tremor of nerves work its way along her spine. Ella raised her chin in the exact expression that Rose and Maggie both wore at times, and Charles smiled at her proudly from his seat in the back. Maggie exhaled, and nodded at her grandmother. Then she fixed her eyes on Rose, wearing the beautiful dress she and Ella had made, and began:

> " 'i carry your heart with me(i carry it in
> my heart)i am never without it(anywhere
> i go you go,my dear;and whatever is done
> by only me is your doing,my darling)
>   i fear
> no fate(for you are my fate,my sweet)i want
> no world(for beautiful you are my world,my true)
> and it's you are whatever a moon has always meant
> and whatever a sun will always sing is you' "

Maggie's throat closed like a fist. In the front row, Lewis nodded at her, and Ella was smiling through her tears, and her father was pushing up his glasses and taking fast swipes at his eyes, and the assembled guests were staring at her expectantly. Under the chuppah Rose's eyes were wide and her lips trembling. And Maggie could imagine her mother, too, a ghost in the back row, the brightness of her red lipstick and gold earrings, watching over her daughters, knowing that in spite of everything both of them had grown up brave, and smart, and beautiful, that they'd be sisters to each other, and friends, too, and that Rose would always want what was best for Maggie, and Maggie would always want what was best for Rose. *Breathe,* Maggie thought, and began again:

> " 'here is the deepest secret nobody knows
> (here is the root of the root and the bud of the bud
> and the sky of the sky of a tree called life;which grows

higher than the soul can hope or mind can hide)
and this is the wonder that's keeping the stars apart'

" 'i carry your heart(i carry it in my heart)' "

She smiled at the crowd and smiled at her sister, and it was as if she could see the future—the house and the babies that Rose and Simon would have, the vacations where they'd visit her and Ella in Florida, where they'd swim together, Rose and Maggie and Ella and Rose's babies, in a wide blue pool under the sunshine, and where they'd curl up together at night on Ella's bed, side by side by side until they fell asleep.

"E.E. Cummings," she said, knowing that she'd done it, that everyone's eyes had been on her and she'd said every word perfectly; she, Maggie Feller, had gotten it just right.